Climbing the Ranks

An Epic LitRPG Cultivation Novel

by

Tao Wong

Copyright

Climbing the Ranks

A Starlit Publishing Book
Published by Starlit Publishing
PO Box 30035
High Park PO
Toronto, ON
M6P 3K0
Canada
www.starlitpublishing.com

Ebook ISBN: 9781778551352
Paperback ISBN: 9781778551369
Hardcover ISBN: 9781778551611
Dust Jacket Hardcover ISBN: 9781778551376

Series by Tao Wong

Climbing the Ranks
Climbing the Ranks Book 1

A Thousand Li series
Book 1: The First Step

A Thousand Li World Novel
The Sundering Blade

The System Apocalypse Universe

Main Storyline – Completed series
Book 1: Life in the North

System Apocalypse – Relentless
Book 1: A Fist Full of Credits

System Apocalypse: Australia
Book 1: Town Under

System Apocalypse: Kismet
Book 1: Fool's Play

Anthologies
System Apocalypse Short Story Anthology Volume 1
System Apocalypse Short Story Anthology Volume 2

Hidden Universe

Hidden Wishes

Book 1: A Gamer's Wish

Hidden Dishes

Book 1: The Nameless Restaurant

Adventures on Brad – Completed series

Book 1: A Healer's Gift

Table of Contents

Acknowledgements

Thank you to all the Backers on Kickstarter who made this book possible.

Especially:

Abdul Hadi Sid Ahmed • Adam Nemo • Agnès Metanomski • Alex Dummer • Alex Grade • Alexander McClement • Andrew Stines • Aris K. • Austin P. • Ben Padbury • Braden Davis • Brent V • Caitlin Pollastro • Cassi Krotzer • Christopher "Zhul" Dean Jr. • Corwin Whitefield • Daniel Schinhofen • Dylan Humphreys • Estelle Rousseau • GhostCat • Giuseppe D'Aristotile • Hadi Zein • J Hughes • J. R. Forst • Jason • Jason Murray • Jay Taylor • Jez Cajiao • Joey Quann • Joseph Hill • Justin Aaron Gross • K.R.S. • Kenyon Wensing • Kim Martin Rasmussen • Kristina • Kyle G Wilkinson • Lani • Lew Kohl • Luke Batt • Mathieu Lefebvre • Matt Weber • Matthew Koleda • Matthew Riley • Michael Ring • Michael Welch • Mike Szewczyk • Nicholas Stephenson • Nigel McCabe • Paul Smith • Princess Donut • Richard Fontanes • Richard Jensen • S.W.H. Garner • Santiago Rosado • Shawn Tarl Treants • Steven Neil Lacks • T. Hise • Tygran • Tyson • Victory D. Walker • Will Whittaker • Zaix Oliva

Chapter 1

"*Cendol!* Best cendol in the city!"

It was always like this. Give Malaysians a big enough space in an event and, sooner or later, roadside hawkers would appear. A lot might have changed ever since the advent of the Towers, but the Malaysian love for food had not altered one iota. Even with the pagoda-like Tower looming over Merdeka Square, the hawkers were all out, offering easy-to-consume and all-too-tasty foodstuff.

Merdeka Square itself—once a giant square of concrete and grass with "the second tallest flagpole in the word!" its singular claim to fame—had changed significantly since the appearance of the Tower. Now, a wall blocked off access to the Tower itself, bisecting the square. Numerous guards with assault rifles stood on the wall and the guard towers, which were built to safeguard from within and without.

Ringing the walled-off Tower were the hawkers, who sold food to tourists, gawkers and Tower-climbing groupies, all of them doing a brisk business. The one-man hawker stalls were often backed up by additional moving vans which resupplied the busy carts, as they dispensed a variety of foods. In the small circle around Arthur Chua, he could spot cendol, fresh fruit, *kuih*, and *goreng pisang* sold as quick snacks and a *char kway teow* man further away with small tables and chairs set up for his customers.

The presence of so many people and food stalls made the air redolent with scents. Sweat, the smell of unwashed humanity, the omnipresent humidity, and the overwhelming heat pressed down upon everyone as sunshine warmed the concrete floor.

Arthur drew another breath, enjoying the smells—even the acrid burnt smell of electric vehicles passing by on too-hot rubber tires—and listened to the conversations that washed over him. The constant honking of electric motorcycles and self-driven cars driven to the extremes of their software combating the careless nature of Malaysian drivers... It was all a reminder of what he was about to leave behind and he wanted to enjoy it, just for a few seconds more.

"*Aiyah*! I tell you, my cendol is the best. Better than that Sungai Besi fella!"

Then the moment was over, as the hawker bickered with one of his customers. Arthur briefly considered eating, just to see—the Sungai Besi cendol-maker was very good—and then his stomach twisted in knots further, reminding him why he was here.

Right.

Food… later. He had packed his favorites anyway, since once you entered the Tower, you couldn't leave. Not until it was cleared. If you cleared it.

Never mind what it did to your appetite and your hunger…

And that led him to the final group of watchers. The ones that no one wanted to notice, to remember. The ones that everyone ignored. The hopeful, the desperate, the abandoned. Parents, brothers and sisters, wives and children; all staring at the Tower gates, hoping they would open and their loved ones would exit.

Occasionally, someone would; but rarely would it be a happy reunion, a figure from those who were waiting and watching. Those who came by every day had little hope left, but what little they had, they clung to with all their might. No one knew how long it would take to clear the Tower. It could be weeks; it could be years. Just the other day, a climber finally exited after 20 years.

And so the crowd hoped, watched, and waited.

No one watched them for long, not even Arthur. They were a stark reminder that all the riches, the promised strength and opportunities within the Tower, came at a price. One that took nearly nine in ten of those that went in.

But still, people got in line just like Arthur, shuffling forward to be inspected at the gates. What else could you do, when the world was as it was and the rich held all the power and most of the well-paying jobs? Everything else, well, the robots did it and you had to survive with whatever odd jobs were available, however dangerous, disgusting or humiliating.

Especially in a country like Malaysia.

Sure, some of the Western countries had concepts like a universal basic income or a daily living stipend. Malaysia was not that rich, not since it had wrecked all its chances with foolish policies and driven the smart, the ambitious, the connected away. Not when tower technology and enchantments drove so much of the world now, when magic replaced a fifth of the world's technology and updated technology from the towers sent whole industries into tail spins.

"*Nama*?" The guard standing before the gate barked at Arthur in Malay, forcing his attention back to him. "IC?"

"Arthur Chua." Arthur handed over his Identification Card, watching as it was scanned. The guard eyed Arthur, verifying it was him, then looked him over with a considering gaze. Arthur made himself stand up a little straighter, his five-foot-ten frame putting him on the taller side for a Chinese Malaysian.

He was, he knew, well-proportioned too; though many of the hopefuls were the same. One of the secrets that had been revealed early on was that whatever body you brought into the Tower was the base you began with.

Everyone who could tried to improve that very base, long before they entered.

"That your only weapon?" the guard asked, still speaking Malay. Even if English was the official language, the Malays who made up the majority of the population and occupied most government positions rarely deigned to speak it. Not when they could afford to shove it in the face of someone like Arthur.

"*Ya*." Arthur nodded in acknowledgement, hefting the simple wooden staff. There were others in line with real weapons, like the biracial man behind Arthur who carried a spear and sword—though the man, a mix of Malay and Chinese was Arthur's guess, was juggling the weapons as if he was not used to them. Probably another rich Dato' who could afford the bribes for proper weapon permissions.

Theoretically, you didn't need to bribe for permits, so long as you put in the right forms. And show that you were going to be joining the Tower. However, Arthur's first two applications had mysteriously been lost, before he gave a sufficiently large bribe to ensure that the paperwork did not just disappear. But they still hadn't approved his permit. He was left hanging, no matter how often he went to check at the office. So here he was, carrying one of the approved weapons for general use by the populace, even if he was fully trained in a variety of melee weapons.

"Okay. Go. Faster." The guard waved at Arthur, sending him in after returning his IC. Arthur walked past the looming walls, glancing backwards at the long line of hopefuls, many of them dressed and armed just like he was, though a few stood out with their real weapons.

He could even see a couple of people with bodyguards, who were carrying guns. Rifles, pistols, and even bows worked in the Tower. But getting a gun license in Malaysia required the prime minister himself to sign off on it, and that kind of clout only the richest had.

It mattered not once they started in the Tower. In the end, you could only rely on yourself, and whatever advantages these people bought by being born to the right parents would be ground away.

Arthur believed that. He had to. Otherwise, there was no reason to keep going on. And hope, no matter how thin, had arrived along with the Towers.

Chapter 2

There was no rushing or pushing to enter the dungeon's main entrance. The Tower was no longer a mystery, and everyone understood that they would be tested the moment they entered. The winnowing stage was entirely solo, before you were allowed into the Tower proper. Of course, when the first Tower arrived, this testing stage had taken a large number of lives since no one had expected to be thrown into a life-or-death fight immediately.

Nowadays, the test was well known. An empty room—blue, white, or sometimes brown, depending on the Tower—with no obstacles or other environmental factors to aid or hinder the testee. Everyone faced the same monster here, the only variation being the type that was dependent upon the individual Tower itself. Arthur knew that in some places, they faced goblins, or red caps or kobolds. However, for those that chose to enter via the Malaysian Tower, they got to fight the *babi ngepet*; as if the tower had decided to offer a nod to local legends.

Standing in a plain white room, its temperature a chill 20 degrees Celsius or so—way too cold for even an air-conditioned shopping mall in Malaysia—Arthur could not help but be impatient. This test was the first of many, but without passing it he could not move on.

A chime like a cellphone alert roused Arthur's attention and made him focus. Somehow, while he was thinking, the ground ahead had given rise to a bank of mist. The mist wrapped itself around a slow-forming figure.

Arthur waited, knowing it was useless to attack the mist until it had finished its job. Besides, he had often heard of people receiving lower marks because they had tried to cheese their way through the test. *Sangat bodoh, nak buat itu.*

Better to wait, then launch an attack and score higher.

When the mist finally parted, it brought with it the sight of the demon boar he would have to face. The *babi ngepet* easily weighed three hundred pounds with overly large tusks and an evil look in its glowing red eyes. Like all boars everywhere, it had a terrible temperament and, upon sighting Arthur, began its charge.

That was the thing they didn't tell you if you lived in a big city, supping on the tender *siu yuk* of their domesticated cousins. Boars were nasty.

Most wild animals—even the *harimau*, the king of the jungle—would avoid humans. They had no reason to hunt humans, and so never attacked. But the *Babi*? They'd attack just because they could. And this was a demonic version.

The loud squeals, compounding off hooves charging forward rose up around the room, filling Arthur's world. He found his heart beating faster, his hands growing sweaty as adrenaline coursed through him. No matter how much training he had, no matter how real they had tried to make it, they could not duplicate the reality of facing something that truly wanted you dead. Legs turned to the left, arms bent forward, staff held in both hands before him. Even as the boar closed in, with each harsh breath.

At the last moment, Arthur jumped aside. A little too late. He swung his staff at the same time, hoping to strike the monster away from him. His timing was off, just a little, enough for it to gore a trailing foot, leaving his ankle bloodied. He stumbled as he landed, the monster staggering aside and turning in a wide circle as it shook its dazed head.

Arthur had landed the hit, but it wasn't enough. Once more, the *babi ngepet* shook his head and charged. This time there was less space between them, less time to gain momentum. Rather than jump, Arthur merely stepped aside as he swung his staff, blow crashing into a front leg and sending the ball off course. A part of him regretted not having a spear, the perfect weapon for dealing with the tough hide and monstrous muscles of this creature. He dismissed the thought and focused.

Three more times, the demon charged him. Three more times, Arthur struck first, making full use of his weapon's long reach. His confidence grew with each attack, even as he felt his sneaker grow ever more bloodied and his leg radiate with pain.

He could do this, he was certain. Until the *babi ngepet* changed the rules.

It shook itself and rather than approaching him, it began to transform. Black smoke swirled up around its body, and Arthur knew he was seeing the second stage of the test. He took a couple of quick steps forward, knowing that he was allowed to strike now. This was the time to finish it.

Except, on his second step, pain shot up his ankle and it gave way. He collapsed, barely stopping his knees from slamming fully into the unforgiving floor by propping himself on his staff. While Arthur got over the flash of pain, the *Babi* completed its transformation.

Standing in front of Arthur was now a five-foot-four man in dark robes. He wielded a pair of knives, one in each hand. One knife was chipped and bloodied, just like the boar's tusk had been. The man threw himself forward, blades weaving before him. Still on his knees, Arthur weaved his own defense with his staff.

The furious battle between the pair sent the clack of staff meeting blade echoing through the room. Arthur's greater range with his staff was compromised by his lack of mobility, while his opponent's second blade constantly threatened to cut his arm. Eventually the man fell back, cradling his injured elbow while Arthur had blood dripping from his lead right thigh where a blade had scored against him.

Taking a brief moment to relax, Arthur pushed himself to his feet, glaring at his opponent. Notwithstanding the injuries, he had the advantage. He limped forward slowly, even as his opponent attempted to pick up a dropped dagger. A jab with his staff caught the man on his collarbone, sending him staggering away. Another spinning attack was blocked by the remaining dagger. Arthur shifted his grip, swinging the bottom of his staff up as he pulled the top edge back, sliding the staff in between the man's legs. Only a quick motion by his opponent allowed his crown jewels to stay untouched. But a blow to the inner thigh was crippling in and of itself.

Slow, careful steps. Carefully placed blows, and the occasional feint, drove his opponent back, back, back. At last, the man had nowhere to go, and Arthur's staff crushed his skull.

Only then, through the haze of pain and concentration that had overtaken him, did Arthur really note his actions, spotting the unseeing eyes that met his own troubled gaze.

The Malaysian Tower was considered one of the most difficult to pass due to its unusual, nonhuman start and the fact that one had to kill a human at the end. Or something that looked human. Too many testees realized in the end that they could not do it. The act of killing another human was anathema to many.

Arthur, still bleeding, wondered what it meant about him, that he felt very little beyond relief. No regret, no pain or sorrow.

No joy. Not yet.

Golden lines appeared before him, within his mind's eye.

Initial tower test completed.

Results are being graded.

Please wait…

Tests have been graded.

Teleportation commencing.

…

Please wait.

Now the joy came along with the shifting of his senses.

Chapter 3

Blinding light. Arthur found himself in another empty room. Beige walls, a light that came from the surroundings without seeming to have a point of origin. The floor was hard but with a little give, like a particularly firm mattress or the sprung wood floor of a training hall.

Immediately, Arthur let himself collapse to the ground. He wanted to cross his knees and enter lotus position, but the injury to his ankle put a stop to that. So instead he sat with one leg crossed, the other pointed outwards. He noticed the bleeding was already stopping and he knew from the training books that he would soon begin healing.

One of the advantages of life in the Tower. Along with that, the swirling morass of energy that surrounded him. It was so thick Arthur could almost feel it brushing against his skin, like static electricity just before it released. Hair on the back of his neck and along his arms stood at attention, and the teenager smiled.

This room was an opportunity, a chance to draw in the energy released by the *babi ngepet* that had died. The harder-than-normal fight was a lucky break since the monster had a higher amount of energy—chi, mana, quantum potential, whatever you wanted to call it—for him to cultivate with.

Of course, he also hurt and ached, another part of the trade-off of having this opportunity offered to him.

Another breath, tickling along his chest and out his mouth. Arthur calmed his mind, forcing himself to breathe slowly through his stomach, to sit upwards in the hollow body position, his spine straight. Everyone who came to the Tower was taught how to do this. It was one of the requirements of being successful.

Cultivation.

Breathe in, draw in the energy.

Breathe out, settle your mind.

Breathe in, draw in more energy with your breath.

Breathe out, contain that energy.

Repeat until such time that the energy dispersed, or you had absorbed it all. Since Arthur had a bog-standard cultivation method, one taught to all children looking to advance, the former was more likely.

Still Arthur could not let that fact discourage him. This was as much test as opportunity, and he would not stumble on the second hurdle.

His breathing sped up, his intake grew shallower as his desire made him grasp what could not be held with force. Energy slipped through his metaphorical hands, escaping with each inhalation.

Arthur grimaced, forced himself to ignore the part of him that recommended he just try harder. Instead he chose to just breathe, to focus on the every day, the very act of breathing. He grounded himself in the humid exhalation, the slight chill on his skin and the growing warmth around his stomach.

He chose to calm himself, even as energy dispersed.

When his mind was stable once again, he returned to cultivating. That heat in his center, just below his navel, grew. His pool of energy, his spiritual sea, the *dantian.*

Interminable time passed until he found the energy around him too tenuous to grasp. Eyes opened and Arthur's lip twitched as his body buzzed with potential.

Then, another glowing series of golden lines appeared before his eyes.

Second entrance test completed.

Results are being graded.

Please wait…

Tests have been graded.

Would you like to review your results now?

Yes! Arthur mentally shouted. He could have waited but the test rooms were the safest place in the Tower to review this information. Best to get to it.

As quick as he thought his answer, new lines of information appeared.

Cultivation Speed: 1

Energy Pool: 7

Refinement Speed: 1

Attributes and Traits

Mind: 3

Body: 3

Spirit: 3

Arthur paused, then found himself smiling grimly. It was not as bad as he feared. A starting stat of three for one's attributes was expected for your average Tower climber. His energy pool was higher than other cultivators, with most others starting with only four or five points of energy.

Not that it mattered much, since he had no styles or skills that he could channel his energy pool into. The only thing he could do was gain enough energy to refine it and, using that refined energy, upgrade his attributes. Even that would be slower, due to his lack of cultivation and refinement manuals.

Nevertheless, for a man starting out with not a single backer, this was not a bad start at all. Before Arthur could revel further in barely surpassing the average, another line of gold letters appeared.

All tests completed.
Teleportation commencing to first level of Tower.
Please wait.

Chapter 4

Arthur blinked, his world lurching as he was teleported. He fought the disorientation and stomach churning that teleportation caused, the churning in his stomach as he went through the equivalent of riding a rollercoaster during a hurricane in the middle of the ocean. His stomach lurched and twisted, and Arthur fought not to throw up. When his eyes finally cleared and he was able to focus on anything but his stomach, he noticed a group of individuals staring at him.

"Well done!"

"*Bagus, bagus*!"

Cheers and congratulations exploded from the spectating crowd, though one voice also shouted, "Damn it, throw up already!"

Arthur finally managed to settle his stomach, enough that he dared to take a step forward on the raised teleportation platform. The entire thing was made of stone and no larger than a couple of feet across and a few inches off the ground, just enough to demarcate the differences.

Stepping onto sandy ground, Arthur could not help but note that there were dozens of teleportation platforms in sight and even more hidden by the buildings that they ringed. The buildings in the center had always been present, though there was a marked difference between the carefully crafted Tower made buildings of stone and brick and the ramshackle wooden housing created by the tower climbers.

The first Tower-crafted buildings were where the few guides and Tower-enabled residences were, while the ramshackle buildings hosted the majority of cultivators. The first level of the Tower—of all Towers in the world—was the only floor that had a safe zone. As such, it was also the place where tower climbers would return to when they grew all too tired of, well, climbing.

Of course, there were other safe zones throughout the Tower for taller buildings, but all those were manmade. There were residences created by tired Tower climbers, even whole cities—places to stop and acquire new equipment, cultivation manuals, and skills. Places to cultivate, too, but all such places were only as safe as the individuals who ran them.

Only on the first floor did the Tower itself enforce safety, not only by providing individuals with a second chance at life if they were injured, but also by the ubiquitous Tower guards. Faceless sentinels in robes, which floated or flew overhead, watching all those who lived within.

"Platform eleven. Platform eleven. Taking bets now..."

Arthur turned to the speaker, a scrawny kid with a floppy hairstyle who stalked among the crowd, pointing in the direction of the aforementioned platform. That one, Arthur idly noted, was glowing a little. Less than ten seconds since the platform started glowing, it stopped and another cultivator appeared, looking the worst for wear.

The woman lurched forwards a little, bending over. Her foot nearly brushed the outside of the platform before she caught herself from tumbling off, eliciting a series of gasps from the watchers. Then, still bent over, she threw up, red curry and brown sludge with a mixture of white noodles spreading across the black platform and brown dirt.

"Yes!"

"Aiyah! *Perempuan, selalu tak guna.*"

"I knew I'd make it all back. Pay up, pay up. *Cepat, cepat lah*!"

"Damn it..."

Curses from all around, even as a robed figure of a guardian swept towards the woman. A wave of its hand and the vomit disappeared, even as she staggered away—just a girl, Arthur realised, probably just old enough for college if she had not chosen to enter like him.

Which reminded him.

He started walking forwards, staff held over his shoulder, gaze sweeping over everyone as he watched for potential pickpockets. They were always a danger, though none of the current residents chose to step closer than fifteen feet near the teleportation platforms. The guardians' presence probably kept them away, ensuring newcomers had a safe entry during their most vulnerable state.

More teleportation platforms had fired, depositing their testees. A few of the ones that came before had exited the safe zone and been met by others. Sect members, members of merchant houses, and runners. The testees handed over their packs and, in a few cases, amulets or rings of dimensional storage, and in turn were greeted happily by their waiting members.

Arthur had considered, briefly, being a runner. He had discarded the option due to the risk. Not to himself—if he did not make it through the test, he would be dead and uncaring about what any annoyed merchant house or triad group could do—but for his family. The only kind of assurance, beyond money that Arthur did not have, that these groups accepted was family. If you failed to bring the goods through, they would take it out on your family. And that, Arthur would not risk. No matter how sure he was.

Still, he did feel a twinge of regret at playing it safe. Those who took the risk now had a head start, paid in contribution points or skills or monster cores or good old money. Tower money, of course, was different from real-world money.

All he had was a single chit...

So deep in thought, he almost did not notice the trio that appeared before him, standing in his way. Arthur frowned, stopping just a little short, then automatically stepping back to clear space. He noticed the smirks among the loutish trio, all of them wearing baggy sweatpants and singlets. *Samseng*, thugs, of the worse kind—the kind that refused to shower regularly.

And worse, looking at them, Arthur could guess exactly what they wanted.

"Eh, friend, got a second, eh?"

"No," Arthur said, stepping to the side.

The trio automatically moved, repositioning themselves.

"We weren't asking," the leader said again, his smile widening but still lacking any real warmth.

Arthur sighed and set himself, knowing he was not going to get away that easily.

It looked like his first shakedown had started

Chapter 5

Three men, all of them in singlets and sweatpants. The leader had a slight sweat stain on his singlet, and the men reeked ever so slightly of stale sweat. The temperature of the first level of the Tower was similar to Kuala Lumpur's if slightly less humid. All that meant was that you sweated less visibly, with the heat causing hair to curl and bodies to overheat.

"I'm sorry, but I should go. I have a place to be," Arthur said, his lips smiling but his eyes cold. He kept the grip on his staff loose, his eyes unfocused on the leader's nose. No need to meet eyes to make it a challenge, but he was not willing to look away either.

"Oh, a newbie has a place to go, eh?" The leader smirked. That was the second time, so Arthur decided to call him Smirkee in his head.

"Yes."

"Why don't you tell me where that is, hmmm? Or you lying, *ah*?" Smirkee said.

"No, I don't think so," Arthur replied. Then, seeing that Samseng One—the thug with the bigger arms and knife in his belt—was trying to flank him, he turned his head slightly to catch Samseng One's eyes. "Don't."

"Wah, so brave!" Smirkee said, but he did note how Samseng One had stopped short, surprised that his sneaking had been caught. "Do you know who we are?"

"A man who likes to quote bad movies?" Arthur said. Around them, the crowd had noticed the problem. And, like gamblers the world over, had chosen to bet on the outcome.

"What?"

"Never mind." Arthur shook his head, deciding not to try to enlighten the other. "Do you not know who I am?"

"No," Smirkee said, freezing a little. The way Arthur had said it, how confident he seemed to be, forced him to eye Arthur again. Arthur could swear he could see the thug calculus going on behind Smirkee's eyes. Non-bladed weapon, so he had no connections to get a better one. No enchanted gear, no armour, a single bag. No ties to a sect, then, or a merchant house. At least, none that were choosing to make their involvement known. And Arthur's own aura was nothing special. Perhaps a little stronger, but nothing special.

"Great, then let's keep it that way." Even as Smirkee re-assessed him, Arthur was moving. He stepped to the side, moving not towards Samseng One but to Samseng Two, the younger boy with the scrawny arms who was obviously the least proactive of the group.

He was nearly past the boy when Smirkee chose to speak. "Oi! Who said you could go?"

Too bad.

Arthur took off, running for all he was worth. Bag slung over his shoulder, staff kept tilted a little and held close to him, he ran. Headed straight for the village center itself and the newcomers' hall, knowing that once he was within sight of it, the thugs would not dare do anything untoward.

Even now, with so many Tower guards around, they dared not actually hit him. They could intimidate, threaten, and promise retribution outside the town. But physically manhandling him would cross the line.

More worrisome was if one of them was a pickpocket. The single chit that Arthur carried had all his funds, real world cash traded on the outside for Tower credits. All backed by the chit. However, until he managed to register the chit, it was unregistered funds. Available for anyone to use.

Arthur ran, tough hiking boots pounding the dirt, grabbing at the loose earth as he threw himself forward. Behind him, beyond the initial shout of surprise, the trio ran silently. The Tower guards were not exactly stupid but they were not, it seemed, entirely sapient. They had routines and, so long as someone did not break their rules, they would ignore all other actions.

Which meant that the quartet running across open ground, dodging around ill-leaning walls and headed for the beginners' village, were left to their own devices. An eye to the left, a glance to the right, a stack of sticks. Arthur dipped the end of his staff one way, catching the top of the pile. They tipped over, clattering behind him.

Curses, muffled, along with the crashing of a body to the ground. Rather than look behind, Arthur bent his head further and pushed on. His breathing grew harsh, his movements slowing down a little as he struggled forward.

Not because he was exhausted already, but because fear and anxiety stole his breath away. He broke clear of the latest trash-strewn passage, the edge of the Tower village appearing in his vision. A surge of energy ran through him and he sped up, never noticing the thrown rock that caught him in his upper back.

Already running as fast as he could, Arthur's balance was disrupted. He stumbled, falling to the ground, his feet nearly entangling with his own staff before he managed to roll to his feet, back hurting from where his backpack and its contents had dug into muscles and ribs.

As he stumbled to his feet, the trio caught up. Samseng Two threw himself at Arthur in a desperate tackle, only to catch the end of the staff in his chest. He fell backwards, a muffled *urk* resounding as Arthur drove his full body weight onto the braced wooden staff.

"I'll kill you!" Smirkee shouted, slowing down a short distance from Arthur and drawing a knife.

Arthur ignored the fallen body beside him, the painful wheeze of his opponent as he pushed himself to his feet. A light squeak of fear from the doorway behind him helped the cultivator reorient himself, even as he grimaced at the feel of mud on his body. Considering the ground was dry almost everywhere else, he did not want to consider why the ground was wet here, near the corner of a ramshackle building.

Even if the scent was a little telling.

"I guess we're doing this, eh?" Arthur said, beginning to spin his staff as he eyed the remaining two thugs.

And he had been so close too.

Chapter 6

"I'm going to cut you until you bleed, boy-boy!" Smirkee snarled.

Even at this juncture, blade aimed at him and Samseng One moving to flank him as he carefully moved backwards, Arthur could not help but groan. Because, really, when you heard someone that cheesy, you either groaned or smirked. And Smirkee was currently pissed off enough that Arthur attempting to take his prize spot on the Smirkee World of Records was just wrong.

"If you're trying to kill me with your language, you're getting close," Arthur said. He spun his staff, closing in on Smirkee, warding him off before he let the wood smack into his hand and rebound, using the extra energy for another spin and thrust as Samseng One darted close.

"*Cilaka*!"

"Yeah, yeah…" Arthur said. "We don't have to do this, you know."

"I'll rip your heart out and eat it."

"With a spoon?"

"What?" Samseng One said, puzzled.

"Old movie. Good one too, but old." Arthur shook his head. "My streaming account threw it up on random and, well, it was good."

"What the hell are you idiots doing?" Smirkee darted in even as he shouted, his blade coming within inches of Arthur's hand. A hasty pull back and a sweep of the staff took a hip in the side, even as the teenager stumbled.

"Always a good time to talk…" Arthur panted. After catching a breath, he suddenly relaxed and stopped moving. "Also, I was delaying."

"What?" Samseng One said again.

"You need a wider vocabulary." Arthur paused. "More words. Learn them. It'll help people not think you're just a thug."

Face flushed, Samseng One took a step forward, knowing he had just been insulted. But he halted when a green light wrapped around him, freezing him and the other thugs in place.

"What?!"

"See what I mean?" Arthur gritted out. The energy was not directly painful, but it set his teeth on edge and felt like a roll of sharp needles was running across his body. The kind of metal pinprick roller used by doctors to check for loss of sensitivity and by others for... other reasons.

"*This guard has noted threats to the life of a cultivator along with physical attempts. As per Tower rules, parties will be suitably punished.*" A flicker and then Arthur was deposited to the ground, the green energy dissipating even as his opponents and the guard flew straight up in the air before disappearing. Arthur caught sight of Smirkee's frozen mask of fear just before they were yanked away to jail.

"Bye-bye!" Arthur waved, before turning away and sauntering off. The entire act was overblown, since he could feel the eyes of the other residents on him. It was better to look overconfident and a smartass than to cower.

Now that the way to the village was clear, Arthur strolled in, brushing himself down idly as he kept walking. There was little he could do about the mud or dirt, or the slight smell lingering on him, but trying gave him something to do while he studiously ignored the gazes on him.

In the meantime, he also had quite a lot to see. The village buildings created by the Tower were a haphazard mixture of architectural styles, unlike the manmade four-sided leaning slabs of engineering mayhem outside the circle of Tower-made buildings. Once again, the Tower had drawn from local culture and then dumped the buildings out like it was asking for an answer from fortune-telling sticks at the temple.

Two-story terrace shops lined one side of the village, though unlike their Malaysian inspirations they were arranged in a curve instead of a straight row. Next to it, a trio of houses. These were raised on wooden stilts like the ones on the East Coast which saw regular monsoon floods. Then, a short distance later, a modern building made of glass and concrete, that was lopped off four floors up.

Of course, the main novice building was British, a colonial style mansion reminiscent of the British High Commission. A rather interesting development, considering Malaysia's history of colonialism. Then again, the Towers were alien; they probably had no idea of the long discussions about colonialism and the massive, ongoing damage it had done to cultures.

Or at least, Arthur hoped not. Or else the aliens were dicks.

Inside the building, crossing stone floor, Arthur worked his way over to four attendants behind their wooden desk. The first three had that glassy-eyed look of Tower-made residents. The fourth was human and, not surprisingly, had the largest number of individuals waiting. Arthur thought for a second and then went to join that line-up.

He might be in the Tower, he might be ready, but right now human interaction was still better. At least for a little while longer.

The line snaked forward slowly but consistently until Arthur finally found himself before the attendant. He offered the man a smile along with his greeting, only for the attendant to sniff.

"What do you want?"

"Newcomer chit please, and I want to register a credit transfer," Arthur said easily.

The attendant nodded, holding a hand out for the credit chit. Arthur was just about to hand it over when a shout arose from the entrance. As one, the entire hall of people turned to look at a very angry thug who was pointing a finger in Arthur's direction.

"You! We'll get you. You think you won this time, but you've won NOTHING!" Before the faceless guards who ran the newcomer hall could deal with him, he dashed off, leaving the entire building to stare at Arthur. At least, the humans did.

Grinning weakly, Arthur waved to the lookers before turning around to the attendant, who proceeded to snatch the token from his hand. He slotted it into a small section on his desk, the jade token slipping in with ease before it beeped.

The attendant's eyes widened as he read the information. Then, looking at Arthur, he hissed. "Eleven credits? You pissed the Suey Ying tong for eleven credits?!"

"Yes."

"*Bodoh ke?* Are you some kind of idiot?"

A pause from Arthur then he grinned. "Yeah."

Stunned silence greeted Arthur's honest confession. Eventually, the attendant burst out into snorting laughter. "Fine, fine. Eleven credits, registered to Arthur Chua."

"Thank you." Arthur relaxed a little, grateful that it went well enough.

"Newcomer chit and your spare credit token." The attendant handed both over to Arthur before he continued. "You won't be able to spend the newcomer credit anywhere but at the newcomer stores. If not spent within 24 hours, it'll disappear. You are also provided residence in the newcomer building for seven days, total. Not consecutive." A pause, as he looked Arthur over before the attendant continued, "Smart people leave an extra day or two unused, so that they have a place to heal up safely."

Arthur nodded in thanks for the tip, while shifting a little impatiently. Rolling his eyes, the attendant waved his hand.

"Quest board is behind you. Take the gathering quests and low-level kill quests. There's no penalty for failing them on this floor, and you never know what you'll find. Any questions?" The attendant finished what seemed to be a regular spiel, already tapping on the table impatiently.

"Yeah. What's your name?" Arthur said, still smiling.

A snort. "You can call me Lai Tai Kor."

There were a few chuckles from behind at the pretentiousness of being asked to be called big brother upon first meeting. Instead of chuckling along, Arthur stored the chits away and clasped his hands together to offer him a slight bow.

"Then, thank you, Lai Tai Kor."

"Smart ass. Get out of here!" Still, Lai was grinning as Arthur sauntered out, before he turned narrow eyes at the man taking Arthur's place. "And don't think I didn't hear you laugh!"

Arthur chuckled, detouring to the quest board to grab the quests—a simple matter of placing his hand on each glowing runic pentagram, getting zapped with a light bolt of electricity. As he repeated the procedure, his interface kept piling up with notifications. At last, Arthur made his way to a side exit.

Best not to go out the main way. You never know who might be waiting. Or what.

Anyway, he had no time to tangle with the tong and their members. He had shopping to do!

Chapter 7

"Boss!" Arthur called out, waving at the fox who stood upright by the side, watching over the small crowd moving through his store. The fox glared at Arthur, but the young man was unperturbed, treading his way closer.

"I know what I want," Arthur supplied helpfully. "If you get it for me, I'll be out immediately."

This time around, the fox's face had a flash of surprise before it was smoothed out, just like the fur along its face. It bowed a little to Arthur, making its way behind glass counters that lined the edge of the shop interior to meet him.

More than a few of the other customers stared at Arthur. He quickly flicked his gaze over the group, assessing and categorising them into three categories. First were the rich, smart, and connected. They were, one and all, well dressed and well armed. A few even had bodyguards. Those would go far, if luck held. No waste of their newcomer credits, not for them. They'd all have secret lists, information of the specialised items that their backers had provided that, combined with other items, were sufficient to give them a head start. They would retire soon enough, cook together whatever special pill they had been told to make, and then spend the next few days or weeks training to increase their cultivation base. When they emerged, they'd be stronger and faster than anyone else, offered a lead that no one at Arthur's stage could hope to beat.

Those fellas had looked him over and dismissed him, having slotted him in the second category: The smart, the ones who had researched and done their best to learn what they could. They had no secret techniques or manuals, no greater knowledge but knew enough than to rely on fickle luck or desperate fate. They knew exactly what they wanted, and if they all received the same damn thing, well...

"A Beginner Special then?" the fox said, brown eyes dancing with amusement as he looked at the bloody scrap of paper that Arthur handed him.

"Yes."

The third group—the foolish, the unwary, the hesitant—were the largest. They might have done some research; they might even have a plan. But now, here in the newcomer shop, they had no confidence anymore. Not in their research, not in their decisions.

The array of weapons, each with their own unique name, the multifarious names of alchemical pills, the cultivation manuals and exercises that tempted them all. So much stuff, that even lists created by others to aid those who came after did not cover them all.

More importantly, in the here and now, life and death had grown all too real. Rather than trust their own research, they leaned one way or another, listened to what people had to say or bought, all desperately hoping to validate their own decisions or reinforce the current meta.

It took the fox only a short moment to return, holding up items from the Beginner's Special. So named because it was the recommended purchase for those who entered, a simple and effective series of items for those without an in.

"Low quality, white jade knives for gathering and skinning," the fox said, dropping the sheathed weapons onto the table, wrapped in leather to keep his glass counters unscarred. A smaller bundle dropped beside it. "Bags and string, for storage."

Arthur opened the knife bag, unwinding the leather string to pull the two knives out. The skinning knife had a tiny hook at the front, the blade thin and all too sharp. The gathering knife looked like a mini-scythe, meant to catch behind a flower or herb to cut with a pull, leaving the roots behind so that they could grow again.

"Good quality," Arthur said. He wrapped the pair up and pulled the bundle across the counter. He made sure to smile when he spoke, not wanting the shopkeeper to mistake the compliment for what it was.

Not that it seemed to matter to the fox. "Focused Strike, chi exercise."

The scroll that followed the pronouncement was wrapped in a red thread. Attached was a leather label: the words were at first in English, then Chinese, and then Malay—the characters shifting as Arthur stared, magic changing the words to languages he understood.

Arthur knew better than to open the scroll now. Doing so would be the kind of insult that would follow him through all the Tower's shops, leading to much lower offers and the occasional lower-quality item. No, you could check the mundane items, but cultivation resources were all sacrosanct.

"And lastly, bag of storage for the first floor," the fox said, dropping the small pouch beside the scroll. "Good only for this floor, two cubic *feet*."

"Thank you," Arthur replied, grabbing the bag and sweeping everything within. Once he was done, he cocked his head to the side. "And the special?"

"The manager's special?" The fox smirked. "Are you sure you wish to gamble upon it?"

Arthur nodded firmly. "I have two credits left. I might as well."

"Very well," the fox reached behind him before dropping a rock in front of Arthur. "One manager's special."

The loud sniggers that raced across the room had him flushing a little, but mostly Arthur was staring at the plain, river-worn smooth stone before him. It wasn't even particularly large, half the size of his palm and rather flat. Maybe good for skipping...

"A rock?" Arthur said incredulously.

"Yes. As you know, the manager's special is always a gamble." The fox grinned. "We do not take returns."

"A rock..." Arthur sighed, picked up the rock and then shrugging, dropped it into the storage pouch. He slipped the pouch into his jacket before bidding the fox goodbye, doing his best to ignore the chuckles. After all, Arthur reminded himself, he was not the first nor would he be the last to get taken by the manager's special.

Anyway, he had his hands on a cultivation technique at last! Even if it was the lowest grade and most common technique ever, it was a cultivation technique. One he sorely needed, if he was to survive.

Staff in hand, he hurried towards the newcomer inn, intent on getting a room and starting his lessons. It was time to get started on his first real lessons as a cultivator.

Chapter 8

Getting a room—literally a room since there was just a sink, a single bed, and a shared toilet and bathroom on the same floor—was a simple matter. He showed them his chit, handed it over, and got his key. Once he was in the room, he took a seat on the bed before he extracted the Focused Strike chi technique scroll.

Biting his lip, Arthur realised his hands were shaking a little. All this time, all this effort to get here. Late nights, hours after everyone else had slept, stolen time from Hypnos himself as he practised forms and katas and exercised, only to get up early the next day to join the gym and get his ass handed to him, again and again. Until he was one of those doing the beating.

Scrabbling for money, for hard manual work that was all too dangerous or finnicky for machines. Pulling jammed metal pieces out, crawling under moving electronics to swap out parts, sorting through waste matter just to find some nugget of old electronics with parts that were of value.

Then, the fight nights, the illegal scraps in underground rings where the best and most desperate fought for the hoi polloi to watch. It mattered not how good you were, just how well you showed off during the fight. Oh, and winning too, though that mattered less with some groups than others, with rigged fights being a common occurrence.

Not that Arthur had bothered with much of that. After his third fight, limping home—a winner but too bruised to train for a week—he realised the kind of training he was receiving just was not worth the pain and the even greater risk of serious injury. A broken leg, broken ribs, even a twisted ankle could set him back for weeks.

No matter how much he could win, it just wasn't worth it. Not to him.

Slow and easy.

Which led him here. Exhale, pull the string, and open the scroll. Why a scroll and not a book or pamphlet, Arthur had no idea. It wasn't as though there was that much information on the scroll, and it wasn't as though it was magically transmitted into him. That kind of spiritual impartation was much, much more expensive and not something that even showed up until the end of the tower.

Unfortunately, plain paper scroll or not, the information within was significantly more complicated than just drawings and words. Staring at the lines of information, the drawings that shifted and twisted before his very eyes, Arthur sighed.

"I knew they said it wasn't that easy, but really?" he muttered out loud. Direction of flow through one meridian to another, concentration of energy, breath and muscle control, even mental imaging was all part of the technique.

A single technique and one of the easiest, but it still was going to take him hours to work it out.

"Well, best get to it," Arthur muttered. Eyes narrowing, he stared at the central diagram, knowing he had to start from, well, the beginning.

His core.

Learn how to pull the energy out, how to direct and move it, priming the energy to reinforce muscles, tendon, and bone. Keep focused on where the energy went, how it transformed, what form it became while pushing into meridians and across the body.

Slip up, even once and—

"Aaaargghhh," Arthur cried out, falling over and clutching his chest. The pain lanced through him, his chest muscles clenching tight in the worst cramps he'd ever felt. At the same time, it felt like a million ants were trying to eat the insides of his arm apart.

Chi feedback.

Whimpering, Arthur forced himself to breathe, to pull the energy that had gone down the wrong way into his body once more. He churned it through his meridians, transforming the energy back into its base state, struggling through the pain until it and the energy subsided.

Pulling himself upright in bed, he wiped the sweat on his forehead. Panting a little, Arthur closed his eyes as he waited for the energy to calm and for his mind to stabilize. A glance at the clock that hung in the room made his lip twist in humour.

Fifteen minutes in and he'd made his first mistake. If everything he had learnt about learning chi techniques was true, he could expect to make a hundred more before he could even begin to understand the basics of the exercise.

A few hundred more to get it right.

A thousand before he could hope to use it in combat.

But that wasn't, unfortunately, the only thing he had to worry about.

A mental command had his interface call up his status screen. There was a single line he had to see, though he could sense the difference within him too.

Energy Pool: 6/12

Yup. Each mistake was going to cost him energy. Which meant he'd have to spend time cultivating, drawing in the Tower's energy to refill his pool. All of which would take time.

And he had a time limit. Seven days.

No. Five. He should do as Lai Tai Kor said. Save a few extra days.

"Five days." A firm nod, then he banished those considerations for another day. Right now, all he could do was practise.

Force energy through the sixth meridian. No, too fast—

"Aaaarghh!"

Pain. Energy running rampant. Calm it, pull it in.

Roll over.

Get up.

Start again.

Reinforce skin first. Gently, let the energy seep in. Too fast and it'd...

Blisters. Growing as fast as he could look at them. The energy he pushed into his body was too heaty for it to control. He drew the energy back, wincing as his hand and arms burnt. By the time he was done, half of his hand was filled with clear, watery blisters mingled with a mixture of dark blood.

"Ugh..." Wrinkling his nose, Arthur wiped the skin clear, hissing a little at the pain.

Breathe, chill out.

Try again.

"Oooh, I'm hungry. So this why they say you don't bottom out your energy pool." Arthur glanced at his status.

Energy Pool: 2/12

Cultivators and Tower climbers didn't need to eat, not while they were in the Tower itself. The energy of the Tower itself fed them, made them immortal. When they left the Tower, that was when they started starving. Even consuming spiritual food—food originating from the Tower, infused with its energy—outside the Tower only worked for so long.

Eventually, climbers had to return to the Tower. And since you could never clear the same Tower again, eventually all climbers died, lost to the never-ending grind.

But that was for another time.

Right now, Arthur needed to cultivate and replenish his energy.

Closing his eyes, he meditated, pulling the abundant energy of the Tower into his body, gathering it to himself.

An hour later and six energy points returned, Arthur nodded to himself. Good enough for now. He'd start alternating meditation sessions with torture—ahem, practice sessions—from now on. That way, he would never run out of energy and could give himself a mental break.

He still had most of the day left to train. And four more days after that.

Gritting his teeth, Arthur dove back into the scroll.

Chapter 9

Standing in the four feet of space between the wall and bed, Arthur set his feet. He was not a huge fan of unarmed martial arts—only idiots thought it was better to fight using one's hands than a proper weapon—but he still learned it. There were a lot of times weapons just were not feasible. Or your weapon broke, or you had to throw someone or, well.

Lots of reasons not to have one in hand.

Which was why he knew how to throw a punch. Angle your body, raise hands to your chest and face height. Breathe in, on exhalation snap leg, hip, shoulder, and arm forward. In that order pretty much, as you dug in and pivoted, throwing backhand into a simple strike.

Of course, there was a new factor to this. He had to channel his chi at the same time, mixing it all together and pushing it forward into a single, explosive blow. He'd reached the standing and punching part two days ago, managing to corral his energy and even learning to release it when he was seated. Cross-legged. After a good minute of concentration and release.

Now it was a matter of learning to speed up the attack, such that Focused Strike was actually a strike. Then the next step, of course, was integrating it into his weapon. And then, well, more than a single limb.

Air shimmered, the explosion of power flaring around his fist as he finished the movement. He watched it dissipate and could not help but grin. It worked. Only took him a second or so of concentration too.

"Yes!" Arthur couldn't help doing a little jig. "*Siapa hebat?* Me. I'm amazing!"

For a few minutes, he revelled in his success. Five days to learn the technique. He knew it well enough now that he no longer needed the scroll. If only it wasn't keyed to him, he could have sold it off. Oh well.

No, five days was good. Problem was...

"I got to get going," Arthur said to himself, slumping back down in bed. He peered at the tiny slip of a window high up in the room, one that showcased not a slip of light coming through. If not for the lights running the edge of the wall—spirit lights, powered by the same energy that ran through him—it would have been pitch black in his room. "… tomorrow morning."

Then, his eyes drifted shut. Adrenaline and stubbornness had kept him awake for most of the five days except for quick cat naps and moments dozing off while meditating. Sleep debt finally caught up and he fell asleep.

"Could have been nicer about throwing me out," Arthur grumbled as he strode out of the beginners' village, skirting around tents that had been built surrounding it. The damn proprietor had woken him early in the morning and tossed him out without so much as a "good morning". Then again, Arthur had to admit, he preferred that to losing another day.

Especially since his eyes were still gummy and his mind exhausted from the days of work. On the other hand, physically he was doing pretty well. One advantage of being a cultivator here, he guessed. It also helped that being woken early meant most of the other cultivators were still resting.

Except for those three men who had strips of red on their arms, striding over to him. Striding with intent.

"Oh hell," Arthur muttered, hefting his staff and glancing around. Seeing no way around it, he took off, headed for the woods.

"Oi!" one of the men shouted. "*Mana* you *pergi*?!"

"*Ting kuai dan!*"

"As if I'll stop!" Arthur yelled over his shoulder, taking a moment to stare behind him. "*Bodoh ke?*"

Idiots indeed. Two of the people rushing after him were Chinese, the other Malay. Not that it mattered what race they were, if they were just going to beat him up, but it was strange to see a mixed-race gang. After all, racial lines were still quite prevalent, perhaps even more now when the government was struggling to pay for all the social programs they were giving out.

The forest line wasn't far, thankfully. It didn't matter how much the cultivators cut down in this land; the wood had a tendency to regrow nearly as fast as they could chop. If not for the fact that there had been a clearing around the village proper, they'd have had to camp in the woods. As it stood, it was only a short sprint away.

The woods themselves weren't Malaysian forests, which Arthur had to be grateful for. Tall trees and less underbrush. Not the crowded, sharp-edged, leach-infested undergrowth he was used to, ready to rip flesh apart.

But that might also mean fewer fruits and berries, and more importantly, it was easier for the men to spot him here, while in a proper rainforest he could disappear from sight after a few dozen feet in. No, here, the trio of pursuers could spot him a good 20 feet away.

"Stop!"

"I'm going to kill you!"

"Yeah, that's going to make me stop…" muttered Arthur as he ran. He wasn't dumb enough to stop, and he certainly had seen the pair of *parang* two of the men held. The third man hadn't bothered with anything that lethal, but a hard-edged stick with a band of metal at the end worked well enough to break bone and crush skull.

"Come on..." Cursing, Arthur yanked his staff, watching as it got tangled up in the nearby bushes. His breathing was beginning to grow a little heavy, even as he ducked and ran deeper into the forest, desperate to escape the trio.

They kept coming and, worse, seemed to be catching up. In fact, one Chinese man with a parang was outpacing his own friends, the gleaming edge of the long blade catching light. Casting one last glance back, Arthur made a quick decision.

He spun around one tree, took three steps and twisted, spinning the quarterstaff and setting himself. A mental count went off in his head, and as it hit one, he thrust forwards, blindly.

Part luck, part training. The tip of his staff slammed into the ribs of the man turning the corner, glancing off his hand to luckily plunge even more firmly into the man's chest. Arthur felt something crack, just a small shock and release on top of the bigger impact as his attack struck home. His opponent staggered back, raising a hand.

Only for Arthur to clip the fingers with a spin, which cracked them open and sent the blade flying to the ground. Another quick flick had the weapon knocked farther away, and before the man could do anything else, Arthur took off.

Leaving his opponent weaponless, gasping for breath and out of the fight.

One down.

But as the shouts from behind increased, he smiled grimly.

Two more to go.

Chapter 10

Tall forest trees, sticky sap on their trunks with sharp pine needles. That's what those were, right? Pine? Arthur heaved and panted, trying to dodge deeper within, missing the dense underbrush of Malaysia now. At least the temperature around here was a lot cooler, meaning that energy would not be sapped from overheating, from sweating.

Luck had him stumble at the right time, a foot catching on a hidden root. He caught himself easily, but a projected blast of energy clipped his shoulder where it would have struck him dead-on. Instinctively, he clutched his staff close as he spun around and fell, barely managing to get his feet away from the gripping roots—holy shit, were they actually moving!—before he crashed to the ground.

"Oh, you idiot! Bodoh! I had him!" The Malay cultivator snarled at the other man, shaking one glowing fist. "If you hadn't tripped him, he'd be down."

"He's on the ground, isn't he?" the Chinese man snarled back. With his parang, he cut off roots that had been moving under his command.

Eyeing the pair still arguing with one another a good 20 feet away, Arthur slowly pushed himself to his feet. It was when he was most of the way up that they turned their attention back to him, giving him a flat gaze as he attempted to sneak off.

"We're going to beat you and take you for everything you've got, boy!" the Malay said.

"Chop off a hand maybe..." the other man said, swinging the parang around with a grin.

"What?!" The Malay turned to his companion. "I didn't sign up for that. Teach him a lesson, sure."

"He cracked my brother's ribs! He's going to pay." The parang wielder stalked toward Arthur.

Seeing his chance, Arthur rushed forward, staff coming down to his hip. He threw the staff out, sliding it along one hand and guiding by the other into a straight thrust that would smack the Chinese man in the face...

Only for the man to casually duck, then slap the entire staff high into the air with his own blade. Cursing, Arthur attempted to control the flailing staff, even as the other man strode forward quickly.

Not quickly enough to stop his mouth from working, though. "I knew you were going to try that, boy. Cowards like you, you'll take every chance to attack those from behind."

"Ah Chu, you can't..." the Malay man protested, not moving to aid either party. Clearly dithering between the level of punishment and old loyalty.

Not that Arthur cared, not with what was happening. Instead, his focus was on the parang being swung at his head. Instinct had him give up on one end of his staff, letting it flop even as he stepped sideways, watching as the staff fell to the ground as he brought his own end up at an angle.

Deflection. Not a good one, since the edge of the parang bit into the wood of his staff, but not far. Heat-treated, hard as sin, the staff would take quite a few strikes before it broke. It still made Arthur wince internally.

No time to retreat. He threw the punch, not at the other man's face or chest, but at the retreating arm. Much closer range, much easier to deal with. It plunged in, energy boosting the attack to glance off the quickly retreating hand. The tip of the parang coming down caught on his own arm, cutting into him, but the shock of his punch made the other's hand spasm.

Remove the weapon, then fight. You never wanted to fight someone holding something sharp, not if you could help it.

Unfortunately, before Arthur could back off farther, his opponent lashed out. A spinning kick to his side caught him in the ribs, a pulse of energy similar to what he had used. A variation of Focused Strike that was stronger than his own, or perhaps the same skill but better executed. He felt two ribs break, his breath driven out of him as he flew backwards.

He hit the ground, rolling over and over, somehow managing to keep hold of his staff all through the fight. The impact of body against rough tree bark sent another lance of pain into a torso already burning with agony.

Chest constricted, unable to breathe, Arthur looked up to see his opponent charging, refusing to give him a moment to recover. As he stood, Arthur slipped his second hand ahead of his lead one that was still gripping his staff, levering the entire weapon upwards. It flicked a bunch of dirt and leaves into the sky, causing the other man to halt.

Arthur rotated his hands, sending the edges of the weapon spinning in a circle as it neared the bare-handed Chinese man. Before Arthur could strike, branches from the tree he was backed against reached outwards, gripping his body and yanking him backwards. His chest flared with pain, as he was lashed tight against the tree trunk.

The other man slowed a little, just enough to time his punch. The blow cracked across Arthur's face, slamming the back of his skull into the trunk. Little stars danced across his eyes. Then another blow, coming from the other side, catching his cheek.

A rain of blows across his face and, worse, his chest where ribs—bruised or broken—drove Arthur to distraction. Curses rained down on him as the other man lashed out, until Arthur lay slumped, blood and snot dripping from his nose, held up by the roots.

"I told you, you'd pay," growled the other man. "Now, you got anything to say? If you beg, maybe I won't chop off anything more than a hand."

Arthur blinked, letting out a low moan. A hand grabbed his hair, pulling bruised and swollen eyes to look up into the Chinese man's face.

"Well? You got something to say for yourself?"

Blinking a little, Arthur had to focus. He nodded a little, forestalling the slap that he could see coming and worked his jaw. He considered spitting at the man, but then chose to swallow the blood and saliva, to clear his throat.

"I... I do." Arthur's croak was barely a whisper.

"What'd you say?" The man leaned forward but kept a good grip on Arthur's hair. No headbutts here.

Good thing that wasn't what he was planning, Arthur thought as he finished channeling the energy in his body to his shins. It was a desperate move, trying to use a Focused Strike when he had not trained it on another limb. Desperate and risky, but pain and fear had driven him to take the chance.

One that sent his leg striking upwards, between his opponent's legs. Eggs were crushed against body and shin, shattering the man's hopes for the future. Even as he slumped over, pelvis cracked, the roots holding Arthur loosened.

His opponent lay on the ground, face white, a growing red stain around his crotch spreading across his jeans. Arthur blinked, only to find his last opponent staring at the two of them. Try as he might, Arthur could not find the energy to raise his hands or guard himself.

Eyes swimming, he wondered what his fate would be now.

Chapter 11

"*Gila. Kamu dua gila!*"

"A little crazy, yes," Arthur croaked out. He was surprised that the Malay man had not moved, either to help his friend or attack him. As he stood there, hands hanging by his side, his chest throbbing every few seconds, he was a little grateful.

"This is not what I signed up for!" the man said, staring at the two. "This… this is insanity! You killed him."

"Not yet, but he was going to maim me," Arthur replied. "Good as killing me, really. I just responded in kind."

"You'll, you'll bring them all on you." The man shook his head again, clenching and unclenching his fists. After a second, he shook his head. "No. I'm not doing this. You, you all, do what you want. I'm out."

Then turning, he strode away.

For a second Arthur waited, knowing the other would turn around. Trick him into lowering his guard. It was not until the other was out of sight that he relaxed, only to see the Chinese man beneath him stir, try to push himself to his feet, then failing that, crawl away. Cultivator strength gave one a significant level of endurance.

Eyes flat, Arthur stared at the man trying to get away. He weighed the options in his mind, the damage he had done, the possibility—no, the likelihood—of retribution. He sighed.

"I really wish you hadn't come after me." A quick bend, his hand plunging his eating blade into the back of the man's neck. A quick, efficient kill. Twisting the knife, Arthur rooted through the body, finding only a pouch filled with some small chits. Tokens for use as credits for trading in town.

Pocketing it, he cleaned the blade on the body and picked up his own weapon. Noise in the underbrush reminded Arthur of the remaining member of the party, only belatedly arriving. That injury to his ribs must have distracted the man more than he had thought. Either that, or he was just really bad at directions.

For a moment, Arthur considered staying and eliminating the threat. Another breath drawn in sent pain flickering through his body and he grimaced. No, he was injured enough. Best get going. Go out, stay out for a while for the others to calm down and relax.

Nodding to himself, Arthur picked a direction and plunged deeper into the forest. He had best get moving before reinforcements arrived. The very last thing he wanted to do was face the rest of the gang.

It would be rather inconvenient.

Two hours later, even cultivator-reinforced stamina had given way. Arthur grimaced, leaning against a tree and touched his side once more. His feet were wet and his pants too, up to his knees. Wading through a cold forest stream for half an hour and clambering up the stony bank so that he could throw off any tracking had been painful and highly uncomfortable.

Nearly as bad as the pain that shot through him with every breath. He'd broken his ribs before, once in a fight, twice more during training. None of the times had been as bad, and in all such cases he had been forced to be extremely careful about moving for weeks on end.

Yet now...

Another slow breath, carefully so that he did not displace healing bones and aching muscle. Because they were healing. This was Arthur's first real experience with the magical, accelerated healing that was part and parcel of life in the Tower. He was as grateful as anything for it.

It wasn't so much magical as fast, though he heard certain cultivation exercises took accelerated healing to the next level. A broken bone, instead of taking six weeks or longer to heal, became something that was fixed in a few days. Maybe a week at worse.

Cuts, inflammation of the body, fever, and common illnesses were uncommon now or they became incredibly deadly. Not much room in there; anything that could survive the Tower's accelerated healing regime was not your usual run of the mill illness.

For all that healing, though, he still had a couple of broken ribs and bruised organs and muscles. Pushing himself to keep moving required strength—strength of mind, strength of will, what have you—and there was only so much one could do.

Arthur now slumped against a tree, head leaning against rough bark. He breathed, waiting for everything to calm down, for his heartbeat to slow, for the twinges to slow. Wrapping his chest would not help, and it was considered bad form these days. Though... that was for everyone outside the Tower. Not taking sufficiently large breaths meant potential for pneumonia over the weeks of healing.

Did the medical advice change because he was looking at only a week?

A few moments of deliberation and then Arthur shrugged. Moving his body now, though it hurt and was even dangerous, was less important than potentially getting pneumonia in the future. Taking his shirt off hurt, but the roll of bandages in his backpack—that he thankfully managed to keep a hold on through the entire skirmish—was easily at hand. Getting it wrapped, though...

Well, those were a few minutes he could well do with forgetting. Especially since he could do little but breathe hard. No cursing, since you never know what was out there in the forest.

Then, after another deep drink of water, some trail rations and a time to just breathe, Arthur made his way deeper into the forest.

Oh, and one more thing. A glance at the compass he carried, so that he could make his way back. Hopefully. If he had not turned himself around entirely while running away.

It was little surprise to Arthur that he encountered the first of his non-human threats soon after. If anything, the fact that he hadn't found any until then had been more surprising. It showed how picked-clean the forest edge was. After all, the Towers were here to test them, and that meant populating the forest with an unusual number of predatory creatures.

Even if said predatory creature was a goddamn group of carnivorous golden monkeys.

Three of them, a small grouping that had probably broken off from a larger tribe. They swung down from the trees, using vines to launch themselves at Arthur. The first monkey's strike caught him by surprise, knocking his head to the side. The second glanced off his chest, sending an arc of pain through him. The third missed him entirely as he fell back.

A tug backwards and his staff swung upwards. He hit the ground, rolled and twisted, spinning his body around. His staff moved ahead of his body, sweeping ahead and impacting one of the monkeys that had not expected the motion.

The blow, however, was not as forceful as it could have been. It struck an arm, breaking it, but it did not push the monster away. Arthur's strength had been robbed by the pain of falling on his back, his still-injured ribs protesting.

Pain rushing through him, Arthur pushed on with much laborious force, his weapon sweeping back and forth as it threatened the monkeys. One monkey took to the tree branches, scrambling upwards. The other two threatened him, even as he backed himself to a corner while still making quick jabs and swings with his staff.

High above, the monkey that had climbed the branches jumped from one to the next, having grown silent even as the ones below shrieked louder. It stalked Arthur, waiting for its chance, getting into position. Baring its fangs, it finally plunged, swiping at him.

Only to be met not with the front of the staff that it managed to dodge, but Arthur sliding his hands downwards, shifting his grip such that the staff's backend where he normally kept grip of the weapon was flipped around. It caught the monkey in the stomach, the full force of its drop driving breath out of its body, bones cracking.

"Damn it," Arthur cursed, having gotten swiped still by a flailing limb. Blood ran down his lead arm, even as the monkey tumbled senseless to the ground. He aimed a kick, driving another monkey back and then brought a foot down hard onto the fallen monster's skull.

That, finally, stilled it. A moment later, even as he shifted his footing to something more stable and brought his weapon on-guard, the dead monster dispersed into light shards and a single core dropped to the ground.

Tower creatures were made up solely of the magic that powered all cultivators. All of them with a core within their body, much like human cultivators.

Grinning grimly, Arthur flicked his gaze down to the core and then waded forwards, going on the offensive finally. Now that the threat from above was gone, he could risk it. Time to finish it.

Chapter 12

The hollow in the slope of the hill, one created by a half-fallen tree, was just about large enough for Arthur to push himself under with minimal strain to his body. The addition of the tarp, a few sticks, and layering of fallen brush and leaves, and the entire place was actually rather comfortable. He needed to add more foliage and debris to the ground if he intended to lie on it for any length of time, what with the way the earth sucked away heat. But for now, this would do.

The new cultivator sat, finishing the *cha siu bao* he had brought with him. Funny, how even though he did not need to eat, the very act of it was calming. Even if the bao was a little stale. Thankfully, the rumors were true and the effect of the Tower extended to increasing the longevity not just of people but even foodstuff brought in.

Swallowing one last time, the taste of the white flour-bun covering and the sweet pork filling lingering in his mouth, Arthur took a swig of water before putting it all aside. His momentary break was for another reason, one he was rather in a hurry to review.

Fishing out the pouch he had dropped the three cores within, he pulled one out, raising the shard of crystalized, refined energy to his eyes. He stared at the orange-yellow colour of the material, then turned it over and over in his hands, dark brown eyes piercing the center.

Inside, the core flickered, ghostly images of the monkey it had drawn from appearing and disappearing, like *wayang kulit* puppets he had seen in school. Shadows cast from an internal light, fading away soon after sketching their minor plays.

"Now, if I remember right, these had a bounty on them," Arthur muttered to himself, calling forth the quest marker. It didn't take him long to find it and the trade-in value. "Ugh. One credit only? Basically worthless…"

He sighed, leaning against the firm earth wall, feeling a little of his heat leach away. He did so carefully, since his ribs were still aching. Damn injuries...

"Better to try cultivating one. I've got three, and it's not as though I need them," Arthur muttered to himself once more, then eyed the opening in front of him. He quickly moved a few branches and his staff, creating a tiny, spiked opening. It wouldn't actually stop anything that was trying to enter his hideout; but it would give him some warning. Good enough for the middle of nowhere.

Crossing his legs and putting himself in lotus position, Arthur placed the gem in between his legs. He closed his eyes and breathed, calming himself first. Then, feeling the warmth pulsing through the monster core in his hand, he began to gently pull upon the energy within.

It came in fits and starts at first, the lancing pain of refined energy hitting his own nerves like a sharp jab. He fumbled the energy grab the first, second, and third time, unable to keep pulling. Eventually, though, he got the hang of it, drawing just enough that he could handle the additional pain, slowly increasing until the draw was steady.

Pulling the energy through his body into his dantian.

A long hour or so passed before Arthur felt the core shatter, breaking up into motes of energy. Nothing left to draw upon, its exterior casing gone.

Opening his eyes, he pulled up his own status sheet again, curious to see what it had to say.

Cultivation Speed: 1
Energy Pool: 5/12
Refinement Speed: 0.01
Refined Energy: 0.01 (0)

Attributes and Traits
Mind: 3
Body: 3
Spirit: 3

Techniques
Focused Strike

Each basic core was worth a fraction of the refined energy then. At that rate, he would need a full hundred such cores—assuming he did not lose any to fracturing—to get a full point of refined energy. Which could be directed to increase any of his own attributes.

Still significantly faster than trying to refine energy himself. With his own basic refinement and cultivation speed, it would take...

"Ten hours for six points of energy, an hour to refine ten points, multiply by two…" Arthur flicked his fingers, working it backwards, and sighed. "Two hundred and fifty hours or so doing it the hard way. Or just a hundred hours the other way."

They always did say that cultivation was a slow process. Especially without proper cultivation techniques and help. Even a couple of more powerful cores would speed up this entire process. No wonder it was so important for the newcomers to get in good with established groups.

"Well, I ducked that shit up, didn't I?" Arthur muttered.

Another shake of his head as he discarded the thought. Not much he could do about that, not at all. Instead, the more immediate question was what to do about the other two cores. The first was for him to establish a baseline. The other two were money or...

"Who am I kidding?" Arthur pulled out the second core. He was not going back to civilisation anytime soon. Not with so many people looking for him.

Right now, he needed all the strength he could get. And if that strength was slow in coming, that was just the way it had to be. He had a relatively quiet and safe location. He had a couple of cores and an injured body.

The best choice right now was to stop trying to find problems. To simply cultivate and heal. Once his ribs no longer ached, he would get to hunting once more.

Firm in his decision, Arthur cast a glimpse outside, ensured there was nothing coming, and then closed his eyes, falling into cultivation once more.

Time to work.

Chapter 13

Eighteen days and dozens of monsters later, Arthur was feeling better. It had started with a lone snake that crawled into his tent and nearly eaten him alive. Most recently, he had been pursued by a pack of tiny cat-like creatures who'd found him while he was picking mushrooms for a gathering quest near his new camp.

No signs of further pursuit by the cats, and now Arthur was left to heal in peace—or as much as one did in the wilderness. Thankfully, the first level of the Tower was set up more as a training ground than a standard Tower level. Unlike upper levels, which were full-blown battlefields, the first few levels of a beginners' dungeon were a gradual introduction to the world of kill or be killed.

All of which meant that monsters, while persistent and common, were not endless. Unless Arthur was looking for them, he could only expect a couple of battles a day at most. Most of the monsters present acted like real animals—even if they were larger and more dangerous—which meant they would choose not to attack someone like Arthur if he left them alone.

All in all, it meant he could spend the time cultivating and reinforcing his own strength. It was what many cultivators did in the beginning, spending time in a Beginners' Tower to maximise their strength.

"But the drain is the problem, isn't it?" Arthur said, turning over a monster core in hand. "I can already feel it..."

Every day, on a constant basis, his energy fled. Used, twisted, and swallowed by his body, consumed just like food. Every time he increased in strength, increased his attributes, the drain would increase. Sooner or later, the drain level would outpace any potential gains from staying on a floor. You had to climb further up to make use of the denser energy.

Artificial limits, artificial boosts, artificial monsters.

"Might as well be in an episode of *Westworld*," Arthur sighed. Still, he should not complain. With a flicker of his hand, he eyed his own Status.

Cultivation Speed: 1
Energy Pool: 5/12
Refinement Speed: 0.01
Refined Energy: 1.03 (0)

Attributes and Traits
Mind: 3
Body: 3
Spirit: 3

Techniques
Focused Strike

Eighteen days to get a single point of energy. Now, he did have another four cores, but each only gave a single point. Going higher in the Tower meant more powerful cores, which meant a larger amount of refined energy for the same amount of time.

For many who had friends and family outside, who could not afford to just sit on the lowest level, it was better to climb faster, even if one lost out a little on the optimal power progression. Otherwise, you could work with teams, paying for cores that others gathered for you so that you could continue one's ascension.

"Can't let the women or parents or kids wait..." Arthur said, remembering the faces of the hopeful, the grief-stricken, the lost in front of the Tower. That was his advantage, the advantage of one desperate enough to walk away from a potential life outside for a few decades.

He could wait, build his strength, take his time. His family, what there was of it, they would understand. Better to survive and progress slowly than never exit.

Shaking his head, Arthur focused on his point of refined energy. It was time, time to pour energy into an attribute and make himself stronger. Better. That was the entire point of refining the energy after all, taking the next step. The question was where.

Mind was useful since it would make his ability to comprehend energy techniques, fighting styles, and cultivation exercises better. On the other hand, he had none of those with him at the moment. The only other thing that would improve along with his Mind stat was his ability to manipulate the energy within him, increasing the amount of energy when he refined.

On the other hand, increasing Body would increase his base energy pool. That meant he could hold even more energy, useful for fights where he used his Focused Strike ability or whatever technique he learned next. It also meant he could build up more energy within himself so that he would not need too long a break when he was refining energy. Of course, there were the physical benefits of increasing Body too, like being stronger, faster, and more flexible than a normal human. Powerful cultivators could be six to seven times stronger than mortals who had never entered the Tower.

And finally, Spirit. It was the speed he could draw energy from within his body, refining it in his core. It also dictated his ability to handle the various energy types. It was, perhaps, the least important attribute at this time since it only directly affected his cultivation speed. But in the future, it was an attribute that determined many important things like poison resistance or aura control.

Biting his lip, Arthur reviewed his options before he nodded to himself, understanding exactly what he needed to do.

Body it was, for now. Until he got to the breakpoint, he would dedicate points to it. He pushed the refined energy in his core, the coursing power that felt like live electricity and that could only be manipulated by spirit and mind together. He ran it through nerves, muscles, and bones all through his body, flooding energy into them and feeling it ripple through him, rebuilding him.

Pain, pushing through him, tearing him apart. He bit his lips, as he was remade. Thankfully, it was only a point of energy so the change, the pain, was not that significant. It hurt him, rebuilt him, and finally... finally! He was done.

Standing up, Arthur looked around, grinning a little. Time to test out his new body.

Chapter 14

"Monsters, monsters, where are you? I'm here to stab you dead and dance on your corpse..." Arthur sung as he walked through the woods. Of course, he was not completely insane. He kept his voice low as he went along, eyes darting in search of more monsters. In the end, though, he was really looking forward to the monsters and drawing them to him was easier than simply stalking around.

Occasionally, he'd look down and scan the ground, searching for tracks. Not that he had much experience tracking, but you did not need to be a genius to pick out the rather large deposits he was following. The fact that they were somewhat fresh meant... well. That they were somewhat fresh. It was not as though he had studied how quickly excrement solidified in a magical realm.

"Is there a difference?" Arthur mused, breaking off his impromptu song. "Is there a guide? And also, if they're magical monsters made of tower energy, why do they eat?"

He slowed down, turning that thought over and searching the surroundings. After a second, he frowned as he looked at a branch slightly more yellow than normal. Something nagged at him as he moved closer to it, the way the colouration was just a little too yellow for the brown branch it hung over, the way it swayed a little as one side drooped. A broken limb about to fall?

No. It was a little too sinuous.

"Ah, hell!" Arthur cursed, reflexively thrusting his staff. The staff tip hammered into the top of the swaying creature's body, knocking it upwards.

Its attempt at an ambush thwarted, the constrictor hissed, pulling itself further up the branch. Arthur was not stopping though, shifting his stance to brace the staff higher before pushing the weapon forward into a thrusting strike. The staff missed the curled body as the snake shifted away, dropping its body lower to swing towards him.

Staff revibrating through his hands after the failed impact, Arthur retreated. A small notch where his attacks had landed showed, even as the swinging constrictor dropped in the air towards him.

"Not so easy," Arthur cried as he stepped backward, swirling his staff around. It struck at the falling constrictor that seemed to swim through the sky as it repositioned itself in mid-air, only to be batted aside by the staff.

Landing on the floor, the monster hissed. Another twist of his hands sent the wooden implement flying at the snake, narrowly missing as the creature dodged. Then it hissed, its body glowing before it blurred, crossing the distance of six feet to Arthur in a flash.

Jerking backwards, Arthur threw himself away from the striking snake. He almost managed to do so, his body moving faster than ever, but the damn thing's ability had caught him by surprise. His reach advantage gone, the snake had managed to wrap its head and the first coils around his lower leg and begun the process of pulling itself towards him, aiming to crush muscle and bone.

The ground seemed to rear up, striking his back as Arthur lost his balance from the new weight. Staff was abandoned as he grabbed the parang he had acquired earlier, using the sharp edge of the machete to swing at the still unwrapped body of the snake.

Once, then again, the blade sliced the glittering snakeskin. Panting widely and kicking a little with his free foot to reposition the snake as it twisted and turned, he struck again and again, blade gouging deep into its body with each attack.

Even as he did so, the bleeding monster kept crawling up his body, gripping as it snaked upwards. His body creaked, his muscles shrieked in agony as they were crushed. But eventually the snake's movements grew sluggish, his attacks taking their toll.

Until, finally, the monster stopped moving, leaving itself wrapped around his lower body, its head around Arthur's hips.

Panting, Arthur flopped onto the ground even as the body began to disperse.

"Bad monster. No cookie for you."

Snakes were evil. Arthur didn't want a snake dropping in on him again, so he kept a closer eye on the sky after that. And so he noticed a stalking, cat-like creature, its presence only given away by chance reflection of its eyes as the clouds parted above.

Clouds in a tower. How strange, but each Tower level was like that. A world in itself. No one had any good explanation for it, though the prevailing theory was that each level was actually a different dimension.

He spotted the cat before it could jump at him, and this time, his staff had been of use. Smacking it away each time it launched itself at him, Arthur managed to control the distance admirably, never allowing it near him.

The *kuching hitam* had no ability to speed itself like the previous monster, only claws that dug into his staff and left carved scars like divots. Annoying, but a few hard strikes were enough to concuss and then kill the monster. Afterwards, he collected the crystal core as usual and moved onwards.

Searching for more trouble.

Birds soared high above: parrots, popinjays, even a hawk or two. Most of them stayed high above the canopy. They were no danger to him; though Arthur still eyed them with some concern.

"Perhaps I should get a bow?" Arthur mused. Taking those birds down would be an easy cheat, though the problem was finding the bodies afterwards. Once they broke up, he would be looking for a hand-sized crystal. "Probably not worth it."

Shaking his head, Arthur dismissed the thought. He was hunting bigger prey anyway. His body felt good, even the bruises from the damned snake had started to disappear. The single point increase to his attributes was telling, but not to the extent that he would have liked.

Faster, stronger, healthier for certain. But it was not like his strength had doubled or even increased by a third. Maybe a tenth more? It felt like that. Just a marginal increase that a few hard, dedicated months of exercise would see. Maybe a year.

The difference, of course, was that it had happened all at once. So some of his reactions were a little too fast, his movements jerky.

Good thing, then, that the bigger monsters he was hunting had yet to appear, the spoor and their broken trails still showing up once in a while to even his own untrained eyes. In the meantime, he could practise on these other monsters that kept appearing, everything from monkeys to cats to—

Giant squirrel with big insane eyes and even bigger sharp front teeth.

"Aaaargh!" Giving up on his staff which the nimble squirrel kept dodging as it snuck in closer, Arthur dropped it and kept his arms close to his body. When the squirrel finally threw itself at him, he punched outwards. The squirrel bounced off his hand, tiny body crunching under his fist before it flopped backwards, rolling in a ball.

Shaking his hand out, glaring at the cuts the big teeth had left, Arthur remained crouched. The giant squirrel chittered at him as it got back on its feet. Then, to Arthur's surprise, it ran off, disappearing into the nearby undergrowth.

"What?" Arthur muttered, eyeing his back and sides.

Long, tense minutes passed before he finally chose to believe that it was gone. Intelligent monsters. Now that was worrying. Nursing his bleeding hand, now wrapped in emergency bandage, Arthur shook his head.

Hopefully not many of the other monsters out there were that smart. Otherwise, this was going to be a problem.

Chapter 15

Arthur's eyes grew wide as he poked his head around the tree. The sight before him was enough to chill any foolhardy thoughts about taking on the monster he had been tracking. A single *babi ngepet* was something he could deal with, but an entire herd? That was guaranteed to end him.

"I need a damn spear," Arthur grumbled to himself as he pulled away, intent on putting some distance between him and the grazing herd. Herd? Was that even the right term? Then again, did he care?

Nope. Herd of *babi* it was. Time to run away, as fast as he could.

Yet, halfway on his careful backtrack, the wind shifted. Earlier he had been downwind of the group, but now it was blowing his scent toward the demon pigs.

Terror ran through Arthur's body. He turned and ran for it. No need to concern himself with noise or attracting attention anymore. He did not bother to wonder if they might smell and attack him. At least one would charge, and the rest would definitely follow.

He ran, crashing through the brush, pushing himself as fast as he could. Leaves and low-hanging branches slapped at his face, unseen spiderwebs caught in his mouth, making him spit and cough. Unseen ivy gripped at his feet, and roots seemed to reach out of the ground to trip him.

Every step, a struggle.

"I'm getting a damn Agility trait when I can!" Arthur swore, pushing on.

Crashing sounds from behind began to reach his ears. It sounded more like a herd of elephants instead of pony-sized pigs, all of whom were hellbent on running him down, goring him apart and eating him. Alive, preferably.

That thought made Arthur look back and his eyes widened, for the sight of the monsters barrelling right through tiny trees, exploding their very substance, was terror-inducing. He stumbled over a root he did not see and sprawled forward.

Years of training had him turn the fall into a roll, and he yanked his head in time to adjust the roll to the side a little, allowing him to bounce off the big tree directly in his path rather than crash into it. Luck, pure luck saved him as that fall and shift in direction caused a suddenly accelerating *babi* to smash into the tree. Shards of wood exploded, one catching him on his cheek as he kept running, but the monster was momentarily caught in a shattered trunk.

"Up, got to go up," Arthur panted, looking around. The next biggest tree had no low-hanging branches. But he had a staff.

Five steps as he accelerated as hard as he could and then slammed his staff into an upraised root, vaulting himself upwards. He hit the second lowest hanging branch in the stomach and arm, losing grip of his staff and crumpling around the branch as breath was driven out of him.

Hanging curled around the branch, he felt it tremble again and again as the monsters caught up, slamming into the tree. Screams of rage as impact shook both the branch and his body, forcing him to slowly pull himself upwards. He was shivering in fear as tiny, hungry, and angry eyes stared up at him.

Quivering and alone, Arthur crawled towards the trunk. All the while, the monsters waited for either Arthur or the tree to fall. The biggest of the *babi ngepet* was goring the trunk with its ivory tusks.

"Immortals preserve me, what have I done?" Arthur whispered as he stared below.

"Monster, monster, monster below. One wants to kill me and another to eat me…" Sing-songing the words, Arthur whittled the wet green branch he had broken off. The *babi ngepet* had chosen to stop attacking the tree since the hardened trunk was mostly impervious to their attempts. "But all I got, is a little spear-o-me!"

Then silence on his part. The monsters were still snorting, tearing up the ground, and occasionally slamming into trees in an attempt to dislodge fruits and flowers to gorge themselves upon.

"Yeah, that didn't work, did it?" Arthur said. "Now, they say you need to fire harden this. But I got no fire, got no reach. Nothing but what my teach... told me? I suck at this rhyming thing."

Below, there was a drizzling sound, a pitter patter of water falling. The smell rose up, and his nose wrinkled as the acrid stench of wild urine made him wince. Now they were trying to fumigate him out.

"Hey! Stop that!"

Of course, the creatures did not seem to care. More importantly, they might even have understood him for they began to do what animals did, pissing and shitting all around the area.

"Seriously, you're magical creatures. Why do you need to do that?"

Again, no answer. But with the branch sort of sharp, Arthur slipped his parang back into its sheath, made sure it was strapped in, and stared at the monsters below. He had an idea. A dumb one. But it was only slightly less dumb than trying to run across the tree branches and jump away. So he figured that was a win.

Looping his legs around the branch, he steadied himself and went over the motions he needed in his mind. Finally ready, he swung himself sideways, using his legs that were wrapped around the branch to force him into a circular spin.

At the same time, he pushed energy into his spear as he channelled a Focused Strike such that he swung around, then extended his arms and weapons. The attack hit the *babi* directly beneath him, the sharpened branch bending a little before exploding through the hardened monster's skin. It plunged deep within, almost halting Arthur's swing entirely.

Using the crude spear as leverage, now embedded in the monster, Arthur swung himself back upward even as he grabbed with his other free hand the branch he was still hanging from as he bent from his waist. He pulled himself back up, the spear making a deep slurping sound as it exited the wound of the monster, moments before the entire tree shook as the herd charged it.

Holding on for dear life, Arthur waited until they stopped attacking his tree before he repositioned himself and looked at his results.

One monster injured, retreated. Another one had taken its place directly beneath him, along with a few others that were goring the tree and attempting to shake it apart. Incensed, they did not seem to care anymore that the hardwood was resisting their efforts.

It looked like it was going to be a race between Arthur and the *babi ngepet* to see who would win.

"Time to swing..." Humming to himself, he watched the one below him until it was in position and swung back down, repeating his attack. "Got to get your groove on..."

Chapter 16

Releasing his feet, Arthur dropped to the ground, staring at the crystals that littered the area. He grabbed his staff as he looked around carefully. Amidst the corpses that were dissolving into crystals were also the shattered remnants of his impromptu stakes, a half-dozen falling to the forest floor as the bodies they had stabbed disappeared.

He had not managed to kill all the *babi ngepet*. He wished he had, for the crystals that they had left behind would have been of great value to him. But the monsters had chosen to leave after a half-dozen died. Then, when he baited another two into rushing him and getting killed by acting like he would come down, they had finally left.

Of course, he was not willing to accept they were all gone. But failing to find signs of their presence, Arthur quickly picked up the remaining crystals and chose to retreat to his cave. It was time to go back with his spoils.

He had pushed his luck enough for the day, after all.

Another *kuching hitam* assaulted him on his way back. The monster even managed to drop down on him, tearing into an upraised arm and leaving long scratches. He had to throw himself into a tree, using his greater weight and ferocity to pummel the monster until it fell down and he crushed its head.

Woozy, bleeding, and exhausted, Arthur managed to make his way back to his cave before collapsing, barely having the energy to cover the entrance to hide his presence.

The next morning, he washed and rebandaged his wounds before taking a seat beside his cold fireplace ring, tucking feet underneath him as he extracted a crystal from the *babi ngepet.* The monsters had been strong, and Arthur could sense the greater strength in these cores.

Enough, perhaps, to push him to the next grade.

Eyes half-closed, he began to cultivate, drawing forth the energy from the Tower crystal. He would not risk his life like that again if he could help it. Time was not the concern, but safety. He had played the fool enough; now it was time to train.

The first time he finished the core, his lips peeled back into a grin. It was as he had guessed: cores from *babi ngepet* were stronger than other monsters'. Not by much, but even a minor increase in strength meant that using their cores was more beneficial than the average monster he had encountered.

Now he really regretted letting the rest of the herd leave, leaving him with only eight such cores. Still, between his earlier hunting and what he could process, he would not leave this cave until he breached the next level.

Checking the brush he had pulled before his tiny cultivation cave, Arthur nodded at the simple safeguards that included a string and bell. He had nothing better, not yet; but one day he would have proper safeguards.

Proper ways to care for himself.

Till then… he would just substitute hard work for wealth.

Days later, Arthur opened his eyes. He did not have enough cores to last his entire cultivation period and had been forced to cycle between cultivation and refinement regularly. Between the depletion of energy that living in the Tower entailed and the lack of proper light in his cave, he had lost track of time. Even worse had been the wearing away at his mind as the boredom of the repetitive cycle had taxed his willpower.

If not for a reminder of his near-death experience, he would have given up long ago. Only the goal of achieving the next tier had kept him forging ahead, until today.

Almost immediately upon achieving a full point of refined energy, he had dedicated it to his Body. Floating before him, sensed deep within, was a greater question. Now that he had achieved the next tier, what trait should he pick?

Attribute traits were what made cultivators different from one another. They were as different as the fish in the sea and numerous as the grains of rice in a cooking pot. There was only one rule: the more general a trait it was, the less powerful it was. A trait like Hardened Form might make an individual more robust in general, but it would not stack up against someone who chose Iron Skin for physical impenetrability. Yet, if they were to receive a palm strike or other blunt damage, they would suffer much less.

Generalisation or specialisation? Some mixed and matched, specialising in traits from one attribute while having more general traits in other attributes. Others even mixed within an attribute. In the end, it was up to the individual and the degree that they expected to grow. For specialisation, in the short-term was less powerful overall.

Arthur had spent months poring over well-known traits, debating with himself about what to take. Among Body attribute traits, specialists favored Lightning Reflexes, Catlike Agility, and Iron Bones. But more general traits like Improved Stamina and Robust Health had their own adherents.

Turning over his own experiences, Arthur deliberated what to choose.

Right now, his greatest threats were the *babi ngepet* that had a tendency to attack in groups. He had no chance of killing them unless he was lucky enough to repeat his trap. Dangerous, very dangerous, for more than once he had nearly slipped to his demise.

Then there were the *kuching hitam*. He hadn't noticed the one which had attacked him on the way back, not until it dropped. If he hadn't gotten an arm up in time and sacrificed the limb, he would have had his throat torn out.

After that, killing it had been easier. It was nowhere near as tough as the *babi*, what with being a cat. But it didn't matter if it left him gagging on a torn throat, now did it?

So, what to do? Faster reflexes would let him get out of the way of attacks, maybe let him shift his spear a touch quicker to strike better. More speed would help him run away. But greater strength or an overall boost to his constitution might allow him to face the *babi* individually without being torn up.

Strength would help him to kill. Strength would end threats with a single strike. But strength required a proper weapon, or else his poor staff would shatter.

No. Not strength. Speed, perhaps, or reflexes.

Yet, he could not help but remember what had happened with the monsters he had hunted, with the cultivators who had found him.

Perhaps his decision was not optimal; it would not make him stronger immediately. Yet, instinct drove him to choose it, knowing he would not have the option of adding further traits until much later. For now, it would suit him.

Making his decision, he transmitted his choice to the system and felt the energy rush through his body, into his head, and he choked back a scream. Pain, blinding pain, drove him into blessed unconsciousness.

Chapter 17

When he woke, he woke to a new world, one that he had never seen before. Everything was brighter, sharper than ever before. Paradoxically he did not need to squint, for his eyes adjusted to the brightness, the vividness of what he stared at without an issue. It only took him a moment to realise that the inside of his shrouded cave now looked nearly as bright as full daylight.

Enhanced Eyesight was the generic version of a specialisation, in one sense. There were other traits, like Night Sight or Infravision, that could be added, but while those expanded upon the base ability of a human's eyes, they were very context specific. Enhanced Eyesight, on the other hand, was an overall improvement, even adding a few colour variants while sharpening eyesight and expanding range.

Just as important for Arthur, the new trait also increased his ability to pick out camouflaged individuals and notice inconsistencies in the environment faster.

For if there had been one thread with all his encounters, it was that if he had known what was to come, he would have changed his actions. Whether it was to block the *kuching hitam* earlier or just to back away faster from the *babi ngepet*, knowledge beforehand would have given him options.

Over the next few minutes, Arthur concentrated on objects close and far, testing out his new vision as much as he could within his cave. When he was finally satisfied, he pulled up his status screen, confirming his current level.

Cultivation Speed: 1
Energy Pool: 5/12
Refinement Speed: 0.01
Refined Energy: 0.00 (2)

Attributes and Traits
Mind: 3
Body: 5 (Enhanced Eyesight)
Spirit: 3

Techniques
Focused Strike

He was on the way, though in other ways he was just beginning. Still, he could no longer spend time in this cave. If nothing else, the stink from sitting still and cultivating had begun to truly bother him, and soon enough, he expected that other monsters would find him.

Indeed, better to exit, wash himself and his clothing, and test out his new enhancement. If he could collect the necessary cores, then he could perhaps find another location to stay and cultivate. But for now, he needed to clean himself and stretch his legs. Arthur grabbed his backpack.

Locating the river was not difficult. More of a hindrance was the hesitation he felt at plunging into the cold water. But after probing the area and waiting for potential waterborne threats and finding none, Arthur finally committed to washing up.

Clambering out of the river, he grabbed at the towel he had set aside, wiping his body of soap and pond water. He wrung dry the underwear he wore, moving over to his weapon and watching around him. Out of the corner of his eye, he spotted movement. A whipping motion with his staff caught the hand-sized spider in the body, crushing it to the ground where poison slowly leaked out.

A second later, the monster burst into light but left no crystal.

"I hate spiders," Arthur muttered. Doing one more slow pivot check, he ensured that no monster was creeping up on him before he shed his wet underthings and climbed into fresh items. He wrung the rest dry before wrapping it up in his backpack.

Clothed, armed, and newly rejuvenated, Arthur slipped the backpack on and began the process of searching for monsters. He moved carefully, making full use of his new trait to spot movement in the distance: the bending of branches and the sway of monsters creeping through the forest.

High in the trees, a *kuching hitam* crept along branches, waiting until Arthur was nearly beneath it. It leapt, paws brushing against wooden branches as it pounced at the cultivator beneath. Claws extended, viciously sharp and aimed at his throat.

The moment the cat jumped, Arthur stopped playing dumb and swung his staff. He caught it high on the neck and front paws, striking it away from his body and into the tree it leapt from. The wet smack of feline body against tree resounded, and the monster attempted to regain its feet as it slid down, one paw broken.

On three feet, it tried to stand but met its end moments later as Arthur's staff crashed down on its body, breaking its spine and ending its defiance. The monster soon disappeared, leaving behind its crystal.

"Score one for Enhanced Eyesight."

Picking up the crystal, Arthur scanned the area once more. More monsters were waiting for him in this forest. Monsters, and who knows what other gains.

Humming a little, Arthur forged in deeper, searching for easy kills. That, after all, was the point for now. No hard fights, no massive monstrous battles between him and a herd of animals or against multiple cultivators.

Perhaps a cowardly way of progressing, but it was also smart.

Chapter 18

Days passed, with Arthur snatching quick moments of rest late in the evening, cultivating the various cores he acquired during the day. He headed for the looming mountains he noticed in the distance, picking his way parallel to the river he had found. It would lead him to the mountains where the greater density of energy would increase his cultivation speed, provide fresh water—useful for keeping his body hydrated, which while not entirely necessary, thanks to the Tower, still felt refreshing—and ensured he had ample hunting opportunities.

If there was one negative to moving close to the river, it was the lack of locations to rest. His best options were under fallen logs and small overhangs where he managed to build a temporary abode. It was on his third night after exiting his latest cultivation spree that Arthur stumbled, literally, as he put a foot through rotting branches, onto another construction like his own.

After extracting himself with curse words in three languages and some difficulty, Arthur spent a little time reviewing the construction of the tiny house. There were numerous little tricks in the construction of the small lean-to that he drew upon: the use of stripped-down vines as a binding material to keep branches together; adding multiple branches of cut leaves to help shelter the interior.

He was particularly happy he had not walked into the lean-to from the side for there was a hastily constructed and now-rotting set of wooden spikes. He had nearly impaled himself on them when he extracted himself earlier. Interestingly, there was yellow-grey sap on the spikes, a colouration that was unusual to the vegetation around.

"Poison? Bodoh. What kind of idiot leaves things like this lying around?" Arthur pushed the stakes away, breaking them, and shoving the ends into the dirt. He had, briefly, considered carrying the spikes with him. But not knowing how old the poison was, if it was still effective, and how to carry it safely had him dismiss that idea.

Even more interesting was the gleam of glass on the ground. Rummaging a bit and extracting it from the earth, Arthur turned the pill bottle over in his hand. A peek into the opening showed that it was empty, a discarded remnant.

"Now I really wish I'd joined the Boy Scouts," Arthur sighed. No way of telling how long ago this had been. A week? A few months? Someone with wilderness knowledge would know, maybe. His own understanding was limited to knowing how to survive and travel through various outdoor environments.

And how much of Nature's rules were different in a Tower, he had no clue either.

"Still…" Arthur rubbed his chin. Maybe he could follow along. Other than the foot-sized hole in this residence, it was not too shabby. It would save him a few hours, to make use of the lean-to. And since it was on this side of the river, there might be other makeshift shelters further up. If he watched for it, followed the same deer path that the cultivator had been using, perhaps he might stumble upon another lean-to.

Preferably not literally.

His staff whirled, striking once, and then again at the *kuching hitam.* It pushed the monster back but did not break bones or throw it aside. This particular beast was nearly twice the size of the previous *kuching* he had fought, its claws shaving the edges off his staff whenever the two came into contact.

"Here kitty, kitty, kitty." Another spin, the top of his staff dipping to crash into the earth. The cat had managed to skip aside, just enough to dodge before it pounced. Unfortunately for it, Arthur had been waiting for that and threw a Focused Strike snap-kick right into the cat's body, sending it flying. He had only received a few light scratches on his arm.

Bones cracked as he kicked the monster again and it spun through the air, managing to get its feet underneath it just before landing. Then it met a full-speed thrust that caught it on the top of its head, staff cracking it open and leaving the monster reeling. Another full-speed strike broke it at last, leaving the body to disperse into light.

"I might have gone too far," Arthur said to himself, tearing the sleeve off his shirt. He wrapped a stained bandage around his arm, sealing the wound, and sighed. Rather than throw bandages away, he had been washing them after his wounds had healed, but even that cost-saving measure was coming to an end.

Scooping up the crystal, he turned it over, marvelling at the pulse of energy he could feel. Much stronger than before. Not quite double, but he was certain it would be at least half as strong as the crystals found from monsters close to the beginner village.

"Forward or back?" Tapping his foot, Arthur breathed. The monsters out here were a bit of a challenge. The last *babi ngepet* he had met, alone by itself, had nearly destroyed the tree Arthur had led it to charge. Only Focused Strikes had worked to kill it. The battle had left Arthur panting, exhausted and sweaty.

On the other hand, each crystal was worth so much more.

Just as intriguingly, he had found more signs of the mystery cultivator over the past two weeks as they travelled deeper in, towards the mountains. Stories of finding hidden cultivation caves and secret manuals had driven Arthur along, but now the danger of continuing was growing.

For a long pause, he debated one way or the other. Then glancing up at the sky, he nodded to himself. It was afternoon now, and he was closer to where the cultivator had likely built his abode for this evening if he went forward rather than back.

He would rest there, and perhaps even stay long enough to finish refining the monster cores he held. After which, he would return to a less dangerous area.

Arthur returned to the deer trail he had been on, keeping a wary eye out for additional problems.

"Good luck or bad?" Arthur could not help but wonder out loud as he bent over the remains of the corpse. He had caught a glimpse of metal as he crept forward along the deer trail, only to be confronted by the torn remnants of the cultivator. Bones had been stripped clean by scavengers, portions of it pulled away or gnawed upon. Only the belt buckle and the ripped backpack lay testament to his death.

"Don't mind me... you don't need these, right?" he muttered to the corpse as he pulled at the broken backpack to poke within. Most of the clothing and other sundry goods had been scattered or tarnished, though he did take the eating utensils, knife, and compass.

To Arthur's greatest surprise, there was also a manual lying in there, untouched by the dirt. Magic must have kept it pristine, though the fact that he could open and read it meant it was not a manual purchased at the Tower store.

"Good thing, I guess?" Arthur mused. "Then again, untested cultivation exercises can also be pretty, well, lousy... But beggars can't be choosers."

He slipped the manual into his backpack before taking a longer walk around. Food, drink, all those were spoiled or tossed aside. Clothing was of no use to Arthur, though the first-aid pack had bandages and other items he could scavenge. However, one rather important thing was missing...

"*Celaka!*" Cursing, Arthur spotted not what he was looking for but something he had hoped to find since he saw the corpse and the first pill bottle. But the creatures that had killed the cultivator had also torn open the bag, shattered the pill bottles within and consumed their contents.

Not willing to give up, he bent down and started digging in the dirt, brushing away glass shards. After all, pigs or cats or tigers, it didn't matter—they had no fingers for delicate work.

Fingers pushed aside earth and leaves, eyes squinting at the soil. It was, to his surprise, not the area around the shattered glass that gave him what he needed but underneath a tree root a short distance away. Something glinted, revealed as he swept the ground before him, a little bit of dirt knocked aside.

Craning his neck, Arthur squinted and there it was: the outline of a pill bottle, one so small that it could only contain a single pill. He extracted it gently. The noise of a single pill rolling within made him grin.

However, he did not open the bottle. Cognizant of potential trouble and seeing nothing else in the vicinity, Arthur made a circle of the surrounding area. He finally found what he had been looking for, a short distance from the body.

Sword and sheath, the weapon half-drawn. Soil, moisture, and rain had marred the half-drawn steel and a quick cleaning was not going to fix the problem. Still, Arthur chose to take it. He attached the sheath's sling to his backpack.

A free weapon was free.

He chose to leave then. Whatever had killed the other cultivator, he definitely did not want to meet it.

Chapter 19

Moonlight. Travelling through the night was dangerous, and not because of the lack of illumination. The Tower's first floor had not one but three moons, each providing sufficient illumination. At times, when all three were high above, it was as bright again as twilight. Even when the moons were moving across the horizon, it was still brightly lit enough that night-time travel was viable.

No, the issue was nocturnal monsters. Normally, Arthur would have avoided travel during this period, but he felt the need to leave the corpse behind. Whatever had killed it was more than powerful enough to end him.

Better to run.

Step after step, he pushed onward at the end of day. Things were moving out there, and more than once, he had to stop and keep his head down while waiting for whatever was out prowling in the darkness to go by him. The occasional scream of dying prey and the hacking cough of a cat or another monster had him tensing before the silence would deepen and he would move on.

Even for all the care that he took, he was unable to avoid encounters. The first was a frog-humanoid monster that came crawling out of the thus-far safe river. It caught him by surprise, forcing Arthur to strike downwards with his staff and crush head and limbs when it bit into his ankle. He found himself limping after killing the thing, the poison that been embedded in its jaws forcing him to move carefully as his leg had numbed.

The speed of his retreat slowed even further with his new limp, forcing Arthur to debate the wisdom of continuing to travel. Eventually, he chose to keep going, figuring that moving slower—forced or not—would help mitigate the increased danger.

Perhaps it was because he was moving more quietly, or because he was used to hunting *babi ngepet*, but he spotted their presence further up the river, sleeping in a small clearing in a circle of mud and shit. That stopped him from stumbling directly into the herd.

Crouching low, favouring his injured leg, Arthur bit his lip. The monsters were sleeping, unaware of his presence. A full herd of monsters were there for him to take advantage of, if he dared. Of course, he risked waking them if he made a mistake. On the other hand, there were over 20 monsters there—a surplus of cores.

Looking down at his staff and then at the sword he had found, Arthur sighed. He was not the most conversant with the sword, but he had been trained to use one. And a sword was better than a staff, at least for slaying something that was sleeping.

Arthur lay his bag and staff down, then slowly limped forward, doing the best he could to ensure that his foot did not drag too much. It was tense work, lifting one foot after the other as he moved closer. The first was a big male pig, snoring heavily.

Forcing himself to breathe slowly, Arthur raised his sword and positioned the weapon about a foot and a half above its foreleg and then shifted the weapon again, down the torso a couple of inches. He did not know the animal's anatomy that well, but he assumed that was likely where the heart was.

His hands trembled a little, eyes darting over sleeping forms all around him. None seemed to be awake, none seemed to notice the quiet killer among them. Then, pushing with everything that he had downwards, Arthur slid the blade into the monster's body, puncturing heart and lung with one swift motion. The monster thrashed a little, but with his full weight bearing down on it, the creature did not move too much.

One down.

Slowly pulling his weapon out, Arthur moved over to the next body, limping with each step. The next was a small baby monster. For a second, Arthur wondered what the point was of having baby monsters in the Tower, but in the end, he knew there was no point asking such questions. All that mattered to him was that the monsters yielded crystals—the baby ones had smaller ones, perhaps, but still crystals.

Sword raised, then plunged down. The pig barely even twitched as he killed it.

Then he moved to the next monster. And the one after. Breathing slowly, adrenaline coursing through his body with each second, Arthur found that the numbness in his leg was fading. The poison was running its course, though so were his nerves.

Each twitch, each muffled snort, it made him wince.

Arthur forced himself to continue, moving from body to body. He was nearly done, working in a circle towards the center where a massive boar that led the group slept. Rather than approach it directly, Arthur had been moving from monster to monster on the fringes since they were more spread out.

Perhaps it was the smell of blood that littered the surroundings, perhaps just the turning of the breeze that alerted the giant boar. Even as Arthur plunged his blade into a sow, the creature kicking and snorting lightly, the herd's leader twitched awake. An eye opened, and then the head turned as it snuffled.

Tiny evil black eyes met Arthur's own brown ones. His eyes widening, Arthur jerked the blade out from the sow as the boar clambered to its feet, mud sucking at its body with an audible slurp. The smell of shit and blood, mud and river water washed over Arthur in sudden proximity as adrenaline, faded from the long minutes of killing, rushed back into him.

Reacting first, Arthur hurled himself into a two-handed lunge, thrusting his sword forward. Targeting the area between the monster's eyes, he threw the full strength of his cultivator body behind the attack even as he triggered Focused Strike.

Surprised and still waking up, the boar managed to turn its head away, long tusks tearing at Arthur's arms. The blade did not stop though, tearing brown skin and glancing off hardened bone in the skull to slip into an eye. His blade penetrated deep, bursting and bouncing off the insides of the eye socket as the monster continued its turn and Arthur was thrown aside.

Arms throbbing, he staggered backwards as blood ran down the torn muscles along one arm. His hand spasmed a bit around the grip, forcing him to clutch tighter with his other hand.

No time to wait though, for the *babi ngepet* was turning back. Already too deep into the fight and with more of the herd waking up, Arthur threw himself back into the fight, swinging the blade around to cut and chop at his opponent.

A couple of good strikes which did nothing but bounce off thick hide and hair, a barely dodged goring, and then Arthur was forced to flip away as the other monsters charged. Retreating hurriedly, he twisted at the last moment to stab down at another boar, an adolescent only half the size of its monstrous leader. A chop took off its front leg, leaving it crippled as Arthur kept backing off into the treeline.

Fight from the trees, that was all he could do. Either that or retreat. But greed had him eyeing the monster cores left behind and imagining the one in the lead boar. He would not give up this attempt, injured or not. Not without a try.

Weaving between the trees, monsters were charging from all directions. Arthur was forced to put the full extent of his boosted attributes to use. He was stronger, faster, more flexible than he had ever been—as good as an Olympic athlete outside the Tower. He could do this.

Or so he told himself, even as he barely managed to dodge attacks. He was left limping and bloody as monsters bowled him over or tore into his back. An unlucky blow, unseen from a wily monster towards the end of his battle, threw him out of the woods and back into the small clearing, forcing him roll and clutch at his injured back.

Their leader arrived, pawing at the ground. Half-blind, it had let the others of its herd chase Arthur around the forest, waiting until he had been cornered before it made its move. Now, with the cultivator only just beginning to recover, it charged.

Still on his hands and knees, Arthur looked up to see the monster rushing him. Time seemed to slow down, even as his gaze sharpened and focused upon the monstrous boar's open mouth that kept moving up and down as it charged. There was a small gap, a tiny space between big lips, heavy tusks, and savage teeth that arrested his attention.

Instinct driven by the unusual focus overtook Arthur and he stepped to the side, into the monster's blind spot. It turned its head, legs shifting as it changed direction a little, but Arthur was not planning on running too far.

No, he was going to follow the flow of monster's movement.

Back hand powering the thrust, lead hand guiding it, he followed his gaze, timing it just right to slip through the tiny gap. Past tusks, lips, and teeth into the soft palate of its throat. Skin within the creature's mouth gave no resistance, and his sword went all the way in.

Then the monster hit him, and Arthur was flying, sword still embedded in

Chapter 20

He woke up a second later, still hurting. He pushed himself upwards, struggling to rise as he gripped the sword. Ribs were cracked, his hip twisted, and his leg bruised from where he had hit the ground and eventually a tree. To his surprise, the monster was dead. But there were still other *babi ngepet.*

Three left. Not the largest; in fact, one was an adolescent, half the usual size. Arthur's eyes narrowed, even as the monsters charged. The first to move forward was the largest of the three, charging in a straight line. Propped up against the tree, Arthur breathed slowly, knowing he had one chance.

Timing. It all came down to timing. Figure out how fast the monster could reach him, figure out when it would be too late to turn, figure out how long he needed to dodge. If he was uninjured, he could do that math on instinct. But leg injured and body tired, he had to guess.

And hope he was not wrong.

Now!

He dodged, and the *babi ngepet* turned its head a little to track the cultivator's fleeing body. A pained whimper as he hit the ground, bouncing off roots and grass before the monster hit the tree. One tusk embedded itself deep in the trunk, the entire tree shaking.

Pulling himself to his knees, he lurched forward and plunged the weapon deep into the boar. A twist of his hand, pulling the blade out and widening the wound. Then he turned on his knees, the rumble of even more monsters approaching making him wince.

Damn it.

Too close. No time to dodge. Thankfully, it was the adolescent. Rather than run away, he stayed focused instead and braced his sword against his hip. He shoved forwards at the last second, locking his body tight as he allowed the smaller pig to skewer itself on his weapon. It still bowled him over, hundreds of pounds of meat and fury pounding into his chest and legs.

Bruising, pain, even worse than before. The only good thing was that the momentum drove the monster off his body mostly, a heave of legs and arms pushing the bottom half away from him. Arthur whimpered and twisted, seeing the monster turn and slow down rather than bowl over its own kind.

It ran past him, buying Arthur time.

Time for him to struggle to his feet, to stand as he desperately pushed. Pain, fury, arrogance. He should never have tried this, never taken the risk. But he would not die here, not when he was so close to finishing this battle.

One last *babi ngepet.* One last fight.

It was charging him, and he could barely stand. He could not dodge aside and had no tree to trick the monster into hitting. All he could do was gamble. Hands holding the sword, shifting his grip a little so that he held it parallel to his arm, he focused his entire body as he hurled the weapon.

Focused Strike but twisted, pushed into his weapon and thrown. The weapon flew, sinking deep into the monster's lower body even as the energy shoved into the weapon forced the creature to stumble, stop, and...

Die.

Arthur's jaw dropped, blinking at the sudden end of this battle.

Exhaustion and pain took over as adrenaline faded, driving both shock and consciousness from him, leaving him to slump senseless on the ground among the corpses.

Waking up was a painful process, one that almost made Arthur choose to fall unconscious once more. Yet, recollection of where he was forced him to his feet, hand scrambling for a weapon and finding nothing. He searched around with bleary eyes, memory of what happened coming slow.

"Right, right... I might have... might have thrown. Thrown... aside a weapon or two." Hunched over broken ribs, he stumbled over to his sword and picked it up. Once, twice, and then a third time he attempted to sheathe the weapon, only succeeding on the last try. Then he bent over again to pick up the nearest crystal and tipped too far, landing on his face, only barely managing to roll a little as his body gave way.

For a time he just lay there, staring up at the sky. Pain pushing and fading in waves. All he was able to do was hold on like a tiny raft of consciousness on the waves of agony. Eventually, the tide swept out and Arthur rolled over to grab and store the crystal in his pouch.

"Bugger dignity… *tak ada duit, guna* dignity."

Suiting words to action, Arthur started crawling around the clearing. On hands and knees, stopping occasionally when the pain was too much, he picked up the monster crystals. Each breath made his ribs ache. Each time he put weight on his left hip or arm, he wanted to cry. Under the light of paired moons, he could see the dark bruising all along his limbs.

If there was one thing to be grateful about, Arthur knew it was that none of the broken ribs had pierced his lungs. Whatever internal bleeding he had was confined. A cultivator could heal—and heal fast. He had never heard of one dying from something as prosaic as a brain bleed or aneurysm.

Still, the faster he collected the crystals, the better off he would be. There was no telling when other monsters would stumble upon him, and he was in no shape to engage in another fight.

Eventually, the crystals were all picked up, the last couple taking him longer than the previous dozen. Between pain and the way his sight kept doubling up on him, Arthur was having trouble focusing. By the time he stumbled over to his backpack and staff, he was ready to collapse.

Squatting, Arthur stared at the heavy pack and winced. There was no way he was going to be able to pick it up and carry it, not with his ribs, not with his hips and arm. Making a decision, he reached over and grabbed the pack and dragged it, headed for a fallen tree he recalled seeing.

Once there, he stuck his staff diagonally across the fallen tree, threw a tarp he extracted with great labour over the top of the entire thing, and then absently threw leaves and branches on top of the hastily assembled camouflage.

Then, crawling into the simple construction, he crashed to the ground and fell unconscious once more.

Chapter 21

Waking was pain, waking was discomfort. A branch dug into one side of his stomach, making Arthur roll over with a groan and whimper. The impediment hurt, his body ached all over, and worst of all, he could feel how his body was reacting to the numerous injuries. Too hot, he was too hot.

"I'm running a fever, it'll be pretty severe..." Arthur pulled at his pouch, extracting a crystal that he had risked his life to get. At first, he considered trying to cross his legs to cultivate and then gave up on it. You could cultivate in any position, but it just wasn't as efficient as sitting upright and cross-legged.

Then again, there were rumors of yogis who put themselves into pretzels and did marvellous things with crystals. Something about guiding the flow of energy through chakras and breaking through blockages.

He had done some basic research into it on the Internet, but with most things, either the secrets were locked under five-easy-to-make payment plans or just untrustworthy as sources. In the end, he was discouraged by the secrecy of it all, that people didn't seem willing to share their knowledge. Add the fact that each individual was unique, and there probably wasn't an approach that worked with everyone. He'd given up on learning the truth of the matter after a few fruitless weeks of searching.

Now, eyes closed, hands gripping the crystal, Arthur could not help but wish he had spent more time on that research. Maybe he might have been able to do something more than just draw on the core in his hands, ever so slowly.

Create a suction force in one's hands to drag the energy out of the stubborn core, pull it through your meridians, and into your upper dantian. Then, push it through your body again to the middle and then lower dantian, each process cleansing the core of the Tower's influence and making it your own.

This was the most basic method of cultivating, one that almost every cultivator had stumbled upon after entering the Tower. Some believed the Tower imprinted that information on human minds, others that it was a natural process of life in the Tower.

It didn't matter for Arthur so long as it worked.

But pull as he might, he could feel pain that threatened to tear his concentration aside, the heat in his head and the fogginess in his mind.

Almost instinctively, he pushed some of the energy into the parts of his body that still ached. It made the pain worse, though at the same time, Arthur felt a greater connection to those areas. He felt the flow of chi enter his wounds, his cells soaking up the additional energy as damaged cells were destroyed and replaced with new ones. Scabs slowly detached, as the platelets and cells holding them to the wound were eaten and replaced by new, undamaged cells.

A small portion of Arthur's mind, the one not focusing on pulling energy into his body, watched the process all across his body. He could feel the way he exuded and dumped the created waste, the way his body hungered for nutrition which came from the Tower and his own body itself. He felt his body growing even warmer; metabolism sped up even further as infection was fought off while his own body worked overtime to convert sugar and fat to energy.

Yet, for all that, it was the Tower energy that supported the majority of his body, that allowed it to heal at that speed. And while force-feeding his wounds with energy did not seem to be the most efficient method, Arthur could not help but notice how the body stole energy from different points of flow to aid itself.

Testing, carefully, he shifted his flow. Sending energy when it was not fully cleared but when it had passed his upper or middle dantian at different periods to the wounds. He had so many wounds to experiment on—old and new, bruising, cracked ribs, split open, bleeding cuts and gashes, internal bleeding, weeping infections and more.

Energy was good, but specific energy taken at different times seemed to work better for each type of injury. Given time, given a refined energy source rather than the raw energy of the Tower, Arthur realised that he could speed up healing—so long as he was careful.

More than once, flashes of pain ripped through him as he sent refined energy the wrong way. Or the wrong time, flooding a wound that was not ready for the flow. Yet, he persevered, testing and pulling, extracting energy from new cores when his initial ones were consumed.

Hours passed as Arthur cultivated the refined energy, pulling it into his body. A small portion of each core went into his dantian, the majority being spent on healing his body. As he processed it all, he found himself improving in use of the energy, requiring less of it each core to undertake the same amount.

At some point, the infection disappeared. The pain reduced, his injuries going from critical to just serious. Enough so that Arthur stumbled out of his makeshift tent, leaving it open to air out while he travelled to the water carefully.

Stripping down to his underwear, sword still strapped to his side, he washed himself as best he could to remove the old blood and gunk across his body. He hissed in pain as the cold water hit wounds, as he scrubbed off dirt, blood, and sweat. Even catching a whiff of his own body had made him want to retch, so doing this was a necessity.

Once he was clean, Arthur stumbled back to his tent and stared at it, debating whether to move it once more. Aired out or not, it still smelled of human for sure. But thinking of carrying his pack, of attempting to leave, made him shake his head in the end.

No.

In turn, he spent a long, laborious hour to properly camouflage his residence before he stumbled within. He supped on one of the travel rations, needing the feel of rice and meat, of crunchy vegetables and succulent meat. A man could survive on Tower energy only, but who would want to?

And then, crossing his legs and propping both staff and sword such that they blocked the entrance, he returned to healing. Yanking energy from monster cores into his own body even as he poured it into his wounds and dantian.

Long days passed, time flowing onwards, until he was mostly healed, and Arthur had refined the methods of healing himself as best he could. Then, and only then, did he open his eyes and stare at the notification that had appeared.

Technique Learnt: Accelerated Healing – Refined Energy (Grade I)

Not a complete waste of monster cores then.

Chapter 22

Days later, Arthur finally chose to break away from cultivation. He had completely used up the majority of his cores and progressed his cultivation a little, enough that he now felt comfortable leaving his hidden residence. Twice, he had to step out to kill a monster that had come a little too close to locating him, once late at night and another time whilst he was in the middle of cultivation. No longer did he consider his hastily-made abode safe.

Not that it really was that safe to begin with, but the mind is willing to trick itself when it has four walls and a roof. Even if that roof was thin fabric and a bunch of cut leaves. Then again, Arthur knew, his safety lay in both the size of the forest surrounding him and his concealment, not the strength of his walls.

It was time to leave, and that meant packing up, stretching, and washing. His clothing looked much the worse for wear. The extra change of clothes he had brought—more tops than bottoms as befitted any good camping trip, and more underclothes and socks than anything else—were both dirty and worn. Living constantly in the outdoors and fighting monsters was hard on clothing.

Staring at the stained and torn shirt he had put on, Arthur wrinkled his nose. Perhaps his plan of staying outside of the beginner village for years on end was too flawed. Unless he chose to be naked, he was going to have to return to resupply.

Pondering his options, Arthur made his way downriver, back towards portions of the forest that were a little less dangerous. He still remembered the fallen cultivator, the pill that he still had stored away. He had considered taking it, but not knowing what the pill was actually for, he had hesitated. Taking the wrong medicine at the wrong time could kill him, or at least damage his body and set him back.

In the end, he had chosen to wait until he could get it analyzed. There were risks and then there were risks—and this one just seemed foolhardy in the extreme. As it stood, the rusty sword that he wore on his hip was a good find in itself. With some care, it would last him a little while longer before it broke. And if it did break, he might still make use of the broken sword head by strapping it to his staff as an impromptu spear.

He actually would prefer that in a way. Spears were nice: they had the reach to keep monsters away and the flexibility of a staff. And, they were useful as a walking stick when you had kilometers upon kilometers of land to cross.

Making his way back through the woods, Arthur detoured when he spotted the occasional monster, taking them out with ease. He might not have grown stronger since his journey upstream, but he had grown more confident and that added a surety to his strikes that had been missing.

Nearly dying and getting a healing technique had both done wonders for his confidence.

It always seemed that the path back was faster than the one into the unknown. Even if he was not retracing his way entirely, Arthur soon found himself in familiar environs. To his surprise, though, he heard voices in the distance, shouts and screams.

He frowned, cocking his head to one side and debated what to do briefly. He was no upstanding hero of justice, but then again, he was not a fan of just walking past like a blind passerby.

Slipping forward, marvelling a little at how much more comfortable he had grown moving in the forest over the past few weeks—months?—since he had been in here, Arthur sought out the shouts and clash of blades. He kept hold of his staff but put away his backpack since carrying that into battle was a bad idea.

Damn, he wanted a portable storage device.

His first sight of the fighting group made him frown. One side was a trio of women, all of them wielding polearms. On the other side were four men, though only two were still standing their ground. These two, wielding parang and sabres were blocking the spear attacks of the three women, while their compatriots kept trying to run away. Interestingly enough, the entire group was a mix of races. The men were Malay and Chinese, while the women were from all three major races in Malaysia.

"*Jangan lari!*" one of the men kept shouting, waving his sabre around. "Stop running. *Kita mesti lawan sama-sama!* If we don't fight together, we'll lose!"

"Bodoh*!* You can die first." Clutching his stomach, one of the other men turned tail.

As though incensed by his compatriot's words, the shouting man shifted aside, opening a gap. Sensing it, one of the women thrust her spear forward, plunging the weapon directly into the back of the running man, skewering him.

"Rani! Keep to the line!" another woman ordered, swinging her own halberd to beat the male leader's swinging sabre aside, barely saving the flinching Rani's arm.

"Sorry, sis!" Rani pulled her spear back and retreated, but the two groups were still locked in battle.

Arthur crouched in the bushes, biting his lip. He wasn't sure who was in the right, who was the aggressor. It was clear the fight was for keeps; both groups were bloodied and willing to kill. In fact, as he hesitated, he saw a hand skewered, a leg chopped, and then the owner impaled in short order, leaving only two men alive—one was their leader, who continued fighting.

"No way. I give up. Mercy!" pleaded the other man. Throwing his parang aside, he clasped his hands together and collapsed to one injured knee. "Please, sis!"

"Fool!" his leader snarled, suddenly reaching to his side and weapon. That motion left him open for Rani to thrust her spear, over-extending again. Because of that, she was caught when he threw powder in the air, purple dust and smoke exploding across the clearing and obscuring vision.

The Indian woman stumbled back, clutching at her eyes, waving her spear carelessly in defense. The halberd-wielder pulled her group back until they were in a tight line, whereupon she hissed.

"Violet poison mist. Low-grade poison. Just take the antidote pill and wash your eyes out. And stop breaking the line, Rani!"

Spluttering out the water she poured onto her own face, her spear dropped to the ground, Rani grumbled. "I hit him! I felt it go in."

"But now he's gone," the leader muttered as the poison mist disappeared, revealing the corpses of those they had been fighting and the thrashing body of the man who had attempted to give up. Their leader was missing.

"Yeah, well. We have other problems." One of the other girls said, turning and pointing her weapon at where Arthur was hiding. "Get out here, you coward. Don't think I can't smell you!"

Cursing, Arthur stared at the aggressive looks the group shot him, debating what to do.

Damn his curiosity and greed.

Chapter 23

Arthur hesitated only for a few seconds more before he chose to stand up. He waved a little to the three women, still holding on to his staff as he offered them the most disarming grin he had on hand. It was a good one too—he'd been told it was a little rogueish and charming. A hint of little-boy mischief in it.

It bounced off the glaring women who gestured for him to enter the clearing.

Once again, he hesitated. His choices were either run like hell right now or talk his way out. And he rather thought he had a better chance at negotiating peace than outrunning the women.

"I'm not with them, if that's what you're thinking," he began immediately. "I just heard the fighting and came to see what was happening."

"And play vulture once we left, right?" sneered the girl who had found him. She was tall, probably of some Northern Chinese descent. Didn't use to have a lot of them early on, since the initial wave of settlers to Malaysia came from the south; but once China had grown more populous, many Northern Chinese arrived.

"If you left anything, yeah," Arthur admitted. "One man—well, woman's—garbage is another's treasure, right?"

"Scavenger." The woman spat to the side and muttered something in Mandarin, too low for Arthur to pick out. Also, his own Mandarin sucked. After all, he was a KL boy after all—a native of Kuala Lumpur— and Cantonese was his dialect. Heck, he could even pick out a word or two of Hokkien, but Mandarin was no longer in much use except by those who'd gone through Chinese public school. And those guys were annoying.

Arthur tried not to look offended. It was not as though he were stealing after all. Or killing.

"He's weak," Rani said. "Come on, if we chase Budo down now, we can capture him."

"You think you can catch Budo?" the leader snorted. "As good as he is at fighting, he's even better at running. By this point, he's probably a good few kilometers away. Anyway, running off to catch the bird in the bush when you have one in hand makes no sense."

Arthur offered them a tentative smile as his grip tightened on his staff. "I'm really not a very tasty bird, though. Nothing much for you to steal, beyond a few crystals."

"Quick to admit you own anything," the leader said. "Not scared we're going to rob you?"

"Scared? Yeah. Robbery's never fun. But you seem rational and in control, so that's a bonus. Better than drugged out or in withdrawal or doing it for the first time," Arthur replied.

"You been visiting Shah Alam a lot then?" Rani said, her eyes crinkling a little in humor.

"Not by choice. But I've done a few deliveries that way before. Almost not worth the money, you know?"

The girl made a face as she nodded in agreement. "Damn tongs."

"Yeah."

"If you two are done?" the leader said, tapping the edge of her halberd against her body. "We still need to decide what to do with him."

"That's your job, isn't it?" the Chinese girl said with a smile.

"I…" she faltered, then sighed and nodded. "Fine. I'll take your word for now. But why the hell are you this far out here?"

Arthur grimaced. "I had a little bit of a run-in with people when I first arrived. The, umm, Suey Ying tong got in my face. So I got in theirs. Been out here, you know, powering up."

"Suey Ying… beginner…" the leader frowned, trying to remember what she had learnt. Then, her eyes widened as she recalled the details in full. "You're the fool who killed three of their people! They've got quite the bounty on you."

"Yeah, I assumed that." He sighed. "Well, thanks for the confirmation I guess."

"If you're idiotic enough to antagonise them, I guess you're not an enemy. But we sure don't want you hanging out with us."

"Now that's just hurtful," Arthur replied.

"Whatever. Stay out of our way, we'll stay out of yours." The leader gestured to the other girls, who had just finished looting the bodies. "Got it?"

"Yeah, yeah."

Rani frowned, looking back and forth between her boss and Arthur before she leaned in. "We can't just leave him here. He's going to get killed."

"Not. Our. Problem." Pushing Rani along, the Chinese girl hissed, "We've got a mission, damn it."

Arthur watched as the group moved off, leaving him in the clearing. He bit his lip, considering following them before he shook his head eventually, leaving them alone. Whatever they were up to, it was none of his business.

He did check the corpses and the bags of equipment that the girls had not taken. Extra clothing, basic hygiene kits, a sewing kit, and a bunch of pots and pans for cooking, along with a pair of tents. He eyed the tents for a second, then replaced his own worn-down one with these better-quality options. He took the rest of the equipment in short order.

No food, which was fine. He could survive on Tower energy, though he was really missing actual food. No first aid supplies, no pills or even a boot knife. Still, even the extra sets of clothing were a boon to him at this point.

Having stripped the corpses of everything the women had chosen not to take, Arthur made his way out of the clearing. He had a little bit of a jaunt in his step.

This was a good day.

Which was, of course, why an hour later he found a sword against his throat and a glowering, angry man staring back at him over the weapon's edge.

Chapter 24

"Seriously, boss, I'm not with them." Arthur gulped, even as the other man finished tying his hands up in front of him. Not that Budo was listening to him. His one major protest had seen him struck across the head, leaving him with a nagging headache and blood trickling from an open scalp wound.

Budo ignored him further, shoving him backwards so that he was propped against a tree as he went through Arthur's backpack. He tossed the stolen clothing, tent, and other camping gear aside with casual disregard. He'd already pocketed the small bag of crystals that Arthur had kept separate.

Luckily, so far, he hadn't searched Arthur's body too thoroughly and had missed the small pouch he'd slipped on the inside of his pants. It held the pill he had found. He didn't know what the pill was, but outside of the disposable crystals, it was his biggest gain. Well, besides his sword—and he couldn't shove that down his pants to hide it. He wouldn't want it nicking the other, more important rod he had down there.

Finished with her perusal, Budo put the tip of his sword against Arthur's neck, making him raise his head. "Where are they going?"

"I don't know!" Arthur said. A second later, he hissed as Budo pushed the blade against the side of his throat until it bled. "Be careful!"

"Mmm... you're right. I should just chop off your fingers instead. Less chance of you bleeding out too quickly," Budo said, moving the sword away from Arthur's neck.

Arthur stuck his tied hands between his legs so that the man couldn't get at them easily. Not that other parts of his body weren't vulnerable. He'd been placed against the tree and forced to sit down, so all he could do was wait.

"I really don't know anything. I never met any of you people before. I was just getting some clothes!" Arthur said, hating how his voice grew higher in pitch as the sword waved in front of him. Even so, he flicked his gaze around, searching for a way out of this. A way to escape. His feet hadn't been tied up, thankfully. And his sword had been discarded to the ground nearby. As he shifted and squirmed, the leaves beneath his body crackled and broke.

"Then you're no use to me." Budo drew back his hand to thrust the blade.

In that small gap, Arthur acted. His feet had dug into the dirt a little and with Focused Strike pushed through his feet, he kicked upwards. Not directly at Budo, but so that he could fling the dirt and leaves at his opponent. For a brief fraction of a second, Budo was surprised before he lashed outwards, thrusting his sword at where Arthur had sat before.

Too late.

Arthur had rolled aside immediately after kicking away, pushing himself into a backwards roll around the tree, knocking his own shoulder on the trunk. He came up on his feet even as Budo tore his sword out of the trunk, sap and bark spraying in an arc as he did so. Then, choosing prudence over valour, Arthur turned around and ran for it, hands still tied.

"I'll kill you!" Budo roared behind him. Yet he didn't chase after Arthur immediately. Arthur assumed the man was busy grabbing his belongings, rather than leaving them behind like Arthur had himself. Or maybe his kick had actually put some dirt into his opponent's eyes.

Either way, it gave him a small head-start and Arthur intended to make full use of it. He skimmed around in a long circle, intent on not running in a straight line. His gaze darted across the surroundings, searching for ways to throw his opponent off.

Kuching hitam over there. Don't get too close. But he wanted to get close enough that it was alerted and started stalking him. He made sure to run by, pounding away as fast as he could. If he did this right, the two pursuers would run into one another and fight.

Not that he expected the *kuching* to do much to Budo. He was not that lucky, not by far. But it might buy him another minute or so.

He pushed himself, jumping over logs, ducking under the branches. Kept pushing. Spun around the giant spiderweb that he barely noticed until he ran through it, wiping at his face with still tied hands. Arthur kept moving, trying desperately to find ways to slow down his pursuer, chart his escape and undo the knots around his hand.

Thankful Quan Yin the idiot had not bothered to tie his hands properly. Probably never thought Arthur would try—and manage—a real escape. Even so, for all his success, Arthur knew he was on a ticking clock. On that note...

"HELP! *ORANG GILA NAK BUNUH SAYA! TOLONG*!" Arthur kept screaming and running. Maybe...

"I'm going to chop you up!" Budo snarled, all too close by.

A quick glance back had Arthur spot the man pounding away behind him. He was fast gaining on him. Arthur held his view for a second more before he turned back around, just in time to dodge a tree, nearly knocked off his feet as he bounced off it and scraped his bound arms raw.

Then, he kept running, counting off in his head. At the last second, he threw himself to the left, a little too slow for the cut that ripped blood out along his back. Still, it gave him a few seconds as Budo got his balance back.

Arthur crashed through thick brush, only to realise there was a steep hill beneath. He had a fraction of a second to take all that into account, before he was running down the steep cliff face, desperately trying to keep his balance as feet kept kicking out.

"Wait until I—Aaaargh!"

Arthur wanted to look back, but he could not afford to do so. He was barely managing to pick out places to put his feet, his enhanced senses spotting dips and twists in the ground. He would have spotted this damn cliff too, if he had actually been paying attention instead of worrying about the man about to stab him in the back.

Large crashing sounds behind him and to the side had Arthur wondering what was going on. A second later he found out as Budo sailed past him in giant leaping bounds to help manage the sudden rush downwards. He was so focused on leaping like a gazelle down the cliff he had forgotten to even swing his weapon at Arthur as he passed.

Not that it mattered since both of them were rushing to the bottom of the cliff face and Arthur had no way to stop his own headlong rush. Not without possibly breaking his feet.

One last jump and Budo was in the air, arcing through the dangerous sleet right at the bottom of the hill, almost recovering some of the altitude he had lost while rushing downwards.

Without thinking, Arthur changed direction a little. He jumped too, hands held out by his side as he hit Budo with his shoulder. It was only at the last second that he found himself screaming, unable to believe he was doing something that dumb: "*BANZAIII!*"

Chapter 25

The pair crashed into one another, Arthur throwing Budo's planned trajectory off course entirely. The pair slammed into the ground moments later, Arthur's initial impact cushioned by his opponent's body. Bouncing off body and ground, they rolled until he managed to stagger to his feet, his arms and wrist throbbing.

Good news. His hands had managed to free themselves. Bad news, that was because he'd broken some bones in his hand and wrist. Further good news: Budo was struggling to get up and looked worse for wear after falling and being crushed. Bad news: he was still standing and looking even angrier than ever.

For a fraction of a second, Arthur debated running. If Budo had managed to injure one of his legs, Arthur might still get away. His own legs hurt, but nothing was screaming broken or twisted at him. Just "slammed into ground and branches repeatedly at high speed."

Then as Budo staggered to his feet, hands bare of weapons and looking angry but woozy from a bleeding wound on his head, Arthur made up his mind. He was done running, and especially done running from that asshole.

Letting out a yell, he charged forward, forming energy around his fist. Budo eyes cleared as his enemy neared, his grin widening in savage glee as he dropped a little and waited for Arthur to reach him.

Only for Arthur to jump and twist, throwing a reverse axe kick that arced up high. A last-minute flinch made Arthur miss his target, leg coming down on Budo's shoulder and neck rather than temple and head. Budo crashed backwards even as Arthur recovered, spinning around with his energy-laden fist ready for a Focused Strike.

Unfortunately his opponent had recovered just as fast and stabbed forward with fingers held straight. They plunged into Arthur's side, sinking into the flesh just under his floating ribs and eliciting a pained grunt. Budo tore his fingers out, blood dripping from them. The pain from the eviscerating strike radiated through Arthur.

His control of the energy surrounding his own Focused Strike disappeared even as his hook hammered into the side of Budo's head. Much of the energy and power had been robbed from the twisting blow, as Arthur's pain and surprise messed up his attack.

Budo still tottered aside, his eyes going blank for a second. It seemed repeated strikes to the head were a bad idea. The pair stepped back for a second, each of them dealing with the wounds they had acquired before they surged at each other as though a start gun had gone off.

The pair exchanged a flurry of blows, jabbing, crossing, and blocking strikes. Within a few rounds, Arthur understood that he was outmatched. Budo was faster and stronger, though he had a bad tendency to flinch when he was hit.

Making a choice, he stepped much closer to Budo. In-fighting was not his preferred method of doing battle, but it had the advantage of not being the preferred fighting range for most others either. Some people actually liked getting close—grappling or aggressive snuggling, as he liked to term it. But stand-up in-fighting with elbows, headbutts, knees, and short-range hooks? Not the same.

Budo reeled backwards, trying to get away to a range he was comfortable at. In-fighting was for the crazy and insane, the stupid and violent. There was nowhere to go, no way to distance yourself from the harsh panting, the breath on your face, the spittle flying and the crunch and pounding impact of blows. No way to escape blows, just mitigate them. Hit harder, push with knees or angle with shoulders and body to disrupt balance.

Power generation was all kinds of weird too; no long wind-up attacks that came all the way from the proper twist of an ankle and snap in the hip but had to form and extend in short, twisting motions. Off-balance, on one foot, using muscles directly from the core or in the back.

Back against the cliff face, nowhere to retreat. Budo was struggling now, losing the most important part of the fight. The mental one, where even if he was stronger and faster, he was beginning to pull in and protect himself, instead of looking for ways to hurt Arthur.

As for Arthur, he kept hitting, hard and fast, shoving hands aside, using elbows to dig in strikes. Down low and then high, always attempting to open up that vulnerable head and temple. In non-subjective time, it was over in less than a minute. For the pair, an eternity.

One that finally had Budo collapsed, repeated elbows at short range to his skull driving him to the ground. Unconscious, if not dead. And Arthur, leaning against the tree as blood dripped down his side and heaving with a desperate need for oxygen.

But for all that... victorious at least.

"Well, well..." the voice behind him was familiar, if unwanted at this time. "You're more than a little surprising, newbie."

His words forced a long-suffering sigh from Arthur as he turned around. It really was becoming that kind of day.

Chapter 26

"If we keep meeting like this, I'm going to want a name," Arthur said, clutching his side. The bleeding wasn't stopping, and he needed to fix that soon. Though maybe making sure Budo didn't wake up was more important. Or perhaps dealing with the three girls in front of him.

Damn. Blood loss really was kicking his ass.

"A name? How about I kick your—" the Northern Chinese girl fell silent as their leader held a hand up, cutting her off.

"Daiyu. Enough." The leader stared at Arthur's bleeding torso, then shrugged. "Sure, why not. I'm Mel. That's Daiyu. Rani."

"Arthur." He offered them a weak grin, then realised weakness wasn't just in his ability to smile. His legs gave way and to his surprise, Rani caught him and helped him slowly sit with his back to a tree. Before he knew it, she had his shirt pulled up and a gauze bandage pushed against his side.

"Press on this," she commanded. "Harder. No, harder!"

Hissing as the woman clamped down on his hand, Arthur found himself unable to breathe. Eventually the spike of pain faded, leaving him able to take slow, hissing breaths. The bandage itself was soaked through almost immediately with his blood. But resting on the ground and with the bleeding staunched a little, he was able to focus better.

Not that the math was hard. Women: not trying to kill him. Budo: tried to kill him.

So, kill Budo.

"Just give me a second. I just need..." Searching along his waist, he finally found the survival knife he had picked up from the forest corpse a few weeks ago. A flick of his wrist popped the sheath open, only for his hand to be clamped down upon by Rani, who had been looking for a bandage to wrap around his chest.

"What do you think you're doing?" she said, her voice dangerously calm.

Maybe he was a little more loopy with blood loss than he had thought. Everything was rather hazy, but he was trying his best. "Going to stab Budo. Make sure he doesn't wake up and finish the job." A pause, then he added. "Of killing me. Trying to kill me." Another pause. "Might have succeeded actually..."

He shivered, from the cold more than anything else. With adrenaline wearing off, he found himself shuddering more and more at how close things had gotten.

"Shit. Shock. I need to warm him up. He needs blood too," Rani spoke up, pointing at Arthur. "If we don't want him dead, we're going to have to give him a Blood Replacing pill."

"No way. Do you know how expensive those things are?" Daiyu snapped. "I'm not paying for it."

"He did get us Budo. Which means we do owe him," Mel said.

"Can't owe a dead man. And he's about to die."

"True."

"You can't be serious!" Rani said, having released him as she had finished wrapping the gauze and bandage around his body during the argument. "I know you don't like men, but he's done nothing to us. We can't just let him die."

"Watch me," Daiyu muttered.

Arthur, having heard the argument, felt something flash in him and he raised a finger, pointing it at the bickering girls. The fact that the same hand was still clutching a knife helped emphasise his point, he figured. Also, he'd forgotten it was there until he started talking.

"Look here. Just take him and leave me. If I find you, we'll call it as you owing me one. Got it? And if I die... well, she's right. Can't owe a dead man," Arthur said.

"Why should we deal with you?" Daiyu sniffed.

"Bold." Mel had a little smile on her face. "Sure. Deal. We'll owe you one, if you survive. Girls, grab Budo. We've got some questions for him."

"I—" Rani began to protest, only to fall silent as Arthur turned his head to her, giving her a tight grin.

"Look, it's the Tower. The strong survive, the weak die. So, you get going and I'll get to showing you all. I'm not weak."

Rani bit her lip but eventually nodded and stood up. "You need to stitch that wound closed, but we don't have dissolving stitches. And if you do manage to survive, cultivator bodies heal too fast for normal stitches, so you're just going to have to suffer. It'll leave a divot in your body, but it should even out. Eventually."

"Gotcha. Now, shoo..." Arthur waved his hand weakly, continuing to stay slumped against the tree. He stayed in that position until the trio had left, allowing him the peace and ability to do what he really needed to do.

"Not much refined energy," Arthur groaned, checking his own core. Thankfully, Focused Strike did not use refined energy but raw Tower energy, so he had not touched his store as yet. That meant all he had to do was focus within, pull it out and begin the process of accelerating his healing.

Except this time, eyes closed, he focused first on dealing with the open wound, closing and stitching together blood vessels and other massively hemorrhaging wounds. At least, that's what he thought he was doing—it was not as though he were pulling skeins of yarn with chopsticks apart. No, that would be easy. This was much more complicated, like picking out different kinds of noodles, while badly blindfolded and colourblind.

On the other hand, accelerating his overall healing replaced some of the blood he had lost, which cleared his head. That meant he was less likely to faint, which made the process he was undergoing slightly easier.

Step one. Stop the bleeding. Between clotting, bandages, and him finally managing to knot split arteries together, he managed that process. It was not perfect, but it was better than nothing. Next step, and the last partial point of refined energy he had left available was to shore up the wound itself.

After that, he was going to have to cultivate and refine energy from the surroundings. And hope that no monster came across his body before it chose to eat him.

Chapter 27

Once he finished using the last of the refined energy in his body, some scrambling around allowed Arthur to find the parang that Budo had dropped. He pulled it along with him as he headed for another spot further along the wall, searching for a way back up. The cliff face was more steep than sheer, and with the amount of greenery growing on it, he could probably climb it.

If he wasn't, you know, sporting a bleeding wound. On the other hand...

"This is a stupid idea," Arthur muttered to himself when he had gotten far enough away from the smell of blood and terror of his initial fight that he felt safe stopping.

He eyed the cliff face, picking out the spots he could get a grip on, and then for a few seconds, juggled the parang location in his mind. Back of pants? Nah. Front of pants, even more of a no. Slung through the back of his clothing or tied off? He didn't have enough scraps to do it that way. In the end, he settled for putting it in his mouth, blunt side tongue-wise, before he began the process of climbing.

Focus on legs, not hands. He couldn't reach very far, not with the wound in his side. In fact, he was better off simply using his uninjured side and pushing with legs rather than manhandle his way upwards like he was used to doing.

His target was a small overhang, jutting outwards due to the remnants of a big tree that had fallen but whose roots still hung on tenaciously. The entire thing was growing haphazardly sideways, with smaller plants jutting out to form corners which offered quite a bit of shade from those casting a cursory glance up. The trunk and branches would stop monsters from approaching him easily.

More importantly, it would make it impossible for the majority of monsters that he knew were on the first floor of the Tower to approach him.

The only problem was getting there.

Slowly he climbed, wincing with every stretch, each time he pushed with his feet. The soil underneath his fingers was crumbly and only slightly moist, the lack of rain over the last few days making itself all too apparent. He had to dig his feet in hard to push upwards, his footing always moments away from giving way.

Halfway up, his concerns played out.

Pushing with his right foot as he began to reach for another handhold, the roots holding the earth tight let go, sending him tumbling downwards. He fell, the hilt of the parang bouncing off his arm and the side of the cliff, making his jaw ache and cutting a little into his mouth. He scrambled for a second, ignoring the shooting pain in his side as he tried and managed to grab hold of an outcropping of rock.

Jerking to a stop, holding on with one hand, Arthur's tender side wound burst open and poured warm blood down his body. He panted harshly, the iron tang of blood on his lips, even as he scrambled with his hanging foot for a stable point.

Eventually, he found one. Not very stable, but good enough that he was able to put more weight onto it. He hung on, wheezing at the pulsing pain in his side and the blade clutched in his mouth. Adrenaline shot through him, making movement hard but at least dulling the pain.

Control was difficult, but Arthur managed to find another foothold, a more stable one via feel more than sight. Then, carefully, he levered himself upward again.

He leaned his forehead against the cold earth for a second, before Arthur shook his aching exhaustion off. The adrenaline of nearly falling and the pain was giving him strength now, but when it faded, he would be even worse off.

No time to take this as carefully as before.

He extracted the parang from his mouth carefully, slipping it past him and then stabbing upwards. Using the blade as a firmer handhold, he began to push onward, his destination a bare twenty feet away.

Stab, push, get new handhold or foothold. Extract parang, push, find new holds. Pull upward. Spit and curse, whimper and push. Look for new handholds and footholds. Find them. Push and reach. Stab and pull. New foothold.

Move.

Step by step, inching his way up, Arthur managed to make his way to the outcropping, leaving a trail of blood behind him. Noisy ants stopped by the bloody soil, testing and tasting before picking up pieces to bring back. Caterpillars searched the earth for carrion and beetles crawled across his face, even as Arthur kept moving.

Until, finally, he was there. A final surge of energy had him sprawled over the edge of the outcropping, legs dangling over the side. It took almost all his energy to flip over before the pain and exhaustion caught up, sending him into uneasy slumber.

Hours later he woke, wiping his face and wincing at his side. Something sharp and twisty in his torso. He searched, fingers brushing against hard carapaces. Quick movements sent away the damn ants that had been attempting to extract blood and flesh, leaving behind itchiness and pain.

Another moment and Arthur managed to get his feet over the ledge and propped himself up against the wall. He had been lucky he had not rolled over while asleep, but it seemed his body was too exhausted to even consider that much movement.

Luck.

Now, head leaning against the wall, he touched the puffy red sides of his torso and winced. Some degree of inflammation there. Minor toxins mixed in there from the damn ants. None of it great for healing.

Yet he had no time to worry about that. He had no refined energy to benefit his body, so he had to concentrate instead on cultivating. Draw in Tower energy so that he could fill his core and then refine it. Only then could he begin healing himself.

No time to waste then.

Settled in as best he could, having adjusted the leaves and branches to hide himself from prying eyes. Arthur closed his eyes and began the process of pulling Tower energy through his body, slipping it into his core and storing it away. It was going to take a while to get enough energy to refine, but it had to be done.

He couldn't exactly walk around with a hole in his side.

Chapter 28

Days later, Arthur finally cracked his eyes open. His side still hurt, but at least he was able to function. The only reason he chose to stop the process of cultivating more energy was a desire to find his missing equipment. Already, it had rained once during the time he had been here, and he desperately hoped that he could at least locate his equipment before it was scattered by wild animals, found by other cultivators, or just destroyed.

"Could have left me with the crystals Budo stole from me..." Arthur grumbled as he hauled himself over the lip of the cliff. What had been a tenuous and dangerous climb was so much simpler now that he wasn't bleeding to death.

Rolling over the edge, he forced himself to breathe slowly, waiting for the ache in his side to subside. Lying on the fresh grass, he could not help but feel the scratchiness of his clothing, the crustiness from all the bleeding he had done, and smell the rancid odour of multiple days of not washing.

They said that once you rose up in the ranks, you stopped sweating and smelling as much. You became closer to a perfect being. He was kind of looking forward to that. Of course, he would have to survive the process first, which was currently a problem. How many times had he nearly died since he arrived at the Tower? Four? Five times?

The fact that he had lost track was a problem.

"Going to get killed,
For the thrill,
By a real monster,
But if I don't,
Then I won't,
And I'll become the monster!"

Muttering to himself, Arthur tested out the rhymes. Well, it was kind of juvenile and basic; and he was trying to become an immortal cultivator and ascend the ranks in the Towers, not be a poet. Also, he was pretty sure using "monster" twice was just cheating.

"What rhymes with monster? Bonster? Lonster? Foster? Mobster?" Arthur continued to mutter as he wandered through the wood, doing his best to backtrack. He was cutting at an angle, watching for problems as he searched for the trail he and Budo had created while running. "A mobster monster. That'd be... weird. I wonder if they'd like cannoli? What is cannoli, anyway? What does it taste like and is it good?"

Talking to himself. A bad habit, but it helped distract from the pain. And he was making sure to keep his voice low, since the only one who needed to hear him was himself. It just helped stave off the loneliness he'd begun to feel.

Meditating and cultivating, healing himself—all that was great and good, and he had the discipline to do that. But when he wasn't actively trying to improve himself, that was when the waves of solitude would crash, driving him to this.

He knew being by himself for so long was not a good idea. Arthur had not progressed to the point where he could sit and cultivate uninterrupted for years at a time. The human brain wasn't built for years of solitude, which was why so many fools who tried to circumvent the world alone got into trouble. Or, you know, prisoners in isolation.

Supposedly it became less of a problem, something about differences in brain waves and chemicals between higher-rank Tower people and those who were not. But he was still starting out; he needed to talk to someone, anyone.

"Good thing I'll be heading back to the starter village soon," Arthur said to himself. He desperately needed to do so, but he couldn't just return without his pack and all the things he had acquired. Even the basic herbs he had collected would help. After all, he had his herb-gathering quest to finish.

"I wonder what their quest was?" he muttered. It was obvious the girls had one too, but... well. He was so not going to get involved in that. Some enterprising protagonist in a book might consider themselves better able to handle the dangers of following a group of angry woman who'd threatened to kill him before, but Arthur knew better.

He had taken enough risks. It was time to go home.

Once he found his bag.

Hours later, Arthur sighed as he stared at his weapons, the parang, sword and staff, dropped by the wayside. The sword at least seemed alright, though the hilt looked even worse for wear after lying around even more in the open weather. The staff had a slight dusting of mold growing on one side, where the storm had come and deposited water on it, but a good sanding would fix that. It still wasn't great, but it would do.

His backpack contents were, unfortunately, worse off. A *babi ngepet* or a herd of them had likely come by and, smelling the collected herbs, torn it all open. The clothes, camp utensils, and tent, things to make life out here easier, were all scattered around. Everything he had collected and meant to bring back was gone, consumed by the damn monsters.

"Damn it..." Arthur ran a hand through his hair, realizing it had grown way too long. He would need to take a knife to it later, so that it wouldn't bother him.

Staring at his scattered belongings, he let out a long-suffering sigh and got to work. First things first, he searched through his belongings before coming up with that most important item for long trips: a sewing set. Came with every beginner kit, with multiple thread sizes including some large enough to take care of fixing tears in bags or tents.

Extracting the rest of the items from his bag, Arthur set to work after verifying that the small clearing he was in was empty. No point in moving away, especially since he had no way to carry anything. He was not a master at darning, having learnt just about enough to fix buttons, holes in pockets, and the occasional ripped sleeve.

Not as though he had much money to spare. When not working as an odd-job man or making deliveries, he trained all hours of the day to prep himself for the Tower. Even if the world had turned and twisted with the advent of the Towers, there were still people who had money or influence and needed their daily desires met by others. Whether it was delivering a cup of boba or the char kway teow from SS2—though the char kway teow in Shah Alam was better, as anyone in their right mind knew.

Finished with the repairs, he tested the new patch on with a couple of good tugs. It looked to be holding, so Arthur took his time cleaning off the remains of his gear and putting it away. Eventually he came to the bags and broken container boxes that were supposed to keep the materials and ended up sighing.

No way to store the herbs and keep them fresh now.

"Can't go back empty handed either," Arthur muttered.

Didn't leave much choice then.

Hefting the contents of his backpack and slinging it over his shoulder, he grabbed his staff and began the long walk back to the village. He would have to see what kind of monsters he could find along the way. If he could harvest a half-dozen cores, he would not be entirely penniless.

And at least he had a place to stay, once he got back.

Plan of action in place, Arthur started limping back, keeping an eye out for monsters.

Chapter 29

A month later, Arthur stumbled out of the woods. Across the clearing of space were the gathering of tents around the newbie village. The ensuing month had seen the creation of even more buildings. Yet, there were still those tents—for those who could not afford more permanent accommodation.

As he wove his way through the unorganized mess of tents, compost pits, and burning campfires, Arthur's appearance was rather bedraggled, even for the hard put-upon group of nobodies that were the commoners and non-elite. His clothing was patched together from multiple pieces, held together by thread and a wish for greater decency.

As for his weapons, those were even more damaged. His staff had been broken during a desperate fight with a herd of *babi ngepet* that had found him in the middle of the night, his sword shattered on the last thrust. Now, he held the broken ends of his staff in either hand as he slunk through the tents, eyes darting from side-to-side on the lookout for trouble.

Arthur watched as more than one individual flinched from his gaze, skirting away from him or watched his passing with wary looks, hands on their weapons. Unknown to him, his gait had grown longer and smoother, and more predatory as did his gaze. Constant weeks under danger had added a dangerous edge to his movements, a coldness to his gaze as he assessed potential threats.

Moving quickly, Arthur managed to get through the tents into the beginner village proper before anyone remembered who he was. Rather than head straight for the Guild Centre, he checked into the beginner residence.

Exiting a hot shower, he ran a hand through his wet hair, trimmed inside the shower. It was not a good job, but it was certainly better now. The scruff around his chin and beard was gone, only a couple of light cuts indicating the toughness of his skin and the bluntness of his blade.

On the other hand, his clothing was a wash. Thankfully, a quick check outside showed that the requested new set had arrived, allowing him to change into fresh clothes. The few coins he had been able to keep from his first kills had been enough to pay for the cheap material.

"Got to get paid. Need more skills, need to train..." Rubbing his chin, Arthur walked over to his bag and extracted the pair of pouches, dropping the contents onto his bed. He watched as the monster cores bounced before sorting and counting the totals.

"Forty-two." He sighed. "Don't know how much the herb boxes are going to be, but probably worth two cores." Moving the two cores aside, he dropped them into his pouch while continuing to speak to himself. "That leaves forty for paying for goods and sundries and training."

Sucking on his bottom lip, he pushed the cores from side to side as he thought. "Half? Half seems like a good idea. I mean, half is easy. Means I get to improve... but not fast."

Cultivation Speed: 1
Energy Pool: 7/14
Refinement Speed: 0.01
Refined Energy: 0.13 (2)

Attributes and Traits
Mind: 3
Body: 5 (Enhanced Eyesight)
Spirit: 3

Techniques
Focused Strike
Accelerated Healing – Refined Energy (Grade I)

Then again, half of the points were only a fifth of a point to an attribute. His time wandering the wilds had given him a little bit of time and energy to refine some of the monster cores for his own use, such that he had gained enough points to add to his pool of refined energy. He would never let the pool drain so low again that he could not make use of his Accelerated Healing technique.

He needed more. Needed to grow faster. Needed more techniques so that he could be a well-rounded fighter. Needed a better weapon.

"Maybe just trade it all?" Arthur sighed. "*Tak cukup duit.* Forty cores would hardly cover it."

He ran his fingers over the cores one last time. Trade it all for gear and techniques and maybe a few more days in this room. Learn whatever technique he bought. Then go out and, this time, stay close enough to the village to actually make some damn funds so he could begin the process of getting to the next damn level.

Rough plan in place, he swept the cores into his pouches and stood up. Time to see what there was to buy.

"I don't believe it. You're alive."

"That I am, Lai Tai Kor," Arthur said, grinning as he propped himself against the counter with an elbow. "I have some cores to trade in." A pair of dirty, messy bags were dropped with a thump. That motion attracted some mild attention, mostly for how dirty the bags were.

"I can see that," Attendant Lai said. His face did not flinch as he opened the pouches, pouring the crystals and separating them on the counter with the speed of long practice. "You don't seem much stronger, for all your time away. Things get too tough?"

"You could say that," Arthur replied. "But how do you know I haven't gotten that much stronger?"

"More techniques out there than you can imagine, boy." The attendant finished counting, then rubbed his chin. "And...?"

"And what?"

"You took the herb quests too? The other gathering quests? So, where are they?"

"Ah..." Arthur hesitated.

"You broke the boxes that came with your newcomer gear, didn't you?" Lai rolled his eyes. "What? You try to stuff too much in? Mix the wrong types of herbs together and make it all melt down?"

"That can happen?" Arthur's eyes grew wide.

"Why do you think we tell you all not to mix herbs when storing things?"

"…"

"Bodoh!" Lai sighed. "Whatever. You want all this converted to credits then?"

Arthur nodded.

"Considering quality, type, and variety, I can give you 48 credits. *Cukup?*"

"You can't do better?" Arthur said, doing his best to be charming. "I've been out for a long time, and this, well…"

"Forty-eight," Lai said firmly. "Or you can take it all back and just use them. Your call."

"Forty-eight it is." Arthur sighed.

"Good man." A twitch of his hands and the man dropped the cores down multiple circular holes built into his desk. Arthur could hear the cores bouncing around as they fell down the funnels, headed to who knows where. At the same time, a sale slip was jotted down and marked and stored in another box while Arthur's credit token was updated.

"Thank you. Pleasure doing business, as always, Lai Tai Kor."

Laughing, Lai waved Arthur off. The man could not help but grin and saunter a little, for now it was time to do the thing that all men enjoyed—shopping for weapons and techniques!

Chapter 30

Entering the armoury was an interesting experience. The armoury itself was connected to the beginner hall, with the two buildings sharing access to the same warehouse. In the early days, a number of enterprising fools had attempted to break into the armoury, only to find themselves caught and slain. Since then, no one dared to even consider stealing from the first-floor guardians. Rather, everyone just lined up quietly while waiting their turn.

The building itself was roughly the same size as the newcomer hall, which to Arthur screamed of bad planning. After all, considering the crowd before him compared to the one before, he could not help but think perhaps dedicating more attendants would make sense.

Then again, at least in the Tower they were able to skip out on one of two major mainstays of civilization—taxes—so perhaps he should be willing to accept long waiting times. Still, it didn't help that the hall he waited in was just the holding area before individuals were brought into small private rooms to make their purchases.

Cocking his head from side to side, Arthur examined the mix of individuals within. About a good half of them were silently cultivating, using the time provided to pour energy into their bodies. The fact that they were willing to potentially miss their slot spoke volumes about the wait times involved. The other half were like him, too tense to cultivate, and either spending the time conversing with others or looking about.

"So, what's your story?" The woman who'd just flopped into the chair beside him asked. Unlike many of the youngsters in the room, she looked to be in her mid-thirties at least. Most startling of all was the missing front tooth she sported as she spoke, though the slightly squashed nose was just as remarkable. If not for those two imperfections, she would have been a decidedly average Chinese female.

"Huh?" was Arthur's intelligent reply.

"Your story." A gesture at him and his haircut. "You aren't a newbie, but I haven't seen you around before. So, you got to be something interesting."

"I really am not." Arthur crossed his arms. "Anyway, what's *your* story?"

"Me? Boring. Mother of two, just another serf. Parents are taking care of my children until I come out, but..." A shrug of her shoulders, a flash of pain. "That might be a while. Still, better than them starving. And the loan of my services in here isn't that bad."

"Serf?"

"Ah. Indentured servant. I took a loan that gets paid off by serving the company in here." She shrugged. "I'm Mei Ling by the way."

"Arthur." He automatically replied before knitting his brow. "Which company?" The use of indentured servants was not unknown. Mostly among more experienced folk though, what with the high death rate among those trying to climb their first Tower. In fact, some guilds had become major companies—or taken over major companies—with the sheer abundance of resources and strength they gained by running the Towers.

Very few companies bothered with newcomers. In fact, he could only think of three. Of which, the worse was—

"Bumikasih." Mei Ling said. She watched him wince, but she shrugged, seeming to be content with the way things were. "So, your story?"

"Why are you asking?"

"You ask a lot of questions without answering. But sure, here's the last answer, free of charge. I'm charged with getting information about interesting people. And you look interesting." Mei Ling said.

"Is this how you get all your information? Just blatantly asking people?"

Mei Ling kept quiet, staring at Arthur.

His head spun as he considered what he should say. Not speaking would mark him out even more as someone of interest. On the other hand, he did not want to reveal his problems with the Suey Ying tong. Or his encounters in the middle of the forest. Still, if she was an information gatherer, they would also be willing to sell that information. And that could be useful.

"I'm not super experienced, but I've been around for a few months now. Mostly working the outer edges, so I haven't really been coming into the village much." Or at all. "Need to stock up though." A gesture downwards, taking in his rather pitiful shoes and the sheathed, weathered sword by his side. "So… here I am."

"You were trained, weren't you?" Mei Ling said, eyes narrowing as she looked at the sword.

"Why'd you say that?"

"Not many like actual swords. Parangs are preferred. Cheaper. Works just as well."

"I took a few classes before I came," Arthur said. "I never understood why others wouldn't."

Holding up fingers, she counted them down as she spoke. "Arrogance. Money. Time. Connections. Bad information."

"Bad information?"

"Oh yeah. Didn't you see the videos about how the parang—or the spear or the keris or barehanded—is the way to go? Like five years ago, it was all axes!"

"That was when Andrev the Ukranian Bear was all the rage, right?" Arthur said. "I remember that a bit."

"How can you only know it a bit?" Mei Ling said, waving her hand around. "And you know what Datok Mahathir wields."

"A parang and keris combination, yes. I'm not completely out of touch," Arthur said. "But I spent most of my time training or working to earn enough money to train." He waggled his fingers at her. "Not many people to talk to, unpacking in warehouses or doing deliveries."

"Whatever." She shook her head, then frowned. "Not even school?"

"Training," Arthur bit off.

"Right, right. Gotcha. You're type B then."

Glowering, he waited for her to clarify.

"Battle fanatic. Always thought you'd be the hero of the ages, trained ever since they were a kid, so on, so forth." Mei Ling nodded along with a grin. "Good, good."

"And why's that good?" Arthur bristled a little.

"Wanna know a secret?" She lowered her voice, though more than a few people leaned in to listen. "People like you are the ones who manage to make it off the first floor and up the Tower fast. The rest of us? We're stuck in here."

"I'm—" Arthur began to protest her words, but before he could finish, his number was called. Looking up at the Malay attendant, who was oddly thin in his arms and legs but also sporting a stomach, he blinked and looked back at Mei Ling. "Got to go."

"Sure, sure. If you ever want to talk, just ask for me on the outskirts of the Bumi enclosure. I buy and sell information, you know." Grinning, she waved goodbye to Arthur before looking around, scouting for her next target.

Rolling his eyes a little, Arthur hurried over to the man, rubbing the back of his neck. For a moment, he wondered what life was like. For those who had not trained, who came in here thinking they could do it, and realising exactly how hard it was to get ahead. He had nearly died multiple times, so how much harder was it for those who did not have his years of training?

Was it a surprise then, that sometimes things got a little desperate? If a way out showed itself, a way to climb upwards with less risk, would he too not try to grasp it?

Shaking his head, Arthur slipped in along with the attendant and took a seat across from the man in their private room. A slight humming spoke of enchantments closing in, allowing them to speak in privacy.

Mei Ling's offer was something to think about later anyway.

Chapter 31

"Let's see, Arthur Chua. Fifty-nine credits total." The attendant was reading the information from the scrolling tablet he had before him, eyeing the information idly before gesturing and handing the tablet over to Arthur. "There you go. Shop items are now listed up to 60 credits. I can expand further, if you want to look at saving up for more; but considering you're brand-new and poor, I'm going with the assumption you need to buy techniques and pills immediately. Fair?"

"Fair enough." Arthur picked up the tablet and flicked his gaze down, eyes widening at the sheer volume of items listed. "This... I... That's a lot."

"It is."

"Can you help?" Arthur said plaintively.

"If you wish," the attendant replied, sounding a little bored. "I will need parameters of what you want, however. What are your goals? Do you even have any?"

Arthur paused, hearing the tone underneath the man's words. Not exactly scorn but dismissal. His eyes narrowed, but he swallowed his pride and spoke. "Vague ideas. Do you perhaps have suggestions?"

A shrug. "What have you done so far? What do you have upgraded?"

"I've upgraded and developed my Body attribute, with Enhanced Eyesight as my first trait. Otherwise, I have Focused Strike"—the man gave a dismissive snort—"and an Accelerated Healing technique."

"Interesting," the man leaned forward. "There's no indication you bought that from us."

"I learnt it myself," Arthur said pridefully. There was a considering look from the attendant before he gestured for Arthur to continue. "My plan was to upgrade my Spirit attribute next, with the goal of increasing my cultivation speed. It's too slow right now."

Another dismissive snort. "They're always too slow."

"Well, that's my plan for now," Arthur replied. "I'm not exactly sure what techniques or equipment I should get. I'm leaning towards buying more techniques, maybe a pill to boost an attribute or increase my energy."

"Forget pills that boost attributes directly. There are only two that you could afford, and I'd advise against them to anyone—the amount of corrosive and corrupt chemicals are too high. Very temporary boost, for those who are too much in a hurry. Not worth it."

"Oh, right!" Arthur remembered and extracted a pill from his pouch, placing the unknown item on the table. "Does assessing what this is cost me anything?"

Lips pressed, the attendant picked up the box and opened it, staring at the pill within. After a moment, he set it down and pushed the pill to Arthur. "Yes, normally. Even if we are unable to tell what an item is, there is a cost. However, since you're poor and I have no idea, I'm waving it." He pushed the pill back to Arthur who caught the open, spinning box in his hand.

"You don't know?" Arthur said. "At all?"

"I don't specialize in assessments. If you wanted someone like that, you should have specified when you got your number. I can tell you, it looks to be a specialized pill, so details will likely be hard to acquire anyway. Probably something either made by a sect or corporation for their personnel."

"So it's safe?" Arthur said eagerly.

"Hah! No. Pills made outside of the Towers are not registered beforehand, so the formulas and processes are secret. However, without the Tower's aid, they are also more expensive to make and might have secondary, unknown effects later on down the line. In addition, many such pills might require a specific cultivation technique or prior use of other pills." The man shrugged. "It's a good way to ensure your work isn't just stolen."

"I didn't steal it!"

"I didn't say anything."

Arthur glared at the man who continued to look unperturbed. Turning the box over in his hand, he sighed and put it away, choosing to decide what to do about it later. "Right, so any other suggestions? Or none at all?"

"Don't get snarky with me. You're the one not giving me much to work with." The attendant rolled his eyes, before shrugging. "I would not recommend too many techniques at your stage. Your biggest problem, as you have mentioned, is your cultivation resources. More than two or three active techniques become a problem. Perhaps a single passive technique at most, though those come with their own problems."

"Reduction in cultivation or refinement speed due to reservation of energy for the technique. And it's hard to find techniques that you can turn off, so once you start, you are stuck until you either upgrade the basic technique or replace it with another," Arthur said, just to show off that he knew something.

"Exactly. So, I'd recommend two to three active techniques—combat focused, of course. And maybe some equipment. Pills to aid your cultivation might be viable, but at your stage, it'd mostly just speed up your current cycle. That, you will have to decide."

"Upgrade now or later..." Rubbing his chin, Arthur considered the question briefly before asking. "How much for those pills that give more refined energy?"

"Depends on the pills. The cheapest costs 10 credits and will increase your refined energy, if you use it well, by a maximum of a quarter of a point.

If you had a technique, it might go as high as a third. If you are not compatible, you might at most break even."

Another damn factor about using pills, even Tower pills. Some pill consolidation techniques, some cultivation techniques aided in absorption, speeding up the process and amount of good a pill did. For people like him, they could only hope for the basics. Which lead him to ask:

"Are there cultivation techniques I can afford?"

"No."

Another grimace but he nodded. Not unexpected. The advantage of Tower cultivation techniques were that they could be used by everyone. The disadvantage was that they were at best mediocre for most people and incredibly expensive. Just like the basic technique he studied, really. Anything better than the basics was just out of reach for now.

"Right. Techniques. Combat ones... Maybe if I'm going with Spirit for my next attribute, something that will boost my Body?"

"Specific or general?"

"Uhh... general?" Arthur said, hesitating. "Yeah, general."

"High-end but costly, or low-cost but low amplification?"

"Low amplification and, preferably, good for long-term."

"Won't be worth it in the long-term, but if we assume long-term means length of Tower stay, then yes, there are a few." The attendant kept tapping away at the tablet, before he continued. "What else?"

"Let's go with gear. I need to replace the herb gathering boxes from the newcomer gear, and I need a spear. Something solid and unlikely to break. Enchanted if possible..." Catching the look of disdain in the man's eyes, he continued. "But not necessary. Armour would be nice too. Or a protective technique?"

"Armour is cheaper for now and probably better. Once you upgrade your body more, you'll step out of the need for armour with techniques, but that should be something you look at on the third floor or higher."

Arthur winced, recollecting what he had read. Right, right. Body techniques for physical improvement like that went down one of two routes:

a general active boost, or a passive rebuilding boost. Since he had no desire to smash himself into trees and fists and what not to rebuild his body, he was happy to make use of active boosts. Anyway, active boosts were stronger later on when he had a higher energy pool and access to better techniques.

"Anything else?" the attendant asked, forcing Arthur to shake his head. Not that he didn't want more, but with only 59 credits to his name, there was a limit to what he could buy.

"Here." The tablet was shoved over again, the list much shorter.

Nodding in thanks, Arthur looked down while idly humming, still excited to see what he could purchase.

Chapter 32

Thankfully, Arthur noted that all the information about techniques was categorized. First things first, he checked the pill information. There were literally only three pills. The cheapest, as mentioned, was worth 10 credits; the other two even more. A glance at the information the pad pulled up showed that he could expect roughly the equivalent level of upgrade in his refined energy, except with the addition of more impurities to his body.

"Why the heck would anyone buy a pill?" Arthur said, frowning.

"It's faster to consume a pill. Only spend a single hour rather than 10 hours absorbing all the crystals. And that assumes you can concentrate for 10 hours straight." The attendant saw Arthur's surprise and he sighed. "Right, right, Tower fanatic. Look, not everyone's like you. Most of those who come here do so because they're desperate. So, cultivating for 10 hours straight? Forget it.

"On top of that, as we said: there's techniques that can help. Make more use of the pills, give you a better bang for your credits. Then you've got the special ones."

"Special?"

"The lucky people who take in pills better or who have a mystic bloodline."

"Those are real?" Arthur's jaw dropped. "I thought that was a Hollywood thing."

"Nah. As real as the Tower. Just a heck of a lot rarer than they showed in the movies. You might be lucky to find one once a year or so per beginner Tower." The attendant shrugged. "But as I said, not worth it for most."

"Right." Armour next, since he liked staying alive. Techniques, while useful in the long term, weren't going to give him an immediate, accelerated likelihood of making it through the day. Anyway, how expensive could armor get?

"This is daylight robbery!" Arthur shouted, pointing a finger at the pad moments later.

"You wanted armour? That's what we have. You can buy cheaper outside; just walk around the lots. Lots of people bring armour with them, sell them secondhand. Have it made by artisans and other fools outside, wear it in here and think it's good enough." The attendant snorted. "Maybe for the first floor or two. But after that? After that, you want this. Better to pay more now."

"*Pok gai*!" Cursing, Arthur read the details.

Mutated Heteropoda Lunula Silk Tunic
Provides superior protection against cutting and blunt damage and minor protection against piercing damage. Will disperse lightning and water elemental damage at an additional 7% rate.
Credits: 42

Hardened, Layered Babi Ngepet Leather Breastplate
Covers torso and shoulders of wearer, providing superior protection against all forms of cutting, piercing, and blunt damage.
Credits: 26

The details went on. Soft leather armour, plated armoured tunic, even a leather skirt in strips. But the cheapest—the skirt—was nearly a dozen credits and the most expensive was the Silk Tunic. After a while, Arthur shook his head.

Better to buy something cheap for now and upgrade later. He mentally set aside a couple of credits to buy something in the tents before he moved on.

Techniques next. This was the meat of the shopping experience, where he expected he would be spending the majority of his funds. Each technique started at 20 credits and rose from there, with Arthur looking to start with the general body reinforcement technique.

Surge of the Dung Beetle

Strengthens and reinforces the user's body, increasing the flow of chi through meridians. Increases Body attribute by 1 at lowest level of understanding. Maximum increase of 3 points.

Cost: 1 Energy per Minute

Credits: 20

"Dung beetle?" Arthur said, looking at the attendant.

"It's a good technique."

"And a horrible name."

All he got was a shrug at that comment.

Still, three points to the Body attribute was significant. That was the equivalent of adding the strength, speed, and reflexes of a well-trained athlete. Which... huh.

"Hey, am I wrong? All the forums I read said that three points in attributes was the base expected number for entrants to the Tower. But you keep saying that most people aren't as well trained as me. So do they get lower traits then?" Arthur said, curiously.

"What am I? Your librarian?" The attendant snorted. Arthur apologized and returned to poking at the tablet, pulling up the next technique.

Heavenly Sage's Mischief

Boosts the Body's natural attributes by a significant portion, increasing the user's abilities. Base understanding of the technique sees an increase of 2 Body attribute points, to a maximum of 5. Cultivator will be fatigued and drained after use, to a degree dependent on length of use of technique.

Cost: 2 Energy per Minute

Credits: 27

"It depends," the attendant said suddenly. "In the forums you browsed, they probably spoke of three points as being the normal; but that's for fanatics like you. Your average human scores around two. Two, two point five, maybe one point five. Of course, the Tower doesn't do decimals for attributes, so it just rounds up or down."

"Thank you."

"Now, make your choice. I have others to work with."

Arthur chose not to answer the man, instead turning back to the information he had been provided, skimming through the techniques. The others were variations of the first two he had read about. The more expensive versions had higher base amounts and additional effects or a lower surge potential, but they also took longer to learn.

Nodding to himself, he moved on to the combat-focused techniques, curious about what options had been given. His eyes flicked across the names, some elaborate like Heaven Splitting Kick while others were simple like Piercing Strike. However, his gaze fell upon the one item that he had not expected to see.

Refined Energy Dart

Project a dart of compressed and refined energy, to strike an opponent at range.

Cost: 0.1 Refined Energy

Credits: 12

"Only twelve?" Arthur could not help but exclaim in surprise.

"It's not that powerful," the attendant replied. "It's only good for taking out small animals."

"Oh, like, literally a dart." Arthur made a face. "Is this upgradeable?"

"Yes. One of the reasons it's included. More powerful options are available."

"Nice..." Back to the pad, he browsed further, searching for options. Finding nothing that jumped out at him, he began to look into details of the earlier techniques. After a moment, he realized he had made a mistake and handed the pad back.

"I need weapon techniques. Or techniques that work with weapons and unarmed combined, if possible. Staff," he added quickly when he realized what he forgot to specify.

"Should have said earlier," the attendant grumbled, even as his fingers flicked over the pad. In a short period, he handed the thing back to Arthur. "Combined weapon and unarmed techniques are expensive. Generally better quality, but expensive."

Nodding, Arthur scanned the list. It was a very short list: only four items listed and only one of those that was a combined technique. He could not help but smile as he noted the name of one of the weapon systems.

Heavenly Sage's Heaven Beating Stick

Staff technique that infuses weapon with energy. Initial stages reinforces staff, increasing durability and damage done, allowing the staff to strike ephemeral and spirit creatures. Higher stages of the technique will allow the projection of energy-infused extensions of the staff.

Cost: 1 Energy per Minute. Must attune to weapon beforehand.

Credits: 12

It was kind of annoying that the basic Focused Strike he had learned really only had two major stages: using it with a single limb, then learning to use the same attack with all the limbs or body parts. He was still working on the second portion, since those with the skill could even use unusual parts of the body like shoulders or foreheads.

Moving on...

Aura of the Stars

Imbues the user's aura with the strength of the stars. Amount of damage depends on level of imbuement. As technique is based off aura imbuement, it can extend to weapons wielded by the user.

Passive Cost: 0.1 Energy per hour

Credits: 20

"Can or not?" Arthur said and tapped the information. "Also, didn't we discuss not wanting passive techniques?"

"We did. Then you asked for techniques that could work with both unarmed and armed." The attendant shrugged. "You'll have to make up your mind."

"Aura control's the only way to extend techniques to both weapons and unarmed then?" Arthur said, surprised.

"Other than specific martial styles, but those we don't sell."

"Oh." Arthur sighed. He had been hoping to get the man to recommend a secret martial style that only those who could ask for it might receive or something similar, but obviously this wasn't a movie. There were no secret scrolls to be bought.

Turning back to the pad at the pointed look he got, he scanned through the rest of the information. There were a few other techniques that caught his attention before he chose to lean back and think, debating what to get.

"You can come back later, if you need time to think about your purchases." The attendant's waspish voice broke Arthur off from his thoughts, making him blink.

After a moment's more hesitation, he grinned. "Nah. I know what I want."

Chapter 33

Walking out of the hall, Arthur made his way straight to the hostel. He paid for an additional 10 days, wincing at the loss of a full credit before he went up to his room. Better to pay for extra time and get a credit on file than to find himself under and thrown out while he was in the midst of something important. And he did have something important to do. Important and stupid.

Maybe it was foolish to try, but he had been thinking about the advantages that all these heroes and special sect members and the rich had—and he had, now in his hands, one of those advantages. So he was going to use it. Even if it might kill or damage him.

Hurrying into his room, Arthur dumped out the technique scrolls he had purchased, set his new fighting spear beside him, and made sure the door was locked and a chair placed in front of it. Not that the Tower guards would allow anything to happen to him, but they were not magical enough to appear immediately. Better to be safe than sorry.

Checking that the bars on the window were engaged, Arthur sat down on his bed and picked out the pill. He turned it over and over again in his hand and then jumped up, stripping to his underclothes and putting a towel beneath the spot where he would cultivate.

Then he sat back down, forcing his right knee from jittering. He could not help but think this was foolish, but...

"Ugh... tastes like bad Chinese medicine," Arthur said, feeling the bitter, muddy flavour on his tongue. "Wait. Is there good Chinese medicine?" He scratched the back of his head, trying to think of any of the concoctions he had been forced to drink by his master, concluding that there really wasn't. All of them had been horrible.

Then, the heat in his stomach began to grow. He had no more time to think about such things as awful flavours, so he focused on breathing and cultivating, pulling energy into his body and churning it around. Not that he had ever used a pill before, but everything he had read indicated the process was similar. Just that the energy he would be pulling would start from his center.

Heat grew in his stomach as the pill broke down and interacted with his body. Not the heat of a fire, but a cold heat, which sent wracking shivers through him. Like a brain freeze, except starting from his stomach. At first it was low, no colder than *ice kacang* swallowed too fast, freezing his stomach as he sat there. Then, it began to pick up, the cold-heat growing with each pulse of energy, as though a lump of frozen energy was being chilled by liquid nitrogen.

Every second, it grew colder. As the chill in his stomach grew more painful, tendrils of energy reached out through the entirety of his body, sending lightning through his nerves and tendons, his veins and arteries. Blood chilled and sung, and Arthur began to sweat as his body tensed and released.

The cold grew too much, the block of ice in his stomach sending liquid nitrogen through his body. His teeth clenched and clenched, and he wished he had grabbed a strip of leather or maybe his mouthguard, just so that he would not break his teeth.

Then, he had no more time for even those thoughts as the pain swept over him. Nerves on fire as cold lightning danced through them, Arthur sweated and struggled, churning his cultivation process as fast as possible, drawing the energy into his stomach, into his dantian where the refined energy could be stored.

So much energy, coming into him at once. More than that, though, he could feel it changing his body, ripping apart muscles and tendons, strengthening ligaments and joints as he sat there, the pill freezing and shattering the impurities even as his new Tower body struggled to fix the damage.

Fuel and catalyst, all in one. Head thrown back, muscles taut, Arthur screamed into the sky, struggling to stay conscious. More than anything, he knew instinctively that if he were to fall unconscious he would damage himself, maybe die.

So he stayed conscious, a bobbing sliver of himself in a sea of pain, bailing the energy back into his center where it rushed out just as fast to heal him.

Innumerable moments passed as the ocean of pain shrunk with every bucket of energy he pulled away. In time, the pill no longer added to it, and the energy—the cold, ponderous, and freezing energy—faded, leaving him to float in an ocean of calm.

Safe, at last, he relaxed.

And collapsed.

Hours later he woke up, mouth dry and his jaw aching. He stumbled over to the sink in the room, draining a cup of water and wincing at the pain that shot through his mouth as dried blood cracked and pulled apart and the cold water struck raw nerves. After a bit, he spat out the shards of a broken tooth, making a face. He stumbled back to his backpack, searching through his camping gear before finding what he needed and returned to the sink with pliers in hand.

For a long moment, Arthur hesitated before he stuck it in. A lot of grunting, muffled swearing, and pain later, he extracted the cracked tooth from his mouth, spitting out a torrent of blood that slowly trickled off as his expanded cultivation body healed the minor wound. It didn't, unfortunately, regrow his tooth, making him tongue the still-sore section.

"Bodoh!" Cursing himself, Arthur stumbled to his seat and winced at the smell he caught of himself. He changed direction, throwing the window open before he got out a camp towel and made his way back to the sink to wipe himself down.

"At least no black gunk. I wonder if that was a lie, or I just didn't manage to break through enough?" he could not help but wonder aloud. Of course, there was no answer; but at least the rank smell of sweat and fear was easy enough to get rid of. He could take a shower, but that would require him to leave the room and he was not ready for that yet.

Eventually he sat on his bed, closing his eyes for a long time before he braved what he had been avoiding.

"Status."

Cultivation Speed: 1
Energy Pool: 7/15 (Yin Aspected)
Refinement Speed: 0.015
Refined Energy: 1.13 (2)

Attributes and Traits
Mind: 3
Body: 6 (Enhanced Eyesight, Yin Body)
Spirit: 4

Techniques
Focused Strike
Accelerated Healing – Refined Energy (Grade I)

"No, no, no, no... that's not good!" Arthur said out loud, staring at the new change. He worked his jaw and fingers—also his mind as he tried to prod the damn software to give him more details about what it meant that he was "Yin Aspected".

It, of course, provided nothing. He groaned and let himself flop onto the bed, staring up at the ceiling. Memory came back, of the corpse in the woods. Had it been a little smaller, a little thinner and smaller boned than what he had expected? Maybe shorter? Were its hips larger? Was it wearing women's clothes?!

He couldn't recall. It was not something he had noticed. Besides, everyone here wore pants and shirts, or robes—not skirts or dresses. And he certainly hadn't seen any female underclothes. But that didn't mean anything. Maybe it really had been a man, who was Yin-aspected.

He didn't know.

All Arthur knew was that, now, he was too. And what that meant, he didn't know.

Chapter 34

"My left nut for an internet connection," Arthur muttered as he continued to stare at the ceiling. He gently prodded his body mentally, reviewing how it felt, how it moved. He could not tell if anything was majorly different. Maybe the world was a little warmer around him? He was himself a little colder? It didn't seem to be the case but...

"Coulda, shoulda, woulda?" Arthur sat up and ran a hand through his hair. Then, remembering other stories, he made his way over to the mirror, grateful to note there was no change in appearance. No white hair or streak of white in it, no pupils that had become ice blue. How weird would that be? A Chinese with blue eyes? Or any pale colour for that matter. He rubbed at the skin on his face.

"Nice!"

Point one for Yin Body—it gave good skin. Probably because he was not too heaty, and that reduced pimples, blackheads, and oily skin. Could also be thanks to the point upgrade in Body that he had received, but he was going to give credit to the Yin Body for now.

His expanded energy pool was important too. In fact, his energy felt different in general, colder. The swirling energy contained in his center now felt more like a slushy than, say, contained lightning. Fascinating, but more importantly, having two more energy points could be useful in longer fights.

Beyond that... Arthur shook his head. He had no idea. But he had a quiet room and time to experiment, so he would. Hopefully, no major disadvantages; though he was certain there would be. He just didn't know what they might be, since Yin and Yang bodies and bloodlines were not subjects he had studied.

Not as though he had planned on getting a Yin or Yang body.

Yeah, he could see how he had been tempting fate there.

An hour later, after a physical inspection, going through his martial forms, and channeling both his acquired techniques, he had a rough idea of what the Yin Body had done. Firstly, physically there were minor alterations. He was slightly slimmer, seemed to have lost even more hair in his extremities, and had that fairer and smoother skin he had noticed earlier. He was also stronger and faster, but that could have been due to the increase in his Body attribute. He definitely did not sweat or grow as warm as he should have after moving through the full series of martial forms.

When it came down to his techniques though, that was where he had noticed a significant difference. The Focused Strike technique had actually failed the first few times. He had to adjust to his new body, to the new pathways of power and how to input energy into the technique. It was hard to describe, even to himself, but rather than slotting in A and B, he had to slot into A only but then divert the extra flow in A to exit point C so that the output amount was the same.

Sort of. Except more metaphysical.

In the end, he had figured it out, learned how to blend the energy such that the energy empowered his attacks again. That additional point to Spirit probably helped, guiding his sense of how energy could and should flow through him.

Externally, the biggest change was the slightly crackling black and blue light that now appeared around the limb that was being empowered and the wash of cold emitted when he struck something. It wasn't yet enough to freeze anything, but intuitively Arthur knew that might happen with more powerful techniques of the sort.

In the meantime, though, he was facing a problem with his other technique. Accelerated Healing was not really that Accelerated anymore. That kind of made sense, but now, triggering it seemed to speed up his healing only marginally. If anything, it made him concerned that his body was now healing at a slower rate than before.

Bad news if so, but not entirely something he could do much about. He could only hope that there were additional benefits to this Yin Body he did not understand. For now, he had done all the testing he could have.

For a brief moment, he considered leaving and taking a place in line at the armoury again to ask for information about his Yin Body. Buying information from the novice library might help, but he realized moments later that it didn't matter. He had too few credits to spend.

Maybe later, after he had picked some herbs and acquired more monster cores. Then, and only then, would he go buying things he could not afford.

Till then, he had a bunch of techniques he had meant to learn. Though...

"Is this new Yin Body going to need me to adjust every single time?" Cursing quietly to himself, Arthur had no answer. That extra point in Spirit had buffed both his refinement speed and his eventual comprehension of energy flows in his body. Of course, Mind upgrades would help him learn techniques faster, but it seemed adapting it to his new body would require both attributes.

Cursing idly again, Arthur pulled out the technique scrolls and spread them across his lap to consider. Now, which should he learn first? Considering the need for adaptation, he might not even have time to learn them all, not anymore.

Chapter 35

In the end, when it came down to buying techniques, Arthur chose to prioritize what he wanted immediately along with saving for the future. Between paying for accommodation and the various boxes, expanding his combat techniques, and potentially having funds for more armour, he had found himself with much fewer resources than he had wanted. In the end, Arthur chose to purchase only two techniques.

Heavenly Sage's Mischief

Boosts the Body's natural attributes by a significant portion, increasing the user's abilities. Base understanding of the technique sees an increase of 2 Body attribute points, to a maximum of 5. Cultivator will be fatigued and drained after use—degree dependent on length of use of technique.
Cost: 2 Energy per Minute
Credits: 27

Refined Energy Dart

Project a dart of compressed and refined energy, to strike an opponent at range.
Cost: 01 Refined Energy

Credits: 12

The first would give him quite an extensive period of use, all the way to the top of the Tower. More than that, the Heavenly Sage series of cultivation techniques all had expansions, such that the next level in a more advanced Tower would have techniques in the same line that he could purchase. Important since it would also reduce the amount of time he needed to train in the technique. Even if there was no time limit for ascension, he could still die of old age.

For now.

As for the Refined Energy Dart, well, he did need a ranged attack. Even if it was not powerful or lethal at present, he could use the skill to kite monsters to him. Eventually, he might have other techniques that complemented or upgraded the skill.

And even if not, something was better than nothing.

Now, the only question was which one to study? Sucking on his lower lip, Arthur gave up on making a decision immediately. He grabbed the first scroll and sat down to glance over the Heavenly Sage manual. He did not try to comprehend it fully or even practice it, but simply skimmed the contents to get an overview of the entire matter before he turned to the Refined Energy Dart and did the same thing. Only when he was done, sometime after the sun had set, did he sit back, rocking on two legs.

To his surprise, even if the Heavenly Sage technique had been more expensive, it was actually easier to practice—at least, at first glance. Perhaps that was because he had already studied the concentration and flow of energy within his body with Focused Strike, on top of the overall empowerment of his body via Accelerated Healing. Many of the concepts seemed familiar.

Whereas the projection of energy outside of himself... well, that seemed more complicated. He did not understand the discussion about projection of energy to his aura, of holding it just within the aura membrane before releasing the built-up energy. Thus far, he had not even practiced with his aura, so...

Heavenly Sage's Mischief it was.

But first: sleep!

The next morning, after a tasty but unnecessary meal of bacon, eggs with soya sauce, and *kaya* jam bread, Arthur got back to practicing. This time, he read over the manual for the Heavenly Sage's Mischief in more detail, smirking slightly at the little monkey drawings in the corner of the manual that were meant to showcase the way the energy flowed. Rather than using a human outline, the manual had that of a mischievous monkey, though thankfully it kept to the usual meridian pathways.

Though, he wasn't entirely certain that they were serious about the one where the monkey was hanging from its tail, upside down and scratching its armpit. That, he figured, was artistic license. He hoped so at least—or he was going to have problems.

Hours studying and practicing portions of the manual, memorizing energy pathways, and falling over as he sent energy the wrong way or too fast or too slow. Sometimes, he spent long minutes curled up, cramping as his muscles rebelled at the sudden surge of energy.

Often, he had to backtrack, decide if what was happening was because he was practicing all this in portions or because he was doing something wrong. More time was spent just whimpering or reading or debating how he was going to enact the technique.

Eventually, a whole day passed, leaving Arthur with the knowledge of the technique in his mind and what he believed was the correct method to manipulate the skill.

Before he could practice the technique in its whole, though, he needed to cultivate. Between wasted energy sources via practice and the need of his body, drained from the Tower, Arthur found himself quite empty.

Seated cross-legged on his bed, he began to cultivate for the first time since his change. Within minutes, he cursed himself, for he realized that there was indeed a major disadvantage to this new Yin Body.

The energy he drew into himself from the Tower was both Yin- and Yang-based. As it flooded his system, the heat of the Yang chi began to make his body ache; his dantian and his meridians increasingly felt on fire. Forced to stop, Arthur could only breathe slowly, cycling air through his lungs as he kept himself calm.

The good news: he noticed that the Yang energy slowly leeched itself out of his body or was converted by the greater Yin energy he held within himself into Yin again. However, the process was slow, even if the energy being converted reduced the pain he felt.

When the agony reached levels that could be withstood, he reviewed the cultivation technique he had been taught, turning it over and over in his mind. Was there a way to separate Yin and Yang chi? Could he block the Yang energy from coming in, thus decreasing the problem and pain?

Arthur was not certain, but he was sure that he should try. If not, this new Yin Body was going to be a real problem. He couldn't stop to cultivate constantly.

A quick thought had him pull up his status, searching for the specific part he was concerned about.

Cultivation Speed: 1 (0.5 Yin)
Energy Pool: 3.51/15 (Yin) (0.42 Yang – Unusable)

Yup, there it was. That had been what had worried him when he started the process. His actual cultivation speed was incorrect right now, and the Tower was probably going to take time to figure out what his true cultivation speed was, if he brought in Yang and Yin chi. More importantly, while the Yang chi did convert, it was at a significant loss.

Overall, he was barely better than half a point of Yin chi for his cultivation speed.

"*Hun dan*!" Closing his eyes, Arthur forced himself to calm. He had been warned, he had been warned. But it worked in the movies and novels and...

Yeah. Okay. He could see where he went wrong.

"Right, got to fix this. Only person who can is you. Because there isn't a gnu. Not that there should be a gnu, but you never know." Scratching his head, Arthur grimaced at the forced rhyme. "Right, right. Cultivation technique alterations... because that's going to work out well."

No more talking. Time to work.

Chapter 36

There were many things Arthur learned over the next few hours. Firstly, altering a cultivation technique was, thankfully, not impossible. Secondly, altering a technique so that it was actually usable was very difficult. Thirdly, every alteration and failure enacted a debt of pain and agony that made pulling Yang chi into his body a walk in the park—a Malaysian park, in the middle of the day, when the sun beat down on you and there was no cloud cover.

Spitting up blood again, Arthur ran water in the sink and staggered back to his bed to flop onto it. He might be a training maniac or Tower maniac or whatever they wanted to call him, but there was only so much even he could take.

There really was not much joy in hurting yourself over and over again for little gain.

He slept for a few hours, waiting for his mental energy to return. On waking, he cultivated to draw in both Yin and Yang energy before he went back to practicing. It hurt to keep pushing at his cultivation techniques, to alter how they moved and drew from the world, to refine the technique to find something that would work with only Yin energy, keeping Yang energy out.

Hours, then days, passed. He only stopped long enough to fill his energy core and practice the Heavenly Sage's Mischief. Hours working on that technique until he ran low on energy and had to start all over again, cultivating Yang and Yin energy and then altering his own cultivation form.

At times, it seemed like he would almost reach an understanding of the changes he needed to alter the technique, only to realise that there was no true path in his cultivation form. It could improve, reducing his Yang intake to only 0.2 or 0.3 of a point, the rest being Yin chi or, sometimes, nothing at all. It made the pain less intense, but it did not get rid of it all.

Still, the Tower never acknowledged the change, a verifiable way to indicate that the technique was broken and incomplete. Whatever improvements he made was insufficient.

So.

He would take the next step and the next, retreating backward or pushing forward with alterations in how the energy flowed, all the while failing. Somehow, something was missing. A way that he touched the chi perhaps, the way it flowed or was cleansed when moving through his meridians.

No matter how much he tried, it was never enough.

That didn't stop him from trying, though. Again and again, his minor successes with learning things like the Heavenly Sage's Mischief was insufficient to remove the growing frustration at his failures, all of it driving him to push harder.

It was after one particularly difficult session, where he found himself throwing up blood again into his chamber pot, that a knock on the door arrived. Arthur ignored it, curled up as he was, but it was insistent, refusing to let him stay on the floor.

"Your time is up! You either pay or get out!" More hammering, and Arthur blinked blearily.

"What?" he whispered. It could not have come, not yet. He had paid for extra days; he should have enough time. There was no reason why—

"Fine, if you won't come out..." A key was jangling in the lock, before the door was opened. The man who came in stared around the room before his gaze fell on the prone Arthur before he spat. "Really? Another one?"

He let out a sigh, looking at the various pieces of clothing and gear owned by Arthur before he strode over, hastily throwing all of it together into Arthur's backpack. Pushing them together, he then grabbed hold of Arthur by the back of his robes and dragged him out, letting his feet bounce off the stairs as he descended.

Arthur, weakly protesting, was unable to stop him even as he clawed at his arm. "Please, I can pay."

"No. I think we're done for today. Wash yourself and clean up, then figure out how to fix yourself," the innkeeper snapped before heaving Arthur through the door. He nearly struck a pedestrian, and the passing Tower climber had to duck as Arthur's backpack landed a few minutes later.

The backpack bounced off his prone body. Arthur weakly pushed himself up, only to collapse again, his eyes half-closing from the accumulated pain.

"Gods, another layabout. And he isn't even fully healed." Snorting, the man walked around Arthur, leaving him to lie there. Nearly all the other passersby did the same, none daring to touch his bag or body.

A good thirty minutes of silence and exhaustion, as Arthur slowly came to himself. Only for a guard to come by, prodding him with his foot.

"No layabouts here. Get up, or we'll throw you out."

"Just five more minutes, Mama!" Arthur said, only to get another boot in the side. His eyes flew open, and he saw the guard looming over him.

"Last warning. Get up yourself. Or we'll throw you out."

"Sure, sure..." Arthur pushed himself up, wincing in pain. He grabbed his bag before the guard could do more than begin growling at him, clutching at his chest as he began coughing again. Flecks of blood were on his lips and the hand he held up.

The guard drew back, glaring at Arthur. "You're not plagued, are you boy?"

"I'm just... injured. Not sick. A cultivation deviation..." Arthur replied, coughing again as he wiped his lips. "I just need a few minutes of rest. Please."

"Not my problem." The guard grabbed Arthur by the scruff of his neck and yanked him up, lifting the 190-pound man easily. When Arthur managed to get his feet under him, he was frog-marched to the edge of the beginner village. A lot of the newbies watched the process with trepidation, knowing that this could easily be them. Still, no one moved to help.

It was a dog-eat-dog world out here, and even if someone wanted to help, you couldn't exactly beat a guard. So the only other option was paying for Arthur's stay in a village, something no newbie would offer to a man who looked to be on his last legs.

More than a few vultures took off running when they saw what was happening. Arthur would make easy pickings once he was out of the village. His goods, his weapon, and yes, himself: a rambutan fresh and juicy for the tongs and gangs that ran the tent village outside.

Knowing that, Arthur forced himself to awaken, grateful he was being allowed to walk. At least this way, he could circulate some of the energy in his body, burning excess energy and pain by the sheer basis of movement.

All too soon, though, they hit the edge of the village where he was unceremoniously pushed out of the boundary. Wincing, Arthur noticed some familiar faces waiting for him already, staring at his pale face hungrily and licking their lips.

"Well, well. Look who we found. And here I thought you'd gotten yourself killed."

"Oh, hey, Samseng One. Nice to see you." Arthur waved weakly, lowering his bag to the ground. No place to run, not with the entire tent village before him and his feet still a little shaky. Which meant standing here, fighting until he was beaten black and blue and maybe killed.

"You really don't know when to shut up, do you?" Samseng said, grabbing the parang by his side and pulling it out. "I'm going to enjoy this."

"And that's something none of your partners have ever managed to say truthfully."

Seeing Samseng's eyes pop out made the coming beating almost worth it.

Almost.

Chapter 37

The first punch hurt. A lot. Not as much as the second one, even as he managed to block the third with his spear. That got grabbed and yanked away by Samseng One. Leaving an opening for his friends to charge Arthur.

He'd managed to send a knife-edge strike into that man's neck, leaving him clutching his throat and trying to breathe around the bruised trachea. Too bad he hadn't crushed it, but he was still a little weak. Also, the entire trachea and neck region was kind of squishy so actually collapsing the thing was harder than it looked, especially when your opponent was flinching in response.

That was Arthur's only real success. Getting dog-piled while exhausted and hurting meant that he managed to land a few more blows that caught at thug bodies, but eventually they wrapped his arms up and kicked him hard enough in the balls that he stopped trying to kick people.

Then, Samseng One made his way back. Throwing punch after punch into his body. Not the face, since working the body left him exhausted and wracked in pain. Each meaty thud elicited a groan of pain and a cough of blood, each cracked rib threatened to puncture a lung. Only the improved body he had developed in the Tower stopped him from receiving a fatal wound immediately, but that was just a matter of time.

Another punch, this one to the face, had his head snapping to the side. Before the next one could snap his head back, a hand had reached out and grabbed Samseng's arm. Samseng looked really surprised, especially since the woman holding his arm was a foot and a half shorter than him, clad in a traditional Chinese flowery blouse and had grey hair with the requisite deep creases on her face to demarcate her age.

"Amah! What are you doing?" Samseng said, pulling at his arm as he tried to free it. "This is none of your business!"

"Yes, yes. You can beat him up later. I just want a word with him first," the old woman said with a smile, eyes glittering. "Now, if I let you go, you wouldn't hit your Amah, will you?"

"You're not my grandmother!" Samseng growled. However, the looks even his own people shot him at his belligerence toward the older woman was enough to make Samseng retract his anger and bow a little. Or maybe it had something to do with the dozen other women surrounding the group of five. "But I don't hit elders." He paused, eyes narrowing dangerously. "Unless they hit me first."

"I only hit my children when they were properly bad." Releasing Samseng's arm, the older woman then carefully lifted up Arthur's bruised face. "So, young one. Can you speak?"

"Speak, sneak, beak." Arthur replied. He frowned, then shook his head. "Meek. I can be meek."

"I do not require any of that. Just information, if you have it. I hear you came in from the east. Deep east." A single eyebrow rose. "Is that true?"

"Uhhh..."

"Answer the Amah, you fool! You think delaying is going to change your fate?" Samseng growled, sticking his head closer, only for the Amah to tut at him and push him back with two fingers.

Once he had given her and Arthur space, she looked at the wounded man and raised an eyebrow in further enquiry. "Well?"

"Which way's east?" Arthur said after a moment.

"Oh my gods, you're dumber than you look. I should have expected that, what with you daring to challenge us!" Samseng muttered.

Even the Amah was a little perturbed before she pointed in the exact opposite direction, right through the village. Or, as Arthur slowly realized, the direction of the woods he had returned from.

"Yes, I think so. Yes." He nodded. Then, worry flashed through his mind, remembering the corpses he stole from. "They were all dead when I found them!"

"All?" Suddenly, the way she had looked and spoke to him grew sharp, the older woman leaning in and fixing him with a steely gaze. "Who is all?"

"A corpse. Had a sword..." He gestured downwards or tried to, then remembered he had left the broken weapon behind. "Uhh, had it..."

"Were they women? Three of them? Where did you find them?" Amah said urgently.

"No! Single corpse, killed and eaten. They were mostly bone... Deep inside. I can show you where?" Clutching at straws, which made Samseng growl in anger, and the pair of thugs holding him up by his arms shook him.

"Only one?" Amah relaxed, shaking her head. "Never mind, then." She turned away, dismissing Arthur to his fate.

Arthur sagged in the hands holding him, his exhausted body aching as he realized his brief moment of hope was disappearing. In the meantime, both Samseng and Amah—and really, would it hurt people to introduce themselves by their actual names?—were exchanging polite words, as though beating up and nearly killing a person was an everyday occurrence.

Maybe it was, in the Tower.

Head hanging, something nagged at him. Something she said. His brain was woozy, repeated blows to it along with the cultivation backlash leaving him struggling to remember what it was. Something about women.

Women. Idiot women, who'd taken his kills, who had not let him steal from the body. "Stupid people... Didn't introduce themselves. What a stupid name too, Daiyu..."

"Wait. What did you say?" Amah turned around, her eyes fixed on him.

"It's a stupid name. Daiyu." Clarity, all too late, as he remembered. "It's who you're looking for, right? Mel, Daiyu. Rani."

"How do you know them? What do you know, boy?" Hands gripped his chin, raising his head again. They tightened on his face as the old woman leaned in, her hot breath laced with stale tobacco smoke breathed into his face. "Where did you see them? When?"

"Why should I tell you?" Arthur said, gasping a little as her fingers tightened. "I'm just going to die anyway."

"I can make it more painful," she threatened.

"And? They went north. South. East. West. They danced in the river and killed members of the Suey Ying tong. They took them prisoners. Tortured them. Ate their flesh—Urk!" His voice cut off as fingers tightened.

"What do you think you're doing, boy?" Her voice had dropped low and dangerous now.

"Telling the truth. Telling lies. I'm going to keep doing that, until you don't know whether the sky's blue or green." Arthur glared back. "Or you can help me out. And I'll lead you to where I last saw them. Let you pick up the trail."

"You little shit. I should cane you until you bleed."

"Sure." Arthur coughed, spitting blood to the side so as not to hit the woman. He sucked at the cut on his lips, and then grinned weakly. "But that won't help you. I'll spout bullshit until you're not sure if I'm lying or telling the truth, no matter how much you're hurting me. I'm real good at talking shit."

Hissing, the Amah stepped back. Samseng, having watched the entire interaction, shifted a little so that he could look at Amah more closely.

"You aren't thinking of taking him away from us, are you? If you want knowledge, we can extract it. We got people. No one talks shit when their balls are chopped off," Samseng said.

"Why is it the balls with you people? Are you all just lusting after them? I mean, sure, Malaysia's still a little backward, but really—URK!" Arthur stopped speaking as another punch took him in the stomach, leaving him heaving and gasping.

"I'm sure you could," Amah was saying. "He might think he's smart, but directions... well, you saw him. He's probably too dumb to have kept a map—"

"I resemble that remark," Arthur wheezed.

"—and we need to find our people."

"I can't let you do that," Samseng said, stepping back and letting his hand drop to the parang he had sheathed.

"Now, don't do something you'll regret boy," Amah said, her head rising. She fixed him with a stern glare, even as the men holding Arthur let him go, letting him fall to the ground. Like the rest, they got ready to fight over his poor, tortured body.

It'd be amusing. If he wasn't hurting so much.

Chapter 38

Arthur was never sure afterward who threw the first blow. All he really knew was that things had been tense, like in a Mexican standoff but with parangs instead of guns, and next, everyone was punching, kicking, and slicing one another up.

Being rather broken at the moment, Arthur was not able to pay full attention to the fight. Though a few things were quite clear, quite fast.

Firstly, Samseng really knew how to run. It wasn't as though he had learnt a new movement technique, unless there were a technique called "throw your friends in front of your enemies" except, you know, with a more flowery title—but he seemed to have an innate sense of when to run and when to duck, so that others could get in the way of the oncoming fist.

Secondly, the Amah was just as she looked. She had a scary level of efficiency at using the cane in her hand, smacking weapons out of knuckles and cracking it across temples and collarbones. The fact that the cane itself was sheathed in some lightly glowing energy probably helped with the smacking.

Lastly, the Suey Ying tong's people here were all thugs. They seemed to have improved their Body attributes in strength and endurance more than in speed. It made them really hard to take down but also slow in comparison to the ladies, who made up for their lack of damage potential by using very sharp weapons.

For all that, when one of the men managed to land a hit—and in a fight, that happened all too often—the women had a tendency to break.

In the end, two corpses, two injured, and one fast-running man were left, along with three tear-stricken faces. The Amah stood around, glaring at the two men she had taken down mostly by herself. Then she prodded her no-longer-glowing cane at Arthur.

"Get up, boy. We can't stay in their territory too long. Ah Choi is good at running and he'll bring back his people fast enough." Looking at the bodies, she barked out a quick series of orders that had them stripping weapons and helping the injured get away. One girl, the largest of the women, grabbed hold of Arthur's bag and then his arm, dragging him upright.

"Move!" She growled. Her voice was husky. Kind of cute, if you liked a low, growly voice in women.

"Who are you people? And what do you want with me?" Arthur muttered.

"Us? We're the Thorned Lotuses. The *Ci Hehua*." She was a bear of a woman; she looked as if she might burst out of the clothes that tightly hugged her dark skin. She kept him moving along the edge of the tent village, following the limping but still fast-moving Amah.

Arthur winced. "Please don't."

"Don't drag you? We got to move."

"Don't speak Mandarin. Your accent is horrible."

"Yours isn't much better!" A voice called out from behind, ribbing Arthur.

"Never studied Mandarin. I'm a KL boy!"

"Uh-huh," said the same woman, smirking. "Didn't go to a proper school?"

"No Chinese schools where I was. Malay public schools all the way," Arthur admitted. What that meant was that he studied in Malay mostly, had a class in English, and no Mandarin at all. If not for some afterschool classes, his Mandarin would have been pretty much non-existent. As for his English, that had gotten a decent boost from his sifu and a dedicated teacher overall.

Ah, the joys of public education, where there was never enough money, never enough good teachers, and everything was taught in a language less than 30 million people spoke, many of them not even well.

"I do have to ask: what the hell is wrong with you?" said the girl holding him.

"I got beaten up."

"Not that. You feel off."

"Ummm, thanks?" Arthur said uncertainly.

"Stop being dense. I meant your energy flows. It's not what I'd expect from a man. You feel like a... a... girl!"

"Oh, that. Yeah..." He winced. "Cultivation deviation."

"So what? You're a girl now?"

"You know ah, I don't let my friends call me a girl, never mind an unnamed woman."

"You can call me Sharmila. Now, stop dodging the question," her voice dropped and grew dangerous. "If you're into some weird dual cultivation practice you read on the Internet—"

"No! Nothing like that." Arthur shuddered. He knew what she had spoken of. There had been a case a few years back: one man who had left the Tower started sacrificing women, using them to empower himself. He had to use Tower survivors, but he had left them as husks. Unfortunately, before he was captured, he'd released his methods onto the Internet. Attempts to scrub the information had obviously failed, so rumors of dual-cultivating cults were always floating around.

Didn't help that other groups like the Golden Sunrise and the Third Pyramid in the US had all chosen to jump on the same cult bandwagon, leaving the entire process with a rather bad taste in everyone's mouth.

"Ha? You very fast to say no, ah!" remarked one of Sharmila's companions.

"You got that right, Jan," Sharmila said.

"It isn't," Arthur said quietly. "I took a pill I found. Thought it'd give me a boost... It was dumb, alright. I knew it was dumb. But it's not as though playing it safe is going to get me to the top."

"Oh, you so *gila* Tower ke?" Jan said, rolling her eyes.

"What? And you all aren't?" Arthur replied. "what's the point of going into the Tower if you don't intend to climb it."

"Just like a man. You men got options," Jan said. "You think we got, ah? You think we want to be here? Some of us come 'cause we have no choice, lah."

"So, what? Come in, hang out, live life and, maybe, ascend?" Arthur's eyes narrowed. "What's the point? You can't even have kids in here."

"And thank god for that!" Sharmila said fervently.

"No hunger. You *mau makan?* Then eat, lah! You *tak mau makan*? Then no need to eat! Have to fight sometimes but can also sleep a lot." Jan shrugged. "Outside got loan shark. Got rent. Got lot of people want something from you. Here, no one come bother you from outside."

"*Ya lah*, that's right. I wasn't going to marry *him*." Sharmila shuddered at some memory. Then she said, "A Tower climber? That's status. And hey, no reason you can't, maybe, eventually ascend."

A lot of nods then, from some of the other women.

Arthur could not help but contemplate their words. It was an entirely different viewpoint about Tower climbing than he had been exposed to. Everyone in his classes had been like him, dedicated to the idea of bettering themselves through the Tower. Using it for its intended purpose which was, presumably, to ascend.

Then again, were they so different? Everyone who entered the Tower was doing so to escape the dystopian world of automation, low-paying jobs, and barely enough welfare income to pay for their existences. Well, except for the rich or connected, who were here to become richer and more powerful.

"Whatever. I just need to figure this out. Then I'll be fine," Arthur said.

"Uh-huh. Just keep telling yourself that," Sharmila said, following Amah as the older woman turned, heading deeper in the village of tents. Soon enough, more and more individuals appeared, women of all sorts, many calling out greetings that were ignored or shushed.

Word spread, and suddenly, Arthur felt himself rather alone in a sea of women. A sea of watchful, angry women.

Chapter 39

They brought him into a building, not the central one but off to the side of it. Amah was already seated, rubbing her knee with a grimace of pain. By the side, a woman was brewing tea.

"Sit. Sit. We don't have a lot of time. We got you out, so talk. And make it quick," Amah said, glowering at Arthur.

"First things first, names!" Arthur said. "I'm Arthur. Arthur Chua. Be nice to know the name of my savior."

"You can call me Amah Si." The old woman's hand moved off her knee for a second, touching the cane by her side as she glared at Arthur. "Now, talk."

"Right, so, I met your girls the first time by accident. They were in a fight with..." Arthur chose to speak, fast, no longer seeing a point in delaying. He owed them for saving his ass after all, but he wasn't out of the fire yet. Maybe edging towards the fire's edge, but he knew what they wanted. Eventually. Thus all the noise he could hear outside, the bodies he could catch in the reflection of the glassed window of people hurrying.

When he finally ran down and finished telling his story, Amah Si stared him up and down. She frowned as she looked over his body, then nodded abruptly.

"Sharmila!" She called out.

The big, dark-skinned Indian woman poked her head around the corner. "What?"

"Take him to get washed and changed. He stinks."

"I... do." Arthur paused, taking care not to sniff himself. Vomiting and bleeding and sweating and exuding corruption while cultivating was not a good smell.

"Well then, stinky. Move!" Sharmila snapped, causing Arthur to jump up. He grabbed at the edge of his chair when he realized he'd moved too fast, wincing as his head spun. Once he had his feet underneath him though, she chivvied him into the nearest bathroom.

Arthur was not at all surprised when he found the bathroom cleaner than most that he had visited. After all, Amah Si did not strike him as an individual who allowed things like uncleanliness or slovenly behaviour to exist within swinging range of her cane.

So, in a clean, pandan-and-bleach smelling bath, he cleansed himself. The scrub and exfoliating brush he found nearby did wonders for his skin, leaving him to marvel just for a second at his transformation as a cultivator.

Of course, unlike a real bathroom, there were no showers, forcing him to go old-school using a pail and barrel. Surprisingly, the cold water was invigorating rather than freezing. He luxuriated for a few moments in being actually clean, before his time of peace was interrupted.

"Mmm... so are you a shower or grower?" Sharmila, standing inside the bathroom with a towel and a change of clothing in hand. She was staring at Arthur rather admiringly.

"Oy!" Arthur spluttered, covering himself. "I latched that door!"

"And?" Sharmila smirked. "You think we let you in alone without a way to get in? You think we're that trusting?"

Still covering his privates, Arthur glared. "No, just a pervert. You know, this is assault."

"I haven't touched you. Yet." She shook the towel in her hand, smiling. "Also, I came here to offer you this."

"Fine. Sexual harassment." Arthur growled, walking over and snatching the towel. "You do realise, if I was a guy doing this to a girl, you'd be screaming bloody murder. Equality means you don't get to do shit like this either."

"Well then, I guess that means you have permission to walk in on me when I'm bathing," Sharmila replied. She even winked.

Surprisingly, beyond the initial shock, Arthur found that he was not as embarrassed as he could have been. Some of that, of course, had to do with having shared quarters and bathing areas with women. Accidents did happen, though there was often a lot more blushing and apologies involved.

Still, her sauciness and outright flirting didn't affect him like it should have. Any other time, he might have grown bolder. Maybe stepped up, kissed her, played the game of daring to see how far he could push it. He had never been sexually shy.

Right now, though, while he could feel his desire, it was at a remove. As though a slight film was covering it, letting him gauge the entire situation with less heat than before. He could see the way her eyes had tracked over his body initially, but now, beyond the over-exaggerated licking of lips and perusal of his body, Sharmila was watching him—his face, his body language—with a different kind of intensity.

As though...

"*Tiu.* You're testing me." Arthur sighed, running a hand through wet hair. He might have flexed a little. He might be weirdly cold about all this, but he was still a man and rather vain about his body. Long hours training meant he was ripped, especially since his meals had become Tower-energy intensive.

"Amah was right." Sharmila said, suddenly relaxing and turning away to put the robes aside. "She's always right. It's *really* annoying."

"Right about what?" Arthur asked, stepping closer.

He hesitated, losing his chance to grab her by the arm. That last inch, that sacrosanct millimeter of space where physical touch became all too invasive between people who lived in crowded cities and stand breathing in each other's faces on packed trains and buses... that invisible barrier stopped him.

And she was gone. Leaving him asking the air, "Right about what?!"

Dressed and dry, he found the woman waiting with Jan. The pair seemed to have chosen—or been chosen—to be his guards. In short order, he was down the stairs, hustled out of the building. When he craned his neck for a glimpse of Amah Si, he was pushed forward with a stick in his back.

"Ouch. And where are we going?" Arthur groused. "I'm grateful for the rescue and bath, but I'm not exactly thrilled at being led around."

"Out. We're headed out," Sharmila replied breezily, her head craning from side-to-side constantly.

"I get that, but where out?" He waved at the few buildings and many tents around him. New buildings were still being constructed by industrious women and the occasional few men. "What's the plan?"

"You don't know, ah?" Jan said, derision in her voice. "It was your plan, *mah*."

"My plan?"

"You show us Mel and others, we save them lah!"

"Right. Of course. My plan." Arthur sighed. Well, it was better than being slowly beaten to death. Still...

"Cheer up. We're going to meet Uswah. She's got a Yin Body like you. You can learn how to cultivate from her," Sharmila said, prodding Arthur again with her stick. "Then maybe you'll be a real man again."

"I'm not......" Arthur threw his hands up. "Fine. Whatever. But I need my bag."

"*Ya, ya, kita dah bawa.*" Sharmila tossed his bag over. "Now move, before the Suey Ying tong stop talking and try bursting in." One more prod and Arthur grumpily caught up with Jan, who had started moving faster. In the distance, he could just about spot the commotion by a tent, where a group of large, burly, and angry men stared in their direction.

Yup. Definitely better than being beaten to death.

Chapter 40

Escaping into the forest edge. It was beginning to become a trend, it seemed. Not one that he was particularly looking to continue, but what was it they said? Once was chance, twice coincidence, and three times enemy action? He knew that didn't make sense here, but then again, maybe fate--or the Tower--enjoyed watching him run.

"Doom here, doom there. Where's the doom you can fear, when the boom comes to adhere?" Arthur muttered as they hurried into the forest.

"Eh, you *cakap apa*?" Jan poked him in the side.

"Nothing, just making something up." Arthur shrugged, unrepentant. "Just wiling away the time, waiting to do some crime. You know?"

"*Dia ni gila, ke*?" Jan rolled her eyes in disgust. "Why we risk our lives on this guy?"

"Just a little insane," Arthur replied, waving his hand around. "But it's just that we're all volunteers."

"Oh God, kill me now."

"Not sure God's around here."

Silence. Arthur turned his head and found Jan glaring at him. "Eh. Don't joke about Him, ah."

"I... right. Gotcha." Arthur nodded though he didn't share her sentiments.

There was nothing in the Good Book about giant Towers appearing all across the planet, or about cultivators developing powers that could only be described as supernatural. No one really knew what to make of it, but hey, they didn't stop trying to. Some people had gotten creative, started a number of new cults. Not that there hadn't been a surplus of them since everything went automated and people started losing faith in, well, everything. Hard to believe in capitalism or your government when every day was a scramble, when the rich just got richer and calls for reform were at best given lip service and authoritarian states proliferated like *lalang* grass.

Shade.

They made it under the canopy and kept moving, a pair of new warriors joining the pair flanking him soon after. Then a few more women, until there was a group a dozen large with him in the middle. Any hope of running away was dashed.

The group picked up the pace, until they were practically running. He had, despite the last few hours of being hurried around from one place to the next, recovered a little from the beating and cultivation deviation. That little was not helping him much, not when he was being forced to run. Each breath was a desperate, painful stab in his side. Each step a stitch as his inners complained. His face throbbed as blood rushed, and he found his focus narrowing.

Yet through all that, Arthur could not help but notice something. He was not sweating, not nearly as much as he should be. The pain from the overabundance of Yang chi in his body was slowly fading, as his body burned it away at a faster than normal rate. The Yin chi cooled his body and clarified his mind with each step.

He moved on and on, hurrying alongside the women as the day lengthened. Eventually, they called for a halt, Arthur stumbling to a stop before he collapsed onto his back. The sun peeked out between leaves, casting long shadows onto the clearing as he cycled chi through his body, refilling energy reserves.

When he caught his breath, Arthur could not help but ponder out loud. "What is a Yin Body? The Yin and Yang are a duality—that's the entire point of the Yin-Yang symbol. You can't have just one or the other. So maybe having a little Yang in my cultivation method is actually right?... Or do I just generate Yang normally? Does a Yin Body actually mean that I'm entirely or mostly made of Yin energy—or just what I'm geared towards using?"

"And why, oh why, are you asking us?" Sharmila crouched beside him asked, amused. When he looked over, she offered him a bottle of water, which he took gratefully. You might not need to eat or drink here, but throats still got dry.

"Is there anyone else to ask?" Arthur said, lips quirking a little as he tried not to smile. "Your supposed expert hasn't appeared."

"Perhaps if you were not so lazy, you might have seen her already," Sharmila said.

Arthur turned his head to the side, staring at Sharmila. Then, he turned to the other side, searching. Nope. That left two directions, both of which would require more work. And seeing as he was flat on his back...

"Later," Arthur muttered. "Or she can come over."

"So Yin Body just another word for lazy boy, eh?" Jan asked, amusement trickling through her voice.

"I had a cultivation deviation and then was nearly beaten to death today before negotiating with a group of angry women for my life before trekking untold miles through the wilds," Arthur said. "I'm allowed to be lazy."

"And what you call laziness is just choosing to make the most of this little break." The unfamiliar voice had, surprisingly, a drawling Australian accent. Arthur frowned. The voice had him searching until he found its source: She was lying on the branch of a tree, one leg hanging off the edge and a hand beneath her head. Not Caucasian, but Malay. And she wore a head covering, an olive green *tudung*.

"Uswah?" Arthur said, hesitantly.

"Yes."

"Huh." Then he flopped back down, his initial burst of curiosity overridden by exhaustion. He would deal with her and his questions later.

Later was, unfortunately, only a half hour away. The group took off, with Uswah the last to join them after dropping from the tree. She seemed to be both idly strolling along and yet, somehow, managing to keep up with the fast-moving group. Arthur frowned, watching her for a long time before he was forced to ask.

"Are you using a movement technique?"

"Yes."

Silence. When he realized she intended not to clarify, he grimaced. "So, I don't know if you know, but—"

"You have a Yin Body. And you want information."

"Well, yeah."

"Why?"

"Um, because I can't cultivate properly with it?"

"Why should I help?"

"I was told you would," Arthur said, his jaw jutting out a little. "They said you would!"

"They did not," Sharmila called out from behind. "I said there was someone with the Yin Body named Uswah. I never promised she'd help."

"You—!" Fuming Arthur turned around and glared. Sharmila simply grinned at him unrepentantly. "Fine. Whatever. I don't need you people." Picking a direction, he started walking away from the group. He had his backpack, his spear. He could and would leave if they would not hold up their end of the bargain.

"Child."

"What did you say?" Arthur turned around, his temper flaring. Still, it guttered out faster than he would have expected, exhaustion robbing him of the energy to be incensed.

"I didn't say I wouldn't help."

Eyes narrowed, Arthur breathed. He forced himself to calm down, to remember what she had said. She was right. Just...

"I'm done being dicked around. By you and everyone else. If you want something, just speak plainly," Arthur said. No heat in his voice, he was surprised to find. Which made it sound... stern? Well, he'd go with stern.

Uswah cocked her head, watching Arthur curiously. "You've lost your heat. Your Yang."

"Told you, half a man," Arthur could hear Sharmila mutter to Jan. "Pity. He's got a cute butt."

"I have not." Arthur frowned. "Alright, maybe I've lost some of my Yang. But I'm still a man. I can still—"

"Don't care," Uswah waved his excuses away. "Your heat, your anger, your Yang—it's been overridden by the Yin. Not a bad thing. But your passion will be subdued, your anger run deeper, your grievances sharper."

Arthur said nothing, and she continued.

"Yin is not lack of passion or movement, but the slow progress of the world. The cooling of the earth, as the world rotates, the changeover from burning enthusiasm to long-lasting coals of dedication. You won't struggle for revenge but patiently plot your vengeance."

A step closer, and Uswah looked into Arthur's face.

"You are Yin now, and we do not give for no reason. Or take without cause."

Arthur shivered, staring into the pools of inky blackness that looked into him. Her eyes were not brown, not the earthen silk of the past, but the abyss. Staring into it, he shivered again and understood.

"Then, let us bargain," Arthur said.

And for the first time, Uswah smiled.

Chapter 41

"Information." Uswah spoke after a brief silence, one the group had filled with further walking. Their short tiff had ended with them left behind, and so the group had hurried to catch up with the scouts.

"I want it. You have it," Arthur said.

"Oh gods, he's rhyming again," Sharmila groaned.

"Flows both ways," Uswah said.

"Really?" Arthur said, eyes narrowing. She could not know about his other skills, unless his expanded healing ability made sense to her. He had not used it, not much since he had not had the hour it would have required. Never mind the fact that the pain had been, surprisingly, more subdued.

Perhaps another side effect of the Yin Body.

"You are the first male Yin. Unique." Uswah raised a hand. "Unique can highlight differences. Help me learn more, about my own cultivation techniques." A slight smile. "Maybe come up with something new."

"I see. That's a little vague, though."

"It is. Information on Yin Bodies is... sparse. Except to those privileged to be in certain clans. Those not born into one, we're forced to learn ourselves."

"Damn," Arthur cursed, though without heat. "I'd hoped you knew more."

"I do." A slight smile. "I know at least how to cultivate properly."

Now she had his attention. He stared at Uswah who offered him a wider half-smile before she continued. "Also. A favour." She held a single finger up. "One big favour. No excuses, no hesitation."

Arthur frowned. "No. You could, you know, ask me to kill a baby."

"No babies in the Tower."

"Metaphorically! And once we're out of the Tower, well, a lot of babies there."

"Okay. No baby killing."

"Wait, was that on the table? Seriously?" Arthur said, stepping away from Uswah.

A teasing smile danced on Uswah's lips in answer. "No horrors. But no promises about it not being illegal. Just not immoral."

Arthur drummed fingers along his staff, using it to prod the ground before him. He was not surprised to see a nearby plant snap upwards, grabbing his staff—and it would have grabbed his leg if he had put it there—before he yanked the entire thing out of the ground.

"Don't destroy that." Behind him, Jan's voice. She hurried over, grabbing at the staff and pulling it upwards as she cut at the bottom of the plant where root and stem joined, extracting a glowing portion in short order. "Good find. Thanks, ah!"

Arthur peeled the dying, limp plant off his staff. "What was that?" He had never seen that portion Jan harvested before. Not that he went around gathering plant parts much, but he was sure he hadn't seen anything like that on the Guild boards either.

"Ingredient. For alchemy. Don't worry, I share," Jan said.

"Not a real answer," Arthur grumbled.

"Secrets. All of us have them." Uswah prodded him. "Now, your decision?"

"Fine, fine. One favour, nothing immoral," Arthur replied. That was still a little too vague for his liking, but at least he was going to be deciding what constituted immoral. It wasn't as though the Tower held people in a supernatural way to such promises.

"Good." Uswah reached into her dress, making Arthur blink. He did not, however, turn away as she rummaged and extracted a scroll, so she raised an eyebrow at him.

"Hey, I'm just a half man."

"Rude man."

He grinned, taking the scroll she handed him. He pulled it open just enough for a peek. "This is your cultivation method?"

"Ours."

"I see." Relief, rushing through him. He clutched the scroll tighter for a brief second, drawing an annoyed squeak from Uswah at the damage, which he guiltily smoothed out. "Thank you."

"Read later."

"Of course." Arthur nodded and slipped it in his bag carefully. Once that was done, he hurried to catch up, turning his attention to the act of trudging along. There were many miles to cover.

And at the end, he had a scroll to read and decipher.

Hours and hours walking before the group finally stopped, pulling into a clearing and setting up a makeshift encampment. Tents, strings strung around trees, and a few stakes punched into the ground were all that was done for protection, besides a half dozen talismans strung on those same strings. Once triggered, they would protect the encampment from being located or breached. Or at the very least, sound a warning.

Despite his resolve to read that scroll, Arthur was unable to keep his eyes open. He did not even manage to do more than crawl into his tent before he collapsed on the bedroll, exhaustion and the drain of healing taking him to the land of Somnus.

Six hours later, Arthur woke, his body humming with energy. He had not realized it before, but his Yin was stronger in the dark of the night. He had noticed the change in cultivation speed at times, but in his old solitary, windowless room, he had had no way to tell the time of day. Nor had he cared to then.

Body thrumming with power, Arthur spent a moment to review his stats.

Cultivation Speed: 1 (0.71 Yin)
Energy Pool: 4.51/15 (Yin) (0.08 Yang – Unusable)
Refinement Speed: 0.015
Refined Energy: 1.27 (2)

Attributes and Traits
Mind: 3
Body: 6 (Enhanced Eyesight, Yin Body)
Spirit: 4

Techniques
Focused Strike
Accelerated Healing – Refined Energy (Grade I)
Heavenly Sage's Mischief

"Oh hell," he groaned. "I forgot to learn Energy Dart. And spend my refined energy point."

Damn it. Every time he got too involved in his cultivation, in anything, he hyper-focused and anything else that was important was driven away. All that he could do, all that he could focus on, was the project that had driven him to this point.

And now, well.

"I really could have done with more points in Body." He really could have. But he had a Body of 6 now, higher than before. And he was one point away from a trait in Spirit, but if he grabbed that...

"My problem's in gathering energy to refine, not in actually refining that energy." He muttered that all softly to himself as he reviewed his status.

On the other hand, a trait could make a difference. He cudgelled his brains, trying to recall the common Spirit traits that he had read about and the one he had planned to acquire. It had been long, all too long since he'd read about them. The things that Spirit changed were not just refinement speed but also aura, killing intent, poison resistances, and even the ability to control and mold energies.

Now, he had not a lot of refined energy-based effects, but perhaps his most important skill, Accelerated Healing, did use it. On top of that, the Energy Dart technique which he had meant to learn used refined energy.

On the other hand, boosting his Mind ability would increase his energy collection speed, help him learn the Energy Dart technique, and deal with things like the rather fraught social situations. He wouldn't necessarily be smarter, but greater comprehension helped.

"Gods, I hate decisions." Arthur sighed, grabbed the scroll from his bag and unrolled it. Better to see how hard it was to learn this.

An hour later, as the light of the sun began to cut through his lantern, Arthur was done with his third read-through. He rubbed his temples, staring at the document, and sighed.

"Mind it is..."

The application of the refined point of energy shot through his body like lightning, tightening his muscles before cold, ice-cold, shock cut through his mind. His brain froze and hurt, lightning arcing through mind and soul.

Teeth gritted; body arched. He whimpered, thrashing around until the point, his first ever into Mind, faded away. Leaving him...

Changed.

Chapter 42

"Oi! You're leveling up now?" Sharmila grabbed Arthur by the ear and dragged him out of the tent. She gestured impatiently for the women to finish packing, then turned on him again. "Don't you know better than to use refinement points in the field? Especially your first point in Mind? You bodoh, ke?"

"I know a lot of things. And shouting at me is not helping," Arthur groused.

"So you're not ignorant, just stupid."

"Oh, and waiting weeks before I can progress is a good idea?" snapped Arthur as he stood up more fully and detached himself from Sharmila. He walked over to a woman who was pulling his spear out of the tent and took it from her. "Mine."

"Aiyoh! Just say, lah. No need to grab like that," she grumbled at Arthur.

"Sorry, ah!" Arthur replied before walking back to Sharmila, who was watching Arthur's tent and his gear get packed with a critical gaze. "Anyway, I'm not that late, am I?" He looked up at the sky. Hard to tell, but he could see the sun coming over the trees.

"Late enough. We need to put more distance between us and our pursuers."

"What pursuers?" Arthur said. "I'm not that important. I mean, sure, a few people got killed but they'd just wait for me to come back and then kill me. Or beat up those of you who are still there. No reason to come all the way out here. Unless…"

"Later." Sharmila's lips pursed. "Take your bag. Let us go." Spinning on her heel, she rushed off, not answering Arthur's own words.

"Suspicious behaviour, your name art Shar!" Arthur cried out at her retreating back.

Sighing, he did as she asked, slipping his bag on and hoisting his spear. He joined the group, falling into the center where they seemed intent on having him. For now, it seemed, they had no need to ask him where to go. Not a huge surprise since they were only a day of hard marching away. Mel, Daiyu and Rani had left word of their route before leaving the larger group.

Well, that sounded like they had a plan. One that they had spoken of and informed the Thorned Lotuses about. Which spoke of premeditation. Which spoke of...

"Why you always frowning?" Jan had suddenly appeared beside him.

Arthur jumped, both feet off the ground, his spear leveled at where Jan had been. She had stepped aside swiftly and was now giggling like crazy. Guffaws came from the other women too.

"Don't do that!" Arthur snarled.

Grinning, Jan sauntered, pushing the tip of the spear aside with her fingers gently. "Keep doing your face like that. Get wrinkles fast."

He growled, but her continued giggles made him decide that complaining would not end well for him.

"Aiyoh! Just ask, lah!" said the same woman from whom he had taken his spear.

"What?" Arthur said. He hated Manglish. Getting beaten by his teacher every time he had used it meant he'd learned how to speak properly—or at least, proper enough that he only got walloped once in a while by that snotty old Brit graduate—and created his own rather pointed viewpoint.

"Ask, lah. You know you want, mah."

She had a point. "Thanks!" Arthur said, then hurried after Sharmila who was at the front of the convoy, his suspicions dancing in his mind.

When he got to Sharmila, he blurted out his theory. "Mel and the others—they learned something. Something important. A hidden part of the first floor, a hidden boss or treasure room. Something important, didn't they?"

Sharmila's brow drew tight as she turned to him. Her long black braid swung around her leather breastplate, which stood out against her darker skin. It struck Arthur that she possessed the severe look of an authentic woodswoman. If she had a spear like his, she'd make a great ranger cut-out.

"None of your business."

"I'm right, aren't I?" Arthur smirked.

"You know, asking too many questions can get you killed."

"By the time we find them or get to the place, you'll all love me and my rakish charms," Arthur said.

"Or want to kill you immediately."

"Or want to kill me." Arthur shrugged. "It's hard being as good looking as I am."

"My dog more handsome than you," Jan had been shadowing him, and she now flanked his left.

"Seriously, do you just hang around, waiting for me to say something so that you can poke holes in my ego?"

"Your ego so big I can poke holes from there." Jan jerked a thumb towards the rear of the group. Sniggers resounded, but she wasn't done. "But you can't hear me there."

"I hate you."

"I know," Jan said.

Arthur frowned but dismissed the woman to focus on Sharmila. "So, you going to answer me or what?"

"I'll take door number two," Sharmila replied.

Lips thinned, but Arthur realised he wasn't going to get an answer. Not right now at least. Still, just because they would not confirm his guess didn't mean he couldn't...

Well. Something.

Long minutes later, while he stewed in silence, Sharmila finally spoke up. "What?"

"Huh?" Arthur said, looking at her.

"You just going to pout because I didn't answer you?" she said accusingly.

"No." He paused, then grinned. "Unless that means you'll answer me."

"Not a chance."

Arthur sighed. "Figured." Then, seeing she was still waiting for something, he continued, "I was just thinking about what else I needed to do."

"Nothing much to do," Sharmila replied easily. "You show us the place you last saw them, we confirm that we can pick up the trail and then, well..."

"Well?" Arthur's eyes narrowed. "Well what? Stopping in the middle of that sentence isn't disconcerting at all."

"Nothing bad. We just haven't decided what we're going to do with you."

"What's there to do? You let me go on my way, you guys go do your thing."

"Oh, and you don't want to spend more time with Uswah?"

"Sure, that's fine. After you guys are done with whatever." He tapped the strap of his backpack. "If I learn this by the time we're there, I'll probably just need a few pointers after."

"And what about your deal with me?" Uswah said as she appeared by his side. Arthur found himself jumping a little.

"How—?"

She just smiled a little enigmatically, waving a finger for him to continue.

"I'll tell you whatever you need, after. I don't want to get involved in whatever you guys are doing."

"Oh, and he was so excited about a 'treasure'," Jan replied from behind, tauntingly.

"As though you'd let me get anything good from whatever you guys are up to finding." Arthur crossed his arms. "I also noticed most of you are stronger than me. Significantly. So whatever it is, it's dangerous." He shook his head. "I'm willing to take risks. But I'm not entirely stupid."

Jan snorted, but Arthur didn't take the bait. He shook his head, saying, "I'll give you the information you want. But I'm not coming with you."

"We'll take that under advisement," Sharmila said.

Arthur pursed his lips but nodded. It seemed his saviours were not so much here to save him. Which meant...

Deep breath. And then he grabbed the document from his bag to read it over once more. If they wanted to drag him around against his will, he might as well let them do the hard work of keeping him alive while he studied.

Because he was going to need to be stronger, faster, sooner or later.

Chapter 43

Studying the Yin Body cultivation menu was fascinating. It touched upon the idea of the aura, the external chi, environment and chi sensing as almost pre-requisites to making full use of the cultivation tome. It spoke not just about the actual process of cultivating but also the environment, mindset, and physicality required to make the most of a cultivation session. There were also details about the kind of apothecary items that were most beneficial and a much smaller section on useful equipment.

Upon being questioned, Uswah had laughed in Arthur's face. At first, she thought he had made a deliberate joke. Then she laughed again, this time in incredulity that he had not accessed anything more than the most basic cultivation manual.

After she had stopped laughing and he stopped fuming, she had gone on to explain that all true cultivation manuals delved into such topics as a matter of course. She had structured her own treatise—along with the information she had already acquired—in a similar manner.

What she provided him, in her view, was but the barest of minimums.

For Arthur, though, it was a feast of enormous proportions that he consumed, deliberately and carefully. Savouring and tasting each morsel of information, intent on making full use of it. He read, he memorised, he practised, and he tested.

And then, to make good on his deal, he related his own observations to Uswah. At times, she would just nod; other times she would correct a misconception. Only occasionally, when Arthur mentioned one peculiarity or another, would she grow silent.

He soon realised that on those nights, Uswah wasn't on guard duty, instead always taking the time off to cultivate. And night was, as he had realised, the best time to cultivate. In the darkness, under the moon, drawing forth the cold energy of the Yin side was easiest.

So much so that he found his cultivation speed had increased significantly. Even though he had not learned it fully, still allowing Yang chi to slip in, he found that he was nearly back to his "normal" cultivation level in the dead of the night.

What was even more useful for Arthur was the other portion of the manual, the method to remove and convert Yang chi into Yin chi. More than once, he would stop amidst his nightly cultivation to process the built-up Yang chi, reducing the growing pain in his body to manageable levels.

It was also during this process, as he focused deeply within, that he saw the churning Yang chi slip into his body, hiding and becoming part of it. After the fifth night of watching how it shifted and hid, he found himself making his way to Uswah.

"Yang chi or Yin chi, the energy – its within and outside of our body, isn't it?" Arthur said. "It's not that we have a Yin Body and it's just Yin. Yin is just what we do best with," Arthur said without preamble.

"Right. If we had only one type of chi, we'd be dead and unmoving. Entirely inert with Yin, Even with fire of Yang, well, fires still die," she said. "And even then, fires fade and die, corpses rot and change."

"So a Yin Body just means we accept Yin into us better, but not only Yin. The minor traces of Yang energy we draw in helps power us, too."

"*Saya dah kata, kan?*" Uswah said, exasperated they were still on this topic.

"Sorry, I just needed to confirm that. But I just don't get it. Why make us, allow us, to grow like this?"

Uswah shrugged at that. "Ask the Tower. Maybe it'll answer."

"You're quoting memes at me?" Arthur said, incensed.

Uswah smiled enigmatically and then sped up, leaving him behind and grumpy. Still, he had his answer. Crossing his arms, he sighed and went back to reading. He wished he could cultivate while moving but if there was a method to that, no one had found it.

Or if they did, they had kept that method secret. Which was not surprising. Moving cultivation would be a huge advantage for anyone who figured it out.

Nearly half a day later, Arthur finally gave up. He placed the scroll aside, having drained for now any and all understanding and knowledge he could have from it. He was certain that, eventually, he might learn more after practice, studying it further, and most of all, giving it time.

Rubbing at the bridge of his nose, he looked around, searching for something better to do. Unfortunately, his usual mode of entertainment—verbal sparring with Jan—was out scouting. A half hour of wandering through the woods, following behind the group, watching them take care of any and all monsters and snatching up herbs from the ground left him bored.

He might be safe in the midst of the large group, but he was also bereft of any chance to acquire monster cores or pick at the herbs necessary for his gathering quests. Which left him:

"Bored. Bored. Bored. I'm bored of being boring, and when I'm bored of being boring, I'm liable to do some rhyming."

"That's not a rhyme," Sharmila commented. She was never too far away.

"It's not that easy, you know, coming up with rhymes on the fly. If it were, rappers would not die."

"I could kill you. No one would need to know."

"But then who'd show you the way?"

"You've not been doing much guiding, now have you?"

Arthur could not help but shrug in acknowledgment. They had not actually been taking the way he had returned, instead cutting a more direct path to their target, which left him mostly useless beyond a nightly verification via map that they were on the right path.

In another week or two, of course, that would change. It would depend on the kind of dangers they would face, but thus far, they were close enough to the newbie village that they had yet to deal with powerful or a large number of monsters. Even the largest *babi ngepet* herd was easily dealt with by a group as experienced as theirs.

"Whatever." Arthur let out a long sigh. "I'm still bored. At least let me fight a bit. I'm going to get rusty if I don't."

"You can train when we stop at night," Sharmila said mercilessly.

"I need to cultivate then. Got to actually get good at this kind of cultivating."

"Not my problem."

"Bored, bored, bored. When we're bored, we make up lore! Did you know, that a *kuching hitam* once ate Ah Ang!"

Sharmila swung her fist, forcing him to duck. A second later, she growled, "Go practise a fighting technique! You have a few, don't you?"

"Okay! I can do that. Just, make sure to be gentle when you carry me, okay?" Grinning, Arthur flooded his body with chi, directing it through his meridians. Heavenly Sage's Mischief would give him a boost in strength for a bit, but once it was over, he was going to be exhausted.

Ignoring the increasingly strident demands for him to explain what was going on, Arthur hopped ahead to the front of the group. Maybe, if he stayed at the front, he would have a chance to attack the monsters before the rest of the group.

Sometimes, being annoying and silly had its uses.

Chapter 44

Being dropped onto his back without warning was painful, but thankfully, he had been exhausted enough that all it meant was that he bounced off the ground rather bonelessly. Looking up at the glaring woman who had carried him the rest of the way, he grinned his thanks a little.

"Idiot." Jan shook her head. "If someone attacks us, then how?"

"I'll hide behind all of you big strong women, of course," Arthur replied. He wasn't going to tell her that he wasn't as exhausted as he acted. He still kept a good portion of energy stored away, just in case he needed to trigger Heavenly Sage's Mischief again.

Rolling her eyes, Jan tromped off, leaving Arthur to pull himself up. He winced and shrugged his backpack off, rubbing at the portion of his back where he had managed to land on the pots and other hard objects.

Gods, what he would do for a storage ring.

Dismissing the thought a moment later, he sat there and breathed slowly, circulating energy through his body to help drive some of the exhaustion from him while also refilling the stores of his energy. He was two thirds through his fifth cycle when a foot made its presence known in the side of his ribs.

Falling over on his side, groaning in pain at being interrupted, he was just grateful it was not during a very critical part of his cultivation. Sitting upwards, he found himself growling.

"What kind of jerk interrupts someone in the middle of cultivation?" Arthur snapped. "You could have—" He trailed off when he realised it was Uswah who had kicked him.

"I checked. Now, go set up your own tent. We're not your slaves." She kicked his bag and left.

"I didn't think she had a temper at all," Arthur said, rubbing at his side through tight breathing.

"She doesn't. I do," Sharmila said. "Next time, I won't ask her to interrupt you. I'll do it myself."

Arthur stared at her for a second, then grinned and hopped to his feet. Or he tried, before his left leg seized and he fell over.

"Just... one second."

Muffled laughter from most of the women around. Except for Jan, of course. She didn't bother even to muffle her hoots of laughter.

It took him a good five minutes of circulating his energy and stretching before he managed to get his leg working again, at which point he began the process of putting his tent up. Luckily, these were modern tents, which meant putting them up was a matter of minutes rather than hours of cursing and wondering which demented god had decided to invent tents.

Without the need to cook dinner, the group fell silent soon after, each member of the team cycling energy to cultivate in turn. Once Arthur managed to top himself off too, he turned his focus—finally—to the other battle technique he had purchased.

Training in Heavenly Sage's Mischief during the day had been more than enough for him. Already, he could tell his muscles were sore and were going to complain about it later, so a period of resting the body was optimal. Anyway, he really did want to learn Refined Energy Dart.

Reading over the technique's scroll once more to make sure he had the full understanding and recollection of the process in mind, Arthur began the laborious process of feeling for his aura and then pinching a portion of it off.

Pinching his aura was sort of like squeezing a water balloon with your eyes shut and a hand that had been clad in oven mitts. Practice made the oven mitts less strange to wear, thinning the material and giving him more control. Practice also meant he could actually find and grip the damn water balloon three times out of ten.

The good news was that this part of the Refined Energy Dart combat technique did not require him to use any actual refined energy. Considering he first had to refine any energy he cultivated, wasting refined energy on practising this was going to be annoying.

On the other hand, in theory, using refined energy meant that it would do even more damage. Of course, that was a supposition since he had no idea how much damage it would do until he actually used it.

When he got tired of grabbing and failing, Arthur opened his eyes. Turning his head from side-to-side, he briefly looked about, finding the silence peaceful. He breathed deeply and took in the forest and the cries of animals late in the evening. Cicadas and other insects, swooping bats and floating heads, trailing intestines, all in the forest.

Peaceful.

He breathed in and out. Then, his eyes widened and he grabbed his spear, screaming, "*Penanggal*! Penanggal attack!"

A floating head moved, yanking its teeth out of a woman's neck—she was one of the forward scouts. Intestine-like entrails connected to the head had wrapped around the scout, who began to thrash and yelp with pain. Another head—which had feminine features and long black hair—floated towards Arthur, screaming. Or it tried to, having no lungs to expel air. Merely vibrating the air in its throat, it could only make a strangled sound.

The women were fast to act, but Arthur was already awake and the first to spot the monsters. Uswah, who happened to be on watch, attacked the floating head that had bitten the scout. An arc of black light flashed, catching the monster on its face, tearing and revealing white skin beneath.

At the same time, Arthur leapt and stabbed his spear at the nearest penanggal. He pushed energy through his body and into his spear. Focused Strike empowered his attack to punch through the head that was darting towards him.

Impaled through its nose, the monster did not stop moving. It merely floated down the spear, eyes gleaming and intestines whipping at Arthur. He winced as he was struck and reflexively threw the entire spear away, taking the creature and its whipping tentacles with it.

Breathing through the pain, he watched the penanggal fly and bounce off the ground. Intestines splayed and curled, before they pushed and slid the bleeding head off Arthur's spear.

Another muted, twisted scream and the monster was now lunging back at Arthur. A pair of throwing knives caught it midway, tearing stripes of skin and an intestine edge off.

Nearby, the first monster screamed as Uswah tore into it with her black Yin chi knives while Sharmila strode up, her heavy maul swinging hard the moment intestines were ripped free from the scout who was first attacked.

Impact shattered the penanggal's skull before it flew, entrail-less, into the distance to crash into a tree, splattering like a rotten egg. Dropping down beside the scout, Sharmila tore at a few stray tentacles and freed the woman to breathe.

Pulling his attention back to his assailant, Arthur was not surprised that the second penanggal, that vampiric ghost, was being dealt with. The rest of the team tore and struck at it until it finally died.

Exhaling in relief, Arthur opened his mouth to make a quip. Only to catch Sharmila closing the eyelids of the scout.

Neither the night nor the forest was as peaceful as he had thought.

Chapter 45

Morning came early that day, bringing with it a somber group. Arthur no longer teased the team or made them carry his body while he practiced his techniques. He understood that such actions would see him receive even shorter shrift, but also... it was just wrong.

Mischief and humour were all right and good, and in fact necessary in the greater view of the world, but there was a time and place for tomfoolery. Today was not one of those. Today was a time for somber thought and grief, long laid within. He felt it too, though much less than the women did. He had even helped to lay the scout's body to rest, his spade digging into soft earth in the early morning light.

A part of him questioned the point of burial, what with the tendency for bodies—human or monster—

to break apart within days. Yet, he chose not to speak his thoughts out loud.

Wisdom, perhaps.

They took off soon after, moving through the woods at a slower clip, more watchful than ever. The scouts pulled in a little tighter, their concerns over the higher level of monsters growing. Arthur kept one ear out for them, but for the rest of the time, he practiced.

The danger they were in pushed him to *jiayou* a little, to try harder. He needed to improve and expand his range of options. He could not increase all his attributes—he did not have the requisite number of points—but he definitely could at least study his Refined Energy Dart.

All day long, with minor pauses, he grabbed and twisted energy, again and again. He did not push the energy through his body, knowing better than to try that with the low reserves that he had. He also knew he needed to preserve a certain amount of it to actually use the skill later.

Lunch was a small number of berries, more something for them to chew upon and a drink of water than anything substantial. While there was no need for it, the act itself helped calm them down, settle nerves. Ritual, a connection that reminded them of who and what they had been.

Five minutes and then they started moving again, travelling through the forest. Once again, Arthur began his practice, only to be interrupted moments later.

"What are you doing?" Uswah, head cocked to the side. She watched the hand that he had been flexing as he imagined the motion of pinching his aura to cast the Refined Energy Dart from it.

"Practicing," Arthur replied. "Aura practice."

"Oh. I hated those," Uswah said. "But you're not doing it for your cultivation."

"How'd you know?"

"Too concentrated." She pointed at his hand.

"I might be trying to focus on one part, you know."

"Maybe." She shrugged. "I don't think so, though. It looks different."

He sighed. And after a second, shrugged.

"Fine, you caught me out. I'm practicing a new technique. Needs my aura to make it work, so I'm practicing how to do that."

"Good to learn other forms," she said after a second. She visibly hesitated then shut her mouth a moment later.

"Wh—" He never finished, as a cry from ahead made the pair look up. Gripping his spear tight with both hands, Arthur pointed it in the direction of the cry.

Ahead of them, a scout was backpedalling fast. Her hands were moving, half-drawing and loosing as fast as she could. But a single arrow—no, even a dozen arrows—would not be enough to stop what was coming. Not *all* of them, which was the frightening part.

"*Semut merah*!" she screamed as scores of ant-like monsters scrabbled into view one after the other. Actual red ants outside the Tower were each about the size of the first knuckle of a pinky, but these were nearly the size of a palm.

She was nearly back with the rest of the team when the first monster got hold of her as she failed to nock and fire fast enough. It clamped its mouth down on her foot, making her stumble. Then the next one climbed on top of the first ant. Then the one after, biting into the leg, the ankle, the foot.

She fell, screaming. They crawled over her, swarming, biting, tearing, crushing. She kept screaming, even as attacks from the rest of the team fell on the ants. Waves of black yin energy that cut into monster limbs. Arrows that punched through carapace and locked them down. Even little touches of flame that licked against a few.

Yet, for all that, they were just first-level Tower climbers. None of them had the power to destroy a swarm with the wave of a hand. They had no way to peel the ants off, not without harming her. Try as they might—and they tried mightily, some even risking their own hides to close in with a stab or jab—they failed.

Writhing body, covered in a carpet of red carapaced bodies. A scream that slowly increased in volume, on and on, then muffled by stabbing bodies and tearing pincers before it ended, cut short by a tearing strike. There were still screams, though, from the other women as they attempted to save her, even as her thrashing slowed then ended.

Arthur was in their midst too, stabbing and thrusting, using his spear to pin ant after ant. He growled as he noticed some crawling up the shaft, some heading for his feet. He fell back, eyes widening as he saw Sharmila wading in towards the body and swinging a parang.

"We have to retreat!" Uswah, cool-headed, at least enough to sense the danger. "She's dead. You got to let her go."

"No!" Sharmila cried.

Arthur swept low with his spear to send the monsters bouncing away. Then, he struck at Sharmila's feet too, driving some of the ants back, attempting to keep her safe. Each monster bounced easily away with each strike; individually their light bodies no match for the enhanced strength of the Tower climbers.

It didn't matter. There were too many.

"Shar!" Jan cried out, jumping in and pulling her back by the scruff of her breastplate. She pulled, harder than ever, making her friend stumble and retreat. "She's dead. And so are we if we don't go!"

Another swipe, another stab. Arthur retreated with the rest of the team, cursing out loud. "Where are they coming from?"

"Nest. We must have stumbled in too close," Uswah said, still calm as she cut with her blades of Yin chi. "They're very rare. Good killing, so long as you don't get too close."

"We're too bloody close!" Arthur snapped. "We got to run."

The group was shaken and backing away. Still fighting, but on the defense. Afraid. No one wanted to die, not that way.

"*Chutiya*!" Sharmila cursed and shook Jan off. Then, waving her free hand and still stumbling from the bites around her feet, she shouted, "Back! Keep moving. We got to back off. Find water."

Together, the group ran, half-stumbling. Leaving one of their own behind, because they had no choice. Leaving the torn, damaged body, along with a piece of themselves. Because that was the way it went in the Tower.

Chapter 46

"Damn it, damn it, damn it!" Sharmila cursed, pounding a fist over and over into her leg as though the pain was but a penitence. "I should have told her to be more careful. I should have been in front..."

"It's not your fault," Jan was repeating, over and over again. For obvious reasons, Sharmila was ignoring her entirely.

The team had reconvened a distance away, having managed to retreat across a swift-flowing stream. Water would not have stopped the colony of semut if they had chosen to pursue, at least not for long, but the ants seemed to consider it a done cause, staying on the other side of the stream even as Arthur and the women ran for it.

Thankfully, the ants were not very good at pursuit, more and more of them wandering off in random directions the further the team retreated. It meant that beyond the initial difficult breakoff, they had not been in any real danger of being swarmed.

Now, they sat and rested, attempting to catch their breath and still their pounding hearts. Sharmila strode back and forth, angrily cursing herself out and lapsing into Hindi at times. Arthur's own knowledge of Hindi was rather anemic, even in the cursing department. So he mostly let what she said wash over him, as he cleaned his spear and checked on the edge, making a face as he noted a nick.

"I never saw any of those things, the last time I was out," Arthur muttered ever so softly to Uswah. He did not want to set off Sharmila again, but this was information he felt he needed.

"*Semut ni...* They're not common at all," Uswah replied after expelling a long breath. "*Kita malang je.*"

With a nod, Arthur agreed they had simply been unlucky. Idly, he noted her switching to Malay. Perhaps even she was shaken. Even with the cool effect of Yin on their minds. He was surprised he was not more scared himself. His breathing was only short because of the run, not because of the hideous image of a woman being torn apart by ants, screaming and screaming and screaming and thrashing...

He blinked.

Or maybe he was.

"So, we're just unlucky to meet the semut merah?" Arthur mouthed the words, as though testing them out. As though saying it made the horror any less... horrible. And finding that it did, a little.

It was something Asians in particular seemed to be more accepting of than the Westerners. Their "first-world problems" meme even made fun of it. They were more resigned to the fact that the world sucked. Fate and the gods really were out to get you, and sometimes shit happens.

Of course, the generation before was even more bitter and twisted. His own generation had grown up with the Towers as a potential saviour, while his elders had grown up with rising inflation, capital flight, the great depression redux forced by autonomous machinery, and climate crisis control and damage, and...

Yeah, maybe they had a reason to be bitter.

"So, now what?" Arthur muttered, watching as Shar kept stalking around, cursing. So many deaths, so many losses. Even people who decided to leave. They were now down to six members of the team.

"We go round the nest."

Well, of course. Sensing Uswah was done with the conversation, he shut up too and focused on cleaning and buffing the nick out of his spear. If things were going to get tougher, he had better keep his gear in good condition.

The group swung wide of the nest, spending nearly an entire day hiking parallel to the location before crossing back to their initial path. They took only a minor deviation, following a Tower compass that only worked in the Tower and charted the direction they needed to go in.

As though the presence of the semut merah had marked the start of a much more dangerous section of the first floor, the group found themselves beset more often by monsters. Even Arthur stopped trying to practice his exercises during the day, as an extra eye out for threats was necessary.

Everything from *babi ngepet* and *kuching hitam* to mutated snakes and more appeared, all intent on ending their lives. As dangerous as these monsters were, the annoying increase of poisonous, thorned, and spore-ridden plants forced the group to move cautiously, slowing down the team even further.

Exhausted more regularly and earlier in the day, they started taking longer breaks and stopping for the night earlier. Regular cultivation sessions were built into those stops to allow the team to replenish the energy they lost battling monsters or taking a longer route to avoid confrontation.

Yet, for all their slowdown, the team continued to make their way to their destination. Eventually, after nearly a week and a half, during which time Arthur managed to learn and put into practice his new Refined Energy Dart technique—though only when holding still—the group reached the location where he had last seen Mel, Daiyu, and Rani.

It had been luck more than careful scouting that had them stumble upon Arthur's old trail. They found a lean-to built hastily into the ground, where Arthur had rested. The trail led them back to where he had conducted his desperate battle with Budo. Stopping in the clearing, Arthur watched as the group spread out, searching for traces of the three women.

Of course, months after the initial meeting, traces of their passage had been entirely wiped out. Leaving the team to stand around, looking a little frustrated and very lost.

"Now what?" Jan was saying to Sharmila. "We lost Kate and Wang Ming. We can't track Mel. Nobody got a tracking technique."

Shar, voice low, cast glances at the rest of the disgruntled team. "No," she muttered. "We thought two would be enough. Two of us could have gotten here faster. Maybe found some trace of them." Cursing, she looked around. "I don't know. If we go on..."

"It's dangerous *lah*, Shar."

"It's a chance for us all, though," Sharmila said tightly.

"And him, *leh*?" Jan flicked a glance at Arthur.

Studiously ignoring the conversation, legs crossed and eyes half-closed as though he was cultivating, Arthur made himself continue to breathe properly. He was not likely to be fooling Uswah, but she hadn't said anything so...

Who was he kidding? They probably weren't that dumb to think he was cultivating while they discussed what to do with him. Since one of those options might be "chop his head off and let the Tower deal with his body".

Still, if he managed to fool even one of them, it might be worth it. In the meantime, he had a Refined Energy Dart half-formed above his clasped hand, ready to throw as a surprise.

Don't trust and definitely verify.

"Kill or trust." Uswah murmured, her voice fading in from a short distance away. "Either way, choose."

Sharmila fell silent, and even with his eyes half-closed and unfocused, he could feel the weight of all their gazes fall on him. Holding the Refined Energy Dart close, he waited to hear his fate from those he had traveled and fought beside for weeks.

Sometimes, secrets were worth killing for after all.

Chapter 47

"Wake up," Sharmila said, her foot prodding at his knee. He opened his eyes, clear and without the fog of ascending from cultivation. She glared at him for a second before she nodded, as though her suspicions were confirmed.

They probably were.

Arthur felt no remorse in doing so. The spear he had on his legs came with him as he stood up, idly placed by his side as he waited. Calm. Almost serene, it seemed, thanks to the Yin Body. A corner of his mind gibbered at the thought of death, but it was a small voice.

Was being killed by erstwhile allies any different than being slain by a monster? Dead was dead and his mangled corpse would not care.

"You're not running? Or fighting?" Sharmila said, an eyebrow rising. He could not help but note that it had gotten a little bushy, now that she had drawn attention to it, the gap between two eyebrows closing.

He did not, however, mention it. Though it might make a useful distraction if he had to fight. "I'll fight if I have to. But I'm hoping I don't."

"Don't think you can *tipu* us, ah. Any trick, you die," Jan said, having edged around to his back.

If she had hoped to startle him, she would be disappointed. Those eyes of his, his only real talent upgrade, were more than sufficient to pick up her sneaking behind him. "You're the ones dragging me around. I'm more strapped to your horse, rather than a willing participant. I've asked to leave, multiple times."

"And then track us, ah? No way, man," Jan snapped.

"Peace." Uswah spoke up, stepping forward. "It's not our choice." Dark eyes, lying heavily on Sharmila. It seems the women, even Uswah, deferred to the Indian woman's decisions.

Sharmila bit her lip, considering. She turned her head one way, then the other before letting out a long, exhausted sigh. "I don't want to kill for no reason. And he's been faithful thus far."

"But..." Jan protested. "He has to promise not to take it then!"

"Why don't I just leave? Before anyone else says anything, eh?" Arthur said, offering a placating grin as he tried to edge away. Of course, that did not work and instead their gazes sharpened, with Jan shifting to block his movement.

"No leaving!" Jan snarled.

"Then just make up your mind. I could be doing something better with my time. Like dying," Arthur said. "Or flying."

"Flying?" Uswah said.

"I thought rhyming would be too on the nose."

Sharmila sighed. "He's too much of an idiot to be a traitor."

"Hey!"

Jan snorted but relaxed a little.

"Okay. Here's how it is. We need to finish the job, find our people, and collect the treasure," Sharmila said. "We can let you go, but then we risk you following us." She shook her head. "We can't have that. So you come with us, but you got to promise you won't keep the treasure to yourself."

"And what do I get out of it?" Arthur crossed his arms. "You've dragged me all the way out here, not let me collect any cores, and what? I get dragged even further into possibly fatal danger for nothing?" He threw his hands up, exposing his chest. "If you want to kill me, just kill me already, lah. 'Kay?"

"He asked." So saying, Jan drew her parang, leveling it at his neck.

Arthur stared right back without flinching.

"Jan. Enough!" Sharmila said before sighing. "What do you want, then?"

Arthur shrugged. "Fair share of the cores. Knowledge of what is to come and, of course, a promise that whatever may happen, you let me walk away safe and unharmed." He paused, seeing them stir a little before adding. "By you. I understand, of course, the Tower is no place of safety."

"And you'd trust us?" Sharmila said.

"It goes both ways, doesn't it? We start, one way or the other. Or we end it. One way or the other."

Still holding the parang to his neck, Jan pressed a little harder, pricking his skin and leaving a thin line. "I still say we kill him now. Kill him and *dah cukup*. We don't need him."

"And I'm still the boss," Sharmila snapped. "So put your sword away. He has a deal. I won't become the very kind of people we're trying to break free from."

"Fine. But I get to say, I told you so, *ke*," Jan withdrew her blade, pushing it back into its simple, soft leather sheath.

"Parang. Not really a sword as much as a machete. It'd be better if she actually had a real sword. More options and length," Arthur said, even as he stepped back and touched his neck. His fingers came away bloody, but the wound had already begun to clot.

"Oi! Who the weapon expert now," Jan said, sarcastically. "The guy carrying a long stick."

Arthur just rolled his eyes, ignoring her comments, and turned to Sharmila. "You gonna explain the plan?"

Sharmila pursed her lips, looking uncomfortable now that the matter was brought to a head. It was Uswah, standing silent until now, who spoke up. "We're looking for a clan seal."

"On the first floor?" Arthur yelped. "Those things don't appear until the tenth, at the least!"

"Normally. But there are cases when such things happen," Uswah said. "And, with a clan seal, we'll finally be able to break free. Make the Thorned Lotuses an actual guild, with the ability to build a guild house in the lower levels, safeguard our people. Even recruit and give guild bonuses."

For once, the usually quiet woman grew excited.

"That's why you sent some of your strongest," Arthur said, remembering Mel and her group. "You need to bind it to her, don't you?" There wasn't much in terms of details about clan seals on the Internet, what with being one of the most sought-after items. However, a few things were well known.

A clan seal allowed the formation of an official establishment recognized by the Tower. Unlike the informal organisations created by the humans who entered a Tower, such an establishment—called a clan, guild, or corporation depending on your location and preference—had Tower-given rights. Among them, as already mentioned, certain types of guild rights.

For example, at the lowest level, a clan seal holder was recognized by the town guard as nobility. They were protected from casual violence while within the confines of the Tower villages. They were allowed to purchase land and create buildings on each Tower level they visited. Those who fell under their banner would receive advantageous prices at the store. Inter-Tower mail, transportation between Tower establishments, and most important, the ability to allow a limited number of individuals to exit the Tower on a limited basis before Tower completion.

Such organisations became powerful very fast.

They were also incredibly rare. In the entirety of Malaysia, there were but two such organisations. In the world, just over a thousand.

"Yes." Sharmila confirmed his suspicions, eyeing him now that their secret had been revealed. "So what do you think?"

Arthur shrugged. "What do you want me to say?" He had to silently thank his Yin Body. Without which, he would appear uncountably excited. Something that would be entirely the wrong move right about now, especially considering the way Jan was caressing her parang hilt. "Is it exciting? Sure. Definitely a secret to kill for. But am I going to do it?" He shook his head. "I'm not dumb. I just got into the Tower. That kind of power means I'm someone's lapdog for the rest of my life. Worse than staying out there."

Sharmila searched his face, lips thin and angry. Eventually, not finding what she was searching for, she nodded. Jan, by his side, relaxed.

Which was why, of course, he decided to push it. "I do have one other condition though, now that you've mentioned this."

"What condition?" Jan was tense, while even Sharmila had shifted the position of her weapon aggressively.

"I get to join you guys." He waved a hand. "And without any, you know, sex change or whatever."

"Do you think we're all women?" Uswah said, a hint of laughter in her voice.

In answer, he just gestured around.

"We have men too, just not so many, " said Sharmila. "And they're not *pondan*, if that's what you were thinking."

"*Ya-lah.* So you can still be a man," Jan chimed in. But she just had to add. "Though, with your Yin Body *ah*, maybe you're not anymore."

"You're a real *biao zi*, aren't you?" Arthur said.

"Yup," Jan replied.

Well, at least she had an understanding of herself. And he, an understanding of what was to come. Even through the enforced calmness of the Yin Body, he found himself excited for the future.

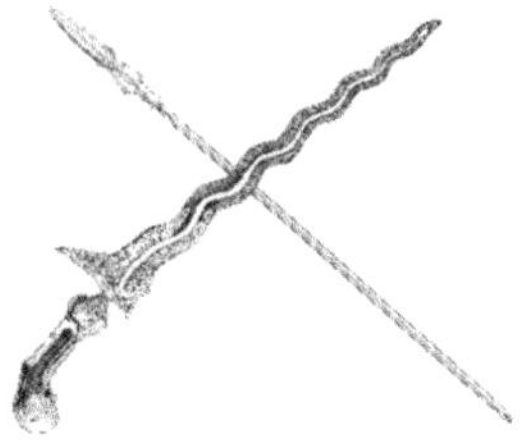

Chapter 48

"I hate this," Arthur cursed, swinging the parang he had been loaned. He was using the damn tool for its intended purpose: chopping his way through the undergrowth. The deeper they pushed into the forest, the more overgrown it grew, with trees towering above and secondary growth having overtaken the lower altitudes. Shrubs, vines, thorny bushes, and low-hanging ferns composed the undergrowth in a dizzying and ecologically improbable array.

"There can't be enough light for all this to be growing," Arthur said, slicing upwards and then using his other gloved hand to rip a vine away before taking another step.

"No, not enough light," Jan said. "But the Tower, no follow normal rules *lah*."

Grumbling for another half dozen steps, Arthur snarled all of a sudden. He lunged forward, parang catching a *kuching hitam* as it leapt at him. The parang, never really meant for stabbing, was still empowered by the full-speed extension of his body. Thanks to that and the creature's own momentum, the blade punched right through it.

A quick twist, a shake of the blade, and the body crashed to the ground a short distance away. The cat struggled briefly before a spear pierced its throat. A few quick cuts and a plunging hand, then he was tossed the beast core.

"Thanks!" Arthur put the core away in his pouch, grateful that at least he was getting something now.

Another few steps before he could not help but ask, "Are you sure we're going in the right direction?"

"Definitely," Sharmila answered immediately.

He managed another half-dozen steps, his shoulder and muscles aching from the constant motions of slicing the undergrowth, before Shar added, "I'm pretty sure. At least in the right general direction."

"Ohhhh no. You did not just say that," Arthur said, spinning around. "What the hell are you talking about? What general direction? Are we just randomly hunting through the jungle? Because that's how you get eaten, you know."

"It's not like that," Sharmila said defensively. "We have a map, a series of coordinates we built up. We're moving in the right direction to the coordinates but the, umm..." She scratched the back of her neck, looking sheepish. "The compass leading to it, that's with Mel's group."

"Can we even find it without the compass?" Arthur's eyes narrowed.

Silence was his answer. Though whether it was a silence of negation or just of unknowing, he was not certain. He wasn't even certain they knew.

"Don't you think it might be better for us to try to find their trail in that case?"

"We will, once we get closer." Sharmila's tone had grown colder, as though she intended to cut off this conversation.

Instead Arthur continued, though he did at least choose to continue to open a way. "And how long is that?"

"That one, we won't tell you lah," Jan snapped. "We let you come with us, but we not tell you all."

Arthur sighed. Well, at least he had gotten something from the paranoid women. It didn't matter in the end; he would learn what he needed to learn. Meanwhile, he could do nothing but play muscle for them and work on rebuilding his own strength.

Later that night, Arthur cycled between pulling energy from the beast cores he had collected that day and practicing his Refined Energy Dart. With his new Mind point, he was able to refine the energy much faster, both from the monster cores and his own energy core. In addition, the Dart skill was progressing well, now that he had the energy to waste. It was halfway through his ostensible watch that he felt the technique click, his formation speed and extraction of energy happening faster than ever.

"About damn time," he whispered to himself, staring at the pockmarked bark of the tree he had been using as target practice. A fully refined and formed energy dart could tear through even the iron-like skin of the tree before him, drilling a half-inch hole into the hardwood beneath.

Against a fleshy opponent, he would expect it to pierce skin and damage organs. At least, so long as they had reasonably low stats in Body and hadn't chosen a physical hardening aspect. Which, sadly, would probably take the Dart's effectiveness from great to just mediocre.

There was also another problem.

Flexing his hand, he grimaced at the aura around his body. He stared, though he could not truly see it. Not yet, though he expected more practice with his eyes and with the techniques would allow him to build up such strength. Even so, what he sensed was ragged, torn, as he had ripped his own aura apart constantly.

"Figure maybe a half-dozen uses before it starts becoming dangerous to use," Arthur said, again mostly to himself. He sighed after a second but nodded. Good enough, especially since it still took him time to refine energy.

Speaking of that… A mental command pulled his status screen into being.

Cultivation Speed: 1.12 (0.92 Yin)
Energy Pool: 9.11/15 (Yin) (0.04 Yang – Unusable)
Refinement Speed: 0.025
Refined Energy: 0.87 (2)

Attributes and Traits
Mind: 4
Body: 6 (Enhanced Eyesight, Yin Body)
Spirit: 4

Techniques
Focused Strike
Accelerated Healing – Refined Energy (Grade I)
Heavenly Sage's Mischief
Refined Energy Dart

"Not bad." He could not help but be proud of the changes compared to when he started. Months ago? Half a year? More? He had lost track of time while out in the wilderness, especially while cultivating.

Was that, perhaps, why so many people outside were left waiting? Not because people had died, but because so many climbers just forgot? They got caught in a cycle of cultivating, refining, and improving, and they never realised how long they had been here?

Sobering thought. If he cared about what was going on outside. But he had few enough ties, thankfully, so it had little import for him.

No, more important was the increased speed in refinement and cultivation. His next goal was to get another point in refined energy and then sink it into either Mind or Spirit to boost the attribute and gain an aspect.

He'd have to consider which attribute, but either choice would be a boon to either study or cultivation progress.

For now, he had the remainder of a single core left. Even if these cores were beginning to give 0.15 points of refined energy per core, it wouldn't be enough for what he needed. Which meant he'd crash once he sucked it dry. After all, he still needed actual sleep.

Huh. Maybe he should get *that* talent next time.

Chapter 49

Four days of travel. Crossing streams, treading moss-covered rocks, climbing hills. Arthur took his turn at the front and at the back of the group. He fought, killed, and dealt with the creatures. As they delved deeper, more and more powerful monsters arrived. Some of them, like the *babi ngepet*, grew in size, strength, and numbers. Swarming the team, forcing them to fight defensively and sometimes run.

Injuries accumulated, even as concerns grew over where they were going. On the fifth day, the group changed direction, traversing at an angle to their initial line of movement to cut across a wider ground.

After another full day of walking and no sign of any trail, they cut backwards. Traversing the same direction, finding nothing, and then travelling another day. They pushed upward, climbing the series of hills that had appeared, dipping deep into the valleys in between.

Tension grew among the group, tempers fraying with each step as doubts simmered about reaching their goal. Of them all, Arthur was the least concerned, having the least invested.

Rather than engage in arguments, he took on more duties, being willing to take on the worst watches at night. He stayed up late and slept less, finding the time in between to train and cultivate, pulling energy from the cores he acquired when he could.

On the sixth day, towards the end of the afternoon as they searched for a place to camp for the night, eyes warily searched for the monstrously large *kuching hitam* that had been tracking them from high above, refusing to engage. It was then that they finally, finally, found the trail.

Sharmila, in the front, cried out loud. She waved up and down, calling them to the faded deer trail. There were few indications the trail had been used, but her grin was still wide and bright.

"I told you we'd find it!" Sharmila said.

"How do you know it's theirs?" Jan said. "Maybe just an animal trail." Sniffing a little, she walked forward and then poked at some scat on the ground. "See?"

"Of course it's an animal trail!" Sharmila said. "They must have found it and followed it." She shook her head firmly. "Don't you get it? This leads in the right direction and it's the only one we've found. It has to be the way they came."

"Also, footprint," Uswah said. She was further up the trail now. "See?"

The entire group rushed over, excited to see, and realised that she was right. A single shoeprint—

or half of one, for it had driven deep into the mud between two roots, imprinting itself as the walker pushed forward after balancing on the root. Deep enough that even after weeks, it still stood.

"I told you!" Sharmila crowed.

"Yeah, yeah," Jan muttered. "So now what?"

"What do you mean? We follow it, of course!" Sharmila said, waving down the trail. "We can't be that far from the goal. A day. Maybe two."

"Exactly," Jan said. ""And still no news from Mel, after so many weeks. Something is wrong lah, Shar..."

The Indian woman fell silent, a look of concern flashing through her eyes as the seriousness of the matter overrode her initial excitement. After a few minutes, she sighed and nodded. "You're right. I don't want to lose the trail though. We go forward, carefully, and look for a place to rest. Then we prep."

Nods from all around, as the group took position on the trail. They managed half a dozen steps before the *kuching hitam*, forgotten in their initial excitement, attacked. It dropped, claws tearing into one of the women on the fringe, its mouth clamping down on her neck. The partner standing beside her managed to swing a glancing blow at the monster, the attack bouncing off the muscular creature who was the size of the woman herself.

Then the dark black cat, muscular in a way that was unnatural, leaped with strength empowered by the Tower and its supernatural nature. As it leaped back toward the tree branches, the woman was dragged along by the neck. She had not stopped striking at it, but she grew ever weak as the powerful feline hauled her up. Only the supernatural strength of a cultivator kept her struggling, but there was a snap, and her neck broke at last. In the midst of arrows and darts, or in Arthur's case, a Refined Energy Dart, the fast-moving *kuching* managed to escape with its prey and minimal damage, hiding in the foliage above.

Leaving them one less person on the trail to the clan seal.

Arthur had rolled over in his bedroll, eyes half-closed as he tried to sleep after his watch. Usually, he would have fallen asleep immediately. And besides, with the loss of another member, their watch hours had increased. However, the excitement from the day kept his mind spinning, and he found sleep elusive. The ground felt harder and colder than ever, every hoot and rustle of leaves, every creaking branch and chirp and buzz resounding in his ears.

Twenty or so minutes of lying down, conversations low and hushed came to him. Not the conversation of those concerned about waking their friends, but the hush and whisper of conspiracy.

"They all asleep, ah?" Sharmila whispered, glancing around.

"*Ya.* The fool was the last one on watch. You know? The moment he finished his turn, he's already sleeping. Hah! He keeps saying he will take the long watch. Thinks he can cozy up to us, is it?" Jan said, harsh and derisive. "As if."

"Don't. He's trying. I told you, it's not useful."

"I don't trust him."

"I know. But we might need him. You know it's going to be even riskier now. If Mel's dead..."

Jan sighed. "Shouldn't have trusted her so much. She's not that good."

"You just wanted to be on the first team."

"If I was, no problem already." A rustle of clothing, and then she paced away, her voice rising. "But you all thought better. So, whatever lah. Still, this fool?"

"We use him. Don't drive him away, okay? If he runs, no guarantee we can find him. And the location, it's got to be dangerous. So we need him," Sharmila said.

"Bait."

"Canary."

Silence then. Arthur realised he was gritting his teeth and forcibly made himself relax his jaw and neck. He had thought that Sharmila at least had chosen to accept him. But it seemed all she wanted was him as bait, as the fool who set off traps.

Well, so be it then. If they were not going to play straight with him, then he saw no reason to play straight with them.

If he even bothered to stick around.

Resolved, he forced himself to relax, cycle, breathing until his muscles unclenched and the bubbling anger faded, leaving him with but a core within. Waiting to burst outwards and splatter everyone, like an infected cyst.

Chapter 50

"A bit on the nose, isn't it?" Arthur could not help but comment, cocking his head to the side as he surveyed the building. "Or do they have a sense of irony?"

"They?" Uswah said, having come up by his side. The Malay woman's tanned skin had grown a little lighter, though it would never truly lose all its lustre. Not like his own. If he kept getting any fairer, he could star in a Chinese drama about lazy young masters.

"The tower builders." Arthur waved at the four-story tower that stood before them, the entire circular building reminding him a little of the Tower of Pisa. He swore he could almost see the twisting staircase in the center of the building between the open gaps. "A tower within a tower? Ironic, maybe."

"That's not ironic," Sharmila said. "It might be literal, but it's not ironic."

"Whatever." Arthur waved his hand, dismissing the pedantry. "That where we have to go?"

"I believe so." Sharmila gestured to the right, where the remnants of a camp could be seen. The abandoned tents, old firepit, and the tossed and destroyed dining table and chairs were indications of old use—and a potential battle. "We should check if it's theirs first."

"Then?" Arthur said, though he knew the answer.

Sharmila did not bother to answer him, already striding over to one of the tents. Jan and the remainder of the team followed her, leaving him alone with Uswah.

"Then we go into the tower, eh," she said.

"Of course. I knew that."

Rather than join the group at the derelict campsite, he chose to take a walk around the tower. Uswah followed, causing him to cock his head to the side. Still, he chose not to ask, and she chose not to tell, so the pair just walked around, surveying the tower and the clearing it stood in.

"Perfectly circular," Arthur said, pointing at the edge of the clearing. They had chosen to enter about halfway, so they had views of both the tower itself and the forest that surrounded it. "The grass is short too. No lalang growing here, or anything."

"Magic landscaping." Uswah could not help but sound amused.

Arthur grinned a little at that too. "*Cepat* rich, eh? Take outside and use."

"Very rich."

He slowed down a little, bending down to try to figure out why the grass was the way it was. No markings near the base of the tower to indicate a magical laser or anything like that. In fact, there were no external markings that he could see around the tower.

"I don't know magic much, but..."

"Not magic. Not this," Uswah said, her eyes growing dark as she gave the tower a second look.

Unbending, Arthur kept walking around the tower, noting at least two more well-used deer trails into the building and a pair of older, less used trails. By the time he circled fully around the building, the other girls were done with their perusal of the camp.

"Where did you go?" Jan said angrily.

"Looking around, lah." Arthur jerked a thumb in Uswah's direction. "She came along too."

"Don't go wandering like that, idiot," Jan snapped.

"And you don't talk to me like that. I'm not your dog," Arthur snapped back. "Got it?"

"You—"

"Jan!" Sharmila broke in, making the other woman shut her mouth instantly. Arthur smirked, only for Sharmila to turn on him. "She's right, though. We don't split the party without a reason."

"Gamer?" Arthur said, raising an eyebrow.

"What?"

"Ah hell. Never mind." Arthur shrugged, realizing she had no idea of the meme. Not that he was much of a gamer himself, but not everyone in his martial arts center had been as obsessed with training as him. Some of them had a life, and they had dragged him to a few VR gaming sessions. Full-body impact suits, bulky head coverings, moving grounds—it all was worth the day's pay to have fun sometimes.

"Idiot," Jan muttered under her breath.

"So now what?" Arthur said, ignoring the woman. "Up the tower? Or we camping?"

He tilted his head upward, eyeing the sky. It was getting late in the day after all, and entering a new building for the first time was concerning.

Sharmila visibly hesitated, looking between Jan and Uswah. The trio passed a series of silent communication between one another.

"Let's... camp here," Shar said finally, waving at the tents. "We'll put theirs aside, recover what we can. Clean out the campfire and get prepped. We go in tomorrow morning."

Jan looked a little unhappy at the decision, but Uswah was nodding. Decision made, the group broke up, processing the various tents while Arthur grabbed a shovel, choosing to clean out the campground and campfire.

If nothing else, he was going to make sure he ate well tonight. After all, there was no guarantee they'd get a chance to eat anything after that.

"Really good kuih!" Arthur muttered around the mouthful of the green and white dessert.

This particular kuih was a Malaysian Nyonya delicacy, made of coconut and mung bean. The recipe itself was simple, but the amount of time processing and baking made it a delicacy that had yet to travel far outside of Southeast Asia. The fact that it required a certain level of skill to bake made it one of those national delicacies that stayed local, despite an explosion of diversity in kuih as people got creative.

"There's an *amah* in the camps who used to run a shop. Once we got her access and a budget, she's been making this for us. One of our exports," Sharmila said around her own mouthful.

Like all good Malaysians, they each had brought some delicacy with them on the expedition from their storage space back at the village. Space might be a premium there, but food—good food—was a necessity. Everyone had contributed except Arthur, who decided to forage for some edible plants. The fact that Jan hovered as he did so was more annoying than anything else.

"And this *nasi lemak*?" He pointed at the bowl of coconut-milk rice and *sambal* chili paste. "Who brought that?"

A shy hand was raised, one of the other women. Arthur made sure to thank her profusely. He noted that his own series of fire-charred vegetables were barely touched. Well, he couldn't blame them. He didn't even have salt.

The meal itself was a success, the group seeming to have come to the same conclusion as him: they brought out items they had been reserving. Sharmila surprised them all by extracting a bottle of whisky from her own pack, pouring shots for everyone.

The meal grew louder and louder, conversations turning to friends left at the camp, old instances of hilarity and grievances. As the level in the whisky bottle dropped, though, the conversation turned to the world outside and those they left behind.

"My brother wanted me out. They said I was taking up space they could use for their own children. They kept hinting about me marrying one of their friends," Sharmila said. "Eventually, they arranged a marriage."

"To Laksh who lacked down there!" Uswah said, with a twinkle in her eye.

"How did... ?" Arthur began tentatively.

"What, you think I'm pure?" Sharmila said with a leering smirk. "Of course I checked. Laksh, who lacked, and who was twenty pounds overweight and was hairier than a bear."

The girls shuddered.

"Really, why won't men take proper care of themselves?" The formerly shy girl said. She leaned over, poking Arthur. "Do you?"

"Do I what?"

"Landscape!" Uswah said, laughing.

Arthur stared at the girls, who all laughed as he turned red at the question.

“"Oi. Sharmila," Jan said. "At least someone want to marry you. Me? That puda never said he already married. Then his wife found out and I got fired!"

"Good job too, no?" Shar said.

"*Ya* lah! I was an accountant! Jan shook her small cup of whisky belligerently. "After machines check the books, I verify." She grimaced and said more quietly, "I liked my job, you know. But now got machines. So they said, 'We going to stop hiring accountants anyway'... Stupid machines."

"Stupid machines." The group echoed her words, raising their cups and swallowing the burning liquid. Arthur copied their motions, but he made sure not to quaff his drink like the others. He was still on his first, unlike most of the women.

"I hated living outside," Uswah offered, her voice low. "It was so boring! There's no more magic in the world. Not outside..."

Fewer nods, though Arthur could not help but echo her sentiments in his heart. Automation had taken away so many jobs, and while some creatives still did well, even the magical items that came out of the Tower were barely enough for the rich, never mind the general populace. Everything from magical combs to weapons or machines created to use the monster cores they all refined needed Tower climbers to run.

The world had changed, but one thing still stayed the same.

The powerful took all, and everyone else was left to scrabble for the remnants.

Chapter 51

Arthur looked over the group, all lying asleep. His bag was packed, his gear over his shoulder. All but the tent which he had to leave behind. He had slept rough before, so leaving the tent was no big sacrifice, well, except to his comfort.

His lips curled upwards in a smirk, as he hefted his spear one last time. A small pang of regret flickered through him when his eyes dropped to where Uswah slept, curled up with a hand and leg thrown out from under her blanket carelessly. Of them all, she had been the most upfront and fair with him. He could almost believe she knew nothing about the others' upcoming treachery.

Almost.

Yet it mattered not. He was not going to stay around and play bait. Let them test the tower themselves. He would return to the camp alone. And if he made them enemies, well, better enemies in the future than dead.

He was half a dozen feet out of the perimeter when a noise made him turn, eyes narrowing at the shaded forest. He crouched lower, leveling his spear in the direction of the noise as he tried to spot what it was. Something high up in the trees was moving.

The hair on the back of his neck stood on end, a sixth sense warning him of the creature's regard. Without thought, he raised his voice. "'Ware! Monsters!"

Thrashing out of their blankets behind him, as the seasoned adventurers woke. The creature shifted, two glinting yellow eyes disappearing for a second. Then, they returned, multiplying.

One, two, three... six pairs of yellow eyes, all of them hovering nearly ten feet off the ground.

"*Oh sial,*" Uswah was by his side, cursing.

"Yeah, you can say that again," Arthur muttered as he began backing off.

"Shit." Sharmila formed up beside the slowly retreating pair.

"She said that already," Arthur replied. "Why aren't they attacking?"

"You want them to attack?" Uswah said. "I'm okay with them not..."

Jan sniffed. "We can beat them."

"Really? And what, exactly, is this 'them'?" Arthur could not help but ask sarcastically. The hair on the back of his neck refused to lower, the twisted knots in his stomach refusing to unclench. Every one of his instincts told him that he wanted nothing to do with these creatures, even if he did not know why.

And his instincts had kept him alive so far.

"Monsters, of course..." Jan's voice trailed off as they finally chose to reveal themselves, stepping into the clearing. Large humanoids with long hair and two long tusks. Their arms hung to the ground, covered with the same coarse fur that encompassed their whole bodies. Even with their fur, which was matted with dirt and blood, it was clear that these creatures were muscular with broad shoulders and tiny waists.

"*Jenglot,*" Uswah breathed.

"Time to go," Arthur said, speeding up his retreat. When he noticed she was not moving, he called out, "Move, Uswah!"

Shocked out of her fear, she began backpedalling, as did the rest of the group.

"What about our gear?" Jan shouted.

As though their retreat was the signal, the creatures tore forward. Their long legs covered the ground quickly, their movements unusual as they bent large, heavy upper torsos forward to aid momentum.

An arrow, loosed by one of the other girls, sunk into the coarse fur where one of the *jenglot*'s hearts should be. The attack seemed to not bother it at all, for the creature kept sprinting towards the group.

Shouts rose up as the group loosed a variety of other ranged attacks. Energy attacks, chi blasts, even a throwing knife went out to meet the monsters. None managed to do more than annoy the creatures and superficially wound them.

Choosing to not waste his breath further, Arthur turned around fully and ran for it. Let the girls fight for their belongings. He was not going to fight those creatures, especially when everything he owned was on his back.

He darted to the tower entrance, losing precious time to shoulder one of its double doors open. Only after he had stepped inside a half-dozen feet did he think to check for traps. Thankfully, there were none, but he still slowed down long enough to scan the room.

Not a moment too late, for a monster was waiting within: another *jenglot*. Except this one was twelve feet tall, hunched over as it stared at the group, hands darting forward for him. Arthur managed to bring his spear out in front of him at the last moment, blocking the attack only to watch the shaft of his spear bend. He fell backwards, the monster yanking its hand back as its skin was split by the shaft's splinters.

"Damn it!" Arthur cursed as he backed away, jabbing with his spear as he tried to keep the monster back.

Out of the corner of his eye, he spotted the open archway and the staircase leading up. Unfortunately, it was an angle opposite him, nearly perpendicular to where he and the monster stared at one another.

Roaring, the monster chose to take a wound as it darted forwards, skin ripping as it grabbed Arthur's spear by the haft and tore it from his grip. Unable to keep hold of the weapon, he let it go and danced backward.

Instinct had him flick his hand outwards, the Refined Energy Dart shooting out of it to strike the monster in the face. He missed hitting the eye dead-on but the monster was so big and with it hunched over and paying attention to its newly acquired spear, the attack managed to gouge the eye and half-blind it.

"Gotcha!" Arthur cried.

Seconds later, he was throwing himself across the ground as the creature stamped on where he was. The ground cracked and splintered. Rolling away, he stuck a hand out to grab his spear from where the monster had discarded it, then got back on his feet.

"Let's try this again," Arthur hissed.

Jumping forward, he stabbed with his weapon, once, twice, thrice. It forced the monster back, before it managed to clip him in the side, spinning him. A sideways drop and roll had him coming up, his arm throbbing after the glancing blow.

Again the monster came forward, edging him backward. Circling to the side, Arthur tried to reach the archway up the staircase, only for the doors to swing open. The *jenglot* turned its head, eyeing the girls who had burst in.

Jan, leading the run in, let out a long scream before she struck out with her parang, catching its thigh muscle. Shoving its leg sideways, the *jenglot* managed to back her away, leaving Arthur a chance. He triggered Heavenly Sage's Mischief, feeling the strength course through him as he leaped forward and thrust the spear. The weapon plunged into the monster's neck before it was pulled out again as he fell, leaving a gaping, bloody wound, hot blood spilling everywhere to stain the air.

"Move!" Jan snarled, shouldering past him as she pushed through. She warily eyed the *jenglot* that had staggered back, clutching its throat as it died.

Arthur, spear back in his hand, glanced at the dying *jenglot* briefly before he turned to the entrance. Just in time to see Sharmila and Uswah stumble in. A pair of *jenglot* came charging in, only for Uswah to grab one by its arm, throwing herself and the monster backwards. She flipped it through the air, using the strength of her fall and her arching legs to throw the monster back out the door.

Sharmila and Jan slammed the doors shut, leaving the final, unmolested monster to Arthur. Trapping the four humans in there with two *jenglot.*

"Yeah, this feels just about right for my luck," Arthur muttered as he charged.

Chapter 52

He ducked under the *jenglot*'s swipe, managing to mostly dodge it. Even the small clip on the top of his head was enough to stagger him, putting him a little out of position for a straight thrust with his spear into the monster's chest. No heart, but it still had a kidney exposed—or what he thought was a kidney.

The spear moved as though it were traveling on its own volition, piercing tough, bristly fur and entering softer muscle beneath. At the last second, knowing he had a clear opportunity to attack, he had poured energy into the spear and imbued it with Focused Strike.

He felt his attack pierce the monster's side, and blood gushed from the wound. Dancing sideways, footsteps crossing over one another in his haste, he lashed out with the sharp spear point, tearing at skin and hair.

"Stupid hair, got to get some flair," Arthur sung under his breath, realizing in short order that the cuts were of little use. The spear was never truly meant for cutting attacks, and the monster's bristly fur was slowing and softening his attack. All he was doing was giving it a trim each time he swung his weapon.

He had made half a rotation around the monster, the creature spinning as fast as him, before the *jenglot* decided to do something strange. It dropped low, extending an arm out beneath and supporting itself using the arm, and kicked like a capoeira student.

Surprise caught Arthur, as did the paired legs of the monster. Thankfully, it was not a technique it had practiced much, meaning that the full strength of the creature's massive legs were not in play. It didn't matter though, since the *jenglot* was more than powerful enough to send Arthur flying through the air. He crashed against the tower's inner wall, cracking his head against stone even as he attempted to curl in defense.

He fainted, for a brief second or two. He knew he had fainted, because by the time he came to, he was on the floor, spear on the ground a half-dozen feet away, his body half-folded like a discarded rag doll. His scalp had opened in the back, blood gushing as dark spots warred in his vision. Blood from his scalp and nose and mouth, where he had accidentally bitten his tongue.

Never mind the way his back, ribs, hips and spine throbbed. If he had been a normal human, Arthur would never have survived. As it stood, he was seriously injured. Eyes searched for his assailant, only to be grateful to find that the monster was battling the girls now instead of him.

Knowing he was useless for now, he delved into his body to pour refined energy into Accelerated Healing. Attempting to fix his most crippling of injuries, that meant first dealing with the concussion that threatened to tear away his concentration.

Searing pain, one that tore a scream from his throat. It pulsed through his head, as blood clots and a burgeoning brain bleed were fixed. Moments later, he found himself coughing and snorting as globs of congealing blood were forced out of his head along with cerebral fluid. When the pulse of healing ended, his thoughts were clearer, though a part of him wondered how bad things had been that spitting and dribbling blood from his mouth was the better option.

Crawling forward, he grabbed his spear and surveyed the battle. It had gone from bad to worse, with the only advantage being that he was not the only one crippled. Another monster was down, one leg mangled such that it was unable to reach the battling trio. His own *jenglot* was fighting at a disadvantage too, with one hand clutched around the open wound his spear had created. It seemed that throwing itself sideways and kicking Arthur had torn something wide open.

Attempting to stand was a failure, his body refusing to hold him up. He crumpled to the ground, unable to stand. Something was not working right in his lower back.

"Tiu..." Arthur cursed as he managed to get back onto his knees. Fine. He had no way of getting into the battle. Didn't mean he was out of options entirely.

Using the spear to prop himself up, he raised his other hand and formed the Refined Energy Dart. He waited for a brief second, making sure he had the right timing down before releasing it. It was not targeted at anything as crude as the head or neck as those moved too much. But a foot, planted onto the ground, used for bearing weight. The knee that supported the entire thing—those didn't move much. Not when the timing was right.

The Refined Energy Dart shot forward, impacting the back of the *jenglot*'s knee. It tore into the extended, outlined muscles, ripped apart tendons and ligaments before the dart ended, power emptied. The monster stumbled forward, then as a parang swung at its head, managed to sway aside. However, when it tried to recover and attack again, it put its weight on the injured leg, and the knee gave way. The monster crumpled, leaving its face open to a return strike of the parang by Jan.

Still it did not die. The monster fell backward, clutching at the open wound of its own face. Seeing the battle turn tide, Uswah shouted.

"Back! Focus on the boss!" She put words to action, pulling the team away and circling towards a wall, leaving the other two monsters to crawl after them. Except...

"Shit," Arthur cursed, realising that the other *jenglot*, the one that had first been crippled had switched directions. It was coming to him now, instead of the women. And in the time he had been watching, it had covered nearly half the distance.

Switching aim, he conjured Refined Energy Dart again. Unfortunately, though launched at the monster's face, the dart caught its shoulder instead when the monster twisted at the last moment. Its shoulder was now bloodied and injured, but still mostly functional.

Too close for him to launch another dart—never mind his desire to keep at least some energy for healing—Arthur switched plans and struck out with his spear. He stabbed once, twice, forcing the monster to defend itself rather than crawl forward.

Blood began to gush down the injured arms, but without his own mobility and having less range to move his spear, his attacks grew predictable. A yank by the monster tore his spear away when a failed strike brought it too close, leaving him weaponless.

"Shit, shit, shit..." He would back off, but he was up against the wall already. He briefly considered getting up and running, but his legs were still half-numb.

Choosing to give up dignity for survival, he threw himself to the side and began crawling away from the *jenglot*, moving as fast as he could. Hopefully the team would get to him before the *jenglot* and its long, claw-like fingers did.

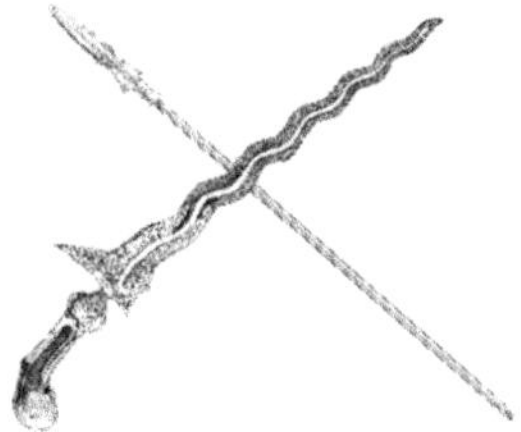

Chapter 53

The screams of the *jenglot* chased after Arthur as he crawled away, both of them moving in a slow circle. He kept his head faced forward, not daring to waste even the fraction of a second required to look behind. Each movement was painful, each pull of his arms driving him forward as he wiggled his hips to help with his crawl. Time stretched; he crossed a half dozen feet, leaving a trail of blood behind.

Then long fingers, hairy and callused, closed around his foot and yanked.

Screaming, Arthur found himself dragged backward. He kicked with his free leg; the other foot being gripped was numb. The strikes did little but annoy the monster as it clamped down with sharp teeth on his calf, punching through his jeans and into the skin beneath.

Another scream, another series of kicks. This time, with his target fixed, the attack did more damage. To himself and the *jenglot* as its teeth tore free, leaving a gaping wound in his limb. The monster swallowed the chunk of flesh it had won, then turned its attention back to him.

Sitting up, Arthur reacted. At first, he meant to throw a punch, already pulling energy from his dantian for Focused Strike. Only to realise he did not have the range to lash out. Refined Energy Dart was the obvious option, but pinching off his aura as he gripped it and poured refined energy into it inadvertently mixed with his Focused Strike. An attack he realized he had not released.

Acting on instinct as much as training, he poured that energy into the pinched-off section of his aura that formed the Energy Dart. The attack warped and twisted, almost escaping his control but desperation and the short distance he had to throw it meant that the entire structure managed to hold itself together as the glowing chi attack struck the *jenglot* in the face as it lunged.

To Arthur's surprise, the attack worked even better than he had expected. The Refined Energy Dart shredded the *jenglot*'s natural aura protection before penetrating into the skin and flesh beneath. It exposed bare bone, which was crushed by the infused Focused Strike. The impact caused the monster's head to snap back.

Of course the attack had not been without cost. His hand ached, his body feeling exposed as a large portion of his aura was torn away. He cursed, fingers numb as he scrabbled for the knife he carried for eating. Pulling it close, he crawled his way to the stunned monster and plunged the knife into its neck, feeling hot blood spurt from the wound onto him.

Again and again he stabbed the monster, wasting energy and drowning the fear that had filled him in the wash of blood. Only after a half dozen strikes did he turn aside, good sense returning as the dregs of his terror washed away.

To find the other monsters dead and the women staring at him, partially in horror and partially in disgust.

Grinning weakly, Arthur could not help but think that the Yin Body's impassive nature had limits. Death by mutilation and cannibalism was one such limit.

"They're not attacking the door anymore," Jan murmured.

Arthur barely acknowledged her words, having just finished wrapping his wounded calf with bandages from his discarded backpack. He did not even remember dropping it, but he must have when he fought the first *jenglot.*

He wondered if the group of *jenglot* outside had meant to drive them in here. Or had the biggest creature been hiding within all along? Or hiding *away*, perhaps? Who knew. Certainly, none of these monsters would be explaining themselves.

"They left, ah?" Sharmila said.

"Probably," Uswah said. She looked about, noting there were only the four of them left, most wounded. She sported a long series of cuts down one side, her dress hanging open in rather bloody rags. Walking over to Arthur's backpack, she rummaged in it before extracting a shirt and his bandages before grabbing at his water bottle.

"Hey!" Arthur cried out.

"I've gotta clean up. *Kita tak bawa apa pun*," Uswah said, gesturing to remind him they had left behind all gear but weapons. "So don't be selfish."

Arthur nodded mutely, especially since the woman began to strip off her tunic right in front of him, hissing as she pulled down her shirt across the bloody, jagged wounds. Sharmila, herself still bleeding from cuts on her arms and legs and a matted wound across her scalp, came over to help. To Arthur's amusement, he idly noted that Uswah had a rather nice, frilly bra on, until of course the women glared at him.

"You did it here!" Arthur muttered, but he did turn away then. Admittedly, he had been looking but not *looking*, as his heart was still pounding from the danger they had all been in. And the usual rush of horniness that should have arrived after the fight was missing. Had been missing for a bit.

Another characteristic of the Yin Body?

It didn't take away his desires entirely, but they were more controlled. Which, really, wasn't a bad thing. So long as he wasn't emasculated, as Jan had teased.

Speaking of her, Jan limped over, one hand fumblingly returning her parang into its sheath by her waist. She was glaring at him, which was not unusual, but this time, it seemed to have a more scrutinizing look.

"Why do you have a bag? Why does it look so full?" Jan said.

Oh. That. "Would you believe coincidence?"

Jan's hand went to her hilt, going so far as to half draw the weapon before Sharmila gripped her hand. The older woman shook her head at her friend before looking at Arthur. "You're not helping yourself."

"Wasn't trying to." Arthur tested his foot and winced. He needed to heal himself, but he could not afford to do so now if they were threatening to kill him. "I was leaving."

"Did you bring the *jenglot* to us?" Sharmila asked suspiciously.

Arthur noticed that Uswah had shuffled aside, putting herself at an angle such that he could only see either the pair before him or her. Tension knotted his shoulders, but he chose not to make any big moves just yet.

"If I did, why the hell would I call out the warning?" Arthur replied.

"That..." Sharmila fell silent.

"Why you trying to leave?" Jan asked accusingly.

"I got spooked." He gestured around him. "Missing members, a silent tower. None of that creeps you out?"

Her eyes narrowed in suspicion, but Arthur just returned the stare blandly.

"Then why didn't you talk to us?" Uswah asked, forcing him to turn to look at her.

"Her." A finger jerked over his shoulder to where Jan was. "I doubt you'd let me just leave, not with your desire for security. Even if I didn't say anything and promised, I bet she'd bitch and complain and force me to come along."

Lies mixed with truth. Best way to lie.

"He's just a traitor," Jan said.

"Good thing too," Arthur said, tugging his bag to him and gesturing for Uswah to give back the water. She had used torn, clean portions of her tunic to clean her wounds before having Sharmila wrap the bandages around them, though the job was only half-done. She was awkwardly holding the bandage roll in one hand, but she reluctantly handed the water bottle back.

"See? This guy only cares about himself." Jan pointed accusingly at his face.

"I'm not sharing with you." Arthur paused. "Until you apologize."

"I'd rather die!"

He shrugged and began to pack his gear, while Sharmila hissed at Jan and yanked her away. Smirking to himself, he finished putting away his bag, only to find Uswah plopping down beside him.

"Yes?"

"Help please." A waggle of the bandage in her hand indicated what she meant. Arthur hesitated for a second before helping her. No reason not to. And having at least one person willing to be partly in his favour might help.

Maybe.

"You shouldn't antagonize her," Uswah said.

"I shouldn't? I wouldn't, if I didn't," Arthur half muttered, half sang.

"She's just protective. Of the Lotuses and us."

"Whatever. We're all going to die anyway."

Uswah lips pursed but she had nothing to say to that, considering their current predicament.

Chapter 54

Arthur had taken to lightly meditating, considering the combined attack he had inadvertently created. He knew it was not complete, not done right yet. If it had been, the Tower would have given him a new technique. So he considered what he had done, trying to remember the feeling of it, the process in exact detail, so that he could recreate the glowing chi attack. He wasn't cultivating, so he was able to keep an ear out for trouble.

Which was why he noticed when Jan stomped over to him, her talk with Sharmila over. Her friend followed a short distance away, Uswah having disappeared into a dark corner of the tower to cultivate. Unlike him, she was secure in the knowledge that no one wanted to kill her.

Lucky.

Jan came to a stop before him, and Arthur could not help but take a slow count of three breaths before he looked up at her fully. The woman was visibly trembling with rage at the delay and only a light touch from Sharmila stopped her from exploding at him.

"I'm sorry," she grated out, once she was certain he was paying attention.

"Huh?" Arthur said dumbly. Of all the things she could have said, that was not one he had expected.

"I said, I'M SORRY!" Jan shouted at him, making Arthur wince.

For a moment, a malicious part of him wanted to rub it into her. However, knowing that he would have to rely on them all if he wanted any hope of surviving quelled that thought. After a certain point, his personal satisfaction at having her humbled was outweighed by the need to not get stabbed in the back.

Not that he expected them to kill him today, but it was better to be backstabbed later instead of right now.

"Fine. I'll share. Not that I have a lot, but the bandages should help." Arthur pushed the bag forward, and Jan snatched it up with a jerky nod of thanks and stalked off. When she was half a dozen steps away, only then did he call out, "You're on first watch though."

She froze at being given an order, but Sharmila stepped in. "Second. I'll do the first. I have the least injuries."

Arthur nodded and closed his eyes, waiting until they were away and on the other side of the room. He debated continuing to meditate, but eventually chose to focus on healing. The pain from his numerous wounds was making it hard enough to concentrate as it was. Better to heal first, then go back to cultivating and meditating.

Plan made, he began the process of triggering his Accelerated Healing technique, trusting they wouldn't kill him just yet. At least, not after Jan had gotten over her initial impulse.

After all, they still needed bait.

Which was all kinds of ironic if you thought about it.

The bite on his calf healed up, not fully but at least it went from agonizing pain each time he stood up to just blinding pain. Once he had cycled a trio of the beast cores he had, he crashed. Hours later, he woke up with his leg hurting a little less and the girls seated on the opposite side, chatting quietly with one another.

Arthur levered himself to his feet, wincing with each movement. Other injuries made themselves known: a pulled muscle on his right shoulder, a stitch down his lower back, a graze along his neck that had opened a little. He didn't even remember getting most of them, but the pain was mostly dwarfed by his foot. Grabbing his spear from where it had lain discarded, he used it to limp over.

"*Apa kita cakap?*" Arthur asked as he neared them. "And how much of it includes me?"

"Just weighing options," Shar said.

"What options are there?" Arthur said. "Up or outside. Even if we choose to go up, we're going outside eventually. Or we're dead. I prefer not being dead."

'Then run away, lah," Jan muttered.

"How many, exactly, of the *jenglot* did you see?" Arthur said.

"We counted a dozen," Uswah murmured.

"Yeah, and it took only three of them to kick our ass."

"We beat them, though," Jan snapped.

"Barely." Arthur gestured around the building. "We're all banged up and exhausted. But they won't come in here. Which means we can heal up, then go out and kill them. Retreat. And do it again, until the group is wiped."

"Except they respawn," Uswah said.

"Except they respawn." Arthur winced. He had forgotten that part. "Then that means we have to do it faster."

"Faster? Just the four of us?" Shar said, shaking her head. "Not possible."

"Then what?" Arthur replied. "Go up and hope to find the ladies you're looking for. Except they're dead, you know."

Jan grabbed the hilt of her parang. She didn't draw it, but her teeth were bared. "They're alive," she snarled.

"Mmm... alive and trapped up here, in this tower. For weeks," Arthur snorted. "Grow up."

He barely managed to dodge the punch and only because she telegraphed her intention by releasing the grip on her sword. Jan tried to punch him again, only to be yanked back by her pants by Sharmila.

"We can't win just by leaving," said Sharmila. "But this... this is probably a dungeon or lair or something special. Which means there might be enchanted tools. And who knows, maybe even our friends, trapped. It's a slim chance, but better than the no-chance out there. In any case, we need all of us. Working together."

"We holding hands and singing songs next?" Arthur said. "Fine. But I'm renegotiating our deal."

"So selfish," Jan said.

"I'm just practical," Arthur replied.

"Selfish."

"Shellfish," Arthur said, just to provoke.

"What do you want?" Sharmila asked.

"Equal share of the loot. You can keep first dibs on the clan seal, 'cause I don't need that kind of trouble. If that's the only loot there is, you pay me an equivalent amount." Arthur tilted his head to the side, considering what else he wanted to say. "Oh, and I get to join the Guild, as a founding member. With all the rights that might entail."

"What! No," Jan said. "It's a women's only guild!"

"Sexist much?" Arthur said. He then ignored her, focusing on Sharmila. "Just consider me an honorary member, then."

Uswah, standing by the side, smiled a little, watching the entire conversation before she spoke up. "You really think we would agree to this?"

"Think, guess, maybe. Believe at least," Arthur said. "Got to, eh?"

Uswah nodded and then looked at their leader. After a moment, Sharmila sighed. "Okay lah, fine. I agree. But no idea what the others will think."

Arthur nodded before he laughed. "All theoretical anyway. Got to survive first, right?"

Sharmila snorted but could not help but nod in agreement.

Of course, Arthur did not miss the way Jan had returned to gripping her parang. Or the thoughtful look on her face.

That one was going to be a problem.

Chapter 55

They took the stairs slowly, Arthur leading the way. He had agreed to do so because of his visual upgrade and spear, making use of the butt of the weapon to test each step as he crept up. He studiously ignored Jan's mutter about being overly cautious, carefully testing each step for pressure plates and eyeing the walls for murder holes and other traps. Yet there was nothing; the ascent to the first floor was peaceful.

Standing at the door that would open to the first floor, with stairs leading farther up, he pushed at it. The plain door gave way with little effort, sliding open a little with only a gentle hiss and grind. He peered within, spotting nothing in the sliver of space offered, hearing nothing as he strained his ears. Arthur waved the team down.

After a moment, no longer under pressure, the door swung back shut as counterweights pulled it close. Eyes narrowing in suspicion, Arthur backed off halfway down the stairs before turning to the rest of the group.

"We need something to block the door from closing," Arthur said.

Fishing into the rubble, Uswah came up with a pair of wood blocks.

"Do we have to go in this one?" Sharmila said dubiously.

"I don't want to get pincered," Arthur said.

Jan nodded. "He's not wrong. Surprisingly."

Arthur flashed a tight smile at her.

"Okay, so..." Tilting his head from side-to-side, he waited. "I go in, followed by the rest of you. Uswah spikes the door, watches for more from the stairs?"

Once he received acknowledgment from the group, Arthur crept back up the stairs. He breathed deeply, calming his racing heart and wiping sweaty palms on his pants a few times before he pushed forward. Best to get this done, and quickly.

The door swung open easily. He stepped in with no incident. To his surprise, it was an open hall that stretched for a good thirty or so meters before ending in a stone wall. Dim light, filtering in from narrow slits, illuminated the vast emptiness that was this room.

Stalking within, wary of invisible enemies, he kept his spear point in front of him as he worked the edges, and the women spread out to the opposite side and middle of the room. They crossed the entire hall, finding nothing but a few particularly dark splotches on the floor before they regrouped in the center. Uswah joined them after making sure the door would not shut.

"What do you think?" Arthur asked.

"Trap?" Jan said.

"Or did Mel and the others clear it first?" Sharmila offered.

"Maybe." Uswah pointed to the darkened floor. "I feel quite a bit of Yin energy in there."

Arthur frowned, not sensing it himself. Then again, she was significantly more trained. "So the guardians were killed?"

A shrug and nod from the woman. They were just guessing after all.

"Maybe it's a trigger?" Jan said, pointing to the door that had not been propped open.

"If so, do we want to trigger it?" Sharmila said.

"Why would we?" Arthur said incredulously.

"Cores. And maybe, to not leave enemies behind?"

"Yeah but if it's not triggered, maybe we'll save ourselves a world of trouble," Arthur said.

Again, another shrug. Guesses. All kinds of guesses.

In the end, the group chose not to push their luck. Injured and tired as they were, they could not afford to run a risk like that. Limping back to the stairs, Arthur took point again and waited until the door was fully closed. Uswah eyed the door, but since it swung inwards, there was no way to bar it from opening their way, not without a lot more ropes. In the end, they chose to leave it be and began their ascent once more.

Three floors, three empty halls.

Tension ratcheted up as they crept higher. Each time, the opening of a door and the revelation of what lay beyond was a stomach-churning affair. No idea if there was going to be something, or someone, dangerous behind. They could only stand ready.

Yet, all their precautions were wasted. No monsters, no traps, and even no friends awaited them. Just empty rooms and dark splotches that might be the remains of an old battle.

It was on the third floor that they first found a clue that the quest for their friends might not be entirely forsaken. It was Jan who spotted it, hidden between the gaps of two stone tiles. She bent low, picked up an ivory-colored object, and called the others. The simple plastic button, perhaps torn loose from a shirt, was all the hope they had.

"Didn't Mel's favorite blouse have buttons like that?" Sharmila said, frowning as she tried to recall.

Uswah picked up the button from Jan's hand, turning it sideways and then bringing it close to her nose to sniff. After a moment, she handed the button back to Jan, who looked puzzled about what to do with it. Eventually, she slipped it into a pocket with a shrug.

"Yes, I think so," Uswah confirmed. "No thread on the button, no smell of blood. Maybe it just fell off?"

Arthur made a face, then shook his head. He had nothing to offer to the conversation, instead squatting to stare at the floor. It took him a bit, but he spotted it. Running a finger along the ground, he murmured, "Blood splatter. I think we can confirm there's been a fight here."

"Against what?" Sharmila said, gesturing about. "If they killed something, why are there no bodies? Where are the monsters?"

"Ah lah! I can't stand it. We don't know anything," Jan said in exasperation.

In reply, Uswah pointed upwards.

Which, really, was answer enough for them all. Because up was the only way they were going to find an answer.

Chapter 56

Two more floors, the same thing. The only change was how long it took for them to cross the floors, as the layout changed from one large hall to a long hallway with multiple rooms. The rooms themselves were empty, devoid of anything but a small slit in the wall that served as a window. No desk, no chairs, no bed frame. Devoid of furniture, just cold and empty cells.

Arthur could not help but say it. "This is creepy, right?"

"Yes. Two dozen cells so far, if the count is the same," Uswah said, turning her head from side to side as she scanned the hallway. "These aren't places to live in. Not really even holding cells, since there's no way to lock the doors."

Arthur blinked, tilting his head to the side as he stared at the doors. She was right. No place to put a bar, no lock or even a hinge to shut the doors tightly. In other words, the doors closed only by virtue of the way they were hung.

"So what are they for?" Arthur said eventually as they finished sweeping the floor.

"Offices?" Sharmila offered. "Except, they've not been moved into. Yet."

"Maybe no one came. Ever," Jan offered.

Uswah smiled tightly. "An empty tower, inside a tower that climbs, found only recently after decades of exploration." She shook her head. "None of this makes sense."

"And the Towers make sense in general?" Arthur said with a snort. "After all these decades, we don't know why they appeared, what they're meant for, or who put them here. All those smart-smart people studied the Towers and what did they learn, *ha*?"

"Nothing," Sharmila said.

"Exactly. Nothing." Arthur shook his head.

"So if you think it's a big mystery that we'll never understand, why ask any questions at all?" Uswah said.

"Because fools like to talk, lah. You know that," Jan said.

"Funny." Arthur shook his head. "It's bloody creepy, that's all. If we can't understand why these buildings were created, can we even guess what we'll run into?"

"Doesn't matter," Sharmila said. "We meet whatever it is, we kill it. And we get what we came for."

Arthur's lips thinned at her words. He still had not agreed to that, but since going up was their only other option other than going out, he didn't object. Not just yet.

"You know, in older video games, these kinds of cells were just spawning points," Uswah said, and they all turned to look at her. "Places where monsters just appeared. They weren't really meant for anything else, so game developers never put much effort into them."

"Don't they have scripts to fix that problem these days?" Arthur said. "I remember reading about pre-built scripts being a problem in modern game design. Because everyone uses the same things, there's no creativity."

"Aaargh. That old complaint." Uswah rolled her eyes. "Next, you'll complain that dating games have no real story, that girls should stay out of FPS, and that you're tired of seeing non-Westerners as bad guys."

"That..."

For the first time, the Yin-bodied woman seemed heated. She stalked up to Arthur and glared at him. “Go ahead. Say it.”

“I just meant to say: how old are the games you’re playing?”

“I like the classics. What can I say?” Uswah sniffed. “Anyway, I can run emulators on one screen while waiting for a raid to start. Takes up almost nothing on the clock.”

Sharmila cut in before things got any more heated: “Arthur, you said those game developers didn’t put much effort in the cells or whatever. But these empty rooms seem like... no effort.” Uswah shrugged. “The game theory of the Towers is a better one than most.”

“Ya-lah, but it’s so stupid.” Jan shook her head in disbelief. "Some aliens made a game and then forgot about it?"

“Or are using us to test it,” Arthur interjected.

“Better than the dystopian theory that we’re all in a giant TV show,” Shar pointed out.

“Like, seriously, why do we think aliens would even care to watch other aliens do stupid things? Humans might. But maybe aliens prefer, I don’t know, watching paint dry. These theories are all so... human-centric,” Uswah said, wrinkling her nose.

“But the Tower is human-centric. The cultivation methods we’re finding, that’s for our use,” Shar said.

“Eh, *jangan-lah.* They don’t need to know you’re a futurist,” Jan said, waving her hand around rapidly.

“You just told them,” Sharmila said.

Arthur smirked but as Sharmila glared at him, he opened his hands wide. “It’s fine, it’s fine. It isn’t any stupider than the ‘we’re all dead and this is God’s test’ version.”

“Allah would not test us in this manner,” Uswah said firmly. “Perhaps—”

That was when the roar reverberated through the tower. The group moved apart, giving each other more space as their eyes darted around. Most of them watched the way they had come, since the sound seemed to be coming from within the tower. Even so, Uswah had her back almost fully turned to the door, watching the opposite direction just in case.

"That sounds like a very big, very angry *jenglot*," Arthur muttered, eyes narrowed.

"And inside the tower," Sharmila said and started moving back towards the stairway. When no one else moved, she spun around and glared at the rest of the team. "Move!"

The trio glanced at one another and in that time, she had already made it halfway down the hallway. The urgency of her movement broke them free from stunned inaction and they hurried after her, catching up as they hit the staircase.

For a second, Sharmila hesitated, casting a glance downstairs and then upward.

Her indecision was broken by another pained and angry howl, coming from high above them. She started running up the stairs, hitting two or three steps at a time. Arthur growled but followed behind Jan who was calling for her friend to slow down, to explain.

Sharmila chose not to, but Arthur was himself still unwilling to jump right past new doors. He slowed down, so the gap between him and the two women widened.

"Go," Uswah said from behind, her voice trembling a little with excitement. "It's Mel. It must be. They're alive. And they need our help."

"Maybe. But we're no use if we get ambushed now, are we?" Arthur said, casting a glance back down the stairs. No sign of monsters, nothing coming out of the doors they were passing. "Got to survive, 'cause there's no revive."

"No monsters have appeared. I don't think they can. If it's a respawn center, maybe they can't respawn while we're here?"

Arthur opened his mouth to answer her but, as he hit another step, snapped his mouth shut. She could be right. Or it might just be a giant elaborate trap. They had no idea and that was, he had to admit, driving him a little crazy.

All that second-guessing, trying to work the safest way out. Trying to survive at least the first floor of this Tower. Because how embarrassing would that be, to fall here?

Then, they were another seven floors up, and the door there was open. Sharmila and Jan had already burst into the room by the time he arrived, panting from the sprint. Hopefully they hadn't entirely exhausted themselves before the fight.

Because from the looks of it, they were going to need some reserves.

Chapter 57

A massive *jenglot* dominated the center of the room, nearly half a size bigger than its three companions. At full extension, it would have knocked its head against the ceiling. Which was probably why it was crouched.

Or maybe it was trying very, very hard to deal with Mel and her team. Despite his pessimism, the trio of women they had searched so long for were all here. Worse for wear, it looked like, but still alive.

Rani's spear was broken, but she still fought with both ends; she had tied broken-off claws to one end as a short makeshift spear. Mel was showing much of her pale skin, most of her clothing having been turned into bandages for the other women. Daiyu looked the worst, her right foot dragging and bleeding as she fended off the monsters closing in on them from behind.

"Hold on!" Sharmila cried out, already running to meet the *jenglot.* She raised her spear, leaping the remaining distance and plunging her weapon into the nearest monster's body. It cried, rearing backwards as it tried to grab its assailant.

Another of the *jenglot* turned away from the fight, growling at the new group. Jan swirled her parang around, gesturing at the monster to close in on her. At the same time, Uswah moved to flank her, leaving Arthur the only one still hanging back.

He scanned the ongoing battle, trying to figure out what was going on as he started shifting to flank the group. Together, Uswah and Jan were fighting a single *jenglot,* wearing it down but unable to land a killing blow. In the meantime, Mel, freed up from handling four monsters at a time, had turned around and focused on taking down one by herself while Daiyu and Rani held off the largest *jenglot.*

Having assessed what was happening, Arthur made a decision. He circled the fight towards Daiyu and Rani, who were struggling to hold off their monster. After all, Daiyu was badly injured, and Rani looked exhausted. Each blow that they blocked made it seem like they were going to fall over.

Once he was in position, he ran forward as silently as he could, keeping himself as low to the ground to dodge the monsters' awareness. Unfortunately, the larger creature seemed to sense him long before Arthur could reach it, bounding backwards and away from the girls.

Undeterred, Arthur kept moving forward, watching as the *jenglot* pulled away from the women, far enough that Rani finally collapsed to the ground, breathing hard and leaning on one butt end of her broken spear. Arthur winced, having hoped for some help but he kept moving. Then he realized that the damn monster had stopped in its tracks.

"Smart bastard, aren't you?" Arthur grumbled under his breath as he planted a foot forward and thrust with his spear, using the full momentum of his movement. The spear shot toward the monster's throat controlled only by one hand.

Only for it to be batted aside with casual disregard by one claw. The monster snarled and strode forward, attempting to catch Arthur off-guard.

But he kept the momentum, spinning his own body and shortening his grip on the spear haft. Swinging the weapon above his head, he blocked a claw attack, then stabbed up at the *jenglot*'s thigh. Now that he was certain of the creature's speed, he poured energy into his body, triggering the Heavenly Sage's Mischief to increase his speed and attack form.

The tip of the spear tore the inside thigh, the empowered attack easily parting monstrous flesh and defense. Arthur stepped away a single step after so that he could put his point at the back of the monster's chest. It stopped the monster from approaching closer, even when it tried to unleash strikes from both claws. Ducking low, Arthur kept moving, using the haft and his positioning to block the attacks.

A half-dozen passes and Arthur received nearly half as many wounds, the claws leaving lines of blood all along his body. Even with his boosted attributes, he found himself struggling. His own return attacks had left a few stabs in the monster's body but nothing fatal or damaging enough to make it stop or slow down.

Bu the battle all around had the group slowly winning, whittling the monsters down. The *jenglot* who were so powerful could not be ended with a single attack, so Arthur and the women had to bleed them, cripple them with repeated attacks that took muscles and tendons and senses with each successful hit.

Yet, the *jenglot* were so strong that a single claw attack could end them if it landed right. It was a dangerous game they played, and Arthur, after a further clash of staff and claws, chose to switch it up.

He reversed his spear and stabbed deep into the monster's foot, causing it to rear backwards. Then, in the gap, Arthur stabbed again, this time sinking deep into the monster's knee, crippling the monster.

Then, before it could recover, Arthur skipped to the side, thrusting again at the monster's raised arm. He stabbed it deep between the bicep and bone, tearing sideways and ripping a gap. He jumped backward then and wobbled on his footing for a moment.

The *jenglot* on the ground threw itself at Arthur, trying to take advantage of the moment, only for Arthur to stabilize immediately and hop up high. Before the monster could claw his legs apart, Arthur swung the weapon down onto its head. He smashed the haft on the back of its skull, crushing the monster's face to the ground. Then, landing smoothly, he sidestepped around the clawing and twitching hands to drive his spear into the monster's neck before retreating the rest of the way.

Looking up, he scanned the group, searching for his next opponent. Mel was already done with hers, the monster on the ground and clutching its chest. On the other hand, Jan and Uswah's was still standing, though Mel was moving to flank it. Which left...

"Hold on, Shar!" Arthur called out, rushing in from behind. The monster looked up at the cry, spotting Arthur and turned to watch as he ran over. Which was what he wanted, because in the few moments when the monster wasn't trying to claw Shar, she managed to bury a knife into the monster's lower body.

The monster reared, the pain from getting stabbed in the back causing it to jerk backwards. Arthur sent his spear into the monster's chest, grimacing as the end wobbled a little to sink into the creature's left lung.

The monster staggered further, then ripped the spearhead from its body before tumbling backward. Shar, moving a little too late, didn't manage to get out before it crashed down on her, trapping her. She let out a cry of pain, trying to scramble out even as Arthur turned to search for more *jenglot.*

Only to find that none of the monsters were still standing. Even the one he'd left injured but still alive had expired in the meantime. Their own team were all alive, none injured fatally.

A situation that Arthur found surprising to the extreme. If gratefully so.

Cutting the flow of energy to Heavenly Sage's Mischief, he found himself flopping to the ground moments later as the battle took its toll.

Chapter 58

Wounds were bandaged, water drunk to hydrate parched throats and clear bloody mouths. Weapons were collected and resharpened, broken knubs smoothed out and checked over, whilst secondary weapons were handed around. All in all, it took nearly a half hour of mostly silent preparation before the group settled after the fight, a tense period in which Uswah watched the staircase for additional threats. In the end, the group gathered near the entrance by unspoken agreement, ready to hear the story of those that had come before.

"Don't worry," Mel said to Uswah. "The *jenglot* never come down from their floors. Not in all the time we've been here."

Uswah nodded to acknowledge Mel's words but chose to stay in her spot nevertheless. Mel shrugged, while Arthur stayed seated nearby, slightly apart from the group.

"How long have you been here?" Shar said. "We saw your camp but..."

"Two? Three weeks now?" Mel said, frowning. "It's hard to keep track of time. And we've been taking turns cultivating and healing."

"Eh! See, lah. Told you, right?" Jan said, smirking.

"Yes, yes, got it," Shar said, and waved her off. Then: "Mel, what happened? What's taking you so long to clear the tower?"

Mel made a face, glancing at the group before she sighed. "It's not that easy. There's a trick to the tower."

"A trick?" Shar cocked her head to the side.

"This is the... third time clearing this floor?" Mel looked over at her friends, where Daiyu nodded firmly. "Third time. We've been up and down, clearing as we go, but they keep coming back."

"And the seal?" Shar said carefully.

Mel frowned, casting a glance at Arthur, who gave her a grin.

"Shar *dah cakap*," Jan muttered.

"Really. You told him?" Rani said, surprised. "Why?"

"We needed him to tell us where you went. He was the last one to see you. And things were getting hot here. Anyway, he knows he's not getting the seal." Here, Shar glared at Arthur. "Right?"

"Ya, ya." Arthur waved a hand dismissively. "I ain't dumb enough to put that big a target on my back. I've already got one group after me."

"See," Shar said.

Mel's lips thinned but eventually she answered the question. "There's sign, but no appearance. We..." Again the long hesitation as she looked at her friends.

"Just tell them," Daiyu said. "We can't finish the tower ourselves."

Rani nodded in agreement, though she still eyed Arthur suspiciously.

"There's no real sign that clearing the tower is the way to get the seal," Mel finally said. "There's no boss monster, no alpha *jenglot* to kill. Just more of them, no matter how many times we go up and down."

"Are we even in the right place then?" Arthur said curiously. "Maybe the tower is a red herring."

"What?" Jan said.

"Red herring: it's an idiom."

"More like an idiot," Jan snapped.

"Neither of you are helping," Mel said, raising her voice and shutting down the bickering pair. Then, with her gaze fixed on Arthur, she continued. "We know we're in the right place. The seal guide says so."

"It says so?" Arthur said.

Another long pause, when all the women looked at one another. In the end, Mel shrugged and reached into her blouse, fishing out a circular amulet. Without removing it from the string around her neck, she bent over to offer Arthur a closer look at the amulet.

Seated as he was, Arthur was treated to a bit of an eyeful which he valiantly struggled not to notice. It wasn't that he was trying to be pervy, but it was just there and... nope.

"Ummm. Can you take it off?" Arthur said, turning his head to avert his gaze.

"What?" Mel snapped.

"Why?" Rani asked at the same time, clutching the spear in her hand tight.

"It's a rather pretty bra, but a little bloodstained," Arthur replied.

Silence, then Mel hissed as she straightened. She glared at Arthur for a second before she pulled the amulet off her neck and tossed it at him. However, she moved too quickly, angered as she was by his words and the amulet flew through the air, off course from Arthur. He jerked away and, expecting a slap instead of the amulet, batted it away out of reflex.

The metallic object flew through the air, bouncing once and then again before landing on the ground and rolling away. It finally fetched up against the body of a *jenglot*, slowly leaking blood.

"*Bodoh*! Why you did that?" Jan snarled.

Arthur scrambled to his feet, only to find a hand coming down on his shoulder. Rani stopped looking vaguely friendly and was now pressing him back onto the ground.

"It was an accident!"

"Sure, sure. We'll just have Mel pick it up, and maybe we won't have you touching it like that, eh?" Rani said. "Just so there's no further accidents."

Arthur narrowed his eyes but sat there, arms crossed. Together, the group watched as Mel and Shar walked over to the corpse. As the pair bent down to pick it up, their bodies blocked all view of the amulet.

Then, Mel's voice, in a tone filled with wonder:

"Well now, *that's* unexpected."

Chapter 59

By the time Mel and Shar made their way back to the group, the other women were practically vibrating with interest.

"Tell, what is it lah?" Jan said. "What happened? Is it damaged? If it's damaged, I kill him, okay?"

Arthur's eyes narrowed, letting one crossed arm rest near the hilt of his belt knife. Not that he intended to draw it, but if things went bad, he certainly wasn't going down alone. He'd have to hurt Rani first though, since she still stood behind him. Backwards roll, put the dagger into her foot, maybe take out the Achilles tendon. Grab the spear with the other hand and toss the knife underhand.

Easy-peasy.

"Nothing bad," Mel said, sharing a smile with Shar. Then, lifting her hand, she showed the somehow clean and unbloodied object to the others. "In fact, he might have given us a clue."

The group frowned, staring at the amulet. Eventually, Uswah called from her position near the door. "Is it not darker?"

"It is. The bronze has darkened, a little," Daiyu said. "It was brighter before. And... is that a teardrop forming?"

"Looks more like a comma to me," Shar said. "But a drop, or teardrop, might be right."

"Deeply creepy. And so not cheesy," Arthur half-said, half-sung. Tension bled off a little, even as he rhymed. Stupid training, stupid rhyming brain. He didn't move his hand from the hilt of his knife, though he did uncross his other arm. "I wonder how much blood it can soak up?"

"You're so weird," Jan said, the tension in her voice fading as well.

"He's not wrong, though," Mel came to his defense, looking at the other *jenglot* bodies. "I think it might be time to see what happens when we soak our amulet in blood."

"Not me," Rani called out, stepping back and giving Arthur his space once more. He glanced over his shoulder to see her holding both hands up with a smile on her lips.

"Not me!" Uswah added. "I'm on watch."

"Same."

Denials rang out from the group, except from Mel and Arthur. The pair exchanged looks before they both shrugged at one another. Arthur stood, and the pair wandered over to the nearest corpse.

"So, how we doing this? Blood pool or... nope, you're just going for it, I see," Arthur said. He watched as Mel dropped the entire amulet right into the gaping wound in the monster's neck where blood had pooled, going so far as to shove it in and swirl it around to make sure the blood had properly coated it. "Well, that's one way of doing it."

In reply, Mel just smirked.

Not long after, the group regathered at the doorway. As they had predicted, no *jenglot* came down to bother them, even though Uswah had kept watch just in case. The amulet, mildly altered, sat displayed on Mel's palm for them to marvel at.

Now that he had a chance to properly examine the amulet, even Arthur could guess at the changes. On the backside were little teardrops. The initial golden-bronze colour of the pendant had darkened to a muddy red-bronze, but even as he watched, that colour faded back almost to the original. But one teardrop darkened. It looked almost like a ruby, so glittering was its countenance now.

"Thirty-four, thirty-five, thirty-six..." Rani muttered under her breath, her finger hovering over the amulet as she counted.

"Forty-eight," Mel stated firmly.

"You made me lose count again!" Rani huffed.

"It's forty-eight, I counted it before. It's the same now," Mel said, jutting her lower lip out. "That means we got to kill another forty-five *jenglot* and soak the amulet in their blood."

"Yeah, but why not forty-four?" Shar said, frowning. "We had four kills here, but only three teardrops filled."

Mel shrugged.

Jan snorted. "Maybe the fool broke it."

"Maybe *you're* broken," Arthur snapped back. "Anyway, ever heard of decay?"

"Maybe my English isn't that broken lah."

Uswah waved at them to stop bickering and focus. "Are you thinking of game mechanics again?"

"Exactly. Monster decay speeds up in games, so maybe we just took too long getting the amulet into the blood," Arthur said. "Whatever it's soaking up might have faded already—and maybe it's not just blood, creepy as that is."

"Souls." Shar shuddered.

"The Allamah says that none of the monsters we meet or kill in the Tower have souls. Their destruction is *mubah*," Uswah said from where she was watching the stairs. "No souls, so nothing to suck up."

"You've seen their eyes, seen how intelligent they are. If not souls, what is it that drives them?" Shar said.

"Malevolence. Demonic forces..." Rani said, her voice pitched a little high, almost as though she was mocking the very idea.

"Energy then," Arthur said, cutting them off. That kind of philosophical discussion could drag on forever, really, and was not something he ever wanted to listen to. "It's absorbing the energy spent on them. The Tower does that, we know it. So..."

"Take too long and there's not enough." Mel inclined her head a little at Arthur. "As good an explanation as any."

"Better than some, which has no real income," Arthur muttered but then grinned when Mel glared at him. Hey, coming up with rhymes on the fly was hard. "So what now? We rest up and get to the fighting later?"

When no one had a better suggestion, the group pulled away from the door, taking post at various locations on the big floor. They wandered into individual rooms, choosing some privacy. Uswah, still paranoid, lay a few simple traps to alert them if someone tried to sneak in through the main door.

Arthur did the same for his own room before slumping on the inside, back against the door so that it would jar him awake if it was forced open. Then, and only then, did he let out a long-held breath, tension bleeding out of him.

It seemed that their long, long journey was coming to an end. Or at the least, the journey's end was in sight. Even if they had a lot more *jenglot* to kill. Still, with seven of them banded together, the danger was significantly reduced now.

Until, and unless, of course, they decided to betray him.

And wasn't that a cheery thought?

Chapter 60

The group tore through the next level with only a minor complication. The four *jenglot* they had found were easy prey for the bolstered group. The problem began with the *jenglot* which had tried to sneak up on them.

Arthur had dispatched it and then taken its core. An argument arose afterwards, when the others realized he had acquired the core. After all, Mel's group had not been party to his initial agreement. On the other hand, they did not try to renegotiate it, a fact that left him feeling a certain degree of goodwill towards her.

And paranoia. After all, if they intended to betray him, there was no reason to renegotiate a bad deal.

It was why, that night, he spent a good portion of the time drawing and churning refined energy directly from the monster cores he owned into his own core, pulling the energy in to boost his own cultivation the moment it crossed over.

Triggering the upgrade from 4 to 5 points in Spirit also meant he got to choose a trait. He had chosen Spirit to increase cultivation speed, which would also increase his energy resources. Since at least two of his techniques used his energy pool to empower them—Focused Strike and Heavenly

Sage's Mischief—it seemed the more important attribute to upgrade at this point.

An upgrade to Body would actually expand his energy pool. But it mattered little if he could not fill up that expanded pool. Hence the need to increase his cultivation speed first, to fill that pool faster.

Admittedly, if he could learn a better cultivation technique, he could probably increase his base cultivation speed, since each cultivation technique he studied would improve upon that. Still, he was rather chuffed that the new Yin cultivation method taught to him by Uswah had improved his speed so far. He was now getting close to his theoretical maximum in cultivation speed.

However, he was not there yet. And whilst he had an idea of what he meant to acquire as a Spirit trait, his new Yin Body had made things a little more complicated.

Spirit traits could be broken into a few major areas. First, willpower-based traits. They allowed individuals to push aside soul attacks, everything from directly-damaging soul attacks to fear effects. Secondly, there were the aura effects. Killing Intent and fear auras, for instance. Even attractive, charismatic or presence-based effects all came under this heading. A powerful aura could be used to deter monsters from attacking you, and when grown enough, the aura could be wielded like a weapon. The third major area involved the formation and management of energy, whether it was manipulating one's aura more easily to unleash attacks like his Refined Energy Dart, or directly speeding up cultivation efforts.

"Got three options, where there's no floptions." Another grimace. That wasn't even a word.

Three options, three ways to go.

"Options three, for there be a tree!" Much better.

While he could pick a specialized trait from one of those three options, he could instead choose general reinforcement of the entire soul with a trait like Flexible Soul, which would provide marginal improvements all across three aspects.

Initially, his plan had been to gain a general energy collection method to increase his cultivation speed. It would benefit him in both the long- and short-term. A trait like Energy Vortex was very popular for exactly that reason.

Unfortunately, he now debated if he needed a second method of increasing his cultivation speed. Right now, he was trying to learn how to properly cultivate *only* Yin chi. Once he mastered the skill as taught by Uswah, he knew his total cultivation speed would increase significantly. As such, he dismissed that particular path.

No. Better to find another method of improvement, which meant one of the three specialized options: willpower- or soul-strengthening, aura improvement, or more manipulable energy.

Aura improvement was an interesting option, though he was not sure if it was useful. From what Arthur had read, it was hard to wield aura at the early stages, since beginning cultivators were just not powerful enough to output much energy. In that sense, it was more often purchased at later stages, which was why things like Killing Intent could only be wielded by higher-level cultivators.

Fear auras were the same, useful for driving away normal animals but not monsters. Not at his current cultivation level. And the same applied for each of the charisma or presence benefits of a powerful aura. He could go esoteric, making use of his aura to chill or warm himself and others. That could make it even easier to wield certain energy types later, but none of it was directly useful.

No, aura improvement was interesting but it very much a later purchase. It would offer him little short-term benefit, so he discarded it entirely.

Willpower- or soul-strengthening improvements were defensive improvements for the most part. Again, useful for the long-term but none of the monsters that Arthur was currently facing utilized skills like soul attacks. In general, creatures like that did not make their presence known until at least the third floor of a Tower.

Which left him a lot of time to purchase something that would aid him in such a case.

If he did not improve his cultivation speed, perhaps he should work on improving his overall control of energy. That improvement came in two forms: either making it easier to control—speeding up his manipulation of energy, such as making Refined Energy Dart fire faster—or making it more efficient overall, thus reducing the energy use.

He could also aspect his energy at this point, or create the beginnings of favoured energies, but making such choices so early on was rather a good choice. It might work out for those cultivator families and rich kids who had the funds to know where and what kind of cultivation to acquire. But for someone like Arthur, his best choice was to wait and see.

Anyway, he was already tied down with Yin energy. So making it Cold Yin Energy or Fiery Yin Energy made little sense. Though it might be cool...

Shaking his head and dismissing casual fancies, Arthur made himself concentrate on what was important: picking out the trait he needed. It was obvious that he needed to work on energy control. The first form would see the most obvious increase in his martial strength. The second form was likely a greater advantage over the long-term.

Thinking about it, Arthur recalled some posited builds that focused on efficiency as the main trait purchase for the Spirit as one progressed. Also known as "spammers" colloquially, these individuals also focused on gaining a large number of low-cost attacks; they would "spam" these attacks on a continual basis, overwhelming their opponents by the volume of attacks rather than any great skill.

So: speed or efficiency?

Considering previous interactions and his most recent fights, Arthur came to a conclusion at last. And made his choice for his Spirit trait, feeling the shift deep within as the Tower System put it into effect. He hissed as the pain erupted throughout his body, and he battled it as he grasped the changes, helping them along as best he could.

"No pain, no gain. And it ain't no movie, that did poorly."

Chapter 61

"Are you done?" Mel asked, cutting into Arthur's slow recovery.

Lying on the ground, he opened his eyes to stare at the woman who stood over him, hands on her hips. Almond eyes narrowed a little into a smile while she watched him struggle back into a sitting position.

"Done with what?"

"Either having a *really* good time or upgrading yourself." Her gaze drifted down to his crotch before she continued. "If it was the first, my condolences."

"For what?"

"Your... lack." A glance at his staff, before she continued. "Of course, that would explain certain weapon choices."

"Are you calling me small?" Arthur said, incensed and bouncing to his feet. "Why, I'll point out that I've never had any complaints."

"Oh, you've had quite a few companions then?" Mel said, teasingly. "I thought you were a Battle Fanatic."

"I'm not! And if you know what happens when a bunch of sweaty, highly athletic individuals get together, you should remember how many condoms they send to the Olympic Villages!" he replied. Then he added, "Not that

I'm a slut or anything. I mean, I like sex and all, but the count isn't in the hundreds or anything."

"Hundreds..." Mel trailed off, arching an eyebrow. "So the count is in two digits then."

"What makes you say that?"

"If it was under, you'd have said it. Since you jumped to the next level after two, and not one, it has to be around there."

Silence followed her pronouncement. Then she smirked and turned to walk back to her pile of belongings and untied her bedroll. "Just so you know, two digits at our age does make you a bit of a slut."

"It's the 21st century! No slut shaming."

"Who's shaming?" She grinned as she lay on a thin bedroll. "Perhaps I'm just intrigued."

"Uh..." Arthur tried to work out what the heck was going on. There were enough changes in both body language and topic that he felt a little flabbergasted. He thought she was flirting with him, maybe even making a full-on overture. But also... not?

"Anyway, it's your turn to watch. Don't cultivate when you're supposed to be on watch." So saying, she rolled over and closed her eyes.

Staring at her back for a long moment, Arthur finally gave up on discerning what the heck was going on. Maybe she was flirting or giving him a hint that flirting was acceptable. Either way, a small empty hall—what Arthur might consider a dining area—was not the place to conduct further amorous pursuits. Not when the rest of the group was a dozen feet away.

Well, not unless you were quite adventurous. Smiling at a memory, Arthur picked up his spear and moved to the main doorway, taking a seat on the chair placed nearby. Rather than splitting up into individual rooms this time, the group had chosen to rest together.

Easier to secure, even if it lacked privacy.

A few moments later, Arthur found himself bored so he pulled up his status. No reason not to see how far he had improved and what his choice had done.

Cultivation Speed: 1.23 (1.11 Yin)
Energy Pool: 7/15 (Yin)
Refinement Speed: 0.025
Refined Energy: 0.14 (3)

Attributes and Traits
Mind: 4
Body: 6 (Enhanced Eyesight, Yin Body)
Spirit: 5 (Sticky Energy)

Techniques
Focused Strike
Accelerated Healing – Refined Energy (Grade I)
Heavenly Sage's Mischief
Refined Energy Dart

Among techniques, Sticky Energy had one of the least marketable names. It was also a deceptive name, as the technique did not create energy forms that were sticky like a certain superhero's webs, but instead made the energy within an individual easier to manipulate.

In the end, rather than go for a general boost in efficiency, Arthur had chosen to go with making his energy easier to manipulate. It would aid the channelling of his Focused Strikes, speed up Heavenly Sage's Mischief and Refined Energy Dart, and even improve Accelerated Healing.

He had chosen Sticky Energy precisely because it affected all of his techniques. He could see it being useful in the future as well as immediately. Before acquiring Sticky Energy, it still took him too long to form Energy Darts. So he could only use them at range.

But how much better would it be if he could unleash an Energy Dart into a monster's mouth at point blank? Or while hopping away?

Arthur entertained several daydreams of the possibilities. Then he shook them off and practiced forming his Energy Dart instead. Better to do that than daydream on watch.

Though... when exactly was his watch over?

Chapter 62

Climbing the *jenglot* tower was a slow, painful slog. Each battle was risky, for the *jenglot* were strong and smart enough to adapt to changing circumstances. Failing to block one of their attacks could easily lead to significant injuries, and so everyone including Arthur fought with care rather than risk accumulating even additional wounds.

Which did help, even if it didn't prevent injuries entirely.

After each battle, the medallion was dipped in the bodies, tear drops of blood slowly filling up. It never stopped being creepy of course, but filling the medallion's many tear drop hollows was satisfying. More so for Mel and her team after the long period of stagnation.

By the time they had managed to make it most of the way to the top of the tower, they had filled three quarters of the medallion in only a few days. However, eyeing the group and the constant battles, Arthur could not help but wonder how much more they could take.

Movies and TV shows often had heroes who could fight tirelessly. Even in most shows about wars, they only highlighted the great battles, the push and pull of death approaching or being cast aside.

Yet, humans were never meant to exist in a constant state of violence. Travelling through the forest was bad, but the attacks only came once every day at most if one was unlucky. That had been no MMO where battles were never-ending and around every corner. In the forest the mind could still rest, the heart-pounding could slow, and constant tension could drain.

Here, in the tower where the next battle was but another floor above, the exhilaration and exuberance of violence never ended. Pulled by the knowledge that their task was finally nearing completion, pushed by their impatience, the group moved from fight to fight with few pauses.

And the toll was showing.

Jan, always the most impatient of them, was hurrying forward and refusing to stop. Bouncing from foot to foot, she clutched her weapons tightly and startled at every loud noise or sudden movement, occasionally sweeping her parang in that direction. The others kept away from her, worried they would be hit, which made her even more agitated.

Mel in contrast looked impassive for the most part, except he caught her worrying her lower lip whenever no one else was looking. She kept touching her chest too, placing a hand on the amulet to ensure it was still there.

The others all showcased minor variations of tension and worry, Daiyu picking at the crusted wounds on her body without end, Shar and Rani bickering and snapping at one another, sending cutting asides before parting ways to sulk. Only to find one another later and begin the process again.

It was, to Arthur's surprise, that only he and Uswah seemed to handle the pressure well. As they rested, he found himself taking a seat beside her, curiosity driving him to speak.

"Why aren't we affected?" he asked her.

"Affected by what?" Uswah murmured. And once he explained, she smiled a little. "What do you cultivate?"

"Um, just the basic cultivation style and what little I've learnt from you." Arthur paused, then added, "Thanks, by the way."

"No, I didn't mean your cultivation style, but 'what do you cultivate'?"

Frowning, he took a moment to find the answer she was looking for. "Yin chi."

"Ya, lah."

"You mean, because of our Yin Body and the Yin chi…"

"We are calmer. Yes. You've felt it before, have you not?" At his nod, she continued. "Cool in battle, calm in our passions. Not coldly logical like a robot, but a faded passion. One worn away from long nights of repeated exposure, but no less true.

"That is the Yin. And because of that, we feel the pressure less."

"Because it's what we do," Arthur murmured, in a slow dawn of understanding. Yang was all fiery passion, the momentary explosion. But that kind of passion had to be built upon ever increasing amounts of fuel, or it would gutter out.

Yin, though, could take the same amount of fuel and keep burning for ages. Providing heat and warmth for hours on end, though not to the same extent as Yang.

Some might think one or the other was better, but it was but a matter of context. Yin and Yang, they moved in tandem, and the mindsets they formed were but mirror opposites of one another.

"Yes. And it's why you need to watch them too," Uswah said. "I know you worry about us turning on you."

"I don't."

"I see your eyes dart to exits, the way you hang at the back all the time. Never leading the charge, always watching for a way to leave." She held up a hand when Arthur tried to protest further. "It's understandable. We are strangers, even though we have shed blood together. And some of us..." Her eyes drifted over to Jan, who was pacing up and down the hallway, "have been less than accepting."

She went on: "But loyalty and trust go both ways. If you are always looking to leave, we will always be looking for you to go."

Arthur nodded jerkily, acknowledging her point. Still...

"But that's not the point I was trying to make. It's this. They are like Yang to our Yin. When they begin to burn out, when their fuel subsides, we must contain them. Make them rest, recharge. Or, if in battle they rage beyond reason, we must step in." She touched her hijab, idly adjusting it. "We must face and fight when they can't."

"Because they've done too much?" Arthur said.

"Yes."

He frowned, looking over the group spread around. Saw the bags under their eyes, the occasional tremble in Shar's hand that appeared out of nowhere and only stopped when she focused. He saw Mel wearing at her lower lip, clutching the necklace.

And he wondered if Uswah's earlier comment about him leaving was really as much an aside as she had meant it to be. Looking over her, the way she sat serenely with her legs crossed, he could not help but wonder. What she believed might be coming, and what she had planned.

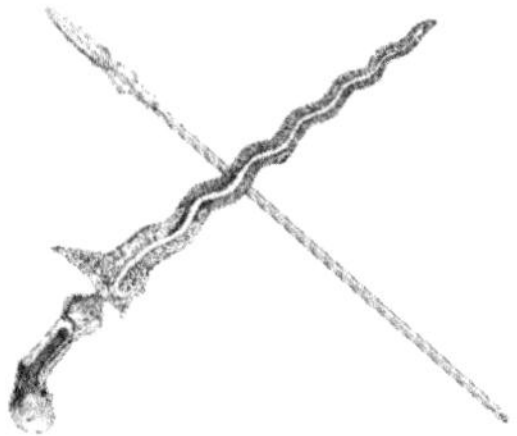

Chapter 63

The attack came from behind, without warning but for the snarls of two *jenglot*. Daiyu, who had been relegated to watching the back was caught by surprise, thrown backward by the claw thrust at her chest and caught on the remnants of her armour. The claw plunged deep into her body, and she was swung aside like a rag doll.

The other *jenglot* lunged at Arthur, who spun out of the way at the last moment. He brought up his spear to keep the monster at bay. At the same time, he formed and pinched off energy in his aura, sending it shooting out.

Not from his hands, which were both holding the spear, but from his forehead, the spot where the third eye would have been in common parlance. The Refined Energy Dart caught the second monster as it stepped into the hallway, tearing a hole through its chest.

This modification of the Refined Energy Dart was something Arthur had been practising for the last few days, ever since the boost in his control of energy had made it possible. Rather than forming it around his hand, Arthur chose to make use of the concentration point above his third eye, giving him a much easier method of firing his only ranged attack.

Best of all, the attack caught most monsters by surprise.

Taking advantage of the monster staggering backward, Arthur stepped forward and thrust with his spear. He aimed up, shoving the spear directly into the softer, fleshy portion of its throat. Focused Strike allowed his attack to slip through the monster's innate toughness, skewering the monster in its mouth and then brain.

Unfortunately, monsters had a bad tendency to last a little even after a fatal blow. The creature thrashed for a moment, throwing Arthur side to side as he held onto the spear. The spearhead twisted in its flesh before popping out with a loud squelch.

The sudden release caused Arthur to stumble and slam into a wall. But the *jenglot* reared up in anger only to suddenly collapse as all the energy driving it ran out.

"Youch, that was an ouch," Arthur complained. Searching for the first *jenglot*, then he froze as he caught sight of what his distraction—necessary as it was—had cost them.

For the monster was standing over the still form of Daiyu, claws buried in her chest as it scooped and tore her innards out. Thankfully, from the way she no longer moved, she had at least expired before the creature got to this.

"*Ham ka chan!*" Swearing in Cantonese, Arthur lunged forward, triggering Heavenly Sage's Mischief. He regretted not using it now, even though he had wanted to save his energy for later. But rage took over reason, and he crossed the distance faster than ever, his cry alerting the monster. But it had barely raised its head before Arthur's spear pierced its throat.

Paddling forwards, he carried them off Daiyu's body, a foot slamming down on a weightless arm as he kept pushing until he had the creature pinned against the wall. He ducked low, feeling a claw rake across his side, tearing up his lower back and hip, before he shook his spear and pushed it higher.

The spear-tip twisted in at last, puncturing clean through, as the monster's health drained away. With a heavy twist of his body, Arthur tossed the monster aside and looked around, searching for someone, something, else to kill.

And finding nothing but a group of horrified women staring at him and their fallen comrade.

It was strange, Arthur thought. Even though he understood, intellectually, that loss and death were part of life in the Tower, this was the first time it had weighed on his spirit. He had traveled alone during his first months in the Tower, and then with the Thorned Lotuses, but none of the deaths so far had really touched him.

He wasn't exactly a stranger to death. The world out there, for those without a family inheritance and living on the meager amounts of a universal basic income, was harsh. Accidents still occurred, triads and tongs with their demands for blood money sometimes took collecting a little too far, and humanity had not learnt how to get rid of the worse kinds of illnesses. He'd burned incense for a school friend run over by an automated lorry gone awry, held the hand of a great-aunt as she passed from complications after a heart surgery, visited the graves of his grandparents.

But to see a friend, a companion, an ally torn apart—that was the strangest thing of all.

He wasn't in denial; he had seen it happen. Even if he had wanted to deny it, perhaps it was just his culpability in her death. Yet, no one else claimed it was his fault. Not even Jan, who blamed him for the sun rising and setting whenever she felt like it.

Instead, they stood around the body, wrapping it up, speaking quietly in a corner, holding hands or looking into the distance. Stewing in the loss, motivation to continue suddenly lost. A room was found, the body placed within and then the door closed; except to those who wished to say last words to their friend.

In the meantime, Arthur found himself a room of his own, where he could play over the last few moments, wondering if he could have, should have acted faster. If he had been a little more wary, if he had killed his own opponent faster, could he have stopped it? Left her injured but alive?

What if she had survived, injured and in need of healing? Crippled in the Tower, alone. Would she have thanked him?

Another strange thought, that. Their bodies in the Tower were not normal. For all the battles they took part in, few enough limbs and extremities were lost. Perhaps the battles were too vicious, the healing properties of their altered bodies too great.

It required specific cultivation techniques and pills to restore limbs. But it was possible and, given enough time and enough energy, an individual could return to climbing the Tower. If they dared.

For whilst the body might be healed, the mind was still scarred.

How many would dare walk through darkness again, having felt their innards torn from their stomachs, limbs ripped from bodies and snacked upon by vicious monsters? And in this Tower, they were lucky. Tower monsters in certain Western European countries were known to indulge in even darker desires.

Pulling his mind away from those thoughts, Arthur prodded his feelings a little further. Morbid musings aside, he found himself grieving in a more general sense. Not specifically for who had been lost, but for the idea of the woman.

After all, Daiyu had been... hostile to begin with. Then, her presence in the group had been quiet, her presence minimized by her injuries and general reticence. She had spoken with Mel and Rani more than with others, and even then, had done little of that.

The hectic push up the tower, the constant wear of battle, and the tension had seen little enough time to speak and build bonds of camaraderie. So Arthur found himself with few enough memories of what, who, she was. No shared meals for they no longer ate. Just brief moments of terror as they fought and then long hours of silent cultivation.

Perhaps that, most of all, was what stripped them of their humanity. Food, time, and companionship outside of the desperate air of battle.

And yet... Arthur found himself wiping away the silent tears that collected in his eyes. Perhaps, humanity and grief itself were not so easy to discard. No matter what the builders of the Towers thought to do.

Chapter 64

Up the tower and seven more *jenglot* murdered in short order. An amulet dipped in blood, until the tears on the backface were filled and there were but two more left to fill. The group stood around the most recent corpse as it slowly dissolved away, staring at one another.

"What happens now?" Arthur said.

"We kill two more *jenglot*," Shar said flatly. "Then we go back, with our prize."

"Don't think they have respawned already, right?" Arthur said.

"Not in this tower. But there are the ones outside," Mel said. "We have to clear them anyway."

"If we can find them, lah," Jan said darkly. "If they hide in the woods, then *banyak susah lah*. Tough for us to fight."

"There's also a lot more than four at a time," Arthur said carefully. "We can deal with four, but when there's more..." He didn't have to finish the thought since they'd recently experienced what happened when they were surprised by the *jenglot*.

"We also have a place we can retreat to," Mel said, gesturing at the tower. "If we work to thin them out as they rush us, and then pull back and fight them in the tower itself, we should be able to contain them."

"Use the doors as chokepoints?" Shar said, musingly.

"Trap them," Uswah murmured. "Including the ground-floor entrance."

"All good ideas," Mel said. "We've got a long climb down. And we won't want to start until tomorrow at the earliest anyway. So let's think about what we can do, and then do it."

"I want my clothes back," Rani muttered, pulling at her blouse that was made of patched-in pieces than anything else.

"How do you think I feel, with you all using my extra shirts?" Arthur complained.

"Probably grateful we haven't discussed why you had your bag ready, when none of us did," Shar said pointedly.

Arthur just shrugged. They all knew by now that he had been planning on leaving. He saw no point in hiding that, even from Mel. He was stuck with them anyway.

"Then we best get moving." Mel gestured to the staircase before leading the group down.

Descending took significantly less time than ascending did. Knowing that the floors had been cleared of monsters meant that the group could skip down the staircase with impunity, never worrying about potential ambushes. And while the memory of monsters arriving from behind still kept everyone warily verifying doorways as they passed them, it was more of a reflex rather than the wary creeping they had undertaken to ascend.

Once they checked the last few floors more thoroughly—an easy thing to do with them being large, empty hallways—the group verified that the final door was closed before choosing to take that time to rest. Spreading out across the bottom floor in their respective spots, one after the other, the team fell into cultivation practice, refilling empty energy reserves.

In short order, Arthur had refilled his own reserves. The new Spirit trait had, unfortunately, not made cultivating itself any easier, since the energy he was cultivating was the Tower's and not his. His trait only made already-cultivated energy easier to handle, making it "sticky" to his senses.

Still, he did not have a huge pool unlike some of the women. One aspect of his Enhanced Eyesight trait, he was coming to realize, was that he was beginning to gain a sense of the strength of his companions. Whether it was just a by-product of being with them so long or an increase in his Spirit attribute, he felt he had a better internal grasp of their individual dantian.

And, boy, was he low on the totem pole. Judging from the glow that someone like Mel had, he was only half as strong as her, and the others were at least as strong or noticeably stronger than him. He couldn't grasp the amount of refined energy they had—probably, a higher Mind stat was required for that—but he assumed they were all at least as strong there too.

Casting those concerns aside, he made sure to wander over to Uswah. He had questions about his most recent cultivation attempt, just like he did after every session. And since she was here, asking her for help was simple enough.

Only when she had finished answering his queries and set him on his next step to getting better at utilising and filtering out Yang chi did he return to his original position to pick out a monster core. He could process his cultivated energy into refined energy, but considering the monster core he held would do the same thing much faster and not knowing how long they'd all be waiting, he felt better powering up this way.

Falling into the routine of drawing power from the core, he was surprised when the monster core finally crumbled that everyone else was done and moving about, putting into action their earlier discussion.

A simple lever trap with an attached parang above the door. Rope—his rope!—being tied up and added to the space across the door, blocking movement. The rope crisscrossed and was anchored in place by the broken portion of a spear, leaving only a small opening to the right that the group could duck through when the door was thrown open. Additional loops were set there, where metal pitons that looked all too familiar were waiting, probably to help hold the door shut.

Where did they get those metal sticks? Casting his gaze around, Arthur's eyes widened.

"My backpack! You tore up my backpack," he cried.

"Firstly, that backpack was given to you by us. So it's more *our* backpack," Shar said, coming over to Arthur as he walked to the shredded item. "Secondly, we needed the materials. It's not as though there's much in here we can use."

Arthur had to grudgingly, if only internally, admit that they were not wrong. After all, the stone slabs that made up the tables were attached to the wall. There were no chairs to be found. On the other hand...

"How about breaking the doors down?" Arthur said. Then, he froze, for he noticed the wide grin on Shar's face. "What?"

"Thanks for volunteering! Uswah is upstairs. You can join her."

Cursing that he had fallen into such an elementary trap, Arthur still found himself complying. Not as though he could do much good here. Without materials, their only preparations were either what they were already doing or more cultivating.

"Fine. But I get another backpack, if we find one outside," he grumbled.

Shar nodded magnanimously, leaving him to tromp upstairs to join Uswah.

Chapter 65

"Remember, the job is to kill the *jenglot* safely. We fall back if there are more than four of them, let the traps and the doorways keep their numbers down. If there's another Elite, you let me deal with it," Mel said, repeating herself once again.

It was a mark of her nervousness, Arthur thought, that she was telling them what they already knew. The fact that she kept glancing back, around, and at the door—all while licking her lips—were indications that she was not as confident as she seemed. It made him wonder how bad that night attack had been that drove the initial team in. That the original group had not progressed much by the time they had arrived.

Or even gone outside.

Oh.

Was that it?

Before he could ask – before he could even consider if he should ask – Shar and Jan pushed open one of the double doors. Mel stepped out with Rani by her side, the pair crouching low and watching the treeline and the surroundings for an ambush.

As always, Arthur and Uswah brought up the rear, once Shar and Jan had cleared the doorway. A dozen steps away from the tower entrance, Mel and Rani waited.

And waited.

And wait they did, for long moments that dragged into an eternity.

Eventually, the group straightened up, no longer in a crouch. You could only stay tense for so long and not lose your edge. Besides, no matter how much Arthur scanned the surrounding forests, he could not spot a single *jenglot*. Not to say he did not see any monsters, having spotted the passing of a *kuching hitam* in the shadows of a tree to their right.

"They all gone, ah?" Jan said.

"Nah..." Arthur began to reply, then stopped when he realised who he was answering. Not that she seemed to care that he had said something.

"You see them?" Uswah, by his side, asked curiously.

"No. Nothing." Stretching a little, he gestured at the trees. "But we didn't the last time, right? Maybe they only come at night."

"Maybe. We were all sleeping when they showed up," Uswah said.

"Then let's collect what we can, while we can." Mel said, then suited action to words as she led the way to the abandoned camp.

Unfortunately, multiple weeks of being left unattended saw everything from the tents to the backpacks within them rather worn down. It seemed that some of the *jenglot*, in a fit of pique, had taken their claws to any tent left standing, leaving large rents in both tents and backpacks.

For all that, the group did their best to scavenge what goods they could, finding and pulling on new clothing, and retrieving the undamaged plastic bags where they could. It left them with more resources than before, especially the basic gear that they had been missing, including pouches, water filters, plates, and cooking utensils. Even if they did not need to eat, the act of doing so was comforting.

By the time the group had collected their goods, the sun was beginning to set. By unspoken agreement, they returned to the tower to deposit their goods before exiting. The group took a semi-circle position near the entrance, though after a moment, Arthur could not help but comment.

"This is silly. We don't know when exactly they're going to arrive." When the others looked at him, he straightened and pointed to the ground. "I'm going to start a fire at the least. Think anyone can grab some firewood? There's still enough light that if we expect them to come at night, we should be fine."

Again, silence greeted his words before Mel nodded.

"He's right. Let's set up a camp or something. At least get comfortable. If they see us ready to fight, maybe they won't come at all."

Now that was a sobering thought, Arthur considered. After all, a group of monsters that could reason out when a team was safe enough to fight was dangerous. Even more so than the sheer strength that the *jenglot* had shown.

Then again, these monsters seemed stuck in the way they interacted, never moving between tower floors. So perhaps they weren't that smart.

Really, figuring out why and how this tower worked was annoying.

Two small fires, set on either side of the tower entrance, flickered as the last of the artificial sun glowed outside—Was it artificial? It had to be. On one side sat Mel, Rani, and Arthur. On the other side, the trio from his original group. As much as Arthur wanted to query Uswah about his cultivation further, he needed time to practise again before further discussion would make sense. Add the fact that Uswah was at best an apathetic teacher, and he preferred to extract those nuggets of information with as much gap in time as he could afford to.

One aspect that was not particularly concerning was getting cultivation wrong. Not that you couldn't do it wrong and reduce the amount of energy you drew in, or hurt yourself if you drew Yang chi in if you were a Yin-bodied individual—like he found out—but concerns about cultivation deviation that were so popular in stories were overblown.

There were very, very few actual cases of cultivation deviation, and in most cases, it was when an individual had sought to take a shortcut that was prohibited. In all such cases, the individuals involved had later reported a sense that they were going down the wrong route—a very wrong route—well beforehand and had to struggle to push through.

Some studies had even attempted to verify such experiences outside the Tower, and the results were somewhat mixed. Still, it was generally accepted that part of the bad feelings—the sense of taking a wrong path—seemed to stem from the Tower itself. This often led to further experiments on correct, or more efficient, cultivation methods within the Tower.

All of which was a long way of saying why Arthur had chosen to hang out with Mel and Rani rather than the initial group. Actually, it was mostly to dodge Jan's dislike. And, he had to admit, a lingering sense of guilt over Daiyu's death.

"You probably would be better off joining them on that side," Mel said, touching the spear she wielded. "We can hold them off on this side ourselves."

"Maybe," Arthur said. "But I figure it's safer here, than there."

"Eh? Why?" Rani said curiously.

"Stronger, remember?" Arthur said. Then, because his brain said so, he half-sung, "Stronger, together. We cannot be torn apart!"

When everyone glared at him, he shrunk in a little.

"What? No one remembers that song?"

Silence.

He sighed and watched as they returned to Rani's question.

"So, you not being passive aggressive at Jan?" Rani said.

"No, lah," Arthur said dismissively. He even flapped a hand in indication.

"Hm..." Rani was unconvinced.

Mel snorted. "I'm still surprised you ended up here. Or that you managed by yourself so long. Last time we saw you, you were barely hanging on."

"Doing better now, no?" Arthur said, smirking.

She held out a hand and waggled it. "You managed to acquire an uncommon constitution, one that's more suited to women than men. And somehow managed to find the one group that can help you with it, at least without asking for an arm and a leg. Or an oath of fealty. On the other hand, you're in the middle of a forest, and you've angered at least one major guild."

Arthur hunched in a little as she spoke, before sighing at last. "It's not by choice." He considered what he said, then added: "Mostly."

"If you said otherwise, I'd smack you." Mel said, lifting her left hand to indicate the action before shrugging. "It is what it is. You seem to have survived and picked up a few new techniques. Maybe you'll survive long enough to pass through the first floor too."

Arthur snorted, rubbing the back of his neck. "Yeah... but truth be told, I was planning to spend more time on this floor before I push ahead. Get stronger before the next floor and all that, you know?"

"Mmm, that's a common tactic. But it's a waste of time," Mel said. "You aren't getting younger staying down here. And a single core from the second floor is twice as good as the ones here." She shook her head. "Get stronger, certainly. But don't waste all your time, because those on the second floor will always be stronger than you."

"Not the people I'm worried about, as much as the monsters," Arthur pointed out.

"Then you're a fool. Considering the enemies you've made, what makes you think that the monsters are your biggest threat?"

That made Arthur fall silent, as he realised the mistake he had made. It was not that he had gone out of his way on purpose to annoy the Suey Ying tong. It just happened. But if they sent word ahead to the second floor, well...

"Crap," he said aloud.

Rather than answer him, Mel held a hand up. She turned her head to the side, as though listening to something the others could not hear. Alerted to potential trouble, Arthur squinted into the darkness, the three moons above shedding enough light that the clearing itself was well illuminated, if not the area beneath the trees.

Even so, he thought he saw glimmering eyes and movement.

Reaching over, he gripped his spear and came out of his cross-legged position into a half crouch. As though his movements were the signal, howls erupted from around them as figures, shadows at first, made an appearance at the edge of the treeline.

Jenglot. And a lot of them.

Chapter 66

"Shouldn't we be running?" Arthur said softly as the *jenglot* came out of the trees. Even as he spoke, he was scanning the surroundings, counting the number of monsters there were. By the time he hit seven he was thinking they should be running, by eleven he was dead certain.

"I want to see what they do first. We're close enough to retreat," Mel said. "Wish I had a bow right now, though."

"Ah." Arthur remembered he did have a ranged skill. Of course, he also had only 0.9 points of Refined Energy, giving him a total of nine shots. Best not to use it at this long range, considering it'd give the *jenglot* more than enough time to dodge.

Maybe, if he timed it right, he could take one down.

"Sure," he said to himself, "and that'd leave ten more to fight hand-to-hand."

"What did you say?" Rani asked.

"Does anyone else have ranged attacks?" Arthur called out. The cramped quarters they had been fighting within had not allowed the others to showcase many such skills, even though he knew for certain none of the original three women he had come with had anything like that.

Uswah's shadow skills might be useful though, except she wasn't exactly hiding away to ambush and garotte the monsters. Shar and Jan's skills were mostly simple, internally-focused ones like his own Focused Strike and Heavenly Sage.

"Mel's got a projection technique that makes her spear longer, but it's not really ranged," Rani said. That was not news. He'd seen Mel make use of that skill in their fights, though she was careful in its application. It seemed to make the spear head sharper too, allowing her to punch her spear through open mouths or rib cages when she had it targeted right.

"And you?"

A shake of the head was answer enough. Especially with another howl, this time from a massive *jenglot* Elite, upon which the entire group of monsters started trotting forwards. They took their time, not sprinting across the distance but still covering the ground at a good clip, some with fingers hitting the ground as they loped forward on all fours.

"Then what the hell are we waiting for?" Arthur snapped, casting a glance back to the doorway. He saw no reason for them to be out, not at all.

Only to be surprised when, suddenly, the third *jenglot* in line fell, a leg disappearing down a hole and a sharp crack echoing through the clearing as one of its bones snapped with forward momentum.

"Traps? When... who... ?"

"You didn't see everything we did," Mel said. "Sometimes, you're a little too focused."

Arthur wanted to point out that he would definitely have seen someone digging a bloody hole in the ground, especially considering none of them had shovels, but now was not the time. For all the work they might have done on the traps, none of the others—and he assumed there were others in the ground—triggered.

"Well, that was a waste of Energy," Rani said, grumpily.

"Now do we run? 'Cause I'm voting we do it like a nun," Arthur said. Even as he spoke, though, he formed an Energy Dart in his hand, raising it upward at the last moment and pointing it at the incoming horde. He chose to pick the second *jenglot* in line, figuring someone else was going to take the monster who had charged well ahead of the rest of them.

His Energy Dart shot out, flashing across the distance. The monster that was his target jerked and stumbled a little. Almost as though she had been waiting for that moment, Mel leapt forward, crossing half the distance and thrusting with her spear. Her body fully extended behind the weapon just moments before she used her technique, the spear extending in energy form.

It caught the front-most monster in the upper chest, missing the heart but forcing the creature to stumble and halt. She yanked the already-shrinking spearhead out with a spray of blood. Rather than stay in the frontlines, though, Mel started backpedalling.

In the meantime, Arthur's next Energy Dart caught his own monster not in the face or upper torso but in the stomach. It tore into the monster's guts, causing it to grip at the wound and howl in anger. It did not, however, stop its rush.

"Damn it!" Arthur cursed. He'd actually been looking to target a little lower, hoping to damage the hips.

Pulling again at his refined energy, he guided it to his forehead and third eye this time. He was backing away already, joined by the others as the monsters drew closer and were now charging. Rani snapped her hands together, then jerked it towards her chest. A hole, one that could have been easily dodged by, suddenly moved forward, the earth rippling as one monster fell. Face slamming into ground, arms caught in the hole, flipped as both arms broke.

"Gotcha!" Rani said. Only Arthur bumping into her and sending her sprawling saved her life, as the next *jenglot* leapt through the air, nearly tearing her head off.

Spinning on his heels, Arthur thrust his spear into its back, catching it low in its torso. Stumbling forward, Arthur kept moving, yanking his spear out to thrust again, catching the monster under its ribs as it turned. Then, as it faced him, he unleashed the Energy Dart right into its chest, watching the energy burrow deep into the body and punch through.

Its heart burst and the monster, already bleeding out, fell over.

"Come on!" Arthur cried, spinning around to face the other charging groups even as he backed towards the tower. Mel was fighting not one but two monsters, her long spear swirling around and darting outward to keep the creatures from surrounding her. She backed away, positioning herself by one of their fires to help split the monsters and keep them from finishing her off.

Rani, looking wane as she finished using her own energy, was clutching the broken end of her shortened spear, and a parang in the other hand. She held ground towards the leftmost flank, jabbing with the longer haft of the spear at the snarling crowd.

Joining Rani, Arthur kept urging the group to retreat. Knowing they had to get in before they were overwhelmed, frustrated that they had not run already. It seemed the monsters were definitely going to follow them in, judging from their frenzied howls and angry faces.

Which seemed stupid, because they only needed two more dead.

Damn it.

Chapter 67

Harrying the *jenglot* that tried to reach them with thrusts and stabs, Arthur retreated in line with the others, pulling back to the tower entrance. On his right, he noted that Shar and Jan were doing the same too on their side of the entrance, with Uswah appearing briefly after having planted a dagger in the back of a monster and then tearing up an ankle. Then, to his surprise, she faded away between one blink and the next, disappearing into the darkness once more.

"Come on back!" Shar snapped, calling the group to reenter. There was a moment's hesitation when they hit the entrance, as the inward-swinging double doors had been propped to allow only a few people through the gap at a time. As Rani and Jan hesitated over who would enter first, the moment's delay was enough to create a gap in their defense.

In that moment, a *jenglot* on the right surged forward, striking with its long claws to tear into Jan's side. She cried out in pain, Shar too busy warding off another monster to step in. Even as the *jenglot* raised its arm to attack again, Rani threw her broken spear end at it, the attack glowing with a slight green colour as it pierced the monster's chest.

Crying in pain, the *jenglot* hesitated, only for its raised fingers to be hacked off by the half-sobbing Jan. Clawed fingers flew through the air, missing as Rani grabbed Jan and pulled her through the entrance.

"Shar! Back off," Jan cried out.

Taking orders, Shar retreated, followed a moment later by Mel and Arthur, their long spears deterring the *jenglot* momentarily. The injured monster that had attacked Jan was struck by Shar on her way in. Shar's spear cut into its ankle and it collapsed sideways, blocking the way for a brief moment.

"Uswah!" Arthur called out, his gaze darting from side to side in the brief moments while swinging his spear to bat aside reaching fingers, claws dripping with blood from repeated jabs.

"We're clear!" Rani cried out, Jan repeating the order a second later.

Arthur, still outside, backed off further toward the double doors. He searched for the Yin-bodied fighter but could not find her. She had chosen to continue harrying the *jenglot* instead of retreating, but this was not the way to do it. As he searched, he and Mel holding off the group, his body burning with strength and speed from Heavenly Sage's Mischief to match the damn monsters, he realised that big Elite was gone.

"The Elite! Where is it?" he shouted.

Disregarding her spear, Mel jumped and snapped a front kick into a monster's lunging face. He watched the *jenglot* fall backward. Mel landed, her head turning from side to side. "It was there... but it's gone."

Then a loud cry, and they found the Elite and Uswah fighting one another in the shadows. Uswah was retreating, one hand clutching her side while swinging her dagger with the other. At the same time, the Elite stalked towards her, moving to cut off her retreat.

"No!" Shar cried out. Sensing movement, Arthur glanced back to see her being held back by Rani.

He could not afford to look too long, for the other *jenglot* were still pressing toward him. He nearly had his head torn off, the momentary distraction allowing a claw to sneak past his long spear. Only a hasty drop to the ground left him with his head intact.

Another scream and Uswah stumbled away. The Elite *jenglot* raised its head, Uswah's torn-off arm in its bloody mouth. Armless and weaponless now, Uswah tried to fade into the darkness, only for the monster to pounce and hold her down. Breath crushed, she thrashed under its foot.

Arthur threw himself at the nearest *jenglot.* This time, it was the monster who was distracted as a scream from the Elite brought its head around. Taking advantage, Arthur poured energy into a Focused Strike to plunge his spear directly into its throat, and it staggered away clutching at a pierced throat. "Got you!"

Mel, meanwhile, had stabbed her own monster in the thigh, forcing the creature to limp away and retreat. That created a gap in the line of *jenglot*, and Mel leaned forward, almost as though she would rush into the throng. Yet, she held off because of the sight that caught all their attention. The *jenglot* were all suddenly retreating, toward the Elite.

"What is it doing?" Shar whispered.

"Playing with her..." The anger that burned in Rani's voice was palpable.

Arthur could not help but agree, for the monster was crouched over Uswah, tracing a sharp finger down the screaming woman's face, ignoring the weakly slapping hand against its leg. Then, the Elite turned its head to stare at the group, its wide, teethy mouth falling open in a lolling grin. Malevolence stared back at them, clearly evil paired with intelligence.

"Why isn't it killing her?" Shar said.

"It's not just playing," Arthur said softly as realisation struck him. "It's taunting us. Trying to make us come out. It knows we've trapped the tower. It's not going to let us have the power."

"No. It can't... it's not that smart, is it?" Mel said, shocked.

He just nodded at the giant figure, who had pinned down the beating arm and pierced the hand with a single oversized claw. Then, drawing the claw downward, it tore the hand open, eliciting another long scream.

"I'll kill it!" Shar shook off Rani's grip, emerged from the tower, and shouldered her way towards where Arthur and Mel stood. Only to pause as she stared at the wall of hairy flesh before her, the *jenglot* having reformed their lines.

To the group's surprise, even as Shar stood shaking in rage and indecision, the Elite let out a barking noise. The *jenglot* hesitated, and the noise was repeated much louder. Moving slowly, the monsters moved into a ring-like formation. Then they parted, opening a pathway toward the treeline. Toward Uswah and the Elite.

"Oh gods, they aren't thinking we'll fall for that trap?" Arthur said, even as he regarded the *jenglot*. After all that fighting, there were still five monsters uninjured despite three worse for the wear in close proximity, and another three crippled but further back.

Too many for their group to fight, but it didn't matter.

Because Shar, even knowing that all this was a trap, was running forward. And right behind her, Mel was following. Even Rani and Jan had reappeared from the tower.

"You have got to be kidding me," he muttered.

"Do-or-die time," Jan said, limping forward with steely determination in her eyes.

Problem was, if they all died, he'd be following them moments later. Offered little choice, he followed after the women, forming an Energy Dart to unleash for when things inevitably got worse.

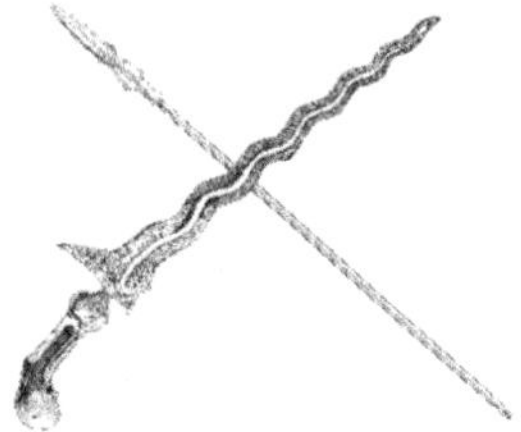

Chapter 68

Stepping between the monsters on each side, Arthur could not help but twitch as the *jenglot* glared at him. Their lips were peeled back, long fangs upon the snub-nose visages. They huffed out diseased, stinking air. Claws hung from dangling hands, swinging with each moment even as Arthur felt the timer of his own cultivation technique tick down.

Slow and tentatively as he might move, the others in the group had rushed ahead. Shar was facing off against the Elite now, parang held before her as she now approached a little more carefully. Not that it helped, for when the creature chose to move, it closed the distance between the pair of them in a blur.

The meaty, solid *thunk*—like an axe-head hitting hardwood—resounded through the air as Shar managed to block the lunge of its claws with her parang. Even so, the woman slid back as the long, single-edged blade backed by the flat of her palm did little to dissipate the large monster's momentum.

On her backfoot, her body began to glow a darker colour, strands of energy forming around her body to give her strength and speed. Not a moment too late for dodging a follow-up claw swing.

The pair danced backwards, Shar entirely on the defensive as the Elite controlled the pace of the battle, its pair of claws almost overwhelming the woman. In the meantime, Mel had skidded to a halt beside the injured Uswah, pulling a bandage out from her storage pouch to create a temporary torniquet around her crippled arm, murmuring words of reassurance.

Uswah was not answering, awake but with eyes staring out into the darkness unseeing.

Behind, Jan and Rani were moving carefully, facing away from one another as they stared at the *jenglot*. Still, none of them attacked, not even when the girls and Arthur managed to exit the ring. Instead, they turned as one and stared at the humans with wide lolling grins as they waited for a command.

Backing away from the ring of monsters quickly, Arthur eyed the Elite that had finally overwhelmed Shar in the brief time it had taken for them to reach them. It now stalked the woman as she tried desperately to scramble away.

"No, not this way! Please..." Shar was half-crying as she tried to get to her feet, her initial anger and impetus torn away.

The others were watching, staring at the monsters that now stood between them and salvation, scared to act and trigger the inevitable onslaught. Unable to watch the murder of their friend.

All but Arthur, who found his mind, cloaked in Yin chi, playing through options. He was scared, he was in fact terrified, but there was still a part of him calmly assessing the options. And that part realised that it mattered little if they angered the Elite now or later; it would be the same in the end.

So.

As the monster turned sideways, he unleashed the Energy Dart he had been holding in abeyance all this time. He was not surprised when the Elite managed to sway aside, dodging what should have been a surprise attack with swiftness as though it had anticipated Arthur.

What it was not ready for was Arthur rushing forward and jumping high, spear in hand. Burning with Heavenly Sage's Mischief, he crossed the distance faster than he could ever have before, moving at a speed that would have put an ex-Tower Olympian to shame.

The spear caught the monster with an upraised arm, tearing through flesh of its upper body and then anchoring itself to the creature's chest. That portion of the attack, driven by Focused Strike, only managed to enter a few inches deep before the *jenglot*'s innate toughness and coarse fur saved it. The spear, as it exited arm and body left a long, bloody wound even as Arthur landed in a crouch.

"DEATH!"

A small part of Arthur was surprised that the command was in English. Another, bigger surprise, that it was uttered by the Elite *jenglot.*

But his Yin-calmed mind took advantage of the moment to thrust the spear again, scoring another injury on the monster's lower torso before he had to back away.

Initial success or not, Arthur had known he was not the monster's match. It was too strong, too fast, for him to tackle by himself. Even with the Heavenly Sage's Mischief, he could barely keep up with the striking claws. Minor wounds appeared across his arms in short order and even a torn flap of skin from his scalp.

Always, he backed off, even as he glimpsed his friends struggling as the other monsters fought on the Elite's command. The three girls, Mel included, stood over the still-unmoving Uswah, doing their best to keep the *jenglot* away. Yet, wounds accumulated and energy was expended.

Even the occasional victories, like when Mel triggered an attack that made her spear blur, tearing into and killing a *jenglot* in a half-dozen flickering strikes, were temporary. Other monsters merely closed the gap. Energy stores would soon deplete, and the end was coming.

For him, if nothing else.

Another block, high. His spear bending, being forced down by the pressure of mighty claws. The other clawed hand pulled back, ready to punch forward; it felt as if Arthur could only watch as death came. A Refined Energy Dart was forming on his third eye but all too slow.

Pinching and gripping the Dart tight, he could only bear it as the Elite punched a hand at his torso. Only by turning at the last second, Arthur escaped a fatal wound. Painful as it was, the claws only tore into one side of his body.

Then, as the creature recovered balance, he finished the Energy Dart and unleashed it right into the monster's face. It blasted half the face off, exposing an orbital lobe and bursting an eyeball. The monster screamed and thrashed as it fell away.

And yet it still lived.

Retreating, finding that one foot had suddenly failed him, blood filling his shoe, Arthur could not help but wonder again if this was the end. A fool's choice, to come out here.

Then again, climbing the Tower itself had always been foolish.

Chapter 69

The Elite *jenglot* was now closing the distance, finally recovered from Arthur's surprise attack. Another Refined Energy Dart was forming around his third eye, but Arthur's thoughts and perception was muddied from the pain in his torso and blood loss. Arthur narrowly blocked the *jenglot*'s swipe with the haft of his spear, turning it aside before lashing back out with the spear tip. Enraged, the Elite chose not to back off but take the attack high on its shoulder.

Spear tip pierced, tearing flesh and muscle. Yet, it allowed the *jenglot* to finally close the distance on him. Unable to retreat quickly enough, Arthur barely dodged the snapping jaws and instead received a headbutt that sent him sprawling to the ground.

A second later, his spear was torn away from his hands, as the monster gripped the weapon by the haft and pulled it from his weakened grip. Another clawed hand rose, but it paused. Even in its anger, the monster wanted to watch Arthur's fear, wanted to savour its victory.

It was its greatest fault. And the reason why, creeping up from behind, Shar managed to land a technique-powered, two-handed strike to the back of its lower leg. Biting through fur, muscle, and bone with one fell swoop, it cut the limb clean from the creature and tipped it over.

Legs coming up desperately, Arthur kicked at the falling monster, sending it flopping away. Rather than follow up on the successful attack, though, Arthur rolled over screaming in pain as the movement had further damaged his own injured torso.

"I got you, you *puda*!" Shar cried, rushing over to lash out at the monster as it tried to clamber to its feet. Meaty thunks filled the air, even as Arthur struggled to contain the pain. Heavenly Sage's Mischief had faded away, making each moment of pain even stronger.

Tuning out the noise, the pain, and the damage, he scrambled within his mind to trigger the Accelerated Healing technique. He could not afford to wait, but he focused the rampant energies that threatened to heal everything at the same time towards his own body, hauling on the sticky energy that coursed through him to focus on the wounds.

To his surprise, the entire process was easier than ever. Perhaps it was the new trait; perhaps it was the multiple rounds of healing and slow understanding of the process. Perhaps it was just the desperate straits that his body was experiencing.

Ragged ends of his open stomach wound, parted muscle fibres, and even separated organs began to pull together, clipped blood vessels linking to one another. The Yin chi that pervaded his body dulled the pain he was facing, making it easier for him to concentrate and patch the wound. In short order, the open wound along his stomach had closed, new flesh and fragile muscle fibres stitched into one piece.

Forcing himself to his feet, Arthur looked around, uncertain how much time had passed.

Not long, for Shar had just finished killing the Elite and clambering off the still body. Its gruesomely mutilated corpse was bleeding into the ground. He spotted Rani unmoving on the ground, two *jenglot* corpses nearby. However, the three other women—including Uswah, for she had miraculously returned to battle, releasing globs of darkness to strike monster eyes with her remaining arm—were hard pressed. Mel and Jan were both bleeding freely from numerous wounds.

Breathing hard, Shar stalked towards the battling group. Arthur made a quick count of the remaining monsters, noting there were only four left: one seriously injured, two mildly injured, and one mostly untouched. The group had improved in their desperate straits, but exhaustion was taking its toll now. He grabbed his spear and followed Shar to join the fight.

Mel was struck; while her raised spear had blocked one attack, she never saw the sweeping leg that hit her high on the knee. Her foot crumpled even as she spun through the air. A descending claw slammed through the spear that gave way, drawing blood that flew against the darkened sky like new ink drops on death's ledger.

Then it was only Jan left standing. She swung her parang around as fast as she could, doing her best to ward off the other monsters as they crowded in. For once, their large size was a hindrance, for they could not all attack her at once.

Pulling another Refined Energy Dart into being, Arthur released the attack into the back of a monster that Shar was already rushing towards. The attack caused the already-injured creature to react, its body twitching uncontrollably as the energy attack burrowed into its back. Before it could recover, Shar plunged her parang into the open wound and tore the blade out sideways, dropping the monster.

Three to go.

Uswah tossed another globe of darkness and collapsed immediately after, never even seeing her own attack wrap itself around another *jenglot*. The monster, face covered, was unable to see. Jan ducked under its wildly swinging arms. Pushing with as much force as she could muster, she leaped and cut an opening in its throat, washing her in a welter of blood.

Two.

The successful attack was costly, though, for another *jenglot* struck out as its compatriot collapsed and Jan landed. Barely getting her weapon in place to parry the monster's claw attack, she lost one of her fingers. Then skin across her face and down her neck was torn, the blow spinning the woman aside. Another claw attack caught her in the back. Jan was now on the ground, moaning piteously.

Before the two monsters could take further advantage, an Energy Dart from Arthur and Shar's parang arrived.

The Dart crippled one monster in the foot. Rushing behind his Dart, Arthur angled himself to catch the monster in the side. The spear-tip sliced all the way down to its ankle. Collapsing to the ground, the monster was easy prey for Shar's swinging blade, though she took additional wounds in return, leaving her bloody and clutching her injured torso.

One.

Checking within his own core, Arthur grimaced. He was nearly out of refined energy. Nearly.

Enough at least to form one more Refined Energy Dart, which was what he pulled to his third eye. No reason to play fair, not when his opponent was bigger, stronger, and nastier than him. However, to Arthur's surprise, the monster glanced around at the corpses of its brethren and then turned tail and ran.

Blinking, Arthur relaxed his grip on the aura that he had been forming, allowing the energy to return to his core. Gripping his burning side, he watched the monster as it fled into the darkness of the trees. Then he looked to the injured group, many of them unconscious and others barely hanging on.

"Well... that could have gone better," Arthur said. Then, mind still spinning, he could not help but add, "If I was a bettor, I could not have sworn, we'd have won."

Chapter 70

Moving quickly, Arthur made to verify the condition of those collapsed. He first checked on the closest, Shar. He extracted bandages from his pouch, pushing it against her wounds to help stem the bleeding before wrapping them around, watching the woman hiss. There was so much blood, and she was half-delirious from blood loss, her eyes glazing over as she entered a state of shock. He was not certain she'd survive. That was the best he could do for now. And she was only one of a few who needed attention.

Moving on, he scanned the group. Uswah was unconscious, bereft of energy and likely overdrawn. Nothing he could do for her. Her chest was rising and falling, breaths coming slowly, but he was certain she was still alive. Good enough.

Rani was alive, knocked unconscious from a blow to her head. Alive and not even bleeding out. He left her immediately after double-checking that her pulse was moving. Lastly, Mel. He found her crouched over a *jenglot* body, swaying on her feet as she dipped the amulet into its blood. Blood filled a teardrop on the amulet.

Coming over to her side, he bent down.

"How is it? It working? Need anything?" he asked, eyeing the hasty bandages the woman had wrapped around herself. Not that it helped, for blood continued to leak out.

"I... fine. Finish. This," she managed to croak out, her eyes focused entirely on the amulet.

Arthur could not help but agree. Letting her get on with it, he noted that there was nothing he could help her with, not with the small strips of first aid left in his pouch. He turned back towards the tower, intent on grabbing the remaining items they had scavenged. More bandages, needle and thread. Probably something to clean the wounds, though infection wasn't likely. Something to do with the Tower itself and their cultivator bodies.

Small mercies.

He only managed to make it a dozen feet before he heard a laborious exhalation and the dull thump of a collapsing body. Spinning around, he realised that Mel was on the ground, unconscious.

"Shit, shit, shit." Rushing to Mel, he checked her over. Luckily, she was unconscious but alive and still bleeding out. A quick check on her bandages and tightening them helped a little, but...

"The amulet."

Now, he was forced to choose. Leave it? Wait? There was at least one more monster left, possibly hiding in the trees. If he waited, one of the others could actually put the blood in the amulet themselves. Though if they had to fight off a large group again, with the team this injured the chances of survival were slim.

The chances of survival for some of them were already low.

Flicking his gaze back and forth between the women lying prone, he resolved to get this done. He scooped up the amulet from Mel's senseless fingers. Then, figuring it was only fitting, he jogged over to the dead Elite's body, pushing the amulet deep into one of its wounds.

That simple task done, he hurried back to the tower to complete his initial objective, finding the first aid kits they had set aside. Finding them quickly enough, he returned to the group outside and propped up Mel to finish bandaging the woman, hauling her back and forth as gently as he could. Even so, he was no trained health care professional, nor did he have help to adjust the positioning of her body.

And yet, for all his rough care, the woman stirred not at all.

Once he had her bandaged and laid back down on the ground, Arthur stood up and eyed the remainder of the group. None of them looked likely to expire anytime soon, so he hurried over to the amulet, plucking it out of the body and pool of blood by its chain. It swung back and forth, and as the blood dripped off, he noticed it seemed to be glowing a little.

Curiosity overtaking him, he grabbed the amulet itself, only to feel an electric shock run through his body upon contact. His hand spasmed tight, and then, to his utter surprise, refused to open again. The electric shock was not the only sensation, for pain spread across his palm as if the amulet were searing it. On the other hand, his fingers that clutched the other side of the amulet were untouched by the pain. But he could not pry them open, not even by using his other hand.

Soon enough, he had to stop, for all he was doing was tearing the skin off his own flesh. His hand was magically bound to the amulet. At the same time, the pain in his palm grew ever stronger, and a smell of sizzling flesh floated through the air as he fell to his knees. More so, the pain radiated from his hand and up his arm, into his chest, and then to his dantian.

Eyes wide with fear as he realised where it was reaching towards, he tried to pull his hand open once again but failed to do so, instead collapsing as the pain reached his center. And then, what had been aching pain grew to blinding agony as it exploded through his soul and mind. He rode the pain like a rising tide until a glowing light in the form of a crest seemed to float before his gaze. A crest in white and yellow light that danced in the sky.

Then the pain overwhelmed his control and he was sent spiraling into darkness. Leaving him to join Morpheus himself in the land of dreams.

Waking was a pain. Literally.

Head throbbing, soul pounding. If you have never had your own soul scoured, imagine a sander taken to the insides of your very being and multiply the resulting pain by three.

But at last Arthur managed to open his eyes a bare slit at the early morning sunlight streaming down around him. His hand ached.

And a parang swung at his face. Well, near his face. It was not, at this moment, being swung at him. Which was good. What was not, was the argument going on above him.

"You can't kill him," Mel said, frustrated.

"Yes, we can. *Pancung kepala dia sekarang*, while he's still sleeping," Jan said urgently, twitching the parang she held. "He betrayed us lah, Mel! Remember what I said."

"We don't know if that's what happened. It could have been a mistake," Mel said.

"He is foolish, but not dumb," Uswah said.

"Maybe he didn't know it would react like that," Shar said weakly. She was seated on the ground like Uswah. Neither of the girls looked up for another fight.

"Doesn't matter what happened. But we need to kill him and get the seal back," Jan said.

"We can't," Mel repeated. "We don't know if the seal will disappear."

"So what? Because of *him* we don't have it anyway," Jan said.

"But maybe we can make a deal," Mel said.

"Or we could cut it off? Maybe that'd work?" Shar offered.

"Oooh, yes." Jan's voice seemed to light up.

"What do you think?" Uswah said. Her question startled the group, and they looked at her, only to follow her gaze over to Arthur's open eyes. Jan's parang twitched again, and only a bump by Mel into her side stopped her from swinging it down on him.

"I think I'd like to not die," Arthur said.

"Then why you betray us?" Jan snapped.

"I didn't! I saved your ass. All your asses," he snarled. The pounding headache had driven some of his control away. He breathed in deep, forcing the pain away. "I don't understand what the hell you're talking about."

Before Jan could say anything, Mel pointed to his hand and said simply, "Look at your palm."

Dread flashed through him, as memory of what had happened before he fell unconscious ran through him. He suddenly had a dreadful premonition of what he might see there. And, as he turned his hand over and raised it—and himself—up, he saw it for what it was.

The branded clan seal, on his palm.

And deep within his soul, he felt the notification waiting for him to look at.

Which he would, if he could convince the damn women from chopping both his hand and head off.

Chapter 71

"I really didn't mean to do this," Arthur said quickly. "I was just trying to make sure all the fighting and death and battle hadn't been for nothing." He looked around, hoping to gesture at the bodies. But since they had disappeared—their cores taken, he assumed—he had nothing to show. "It's not as though anyone was awake for me to ask."

"So you just accepted the seal when it was ready. For our good," Mel said, irritation in her voice.

Waving his branded hand in front of him, and then yanking it back when Jan's parang moved towards it, he growled. "It didn't ask if I wanted it! It just triggered the moment I had it in hand. It burned the seal into my hand, and I didn't even know it could do that." He snorted. "I didn't even know it was a brand. Not as though anyone told me that."

There was a silence at his words before Uswah nodded a little. "That tracks with how I found him. He was screaming and twitching and trying to get it off."

"Weak. This guy can't take pain," Jan said.

"Now that's a little much," Rani finally spoke up. "I don't care if you kill him—though I think we should hold off until we know if the seal can be transferred—but he's not weak. Not from what we've seen."

Jan shrugged, unwilling to take back her words.

"Can you transfer it?" Mel said, ignoring the byplay as she focused on Arthur. "What does the Tower say?"

"I haven't checked." Arthur pointed at the parang. "I'm not exactly looking at taking my attention away from *that*, you know." Then, as a thought struck him, added: "Anyway, what makes you think I'd tell you the truth if it was transferable."

Silence expanded between them all, the women looking at Arthur with looks of contempt, pity, and incredulity in turn. Once his brain caught up with his words, Arthur cursed himself out too. Him and his big mouth.

Sowing doubt further was not a great idea.

"I'll look, I'll look. Just promise not to chop me up while I do so, eh?" Arthur said.

"*Yay a, Cepat-lah.*" Uswah waved a hand for him to do it faster. When he got agreement from Mel too, then and only then did Arthur look at the notification. He could, he believed, trust them not to go too far out of their way and kill him right now.

Congratulations! You have acquired a Clan Seal.

This is a Tier 1 Clan Seal and will allow the establishment of a Tower-Approved Clan.

As a Tier 1 Clan, you will:

- *Be able to establish a Tower-Approved Building in the Safe Zone*
- *Appoint 1 Officer per Tower level to administer the Clan Building*

Aspects:

None

Sigil:

None

"Shit," Arthur said softly.

"What? What happened?" He felt a hand drop on his shoulder, and his body forcibly turned with a worried Mel hovering over him. She glared into his face, demanding an answer.

"It's not a Guild seal, it's a Clan seal."

"Oh jeez." Mel relaxed a little at his words.

"*Puta!*" Jan swore, then threw both parang and her other hand up at the sky. "I cannot lah. I just can-*not*." Then she stalked away.

"What did I do now?" Arthur said.

"Nothing. There's nothing wrong. Clans and guilds are the same thing," Shar said. "Mostly."

"Really?" he asked, relaxing a little.

Mel nodded. "'Guild' is the term used most often by Towers. It's what the Westerners get, so it's why we all use it colloquially. But 'Clan' is what we actually get, over in Asia."

"Mostly," Uswah said idly. "Some of the Japanese and Koreans get guilds too. Those Towers are more gamey, though, and follow more Western tropes."

"Mostly," Mel corrected, glaring at Uswah who just offered a tight smile. She played her fingers along the missing portion of her arm, along the edges of the bite and the bandages around them, making Mel look away to focus on Arthur. "It's mostly the same. Clans are harder to grow, but harder to leave. We get more control over our members than guilds, but it's the same in the Tower enabled building aspects."

"Oh. Duh." Arthur did not need to ask why they'd switched over to using the Western term, even if it was inaccurate. It likely had as much to do with laziness and the dominance of Western media than anything conscious. People were lazy, and unless you needed to know the difference—and so few people did with clans and guilds that it might as well not matter—that it was no surprise the terms had just become synonymous.

"Well, what else did it do?" Mel said.

Arthur hesitated but then eventually shrugged and read out what he had displayed before him. There was nothing in there that he thought was dangerous to reveal, sparse as it was. He was curious though...

"What are Aspects and Sigils? Are those the guild—sorry, clan—bonuses that people talk about?" Arthur said.

"Exactly. In a guild, they're called Perks and Titles," Shar said. "I think that helps?"

Arthur shrugged a little. "A bit. Guilds weren't something I paid that much attention to. Perks are overall bonuses that affect guild members. They're pretty common and, I guess, get added as a guild grows in strength." Mel nodded and Arthur had to push down the flush of happiness that acknowledgement had created in him. Not the time. "Titles are rarer. Requiring you to do something unique. They're also limited, aren't they?"

"Exactly," Mel said. "As I understand it, clans and guilds have slightly different Aspects and Perks to choose between. The guild Perks are much more straightforward and specific in description, like the Merchant which gives a 10% trade bonus. Whereas a clan Aspect might be something like Wealth, which will influence not just trade but also rewards."

"Specialists versus generalists," Arthur said. "Because humanity like their lists and -ists."

"Clans actually have more leeway with Sigils. We get to combine them, unlike the limited number of Titles that guilds get. But clans are limited to a certain extent by the kind of Sigils we choose in the end," Mel continued. "It makes for a more flexible use, but sigils are consequently harder to acquire. Some can only be acquired by killing the previous holders."

That made Arthur frown, before she waved a hand. "It's not important. Not right now."

"Good to hear." Arthur ran a finger along the palm of his hand, frowning as he felt the irregular bumps. He shook his head after a moment. "So, is there a way to hand this over to someone else?"

Mel shrugged. "If it didn't say so, I'm assuming not."

"Stupid way of creating a reward," he could not help but say.

"*Tetapi kau yang sentuh,*," Uswah remarked.

"I really didn't know it would do it. I was just trying to do right by us all," Arthur groused. "I already apologized, damn it."

"Actually, you haven't," Shar said.

"Huh?" he said, dumbly.

"You haven't apologized," Shar repeated, arms crossed under her bosom. Or maybe just clutching her injured ribs.

"I..." Arthur fell silent, reviewing the earlier conversation. Realising he had never actually said sorry and just tried to find excuses, justifications, he grimaced. "I'm sorry. I didn't mean it to happen."

Shar nodded shortly. "I know."

He eyed the group, barely bothering to look at Jan who sniffed. Rani looked out of it, focused inwards on her own injuries more than anything he had said. Uswah, the one who possibly should have been the most concerned with their injuries, just shrugged fatalistically. It was Mel whose gaze he found regarding him, crouched as she was next to his still-seated form and all too close to his head.

He returned her regard silently, curious. She had been vacillating between being reasonable and making the occasional biting remark. She was obviously trying to stay focused on the objective. But he could see the frustration boiling within her eyes. In truth, he understood.

Of them all, Mel had likely given up the most. And to come so close yet fail at the end. Knowing that the prize had been hers...

He wondered, if the option was available, would she have killed him to take the seal? He wondered, if the option was even viable, if he would ever have awakened.

In the end, Mel rocked backward and stood up. "Whatever. We're stuck with you. But... you're stuck with us too. Got it?" she said with an edge in her voice. Shar, too, stared down at him menacingly.

A growl erupted from Jan, and Arthur said quickly, "That's fine. But: I kind of might want to make a few changes..."

"Changes?" Mel's voice dropped a pitch, growing colder.

"Like membership. I mean, a few guys might be good. I don't exactly want to be accused of running a harem, you know?" Arthur said.

Uswah let out a little laugh, and Jan growled louder. She muttered something about hurting him a little, but Arthur tuned her out. It was more the snort from Mel that had his attention, as the group leader sighed.

"We can talk about it."

Smiling, Arthur relaxed. It seemed, at least, that things would work out with the Thorned Lotuses.

Which, of course, was when things went wrong.

Again.

Chapter 72

The Suey Ying tong members who emerged out of the darkness, stumbling out of the boundary forest around the tower, were not looking for a fight. Instead, their eyes had been locked on to the flickering flames that made the tower a beacon to their entry.

It took them long moments to notice Arthur's group, even longer to pull themselves together. It was obvious that the five members that survived of the group were the worst for wear, with one of their members dragged along by another and two others limping, their breathing harsh and ragged.

Even under the matte of dirt and blood though, Choi, the samseng that had harassed Arthur when he first arrived, was simple enough to pick out. The big nose, the lined face, the thuggish swagger that had not disappeared even in his exhaustion were burned indelibly into Arthur's mind. More than that, the voice...

"We found you. Found you now..." Choi said, grinning madly. He straightened up a little, then flinched and collapsed as he clutched the lower part of his ribcage. "I'm going to kill you people."

"How did you find us?" Shar said, edging away from Arthur as though she had already made up her mind to dissociate from him. Arthur noted that, even as he glared at Choi and her.

"Had a tracker..." Choi said, grinning. "Thought you were smart, eh, but you left a trail for us. Now let's see that treasure you got."

"We didn't get anything," Mel said, gesturing at the tower. "You're welcome to try, but clearing it got us nothing. Just a lot of *jenglot* to kill."

"Then you got cores, don't you?" Lowering his wounded friend to the ground, another man said greedily, "Figure that's good payment. Just drop it all."

"No way," Jan said. "You stupid, ah?"

"You want to die?" Choi said, gesturing for his pitiful group to split and flank the women. "You kill us, we're going to war. And your people can't beat us."

"Who's to say what killed you all the way out here?" Mel said, confidently.

"Doesn't matter. My brother will start the war anyway," Choi replied. "So you should just give us all we want and escort us back. Unless you want to go home and find all your precious members dead."

The group fell silent, Mel looking at Shar. The pair traded a long glance, one that spoke volumes to those who could read the subtle language of old friends. As for Arthur, he didn't have that deep knowledge, but he sure as hell knew a bad deal.

"Not happening," Arthur said, pushing himself to his feet. He hurt, in an indefinable way, inside himself. His soul was still scarred, and as he tried to form a Refined Energy Dart, he found himself bending over as his whole body cramped. Pain, as his soul seized up.

Raucous laughter, as he collapsed after attempting to trigger his technique. He writhed in insubstantial pain until he managed to gain control over himself, struggling to his knees just in time to realise that the other group had closed the distance, now only a dozen feet away.

Weapons were leveled. The battered teams stared at one another over bloody instruments of war.

"Can we not talk about this?" Uswah said. "Fighting now, a lot of us are going to die. And we still have to get back through that forest alive."

"Oooh, the creepy lady is scared of death." Choi laughed. "Crippled and creepy. Make a horrible wife now, won't she, boys?"

"I'm going to kill him," Jan muttered under her breath.

There were a few nods from the women, and both groups fell silent. It was the quiet Rani who chose to act first, conjuring a hole under the feet of the approaching men. She did so under the entire line of them, though Choi in the vanguard jumped over while his nearest companion stumbled into her trap.

It was not a deep depression, barely a foot and a half. However, it forced them to separate, leaving Choi alone at the front. His companion's momentum caused him to fall over. Uswah, triggering her own shadow technique, had tendrils of darkness reach out and grab the fallen man, yanking his foot in the hole harder whilst pulling his face into the dirt, muffling his screams.

But Rani and Uswah's actions had a cost, for the pair of cultivators had expended what little energy they had regained before the Suey Ying showed up. The two women sunk to the ground, faces pale, leaving the rest of the gang to deal with Choi and the men before them.

Mel rushed Choi, followed along by Shar. They wanted to take the leader down fast. That, unfortunately, left Jan and Arthur to deal with the two thugs who had jumped over the gap in the ground and the injured fella at the back who had a pinched look on his face as though he'd had a really bad curry.

Making a quick decision, Arthur heaved his spear, throwing it at the last member of the party. Too weak to dodge, the spear skewered the man in his lower body, disrupting whatever cultivation technique he had meant to use.

"Jeff!" shouted one of the thugs. He turned to Arthur and screamed, "You bastard! Attacking the wounded? I'll kill you."

Resolved, he rushed Arthur, choosing to avoid Jan and the others.

Without a weapon on hand, Arthur chose the better part of valour and turned around, legging it for the tower entrance. He glanced at the guttering fires, remembered the rope strung across the open doorway—which unfortunately was meant to deal with *jenglot* and not humans—and ran in, closely followed by the other man.

Lungs burning and his side aching from the run, Arthur grabbed the edge of one door and ducked to the side. He dropped himself flat the moment he did so, letting his body fall against the propped-up barrier that had been built there: above were makeshift wooden stakes pointing outwards.

Behind him, the man followed Arthur's example, spinning around the door. He did not, however, drop prone like Arthur, having missed that action as the door blocked his view.

Instead, he ran directly into the stakes. The first missed entirely, but the second caught him in the right part of his chest, piercing muscle and glancing off bone. He howled and pulled away, shocked by the ambush, but his cultivator-strengthened body saved him from being pierced all the way through.

Only for Arthur to rise, grip hold of his shirt and pull the man forward as he thrust his own body backward, using weight and angle to pin his opponent on a stake. This time, with the added weight of both parties and the initial injury in play, the stake pierced the body.

Even then, Arthur's opponent refused to die. Lashing out with fists and knees, as the sickle he had been wielding had dropped to the floor, he battered at Arthur's body even as Arthur hugged his torso close, blood falling upon his head and face as his opponent bled out.

Eventually, movements slowed, the strikes growing weaker with each passing moment until they stopped. He extracted himself from under the body, scooped up the man's small scythe, and wiped the blood off his face.

Then listened, for trouble.

It was quiet out there. Too quiet.

Chapter 73

Stepping out of the tower, scythe held by his side, Arthur searched for opponents, his eyes darting left and right. What he saw shocked him. Choi was standing over the bodies of Mel, Shar, Jan and one of his own team members. He had just pulled a kris from Shar's throat.

"How..." Arthur gaped. Eyes darting wildly from body to body, he noted that Mel and Jan's bloodied chests were still rising.

Alive then.

Choi laughed as he turned to focus on Arthur. "So the rat is here. Alive. Good at scurrying away, aren't you?"

"How'd you beat them?" he said forcefully. He hoped the other two, Uswah and Rani, were still alive. He saw no sign of them.

"I had help," Choi said, laughing as he kicked the body of his own teammate aside. He peered past the tower entrance, stared at the blood that dripped from Arthur's head and sighed. "Just you and me, eh?"

Arthur gulped, stepping away from the tower's double doors. He held the scythe uncomfortably, eyes darting across the ground as he hunted for a better weapon. Only to find nothing near him; the closest weapons were behind the slowly advancing Choi.

Movement in the periphery of his vision as Choi raised his hand, the wavy blade of the kris reflecting light from the guttering fires. The blade was gunmetal gray, almost black in the deep of the night. The traditional short sword seemed even more sinister in the hands of leering Choi as he advanced upon Arthur.

Feeling within himself, Arthur dipped into his energy stores. He had not used the Heavenly Sage's Mischief much, and so he had a decent amount of unrefined energy left. But his soul still ached, and somehow he knew that he lacked the ability to access it. Not for a day or two at the least.

No help from his techniques. Wielding a weapon he had little familiarity with. And being chased by a man who was stronger than he was and certainly more vicious. Panic clawed at Arthur's chest as he faced his opponent, freezing his feet to the ground and locking his muscles.

"That's right. Just hold still and I'll make it quick," Choi said, his smile growing wider. Again, the blade that he held in his hand waved, drawing Arthur's eyes. He could not help but stare at it, as it waved back and forth hypnotically in front of him.

Another step, then another. Each moment, Choi neared but Arthur found himself unable to move. Frozen by the hypnotic flicker of light on the blade, the way it moved. Fear, too, kept his gaze locked on the weapon.

Then, a drop pooled from the blood that had fallen on his head earlier, collecting on his brow. It dropped into an eye, and he shut them both reflexively. The moment his eyes closed, the spell was broken; the unnatural fear disappeared.

Understanding rushed through Arthur's body as he realized what had happened. He squeezed his eyes closed even harder, not daring to open them. Cursing his lack of vision and his choice of traits. What could he do? What should he do?

The man before him was no longer walking but running. Almost without thought, Arthur reacted, throwing the scythe he held in hand at where he had last seen Choi. And then, rather than fight his opponent, Arthur turned around and ran. A muffled curse resounded behind him, but Arthur never looked back.

Couldn't.

Back into the tower, back to where death lingered. Away from the man who stalked him with his enchanted blade. Fleeing until he had time to come up with a better plan.

Or any plan at all.

Running away was the plan, and so there was only one way to go. Arthur fled up the winding steps. He took them two to three steps at a time, the steps barely visible in the gloom. The paltry moonlight coming in from open windows above and the pair of torches left on the ground floor did little to illuminate the surroundings.

Even so, his Enhanced Eyesight drank in what light there was, allowing him to tread his way upstairs in leaps and bounds. Beneath, he heard Choi run after him but then hesitate and follow Arthur more carefully. A bobbing light reflecting off stone walls spoke of the man having picked up one of the torches.

Arthur cursed a little, having hoped his opponent might chase after him in darkness. There, his Enhanced Eyesight might have provided him with an advantage. At the very least, it would allow him to even the score a little.

Too bad that Choi, for all his uncreative taunts, was not a complete fool. Though...

"Oi! Hurry up, lah. I wanna show you how to die," Arthur called out. "You got the smell, but it's not worth a bell!"

The steady plod and the bobbing light continued to follow him, pace unchanged. Choi hadn't even bothered to answer his provocation. No surprise. It was not a very good one at all. If there were a class in taunting, even Arthur would have given himself a fail.

"*Hun dan,*" Arthur cursed and kept running. He passed the first-floor door, not even bothering to glance at them. If he was to win this, he would need more than just a plain, open floor.

He would need surprise and a way to neutralize that damn kris. In the meantime, all he could do was run and hope that his brain came up with something clever before his body gave away. Because tired as Choi might have been, so was Arthur. He'd already fought one life-or-death battle, had his soul seared and flayed and put back together, and now...

Now he had to deal with a psychopath following him up the stairs.

Just another damn Tuesday in the Tower.

Chapter 74

Second-floor doorway. Third. Each breath was an ache. A stitch grew in his side as he was forced to slow down his headlong rush. Cudgelling a brain already dull with pain, he was still unable to find a suitable plan. He had the beginnings of one at least.

Step one, get rid of the kris. He could not fight Choi when the man was waving that damn enchanted blade around. If he froze again, Arthur could not expect luck to save him a second time. On that note, he wiped at his face, trying to shed more of the blood before it ran down, leaving his arm streaked with the liquid.

Step two, kill Choi after disarming him.

Really, to call what he had a plan was to consider a child's dream to be Prime Minister a plan. It had the barest sketching of an idea there, but it needed more concrete steps.

Gulping down air, Arthur had to stop, breathing hard as he looked downward. Not backward, not to where he might accidentally spot Choi and his blade, but down at his feet where the bobbing light moved. He gauged its distance, strained to listen to the man ascending.

Damn thug moved lightly. If not for the torch, his progress would have been hard to gauge.

So maybe step one-point-five was to get rid of the light.

Arthur patted himself down to verify what he still had on him, make an assessment of his resources. Not much, in truth. He had the starter pouch which contained all the remaining beast cores. He had his belt, the sheath for his belt knife—but no knife because that had fallen off somewhere. Clothing, of course, and boots. Half his energy resources and a couple of points of refined energy, but none of which he could actually tap into without crippling himself.

The light began bobbing up the stairs faster, as though Choi sensed that Arthur had stopped. Then, to Arthur's surprise, Choi's voice called out.

"You should have just given up, boy. The payment would have been over. But no, you just had to make it hard on us, didn't you?" Choi said, his voice echoing as it bounced off the stone walls, stopping occasionally as he caught his breath. "Now, I'm going to take your life, your friend's treasure and all the cores you've acquired."

After a breath, he added: "I'll keep the pretty one alive though. We can always use another slave."

Arthur growled but chose not to answer. Instead, he saved his breath as he began climbing again. Even if Choi was doing his best to hide it, Arthur could tell he was tired too.

"*Kuching* got your tongue, did it?" Choi said, after a few minutes of further silence.

"Maybe I'll make *you* a slave, you knave!" Arthur gave in to an impulse to speak as he checked the next door.

He almost turned around to deliver his retort, before remembered the kris. Instead, he pushed onwards to the next door. Beneath him there was laughter as Arthur's continued failure at taunting missed its mark.

"Stupid, greedy, idiotic, smelly..." Arthur breathed each invective out as he climbed. Each word was punctuated by another step, as Arthur no longer ascended by the steps in twos. He was exhausted and needed to make a choice soon. Or else Choi would not even need to fight him to finish this, just plant the kris into Arthur's prone and exhausted form. "Greedy *babi...*"

Why did he keep coming back to greedy? Arthur shook his head, wiping at sweat again and letting his hand fall to his side. It brushed against his pouch. Arthur blinked.

Greed.

Distraction.

Poor eyesight.

And floors above that weren't open spaces but composed of small rooms.

A plan began to play through his mind, options to distract, strip the kris, fight and end this battle. To get away from the man chasing him.

It was risky, it was simplistic. At the level of a child's prank, really. On the other hand, he had few resources and even less time.

Making his decision, Arthur pushed himself harder. He had to get to a suitable floor. And then, he needed enough time to prepare the trap. Which meant he needed to speed up.

Again, he took two steps at a time until he hit the next level. Pushing the door open, he ducked into the hallway that he remembered. A sudden thought struck Arthur, as he reached for doors within the room, throwing them open as he passed or shoving them ajar just enough that it might seem to Choi he might have entered.

It would just be his luck to have a *jenglot* respawn now behind one of those doors. Still, the thought only brought a moment's hesitation as he continued to open doors, headed for the second to the last room.

Anything to slow the enemy coming after him. Anything to buy him the time to finish his trap. All he needed, in the end, was a few seconds of surprise. And then, it would be over. One way or the other.

Chapter 75

Choi Yuen Mak ascended the stairs slowly, his arms, ribs, and legs hurting as he did so. He had drunk the healing elixir his brother had pushed upon him before they had stumbled into the clearing. The liquid patched him together in its magical way whilst robbing him of some refined energy. Even if he never said it, he was rather grateful to his brother for giving it to him.

His brother...

Yuen Mak hissed in frustration. His brother was the reason he was out here, alone, with lousy backup. His brother, who was the head enforcer on the first level for the Suey Ying tong. Not even a proper triad, just another group of gangsters that had hopes of becoming something more. The only advantage they had was that they were connected to the Ghee Hin triad and thus partially protected.

Partially. That was the thing. They were not even real members, just extra people used to do the kind of things even the triad didn't want traced back to them. And considering the Ghee Hin was happy to dirty its hands with prostitution, drugs, blackmail, and other forms of exploitation, it said a lot.

Then again, the triads were still careful of the Towers. Not in using them, no. They sent their people through, just like major corporations and clans and families did. Some of the Tower clans were even hidden branches of the triads.

No, what they were careful about was exploiting Tower climbers. Everyone had learnt that lesson a decade ago, when the Parusa had cleared three Towers and then decided to show everyone what happened when you abused the wrong person. He was still being hunted for mass murder by the Filipino government. Rumor was, he had escaped to Australia or America and was clearing their Towers one by one, until he got powerful enough to deal with even more of the gang who had wronged him.

Once they realized the kind of danger they had made themselves liable to, the various organized groups had quickly moved to an arm's-length approach to all this. It was why Suey Ying's connections to the Ghee Hin were kept occluded to the highest levels. Like him and his brother.

After all, he was supposed to be the inheritor, the second in command after his brother. He was supposed to be the one they listened to, that the others looked up to and took orders from. Not Ah Yam, that useless, preening fellow who thought he was all that because he graduated from university.

And not even an overseas one, even if he told people that. He'd gone to a twinning program and gotten a degree from an Australian university, though he spent all four of those years in Malaysia. If he'd wanted, Yuen Mak could have gotten a degree like that too. But what was the point?

No one needed to know about organizational structure or accounting. You stood around, waiting for new Tower climbers. Then, when they got here, you shook them down for their stuff. You kept an eye out for those who couldn't be shaken down, people with the right connections, with the right backing. And you kept shaking them down, so that they never got too strong.

No need for a fancy degree to do that.

And still! Some of his people, his brother's people, had started listening to Ah Yam. They had started acting as though that man had more right to make decisions for the Suey Ying tong than he did. And his brother, his damnable brother! He had done nothing when Yuen Mak had complained.

So now he was here. With his brother's favorite kris, to prove him wrong. That he could deal with the problems of the tong like the Thorned Lotuses getting ahead of themselves. Damn women.

He dealt with them though. All of them. Now he just had to finish off that idiot boy...

Laboured breathing above him had stopped, and he looked up. His arm carrying the torch had grown tired. He switched it to his other hand, putting the kris in his off-hand for the moment. It wasn't the best option, but better than dropping the flame.

He saw the silhouette of the fool bent over. Maybe a good couple of floors ahead of him. He would have considered running for it, catching up with the boy. But his own legs were wooden, and exhausting himself before a fight was not the point.

Anyway, the boy looked exhausted too. The young ones were always like that. Thinking too much of themselves. Thinking they could climb the Tower, be the next ranked climber. They pushed and pushed and pushed themselves and everyone else; and led others to their death.

And always tired themselves out.

So he climbed. Slowly. Steadily. Because that was what those who were smart did. Not the book-smart like Ah Yam, but the street-smart, the fighting-smart down in the alleys and gutters of Shah Alam. That's how he'd win.

He spotted the open door as he reached the landing and hesitated. Then, he switched hands again, for the third time, putting the kris in his main hand. He knew, instinctively, that the end was coming now. The boy was tired, just like him. But he'd hurried ahead trying to get away, exhausted himself out.

Now all Yuen Mak had to do was find him.

There was going to be a trick. All the smart ones, the ambitious ones, had one. They all thought they were so smart, playing their tricks. But it was easy for him to figure it out. After all, he'd seen all the tricks. All their special ideas, their smart thoughts, were nothing new.

No.

He'd be careful, check behind all the open doors, see if the boy was waiting for him. Fool boy, he had opened every door, so he was sure he was near the back. Didn't matter though. It would be just like him to run all the way to the back, then come to the front to hide, hoping that Yuen Mak might overthink things just like a college boy.

No.

He'd check. Do it right. Just like he had been trained. He pushed each door open, thrust the flame at arm's length before him so that he could not be struck as easily. And then he stepped in carefully to scan the area, including the back of the door.

Once that was done, he moved to the next room and the one after that. Step by step, he would continue on the same way.

Still, even after he opened the first half-dozen doors on either side, Yuen Mak found nothing but annoyance and impatience building up. Yet, he forced himself to move slowly, carefully, pushing each door open with torch end first and then stepping in, not allowing the boy to escape him.

Three doors before the end, it happened. Fool that he was, the boy thought the sight of a half-dozen beast cores scattered across the ground would be enough to make him lose caution. That he would just pounce at the cores as though he were a greedy *babi*.

Instead, Yuen Mak slowed down further. He cast a glance at the door right behind him and then the one ahead—the remaining doors facing down the hallway, all three doorways along the wall. All three propped open a little, with the baited one the widest.

Yuen Mak could understand what the boy was thinking. What he planned.

Have him hurry down the hallway, scooping up the cores. From one of the other two doors, the boy would jump out, attacking him while he was distracted.

A child's prank.

Snorting, Yuen Mak shifted his body positioning so that he could see ahead. He could not guess which of the two doors the boy might be hiding behind, but all it would take was a good push of each door to quickly see if the rooms were empty. Yuen Mak would still be at arm's length even if the boy jumped out from behind a door.

Switching hands again, he readied his weapon in his off-hand. He would need it to strike as the boy jumped out. Better than crossing his body and facing the wrong way. So with his main hand, he pushed the torch against a doorway.

Only to feel extra resistance. A moment of realization, his body pulling back already, but too late to entirely save the torch as boots filled with water tipped over from the top of the door.

Dousing his flame and plunging the surroundings into darkness.

And that was when a door creaked open, and the boy came for him.

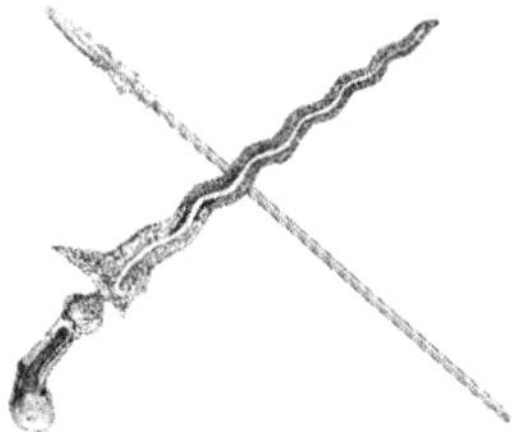

Chapter 76

Barefooted, weaponless, head bent low and coming in at a full lunge, Arthur exploded out of the door. He watched as the kris swung before his eyes, nearly catching the top of his forehead. But in the sudden darkness, the samseng was blind. His eyes had not adjusted to the tiny amount of illumination offered by the rising moon, not yet.

Ducking under Choi's swinging arm, Arthur hit the thug with his elbow, driving it into the man's bladder with Focused Strike empowering his attack. He had missed the hip joint as the man turned, leaving him with a more solid but less crippling attack. It still worked, however, to double his opponent over as the man let out a grunt filled with pain and surprise, and warm liquid exploded from a full bladder.

Rising from his crouch, Arthur wielded the top of his head as a weapon, smashing the crown into a descending jaw. He heard jaws crack together, a tooth crunching even as a shooting pain went down his body and he felt a little faint.

No time for that, for the kris-wielding hand was returning, turning to plunge the blade into him. Both of Arthur's hands came together into an X-block, leverage applied to his opponent's hand. He felt the blade press sharply against one side of his forearm, cutting a little, but then he had a firm grip and it had nowhere to go.

Deadly weapon hand controlled, his opponent stunned and injured, Arthur knew he had to keep moving to gain the upper hand. It would only take a little while for his opponent to regain his senses fully, to break out of the constant disorientation that Arthur kept him in.

So.

Twist the arm, leveraging the flat of the blade that was against it as a pivot point. At the same time, release his other arm and slide it down Choi's attacking hand, grabbing at his elbow to keep it turning and apply pressure to increase the angle. After that, it was but a matter of physics.

The kris popped out of Choi's fingers, pried apart by the opposing forces as his own elbow was twisted away and the strength from his fingers gave away. The moment the kris dropped to the floor, Arthur took the chance to kick it away, defanging his competition. The blade skittered away into the hallway, clattering and bouncing off a wall.

The time taken to send the weapon far away cost Arthur, though. A hammer blow came down on his lower back, once and then again. It cracked a rib, sent him sprawling to the ground with one hand extended. Long enough for another glancing kick, thrown blind, to hammer into his thigh. Pushed sideways against the wall, Arthur scrambled away, back through the doorway for a moment.

Choi followed, reaching blindly for the doorway, fingers finding the edges of the entrance. He hauled himself in, only to flinch as Arthur threw a haymaker into his approaching face. Unlike Choi, whose sight was beginning to return, he could see all too well.

He felt the punch connect, bouncing off and ringing his opponent's head. Reeling back, Choi brought his hands up to defend himself, snarling imprecations that Arthur had no time to listen to. Instead, he lashed out with a shin kick at Choi, turning his heel a little just before he connected so that he hit the planted foot with the side of his leg. Scraping his bare foot along his opponent's pant leg, Arthur hissed in pain as his own foot throbbed.

For a moment, in the middle of the fight, he had forgotten he was no longer wearing his boots. What should have been a heel scrape that crippled his opponent had instead injured himself too, though it sent Choi retreating to the bait room.

Now the man was trying to buy time, fingers blindly questing for the doorjamb to slam it shut. Arthur knew that Choi, with time and sight returned, would likely win the battle. He could not afford to let up, so even on his injured foot, Arthur threw himself forward, shouldering the door to keep Choi from shutting it.

Once more, he went in hunched low. Another Focused Strike, draining his own energy dangerously low, allowed his tackle to hit his opponent with enough force to take him off his feet, allowing Arthur to raise him the much-needed inch before he dropped Choi to the ground.

The thug fell hard, even as he grabbed at Arthur's head. Choi managed to snake a hand around Arthur's neck, attempting a full neck crank but having his grip dislodged as he landed on his back... on a cluster of sharp-edged beast cores.

The preternatural objects did not break, not under such mundane forces like a slammed body. The energy, however, of his body slam had to go somewhere and it did so by breaking ribs and driving the cores into the body. Screaming in pain, his grip around Arthur's neck spasmed, allowing Arthur to grasp further up his opponent's body.

A moment of groping found his opponent's head, and Arthur yanked the head upwards savagely. He brought it back down, hard, against the unyielding stone floor, hearing the dull thud and crack of skull and stone. His opponent still lashed out, punching him in the guts, the ribs, forcing pained spasms of Arthur's own fingers on a sweaty skull.

He refused to let go. Instead, he raised the head again and slammed it down, fingers digging into the sides of the face that twisted and attempted to pull away. A blindly flailing hand hit his face and smashed his nose, but another slam of head against stone slowed the questing fingers.

Then another.

And another.

The figure beneath him stopped struggling after the fourth, stopped moving after the sixth. Somewhere along the way, Arthur lost count of the number of times he repeated the brutal motion, the skull in his hands a squishy remnant as he choked under the onslaught of adrenaline and desperate fear.

Leaving him to collapse on the corpse of the man that had harried him since the first day he had arrived in the Tower. Breathing hard and in pain, but victorious.

If you could call this a victory.

Chapter 77

When Arthur finally managed to haul himself off Choi's body and put his mind together, he had the unenviable task of frisking the body for supplies and goods, extracting the beast cores he had used as a distraction from the now-cooling body and then, finally, find the kris that was dangerously glinting in the dark.

The fact that his arm throbbed where the kris had cut into it, alternating with cold chill and flushing warmth, worried him. It felt similar to something he had experienced before, and since he finally had some time and mental wherewithal, Arthur pulled up the notification he had suppressed until now.

You are poisoned!

Currently under Toxic Yin Chi Poison effects.

- *Minor increase in fatigue*
- *Yang-based cultivation skills cost doubled*
- *Trivial on-going damage effects*

Yin Body Resistance in Effect

Poison effects reduced by 39.5%

Arthur blinked, rubbing at his arm where it felt both so cold and warm. Intuition told him that if he had the time to actually cultivate, he could drive and subsume this chi within himself. As it stood, the poison was having only a minor effect on him, and the on-going damage was negligible due to the insufficient amount of poison that had found its way into his blood.

When he made his way over to the kris and picked it up, Arthur could not help but turn the weapon around. Try as he might, he could not bring up any details on the kris, lacking the cultivation skill to analyze the weapon properly.

Pity that.

Sheathing the kris—after cleaning it off on his pant leg—in his newly acquired sheath, Arthur made his laboured way down. He forewent the torch, not having a way to relight it. Also, illumination from the windows was sufficient to let him see.

The journey down the stairs was agonizing. He limped in squishy footwear, having reacquired his wet boots, the bruise from his earlier attacks making itself known all too well. Each breath was laboured, the cracked ribs shooting pain through his body each moment.

Every other flight, Arthur had to put a hand against the wall, using it to support his exhausted body before he made his way further down. Eventually, though, he managed to find himself at the bottom of the staircase and able to survey the destruction that he had left behind.

To his surprise, Arthur found Jan pointing a parang at him. She blinked wearily, looking Arthur over before snorting.

"Still alive? Of course."

"It's nice to see you too, my beautiful loo," Arthur sing-sung, walking over to her warily. Still, she had lowered the parang, so he was somewhat less wary. His gaze drifted over the bodies she had pulled over, laying them out in the row. "How bad is it?"

"Bad. *Bu huai.*" Jan closed her eyes, bending beside the nearest body and letting her parang fall to the ground. She touched Shar's dark skin, tracing a finger along the cleaned face. "Good woman. The best. Always taking care of me."

After a pause: "What am I supposed to do? Without her?"

That's when she broke out crying. Followed by big heaving sobs that wracked her body. For a long moment, Arthur just watched before he carefully moved over, to put a pair of arms around the woman. Holding her, offering comfort.

Eventually, she pushed away. Much less roughly than he had expected. For a few moments, he stood awkwardly, unsure of what to do, before a rasping cough beneath his feet brought his attention back to the other bodies. He realized that Uswah was waking and scrambled over to her side, only to cast around for water.

"Here." Jan shoved a flask at him, which he gratefully took and fed to the woman, then helped Uswah sit up. At first, the water dribbled down parched lips, but she eventually managed to drink and clear her throat, enough to speak at least.

"What happened?" Uswah asked.

"We won, I guess." Arthur said.

"You guess?" Uswah muttered.

Jan could only mumble, "Shar died. And Rani."

Uswah flinched at that, while Arthur's own eyes grew wide. He had seen Shar's fatal blow but not what happened to Rani.

"How?" Arthur asked tentatively.

"Overused energy," Jan said. "I think. Ya... I think she overdid it."

Arthur winced. That could happen all too easily. Certain cultivation exercises allowed one the chance to "burn lifeblood" as the old stories called it. But in reality, it just sacrificed one's own health for strength. Some cultivation techniques even taught people how to do that in a safer manner, making it almost a hallmark of their style.

It was something the desperate or the needy did, and it was supposedly said anyone who was desperate enough could learn. Obviously, Rani had been desperate enough.

"I'm sorry. For your losses," he said.

Jan lowered her head, biting her lip as a new wave of sobs rippled through her. To his surprise, it was Uswah who grabbed his hand and growled into his face when she hauled him closer.

"You better make it worth all this."

Arthur was at a loss for words, knowing it was not his fault this had all happened. Yet, he could understand how they could lay the blame and the expectations of a brighter future on him—when he had benefitted the most and lost the least from this mess.

Knowing all that, and understanding how precarious his own position continued to be, he could not help but nod in affirmation.

Then, and only then, did Uswah release her grip on his arm as she slumped back onto the ground, her eyes drifting shut. Exhaustion took her consciousness, even as she finished extracting the silent promise.

And silent or not, under duress or not, Arthur could not help but feel obliged to fulfill it.

A better world...

He could get behind that. Even if the world itself might not be exactly the one they envisioned.

Chapter 78

It was a tired and silent group that left the tower. No one wanted to stay at the landmark, not when it was so easy to pick out. Determining that safety lay in the deep wilds, the group packed everything they could find, stripping the bodies of the tong members and their own friends with equal ruthlessness before leaving.

As one of the least injured, Arthur led the way. He kept an eye out for the monsters, not surprised to find that he had to dispatch a *kuching* within a half-dozen steps into the forest, and then a hanging green snake waiting for their inattention. Removing them with the spear he had retrieved, Arthur kept a wary watch in the dim light cast by lanterns the women carried.

The group moved slow; Mel's nearly insensate body helped along by the injured Uswah. The pair moved like a three-legged, drunken pirate, weaving back and forth with each step as they aided one another. Jan brought up the rear, being the only other member of the group who was actually able to fight.

It took them nearly an hour before they managed to make a good few hundred meters from the tower. As though the group had crossed an invisible boundary, a loud rumbling behind caused them to turn around wearily.

Through the gaps in the treeline, the group watched as the moonlit tower crumbled, crashing to the ground in a resounding, calamitous heap. A dust cloud billowed in the air, rising high in the sky and clouding the moon.

"*Eh, kenapa?*" Uswah said, startled.

"No idea," Arthur replied. "Though, if I had to guess..." He trailed off, eliciting a growl from Jan to finish his thought. "It's done, isn't it? The quest. So no need for the tower."

"It's like... this Tower is alive," Jan said, a hint of fear in her voice.

"Alive, programmed, organically constructed and varied..." Arthur said and then shrugged. "Doesn't matter much, does it? The Tower isn't talking, and it sure isn't walking. Its owners are silent, and that's just brilliant." Then, he sighed and dropped the rampant bad rhyming. "All we can do is climb it and survive."

"Survive..." Mel repeated.

The group hesitated, staring at the woman and wondering if she was going to say anything further. When the poisoned, delirious woman stayed silent, the group let out a long sigh.

"How is she?" Arthur said after a moment.

"Sick." Uswah shook her head. "I can't fix her, that's not how my techniques work. But I think she'll be fine. Given enough time, the Yin poison will eventually break down."

"Then let's move." There was no point in further conversation, so Arthur waved the group onward. If anyone was around to spot the tower, they were definitely headed toward it now. Out of curiosity if nothing else.

The group trundled on for another hour, until they finally came across a clearing. Noticing how even Jan was swaying, Arthur knew they had to stop. The group had to take multiple breaks over the last hour just to make their way across a short distance.

He waved the team to rest after he made a preliminary circuit of the clearing, then pulled out the tents and set them up. He only set up two though, eschewing privacy for safety.

"You taking first watch, ah?" Jan said, hesitantly. She was swaying on her feet as it was, but too stubborn to accept the fact that she was more tired than Arthur.

"No." Arthur reached into the pouch by his side, pulling out a trio of yellow talismans. He waved them around, before wandering towards a tree near the opening of the clearing. He slapped the first one on it, then checking himself over, plucked at a dried scab until fresh blood welled out. Wiping the blood on the talisman, he watched as it glowed to life before repeating the task at two other corners of a rough triangle.

"From where?" Jan said.

"Samseng," Arthur replied. Then, not caring to say anything further, he walked right into a tent, pulled out his bedroll and rolled it out before flopping onto it. Dirt, grime, and blood or not, he was too exhausted to care about cleaning beforehand.

Even if it was going to leave a mess when he woke.

Eyes drifting closed, Arthur felt a body roll up against him. Warm flesh and a snoring noise briefly interrupted the inexorable pull toward sleep. He cracked his eyes open, just long enough to realise that it was Uswah curled up against him, drool already rolling down one side of her mouth, then his eyes shut.

Resting, finally.

Waking up the next morning was a stifling experience. Not just because of the woman who had rolled over onto him, but also because of the warmth of the tent and the encompassing stink of dried blood, guts, and sweat mixed together with unwashed bodies in close proximity. Uswah was barely moving, so Arthur struggled free and fought the sluggishness of his own Yin Body to pry the zipper open and emerge into the morning sun.

Finding himself alone in the clearing, Arthur picked up his bag and spear, and proceeded to a nearby stream to deal with the mess caked all over his body. After checking both up- and down-river for potential threats, he stripped down to his underwear and began the process of washing himself, wincing as the cold water hit inflamed flesh.

Catching sight of himself in the water, he could not help but stop for a moment to note the difference that time on the first level had made in him. Scars, obviously, but also his body had grown more muscular and leaner, the minor amounts of fat having burned off.

A part of him worried about that for a moment, knowing that fat was what gave one strength, energy. How ironic that people wanted to rid themselves of fat. When they looked their best, they might in fact be at their weakest... Arthur shook off thoughts of the world outside. What did it matter now?

He was not exactly human anymore. He no longer ate, not real food at least. Though he longed for a good char kway teow or some satay. Crispy, fatty satay with peanut sauce and crunchy raw onions and cucumbers on the side.

His food, his sustenance, was the energy of the Tower now. The beast cores he carried and the energy that surrounded him. Feeling within, he winced as he realized exactly how low he was in his dantian reserves for both. The entire fight had drained him, as had the running of his body through the night…

Dismissing the scars, the new wounds, and the chiselled body from his mind, Arthur finished washing up and set aside the bar of soap. After dressing quickly in a cleaner set of clothes, he beat his old clothing as best he could, scrubbing out what dirt and blood would come out before wrapping it all together in a wet bundle and making his way back to the camp.

To find that none of the others had woken yet.

Letting out a huffing breath, Arthur placed his clothing to dry before digging into the dirt in the middle of the clearing, well away from the two tents. Soon enough, he had a makeshift campfire within a ring of small stones to help contain the flames.

Piling dry leaves, small twigs, and discarded fluff, he set the entire thing alight, knowing that for the time being they were protected by the talismans. A part of him ached for the comfort of warmth and flames, for a chance to sit and soak in the false protection of the ring of fire.

So he did.

While waiting for the teepee of wood he had built to catch and burn properly, he sat cross-legged, spear by his side, and began the process of cultivating Tower energy. No point in waiting for the others to wake. And while he wished to review the seal on his hand in more detail, survival came first.

Which meant energy for his gifts and to heal his wounds. Even now, his body throbbed and ached, and he could tell that a portion of his lower back had opened, soaking his shirt in blood once more. Still, he needed to replenish those energy stores, at least by a few points.

Then he could refine some healing energy from the beast cores and fix himself. After that... well, after that, the Thorned Lotuses would be awake. And wouldn't that be a talk.

Chapter 79

Having replaced some of his lost energy, Arthur was now in the process of pulling refined energy from one of the many cores of the *kuching hitam*. The power of the beast core thrummed through his body, flooding it before diving straight into his wounds after being processed by his meridians to hasten the healing process.

The first few minutes had been painful, especially as some of the cloth and dirt that he had missed was ejected from open wounds, pushed out by the supernatural healing. Burgeoning infections faded as flesh stitched itself together.

Unfortunately, he was only half done, the entirety of one beast core consumed and another well on its way when the survivors began to stir. The first to stumble out of the other tent was not, to Arthur's surprise, Jan but Mel.

The woman moved with haste, looking around carefully while gripping the short sword by her side and gripping a spear with the other hand, ready to block. Seeing no danger, and spotting Arthur cultivating quietly, she stared at the only other tent with dread.

Jerking into sudden motion, she pulled the flap open and stuck her head inside before retreating with as much haste. "No," she moaned and stumbled away, casting her eyes around for others. When her gaze landed on Arthur again, who was putting aside the core, she said harshly: "The others. They're just... out washing, right? Right?"

Mutely, Arthur shook his head.

"No! They can't... they can't—" Mel's voice broke, hiccupping a little as sobs threatened to break out. She shuddered, fighting the grief that threatened to overwhelm her, the tears that leaked from her eyes as she sank down beside the fire.

Automatically, she held a hand towards the flame, seeking warmth. Fresh blood seeped from newly reopened wounds, though she may not have noticed in her grief. When she could control her voice a little more, she whispered, "How?"

"You and Shar fell to the kris." He gestured down to the sheathed blade. "It's enchanted. Very powerful. He killed her while I was finishing off my own opponent. Rani... overdid it. Burned all her energy out and, I guess, died when the Tower needed more from her."

"So that's it. They're all dead. My sisters." Mel shuddered. "I failed them. Failed the quest." Anger flared in her eyes, focused on Arthur. "And gave the prize to you. *Untuk apa, hah?*"

"Your *Bahasa*'s coming out, eh?" Arthur said, idly.

Mel continued to glare at him, though exhaustion soon robbed even her anger of its intensity. She curled up further, pulling her knees to her chest, wincing with each motion. In a smaller, younger voice, one that belied the hardened features and spoke of her true age in her twenties, she asked, "What now?"

"Now?" Arthur hesitated, caught in surprise at being thrown into a position of leading for once. It wasn't his way, not by choice. He liked doing things alone, but it was obvious that she was not in the mood or the mind to lead. "Now, you get up and take a bath. Wash your wounds, take some of the healing pills we found. We rest for the day until the talismans burn out, and then we start heading back."

"That's it? That easy? Just... go on?"

"What other choice is there?" Arthur said wearily. He closed his eyes, the faded memory of his parents flickering to mind for a moment. How strange memory was, that what he remembered was not scenes of them but photos. They were a blur to his mind after so many years, after so much time and heartache. A blur of impressions, of a warm hand holding his own, a smile that he remembered from the way it made him feel rather than the way it actually looked.

Sense impressions, rather than the clear-cut images of blood spilled or the wide open eyes of Choi as his life leaked out, pain and rage, and finally, emptiness...

He shuddered, shaking his head and pushed the thoughts aside, meeting Mel's own knowing gaze when he looked up.

"We go on. Because otherwise, the choice is to fail. And I'm tired of failing," Arthur said.

"Can I... can I just sit here for a bit?" Mel said softly as she stared into the fire.

He briefly considered joking, that she was welcome to do so since she was downwind, but discarded the words. There was a time for his humour and this was not it.

Instead, he picked up the beast core again, knowing he had more work to do. He had a feeling that, soon enough, he'd be having the same conversation with the other women.

Evening fell, shedding dim moonlight on the quartet of cultivators seated in a semi-circle by the dying light of the smoky fire. Arthur cracked his eyes open, dropping the last of the beast cores he had been using to the ground, watching as it crumbled into dust. The others were in varying stages of their cultivation cycle, though he could sense that most of them were nearly done.

He traced the energy connections within himself before flashing his own status open. A half dozen energy points and another 0.4 points of refined energy ensured that he at least had the basic amount of energy required for another few days of travel. Most of his wounds had scabbed over, the majority even closing up such that they were unlikely to tear open unless he did something vigorous. Like fighting.

Arthur snorted.

Pushing aside that thought, he turned to the seal on his palm, bringing it up to his face. He traced the outlines of the burnt skin, then he pulled up information on the seal once more.

{Unnamed} Clan Seal

You have a Tier 1 Clan Seal which will allow the establishment of a Tower-Approved Clan.

As a Tier 1 Clan, you will:

- *Be able to establish a Tower-Approved Building in the Safe Zone*
- *Appoint 1 Officer per Tower level to administer Clan Building*

Aspects:

None

Sigil:

None

NOTE: Further benefits require the establishment and registration of the Clan at a Tower Administrative Building.

Arthur grimaced, poking at the information inside his head a little more. He kept trying to call up additional information on the Aspects or the Sigil, but the seal stubbornly refused to divulge anything further, much to his frustration.

He really did need to know what the difference was between Aspects and Sigils. He knew they gave different kinds of bonuses, depending on what he chose, but he just did not understand what they each really meant.

Letting out a long sigh, he pulled his fingers away from his palm where he had been prodding the brand. He looked up only to meet Mel's quiet and firm gaze.

"Time to talk, ya?" she said.

"Long past time."

Chapter 80

Instead of speaking immediately, Mel fell silent for a moment. When Arthur made a frustrated noise deep in his throat, she shook her head a little, dismissing whatever thought had taken her away from the moment.

"Clan seals allow you to establish a clan. You need, however, a clan building—one, minimum—to activate the majority of functions in the clan. Until you establish that first building, a lot of the abilities will be locked out for you."

Arthur nodded, having guessed that much at least.

"There's a second lock in place, until you clear your first Tower. And, as we understand it, there are thresholds for new buildings that allow the activation of additional abilities. It's certain there's a difference between those clans or guilds that clear a second Tower—"

"Multi-tower guilds," Arthur added. He knew that was one of the ways people looked at guilds in the real world—how many Towers they had influence in.

"—and there's likely other thresholds beyond two. We just don't know what they are." Mel paused, then added, "Yet."

"Okay, so establish a guild building here and then on each floor and get another unlock when I'm done with this Tower. Got it."

Mel pursed her lips, before continuing. "There are two other things you might see right now. Aspects and Sigils. Yes?"

Arthur nodded, confirming her guess.

"Aspects are unique bonuses for a clan or guild. There is some overlap, but for the most part, each Aspect is different for a clan or guild. The combination of Aspects makes a guild unique and often dictates the long-term goal of the clan." Mel turned her hand one way, then the other. "You can have Aspects that relate to creativity or bonuses to healing. Or that improve training time, or the speed that individuals learn new cultivation techniques."

"Or increase their likelihood of getting unique beast cores, or stumbling across rare or hidden aspects of a Tower," Arthur said. "Combat, exploration, crafting, healing, guardianship..." He ticked his fingers off, recalling the big drop-down forms that were used to sort out guilds that he occasionally perused for fun.

"Exactly, though Aspects—like Perks—can also affect things that are less visible than Sigils. So, creative Aspects, trickster or charm-based ones, mercantile Aspects or blessings... Of course, there's arguments about exactly how powerful some of these less numerically-specific Aspects are, but it's clear they have some effect."

Nothing new there. It was well known that the most powerful Perked Guilds were mostly quite specialized. All but Valorant, of course, which had the advantage of being the first mover and having very deep pockets, thus managing to offset their lack of specialization in Perks by just hiring the best.

"I got that, but how do I get an Aspect? Do I need, perhaps to inspect the Aspect?" As usual, his audience did not get his wit.

"We believe the first one appears when you register the clan," Mel said.

"And the others?" And there were only five such Aspects or Perks available. After that, the other Aspects or Perks would no longer be active, though they might still be gained. Rumors were that even non-active Perks could provide a bonus, with such Aspects combining to become a lower-grade Aspect or Perks of the same sort. That was the base assumption anyway, from reviewing the various Perks guilds had shown, but it had yet to be confirmed.

"Unknown. Probably at each step unlocked," Mel said.

"So the first one chosen is going to be very important," Arthur said with a nod. If they weren't going to get another one until he cleared the Tower, he could expect the first Aspect to weigh most heavily.

"We were going to choose an Aspect of guardianship or safety," Mel said, before Arthur could push her for more details on Sigils. She met his gaze, flatly. "Even if we managed to clear this Tower, and that was a big if, the influence of such an Aspect in the outside world could be significant. If nothing else, because of the reputation we could garner."

Arthur bobbed his head. He was not completely ignorant about some of the politics around women, the misogyny they faced, especially in Malaysia and after the shift towards a UBI. There had been significant pressures placed upon them to take up more traditional roles, as homemakers. Not just among the Malays and Indians, but even the Chinese population—which had a hardline, old-guard group.

The argument to push women back into the house had increased significantly, because there was no need for two incomes now, each individual's basic needs were supposedly taken care of, and there was an increased demand for stretching every dollar. That the logic almost made sense, when one didn't look at it too closely, had made the pressure ever greater.

Thus groups like the Thorned Lotuses. Thus their departure into the Tower. But such escapes were only for the few and brave, the lucky who managed to sneak in without being stopped by parents or husbands or "caring" families.

And even then, as evidenced all too recently, there was no guarantee that being in here was any safer. At least the Tower seemed to have an overall sterilization field running, since Arthur had never heard of a single child born within the Tower.

Which, of course, led to the stories of women being bounced off the Tower when they tried to enter it while pregnant. Sometimes to their dismay.

"Will you do it?" Mel's voice came now, more insistent than ever when Arthur had stayed silent too long, thinking this all over.

He blinked, trying to recall the thread of the earlier conversation, the question that she had asked. He remembered it now. And truth be told, it was not entirely surprising that she had asked it.

"Will I take an Aspect like that?" He paused, looking at the much diminished group. Remembered the lives lost, stared at the wounds that covered the others, Uswah's lost limb, and the ragged tear along Mel's torso that was barely held together by a badly stitched patch. He weighed his options, his answer, and his own needs.

Thought about the allies he required if he was to survive, thought about the target that was now branded on his hand. And most of all, he thought of the kind of world and the kind of person he wanted. Because, for the first time, it was not just about making do for himself. He had a chance to make a real change, affect more than his own survival.

And wasn't that a thought?

"Yeah. Yeah, I think I will."

Chapter 81

"If you don't, I'll kill you!" Jan said, eyes opening fully after his announcement.

Arthur snorted at the threat. "I'll come through on my side. Haven't I so far?" He opened his hands sideways. "Also, you suck at hiding coming out of cultivation."

Jan sniffed, but reluctantly inclined her head in acknowledgement of his point. He had, after all, done everything he had said. Even if it had not always been to their benefit or as they envisioned.

"Thank you." Mel's voice was quieter but filled with emotion.

"*M sai.*" With a hand, Arthur waved away any need for thank-yous. Then he tapped the brand on his palm. "Alright, so that's Aspects. And I know Sigils are bonuses with more concrete numbers. They come from a variety of sources and can be quite different in goals from Aspects." Cudgeling his brain for what he knew of the various guilds' Titles and Guild bonuses, he eventually just shrugged. That was about all he had.

"That's a start," Mel said. "Clan Sigils are more limited in some ways than Guild Titles. Guilds can have a variety of bonuses, including multiple Titles, but each bonus is often significantly less powerful than a Sigil. And that's a good thing: as a clan, we get to add up to four or five Sigils to our clan seal. Maybe as few as three, though, depending on the size of the Sigil."

Jan, listening in, was silent. She had managed to find a water bottle and was sipping on it, head propped against a tree. She startled a little when Uswah smacked her arm to ask for a drink.

"You two have anything to add?" Arthur said.

"Not my place," Jan said.

"No," Uswah said curtly.

Arthur frowned, noting how the woman had grown more silent and curt over the last few days. He assumed it happened when the initial shock of losing her arm had faded and the reality of her new situation had sunk in. He hoped that she was not spiraling, though he had a feeling she might actually be somewhat protected by the Yin chi that suffused her body.

It certainly helped him from becoming a complete gibbering wreck. But he wasn't going to tell anybody that.

"This kind of information isn't exactly something we have been passing around," Mel said. "Anyway. Sigils, they're more powerful but limited. You can add swirls—they're additions to a Sigil—but only if they combine right."

"And how do you tell if things combine right?" Arthur said, intrigued.

Mel could only shrug. "Remember, we're getting all this information secondhand. It's not as though most of this information is passed around in general, so we're just making do." When Arthur nodded, she continued. "In general, the Sigil—and the clan crest—will appear on every upstanding guild member, giving them the bonuses that they confer. It can be different from the Aspects, but they almost always deal with our stats."

She hesitated, then added, "Sigils also have one extra benefit, or so we've been told. It's... unknown if it's true."

"Go on."

"They can allow the passing on of cultivation exercises rather than direct bonuses."

Three indrawn breaths, slight hisses of surprises from the group.

"Really, ah?" Jan said, the first to recover.

"It's a rumor. We think it's likely and would explain how some clans all seem to pass on certain techniques," Mel explained.

"Clan libraries explain that too, no?" Arthur said.

"Ya, of course. But so do Sigils that let you pass on techniques," Mel said.

Arthur nodded, conceding the point. More importantly, "How do you get a Sigil added to the seal, then?"

That was when Mel grimaced. "We're not sure. Maybe you'll get more information when you establish a clan building?" She shrugged. "If it's like the guilds in the West, then I would say you get a Sigil when you—or the clan—does something noteworthy. But..."

"But that's guilds and we're a clan," Arthur said, rolling his eyes. "Yay, we get to be exotic. Which idiot decided that?"

"Probably the same kind of person who dumps a Tower in every major country but still misses Singapore," Uswah said, snidely.

"Well, that worked out for us, no?" Arthur could not help but remember the initial cries of relief when Singaporeans realized they'd been missed by the sudden appearance of the Towers. And then, later on, the even louder cries of dismay when they realized what the lack had caused.

Negotiations for Singaporeans to gain access to the Malaysian Tower in Kuala Lumpur on a regular basis had been just as tense as the water supply negotiations, with all the requisite threats about invasion and economic sanctions involved.

Luckily, cooler heads and the sudden acquisition of a few luxury cars and residential properties in the US by certain Malaysian politicians had prevailed. Now the Singaporeans got their own slots to enter, flooding into the Tower about once a week and moving in groups to everyone's chagrin.

Of course, it wasn't just Malaysia's Tower that they entered, having organized entry into multiple countries for initial slotting. Still, being one of the easier Beginner Towers, the Kuala Lumpur one certainly saw a dedicated presence of the Singaporeans.

"Huh. Didn't see any Singaporeans, though," Arthur said, realization striking him.

"What? You literally talked to one as your attendant. Anyway, most of them hang out around the Suey Ying tong. Being, you know, Chinese."

Arthur nodded. That made sense. The racial lines might blur a little, but this was Southeast Asia. Racial cliques never really went away. He wasn't looking forward to having to try out other Towers in other countries. At least, in the Indonesian Tower, he could understand them since Bahasa Melayu—that is, Malay—and Bahasa Indonesia were somewhat mutually intelligible. Thailand would suck, big time, in that sense.

"Whatever. I'll deal with the Singaporeans later, if I have to." Annoying *kiasu.* Kiasu is what Malaysians called their southern neighbors: overly competitive. Arthur himself subscribed to the belief that the Singaporeans thought themselves better than others, always needing to one-up everyone else "So. Sigils. We don't know how to get more, we don't know how they fit, and we don't know how to optimize them. Is that about right?"

Mel made a face but nodded in agreement at that summary.

"Yeah, fine. So, I think that's the talk, right? I'll pick something useful for the Aspect to help safeguard everyone, make us tougher or something." Mel looked like she wanted to object, but then bit her lip and nodded. "And as for Sigils," Arthur continued, "we'll just work it out when it happens. Or I will, I guess."

"I'd like to advise, if possible," Mel said, offering Arthur a tentative smile.

Arthur nodded. Then, suddenly, he grinned. "Well, I'll need a trusted lieutenant anyway."

"Trusted lieutenant."

"Evil overlord," Uswah replied, rolling her eyes. "You're not trying to go evil, right?"

"Who said it has to be an evil overlord?" Arthur protested. "I could be a generous and wise king."

"*Jangan, lah.*" Jan hooted, clutching her side and waving a hand. "Stop. Please. Your jokes are getting worse."

Arthur turned to stare at Mel and said, "But seriously. I'll need help, and it seems you know more of this than I do. So when I can, I'll ask. Otherwise, you run interference with your people. Deal?" He stuck a hand out, waiting.

To her credit, she only hesitated for a second before she shook his.

"Good. First thing, you get to explain why we're letting in men too," Arthur said with a grin.

Chapter 82

Days later, the group was making their way through the undergrowth of the deep wilds. They moved slowly, having been forced by injuries and their lack of provisions to take extra care. Considering the potential dangers they faced, the group had elected to go slow and carefully rather than rushing back, even if the rest of the Thorned Lotuses might be growing concerned by this point.

"They won't send a second party out," Mel muttered, limping alongside Arthur as she answered his question. "We don't have enough fighters to risk losing more." Grief flickered across all their faces, before she pushed ahead. "As it stands, they'll be hard pressed keeping things stable."

"Which is why you need more men," Arthur said, returning to an old argument.

"Hah! Because men are better?" Jan said, calling from behind the pair.

"No. Because men are stupider."

"Can't argue with that," Mel said, laughing a little. "But maybe you can explain your thinking?"

"Men are dumb. They'll want to protect you. They also mostly go for fighting classes. You can use them as guards, as gatherers for monster cores.

You know, all the things that are dirty, disgusting, and dangerous," Arthur said.

"Alliteration," Uswah said. "Where, exactly, did you study?"

"Government school. And under my master," Arthur replied. "He was old school. Thought we all had to be 'traditional Chinese gentlemen'."

"What does that even mean?" Mel said.

"Music, scholarship, strategy, martial arts, and painting," Uswah said.

"Technically, martial arts isn't part of the count," Arthur said, raising a finger to correct her. Uswah turned fully around and raised a single eyebrow, so he explained. "Well, it's true. Traditionally, a Chinese scholar-gentleman only needed to know the four arts. It's bad Hong Kong movies that added martial arts to it."

"Take that back," Mel said.

"What?" Arthur looked perplexed.

"There's nothing wrong with 90s Hong Kong movies. Jet Li and Stephen Chow are gods," Mel insisted.

"Wah, you really like the oldies, ah?" Jan said, looking perplexed by the entire conversation. "*Ei*, did you even watch anything new? Ben Wu is sooo much hotter."

"He's also, like, fifteen," Mel said.

"Nineteen!" Jan retorted.

"I prefer Junada Ali myself," Uswah said. "More manly."

Arthur chose to keep quiet, not seeing a point in getting involved in that discussion. Not as though he spent a lot of time looking at male celebrities. Other than to grouse and bitch about unattainable physiques for your average male.

Though, considering what he had seen in the river the last time he had looked... maybe he shouldn't complain so much. It seemed there was an alternative route to celebrities' sacrificial diets and hours of exercise. One could simply be a cultivator and achieve the same results.

Maybe he'd write a self-help tell-all when he got back...

"Your sifu got teach you Chinese?" Jan asked, interrupting his thoughts.

"English," Arthur said. "Queen's English, as he called it. You learn fast, then you have to do fifty push-ups per infraction. And he doesn't take fractions."

"Fifty push-ups!" Mel said, surprised.

"Mm-hm. We were allowed to substitute for squats, but we could only do one kind of exercise. So if you failed to do all fifty push-ups, you had to restart at one with the squats." Arthur shuddered. "Old school, you know?"

"Abuse," Jan said.

Arthur could only shrug in reply. She was not wrong, but on the other hand, it had been effective. And when you got down to it, it also meant that a large number of those he trained survived their first Tower entry. Not that his *sifu* had any desire for them to actually enter the Towers. It was one of the things he generally discouraged, even if he expected most of his students to ignore him.

And this entire conversation reminded Arthur of the one thing he hadn't done.

"Oh, I'm in so much trouble," Arthur murmured to himself. "Got to come up with an excuse on the double."

"What?" Mel asked.

"I forgot to look up my martial brothers and sisters." Scratching the side of his jaw, he shrugged. "Probably doesn't matter. "I was the last of my batch to come in. And I was a few months behind, so they've probably cleared this floor by now."

"Would we know them?" Mel said.

"Probably not. They're not really flashy," Arthur said. "They'd mostly keep their heads down. Well, except Ah Hui. He has orange hair. Or had, not sure how it'd do without his usual treatments."

"Wait. Orange hair, done up like an anime character?" Mel said, cocking her head to the side. "Uses a pair of tongfa as weapons?"

Arthur nodded.

"Well, he's definitely not here. He blew through the first level in two months, nearly a half year ago," Mel said. "Made quite a few cores in the semi-annual tournament. He was runner up. Then hid in his room until he ranked up enough to pass to the next Tower level."

"*Ya, ya*, I remember! People hate him. If he didn't leave this floor, sure *kena pukul sampai mati* already," Jan said, emphasizing her point by grinding one fist into another hand. "Your *sifu* train troublemakers, ah?"

"No way. I mean, I bet you never noticed my elder sister. She's the latest who came through, three months ago." Arthur shook his head and corrected himself. "Three months *before* I came in."

"Her name?" Mel asked.

"Claudia Wu. Long black hair, nice eyebrows, umm... about five-four?" Arthur waved his hand around the proper height. "Fights bare-handed mostly, except when she gets serious. Then she uses long knives."

"Pretty?" Mel ventured further.

Arthur shook his head and then froze, wondering what would happen if his frank assessment got back to his elder sister. Would she smack him around? Or just laugh it off, because she knew she was no actress? Then again, knowing yourself and having someone frankly assess you were entirely different things.

After all, humanity survived off its dreams and delusions. Without them, most humans could not function.

Not well, at least.

Thankfully the girls did not seem to notice. They passed looks around, but none of them recalled his sister. Which was for the best.

After all, his *sifu* would really be annoyed if they all managed to get a reputation for being difficult.

"Maybe we should just get your master to come in and teach our girls, eh?" Mel said, returning the conversation to the point. "Then we don't need more men."

"Too long. Anyway, my clan, my rules." Arthur raised his chin. "You can put together a good criterion for rejecting the idiots, but we're still taking in men." His lips thinned. "It's hard enough out there, without creating more divisions."

"And the safety of our people?" Uswah said, softly.

"Will be paramount. But we will figure out a way for everyone to be cared for. Even if we have to weigh more heavily female. To start with, at least," Arthur said.

That got some reluctant nods of agreement, which made him smile. It was going to be a long walk back, but at least he could work on convincing this group of his way of thinking before they reached the beginner village.

Though, he knew, the real fight was going to be when they finally made it back. For the final boss, Amah, awaited.

Chapter 83

The change in undergrowth as they moved out of the deep wilds was telling. From semi-regular fights with groups of first-floor monsters, the team started to see more individual groups. Over the course of the journey, wounds were healed and beast cores were used at a significant pace. Stolen bounty from the corpses of the Suey Ying tong attackers and the monsters they fought provided more than sufficient quantities for all their use.

If anything, what the group lacked was time, for they began travel early in the morning when dawn's light had begun to spread and stopped only when darkness threatened to make further travel dangerous. In the few hours of darkness they had, the group turned to cultivating, healing, and pulling refined energy to bolster their bodies.

All those resources saw a significant change in Arthur's own status. Able to do what he had set out to complete on the first floor, he refined his skill with the cultivation techniques he had purchased and increased his attribute points, pushing his reserves and comfort with his altered body to ever greater heights.

Having access to Uswah, and having her willing to answer his questions without holding back, helped him understand the new cultivation technique she had taught him. It improved his cultivation speed, leaving him with no Yang chi entering his body and causing pain or requiring purging. This change in particular was the one he most gratefully accepted.

A bare two days before they arrived at the beginner village—according to Uswah and Mel who knew the grounds surrounding the village much better than Arthur himself—he chose to survey his status once more. After all, it was about time to dedicate a point of refined energy.

Cultivation Speed: 1.23 Yin
Energy Pool: 11/15 (Yin)
Refinement Speed: 0.025
Refined Energy: 1.81 (3)

Attributes and Traits
Mind: 4
Body: 6 (Enhanced Eyesight, Yin Body)
Spirit: 5 (Sticky Energy)

Techniques
Yin Body – Cultivation Technique
Focused Strike
Accelerated Healing – Refined Energy (Grade I)
Heavenly Sage's Mischief
Refined Energy Dart

"What do you think, my drink?" Arthur asked Uswah, leaning against the tree the pair had stationed themselves at for watch that night. He was not meant to be awake at this point, having the last watch of the day; but he felt the need to commit the point now before he slept.

"Hm?"

"Enhance my Body further, or improve my Mind to keep the balance and get another trait?" Arthur said.

Uswah wrinkled her nose in thought. "If you were reaching your *second* transformation, I would say balance for sure."

Arthur nodded. Second transformation happened at the ten-point range, where your average individual was three times as strong and fast as your average mortal. Raising all three attributes to ten points each triggered the second transformation period which refined the body further, increasing an individual's strength significantly but also increasing the amount of Tower energy they needed to consume.

It was partly why certain individuals never progressed further, not wanting to be pushed too deeply into the endless grind of Tower climbing. With judicious contacts and money, it was possible to stay a low-powered cultivator in the real world. Reaching second, third, and further transformations saw a significant jump in strength but once one began that process, it was hard to stop Tower climbing in earnest.

Of course, some people had tried to game the system, building up points in one or two different attributes without crossing the threshold in other areas. In many such cases, the transformation would happen anyway. And in a few rare cases, where there was significant imbalance between cultivation techniques and the body involved, explosive and graphic endings occurred.

Often with innocent bystanders having to clean up the resulting mess.

Still, such imbalances were incredibly rare. So it was not surprising that cultivators often safely achieved second transformation with a significant difference between attribute points rather than a balanced stat allocation, since the needs of the individual—and various cultivation exercises and technique boosts—altered that equation.

Rumors were that after the second transformation, subsequent transformations were a little more arbitrary and happened at varying levels of improvement. They were roughly at the thirty-, fifty-, and one hundred-point range. Rumor also said there were up to seven levels of transformation, but threshold discussions at that level were clouded by speculation. Humanity just did not have enough cultivators at those levels to yield enough information, not even after so many years.

"Right, so not hitting my second transformation, the first threshold, and getting up there balanced, or close to balanced, isn't a horrible idea," Arthur said. "Though, I've liked having a higher Body stat. More directly impactful."

Uswah nodded.

"And there's no guarantee things are going to be quiet for the next bit," Arthur said. "Not when we get into the village. So upping my Body would be a smart thing to do. Makes me stronger, faster."

Another nod.

"But increasing my Mind will improve how fast I can think, what I notice, my refinement speed."

"Have lots of cores now."

"Those run out, though." A pause, then he tapped the pouch by his side. "I could also maybe take a trait to make better use of cores. Be a good long-term benefit."

She nodded.

"What did you take?" he asked.

Uswah just stared at Arthur, making him shrug. "I know it's rude. But you know a lot about me."

"You won't stop telling me."

"I needed to for the training!" Arthur said.

"Still."

Making a face, Arthur crossed his arms. The pair fell silent for a long time, Uswah continuing to watch the shadows, Arthur staring at her to make her crack. Eventually, she sighed.

"I took Calm Mind."

"Oooh, classic. Really fantas-tic." Arthur elongated the last vowel, just to make it rhyme before he tapped the side of his leg idly. "Our bodies..."

"It boosted the properties of the Yin chi, yes."

"Nice!"

A nod.

Arthur leaned back, rubbing his chin. "Or I could go with something social. Maybe Empath or Truth Seeking or something like that, to help me read people and social situations better. Being the Clan Head and all that."

Silence.

"But it's not much use if I'm dead. And I should try, at least, to be strong. That's what all the Clan Heads out there are, right? Guild Leaders, Clan Heads, they're all quite powerful."

"More than one kind of strength."

"Yeah, but..." Arthur paused, then shook his head. "No, you're right. I guess I just want to be strong still."

"Not wrong."

Arthur smiled at that, before he tapped the pouch by his side again. He had enough cores in there to get a second point, almost certainly. All they had to do was wait. In fact...

"Why don't we just do that?"

"Do what?" Uswah said, frowning.

"Wait a little, let me cultivate and get my second point. I can then have the best of both worlds."

"Too long. We've been gone for months," Uswah said. "Our friends are waiting."

"You all could go ahead?"

She shook her head violently at that suggestion, making Arthur raise his hands in acknowledgement. "Still, it's not even a full day. I could just refine the energy and we could delay just by a day."

"Or you could put it in Body and worry about the rest after you establish the clan," Uswah said. "You could refine in a protected place, rather than out here."

"Oh. Yeah, I guess I could do that," Arthur said. Still, while that seemed like a good idea, he had a feeling that their life was going to be significantly more complicated than just wandering in and putting up a new clan building.

Regardless, more strength was never a bad thing.

Making his decision—a decision Arthur had to admit that he probably made long before speaking with Uswah—he selected the refined energy in his body and pushed it towards his Body. Feeling it throb through him, ripping muscles and tendons apart.

Till he was stronger, faster, sturdier than ever.

Because, really, you never knew the kind of problems you could run into.

Chapter 84

The village had grown. Not the beginner village that the Tower had created, but the tent village outside that had been added on by cultivators. Permanent structures of wood and clay, and more temporary abodes of cloth and leather. The growth was subtle, but the clearing in the forest had widened. Sap was still fresh on some tree stumps, and newly trod land around the linen tents still bore grass.

The group had stopped near the clearing line, Uswah having scouted a spot that had been untouched for a few days. They hid under the shadows of the trees, watching the comings and goings in the tent village, searching for clues. Individuals lounged about, some mending holes in socks and pants, sharpening spear heads or parang edges. Others cooked food or walked between the tents, headed out to hunt or came back limping and wounded.

To Arthur, any clues were pretty obscure. He had no idea what to look for, though they had skirted around the village to the north until they were opposite the newbie teleportation squares. They were not where the Suey Ying tong was encamped, nor where the Thorned Lotuses had taken residence. Safer that way, though he wondered if it was too easy a choice.

"Doesn't look like there are watchers," Mel said finally.

"It's been months. The tong is many things, but disciplined is not one of them," Uswah said.

"But they don't forgive," Jan said.

"And Ah Choi was his brother, you said? Someone important," Arthur said softly. "Hate can go a long way."

"For a person." Mel waved a hand at the tent village before them. "For a tong? That's another story."

"So much for loyalty," Arthur said. All that for nothing, or at least, nothing to his eyes. "Now what?"

To his surprise, the group turned to stare at him. He blinked, putting a hand to his chest, before he shook his head hard. That was the point, really. He was the Clan Head, the patriarch, the crest holder. He was leader of the yet-to-be-named Clan and, at some point, he would have to make the decisions.

And it looked like that point was here.

"We go in," Arthur said decisively. "Straight, no hiding. We're just another team coming back. We don't talk to anyone we don't have to, we don't stop for any reason. We keep moving until we get into the beginner village and the administrative sector."

"And what happens if we do get stopped?" Mel said.

"We run like a nun," Arthur said curtly.

"What do you have against nuns?" Uswah asked curiously.

"Nothing. They just rhyme."

"If we can't run, *leh*?" Jan said.

"Then you buy me time. Alright, we go... in this order." He gritted his teeth, pointing to Jan, then Uswah, and then Mel.

"Me first, ah? You don't like me?" Jan said.

"I'm pretty sure you don't like me either," Arthur said, lips twisted in a wry smile. Jan just grinned. "Uswah in the lead, then. Me in the rear. Any questions?"

The group shook their heads and Arthur stood up. Uswah, without a word, led the way forward, the group trailing after her. They had their weapons slung or in their hands in the case of the spear wielders, but they looked from side to side as they meandered through the tents.

At first they garnered only cursory glances, idle curiosity. Perhaps a little more than that, what with their group looking the worse for wear compared to many of the other returnees. Their clothing was ragged, patched together with pieces of other clothing. Their weapons and other equipment looked worn down and ragged too. Dirt and an ever-persistent smell of mildew and human stench wafted from their group, a presence that Arthur only noticed when he saw others edging away.

Most of the teams that left to hunt for beast cores never ventured far. A few hours out, just distant enough to find monsters and still be able to make it back in a day. The more adventurous might stay out for a night or two, enough to build up a good hoard of cores before returning.

Only a small group of deep venturers would stay longer than that in the forest. Delving into the wilds, in search of hidden nodes, powerful monsters, and regular battles. Hunting for secrets, cultivation caves, or spirit herbs to fulfill quests.

The regular work of the ambitious and the adventurous. A world that, Arthur mused, he had missed out entirely with his own uncommon journey. He could say, without fear, that he had seen deeper into the forest and fought more than most first-level dwellers.

And yet, he had almost no knowledge of the culture of the world he had stepped into. Except for any knowledge gleaned from forum posts and autobiographies. Which was a thing.

"To the left." Uswah's voice cut through his musings and spiralling doubts, forcing Arthur to glance over. Four men, angling towards them. Probably not Suey Ying since all four men were Malay. Still a gang of some form, though Arthur could not guess if they were part of a greater organization. When in doubt...

"How much of a problem?" he asked.

"They might be part of the Double Sixes," Mel said.

"I go talk, lah," Jan said. She hurried past to meet the incoming quartet, holding her hands sideways to show she had no weapons. And also, Arthur noted, blocking their way. Politely, of course, what with being outnumbered.

Uswah, meanwhile, had sped up, forcing Arthur to hurry to keep up. Their hurried movements would force the Double Sixes to cut backwards a little from where they had come if they wanted to intervene.

On the other hand, the Double Sixes had stopped in their tracks, thanks to Jan. She was flashing some beast cores at them in one hand, speaking rapidly in Manglish.

Bribery. Always a useful tool in Malaysia.

Chapter 85

Glancing over his shoulder, Arthur saw Jan in a serious talk with the four men now. She was pulling more cores from her pouch, leaning in, and speaking animatedly, her words drowned out by distance and the din of the tent village around them.

Mel, behind him, caught Arthur's eyes and jerked her chin forward. When Arthur nearly tripped from trying to watch Jan, she spoke curtly: "You said it. Keep moving." Seeing the pursing lips, she added, "Trust us."

Twisting his head around to fix his gaze forward, a part of him wondering why he gave a damn about the verbally abusive, grumpy woman who had threatened to kill him multiple times. He kept moving, though, dodging around strung tent lines as he followed Uswah toward the beginner village's threshold.

Maybe caring, whether it was smart or not, was part of the human condition. The same reason why parents could not give up children spiraling into drugs or crime, or why lovers lingered, caring for terminally ill partners. Caring, even when it was not smart or logical, separated humanity from beasts. And machines.

"Left. Again." Uswah's voice cut in, making Arthur search for the incoming threat.

He found them after a bit, the group of a half dozen men bearing in on them. White singlets or T-shirts, with khaki shorts. Parangs in hand, death and mayhem in their eyes. The leader, a familiar-looking face, had his eyes locked on Arthur, idly striking an innocent who had scrambled out of the way too slowly.

No. Not eyes on him. But on the kris he carried.

"Shit. Suey Ying, right?" Arthur said, speeding up. He was not running, not yet. Mostly because the other party was not running. Yet, he wondered if it was time to do so.

"My turn," Uswah said. She gestured with her free hand, the stump on the other arm moving at the same time to mimic the motion. Shadows cast by nearby began to move, twist, and solidify; they grasped and tripped three of the Suey Ying thugs.

As though her attack was a signal, the tong members unleashed a wordless roar and charged. They tried to keep to a single line, but an unseen tent string caught one man, sent him sprawling onto the side of a tent. He crashed down hard, bouncing off the ground, and a bystander outside spun around, hand falling to the knife by his side as he roared, "My tent!"

Even then, there were five more coming at him. Arthur took off, sprinting for all he was worth as he sought to cross the distance to safety. Uswah stayed behind, her face furrowed in concentration as she attempted to slow the group down with her shadow skills.

Arthur pelted ahead, knowing better than to look back or sideways. Not with the number of impediments in the way. He ran, the extra point in Body showcasing its effects. He was faster than ever, his feet digging into the dirt, his eyes picking out motion in his peripheral vision and ahead of him. He jumped, instinctively, leaping over a spear that emerged from a tent, skipped around a thin fishing line that had been used to work down a peg. He skidded around another tent that had been plonked in the middle of the walkway, leapt over the cooking fire without hesitation and nearly kicked the cook in the face.

Chased by the cries of the outraged, Arthur ran. His spear was held over his shoulder, slowing him down, threatening to get tangled. Cursing his choice of weapon, he still kept hold of it, leery of losing his own defense.

"Spear!" A roar from behind him, a woman's familiar voice. Instinct, honed over weeks working together, entrusting his life to them and theirs to him, kicked in. He tossed the spear backwards. Trusting that she would catch it.

Of course, Arthur being Arthur, he could not help but add: "Dear!"

Then he ducked his head low and kept running, even as he heard Mel's footsteps slow and then come to a stop. She was going to block the way, to buy him time.

Ahead of him, the threshold. The beginner village. Wooden buildings, manufactured by the Tower rose from the perimeter. A Tower guard, moving with the eerie grace of the unnatural, patrolled the boundary. A crowd of cultivators formed in front, slowing him down. Curiosity in their eyes, innocent in their motives.

Mostly.

Barreling forwards, hands stretched outwards, he swam through the group. Shoving and pulling, intent on not losing any of his momentum.

Ten meters.

Eight.

He could hear the shouts, the grumpy noises. Feel how the crowd parted behind him as he pushed through, curiosity making them turn.

Five.

He could almost taste freedom now. Then, louder shouts from behind him. Cries of pain, of surprise, the bellowing shouts of a man for the crowd to part or suffer. Arthur pushed faster, forced to shove and elbow, to tear a tent peg out as his foot got caught by an unseen line.

Slowed down. But making his way.

Three.

A hand, unseen, gripped his elbow. He let the hand grab it, but twisted his body to slam into someone's ample stomach. Then he swung the knuckles of his hand upwards, crushing a nose. Not enough to kill, just enough to bloody a nose and cut his own hand on dirty teeth.

But it was enough to make the other let go.

Two meters.

He could do this. Breath coming harsh, sweaty bodies around him. He felt the pressure lighten up behind him, could almost sense the crowd parting. And then, suddenly, no one was trying to block his way.

One meter.

He jumped forward, giving up dignity. He hit the ground ahead of him, rolled and came up, spun around as fast as he could so he could see who was coming for him, even as he kicked backwards, backpedaling.

Wanting to get as far into the safe space as possible.

Only to blink and realise that he had that space. A few meters outside the boundary, the same eyeballing crowd had stymied his pursuers.

Arthur could almost laugh. If not for the cries of pain and surprise, the way the crowd was backing away as his pursuer was revealed.

Just one man. Just the one who had glared at him, looking at the kris he had sheathed.

Arthur kept moving back, then found himself bumping into a wooden building. The wall of one of the permanent establishments. It didn't matter, he was inside the zone.

"Stop! You coward. Thief." The voice that erupted from the glaring man was familiar, having shouted imprecations and orders for the crowd behind. The voice of one used to being listened to.

Arthur looked sideways, spotted the edge of the wall, and kept creeping that way. The guards might put an end to any fight, but if he was killed before they arrived... well, he was dead. What did it matter what happened to his assailant then?

"I said stop!" The man was inside the threshold, unhindered. The crowd was behind, watching. All curious.

Bloody rubberneckers.

"Yeah, yeah. I'm here, aren't I?" Arthur said, hands held out in front of him and sideways. Just far enough that he could block, if he had to. No weapon in hand, though. Then again, neither did his opponent. But that didn't mean Arthur was out of danger.

"Where you get that kris, ah?" the man snarled.

"What's it to you?" Arthur asked, still edging for the corner of the building and the road beyond.

"It's mine." A hand raised, beckoning to Arthur. "Give it. Or else I take it."

"We're in the beginner zone."

"You not gonna stay here forever."

"No, but maybe for a day!" Arthur half-sung, then sighed. Of course no one knew that song either. Wait. Did that rubbernecker grin?

Nice!

"Are you stupid?" the man said.

"Of course I am. I'm an Ascender." Arthur smiled, his back foot no longer finding the wall. He had a way out. "I'll think about it. Just, let me see the admins first."

The man snorted, gesturing to the side and backwards. "Ei. I tell you: We got all your little *kawan*."

Arthur froze then.

"You don't give me the kris and tell me *what happened* to my brother... I will cut them up in front of you." He suddenly grinned wide. "Send you present every day. One finger. One toe."

"You wouldn't."

"I will. So, boy. How?"

Chapter 86

"Who the hell are you?" Arthur could not help but ask, staring at the man. They had less than a dozen feet separating them, a short enough distance that either one could have jumped at the other and struck out. Yet the presence of the patrolling guards, the knowledge they would be killed for breaking the peace, stymied physical violence.

Leaving only the verbal and emotional. The truly dangerous, painful ones being wielded. Now it was a battle of threats.

"You don't know me? Hah! Maybe that's why you dare steal from me. I'm Boss Choi." Smacking his chest, he leaned forwards. "How you get my kris?"

"Picked it up along the way," Arthur said blithely. He let his hand fall onto the hilt, running a finger along the filigreed handle, feeling the carvings of the wooden hilt pressing into his bare fingertips. The cold of the metal and the enchantments pulled away at his Yin-dulled body heat.

"Don't *lie*."

Arthur shrugged. He kept his left hand turned away a little, fist clenched to hide the seal. Not that it was easy to spot, not with the bandage he'd wrapped around it, stained with dirt and blood. He knew better than to allow such information to escape, and the simple bandage was both innocuous and practical.

"Okay. You don't answer me, I cut answers out from your little friends," Boss Choi said, grinning.

"You do that, you declare war with the Thorned Lotuses." Arthur's voice was cold.

To his surprise, Boss Choi just laughed. When he finally stopped and noted Arthur's puzzled mien, he shook his head. "Ants. I can crush them anytime."

"But why start a fight you don't need. Let them go. We can discuss the return of your kris. For a suitable reward," Arthur offered the man a tight smile. Maybe playing mercenary might work here. He certainly wasn't giving away the powerful weapon for nothing. Not when, he knew, they'd be warring with one another anyway after Boss Choi learned what happened to his brother.

"No bargaining. You give it back and tell me where is my brother."

"I told you, I picked this up," Arthur said.

"You lie again, and I start cutting fingers," Boss Choi snarled.

Arthur surveyed the crowd of onlookers behind the thug. Some looked disgusted, others a little embarrassed that they were not saying or doing anything to stop this. Mostly though, they just looked curious.

The Tower was a hard place, and whilst torture was uncommon, most knew better than to get involved in other people's business. Better to focus on themselves and their own survival. Or end up floating down the river, a kris shoved in their back.

No help from there then.

Also, no sign of his friends. Captured or not.

"Why should I believe you've got my friends?" Arthur said, branded fist closing and opening in nervousness. Could he risk it? Would he risk it?

"I no lie lah, not like you." Smirking, Boss Choi took a step forward, only for Arthur to back off two steps. He stopped, eyes narrowing. "Lying is bad, for us leaders."

"Tell that to our politicians," Arthur muttered.

"We are cultivators. Better than any politicians," Boss Choi snapped. "You can say I lying. But you run, and I hurt them. And then, I'll get my kris. And the truth."

Commotion, from the crowd. Arthur's eyes narrowed, seeing a guard turn the corner, moving towards the two. He hesitated for a fraction of a second. Could he, would he, wait? Give up the kris, solidify the enmity?

Or do what he had said he would do. He had ordered.

When put that way, what other choice was there?

He turned and ran as the guard approached, chased by the shouts and curses of Boss Choi. It was time to get this done.

And trust in his team.

"Lai Tai Kor!" Arthur skidded into the room, sling-shooting himself through the door with one outstretched hand as he waved the other maniacally. He barged right past the queue of beginners, more than a few glaring at him. Attendant Lai was busy working with a customer, but he looked up at being called.

"Who... oh, you!" Attendant Lai exclaimed in surprise, as Arthur pelted forward.

Before Arthur could speak, he found a hand landing on his shoulder, pushing him back. The man who had just been served growled at Arthur, breathing right into his face, which made Arthur flinch. Someone needed some fresh mint gum.

"Eh. You doing what? Go line up, lah," the customer barked.

"I got to ask him a question." Fishing into his pouch, Arthur grabbed a small handful of beast cores and shoved the handful into the customer's chest. Automatically grabbing at the sharp objects, the man's jaw dropped as he stared at the handful of cores, then bent over quickly to snatch at the couple that had slipped his fingers and bounced on the ground. Already, others were diving to grab at the cores, forcing him to pay attention to the potential thieves rather than Arthur.

"I see you've done well," Attendant Lai said.

"After traipsing through hell." Arthur paused, then inclined his head. "But I have got something important to ask. And register." He hesitated for a second and clenched the fist of his bandaged left hand. The knowledge would escape soon enough, no matter what he did. Might as well go on as he meant to. "But I need you to tell me how to do something."

"Of course. That's my job."

"How do I register this?" Yanking the bandage off, which tore at his skin a little, he opened his fingers wide to display the clan brand on his skin.

"Is that—it is!" Jaw dropping low, Attendant Lai leaned forward and grabbed at Arthur's hand greedily, peering closely. "This is real? Because I tell you, if you are trying to cheat..."

"It's real."

"*Taai si. Hou taai si.*"

"I know. Now, how do I register this?"

The attendant frowned, before he inclined his head. "One second. This... I can't do. I'll get someone who can."

Arthur nodded, and Lai waved a hand behind the desk. Then, shooting one last incredulous look at Arthur's still extended hand, he hurried away, stopping only long enough to speak briefly to a guard that had appeared from another room before moving deeper into the clan center.

Leaving Arthur to stand alone, watched by the suddenly very curious group of cultivators. Many who were now eyeing him with significant, predatory interest.

Chapter 87

Shifting from foot to foot impatiently, Arthur let his gaze bounce from individual to individual. Not long afterwards, Boss Choi had made his way in, glaring at Arthur. Now that he was forced to wait, along with many others already crowding the registration hall, he realised that Boss Choi was significantly shorter than he had appeared. Presence of body had made him seem taller, but standing next to the others here, Arthur pegged him as no more than five four at most.

"Small man attitude. Shit," Arthur said to himself under his breath.

Further musings were interrupted, as the man he had bribed to take his place came up to Arthur. Unlike Boss Choi, he was on the larger side, over six feet tall and built like a gym bro. Broad chest, muscular shoulders, and even an enlarged neck. So much so that Arthur almost asked if he was on steroids.

"*Ei*, you. What's that?" He gestured at Arthur's branded hand.

"None of your business," Arthur said.

"Ohhh. Something important, huh? Something dangerous? Get you in trouble?" the man said.

"Maybe."

Turning his head slowly and obviously, his gaze trekked towards Boss Choi who was glaring at Arthur. Then, the gym bro turned his gaze back to Arthur. "Maybe. Hah."

"So what?" Arthur said, lifting his chin. "I'm safe here." A nod to the guard who was standing by silently, watching over the proceedings.

"Here. But not outside, right?" For a second, the other man hesitated before he thrust his hand out. "My friends call me Yao Jing."

"Arthur." Shaking Yao Jing's hand, he let it go once he could, casting a glance for the attendant. Nothing yet. "I didn't think we were friends."

"Well, my new boss also can call me that," Yao Jing said, crossing his arms and subtly flexing his muscles.

"Boss?" Snapping his head around, attention fully focused, Arthur stared at the man. "What?"

"I smell opportunity. Real good one." Yao Jing tapped his nose. "So I want to get in, early."

"And what, exactly, do I need you for?" Arthur said.

"I think it's obvious."

Arthur eyed the muscular man. "Fine. You can be in. Though this might become a whole... *thing*."

"Okay, got it." Yao Jing looked at Boss Choi, his lips curling up in a sneer. "They don't scare me. Not one bit."

"Problem is, it's not just one person, you know?"

"If you mean the tong—" Yao Jing started, only to find that Arthur had spun around, his eyes entirely focused on Attendant Lai, who had stepped in with another man, the most beautiful individual he had ever seen, his skin tan and dark, his nose perfectly proportioned.

"Cultivator Chua. I was wondering when you would arrive. Some almost thought you had been lost to us already," the man said, taking a position behind the counter beside Lai.

"Not lost, not at all. Just got here," Arthur bowed. "And you are?"

"Cultivator Ibrahim. I'm the head attendant on this floor."

"Arthur Chua. A pleasure to meet you," Arthur said.

"Is it, really?" Ibrahim laughed. Arthur shivered, for there was something dangerous in that laugh. "An interesting weapon that you carry there, by your side." A head lowered, indicating the kris Arthur kept.

"I... just something I picked up," Arthur said, glancing over to where Boss Choi still stood.

Ibrahim's eyes flicked over to where the short man stood, a smile dancing on his lips. "Well, if you find that it is something you might want to put down... I am a collector of sorts."

"Thank you. I'll keep that in mind," Arthur said, shifting uneasily. Small talk was all well and good and important, but he could not help but remember the threat that Boss Choi had leveled. Even if the man was here, rather than outside torturing his friends, Arthur could not help but hope to get this done quick.

After all, he had the entire thing hovering over his head for weeks now. With the final finishing line in sight, he wanted—no, he needed it—finished.

Ibrahim gave a small, disquieting smile at seeing Arthur's impatience. Holding out his hand, he spoke. "Now, the clan seal?"

Low gasps from those around, even Yao Jing's eyes widening ever further. Arthur ignored it all, only noting that Boss Choi had tried to move closer and been blocked by Yao Jing.

Arthur focused on raising his branded hand, offering the seal to the head attendant. The moment Ibrahim gripped his arm, though, the seal began to glow and warm, heating up until it hurt. He hissed as the pain increased with each second before the clan seal burst into life, a projection of the seal rotating in the air itself.

Arthur blinked. The details of the seal—unnamed, unregistered—were revealed to everyone. Ibrahim stared at the information before he snorted. Further energy was pushed into his hand and Arthur hissed, and a new prompt appeared in his head.

"Name your clan," Ibrahim said.

"I..." Arthur hesitated. "Is the rest of the information going to show? When I make my choices?"

"Of course not. But the registration of a clan, that is public. That will change the Tower," Ibrahim said. "That is what we will do publicly, for the world will know. Every clan might change the Tower and see our dreams come true."

"Dreams?" Arthur said.

"Your clan. Name it."

Arthur paused, options whirling through his mind. It was not the first time he had considered what he would name his clan. The obvious was to name it the Thorned Lotuses, to give back to them that had given him so much. Yet, that brought with it a whole series of concerns about branding.

How many, knowing what the Lotuses were right now, would still join them? How many enemies would they gain, just by naming themselves after that organisation?

Better to begin anew.

He'd played with other ideas, common childish naming conventions. Tigers and dragons, lions and cranes, storks, pigs, sharks, and salmon. Animals of all kinds, combined with other variations of precious metals or colours or fortuitous numbers. The Red Eights. The Black Tortoises. Jade Dragons.

All too much for someone like him. And maybe he could have switched to a different language, but he was still most comfortable in English and...

"Your clan name, Cultivator."

A pulse of energy, pain tearing at his spinning thoughts. He heard a noise, Boss Choi shouting at him, even as the guard moved to kick him out for being disruptive.

But a name, perhaps a silly one, but all too true to who he was, clarified in his mind.

He spoke, and the words appeared as a notification in the air by his projected seal.

"The Benevolent Durians."

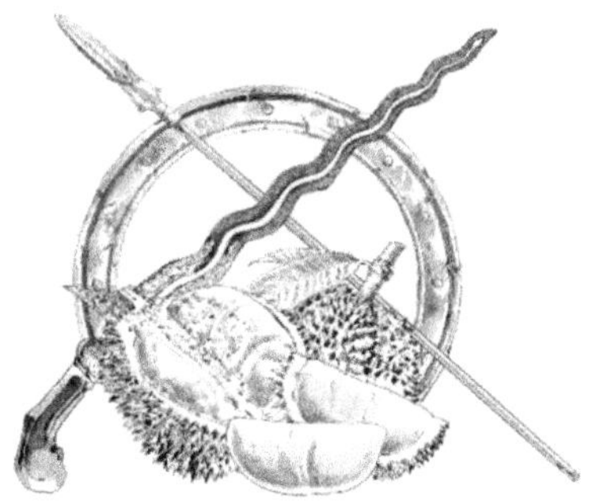

Chapter 88

Laughter. A lot of it. His hand released, Arthur staggered back, even as Head Attendant Ibrahim, Master of the First Floor stared up at the fading clan name and could not help but shake his head ruefully.

"Benevolent Durians?" Ibrahim said. "That is... new. And unusual. I must ask, for my own curiosity. Why name it that?"

"Yeah, boss. I'm not sure I wanna be called a durian," Yao Jing said.

"Why not? The King of Fruits and utterly delicious—if you have the taste for it," Arthur said. "And if not, well, repellent enough to drive away those who aren't right anyway. An acquired taste, much like me. Also, hard bodied and spiky, powerfully protective for those seeds it contains within."

Yao Jing sniffed. "I... whatever. It's just a name, right?"

He still sounded dubious, but with Boss Choi having been kicked out, Arthur had no time to deal with the man's concerns. He had friends to care for.

"I need to finish this," Arthur said. "The building for the sect: where do I, how do I, designate it?"

Ibrahim's hand rose and flicked to life a map of the beginner village. "You don't mind that we do this part publicly, no? After all, your clan hall will be public."

Arthur shook his head. The wireframe diagram of the beginner village hovered above him. A half dozen buildings glowed orange. There were scattered throughout the village, about four of them near the center of the village. Two of them were right next to the administrative building itself.

"Choosing here doesn't lock me up, right? Beyond this floor that is," Arthur said.

Ibrahim shook his head.

There was no real difference in the buildings, all of them roughly the same size. All three floors tall, all roughly with the same design: either old-school office buildings or hotels, sporting many windows. He spun his finger around, checking them out one after the other and noted two of the closer ones were actual office buildings. The third, a motel.

His choice of clan name hadn't taken his allies' opinions into account, but now he considered what they wanted, what they needed. He tapped on the motel, amused by the way the entire wireframe worked. Then, he hesitated, unsure what to do.

"Pour your energy into it. Intention is enough, the Tower will do the rest," Ibrahim said, as though he read his mind.

Arthur followed his instructions, hands raised as he poured energy into the wireframe construct. He watched as the orange glow deepened, then solidified. A moment later, he felt something snap together, connecting his building—and it was his now—to his seal and something deeper. It felt part of him, a connection that ran through his entire body but also out of it.

His soul perhaps, or whatever it was that connected him to the Tower and that provided his status. Arthur could not say for sure, but he felt the connection, the same way he could feel where his status was, whenever he wanted to bring it forth.

A moment later, that connection stabilised entirely. He got his second notification of the day, after the Tower had prompted him to name his clan.

This one was longer, more detailed, and he knew, as the wireframe disappeared from above him, that no one else but him saw it.

Objective Complete: Clan Building Selected
Building Type: Residential
Residence Bonuses Available: Guardian, Security, Recuperation, Adventure
Do you wish to select your residential bonuses now?

On top of that selection, Arthur could feel additional choices waiting for him. He debated answering no, but considering what he intended for his residence, the enemies he had made, the option seemed pretty clear to him. Selecting a security bonus, Arthur's eyes widened.

Residential Bonus Selected: Security.
Tower has assigned one Tower Guard to your residence at this time.
Additional security benefits available as Clan grows in strength.

"That's... surprising," Arthur muttered.

"What?" Yao Jing asked.

"We got a Tower guard assigned to our building. No one's going to be bursting in anytime soon. Not without becoming a misting," Arthur said. The rhyme didn't work, but it got the idea across.

He wondered if that meant that all first-floor guards would be alerted if things went bad. That would be amazing. Even if they didn't, a single guard was more than sufficient. They were a little overpowered for their floors after all.

Shaking his head, ignoring the implications for now, he let the other notifications that had been waiting pop up. All the while looking at Ibrahim, who was in turn watching with a little amused smile on his face.

"Hey, can I ask a question?"

"Of course, Clan Head Chua."

Arthur hesitated at the new form of address before pushing it aside. Not the time. "How do I add people to my clan?"

"You need only inform the Tower. The same way you did before, with the naming of your clan."

Nodding at Ibrahim, Arthur considered asking if he needed to be in proximity to would-be clan members, but chose instead to simply try it out. Better to learn by doing than rely on the head attendant. After all, the man was stupidly powerful. No need to act dumber in front of him than Arthur needed to.

Yao Jing, standing before him, was a good first option. Yet, he hesitated. If there was someone who needed and deserved this, it was Mel. To his surprise, he felt the Tower answer him, a new notification superseding the previous ones that were on their way.

A Party Has Been Detected. Would you like to extend Clan membership invitations to current party members? Current party members include:

- *Mel*
- *Jan*
- *Uswah*

Arthur blinked, staring at the information. Then he grinned. Creepy and Orwellian as the damn Tower might be, sometimes it worked in his favour. In this case, pulling information from his mind.

Approval flowed through his mind and up the link to the Tower. He felt the Tower's confirmation, and even more strangely, a connection that reached outward from himself—three connections. It gave him no information, but feeling those connections was itself enough to make him shiver.

"Ei, what's wrong?" Yao Jing said.

Eyes tracking over to the man, Arthur hesitated. He knew nothing about the other. Had no idea if he could kick him out, how much information he would give away by making him a clan member. Adding him to the clan could be extremely foolish.

But there had to be ways to remove someone from a clan. And though paranoia said that Yao Jing could be a plant, a spy... paranoia was just that. Irrational fear. Logically, it would have taken a level of planning and chance that defied even a Bond villain to put the man where he was.

Which meant that he might just be what he looked. A mercenary looking for a way up. An opportunistic individual. And...

"Don't get the wrong idea, ya," Yao Jing said, eyes narrowing a little. "I don't swing that way, okay. Nothing wrong with that, of course." He gestured quickly, intent on not getting into trouble. The number of gays and other individuals indulging in "alternate lifestyles" in the Tower were well known to be at a higher percentage than outside, where they were still prosecuted by the Malaysian government. "… But that's just not for me. Yah?" Yao Jing finished.

"Not that, you idiot." Sometimes, you just had to take a leap of faith. And if not, well, there really wasn't much that was going to be revealed that wouldn't be. Eventually. "Here," Arthur said.

And with that, a fourth—fifth, if he counted himself—member was added to the Benevolent Durians clan.

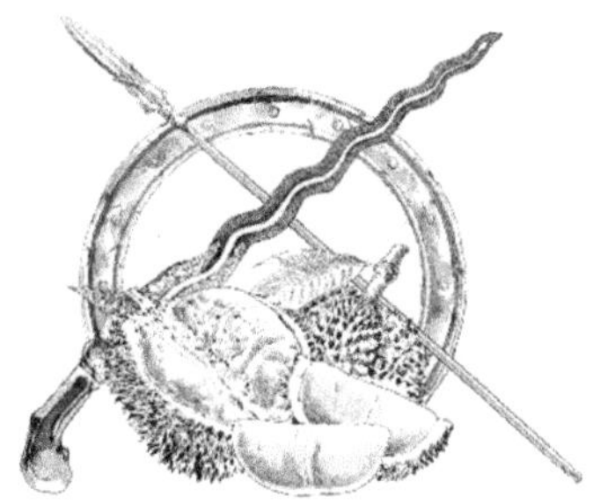

Chapter 89

"Waaah," Yao Jing whispered, staring into space as he received and accepted the invitation to membership.

In the meantime, Arthur turned away, the Tower notifications burning in his mind. He knew that they needed answering, and soon. His left hand had begun to burn again, the seal throbbing against his flesh.

"Is there a private room I can use?" he asked. "Somewhere... private?" Words eluded him.

Smirking, Head Attendant Ibrahim turned to his assistant Lai and nodded. The crowd, so intent on watching them thus far let out a disappointed sigh when Lai gestured for Arthur to follow him. Together, the pair—for Yao Jing was quick to follow—moved after the attendant, skirting around the counter to head behind the scenes into a nearby meeting room.

"I'll bring some water. Though, I would not overstay your welcome," the attendant said, before he shut the door on the pair.

Arthur flopped himself into a nearby chair, managing to blurt out a command to Yao Jing to watch the door, before he gave in to the pressing notifications. He knew that if he kept them away any longer, the Tower would have extracted its own pound of flesh.

Benevolent Durian Clan Has Been Formed
Organisational Ranking: 182,771
Number of Towers Occupied: 1
Number of Clan Buildings: 1
Number of Clan Members: 5
Overall Credit Rating: F-

"Harsh! F rank is not great for the bank," Arthur said as he read the notification. What the heck was a credit rating and why did the Tower inform him of that? He could have understood a star rating—the outside world used that to rank most of the guilds and clans—but a credit rating?

He shook his head after a moment, discarding the thought. It was another mystery to plumb the depths of later. Right now, he was driven by an urgent request to let additional notifications appear, as well as concern over his friends—and yes, that even included Jan.

Clan Building Established in Floor 1 of Tower 2895 by Benevolent Durians
Requirements Met for Completion of Clan Activation
A Founding Aspect May Be Chosen.
Aspect Choices:

- *Safety*
- *Guardianship*
- *Recuperation*
- *Courage*
- *Adventure*

"What the hell is Adventure?" This was the second time he was seeing it. It annoyed Arthur that there was so little information provided. And somehow, he was supposed to make a choice that would define his clan forever. "I swear, if there's no do-over button somewhere, I'm going to be pissed."

There hadn't been one thus far. Maybe it was some weird Tower metaphor for life: you rarely got a chance to do over your mistakes. You made choices and lived with them. If they weren't perfect, you made do.

For that matter, wasn't that the purpose of life? Making do with whatever hellscape fate had thrown you in? To Arthur, hell was growing up now instead of a hundred years ago, when the world was still bright and shiny and the economies of the world had yet to be taken over by nearly-intelligent robots and automated factories. Back then smart cars were smart enough to drive you everywhere but not smart enough to recognise that your average monkey was going to yeet a rock at you, just because it could.

Speaking of wild monkeys, the number of stray dogs and cats had increased vastly, finding food among the improperly packed dumpsters now serviced by automated garbage trucks that had not the sense to clean things up before turning the world over.

At one point, Malaysia—and the whole world, really—had been a bright shining oyster. And then all the world's birds came home to roost, often in climate-changed deserts that had never been there before, and now they paid humans to just exist, calling it Universal Basic Income or the like. Magical, perhaps alien, Towers stood above them all, offering the only promise of salvation or escape.

He sent a mental prod, only to find that the Tower had no answer for him as to what an Adventure aspect was. Somehow, he had expected that, but he still tried it on all the other Aspects in a vague hope that it was an error. Unsurprisingly, no response. All he could read about the Aspects were their single-word names.

Once again, Arthur felt entirely out of his depth. He had probed Mel for everything she knew, but that had been rather sparse as well. No one had expected to need information on how to set up or run a clan or guild. It was so far outside expectations for your average cultivator that it might as well have been like attempting to catch the jade rabbit on the moon.

Which meant that whatever information Mel had was cobbled together from vague memories, occasional comments on forum posts, and a basic primer about what clans and guilds were for. None of which was particularly useful in setting one up.

In the end, all Arthur could do was go with his gut and his intention. In some way, he wondered if that was the entire point of giving so little information. Maybe the Tower wanted cultivators to focus on big-picture concepts and desires, rather than attempting to min-max their system.

That is, if the Tower or its creators even had specific desires and plans.

Arthur knew his mind was bouncing around to simply put off making the decision. He should be attempting to analyze the names of the Aspects to work out their subtle nuances. But how much could you analyze with a single word? Obviously, Guardianship meant more protective works, which marked it different than Security, which likely meant a way to safeguard oneself rather than others. And Recuperation was likely some form of healing or recovery, perhaps useful for those with a medical background.

Nothing about money here. But so far he had been led to believe that many of the choices offered now were determined partially by the choices he had made before. A hotel with Security as its first Aspect might offer different options than an office building. Arthur wondered if he should have picked a different building. Maybe he would have been offered an Aspect that helped generate income?

He liked money, but Arthur had always believed that so long as one survived and moved on, chances to find and grow one's wealth would always appear.

Still, some of the options left him puzzled. What did Courage do? Was it a boost to mental willpower? Did it perhaps make risky cultivation techniques easier to learn or even available via the Tower? Did it increase the chances of meeting powerful monsters on a floor, with the resulting benefit of stronger cores?

Adventure at least made some sort of sense, if one considered his most recent, well, adventure. Was it one of those Aspects that subtly influenced how the Tower offered quests or guided cultivators? If so, it could be both a boon and a bane at the same time.

As the saying went—one wrongly ascribed to the Chinese—interesting times were almost always a curse.

"Boss?" Yao Jing called out, pulling Arthur from another damn random thought.

"Just thinking. Big decision."

"From now on, boss, you gonna make a lot of big decisions. You know what? Best thing is: Just get it over. That's what I always say."

"No thinking, no consideration?" Arthur said, amused.

"The heavens like to give us a good kick in the butt," Yao Jing, "No matter what you choose, you're gonna make mistakes sometimes. Better to make a lot of decisions, then maybe more will be good ones."

"You're the kind who never studied for their exams, eh?"

"Yup. My mum always angry with me," Yao Jing said, grinning. "But I got better things to do."

Arthur snorted. But Yao Jing was right. At least, in saying that Arthur had a lot of other big decisions to make. And this one, it needed making fast. He kept forgetting—or ignoring—the threat that Boss Choi had leveled. So. If he could make a choice, for now and forever... if he wanted something for the Clan, for himself...

He'd choose a world that was better. For him, and others.

Guardianship.

When his decision flowed up the connection to the Tower, he felt it snap into place. And his palm, his body, electrified. Down his palm, into his soul, and then outward to all the other clan members.

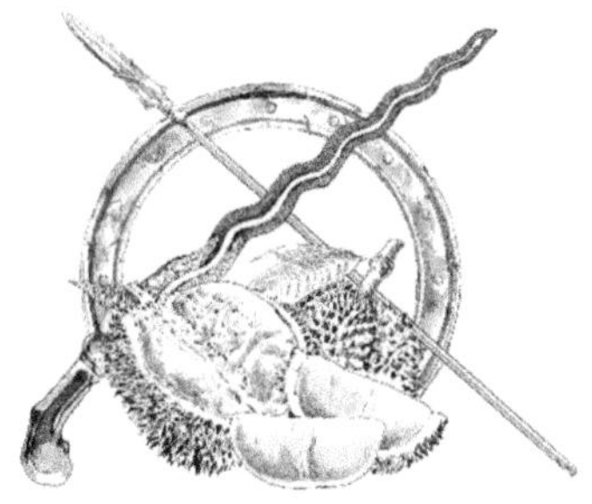

Chapter 90

Aspect Chosen: Guardianship
Five Clan Members Located
Applying Aspect Effects to Clan Head and all Clan Members
Aspects Being Applied. Please Hold.

The words flickered past Arthur's gaze, too fast for him to truly read them. Instead, his body arched as he felt pain pour through him, his teeth gritting harder than ever as the Tower reached within him and altered...

Something.

He could not, now or in the future, put a finger on it. It went deeper than the physical and was more intense than even the alteration of his body to that of a cultivator. That first alteration, when he had entered the Tower, had just been physical and preparation for ongoing evolution as he drew in power from the world of the Tower.

This time it was not just physical but within the mind and soul itself, a pouring of power that altered not just who he was but how he interacted with the world. It was closer to the Yin Body alteration. The pain swept through him, encompassing all that he was, and then left, leaving him panting.

When he managed to recover enough to look over at Yao Jing, he found the big man slumped against the door, his eyes a little glassy. However, the man looked a little better off than he did. Arthur wondered if that was because he handled the pain better or if he had received a smaller dose of the change, what with being only a clan member and not the Clan Head.

That thought brought with it a new notification, details about the Aspect's recent addition.

Aspect of Guardianship Chosen
Aspect Bonuses Applied

- *Minor increase in effectiveness of protective, healing, and shielding cultivation techniques.*
- *Trivial increase in effectiveness of precision, speed, and bonding cultivation techniques.*
- *Variable increase in cultivation and refinement speed dependent upon the number of Clan Members within close proximity.*
- *Tower Quest types have been expanded.*

Share Aspect Bonuses with Clan by default?

"That's... a thing," Arthur said, with surprise. He was not entirely sure how he felt about the bonuses, couldn't even say if it was good or bad. However, the benefits for protective, healing, or shielding techniques were nice. He didn't have protective or shielding techniques, but his Accelerated Healing technique would certainly benefit.

And more speed was never a bad thing. As for bonding techniques, they could be useful. Certainly more than one cultivator had bonded with spirit animals, using them to gain significant power. There were disadvantages, though, what with having to feed and share beast cores, slowing down the cultivator's progress. On top of that, the bonded pair often took characteristics from one another.

Still, the trivial increase in effectiveness probably meant it didn't matter much. Of course, the entire thing about their Clan being ranked so low, and having such a bad rating might mean that they could, eventually strengthen that Aspect.

Certainly, the growth and synergy of additional Aspects and Sigils were a known factor even to him. Of course, it was more a discussion of the strengthened perks of being in a Clan, along with the varying degrees of strength an individual could get depending on their rank within the Clan.

"No ranks, or designation of ranks," Arthur muttered as he acceded to the sharing of the aspect bonuses clan-wide and dismissed the latest notification. At least, not yet. Somehow, he had the sense that there were none to offer.

Not yet at least.

Which kind of made sense, what with there being only five people in the entire clan. He had thought there might be a rank for the person in charge of this floor's clan building, but perhaps there were other requirements they had not met.

"Is this real, boss?" Yao Jing said, drawing Arthur's attention back to the present.

"The Aspect bonuses?" Arthur said. "Of course. Why wouldn't it be?"

"I mean, I offered to be your bodyguard and then—boom! I get all this bonus."

"It's for everyone." Arthur gestured with his open hand, even as he extended his own senses to that weird connection he had to the Tower. It felt more prominent now, as though getting a clan seal and activating it had made the invisible connection more visible. Perhaps that feeling of connection would fade, now that the Tower was done altering him so violently. "We're kind of focusing on being the good guys," Arthur said. "Protecting people, that kind of thing."

"Like, ah, white knights?" Yao Jing rubbed his nose. "Okay. Better than being a bastard, I guess. Though less profit."

Arthur snorted. "If we get good at protecting people, maybe we can work that out too. Lots of merchant clans out there, you know."

Yao Jing grinned at that. "Oooh, I like it."

Arthur smiled in grim amusement. That grin disappeared the next moment when Yao Jing continued.

"But what do you mean 'us'? I thought it was just you and me, boss." Yao Jing tapped his chest. "Also, this connection thing feels sooo weird."

"We have other members. People in my party." He hesitated for a second before continuing to explain. "All members of the Thorned Lotuses. In fact, they're going to be our main allies and clan members."

"Nice! Real ladies' man, ah?" Then Yao Jing frowned. "Unless they're the ones that don't like men. The angry type."

Arthur could not help but snort. He had heard of them: they were said to be lesbians, as well as men-haters. Mel and Jan had both brought up that faction within the Lotuses as a potential problem, since Arthur wanted to integrate men into the Durians.

Not to say all lesbians hated men; Arthur wasn't that ignorant to think so. But that faction banded together and...

"Not right now," he said, more to himself than Yao Jing. "We got to go save them. My party, that is. Boss Choi threatened to torture and kill them. I figured if I could create this clan, we could get more help to stop him."

"And boost your friends, right?" Yao Jing said, grinning. "Smart."

"Yeah, that too." Arthur shook his head. "I don't know how much it'll help, but it has to be worth something. Now, one last thing." He breathed in and out, then allowed the last notification that had been waiting for him to flow through.

Sigil Option Detected.
View Sigil Options?

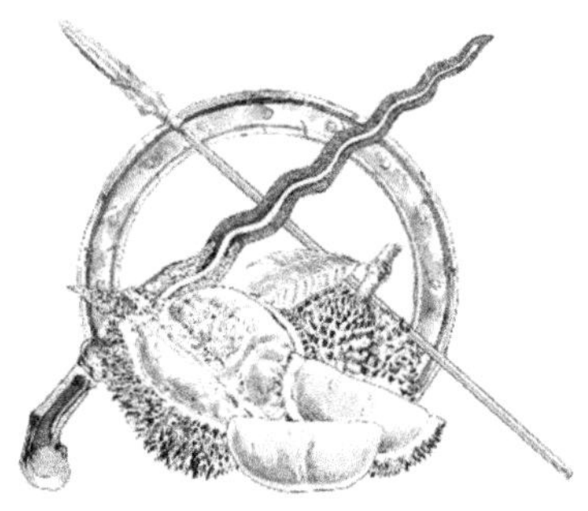

Chapter 91

Accepting the notification and agreeing to it was just a matter of relaxing his mind. Arthur let the Tower display the information he had been waiting for. The Aspect might have given them an overall boost, but he had ideas for the Sigil—and this one he intended to use for himself. Even if it would benefit everyone too.

Sigil Options

- *The Dauntless Shield*
- *The Two-Tailed Fox*
- *The Flame Phoenix*

"What the ever loving, stinky tofu is this?" Arthur cursed.

"Problem, boss?"

Arthur shook his head, choosing not to answer. Mostly because he wasn't sure what the point was. Of course, a swift poking at the Sigil options gave him no additional information. No surprise there. Which meant he had to do all the guessing purely from the Sigil names presented.

What the Dauntless Shield did was at least clear enough. Protection. Probably another bonus to protective cultivation techniques. Very useful if he had something that boosted the toughness of his skin, or made his bones harder to break, or anything like that.

But he had no protective techniques and no idea when he could acquire something like that. The Shield did, however, have the advantage of working in close conjunction with his Aspect, so both of them boosted together could make for a very powerful combination. Something to think about.

For later. Not the most useful now.

Moving on, the idea of foxes having more than one tail was a very Japanese thing. He wasn't sure that it was something present in Chinese culture. Then again, Malaysia had been a melting point of cultures for long enough—and a certain highly popular anime with nine-tailed foxes had influenced large swathes of kids—so that was not too surprising to see. The question was this: Was this Two-Tailed Fox a creature of strength or one of wily cunning? Because traditionally, that was what foxes were. Tricksters.

Arthur found himself drawn to the idea of a trickster Sigil. It could provide many benefits and aid him in ways that didn't require direct confrontation. Sure, his life might have become one of constant violence, what with the hunting of spirit beasts in the Tower, but he certainly hoped that it wouldn't remain just that.

Otherwise, the kind of person he might become was not worth thinking about.

Still, there was another option in there and it was intriguing. Again, there was a slight problem of cultural bleed. Was the Flame Phoenix spoken of here the western phoenix, a creature that died and was reborn? Or a Chinese phoenix, which was immortal but kept itself hidden? Did he gain strength in healing and resurrection perhaps, or could he hide and influence luck or fate itself?

"Never going to make it easy, are you?" Arthur muttered under his breath.

No answer from the Tower, of course. That was the way it went, he guessed. Either way, the phoenix was a powerful mythical creature in either culture, ranked as strong as a dragon in Chinese culture. Perhaps not as much in the West, though he had heard some people compare phoenixes to thunderbirds in Native American mythologies. And those were strong too.

More importantly, at least to Arthur, he had a powerful cultivation technique that focused on healing. An aspect that he could see the phoenix being part of. If it boosted his Accelerated Healing technique, he could maybe upgrade his healing skill further.

How cool would it be to wander around, getting stabbed, head chopped off, and limbs broken, all the while cracking jokes? He'd have to work on his witty repartee of course, but a man had dreams. And not just about Ryan Reynolds' ass in spandex.

Moving on.

Arthur flicked his gaze over the three options once more. He wished he had more time to decide, but perhaps it was for the best. If he had more time, he might get stuck with analysis paralysis, trying to discern greater meaning from insufficient information. Outguessing the turning of luck and fate to no avail.

It was the thought of second chances that drove him on to his decision. Second chances, advantages to being regal and righteous, and the healing technique he already had. "Maybe I'll get another chance if I guess wrong," he murmured.

Decision made, the Tower's workings pulsed through him. Tearing his body apart, connecting his clan crest to the other members. This time around, the pain was less than before. For him, at least. To his surprise, now that he was not the one screaming his head off, he managed to watch as Yao Jing slumped, pounding both hands against the door as the pain coursed through him.

Long before Yao Jing recovered, Arthur found new notifications appearing before him.

Sigil Chosen: The Flame Phoenix.
Complimentary Cultivation Technique Located.
Cultivation Technique Absorbed by Sigil.
Sigil Bonuses (Clan Head): Accelerated Healing – Refined Energy (Grade I) improved to Accelerated Healing – Refined Energy (Grade II).
Sigil Bonuses (Clan): Cultivation Exercise – Accelerated Healing – Refined Energy (Grade I) has been imparted to all Clan members.

"That's it?" Arthur muttered, surprised. He had hoped for more, though he had expected this much. Even hoped for this much, though he had desired a greater change. Still, an improvement in his healing technique was amazing, and a mental prod brought up further information on that.

Accelerated Healing – Refined Energy (Grade II)
Passively increases base Tower healing rates by 47.3%.
Active use of technique increases base Tower healing rate by 138.9%.
May not replace lost limbs or other permanent injuries.
Active Cost: 0.1 Refined Energy per ten minutes.

"I wonder what it would take to get there? From here?" Arthur muttered.

"Get where, boss?" Yao Jing asked.

"Oh, umm, regeneration of limbs," Arthur said.

Yao Jing grinned, rubbing at his left shoulder. When Arthur raised an eyebrow, he shrugged sheepishly. "Clan crest still hurts."

"It's on your shoulder?" Arthur said, surprised. He had wanted his crest on his shoulder. Now that his attention had been brought to it, he found himself flexing the fingers of his left hand, the burning sensation still subsiding. Hopefully nothing else would require the Tower to burn more imprints on him. His nerves, his soul, still felt a little raw.

"Better than my back, right?"

"You get to choose?!" Arthur froze, noting how his voice had kept rising as he spoke. He forced himself to cycle his breath a few times, pushing down the irritation. While he did that, Yao Jing's own gaze had flickered away, tracking information he received.

"You sure you not a dream, boss?" Yao Jing said.

"What? No. Why?"

"Just, this is the kind of thing I wanted to learn," Yao Jing said. When Arthur stared at him inquiringly, Yao Jing shrugged. "I got reasons to learn healing magic. And to answer your next question: To grow back limbs, you need Grade Five healing techniques."

"Five?" Arthur shook his head. That was a long way away.

"If you want to regrow limbs on other people, then you need a different technique," Yao Jing added. "This one won't let you heal others, only yourself."

"I know," Arthur said.

Yao Jing nodded, shrugging. "Still good to learn. Complimentary, right?"

Arthur nodded in agreement. Seeing that Yao Jing was recovered and done reading his own notifications, Arthur gestured at the door. His companion raised an eyebrow, prompting him to explain.

"It's time for us to get going. Got things to be doing. Allies to gather and threats to shatter," Arthur said.

"Going to smash the Suey Ying?"

"If I have to. Or make them back off." A hand reached down to brush the kris by his side, a part of him wondering how likely that was going to be.

Probably not likely at all. But he had to try. Or kill them, trying.

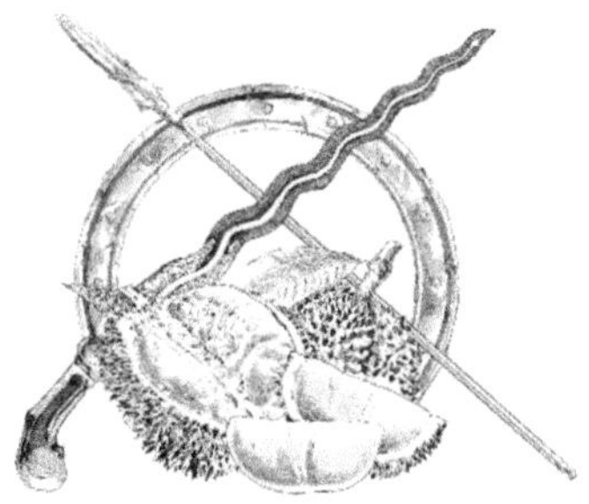

Chapter 92

Exiting the administrative building was mostly a matter of Yao Jing glaring at everyone until they got out of the way and a lot of hurried steps. Since no one wanted to physically accost them, it was a matter of simply ignoring the cultivators shouting for Arthur's attention and favour. Which anyone walking through a night market had learned to do long ago. Especially if you had to play guide to the occasional white tourist with their overfilled pockets.

"Where to, boss?" Yao Jing said, once they managed to get half a block away from the building and cleared themselves of the majority of persistent cultivators. There were a few who hung around on the periphery, but none seemed ready to do anything but watch.

Arthur started to say something, only to fall silent when his least favorite party member appeared. Accompanied by a dozen others, including a few of the Malay thugs that had blocked their way earlier. "What the hell?"

"I got help," Jan said, grinning wide. "These guys are from the Double Sixes."

Yao Jing frowned. "The what?"

"Double Sixes. The gang, lah," Jan said. "Not really a triad, just a gang."

"Oi! We're more than just a gang," said a youngster, who looked barely twenty. He shoved Jan, only to be slapped on the back of his head by an older man, one who had a pair of tattoos crawling up his arms into his raggedy shirt. The older man was a little on the pudgier side, wide and broad like a former construction worker who had gone to seed.

"*Diam!*" he silenced the boy. Having finished, the older man turned to Arthur, the glare on his face fading slightly, and asked, "You registered your clan?"

Shooting a look at Jan who simply nodded, Arthur answered. "I did."

"Then we will help you, and in the future, you will help us. *Boleh*?" the older man said, the frown still lingering on his face.

Again, Arthur looked at Jan, who nodded firmly. Feeling a little lost, but realizing he probably needed whatever help he could get—even if it was on the more notorious side.

"*Boleh*," Arthur replied, nodding in agreement at the Double Sixes.

"*Bagus!*" said the old man loudly, pleased despite his grim expression. He stuck a hand out to shake and pumped Arthur's hand so hard that Arthur nearly toppled over. "I am sending these three to guard you. I will call others to come. You plan to confront the Suey Ying?"

"Yeah. We need to get the Thorned Lotuses—" Arthur began, but Jan interrupted: "Uswah already gone to call them. She will come soon."

Arthur let out a little sigh of relief. "That's great. That's good. Mel?" Of them all, he had hoped Mel had escaped. He could use her knowledge and competence.

Jan shook her head.

Disappointed, Arthur tried to rearrange plans in his mind. Having the Double Sixes with him and the Thorned Lotuses should add significant weight to his demands. Of course, people in grief could be irrational and Boss Choi was not the kind to step back.

"And who is this?" Jan barked, interrupting Arthur's thoughts.

"Yao Jing. You can talk to me directly, if you want," Yao Jing said with a snort.

"Ya, ya," Jan said dismissively. "Why are you here?"

"I added him," Arthur said.

"Why?"

"Because," Yao Jing said, drawing that word out long and hard, drawing stares from Jan and everyone else . When he was certain he had their attention, he finished the sentence. "I. Am. Awesome!"

Arthur choked on his laughter. Jan began berating Arthur for adding another idiot to their group. Yao Jing talked over her, insisting on his awesomeness.

Arthur cleared his throat loudly and snapped his fingers. "Right, we've got people. Now we need information." He turned to the old man, who looked appreciative of Arthur's focus on the situation at hand. "Who are you, anyway? I'm Arthur. Arthur Chua. The Clan Head of the Benevolent Durians."

"The what Durians?" the man said.

"Benevolent," Arthur said. "It's sort of like, um, charitable? Good-hearted at least."

Silence greeted his explanation and for a moment, the man looked like he was regretting his choice of allies. Then he tapped his chest a moment later. "Mohammad Osman bin Awang. I lead the Double Sixes."

Arthur chose not to comment on how common those names were. Real names or not, it was not something he cared to follow up on. Not when he had more important things to do.

"Scouts," said Arthur. "Can you find out what the Suey Ying are up to?"

Mohammad Osman nodded, turning his head to the side and meeting the gaze of two Chinese members of his gang. Like some of the bigger gangs, the Sixes were not built along racial lines but drew from all across the board. In this case, the Sixes were dominated by Malays, but there were advantages to having other races.

Such as spying.

Arthur watched the Chinese pair part ways, heading off in different directions to learn what they could. In the meantime, he scratched his chin, considering what else he could do. Should do. He really wanted a weapon other than the cursed kris. And he needed to meet up with the Lotuses when they came looking for him, though he assumed they'd do what Jan did and come for the administrative building. Or perhaps...

"Can you lend me one more man?" Arthur said. When the older man gestured for him to continue, Arthur added, "Leave him here, or maybe even meet with the Lotuses as they come in. And lead them to my Clan building."

"*Boleh.*" A slight pause, then Mohammad Osman asked, "Where is your building?"

"Shit. Right, right..." Arthur paused, about to offer an explanation before Jan walked over, smirking as she left Yao Jing clutching his arm and glaring at the woman.

"I stay and wait for the others. You bring Mr. Osman to the HQ," Jan said.

"You know where it is?" Arthur said, surprised.

"Ya lah. In my head." Jan tapped her temple. "So weird. But it's here."

Silence greeted her words, while Arthur contemplated how the Tower might engage in mind manipulation. Then, discarding that concern, because he just did not have time to worry about it, he waved for Mohammad Osman and the Sixes to join him.

As they walked through the streets, headed for his own Clan residence, Arthur could not help but glance over at his newest ally. Another niggling thought had crept in.

"What do you want, for being our allies?" Arthur asked, curiously. "What did Jan promise you?"

Mohammad Osman grinned at that, tapping the sheathed kris by his side. "What else? Money. Or cores. New clans make a lot of money, you know." A slight pause before he added, "Eventually."

Arthur had no answer for that. He really had no idea how they were going to end up with the money that Mohammad Osman thought they would generate. But he wasn't going to say so.

That was a problem for the future. Right now, he would take what allies he could get. And hope they were true.

On that rather morbid thought, Arthur turned the corner to finally set eyes on his clan residence for the very first time. He could barely see the entrance, what with the sheer volume of rubberneckers in the way, but what he did see was enough to explain their interest.

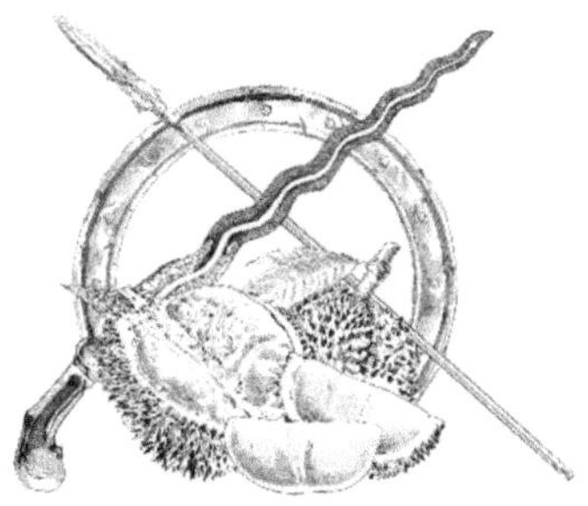

Chapter 93

The clan residence was three stories tall, and from what Arthur recalled, should have looked almost exactly like most of the other buildings on this block. The general pattern was a big structure, but unlike the office buildings, these hotel types had small Juliet balconies—plus bigger balconies for the top floor—and a single main entrance. Not much in terms of decoration, just a wood-and-brick outer layer with some clay cladding and grey paint. Boring as hell.

Overall, their clan's new building was similar to that general design, but it was in the details that made it look so different. Rather than wood and brick, the structure was made of gray stone, each block thick and imposing. The balconies railing were metal instead of wood; the filigree added a little aesthetic touch to them as well as to drain pipes and gutters along the roof.

Even more startling was the entrance: double doors so tall they nearly stretched to the roof, and impressive golden knockers upon the banded metal. The entire building screamed of both security and comfort.

"What does it say on the top?" one of the bystanders asked her friend, peering over the heads to read the inscription above the doors.

"Uhh... I can't be reading that right," her friend said.

"Why? What's wrong?" the girl asked, elbowing the man. "Tell me!"

"The Benevolent Durians." Frowning, he shook his head. "I'm sure that's what it says but... durian?"

"I like durians!" she said.

"Yeah, but do you want to be a durian?" the man said.

Arthur shook his head. He had no time to deal with these people or their thoughts. Rather, he wanted to check out his building and the Tower guard that was supposedly assigned to it. Perhaps he could make use of the guard.

So thinking, he pushed his way through the crowd. Yao Jing moved past him after a few feet to help guide the group through. Their large number of thuggish-looking men moving through with purpose was enough to make the crowd part, few wanting to start a fight. Or perhaps the crowd wanted to see what would happen when they arrived at the entrance.

After all, entertainment was always hard to come by, without the Internet or TV.

Breaking through the crowd, Arthur noticed Yao Jing step aside to let him take the lead now. He came up to the door and then pushed on it. The door refused to budge, nor was there a visible lock. Cocking his head to the side, ignoring the jeering suggestions of those who had tried the same, he eventually used the knocker.

"Who will answer, you think?" Mohammad Osman said curiously beside him.

Before Arthur could reply, the door swung open without a word. Standing behind was one of the Tower guards, dressed in his breastplate and armored uniform. The most striking aspect of the guard—other than the fact that he actually had a face, unlike the shadowed, faceless figures that patrolled the Tower otherwise—

was just how tall he was. He stood nearly a foot taller than Arthur at what must have been close to seven feet.

"Oh, wow," Arthur said, then quickly correcting himself, added, "I'm Arthur Chua. The, uh, owner of this place?"

"Yes, Clan Head. I have been so informed and have been awaiting your entrance." The guard's face was entirely impassive. "You may address me as Guard Shu." Then moving aside while pulling the door open, he waited for Arthur to enter. "You will need to acquire servants or other individuals to handle the entrance after today. This is not, obviously, my duty."

"Right. I didn't see a key or anything…" Arthur trailed off, for as he stepped over the threshold the Tower had sent him another series of notifications.

Benevolent Durians Clan Building (First Floor, Tower 2895)
Type: Residence
Building Bonus Chosen: Security (Town Guard Shu assigned)
Total Number of Floors: 3 + basement
Total Number of Residents: 0
Total Number of Residences: 28 (8, 12, 8)
Would you like to review the layout?

A mental confirmation was all that was required for the Tower to give him the layout. At Yao Jing's rather gentle urging, Arthur made sure to move away from the front entrance while he scanned through the wire diagram floor map that appeared in his view, allowing Yao Jing to pass the threshold. Even as he walked in, he remarked on the greater concentration of energy within the building, similar in some ways to the beginners' inn but less dense.

Maybe if they upgraded the building or the clan, that density of energy would grow stronger?

At the same time, Mohammad Osman and the rest of his people had been gently but firmly barred from entry by the guard. To his credit, Osman made no move to hurry the matter along, even if he curiously eyed the inside of the building.

"Huh. Keys," Yao Jing said, scooping up one key. "I guess that explains one thing." He put it in his pouch, only for Guard Shu to appear beside him, glowering. "What? I'm a Clan Member."

"There are protocols that you must know of. The Tower supplies a number of such keys equal to the number of rooms available. Upon loss, keys must be repurchased at the Administrative Building. Each key is individually designated for its current owner and only the Clan Head or his representative on the floor will be able to remove such allocation," Guard Shu said.

Arthur had a rough idea of the layout now: Lots of residential rooms on the first floor; fewer but bigger rooms on the second floor; and lastly meeting rooms on the ground floor, plus a few residential rooms. Exiting the map, Arthur ran through Guard Shu's explanation in his mind.

"Is this normal, for clan buildings?" he asked.

"No. You have chosen added security features, and as such, the building includes some minor benefits to myself. The keyed keys are another benefit. As the Clan and the building itself improve, additional security features and other bonuses may be applied," Guard Shu explained.

"Thank you. For being a frank you." No response from the guard. So. Another critic of his humor.

So many critics.

Arthur's gaze tracked outside to where the Double Sixes were waiting patiently. "How about guests?"

"They may be allowed entry by any key holder. You may inform me if you wish to place specific limits on the number of guests. Those overstaying their welcome or attempting to enter without permission will, of course, be ejected by myself." Guard Shu grinned, a little malice glinting in his eyes. "As expressly and quickly as you may desire."

"Umm, let's not start any wars. So no deaths," Arthur said. Seeing the slight disappointment in Guard Shu's gaze, he added, "Except those of the Suey Ying tong. Those you can kill if they try to break in." Another pause. "You know who they are, right?"

"I do."

"Good, good." Arthur then gestured at Mohammad Osman. "Let them in. And if any of the Thorned Lotuses come, let me know. I'll want them in too. Maybe let Jan and Uswah know, when they arrive?"

"Of course, Clan Head."

"Thank you." Having said his piece, he waved Mohammad Osman and his people in before gesturing towards the hallway. He did so with his hand closed, using his thumb instead of his index finger to point the way, as he assumed was culturally polite to Osman. Once the Sixes were through the door, he walked off quickly to the nearest meeting room.

The meeting room was outfitted with a boardroom table and chairs, a nice surprise. It would have been problematic if he had to actually furnish the entire place, what with his lack of funds. He hoped that the rest of the building was furnished, especially the residences. If so, it would save him a pretty penny.

His mercantile thoughts were pulled apart as Mohammad Osman stepped into the room, his eyes sweeping the insides before taking a seat near the head of the table and keeping an eye on the door as he sat.

Arthur, leaning on the middle chair of the table, smiled a little at the paranoid nature of the man's movements but chose not to comment. Instead, he waited until the others had filed in, Yao Jing being the last to enter and take up post nearby.

"So, Clan Head, what are your plans?" Mohammad Osman said.

"Hard to plan without information. But if Boss Choi is to be believed, he has captured a friend of mine. And might have acted against the others in the Thorned Lotuses." Arthur paused, considering his next words before continuing. "I cannot allow that."

"What are you going to do? Declare war?" Mohammad Osman's eyes narrowed. "War is expensive."

"It is," Arthur said. "And my clan is small, for now. But once the Lotuses arrive, that will change."

"And my people?" Mohammad Osman said.

The words made Arthur freeze, staring at the other man. Of the things the man might have negotiated for, entrance to his burgeoning clan had not been part of it. His mind spun, searching for an answer, his instincts screaming against answering in the positive. And yet...

"I did not think the Double Sixes were looking to tie themselves so tightly to a clan," Arthur said, stalling.

"Things change. A true Malaysian clan is rare. Especially one not controlled by the corporations. Or politicians."

Those words brought more than a few grimaces to the faces of those around. An unfortunate fact of life that the politicians and their cronies—many of whom ran large corporations of their own—had the majority control of clans here. They made up the cultivator families, the sects, and other groups that controlled information that ran through the Tower. But apart from these groups with powerful backing, rarely were there multiracial clans that better represented the diversity of ethnic-religious groups in Malaysia: not just the Malays and Chinese, but the Indians, the indigenous tribes, and the more recent immigrants.

Thus far, the powerful clans had left Arthur alone. Why would they care for the scrambling of those who were guaranteed to be weaker than them? But now that he had an actual clan? Now he was a threat. And Arthur could not help but realise it at that moment. Perhaps his enemies were larger and bigger than the Suey Ying tong. Even if they were the ones he had to deal with first.

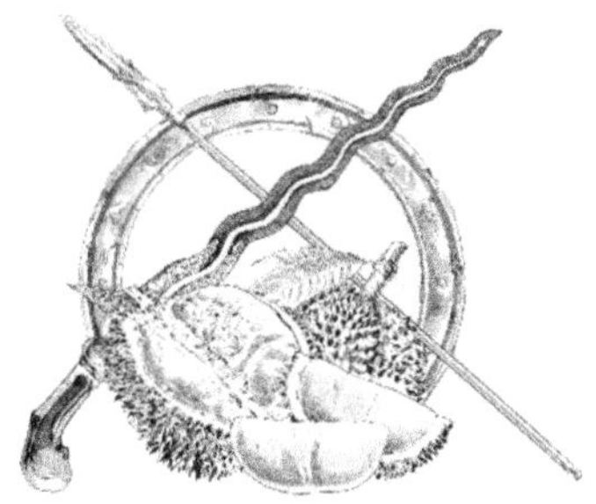

Chapter 94

The silence from Mohammad Osman's simple truth bomb lingered in the boardroom for a long time, until Arthur pulled his thoughts together.

"You are not wrong. And perhaps we might have need of more allies than I considered." Arthur made sure to take a deep breath, banishing the growing tension in his chest as he continued. "However, I still think you need to speak with your big boss, *yeah*, before making a commitment like that. I will, however, take your alliance on this floor wholeheartedly. And if you prove yourselves true, further discussion on acceptance into my clan can continue."

He still did not want to accept them directly. His mind whirled as he realized why, partly, he had chosen not to accept the offer immediately. First there was the possibility of Mohammad Osman overreaching his own position, and the fact that the Double Sixes were a real gang, much like the triads, and thus dabbled in the worst kind of criminal activity.

But mainly, Arthur wanted—no, he needed—more people like Yao Jing. Individuals he had recruited himself, people who were loyal to him. If he brought in both the Sixes and the Lotuses, nearly his entire clan would be made up of people whose first loyalty wasn't to him.

That was a recipe for disaster. It was a recipe for him to become nothing more than a figurehead. Other individuals, those with significant personal strength, might ignore his concerns. He had neither significant personal power nor a third party to help balance his strength out.

No, what Arthur needed was time. Time to hire people who were loyal to him. Time to gain his own strength, such that he might not be abused or otherwise forced to bow to others. If he continued ascending the Tower, he could not only keep the clan functioning but also grow it. Only ascension could give him an advantage over others.

But there were ascensions and then there were ascensions. Being carefully guarded, brought from Tower level to Tower level and never facing danger head-on would just make him a hothouse orchid. And those wilted all too easily when faced with a real-world problem.

No. Arthur would not become one of those.

"Very well," Mohammad Osman cut through his thoughts. "But this building is comfortable. And I am tired of living in a tent."

Not for a second did Arthur believe the man stayed out in a tent. At the worst, he probably lived in one of the fabricated buildings. More likely, he stayed in a beginner hotel, using payments from his people to fund his residence.

Still, if the man wanted to act humble, Arthur would not gainsay him.

"For your aid, today, I can offer a room on the top floor and... four rooms on the second floor," Arthur said, calculating quickly.

"A single room on the top floor... No. Two. And eight rooms on the second floor," Osman rebutted immediately.

Even if neither man spoke of it, they both could tell that the energy in this building was more concentrated than anywhere but a beginner hotel. And it was continuing to grow, though Arthur assumed that there had to be a limit. It was not ever going to maximise like the outer portions of the floor, not unless he managed to level up the building or the clan further. A factor that he would need to look into.

But it was still better than hanging outside, drawing on the energy so many others tried to soak in at the same time. Which meant these residences were going to be important. Not just because of the added safety of the floor Guard.

"Two rooms, top floor. Four on the second floor," Arthur said. When Mohammad Osman moved to speak, he added, "For a month. However, if you agree to an ongoing alliance, we can do two rooms and six."

"Not much difference," Mohammad Osman said.

"Might be the difference between a war fought today, or a longer and more considered talk," Arthur pointed out easily. Already, his mind was spinning through options, considering what he could do with the minor army.

The last thing he wanted was to start an all-out war. However, if they had to fight, having a base of operations that could not be assaulted would leave them in a much, much stronger position. And they could likely cram a lot of people in their building, leaving the Suey Ying tong one step behind in their defenses.

A castle and sortieing knights would always be a problem, especially when one did not have the army to besiege it properly. Add in the fact that those within the castle could grow stronger while remaining indoors, even without food supplies.

Which was what Arthur hoped could drive Boss Choi to the negotiating table.

And if not, then perhaps a change of leadership. But if that was the case...

"Agreed. Two and six," Mohammad Osman said into the silence while Arthur kept pondering strategy.

Smiling at the easy agreement, Arthur could not help but lean forward. "Right. So here's what I'm thinking we need to do. If we want to win..." Lowering his voice, he continued talking.

Sometimes, what you hoped for could only occur if you planned for it.

Amah Si arrived twenty minutes later, after a couple more of Mohammad Osman's men had disappeared out the doorway to carry out his orders and Arthur's. The old woman was accompanied by both Jan and Uswah, and she looked equal portions amazed and upset. When she arrived, she surveyed the room, frowned at the sight of Osman's presence, then stomped over to stand before Arthur, raising her cane to prod him in the chest.

"What did you do?" she snapped.

"Nothing, Amah," Arthur said. "It was all the Tower." Then, pushing the cane aside firmly, he continued. "I understand you're angry. This isn't what you wanted. Heck, it isn't what I wanted. But it is what we have now, and we got to make do."

Then, since she was standing before him, he prodded the Tower connection. The older woman startled as the notification flickered in front of her eyes.

"No negotiating? No arguing?" Amah said, suspiciously.

"I understand gratitude," Arthur said, simply. "I won't just add everyone from your group without at least talking to them first, but I'm willing to work with you all." He shrugged. "At the least, you should be bringing your people into this building. Keep them safe. The most vulnerable ones, especially."

"The Suey Ying are out for blood, no thanks to you."

"Yes. Now, you going to accept or..." He trailed off as he felt another connection snap into place, physical proof that she was now one of his own. The older woman sucked in her breath in surprise as she received the notifications and had the Tower's changes rip through her, but beyond that single sign she gave no other indication of pain.

Tough old bird.

"Jan, Uswah... your people. Dependents on second floor only," he said to the pair while Amah recovered and read through the new notifications. "Fighters on this floor."

Jan snorted at being given an order, going so far as to take station opposite Yao Jing. Uswah, however, was ever practical and headed out immediately, barking orders at women crowding in the hallway, sending them upstairs to put themselves out of the way.

With the reinforcements dealt with, Arthur then ordered Yao Jing to explain the keys to Jan. He had just about finished organizing that when Amah Si prodded his foot, rather more gently, with her cane.

"You didn't do too bad then. But what is the plan for the tong?"

"Funny you should ask that," Arthur said. "Now, this is dependent upon more information, but here's what I'm thinking..."

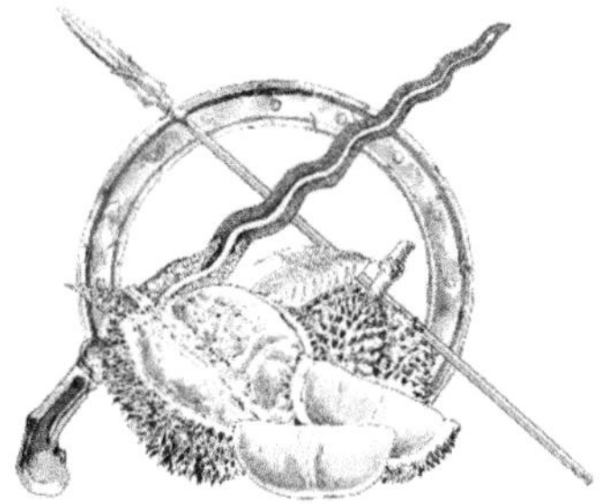

Chapter 95

Once he had finished listing his thoughts out, Arthur let his gaze run over both leaders, trying to gauge their thoughts. Mohammad Osman already knew most of what he had talked about, though in explaining his plan a second time, Arthur had refined some of his thoughts further. As for Amah...

The older woman let out a long snort as she leaned back, looking around and then tapping the table impatiently. One of her attendants scrambled to grab the tea set nearby, only to look disappointed when there was no actual tea within. She did not say a word of reproach, though, but hurried out the door, obviously searching for something to quench the older woman's thirst.

In the meantime, Amah Si was speaking to Arthur. "Your big plan is to negotiate for the release of Mel and any others he might have captured, but failing that, you're going to build an alliance large enough to force Choi to give up or that will finish him off in a fight. Is that it?" Arthur nodded. "And you want to do this *all* today, because you don't want any of the real powers to know about what is happening, or take action."

"Yes. Once the sects or corporate cronies or families get involved, it's going to be a mess," Arthur said. "If we can take care of this problem first, and maybe forge an alliance beforehand, it'll make any pressure they bring to bear less."

"Real powers: you should sign up with at least one of them," Mohammad Osman said. "Or else they will still crush you. And your new friends will run."

"We won't," Amah Si hissed. "And any friend who runs, is no real ally anyway." She shook her head. "None of the powers, the mover-and-shakers, the cronies or families ever gave a shit about us. We won't give a shit about them."

"Then you will die," Mohammad Osman said, bluntly. "They will bring in their people: cultivators who have ascended two, three towers. Who have passed their second or even third ascension. They will crush you all."

"You think we don't have friends of our own?" Amah said, sniffing. "You think we're completely unaware?"

"It's unimportant right now," Arthur said. "We got to fight, soon. Unless you know anyone who can help us out and would be a good fit, we're going ahead with what we have. Deal with the problem in front of us, quickly and effectively."

The pair of leaders were forced to reluctantly nod in agreement.

"So what do we do now?" Amah said. "You want me to send my people out? Ask around and make trouble?"

Arthur hesitated, then shook his head. "No. I think you need to bring in those you trust. I'll interview them. Mr. Osman is getting more information about what the Suey Ying are doing now. Once we know, we'll send someone to tell them we want to talk."

"If they don't send someone here first," Mohammad Osman said.

"Fine." Amah Si barked a couple of orders to her attendant, the first having arrived and busy brewing them all cups of tea. Seeing that there was nothing much else for him to do, Arthur flopped himself down onto a seat, even as Uswah came to report that the Lotuses were settling in.

"You got most of your people here, right?" Arthur said.

"The vulnerable. We have a few still watching over the things we can't pack up." At Arthur's frown, Amah waved a hand dismissively. "It's fine. We hired Bintang to keep an eye on them. Even Boss Choi won't start something with them. Can't afford them for long, but it'll do for today."

Arthur nodded. The Bintang Group was a corporation, mostly focused on running security inside the Towers. They usually worked for families and sects who could afford them but couldn't afford a dedicated security team. Who wanted to deter attacks from other groups that might sully their reputation, make them lose face. Losing face was dangerous and often called for a vicious response.

"Good." Arthur reclined, only to lean forward a moment later when the second attendant started bringing people in. Just over a half dozen women, all of whom carried themselves with the earned confidence of a regular combatant.

"This is the first batch of those I'd have you add," Amah Si said. "Mostly our protectors and core collectors."

Arthur nodded and glanced at Mohammad Osman. The older man stood up immediately, making excuses to leave and take a room on the other end. As he left, Arthur gestured at Uswah, pointing to the man's back.

The Yin Body cultivator smirked at Arthur before following Osman, both to keep an eye on him and to offer any help she might have. It was rather annoying for Arthur to have things move so fast, but he would do the best he could.

On that note...

"Thank you all for coming," Arthur said once the door had slid closed. "I won't keep you here long. You all know that I am the new Clan Head for the Benevolent Durians?" He ignored the snort of laughter and the wide grins that appeared on a few faces. "Well, I am so only because of the sacrifice of your people. So I'm going to be filling my clan with many of the Lotuses." He paused, putting to words what he had discussed with Mel and the other girls in the past. "This clan won't be made of the Lotuses only, though. We need allies, we need more fighters. So we'll take in everyone who fits us.

"But I won't be accepting just anyone. We're here to help and grow those who have been trampled upon, to give shelter and space for individuals who have struggled to make it through the Tower. And eventually, we'll be a power in the real world and do the same out there."

"So you want to be a charity?" said one of the prospects, a charcoal-skinned woman of south Indian descent. There wasn't exactly scorn in her voice, or distaste, but something related to it that Arthur could not place. Doubt perhaps? Either way, she stared at him severely.

"No charity. You join us, you work. But I believe, given enough space and training, people can make something of themselves. We're going to give people that," Arthur said. "It doesn't have to be the rich or the fortunate who get it all. We will give people a helping hand, we'll guide them when we can, but if they refuse." Arthur shrugged. "There's only so much we can do."

"A charity still," the woman said, while Amah sat in silence. Arthur swore he caught a slight nod of approval from her though.

"A clan," Arthur said. "One intent on building up those within. And to some extent, those without. Because we're stronger together. I won't justify my vision, just letting you know what it is. If you don't like it, don't join." His eyes swept over the group, his voice firming. "That goes for all of you."

"Any other rules we should know of?" the woman said.

Arthur held up a hand and pointed a finger at her, knowing how rude it was. "What's your name."

"Rubini Arumugam."

"There are two rules right now. There'll be more," Arthur said. "Rule one. Tyranny, not democracy. I run this clan. You don't like it, you can leave. Or be booted." He felt Amah stir next to him, but he chose not to temper those words. He knew that with allies like her or Mohammad Osman in play, he needed to be firm. Otherwise, he'd just be run over by their strong personalities. "Two. Don't be a dick. Any other questions?"

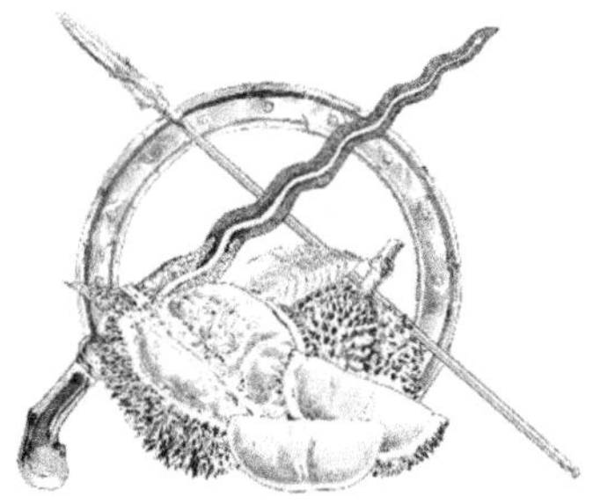

Chapter 96

Of course there were other questions. Arthur fielded them as best he could, though he often found himself using three particular answers. "I don't know. We'll talk about it later," "You're an adult, figure it out and refer to rule two," and lastly, "Maybe."

In truth, he had no answers for them. He did not even have much of an idea of what he intended to do, having little experience running an organization. Being at the bottom and looking up might give you a different perspective from the CEO looking down. But if one was not even bothering to look up, but setting eyes on a different vision, one certainly might make a few good observations.

Arthur had been focused on the Tower the entirety of his life, the imposing structure a means of his own escape. He had not thought about running a corporation or clan, or even a small business. He had vaguely expected to eventually grow to a point that he might be hired by another person, perhaps join someone else's organization.

Not build one.

Eventually, he took their oaths as the first seven Lotuses to his clan. They were merely promises, no Tower enforced contracts involved. But immediately, the Tower sent a notification that the Benevolent Durians had achieved its first milestone.

Beyond the single congratulatory message, no further improvements were offered. Annoyed, Arthur sent the seven to watch over the house and other duties, promising to go into more detail later. Just as he was readying himself to repeat the same damn thing, and regretting that he had not designated one of the newcomers as an official "answerer of dumb questions," the first of Mohammad Osman's scouts arrived.

Yao Jing led the man in himself, having first cleared the annoyed Tower Guard. Waving the scrawny fellow over to a seat, Yao Jing returned to his position at the back of the room, arms crossed.

"Well? You going to make me wait a bell?" Arthur said, impatiently.

He noticed Amah Si shoot him an annoyed look, as though he should have waited for the other to speak first. Arthur made a mental note to ask her about that, though he assumed it had something to do with showing off his impatience and giving away information. But he needed an answer, damn it.

"They gathered their members: nearly twenty fighters. And they have your girlfriend, boss," the wiry man said after glancing over at Mohammad Osman to confirm he should speak.

Arthur knew that calling him "boss" in this case was no more significant than calling a restaurant owner "boss" while ordering a meal from him. A bad translation and colloquial use of the Chinese *laoban* had turned into common parlance and an indicator of respect.

"Is she hurt? Did they hurt her?" Arthur said, urgently.

"Yeah."

The growl he produced surprised even himself, his fist coming down on the table. The reinforced Tower wood creaked under the attack, and the scout shrunk back. When Mohammad Osman waved at him urgently to expand on the report, he reluctantly added:

"It's not anything bad. Some cuts, bruises. Her arms are bandaged, and I think they might have broken a few fingers." Each word was a knife dug into Arthur's chest, but the scout continued, oblivious to Arthur's own thoughts. "I think she must have fought like hell, because there were a couple who were as bad as her. And there was talk of others wounded."

"Any other hostages?" Amah asked calmly but firmly.

Taking the moment to calm himself while listening to the other question, Arthur had to choose to accept that the wounds she incurred might not be a matter of torture. Broken fingers happened when you wanted to disarm an opponent without killing them. Fingers could be caught in the twisting when a weapon was violently yanked out of one's hand or broken with a well-placed strike by a club or flat of a blade.

It could also be torture of course...

Clenching his fists, Arthur forced himself to listen.

"… maybe a few more, they guarded the tent closely. Too dangerous for me to look any closer."

Amah nodded in thanks, accepting the scout's assessment. Mohammad Osman continued to question him, asking for details of the force, weapons, and where they were located—which was in their own circle of tents on the outer edge of the village, as their proper residence was still being built.

Arthur paid minor attention to all that, knowing he would need the information. But more importantly, he needed to know, "Are they sending other people out? Are they going to come fight?"

The scout shrugged. "Don't know what they doing, but Boss Choi, he's talking lots with his own people."

"They might be willing to talk, instead of starting a fight immediately," Mohammad Osman said, smiling. "Did you see others going out?"

The man nodded. "Runners, like me."

"He's looking for allies," Amah said. "And we're sitting here." She looked at Arthur pointedly. "When we should be acting."

Arthur hesitated, before he nodded. "You're right." He rubbed his chin, considering. "Let's do both, then."

"Wait *and* act?" Jan said, amused.

"No. Act and look for allies." He glared at her, and she grinned unrepentantly. "Amah Si. You know people here. Think you can send them around, see who else can help?" He glanced at Mohammad Osman. "And get me another half dozen of your fighters? I'll add them to the clan while we walk. The rest of us will head to the edge of the village."

"You want to surprise them, ah?" Yao Jing asked. "'Cause I bet they got a few guys watching outside this building. Maybe I can find them, and..." Yao Jing grinned. "Delay them."

"No fighting in the village, lah," Jan said, scornfully.

"I don't have to stab them. I got other ways of dealing with people. Unlike you," Yao Jing replied.

"Stab them? I'll stab you!" Jan growled.

Cutting in before it could devolve, Arthur spoke firmly. "We're not going to hide. We need to speak with him first, not kill him." He paused, considering. "We'll try to get Amah enough time to get any allies together too, so we'll go slow too."

"Wah, like a 90s gangster movie, ah?" Jan said. "Big showdown?"

"Maybe no fighting, though," Arthur exhaled. "Hopefully no fighting. But I won't abandon our people."

There was a nod from those around, before Uswah spoke up. "And the tent?"

"The one with other potential hostages?" Arthur said.

She nodded.

Arthur could only hesitate before making up his mind. "Think you can get in with some help and check if there really are more hostages? Or maybe get them out, while we distract Choi's men?"

Uswah smiled at his question before nodding. Immediately, she slipped out of the room, not bothering to ask for further directions or recommendations.

Not that Arthur had any intention on offering her any.

With her gone, he glanced around the room. When no further comments or suggestions were forthcoming, he walked around the boardroom table, straightening his back a little as he did so. He turned to Jan and spoke, his voice filled with command.

"Find me a spear. If we're doing this, I want to be properly armed."

And for once, she didn't argue.

Chapter 97

It took the group just under twenty minutes to get out of the clan building. The time passed in a flash, with orders, questions, and minor details of management dealt with by Arthur as he stood in the entrance hallway impatiently. However, organization was important: everything from informing new recruits of his two rules to ensuring everyone was properly armed and armoured.

He even spent all of five minutes washing away the dirt off his skin and redressing in new clothing to ensure he looked presentable. He had even taken the edge of a razor to his scraggly beard.

Under the pounding water, streaked with blood and dirt and other unmentionable grime, Arthur had had a brief moment of peace from the insistent questions. In that moment of silence, he felt the burgeoning panic rise up, threatening to send him spiralling away. Only by focusing on the needs of Mel, captured and likely being vigorously interrogated, could he stem the emotions.

He knew there would be a cost to pushing all this aside. At some point, he would need to stop and think, to deal with the mounting concerns and panic rising within him. That moment was not now, however, and he managed to exit the bathroom both clearer of mind and cleaner of body.

The spear that Jan managed to acquire for him was slightly shorter than his own preference, its standing height just under his own eye level. However, to his surprise, the gleaming metal head had a watersteel pattern. Down to its tip, the spearhead was overlaid with wavy segments of various metal types. It suited the spear's black haft.

The moment he took the spear and inspected it, he received a notification which brought a raised eyebrow. After all, he had no skill to analyze such information.

"I bought it from the Tower," Jan said. Noting his surprise, she added, "It's for you. I transferred the ownership already."

"Huh." Arthur paused, then realizing what he had done, added, "Thank you."

"No need. Just get Mel back, okay?" Jan said. "And then pay me back."

Arthur could not help but laugh a little. He had begun to worry a little about her being so nice to him, but this was more like Jan. He nodded in acknowledgement of her words. He did intend to pay her back too. Speaking of payments, the 'Clan tax' was just another thing on the long list of things he needed to deal with when they got back.

"Everyone ready?" Arthur asked, looking around. There were a few objections, people wanting to ask some final questions, but he ignored them studiously. Worrying about how and where people would stay, what food to serve, or the kind of defenses they should acquire was for another time.

The moment he led the group out, into the waiting crowd—much grown, it seemed—Arthur knew that his urgent march to the boundaries of the beginner village to reacquire Mel was going to have to wait. He needed to sort these people out first.

"Silence!" He raised his voice, but it was drowned out by the hubbub. Even if the majority of the crowd wanted to hear him speak, those behind could not see him and thus had no reason to quieten.

Yao Jing, seeing the problem, grabbed his sword and struck the blade against the metal buckle of his shield repeatedly. He did so with such vigor and speed that it rang shrilly, forcing the crowd to pay attention. Even when they were mostly quiet, Yao Jing added a shout: "SHUT UP, you idiots!"

Into the silence, Arthur raised his voice. "I know you all have questions. I have only a few answers. More will arrive in time, but here is what you need to know." He paused, drawing a deeper breath so he could continue without stopping. "I have established a Clan on the first floor of this Tower." He felt the ripple of those words carry through, for a new clan hadn't been established for some time. "We are currently allied with the Thorned Lotuses and the Double Sixes. We are accepting applications from the Lotuses. We *will* be accepting applications from others in the near future, looking for fighters and others who are willing to be loyal to the Clan.

"Our goal as the Benevolent Durians is to offer sustenance to all who join us. All those who attempt to take what is not theirs will be pricked and cast aside by our thorns." He paused then, not because he needed a breath but because he wanted this to be clear. "Like the Suey Ying tong. They have taken one of my clan members and they will return her. If they refuse to do so, we will destroy them."

There. That was enough. The declaration of potential war would cause many in the crowd to step aside. No need to join a sinking ship, after all. Though perhaps a scant few might join Arthur because of a grudge against the tong, or because they were simply mercenary enough like Yao Jing.

As for spies from Suey Ying and other groups, they would scurry off soon to inform their people and watch what was about to happen.

Now, it was up to Amah and her people to convince some of them to join Arthur's cause.

And if not, well, he had enough people. He hoped.

Casting doubts aside, Arthur strode forward. Yao Jing and Jan anticipated his movements long before and pushed ahead to split the crowd. Other members of his newly formed clan joined them, pushing people away so that Arthur could travel unmolested.

He still watched for potential assassins, though, people looking to end him before he met with Boss Choi. The large crowd meant that, even with his bodyguards pushing people aside, he only had a few feet of space between him and the crowd.

It was no surprise to him, or his bodyguards, when a man lunged out of the crowd, intending to sink a knife into Arthur's torso. A last-minute, desperate twist had the blade cut along his side, injuring but not killing Arthur.

Not that a single knife stab was likely to kill. The human body had enough resilience that it would not fall immediately to one stab, and a cultivator's body more so.

In the meantime, Arthur's body had acted on instinct. He caught the arm as it passed his body, gripping the assassin's wrist while pulling the elbow in tight to his body, leveraging the body and forcing him down. Then, his other hand swept out to catch his opponent across the jaw. Arthur stretched the man's neck and arm in opposite directions with the elbow as a fulcrum point.

His opponent fell. The sharp pain against the elbow forced the hand to open and the weapon to drop. Before Arthur could transition to another attack, the nearest bodyguard had stepped forward and struck the assassin's head twice with the hilt of her parang. Bonelessly, his opponent slumped, stunned.

Releasing his opponent, Arthur watched as she frog-marched the stunned man towards the clan building. Only then did the shouts of surprise and excitement make themselves known to Arthur once more, as did the blood trickling down his side.

"You're hurt." One of the guards hissed. He waved her away, bending to pick up the assassin's dagger as he breathed slowly.

"It doesn't matter. I want answers as to who he works for," Arthur said, wiping the blood off the knee of his pants before sliding the knife away in his belt. "We still have to go."

No one objected, though they were all more aggressive at pushing the crowd away.

One foolish assassination attempt down. Who knew how many more to come?

Chapter 98

He had stopped bleeding by the time they were out of the crowd. His shirt was still stained with blood and stuck to his body as he moved, the dark splotch showing up against the tan brown of the shirt he had been given. Not his favourite colour. He much preferred black, for reasons like this.

Well, that and splatters from eating black-sauce *hokkien mee.*

"You okay?" Yao Jing said, the big man having fallen back to speak with him. "I can find a small alley, block it off for us to look at your cut."

"Bleeding's already stopped. We should keep moving. Just take your time, eh?" Arthur said. Then, glancing backwards to a commotion from behind, he noted three individuals wanting to break through. The leader was an Indian man, somewhere in his mid-thirties and with a turban on his head. A Sikh then, Arthur mentally corrected himself. All three were, actually.

"Let the leader in," Arthur called, waving Yao Jing aside. He did let his hand drop idly to his kris though. Everything he knew about the Sikh—some of whom had taken up the warrior culture in their history with gusto—said they were not likely to be dishonorable assassins. But that was in generalities.

People, as individuals, could be idiots.

The Sikh leader stopped in front of Arthur, a hand resting on the kirpan by his side. He did not draw it, but let his limp wrist lie just on the hilt of the curved, single-edged sword-dagger; this particular one was a practical weapon that sat in size between a short sword and a dagger. Ever since the introduction of the Towers, the entire religion had shifted again, from symbolic wearing to actual training and use of the blades as weapons.

"Thank you for speaking with me. I am Hartaman Singh." Gesturing behind to where his people stood, he said, "We have come to join you."

"Why?" Arthur blurted out, not expecting such a blunt offer. "Do you want to die?"

"The Suey Ying tong is a blight on the people. As warriors of honor, we would seek the return of your woman," Hartaman said.

"What do you know?" Arthur said, a little heatedly. Unconsciously, he'd stopped and was glaring at the man, his hand tightening on the spear by his side.

"Nothing that is not public," Hartaman said as he gestured around at the crowd. "The rumors have flown. They have taken your woman, intend to torture her until you yield to them." He shook his head, and the green turban he wore bobbed with each word and gesture. "This cannot be accepted. Nor can we allow a new clan, one that has so much promise, to fall into their hands."

Arthur hesitated, staring at the other man's face. The Sikhs were generally well liked, being a mostly peaceful and kind group. Of course, that was not always the case, what with the younger crowd breaking free from religious constraints in search of money and fame. But the Tower had been, in a way, a boon to them.

As it had been for others like Arthur.

Now here they were. Offering to act as the virtuous warriors they had been brought up to be: kind and compassionate at the same time as fearsome. Maybe dreams did not have to die, with the coming of the Tower and new technology.

"Accepted." Arthur offered his hand for the other man to shake. "I won't accept you into the clan right away if that's what you're looking for," he said and noticed a slight twitch in the man's expression, supposing it was part of the reason he had offered to help. Arthur added, "But we can talk about it. After."

"Good, good," Hartaman said, then glanced back to his people.

"Why don't you and your men join the front of this group?" Arthur pointed to a place near Yao Jing. "Send my men—well, my women—over to the left, and you take the right." It also meant that if he needed to strike at them if they betrayed him, they were on his stronger side. "Hold that position and spread out when we get to the boundary."

"And then?"

"Then we talk," Arthur said firmly. "Talk first. War, if negotiations are not possible."

Hartaman nodded, agreeing to the suggestion immediately. Arthur could not help but be grateful that so far, none of those he had picked up were aching for a fight. Well, other than Jan, but she always looked like she wanted to bite someone's head off.

Once the group had rearranged themselves, they made their way forward. Yao Jing, having been sent back to him, was tasked with planning additions to the group. Arthur made a snap decision to make Yao Jing in charge of talking to potential recruits along the way. Unless they represented a larger group, like another clan or a family.

Thus far, though, none had offered to help. That was no surprise to Arthur, for such organisations did not survive by jumping into every worthwhile crusade. Nor were there any familial or friendly ties between him and them. Such bonds took time to build, and it was why people like Amah Si and Mohammad Osman were in charge of finding them additional help.

It did mean, Arthur had to admit, he was going to owe Amah and Osman. But everything had a price.

With interruptions delegated to Yao Jing, the group kept moving forward. They managed to make it most of the way to the boundary of the newbie village, followed by a crowd of curious onlookers and gathering another dozen or so volunteers before another group, a full dozen men and women, came to a stop near them.

All of that group looked bedraggled, some clutching clubs as their weapons. There was an intense passion in their eyes that belied their torn and dirty clothing. The Durians and their allies were forced to stop as the new group blocked their path. Their leader wielded a carved wooden staff.

"Arthur Chua!" the man roared, hammering his staff on the ground. "We want you speak with us."

Hartaman, being at the front, shook his head. "No one demands anything. Especially not people who don't announce their names or intentions." His hand caressed the hilt of his kirpan, but he did not draw it, cognizant of the Tower guards around.

"We are the beggar clan!" the man snapped, stamping his staff.

"Bullshit!" another voice cried out from the crowd. "There's no Beggar Clan in Malaysia, you idiots."

The other man hesitated for a moment before he spoke, a little less harshly this time. "We're not The Beggar Clan. We have no affiliation to them. But we're beggars, and we work together. So we are a beggar clan."

Arthur snorted as he pushed forward to the front. He could understand the man's sudden reversal. No one wanted to annoy the real Beggar Clan. Their leaders were powerful cultivators, all based in China and Hong Kong, individuals who luxuriated in wealth and might take offence at their clan's name being taken by another. Though no longer beggars, they still kept to their roots, allowing anyone to join them so long as they tithed a portion of their income to the clan.

"Might want to change what you call yourself," Arthur said. "You don't want them smacking you down, just 'cause." Then he waved his hand, cutting the man off before he could rebut. "Don't care anyway. That's your problem. What do you want?"

"You are Arthur Chua?"

"Last time I checked. I could ask others, though." Arthur looked at Hartaman and raised an eyebrow.

"I just met you, so if you say you're the leader of the Durians, I will accept it. It would be rude otherwise," Hartaman said immediately.

Arthur snorted, then looked at the beggar. "There you have it, nameless beggar."

"I'm not nameless. But I might as well be, to you people who walk by us, spitting at our feet..." the man began to rant, only cutting off when the woman who had been standing by his side shoved him in the shoulder. The man glared at her, but the middle-aged woman did not flinch and only glared back. Eventually the man let out a long sigh. "I'm Joe."

"Joe the beggar. What do you want?" Arthur wondered if he had really been named Joe or had chosen such a pedestrian name.

Joe snarled, slamming his staff into the ground again. This time, though, a puff of earth erupted from the attack, causing the cobblestone it struck to crack. He fixed Arthur with his gaze. "Are you mocking me, boy?"

"No. I thought I was doing the opposite," Arthur said quietly. "You didn't give me a name, and you wanted to be called the Beggar Clan. But that doesn't matter. I ask again. What do you want? I have another group to deal with, and since you're meeting me here, where we can't fight, I'm assuming you aren't here to fight. Right?"

The no-combat rule of the beginner village encouraged hot-headed people to calm down and use their words instead of their fists. But Joe didn't seem one for calm, rational discussion. Nor were his emotions particularly well hidden, for the anger he had pointed at Arthur now changed targets. He spat out, "The Suey Ying tong. They pick on my people, attack and steal from us. Half of those who joined us—and there are more than you can believe—were killed by them. We will have our revenge. I swore it."

"We'd also like friends too. If you're looking for those," the woman who had struck Joe said. "I'm Suriani." The tanned woman inclined her head.

"I like friends," Arthur said. "And I like passion. But too much can be dangerous."

"Let them join, lah," Jan said. "These fellas are good people. Though idiots, sometimes. Like someone I know."

Arthur glared at the girl, then suddenly grinned viciously. Reaching over, he grabbed her arm and propelled her forward. Jan looked affronted and surprised at being randomly touched.

"This is your boss," Arthur told the beggars. "She'll give you orders. You listen to her, got it?"

"What?! I'm no boss," Jan yelled.

"Too late. You opened your mouth." Arthur gave her one last push, before he waved the rest of the group forward. He let the bodyguards envelope him again before he took off walking. Jan let a little squawk of outrage as she was pushed ahead by an evilly grinning Yao Jing.

Unfortunately, all too soon, they reached the border. And that put an end to all fun and games.

Chapter 99

Arthur was not surprised by what greeted him as he stepped up to the invisible border between the beginner village and the tents outside. The change in buildings and the strip of cleared land—forcibly cleared by the Tower guards when someone accidentally built upon non-authorised land—was where Arthur's clan met Boss Choi's tong. This liminal zone between the Tower and the Choi's own lands were where groups often met to negotiate tense and important agreements. So it was here that the Suey Ying tong waited.

Two dozen individuals, more than what Arthur had expected but fewer than he feared. He could not help but smile a little, knowing that the tong was significantly outnumbered. Of course, a small part of him wondered how many of his "allies" were truly that, but even so...

"Finally, you came," Boss Choi said, standing in front of his people. "Ei. You there or not? Or hiding like a coward?" He proceeded to peer between Arthur's guards exaggeratedly, drawing mocking laughter from his men and a few genuine ones from the onlooking crowd.

Arthur shook his head, knowing the other man was mocking only to draw him out. That it annoyed him a little was even worse, though he did his best to push that emotion down. Now was not the time to act on his impulses, not when Choi held Mel.

Still, he did make his way through his guards, ensuring that he could stand clear of them and be seen by all. It would certainly not do to hide behind and shout over their heads in a negotiation. It would make him look too weak.

"I'm here. Maybe you should consider glasses, if you can't see me," Arthur said, leaning a little on his spear. "Where are they?"

"They?" Boss Choi said, smirking.

"The people you took prisoner," Arthur replied, ignoring the man's provocations. "You must know that we know. And that you can't win this fight." He gestured to his accompanying men. "Even if you seem intent on having one."

"Why you say that?" Boss Choi said, stepping forward. "Maybe I just want to talk."

"If you wanted to talk, you'd have met us inside the village." Arthur hooked a thumb backward at the village behind him and the crowd that had begun gathering, though at a distance. None of them wanted to get caught in the inevitable battle. "No reason to meet here otherwise, I would think. No?"

"Smart boy. But you have to be smart... to kill my brother and steal his kris," Boss Choi said, his voice low and angry.

"Please. Not like you ever cared much for him." That much, Mohammad Osman had mentioned to him on the walk over. Along with expanding on some of the internal politics and fractures the Suey Ying tong was facing. He did his best not to flick his glance to the right, to where Ah Yam, Choi's lieutenant, stood. No word if he was willing to betray his boss. Or even consider it.

"He was my brother," Boss Choi snarled, stepping forward. "Maybe an idiot, but which family got no idiots?" He threw his hands open, speaking to the crowd. "I don't care about your people, but you... I want *you*."

"Really..." Arthur's eye twitched then. This was a new tactic. Not one he had expected. He had anticipated demands for him to bow down, to accept Choi as his boss. The return of the kris, maybe. Or even acceptance of the Suey Ying into Arthur's clan if he went that far.

Not an attack and an appeal to family.

The worst thing was that Choi's tactic was effective. Arthur could see more than a few people giving him looks of askance. The way the public mood had shifted, the way they stared at him. The bonds of family were strong, and revenge for a brother—unliked or not—was a compelling case.

"Yes, really!" Choi echoed.

"Then why did you take my friend?" Arthur said. "Why hurt her?"

"She hurt us! Killed one of my people. Sent two more to hospital," Boss Choi snapped. "We took her alive; we even bandaged her wounds. See!" A gesture had his men bring Mel, whose arms were tied up in front of her. Indeed, her fingers and other wounds had been bandaged. In fact, other than the bruises and bloody bandages, she looked relatively put together. Someone had even taken the time to wipe down her face, though a gag kept her from speaking.

Mel growled through her rag at the pair. Arthur met her gaze, tracked down to her wounds and broken fingers and then up to her eyes again. The woman could only shrug a little. She then struggled to loosen her arms slightly from the tight grip of her captors.

"Well, I'm here," Arthur said. "Let her go."

"You think I stupid, ah?" Boss Choi gestured at the village. "I let her go, you run away and hide. I don't get my revenge. Then you send your shadow killer, try to kill me." Arthur guessed he meant Uswah.

Boss Choi sniffed. "No. She will stay with me until we finish this."

Trapped. Damn it. Everything he said was reasonable, which was the most annoying part of this. The crowd, even Mohammad Osman by his side, was nodding along. The Sikhs on his other side, just past where Yao Jing stood, looked perturbed. The only people who didn't seem to care were the beggars, whom Jan had to constantly growl at to stay contained.

"So, what? You want the kris back?" Arthur shrugged. "I don't think so. It's a deadly instrument. And your brother, he used it on me. On my friends. Attacked us when we were getting our clan seal, right after we had fought so many *jenglot* to get it. He attacked us when we were already exhausted and hurt. Your brother killed those he could have spared... so I won't say I'm sorry that I killed him."

Silence greeted his words for a moment, and Boss Choi trembled with contained rage. Where he had seemed steady before, now he looked almost unhinged. His eyes grew bloodshot from unshed tears, and he gripped the handle of his weapon tight.

"So you did kill him. It was *you*." Boss Choi spat to the side. "Wasted my time on this stubborn girl, didn't open her stubborn mouth."

Mel struggled again, pushing against the bonds before she glared at Arthur. He cursed himself a little, for falling for the oldest trick in the book. Yet, he could not feel too bad about it.

"Doesn't matter. He needed putting down. He was a rabid dog that came after us, and I don't regret it," Arthur said, letting his voice harden. "I'll do the same to you and your tong if I need it. Let her go. Let all of your prisoners go." He drew a deeper breath and added. "Then, break up."

"What?" Boss Choi said, caught out for once.

"Break up. The Suey Ying ends today. Join other groups. I don't need you all to die. But I want the Suey Ying gone." His words brought forth a roar of approval from some in the crowd, but mostly from the beggars and his own people. "This ends. Today."

"You want me to give up my people? Give up my revenge?" Boss Choi returned to his line of appeal, shaking his head. "NO! I won't give up my people. Come out and fight me, boy."

"And get swarmed by your people?"

"Scared, ah?" Boss Choi gestured at the two dozen he had and then back to Arthur's larger group. "You got so many, still scared ah? Little boy."

Again, murmurs of disapproval. Arthur knew that as many as allies he might appear to have, they were newly forged friendships. There was no guarantee they would fight for him, or that there were no spies and traitors within. If it came down to an actual fight, he was not certain of having the upper hand.

After all, one party was fighting for survival. The other, for revenge.

That, of course, was the knot. And the solution to this predicament. If he was willing to risk it.

Chapter 100

Drawing another breath, Arthur stepped forward toward Boss Choi. Beside him, Yao Jing stirred, surprised. He did not bother to explain himself to Yao Jing as he put himself in ready stance. His legs were wide apart so he could move quickly, one foot before the other so he could bounce backward if necessary. He was still within the boundary of the beginner village, but caution was important.

"Okay," Arthur said, opening his hands slightly. "You want to fight? We can fight. But you release her first, you let her stand to the side of your people. You do good, because I don't trust you to be good. Because you just might change your mind."

"You want me to give you something, but what you give me?" Boss Choi said. "You think I give you everything for nothing?"

"No," Arthur said. "We'll do this, farther back. In your area." He could hear his friends hiss in protest. "If you win, you get everything you want. The kris, your revenge. But if I win, your people break up. Got it?"

He could see young Ah Yam, Choi's second-in-command, glare now. Unhappy at Arthur's insistence on these terms.

Boss Choi snorted. "Fine, whatever. If I lose, I'm dead already so why should I care?" Then he grinned viciously. "But I won't lose, boy."

Arthur nodded. Just as he was about to speak, a disturbance in the crowd had him turn. To his surprise, Amah Si stood there with a crowd of armed men, all looking ready for a fight. They stood in the no man's land. Amah's wise gaze flicked between the two leaders.

"What foolishness is this?" Amah said furiously.

"We're talking about a way to get Mel back," Arthur said. "He's challenged me to a fight."

"*Bodoh!*" Amah hissed. "You were going to accept?"

Arthur nodded, turning to focus on Boss Choi again. The man had been studying Amah and the others behind her and now raised his voice. "This not your business, amah. He kill my brother, I must kill him."

"Like you killed some of theirs?" Amah Si said, gesturing at the beggars. "Like you trampled on others, because you were strong? You stole and kept stealing from them, so that they had no place to go, no time or cores or peace to strengthen themselves. What of their revenge? Of their justice?"

The beggars roared in approval, cheering the old woman on. Boss Choi's lips curled up in derision. "Revenge, anyone can have. If you're strong enough, then do so. Just like I'm going to."

He stepped forward again, slamming his foot into the plain earth. Arthur eyed the distance between them, noting it would only take a few seconds to cross the distance. Still, he was safe enough, he thought.

"Seems like things have changed, again." Arthur gestured to the group around. "You might be willing to kill my friend. But if you do, we'll fall on you and your men. And I don't think your men are as willing to die, are they?"

Boss Choi hesitated then and glanced back. There were a few who nodded back firmly, shouting their willingness. Yet, at least half seemed to avoid his eyes. To Arthur's surprise, the tables had indeed turned in a way. The Suey Ying themselves were concerned about traitors in their midst. They, too, had been infected by the fear of potentially losing. More importantly, Yam Kok See, the second-in-command of the Suey Ying, was edging to the side.

Choi released a litany of curses on his men. "I brought you all up! Feed you, train you, give you women. Still you dare to backstab me?" Some of his people backed away as he raged on. "You think you can get away? My *tai kor* will get you, ah. All of you who dare touch me!" He pounded his chest. "My *tai kor* very big in Ghee Hin. You touch me, they chop you all up!"

Arthur shook his head, ignoring Boss Choi now and looking at Ah Yam. He met the other man's eyes, then flicked his gaze to where Mel was still being held. One of her two captors was looking very doubtful, but the other had gone so far as to draw his dagger and push it against Mel's side, forcing her to stand still.

"But truth is you have no guts, all of you," Choi said, when he noticed that no one was contradicting him. "I got your girl. You won't let her die."

Amah looked at Arthur, who stood silent. Waiting. Then she looked at Boss Choi and the way the crowd shifted, restlessly. They had come for a show, and while there had been a lot of shouting and chest-pounding, it was not the kind of bloody show they had been looking for. Judging their mood quickly, the old woman spoke.

"He might not. But I would," Amah said, stepping forward. As she did, the group of armed men she had at her back moved with her. "I would hate to see her die, but I gave up on her already. Long ago."

Now, Choi hesitated. He could read the resolve in her eyes, the way her people moved with her. And the eagerness of the beggars who had broken free of Jan's tenuous control; they edged forward toward the boundary, ready for his blood.

Arthur could see it now. The future. The blood that would be spilled within moments. Amah was not going to stop. She would not let the Suey Ying get away. She would crush them, because she wanted revenge for those she had lost. Because she would destroy the danger to her people, immediately.

Boss Choi would not back down either. He would call for death, and his men would do it. Because they did not know how to do anything but follow the man who had indeed fed them. Some would run, but not the one holding a dagger to Mel, the blade pricking her side—Arthur saw the way his eyes sparkled with glee at the thought of hurting another. He would not hesitate.

And once that happened, it was over. Violence. Death. Murder.

He could see that future stretch out before them all. And he could not stop it, except...

"WAIT!" he shouted. "We don't have to do this. Look!" He pulled the kris from its sheath. At the same time, he reached into his aura, manipulating it. He flipped the kris over, offering it hilt first towards Boss Choi. It lay on his open palm such that he would be unable to throw it.

His words, his actions, had the desired results. Boss Choi froze, as Arthur moved forward with this offering, crossing the ground between them. Choi tracked his nearing steps, a wide grin appearing on his lips. At the same time, Amah froze, her eyes tracking Arthur too. Her slowed movements meant that those with her refrained from engaging in battle without her orders.

Each step for Arthur took him closer, such that he passed the middle point of the distance between the two. Even as he did so, he continued talking.

"There's no need to fight. You want the kris back, right? So, just take it. You want to fight me? We can talk about that. But all this death, all this fighting, what's the point?" Arthur shook his head. "Please. Let's find some other way around this."

Amah Si was shouting now, telling him to stop being an idiot. She was moving forward again, waving her people to close in. The man holding Mel was looking to Choi, searching for a signal. But the leader of the Suey Ying tong was focused on Arthur, the kris he held, and the distance between them.

Another step, then another. Arthur was barely a hand's breadth from the other, when Boss Choi seemed to make up his mind. He lunged forward, grabbing for the upraised kris.

That was when Arthur released the Refined Energy Dart that he had been holding in his other hand even as he pulled the kris away. Too slow on the latter, for the kris handle was grabbed by Choi, the light swipe by the weapon on his retreating hand leaving a trail of blood.

Too late on the latter, but the former arrived in time. Striking his target.

All as planned.

Chapter 101

A single attack, a Refined Energy Dart released from a hand clutched low and pointed at its target, the spear tip that the hand held dipping to point. The clipped off portion of energy and aura, spinning through the air to flash past Boss Choi cut inches away from his body.

All on its way to its final target.

A hand, clutching a blade. It struck hard, splitting open skin and breaking tiny bones in the hand as it did so. The blade held pressed against Mel spasmed open, the weapon digging in at first a little deeper into bare skin before falling aside.

Mel, having waited so patiently for a chance to escape, reacted. The arm holding her loosened and she sunk an elbow deep into her captor's stomach.

Retching from the pain, her captor doubled over. The other man clutching her had released her hand and turned to flee, for Amah Si and her people, along with the beggars, had charged at the Suey Ying when they realized Boss Choi was attacking Arthur, forcing him to back off. He bounced away and reached backwards, his spear landing in his hand as it was tossed to him. Initially stunned, they had unfrozen and were now unleashing their vengeance.

Even with her bonds, Mel fought, raining elbows and knees on her remaining captor. So doing, she managed to set him on the back foot, free of his interference. A particularly hard strike to the back of the neck left him choking, larynx shattered. As she got ready to run, another pair of Suey Ying cultivators sought to block her way.

All this Arthur took in as he ducked and weaved, his spear now rising and falling as he attempted to create space to fight at his preferred range. Boss Choi was too canny to allow that, forcing himself forward with each step, taking the occasional glancing blow of the spear shaft to close the distance. In the meantime, Choi's dark kris scored along Arthur's arms, depositing its poisonous curse.

Yin chi flushed through his body, combating the poison. His vision wavered a little as the invading energy—itself Yin—attempted to make him sleepy and lethargic, while his own chi tried to subsume the foreign energy. Thrumming through his body, acting on an instinctive level, his cultivation exercise flowed, acting against the invading energy in a way it had not before.

Thankfully, the minor change was only slightly distracting. Nowhere near enough to keep him from doing his best to defend himself against Boss Choi. He was also deeply grateful that he had put that extra point into Body, for Boss Choi was still significantly faster than him. If he was a seven, his opponent was at least a nine.

The only thing saving him was the fact that, for all his aggressiveness, Boss Choi was both distracted and less trained. The distraction was understandable though, for in the handful of breaths that they fought, Arthur's men and Amah's had closed half the distance.

"Just die lah, you!" Boss Choi snarled, throwing himself forward into an extended lunge.

Ill-conceived, for Arthur managed to sweep the kris point away and then, shortening his spear, brought its tip to point at the other's chest. Only a heroic twist at the last minute saved Choi, though a long tear across clothing and flesh spoke of the danger he had been in.

Choi rolled on the ground and came back lithely on his feet. He pointed his weapon at Arthur, daring him to close in even as he backed away, eyes darting towards Arthur's freely bleeding wounds and the creeping darkness on Arthur's skin. A savage grin of satisfaction crossed Choi's face, even as his opponents moved to surround him.

Arthur read it in his eyes, the way he shifted his feet and had begun to turn his head to verify what was behind him. In that moment, Arthur resolved to end it, throwing himself into a high leap and raising the spear above his head. At the same time, energy surged down his body as Heavenly Sage's Mischief empowered him and increased his speed.

At the same time, Focused Strike empowered the spear, flowing more easily than Arthur had ever expected. He swung his weapon down with everything he had, unleashing a shout of anger at the same time.

"CHOI!"

Boss Choi looked up, then brought his hands and kris together in defense. However, it was not enough, not against the twice-empowered attack. Wood crashed into metal and the slim kris's handle slipped out of Boss Choi's fingers as the impact made his fingers numb.

The blow had not finished. The spear shaft cracked against Choi's defense and broke it, before coming down on his collarbone. It shattered the delicate bone, forcing him to his knees.

A wave of weakness flowed up Arthur's arms and threatened his balance as he landed. At that moment he was vulnerable to a counterattack. But without a weapon, the kris having fallen to the ground, Boss Choi had a single option.

He used it.

A glowing redness enveloped Choi's fingers as he thrust them forward with his uninjured arm. It sunk deep into Arthur's side, the penetrating strike puncturing his body. A savage twist of his hand and a slight curl of his fingers as he exited allowed Choi to leave a wider wound on exit. Arthur collapsed.

But in his quest for vengeance, Boss Choi had forgotten his other opponents. A running tackle from Yao Jing took him in the side, forcing him off Arthur. The pair rolled on the ground for a second before Yao Jing used his feet to launch Choi off his body.

A shimmering field of energy had formed around Choi in the meantime, and a few stray ranged attacks bounced off him. As he landed and rolled aside, letting out a long cry of pain as it jarred broken bones, the beggars descended.

Makeshift weapons rose and fell, slamming into the protective shielding that flickered. Blood flew as Boss Choi empowered his attacks, but he was only a first-floor cultivator. He had not the strength to endure such an assault for long. Beneath the gleeful blows rained upon him, Boss Choi's shield faltered. And died.

Much like the leader of the Suey Ying tong soon after.

Chapter 102

Arthur clutched his side, breathing hard. He felt his life's blood pumping out, the warm slickness of the liquid slipping between his fingers. Every short and fast breath he took made Arthur all too aware of the broken ribs.

"You fool!" Amah Si was by his side, skidding to a stop. "You stupid idiotic man! I had it!" She yanked a bandage from her bag, pushing his hand aside as she forced it on his wound.

"You. Had. Nothing," Arthur snarled. "I won't. Let anyone. Die."

"Then you'll let *everyone* die. Eventually. You're a leader, not a damn hero!" Amah snarled back, shoving the bandage even harder and eliciting a cry of pain from Arthur. She kept it pressed tight, even as his breathing deepened and energy began to flow from her arm.

"I. Can be. Both," Arthur panted around the pain, even as he felt the healing energy suffuse him. "Have to be both." Then, as the pain subsided a little, added. "You can heal?"

"A little. Not enough..." Amah's voice had trailed off, for her energy was questing in him. Mingling with his own Accelerated Healing method which had already begun the process of fixing him. Blood had clotted fast, split ends of capillaries and veins and arteries having curled up, compressing themselves to decrease the loss of blood. "What is this?" she asked.

"Accelerated. Healing." Arthur had to close his eyes, for the loss of blood was making him weak. He found himself pouring refined energy into the technique, attempting to heal himself. But the technique was only at Grade II level, its method unrefined and unfocused. It tried to do too much at once, not just heal his wound but also fight the poison within him.

Sinking deep into his body, sensing the cultivation technique he was wielding with greater alacrity, Arthur embraced the pain and the floating sensation. The coldness of a Yin Body allowed him to clinically judge the situation, to grasp the greater danger.

Now, he just had to fix it.

Ignore the wounds on his arm or the creeping Yin-based poison that was leeching his energy and attempting to put him to sleep. Contain it, to where it could not do greater harm like reaching his heart or brain. Instead, focus on the still-bleeding wound in his side.

He felt the strands of energy weaving themselves. At first, Arthur attempted to stop them from flowing to his other wounds, using blocks like the one he formed for the poison to reroute the energy.

The energy built up, growing more intense behind the barriers he had created, eating away at the blocks he had created. At the same time, the pain in his arms, and along his hip where he had picked up a cut, somehow intensified. He groaned, collapsing at the same time as the blocks gave way.

Shouts from above, outside him. He felt warm hands gripping him, laying him down, but Arthur's focus was not on them but deeper within. The blood at his side kept flowing outwards even as it failed to clot properly.

Not blocks then. Guidance?

He reached for the energy as it exited his dantian, attempting to grasp and lead it directly to his wounded side. Not all of it, for the mental grasp he had of the energy was slippery. Prone to escaping as he worked to move it in the direction he needed.

More than once, he would pull and pressure the energy upward from the dantian to his side, only for it to fall away. Yet, as it did so, he noticed that the energy kept moving, branching along unseen meridians to keep flowing.

Meridians...

He reached into them then, knowing that the flow of energy through the meridians in his body was how it shifted, changed to become more or less aspected for certain kinds of uses. He tugged at the lines that glowed brightest, opening up the channels that led to his wound.

The energy that had struggled against his grip earlier slipped through his meridians with ease. It no longer needed his bidding, a portion of the energy itself seeming alive and hungering to do its job. It reached the site of the wound. Injuries that weren't along its path slowed in their self-healing, because he could only dedicate so much refined energy at one time.

The blood that had been pouring out of his side slowed and then stopped, the wound beginning to stitch together. Realising what might occur, Arthur moved to push Amah's hand away, only to find the older woman already extracting the bandage herself. At the same time, Amah Si had her head cocked to the side, as if listening to the wound itself.

"Fascinating," she muttered, her own energy pulsing through his. Her energy flow had slowed, trickling to a much-reduced rate as Arthur himself took over the work of healing his wounds. Her lips moved wordlessly, and even if Arthur had the presence of mind to try lip-reading her, the occasional audible word indicated she was speaking in Malay. And rapidly too.

More importantly, Arthur was battling his own body. While the pain had decreased as the body healed, he found himself with an entirely new problem. Forcibly prying open portions of his own meridian network had created a gap that his own energy rushed to fill. He could feel the refined energy within his core trickle away, disappearing at a rapid rate as more energy than ever flowed through him.

Right now, it was healing him, but what happened when the initial injury was over? What happened when all the injuries were healed? Would the energy continue running, without pause? Isn't that how cancer happened? And that aside, what would happen when his core ran out of refined energy?

Would his core break? Or would it attempt to drain unrefined energy directly from his body and soul?

Rather than answer those questions directly, Arthur did his best to forestall the need to find out. He worked on his meridians, attempting to close a smaller branch off from the gushing energy. At first, pushing against the energy did not work; the energy simply poured around his mental block. Only when he pinched his meridians shut, the action a weird flexing of muscles he had never even known he had, did the energy pouring through him slow down.

Noting that the majority of the damage to his side had been dealt with, the veins and arteries stitched together, Arthur turned his attention to the rest of his body. He worked as quickly as he could to slow down the gushing energy, gripping and squeezing meridians one after the other even as his refined energy levels dropped precipitously.

Moments before it was entirely drained, he managed to shut down the runaway cultivation exercise, leaving him to release a long-held breath of relief. As he relaxed, exhaustion and blood loss swarmed him, pulling him down into the land of noctis.

Just ahead of a notification that the Tower was pressing upon him.

Chapter 103

Arthur woke up groaning. His head pounded and his stomach—his core—pulsed from the strain of his earlier actions. His side still ached too, and the cuts on his arm pulsed in slow, aching rhythm in counterpoint to one another.

Hissing a little, Arthur tried to sit up, only to fold back down on the bed even as his eyes struggled to open fully, the world a blurry outline of dark blues and browns. Memory of his battle with the gang leader and his own wounds clamoured for attention, even as he delved within, searching for the poison.

A poison that had grown quiescent. He could not feel it at all, a rather disturbing notion. Rather than worry, he sought illumination, allowing the notifications that the Tower served to spring to mind. Somehow, he doubted he was in danger. Considering how he had fallen asleep. Not just yet anyway.

> ***Skill Improved: Accelerated Healing – Refined Energy (Grade II) -> (Grade III)***
>
> *Passively increases base Tower healing rate by 71.9%.*
>
> *Active use of technique increases base Tower healing rate by 213.1%.*

Healing may now be directed.

May not replace lost limbs or other permanent injuries.

Active Cost: 0.1 Refined Energy per 10 minutes.

Well, that was better than he had expected. He could not help but do the math. In general, a single cleanly broken bone could take three to four days to heal, depending on the size of bone and the Body component of the cultivator. A base seventy percent increase to that meant that an injury with a four-day healing period would fix itself in three days now.

Strained muscles would be gone within a matter of hours, if not minutes. Torn ligaments took around the same time to heal as broken bones, though that depended on which ligaments. Obviously, hamstrings and ACLs were going to be a problem.

Which made Arthur wonder if increased stiffness and wasting was a problem now. Would he need to stretch and move normally in those few hours, just so that he did not harm himself? Or was the magical, unnatural method of healing by the Tower already taking care of such minor inconveniences?

Putting that aside, the doubling of his healing speed while concentrating and actively using the ability meant that he would be on his feet within days rather than bedridden for days on end. Taking all that into mind, he gauged the damage on his side, trying to remember how much of it had been healed during his more intensive process.

In the end he gave up, not able to work out how much time had passed.

"Perhaps in the future. I can work out the speed. With a pedicure. For it is a need." Even Arthur winced at that one.

More interesting was the ability to redirect the healing process to damaged portions, and to speed and overcharge the healing. It had saved his life before, and he expected it would do so again in the future. If he managed to get this healing process to even higher levels, it would make him a truly formidable opponent.

"Wolverine, here I come," Arthur muttered to himself. Reaching up gingerly, he rubbed at his eyes, clearing the sleep from them and cracking his gaze fully open. The blues and browns resolved to the wall colouring and ceiling beams, though the room held no clues as to where he was.

Prodding at his notifications even as he looked around at the empty room, Arthur read through the remainder of notices quickly. There was little of note, ranging from an indication of a strain to his core—

which explained why it throbbed—and an estimated healing time—in mere hours now—as well as a warning that his store of refined energy was dangerously low.

Again, not surprising.

He would need to cultivate and restore some of that energy, but it was more important for Arthur to work out where he was. Somewhere safe, he assumed. Then, smacking himself on the head, he walked over to the window and peered out, edging around the corner just in case someone wanted to shoot him.

No arrow or crossbow bolt went for his eye, and the view was sufficient to confirm his suspicion. He was in his own clan building.

Paranoia set at ease, Arthur made to explore his rooms again. The bedroom itself was of modest size, with the bed and desk taking up the majority of space within. Two doors led away from the room, the first to a living room with an attached kitchen where Yao Jing lounged. Arthur could not help but snort, spotting how the man was lying on the sofa with his legs up on the table, mouth open and snoring.

"Some guard you are," Arthur muttered.

Closing the door silently, he made his way over to the other door. No surprise that it turned out to be a washroom, one that he made quick use of to wash away dried blood, dirt, and sweat.

Was it strange that even now, he still had to brush his teeth? If the Tower could take away anything, change them so massively that they no longer needed to eat or defecate, could it not fix bad breath? And if it could have and chose not to, what did it say about its makers?

Lazy? Uncaring? Slobs?

Pondering these deep and meaningful thoughts, Arthur searched through his closet for clothing, grateful that whoever had dumped him here had at least planned ahead for his waking. Dressed soon after in new clothing, mindful that he had just destroyed his last new piece of clothing in the fight with Boss Choi, he grabbed the kris—which had somehow been returned—and his spear before exiting his bedroom.

"Wake up! Time to break up!" Arthur shouted when Yao Jing did not stir.

The poor cultivator nearly leapt out of his seat. He stumbled and fell as his legs got tangled in the table and then managed to sit up enough to put his hands up. To Arthur's surprise, rather than reaching for a weapon—in fact, did he never wear one?—Yao Jing's arms were glowing, aura sheathing his arms.

"Betraying me already?" Arthur said, looking hurt. "So quickly do you turn on your benefactor."

Silence greeted his words, as the other man breathed heavily. Then, slowly, he straightened, eyeing Arthur askance. "You always like this, ah? When there's no crisis happening?"

"Like what?"

"An idiot."

"If I'm an idiot, why are you following me?"

"An even bigger idiot, of course."

Arthur laughed then, and Yao Jing joined him a moment later. Tension left Arthur's shoulders as the earlier sentence filtered into his brain, reminding him that finally, finally, all the present crises were over.

"Alright, enough fun and games. Tell me how long I've been out, where everyone is, what happened while I was unconscious, and what new problems I've got to handle."

Now, he just had to deal with the upcoming ones.

Chapter 104

The briefing was quick and precise, Yao Jing able to concisely describe the happenings over the last seven hours. After he had fainted, Arthur had been brought back to the clan building under guard while the remaining members of the Suey Ying tong had been killed or taken prisoner. The impromptu alliance had then split apart, the immediate demands of the alliance fulfilled.

"But they still want something, right?" Arthur cocked his head to the side as he led the way down the hallway, searching for the exit. Thankfully, finding the staircase down was not hard and he still recalled details of the map well enough.

"Of course," Yao Jing said. "Who gives anything for free?"

"Captain America?" Arthur said, wryly. "Spiderman?"

"They're not real, lah."

"Mother Theresa?"

"Heard she's not nice, actually."

Arthur stopped halfway down the stairs, hand on the railing—he was being careful on his way down. He looked back at Yao Jing, frowning. "Really?"

"*Ya.*"

"Shit." Arthur shook his head. "You going to tell children that Santa Claus isn't real, next? How about taking my UBI fix, dick."

"Do I need to?" Yao Jing snorted. "That's a Western thing, you know. As if we have chimneys. Aircon ducts maybe."

That brought a laugh to Arthur, only for him to grip his side in pain as it sent arcing tendrils of agony from his wound through him. Still, the image of a portly Santa Claus trying to squeeze his bulk through air conditioning ducts like a wizened, bearded John McClane was hilarious to him.

"You good, boss?"

"I'll live." A slow deep breath as the laughing stilled, and then he kept going down. Meeting rooms on the bottom floor, his own residence at the top. Why was it that the more "important" you were, the more walking you were supposed to do?

He was nearly to the ground floor when Uswah found him. He blinked, remembering the mission he had assigned her, to find and save the prisoners. "How'd it go?"

"Easy." Uswah shrugged. "We found them."

"How many? Any, uh..." He trailed off, not wanting to describe it.

"Four. Three of ours, another random that got swept up because she was a woman," Uswah said in return. "Two guards. More intent on watching one another than us."

"Really?"

"Yes. Problem?"

Arthur considered that question, his own feelings. Truth was, it mattered little to him. A small part of him, the part that had grown up in Malaysia was a little disgusted. Mostly though, he found that his feelings were cold, dispassionate. He cared not what they did, not in this case.

"No. You got them out, right?" Arthur confirmed.

A nod, and Arthur gestured down the way. Uswah stepped aside, following him down as she continued her report. "We got them back. Amah's handling our allies, but it's all breaking apart. Now that the Suey Ying aren't a target..."

"There's no reason to be with us," Arthur said. "And we aren't strong enough, not ourselves, to keep them together. Not when other trouble might be coming."

"Pretty much."

"Then what do we do?" Yao Jing said from behind the pair.

Uswah shrugged, not having a suggestion. Nor did Arthur, not at this moment. Everything that happened had been a headlong rush, from one crisis to another, and then nothing. Now, he had time to plan, and Arthur realized that he really sucked at it.

"You have no idea what you're going to do, do you?" Amah Si said, arms crossed in the meeting room. There were only clan members in here, a good hour after Arthur had finished adding a slew of other members of the Thorned Lotuses to the clan roster. No improvement to the clan stats, though, nothing beyond a minor upgrade in their Credit Rating, and he still had no clue what it did.

"Nope," he said. There was something freeing about being brutally honest. And in here, with Amah and Uswah, Mel, and Jan, nothing else but frank honesty would suit him. Even Yao Jing had been relegated to the outside of the room. "Do you?"

"We need allies. You risking your life, risking the clan because of some foolish, juvenile notion of heroism—that set us back further than you can believe," Amah said, scathingly.

"Really?" Arthur said. "Or was it the fact that you were willing to let one of your own people die, for nothing more than a short-term gain?" His gaze trekked over to Mel. "Sometimes trust, once broken, can't be repaired."

Mel's face was stoic, showcasing nothing of her feelings or inner thoughts.

"And if you had died? The clan would have gone. Just like that. After everything we sacrificed," Amah bit back.

"They sacrificed."

"Now, you want me to plan for you. Figure out what we're going to do, when you can just destroy everything I'm working for in moments."

Ah. And so here it was. Arthur let out a long sigh, knowing that it had come to pass now. The struggle for supremacy, between him and her. Who really ran the clan? For a moment, he regretted having let her in, having so easily given her what she wanted. Not without knowing how to kick her out.

And yet...

"Yes. Exactly," Arthur said. "And if you don't like it, I recommend you leave." Arthur leaned forward, wincing a little as his side throbbed. "This is my clan. I told you that. I told your people that. I'm sorry it happened this way, but there's only one way this is going to work, and you know it."

"You think you have a clan without me? Without my people?"

Arthur cocked his head, looking over to Mel, Uswah, and Jan who sat around the table. He looked at them, people he had fought with, suffered with. Then he took a gamble and gestured. "Why don't you ask them?"

His words shocked the older woman. She turned then to her people. Or what she had thought were her people. In her eyes, there was a trace of doubt now as she awaited judgment.

"I'm with you, Amah. Always." Jan fixed Arthur with a flat look, but she was no surprise.

Uswah spoke next, her voice soft. "I joined to climb." She raised the stump of her arm now. "That doesn't seem possible, not if I follow you, Amah. I'm sorry. At least he's got a way. Maybe."

Amah growled, but eventually nodded. She understood. How could she not? Then, there was one left. And this time, Mel stared back at Amah, her gaze weighing against the other. Recollection of all that had been said, all that had been done, reflecting in both their eyes.

"Do you need me to say it?" Mel said, eventually.

Amah Si held the other woman's gaze for a long beat more, before she ducked her head.

Into the uncomfortable silence, Arthur forged on.

"Well, that's that then. Can we move on to something more productive?"

Chapter 105

Amah Si sat silent and sullen for a long moment after the tiny rebellion against her. But both she and Arthur knew that the trio of followers within this room were not necessarily representative of the world outside. He had bled and fought with these three, whereas to many others he was just a lucky novice.

Yet, they were her people too. Her strongest and most trusted. More so, while she might throw a fit, she needed him to grow stronger, to progress himself and the clan consequently. She could not just throw him into a prison cell, allowing him only the task of inducting new clan members every once in a while.

Into the silence, Arthur could not help but extend an olive branch. "I can't do this without you. I'm not that arrogant. I need you, Amah, if you'll take me. We just have to learn to work together."

"With you the boss."

"And the target."

That brought a smile to Jan's face and then Amah's in turn. He snorted, but it was true enough.

"Fine. But you have to learn to deal with those heroic impulses. You're no wandering hero," she waggled a finger at him. "You die, we die."

Arthur nodded. "So what now?"

"We formalize our alliance with those who will take us." Amah Si paused, then raised a single finger. "The beggars. They need help. Many of them are weak, but they're strong in here." She tapped her chest. "We give them a chance, they can become strong outside too."

"Huh. I thought you were going to speak of the Double Sixes."

"Your problem." Amah Si crossed her arms. "You wanted that alliance. I wouldn't have worked with thugs like that."

Jan, who had formed the initial agreement flushed red, ducking her head low at the indirect criticism. Curious, Arthur thought, that the normally self-assured and annoying woman felt like that. Arthur made a mental note of it but moved on.

"Sure." Arthur stood up, walked over to the door, and opened it, finding Yao Jing leaning against the wall. "Find Mohammad Osman. Let's organize a more formal meeting. If we're going to be allies, I need to know what I owe him. And what else he wants."

Yao Jing frowned, opening his mouth to protest being sent as a messenger, only for Arthur to glare at him. He bobbed his head and left, allowing Arthur to close the door and walk back to his seat.

"Done. So, take as many of the beggars as we can." Arthur looked at Jan, then grinned evilly. "Jan, you know the fighting groups. Break them up, put them in with our harvesters, once they're in? We can help them get experience at fighting that way."

Mind spinning, Arthur considered the ways and methods he needed to grow the group before looking at Uswah. "We need a library. And a schedule."

"Schedule?" she said.

"Harvesting, training, and cultivating." Arthur ticked the words off each finger. "The basis of all growth in strength in the Tower, right?"

Mel nodded, humming a little. "The Three Pillars."

"Right. Cores, Skills, and Cultivation. We need a way for people to grow in strength, and we need to figure out an organization for those who don't want to progress and are content to play support for the rest who do," Arthur said.

"We have that," Amah Si said, cutting in. "Just put them in our system."

"Maybe," Arthur said. "You got it written up? You write it, I green-light it."

The old woman rolled her eyes at Arthur's rhyming.

"Really. I need it written down. So I can read about it."

"You're asking for paperwork?" Amah said, surprised.

"I guess I am." Arthur shrugged. "Is that a problem?"

"Your *head* got problem," Jan interjected.

That got everyone to glare at her and she subsided sulkily.

"No. I'll have it written up."

"In the meantime, do you have any cultivation exercises you have written down that can be shared?"

Cultivation exercises given out by the Tower disappeared, but it did not stop cultivators from copying what they remembered down. Of course, there was a difference between Tower-aided learning and work written by mere mortals. But it did mean that you could eventually save on Tower credits.

Which led Arthur to another depressing thought: he had almost no credits at all in his individual account. After all this time, he was still as penniless as when he had started out.

"What's wrong?" Mel asked, her voice gentle.

"Just thinking about my lack of points." Arthur sighed.

"We'll fix that," Uswah said, speaking up. "A tax should do the trick."

"I don't know about that..." Arthur trailed off. It was an uncomfortable feeling, taxing people for his own gain, especially when he was offering them so little.

"The stronger you are, the stronger we are." Amah pointed to his hand on which the clan seal lay branded. "Literally."

"Right," Arthur said. "Almost makes me want to lock myself up in the building for a few months, doing nothing but cultivate." His words were met with an uncomfortable silence, at least to him. Looking from woman to woman, Arthur let out a low groan. "Really?"

"At least a cultivation exercise to strengthen your body," Mel said. "And you should cross the first threshold."

"That's... months!" Arthur replied. "I don't even think we have enough cores for that."

"Probably not."

"Anyway, the moment I hit first threshold, I'm on a timer," he said, gesturing around. "There's not enough energy on this floor to deal with the drain, so I'm going to have to go up."

"Ei, not necessarily. You just spend more time cultivating, lah," Jan said, waggling a hand. "Look at Amah Si. She's fine." When Amah glared at Jan, she lifted her chin a little. "Allies, right?"

Amah bobbed her head after a moment, grumpily. Arthur could not help but smile a little, at having acquired a secret of Amah's. Then he snapped his fingers suddenly. "Library items. You distracted me!"

"I think you distracted yourself," Mel pointed out.

"Library items."

"There are not many," Amah said, interrupting the burgeoning argument. "Of those, you already have two that are similar. Focused Strike and a close derivative, Precision Blow. And then an elemental form, known as Flaming Fist. We have three cultivation exercises we're still writing down. One close to finished, I think, but the other two aren't."

"What are they?"

"Bark Skin. It's in a line of skin reinforcement cultivation exercises, going up to Copper, Iron, Steel Skin, and so forth." Suddenly, Amah's lips twitched. "We're not sure if Jade Skin is meant to be part of the same line, or if it's just a cosmetic bonus. Or both. It's expensive either way."

"I'll... let someone else experiment on that," Arthur said.

The girls laughed at his hesitation, before Amah Si continued. "Bark Skin's the closest we have to being finished. It was nearly done when..." She trailed off, shaking her head. "Well, the people who had it died. And the last person we have I ummm…. Not really good providing more info."

"Still, if it's not a lot of credits..." Arthur hummed to himself, thinking. He could pick up that cultivation exercise and add to it once he learned it well, providing a boost to his clan. Anyway, he needed some form of protection.

"Exactly," Amah Si said. "The other two exercises we have are a movement method and a weapon technique for slings."

"Slings?" Arthur said, surprised.

"Yes. It can be used for other things, but it imbues an object with chi before it blows up."

Arthur's eyes sparkled, suddenly licking his lips. Now, that was something he could get behind. If he could combine that with his Refined Energy Dart technique...

"I'll want to see that. And the Bark Skin technique," Arthur said.

"Then you'll stay hidden and train?"

Arthur hesitated, then sighed. "I'll stay in the newbie village and train. I still need to add the beggars and speak with Mohammad Osman, but as you said: The stronger I get, the stronger the clan gets." He chuckled suddenly. "Anyway, I think I'm done with walking through forests for a bit."

"Just a bit," Mel chimed in, holding her fingers slightly apart.

Chapter 106

The meeting went on for a little while longer, with some basic details explained about the organization of the Thorned Lotuses—now subsumed by the Benevolent Durians. After that, Uswah returned with documents for the two techniques that Arthur was particularly interested in, warning him not to lose the copies. Without photocopying machines and the like, the documents had to be handwritten, leaving them with only a few precious copies.

"I got it, I got it. No losing them," Arthur said. "Not as though I'm going anywhere."

Uswah just glared at him until he bobbed his head in an agreeable indication before she left, allowing the next group to arrive. In this case, more members of the Lotuses. Thankfully, they had all been briefed about asking further questions, though Arthur made sure to reiterate his rules and watch for any rebelliousness.

No surprise that his first rule garnered minor indicators of dislike. Yet, no one protested. All he could do, Arthur knew, was prove himself. Coming into an existing organization was never easy and it would take time for them to know him, to trust him. And for him to earn their true loyalty.

He just hoped he didn't have to bleed and die with them for that to happen. He was a little tired of constantly being in life-and-death situations.

"Alright, that's the fifth batch. Exactly how many more do you guys have?" Arthur asked, eyeing the notification in the corner of his gaze.

Clan Members: 88

"Just over two dozen more, but they're all out of the building right now. We'll sort them out tonight," Mel said.

Amah had disappeared, heading off to speak with their former allies to smooth matters out. Arthur had asked if he should go but had been turned down. Initially, she muttered that she wanted to feel them out. More formal meetings would happen later, when expectations had been worked out.

As always, taking time to discuss matters slowly and privately, in advance of any public meetings, would help prevent the clan from collapsing in on itself, A risk even Arthur had to admit was quite possible.

"Now what?" Arthur said.

Mel shook her head. "Jan's looking for the beggars. And Yao Jing hasn't returned yet. So I think we're good." She pointed to his books. "Maybe read those? Or cultivate? You're still a little..."

"Bare? A lousy brood mare?" Arthur said, grimacing as he touched his chest. "I'd say you're right but I'm not sure I'll stay uninterrupted long enough. So I'll read."

"I'll leave you to it. I'll be outside. Call if you need anything."

Waving goodbye idly, Arthur was already reaching for the contents of the library. He hoped he could find something useful, something that could spark further refinement of his abilities. Or hell, teach him how to protect himself better.

He was getting tired of being beaten up, even if that process had helped him gain his most powerful skill thus far: Grade III of Accelerated Healing. Then again, that was life, wasn't it? Everything had two sides, if you looked at it properly.

Just a question if you were willing to look at it in the right way.

Though, thinking of Uswah, he could not help but wonder what kind of silver lining losing an arm might have.

The Bark Skin technique recorded by the Thorned Lotuses came in a series of manuals, with repeatedly crossed out words, sections taken apart and disputed by other scholars of the technique. It was a real mess, and after attempting to read through the first few pages as a study guide, Arthur switched tactics. He proceeded to skim the entire document, searching for an overall understanding of the technique rather than studying it in detail.

Perhaps then the various passages would make more sense.

Once he had finished reading through the documents twice, skimming once and closely reading once, Arthur could not help but sit back to contemplate the technique. That is, after the latest interruption, a question about the treasury which was, well, something to be dealt with.

In theory, Bark Skin was simple enough to enact.

Like all other Skin techniques, this was about reinforcing the outermost layer of protection in an individual. There was a whole section in the notes talking about the multiple layers of "skin" a human body had, and how this particular technique seemed to only reinforce the outer layer. The notes included speculation that other methods both improved the kind of reinforcement and the number of layers.

Arthur had found the idea intriguing and potentially even correct, but since it was all speculation, had dismissed it. Really, outside of the speculative elements and discussions and arguments about the right way to make the technique work, basics on how to perform the actual technique could have been summarized in a few pages.

Upon that realization, Arthur made his way to the door and requested pen and paper. It took nearly a quarter of an hour for the simple request to arrive, along with some tea. A testament to the degree of disorganization in his supposed organization.

Thankfully, when Arthur poked his head out again later, he noticed that Mel was seated outside, literally with a desk in place and barking orders at people. It seemed that some form of organization was being put in place.

Along with her playing his bodyguard, he assumed.

Over tea, he read over the cultivation exercise again and organized his thoughts. Then jotted down his own streamlined notes for the Bark Skin technique.

The entire process took him over an hour, but he had to admit that it was worth the effort. As any good student could tell you, writing the technique down helped embed the information in his mind even further.

In the end, when Arthur stood up, cracked his back, and was ready to actually start practicing the technique, he was certain he understood the rules quite well. Even more than the Focused Strike technique he had studied as his very first technique.

Which was, of course, when he was interrupted.

Chapter 107

"*Pao*?" Yao Jing asked as he entered the room, proffering the large white bun. The hulking cultivator looked quite smug and happy with himself, which had Arthur squinting at the other suspiciously. Even if the two of them had fallen into a comfortable routine, almost a friendship, with surprising ease, Arthur still could not forget that they had only known one another for a few days.

"Which kind?" Arthur asked.

"*Tai pao*," Yao Jing said. Arthur eyed the double-sized pao and snorted. He should have known. There weren't many white buns that came in that size.

"Why'd you buy one?" Arthur said, curious. "You know we don't have to eat."

"Need and want are not same," Yao Jing said.

"Also, how? I mean, the ingredients..."

"Can be bought from the Tower. So you better enjoy it, because that pao is worth one whole core."

Arthur winced but took the pao gratefully. Sitting back, he peeled the leaf that had been used to cover the bottom of the pao in place of the usual rice paper and split the still warm pao apart. Inside, bamboo shoots, sliced pork and chicken, yam beans, and a boiled egg were revealed, all giving off the rich smell of soy sauce and oyster sauce. Arthur's tongue began to salivate almost immediately, having not had actual food to eat in ages.

However, he held back long enough to say, "So, what else?" before he put half of the pao in his mouth and chewed.

"You sure you don't wanna eat first, ah?"

Arthur shook his head, even as he took his time chewing. The warm, soft, and bouncy outer skin mixed with the rich taste of the savoury filling, the chewiness of the cooked egg a subtle difference compared to the well-cooked sliced meat.

"Okay." Looking mournfully at the food in Arthur's hands, Yao Jing continued. "Took some time to find Osman and his gang. They had some trouble in their area, during the time they brought so many people to help us." Yao Jing frowned. "They're not so strong as you think. They got the usual gambling halls lah, brothels lah, and moneylenders lah—I mean, core-lenders. Anyway, trouble. That's why it took so long." When Arthur simply nodded, Yao Jing sighed a little.

Arthur made a note to praise the man more. Obviously, he was one who liked verbal and other forms of recognition. A smack on the back of the head and simply giving orders didn't motivate people enough. Arthur's sifu would have called them lazy, but Arthur figured people just were people.

Mostly.

"Osman's people are getting pushed out from their area. At first by the Suey Ying," Yao Jing said, which surprised Arthur since the Suey Ying had actually been smaller than the Double Sixes. "But now, some of the other triads are also pushing them. Osman's strong people went up to the next floor already. I think that's why, now, Osman wants to use your rooms, build up his people here. Safe and cheap-cheap, right?"

It made sense. Sticking around in newbie inns was expensive, even if it was the safest method. Doing cultivation in other locations, especially in areas that might be attacked, was less optimal. Arthur's clan building, on the other hand, provided peace of mind—which facilitated cultivation and training—as well as an environment with denser energy.

"Anyway. They have a few people ready to cross the first threshold. In a few weeks' time. But until then..." Yao Jing waggled his hands in concern.

"Hmm..." Arthur chewed on the pao, mind flicking over possibilities. There might be an opportunity there. A very good opportunity to not just build up the clan but also bind the Double Sixes to them. "Any other news on the kind of things they do? Drugs? Blackmail and slavery, murder and torture, that kind of thing?"

"No drugs. There's no supply. Tower doesn't sell anything. Kinda impossible to get regular supply of *anything* from outside."

"Okay fine, no drugs. *Summore*?"

"Murder: more killing than usual, lah. Sometimes beating people up, the usual thing." Arthur frowned at that, but it was not as though he didn't know what he was getting into. "But not like horrible, horrible."

Not the best of results, but not the worst. So long as they limited the alliance to this floor, it shouldn't be too bad. Maybe creating new alliances and groups on each floor made sense, rather than tying themselves to any organization as a whole.

It might make them a little more vulnerable though.

"When we meeting them?" Arthur asked before he took another bite, surprised to see that he had finished most of the pao already. He also noted that he'd switched back to Manglish. All too easy when you spent a lot of time with people who spoke it.

"Two days' time. They come here. I think they want to move in on the same day."

Arthur winced and then pointed to the door. "Okay. Sort the spacing out with Mel? We need to empty out this place anyway. Or figure out more places for people to stay. I don't think we can keep all the Thorned Lotuses here, and I'd like us to get to the point of only Clan here." He paused. "Or as much as possible, what with my earlier deals."

"Got it, boss." Giving a wave with two fingers, Yao Jing exited the room, leaving Arthur to the remnants of his meal and his documents.

All in all, that could have gone worse. Arthur still had lingering doubts about Yao Jing, but if he was going to expand the clan beyond the Lotuses, he was going to need to trust others. He just didn't have the time to take it slow.

Case in point: almost right away, there was a knock on the door. A group of rather furtive-looking individuals were hanging around outside. They had been cleaned up, faces and hair washed so that the dirt stains and blood were gone. Nothing could be done about the threadbare rags they wore though, which earmarked who they were.

Not that Arthur had anything against threadbare clothing. He recalled his own return to the village just a few days ago, his own clothing barely hanging on.

"Ready or not?" Jan said. Not that she had given him much opportunity to say no, what with the crowd already filing in. But at least she had asked.

Shrugging, Arthur pointed for her to enter and eyeballed the ragtag group. Now, how did he want to handle this?

Chapter 108

The beggars who filed in and stood before him were just over a dozen in number. They were all, uniformly, thin with a put-upon expression on their faces and haunted looks in their eyes. Movement, from Arthur, from Jan, from each other, caused them to shrink back a little or flinch, as though they were expecting to be struck or they were gearing up to run. Probably a little of both really.

How did you keep cultivators down? You took everything they earned or had, you harassed them until they were unable to sleep or otherwise rest peacefully. And you always kept them moving, so that they had no chance to cultivate at all.

It took a level of callous cruelty that sickened Arthur to think about, considering they were in a system that was designed to progress people if they even put in a little work. Yet, seeing the results of that cruelty before him, he realized that he too would have to be cruel as well, to some extent.

"You have been informed, I believe, about what I am offering?" Arthur said, sweeping his gaze over the group and alighting on Joe and Suriani who stood side by side.

No surprise that he was the one who answered, even going so far as to move forward a little and lean on the table to speak to Arthur, who had stayed seated throughout the entire process. "We heard. What makes you think we want it?"

"A guess," Arthur said with a shrug. "You don't have to take it. The Suey Ying aren't holding you down anymore. You might be able to cultivate and grow stronger, even break through and climb the floors. But... just because the Suey Ying are gone, it doesn't mean everyone who saw what they did are gone too. Some might be even worse."

"How could they be worse?" Joe snarled, the shaggy, messy black hair that might once have been a fashionable cut but not just looked like it had been hacked apart shaking.

Arthur just raised a single eyebrow, waiting.

"Murder... isn't acceptable," Joe said.

"It's not against the rules either," Arthur said. "As we found out. Maybe they won't do it to people when they first arrive, but later? Nothing to stop them, beyond the fact that no group here wants a bunch of murderers running around. Hard to keep a society running—and we do have a society here in the Tower—not if everyone kills everyone just for the heck of it."

He jerked a thumb over his shoulder. "There are others too who might object to a lawless society. The real powers, the ones who climb the Tower. They might not care as much about the first few floors, but eventually if fewer people ascend—"

"They'd have fewer to exploit," Joe filled in.

"Yes," Arthur said. "It might take a while, what with communication between floors only really going one way, but eventually they would act. And the last thing any of us want is them trying to take over the first few floors."

"Won't last long, lah," Jan said. "Some groups tried before, but not worth the money. Or their people."

Arthur had to admit she was not wrong. There was a reason the Suey Ying tong and other proxies were used. It was not worth controlling the first few floors oneself, especially when it meant delaying one's own ascension.

"You explaining why we shouldn't worry, no?" Joe said.

"Except it's a chaotic time now. And in the chaos, idiots always arise," Arthur said. "Or do you want to chance that everything is fine?" He shrugged. "In the end, what I'm offering is an opportunity to grow, relatively peacefully. Heck, maybe get a few points into your body in relative safety before you have to make it out."

"And what do you want for that?" Suriani spoke up. She had a little of the lilting but muted accent common to Malaysian Indians.

"Loyalty," Arthur replied immediately. "You'll have duties to the clan of course, things you should do to help build it up. But end of the day: loyalty. We aid you now, you aid us when you eventually grow strong."

"Forever and ever? Seems like a bad deal," Suriani said.

"All loyalty and respect eventually fades if it is not renewed. It's not like we'd provide nothing back in return all the time. But neither do I expect us to have to battle for your loyalty all the time."

Suriani smirked, while Joe was shaking his head. He pushed off the table, growling. "I won't be your hunting dog. Or anyone's dog. I didn't do it for the Suey Ying, and I won't do it for you."

"Is this why you got into so much trouble with them in the first place?" Arthur said, making Joe growl again. "No one said anything about being a dog. Or bowing. Or anything like that. Just that I expect loyalty."

"Like a mangy animal, cowering at your—agh!" He fell over coughing as Suriani extracted her elbow from his stomach. She smiled brightly at Arthur before turning to her people.

"Okay. You heard him. Swear or not, I don't care. *We* are not a formal organization, no matter what this idiot thinks." So saying, she smacked the back of Joe's head.

"One moment," Arthur interjected.

"What?" Suriani said, frowning.

"I have questions. Most importantly: what level are you all? How many points have you all invested?" Arthur said.

"Why does it matter?" she demanded.

"Everything," Arthur leaned forward. "If you're as weak as I think, it's going to be quite a bit before you can power up. And that's going to cost us." He drew a deep breath and let it out. "We'll still do it, but I need to know."

"That's..."

"Acceptable," Joe interrupted Suriani, straightening up as he rubbed his stomach. When both of them stared at Joe, he could not help but shrug and ask, "What?"

"I thought you would object to that question too," Arthur said.

"Why?" Joe said, still rubbing his stomach. "I had to see how far I could push you. But asking how strong your recruits are makes sense."

Arthur could not help but eye Joe more keenly now. He remembered his words, the way he spoke and moved. "Were you part of the army at some point? Did you go barmy there?" Arthur asked with a frown.

"Yeah," Joe said with a sigh. "Eleven years, before I got discharged. Dishonorably."

The man had jutted his chin out at that last word, which deepened Arthur's frown. Obviously, he was daring Arthur to make a thing about it. And curiosity demanded Arthur do the same. At the least, he wanted to know. "Why?"

"A superior officer was stealing all our supplies to sell off. So I gave him a good punch," Joe said, a wicked grin on his face.

"Well, I'll make sure not to get caught then," Arthur said.

Suriani laughed and then when she caught the put-upon face displayed by Joe, she laughed even more. Jan was smirking a little too, though she would not deign to actually laugh at one of his jokes, Arthur knew. That'd be giving him too much credit.

"Most have one to three points." Joe tapped his chest. "I have six points invested. Suriani's got five."

That was better than Arthur in terms of point investment though not in total points used for most of those. It was also, once again, a rather dire reflection of how underpowered Arthur was as a Clan leader. He really needed to spend some time training.

"This is going to be a pain," Arthur said with a sigh. "Jan..."

"I'm not a babysitter," she said before he could finish.

"Get them organized, at least. This is not a request." He then gestured to the door. "Now, I'm sure you've heard my rules, but here they are again. If you have a problem with them, leave." So saying, he reiterated his two rules, knowing that eventually he'd have to add more.

Eventually.

"Tyranny, not democracy. Heh." Joe crossed his arms, then nodded. "I can live with that. So long as the tyrant is benevolent."

"So says the name which is the same," Arthur said.

Laughing, the man gestured for Arthur to carry on. It did not take him long to add them to the clan, and for the beggars to receive their invitations via Tower system. Watching the group file out afterwards, to be organized and sorted out by Jan and Mel, Arthur could not help but smirk a little.

It was good having minions. Especially when so much of the work coming up was rather banal.

Chapter 109

The next few days passed by quickly enough. Barring a single visit to the Administrative Building that had required more co-ordination than he liked to get through the crowds, Arthur found his time taken up by studying the cultivation exercises and just cultivating. Even the visit to administration to learn more about his clan building and potentially upgrading it and his clan had been a waste of time. There was no information to be had, at least on this floor. Any enquiries were met with either a shrug or a reiteration that further information and upgrades were available on a higher floor.

In some ways, this was not too surprising. He was on the first floor of the most beginner-level of Towers. It spoke of the need to climb the Tower, but to do so he would need to strengthen himself.

Which was the entire point of his next few days. Other than sleeping and the occasional meeting when decisions could not be put off—or when he got too curious about clan matters that he asked for further information—Arthur focused on cultivating.

It was rather peaceful in his rooms, especially knowing that his suite was guarded at all times by others. Yao Jing, Jan and Joe, the trio of Js—as he called them in his head—took turns watching over his rooms. It amused him a little that the Js had decided to take on this role, but he assumed Jan was doing so under Amah Si's behest to keep an eye on him. Allies or enemies, keeping them close was smart.

The Bark Skin technique was an interesting experiment to apply. However, after the third attempt at making use of the notes, Arthur had placed it aside for later use. There was a reason that Amah Si had called it an incomplete technique, for even if he thought he had the exercise done right, the sizzling pain and cramping muscles of his arm had been a painful backlash.

Better then, for now, to focus on pushing ahead to the first threshold and achieving his second transformation. Using the last of his own share of the beast cores and staying focused, he managed to break through before the end of the second day, hours before he was to meet Mohammad Osman.

Glowing with happiness at his progress, modest though it might be, Arthur could not help but call up his status. It amused him that thanks to the Yin Body, he had a higher total number of points in attributes compared to his actual investment than others at the same threshold. So even if it seemed like he had not gotten far after all these months, he really had.

Or at least, he so told himself.

Cultivation Speed: 1.23 Yin
Energy Pool: 14/16 (Yin)
Refinement Speed: 0.035
Refined Energy: 0.00 (5)

Attributes and Traits
Mind: 5 (Multi-tasking)
Body: 7 (Enhanced Eyesight, Yin Body)
Spirit: 5 (Sticky Energy)

Techniques
Yin Body – Cultivation Technique

Focused Strike
Accelerated Healing – Refined Energy (Grade III)
Heavenly Sage's Mischief
Refined Energy Dart

Dropping the point into Mind had been a simple choice, though the restructuring and pain that came with the change had made him slip into unconsciousness for a few moments once more. Thankfully, it had been less of a shock for his system than before, since this was the second such upgrade.

The choice of a Mind trait, on the other hand, had taken him a little longer to decide. While Arthur had considered the straightforward choice of Calm Mind, which would have boosted his ability to deal with shocks and analyze fights like Uswah did, he hoped that with better planning such instances would be less common.

Empath and other social traits had been tempting, but with his experience of the past few days, Arthur leaned away from them. After all, it was better to allow others to manage people problems for him. So long as he could trust them to work for the clan, he could avoid managing people more than necessary.

No, what was best for the clan was improving himself. There was never enough time, though. And one thing he had noticed was that the demands on his time kept increasing.

So, it seemed like a good idea to get better at splitting his attention between thinking and doing things, whether in a fight or while talking to others or reading or whatever. Multi-tasking was only a single trait increase, but if he devoted enough traits to it and perhaps found a proper cultivation exercise, Arthur had high hopes of actually being able to process two things fully at once.

Maybe even cultivate and talk! Now, wouldn't that be amazing.

Till then, at least he could listen and read, fight and analyze, or otherwise split his thoughts a little easier. Multi-tasking might even make a good combination with an Ambidextrous Body trait, which granted the ability to dual wield properly. Future plans, future traits.

All good and well to plan, but he knew that something would crop up to throw all his plans in disarray at some point. It always seemed that way at least.

Bath, then an hour more of refinement to fill that yawning abyss of energy in his core, and finally Arthur made his way down to the meeting rooms, half an hour early. It was there that he took the first real report from Uswah about their resources, reading over the information received and tapping on it after a moment.

"Tax rates of one in twenty cores?" Arthur said, surprised. "That's pretty low, isn't it?" After all, even the government took a fifteen percent tax rate. Or others a tenth.

"We don't have much to offer yet. Also, you're the one who wanted to grow our people faster," Uswah said grimly. She pointed further down the document. "We still get a decent amount anyway."

Tracing his gaze down as indicated, Arthur had to admit she was not wrong. "One core per group per day, with seven groups ranging out there. So fourteen cores in two days." At that rate, it would take less than half a month for him to go up a full point if he took the entire thing for himself. "Not horrible at all." No wonder clans—and being clan head—were so sought after. "How are we distributing the treasury then?"

Uswah shrugged.

"What? You don't have a suggestion?"

"We do. But what do you want to do?" Uswah said pointedly. "Sometimes, you should consider asking that, no?"

Arthur sighed but nodded. He hated making such decisions, but she was right. He really should decide on this. "One in ten to me. Two to the people who are bureaucrats, as their salary. Two for reserve." He spoke out loud, using his fingers to count things down. "Five more... we invest?" He rubbed his chin. "Use it to push up people? Or give out loans?"

Uswah cocked her head to the side at his words.

Encouraged, he continued speaking out loud. "Clan loans. We offer three out of the ten as loans to people, and they have to pay us back. Three to one—so we get four back. We loan a maximum of, maybe, ten per person before they pay us back. And the last two out of ten, we use as direct bonuses. No repayment necessary, just an overall boost to our people."

"How do we decide who gets a bonus?" Uswah said.

Arthur shrugged. "Rotation and best clan members? I'll leave that to you to figure it out." At her glare, he shrugged. "Hey, I made the call. Now you can work out the details. But I think this works. We have ways for the ambitious to grow. A bonus for clan members. A way to compensate those who are stuck doing the admin with an upgrade. And to reward those who do particularly well. Maybe we only give a small portion of the bonuses out immediately, and the rest when someone does something amazing."

"Employee of the month?"

"If it works."

Uswah snorted but before they could get into it, a knock on the door stopped them short. Yao Jing popped his head in to warn them. "Mohammad Osman, incoming."

"Thanks."

She was already gathering up her materials, while Arthur made sure to flip over the few documents he wanted to keep, hiding the notes. Lacing his fingers together, he drew a deep breath and let it out.

Time to see how deep a hole he'd thrust them into, working with Osman and the Double Sixes.

Chapter 110

"Have you settled in well?" Arthur asked Mohammad Osman, minutes after the pair had finished their introductions and small talk. Nothing of importance had been said, and Arthur hoped that nothing major would arise.

"We have. The rooms are slightly small and cramped, but otherwise, we are well."

"All too true. Though yours is a decent size, no?" Arthur said, his smile not reaching his eyes. After all, he knew what the man was angling for, and he was certainly not going to offer any additional rooms.

"It is fine," Mohammad Osman said.

Silence, slightly uncomfortable, stretched out between the pair. Now that there were no looming crises, Arthur was not sure what they had to say to one another. He found himself reviewing his earlier thoughts, his goals for this meeting.

Firstly, find out how bad things were for the Double Sixes and what, if any, kind of help they expected from the Benevolent Durians. But Arthur wanted to ensure his clan was not drawn into the fight, if possible.

Secondly, outline any additional help that the Sixes would offer the Durians for their ongoing alliance and provision of rooms. Or, to put it another way, to flesh out what the rental agreement looked like.

Thirdly, see if Osman's group had any resources or manuals he could trade for.

"Your..." Arthur began to say.

"We..." Osman said at the same time.

The pair stopped, trailing off. Arthur flushed, a little embarrassed, while the older man smirked and gestured at him to continue.

"Your group. All goes well?" Arthur said, choosing to be blunt. Or bluntish.

"As well as can be. Some minor issues, but they are being handled. We will show them the error of their ways," Mohammad Osman said. "A small matter."

Arthur nodded, letting the topic drop like the man so obviously wanted. His goal was not to have the Durians dragged into a fight after all. Everything else did not matter too greatly.

"Good. Then about the ongoing payment for your presence," Arthur said, leaning forward. "After this month, of course, which you have earned."

"What do you wish?"

"People." Arthur ticked his fingers off. "A promise of help, if some other group starts causing problems again." The older man merely nodded, dark eyes glittering with suppressed amusement. "Perhaps a trade of your cultivation exercises that you might have written." He paused, then added. "Beast cores."

"You are asking for a lot."

"I'm offering the only truly safe location in town—apart from Tower-controlled buildings. I think there's a lot that I'm giving here."

"And that makes you the tallest *lalang*. The one which irritates the most."

"Maybe. But there's only so much they can do to us, inside the zone." He waved his hand around himself. "Worst case, we sit inside and grow strong and then come out."

The older man nodded, rubbing his chin. "If that is the case, why do you need us then?"

"Because I'd rather we be proactive, no?" Arthur shrugged. "If we can keep our people safe and hunting monsters for their cores, we can grow faster. And we'll need that strength when we move upwards."

"To the next floor."

"Exactly." Arthur smiled grimly. "Not ideal to stay holed up in my own building. Simply cultivating, without cores... climbing each floor would take forever. Though it is possible."

"Not ideal, as you said."

"And I don't want to go stir-crazy. So here we are. Trying to figure out a way to ensure none of that is required."

"I cannot speak for those above me."

"I don't expect you to. An alliance on this floor, for now, is sufficient."

Now it was Mohammad Osman's turn to grow silent, as he considered matters. "We have a few cultivation techniques here, meant for our people. We can allow you to have a copy, but that will be a separate deal—outside of our regular rent."

"Even if we reduced your rent for months?"

"Yes." The man smiled grimly. "I will risk my neck, simply by offering our techniques. As you know, written techniques are rare. So the only way forward is to trade techniques: ours for yours."

"Ah..." Arthur let out a long breath as he began to realize the man's goal. Still, better to ask than guess and get it wrong. "And the techniques you want are?"

"Your healing method."

Of course Osman would want that. Healing techniques were hard to get and, of course, in demand. No one wanted to stay injured. The ability to fix oneself fast meant getting back to cultivating and hunting for cores...

Well. In the long term that could make quite the difference. Already, Arthur knew that it was likely helping people like Mel and the others injured in the big fight get on their feet faster. Hunting groups could stay out longer, return to the hunt faster.

"Two problems with that." Arthur held out his fingers. "My healing technique is not written down, yet. And it's pretty rare, isn't it? So you're going to have to pay up if we start on this."

Mohammad Osman frowned. "I have heard reports that..." He trailed off, staring at Arthur who refused to elaborate further. Eventually, the man nodded to himself as though a suspicion had been confirmed. "I do not think you have anything else to offer us, then."

"Well, before we end this, why don't you tell me about what you have," Arthur said, turning his hands sideways. "Writing down the cultivation exercise might not be a bad idea, and giving you a copy might be viable." He scratched his chin. "Or we could train one of your people. And they could pass it on eventually."

Mohammad Osman's eyes narrowed in thought at that second suggestion. Obviously, the first person to be trained would be him, at first blush. But if Osman wanted to keep climbing, staying around long enough to impart the exercise to the next person might take too long. Though, Arthur could not guess if he was like Amah, content to stay on this floor.

Then again, Osman was middle-aged. The old and worn usually did not have the burning ambition of youth.

"And you would wait? To take that long to train another?" the man challenged Arthur.

"I... well, others could do it too." Arthur shrugged. "I won't be staying any longer than I have to."

"As I thought." Arms crossed, the older man shook his head. "No deal."

Arthur let out a huff. Perhaps they could revisit this conversation later. That is, after Osman had given up on the idea of gaining Arthur's healing ability. Even if the Double Sixes had nothing that was particularly powerful or unique, Arthur still felt it would be good for the Durians to expand their options.

"Let's talk about the rent then. Without library access or cultivation techniques in play," he said, moving on. And boy, did they have to figure out how to keep those things under better watch and distribution. Making a mental note to have a conversation with Uswah and Amah Si about that, Arthur focused on the next discussion with Osman.

If they were not going to get cultivation techniques out of the Sixes, then Arthur would have to squeeze all he could get out of those rentals.

After all, he really did need to keep growing.

Chapter 111

To Arthur's surprise, the Benevolent Durians were left alone for an entire week before they faced their first challenge. What currently had Arthur feeling superfluous was the fact that the entire event – and resolution – had happened without him being informed. Now, late in the evening, Yao Jing, Mel, and Jan were standing before him, under his glaring eyes.

"So, after they beat up our third hunting team, you thought the best way to deal with them was to put together your own group, hunt them down and thrash their place while stealing all their cores," Arthur said coldly, sweeping his gaze over the stolen goods placed before him. "Is that right?"

"Ah... yes?" Yao Jing said, hesitantly.

Turning his gaze away from the man, it rested on Jan who gave a curt nod. Arthur rubbed his face before fixing his eyes on Mel. "And you knew about this?"

"About the reprisal attack? Yes." Mel inclined her head. "I didn't give orders to rob them, though." Her voice grew wintry.

"Yes, about that..." Arthur drew a deep breath and then released it. He really did not have time to deal with this. "Later. Let's tackle this one thing at a time. Starting with why I wasn't informed about our teams being attacked."

"You were cultivating. It didn't seem important enough to disturb you," Mel said, shrugging.

"It wasn't important enough? People attacking ours isn't important enough?" Arthur growled.

"We've had outsiders testing our people the entire week," Mel growled. Seeing Arthur's look of surprise, she waved a hand. "It's expected. We're the new power, and they want to know how much we've got. So they're probing. It's all individual challenges, all taunts to see who is what."

Yao Jing was nodding right alongside before he added, "Ya, ya. Lots of people want to fight me all the time. I tell them to go fly kite, but they still wanna pick a fight. *Haish!*"

Jan grinned. "Same here. I just beat them until blue-black."

Mel growled at Jan who shrugged unrepentantly. "We have some of our better fighters taking the occasional challenge to try to head this all off, but obviously it hasn't worked. Since they were still a small group, we chose to make an example of them."

"Why is this the first I'm hearing of it!" Arthur threw his hands up. "I can't be your boss if you won't tell me what's going on. That's what you're supposed to be doing every morning."

Mel shrugged. "Again, it wasn't important. I can handle such things." She crossed her arms. "We always had challenges like this when we were under Amah. People trying their luck. Trying to see if they can take advantage. It's just more of the same thing. I didn't tell Amah, so why should I tell you?"

"Did she know it was happening?"

Mel reluctantly nodded.

"That's why you should tell me!" He roared, slamming his fist on the table. "I'm not her. I don't know what the hell you people are doing. I need to know."

Silence greeted his shout until Mel eventually nodded. Arthur flopped back in his chair, rubbing his face again as he tried to regain control of his temper. After a moment, he said, "I'm sorry about the shouting. But I need proper debriefs."

"You also need to grow stronger." Jan pointed a finger at him. "Best thing you can do is cultivate."

"I know that."

"Really, ah? 'Cause someone going to challenge you soon, you know."

"What, who?" Arthur was taken aback, but neither Mel nor Yao Jing reacted to Jan's words. "You think so too?"

"Yaaa," Yao Jing said, as if Arthur should have known better. "Attack our members, attack our groups, then finally, attack you. See if we have the strength, lah."

"Shit, shit, shit," Arthur cursed. "I can't beat someone past the first threshold. And that's who they'll send, right?"

"Probably." Mel shrugged. "It's why we're trying to gather as many cores for you as we can." She looked at the two standing beside her. "Probably why they stole all this too."

"Not stealing. They were assholes, they deserved it," Yao Jing said.

"Spoils of war," Jan added, with a smirk.

"Big words, coming from you." Arthur shook his head, pointing at the stack of beast cores. "Return them."

"All of them?!" Jan let out a yell.

Arthur paused, considering. "How bad was our group hurt?"

"They'll heal up in a day." A slight smile on Mel's lips then. "Thanks to the clan boon."

"Then set aside enough cores for two days. Return the rest," Arthur decided.

"Why? They attacked us first!" Jan raged.

Calmly, doing his best not to let her own temper trigger his again, Arthur explained. "We're not bullies. We aren't thieves or robbers either. They attacked us. We attacked back. And took fair compensation. Now, they're stuck healing and with losses." He paused, then added, "Deterrent, not vengeance."

"I don't like it," Jan said mulishly.

"And you?" Arthur looked at Yao Jing.

He shrugged. "You the boss."

"It's a decent proposal. I'll get it done," Mel said before he could ask her to oversee the return of cores. "And we'll keep you informed. But you need to keep cultivating. We need you strong." She paused, rubbing her chin. "Maybe put your next point into Body."

Arthur sighed. He had been careful about the use of the cores coming in, only using the one he had set aside for himself. He'd been cycling between cultivating and refining, pouring energy into himself so that he could begin the process of growing stronger.

He'd also been considering purchasing the Bark Skin technique, thinking he had more time to learn it. But if these fights kept escalating in speed, that idea would have to be put aside.

"Yeah, yeah." Waving the other two away, he kept Mel behind long enough to ask her the question he'd been wondering about since she brought up potential fights. "How strong are you?"

"Me?" she said, surprised.

"Yeah. You're not at first threshold, right?" She shook her head, confirming his guess. "But how close?"

"Very."

"I thought so." Arthur let out a long exhale. "I think you should start focusing on your cultivating too." When she frowned, he waved a hand. "I'm thinking of using Jan and you as my champions to start." He frowned. "Maybe Amah Si?" When Mel shook her head, he gave up on that idea. Even if someone reached the first threshold, there were still considerations about fighting ability and techniques. You couldn't just throw a random cultivator into a fight and expect them to win, even if they were theoretically stronger. "You two then, and maybe Yao Jing. If you are strong enough, maybe we can buy me time."

"To grow stronger."

"Exactly."

She nodded after a moment of further thought. "I'll start putting more time into cultivating." A longer pause before she added, "But we might need to go out, to do our own hunting run too."

Arthur let out a long breath but nodded. She was right. They had set up the clan to divide the income coming in, but the majority of it still went to those who did the work. Which was fair and right, but it did mean that if Arthur wanted more resources, he ought to venture out himself on hunts.

"Tomorrow," he said.

Mel nodded, and then seeing that Arthur had nothing else to add, left him to his thoughts. His mind scurried for a few minutes, concerned about all the things that needed doing, all the strength he had to gain. And then he squashed the thoughts.

For right now, he needed strength more than anything. And the only way to get it was cultivating.

So he got to work.

Chapter 112

The problem with being the head of the largest—and only—official clan on the first floor of the Tower was that you became quite recognizable. The one time he had gone out, Arthur noticed quite a few people pointing him out to others. He knew it would only get worse. And he wasn't the only newly famous; the faces of Yao Jing and the girls who formed his regular group were even more well known.

So the next time he left the building, he did so in the dead of the night, head covered under a *songkok*—which was more common in this Tower than you'd think—and a pair of glasses on his face. Wearing someone else's clothes, he also left with a group so that picking him out was harder.

After his group dispersed, his only company—if you could call it company—was Uswah in the shadows. Attempting to follow her movements was difficult, as she drifted between darkened spot to darkened spot, and Arthur gave up on trying to mimic her movements while he was in the beginner village. It was too well lit for his poor stealth skills.

It was only when they entered the no man's land and the tents around, many of which were already darkened as individuals slept, that he attempted to hide. He moved between tents, casting looks to ensure he was not being followed.

To his surprise, his attempts at stealth paid off, as he managed to make it all the way to the treeline and his objective before Uswah popped up.

"Wrong way." A finger raised and pointed in the correct direction. Arthur let out a long huff, following along. He was not carrying his spear, what with it being a little too prominent. He just hoped that the team would have it when they showed up.

Eventually, after a couple more pointed directions, he found the tiny clearing where they were to meet. Flopping down, Arthur rested with his back against a tree, eyeing the dark. Out here, at night, it almost felt like the Yin chi was so much closer to him, even compared to the clan headquarters.

"How are you doing?" Arthur said, turning his head to where he believed Uswah to be. She had disappeared into the shadows the moment they had arrived, so he was forced to guess. Thankfully, Enhanced Eyesight and her not actively manipulating the shadows right now meant that he was mostly certain he was right.

"*Bagus.*" Her voice drifted down, a little more to the right than he had expected.

Arthur took the compliment silently, then asked, "How are you *really* doing?"

The shadows shifted a little, and Arthur guessed she must have shrugged. He waited, wanting to make his point with silence. Sadly, the silence game was a losing one with Uswah, who was more than happy to let it linger on.

Eventually, he broke. "Really. How are you *doing*?"

"I am missing a hand. I've been relegated to administrative tasks and the occasional scouting mission. Most of the other groups won't take me, even if I'm stronger than them," Uswah said, her voice dispassionate as always. "It is not ideal. But I make do. I save up."

"For what?" Arthur asked, then shook his head after a moment. He could guess. The fact that she did not bother to answer him was clear that she knew that too. "I'll fix it, if I can."

"Not yours to fix." A slight pause. "Thanks anyway."

"So. We got nothing to do for a bit..." He trailed off.

Uswah met his leading statement with more silence.

"Want to talk cultivating?" Arthur ended up asking, almost helplessly.

Again, silence greeted his words. Almost to the point where he thought she would not answer and he got ready to begin cultivating himself. Then, she spoke up.

"Yes."

Smiling a little at the minor win—both for getting her to share her knowledge of the cultivation method and for getting her to come out of her shell more—he leaned forwards. "So, I noticed something while cultivating…"

It was the early hours of the morning when the rest of the group finally made their way over. It was later than what Arthur had expected, but when he questioned them about the delay, the reformed group explained that their watchers had been a little more persistent than normal. After retrieving his spear, he had the group travelling fast and away.

They would be gone for two days total, with the goal of harvesting as many beast cores as they could. A longer trip would have been more desirable, but the pressures of running the clan kept them from that option. As it stood, Mel was worried that even the two days might be too long.

Moving swiftly, the group headed into the deeper parts of the forest surrounding the village, Yao Jing at first struggling to figure out how to fit in with the well-oiled group. Eventually, he gave up and just jogged alongside Arthur.

It did not take the group long to find their first prey: a *kuching hitam*, who jumped from a tree at Jan holding the back of the line. She swerved easily, catching the monster by the scruff of the neck and throwing it into a nearby, thorn-ridden tree with spine-breaking force. The monster fell limply in pain and was quickly dispatched, its core retrieved before the group moved on.

There was no pausing or hesitation, the intent for the next few hours to find herds of *babi ngepet*. After all, the monstrous and ill-tempered creatures would be the best source of cores, though Uswah who was leading the team was not averse to straying the route to deal with the occasional monster as they searched.

It took them nearly half a day before they came across their first herd, having travelled a good distance. Far enough away that most teams from the village would not venture this far out, leaving these surroundings much less picked over.

The herd of *babi* was moving as a group, but they heard the humans before the humans spotted them. A hissed warning from Uswah came only moments before the sound of crashing undergrowth.

Arthur and Mel moved together, creating a shortened line anchored on Mel's end by a tree of pointed spears. Lowering them to the ground, the shaft planted in place, the pair braced for the monsters coming directly at them. At the same time, Jan scrambled up a tree, pulling her parang out to strike from above when the monsters were forced to slow. Uswah was, as always, nowhere to be seen.

It was only Yao Jing who dithered until Arthur shouted a command. "My left and behind. When they stop, swing out."

Then, there was no more time. The herd arrived, eight creatures in total, breaking apart tiny trees and pulling vines down. The first creature to see the problem swerved far right, around Mel and the tree. The others kept coming, with the second and third monsters impaled on the spears. The pair of cultivators were pushed backward even as the spears bent, but Body-enhanced strength and good positioning kept them standing. Monsters at the back of the herd had slowed down, as magical tentacles tripped the middle of the pack, leaving time for both Jan and Yao Jing to jump in the fray.

Finding his spear stuck in the corpse of a *babi ngepet*, Arthur chose to drop the entire thing and yank out the enchanted kris. Swinging around the fighting group, he joined Uswah's darting in and out, laying in quick attacks that damaged the monsters and began the slow leaching of energy from the massive creatures. The fight was hard, but not unusual. With the addition of the muscle-bound Yao Jing whose chi-enhanced punches stunned monsters, the group eventually put the bigger monsters down.

Grinning, Arthur could not help but look at the dwindling herd, thinking how far he had come. Not so long ago, he would have had to pull out every single trick in the book. This time around, other than infusing Focused Strike into the initial charge to drop the first monster, he had not required his cultivation exercises at all.

All the better really. After all, he needed his energy for ascending.

On that sober thought, he gestured for the team to get to work extracting the cores. There was a lot more hunting to do before they got back.

Chapter 113

Arthur cocked his head to the side, watching as Yao Jing threw an uppercut. His closed fist, filled with energy, shook the monster and snapped its ursine head back. The creature roared, clawed paws striking but blocked by the man slipping away with dexterous movements. Feet shifted, putting him out of reach with one particularly smooth weaving motion before he pounded the bear's ribs again with his hands, driving it back.

In the meantime, the rest of the team stood back, Uswah watching the surroundings for potential problems while the rest of the team observed Yao Jing having his solo duel.

"Exactly how did he convince us to let him fight it himself again?" Arthur said, half-puzzled, half-amused. Spittle flew and landed on the surroundings, blood mixing with the foaming froth of the angered monster as Yao Jing kept pounding away.

"He said it was necessary for his cultivation," Mel said.

"Right, right. All for the might. But how does that work, exactly?"

The pair of women could only shrug, leaving Arthur snorting. Still, they had time to watch as the cultivator continued to pound away at the monstrous bear. The creature was a small ursine monster, barely taller than

Arthur's own shoulder even when it reared up. It was, however, massively strong and well-padded with muscle and fat. The powerful, bone-crushing blows that Yao Jing dished out merely wasted strength on its defences.

A day and a half later, Yao Jing had mostly managed to fit into the team. It was not a smooth integration, but it was good enough that he had a rough idea of the roles the group had formed for itself. It was a fortunate addition, since Uswah had pulled even further away from direct confrontations, lurking in the dark and using her shadows to pull monsters aside and occasionally launching an elemental version of the Refined Energy Dart.

Still, powerful as Yao Jing was, and confident as he seemed with his boxing—and it was very much boxing, rather than the mixed martial styles that so many other ascenders made use of—he lacked the pure power and strength required to put the bear down. At least, not quickly.

Then again, his latest companion was technically weaker than Arthur. Yao Jing was new to the Tower, only having his human strength to make use of and some surprising cultivation techniques and secrets. The fact that he needed to battle the monster on his own to build upon cultivation was strange, but it was not something Arthur felt it was his place to probe.

"What, exactly, is that thing anyway?" Arthur muttered. "I never knew we had bears. Or myths of bears."

"Malayan sun bear," Jan replied. "Real one very rare. And not so big." She nodded at the bear, who having failed to crush Yao Jing again by rising up on its hindfeet and coming down with its paws, threw its head to the side, briefly exposing the patch of white underneath its fur. "See. Sun bear."

"Huh." Arthur rubbed his chin. "Are there legends about it?"

His question received only shrugs. It was unusual to find a monstrous creature that fit their country but not their legends. Even the snakes they fought often had some form of urban legend, if not older myths attached to them. So to see the sun bear, a creature he had not even heard about, running around was interesting.

"How come we haven't seen one before?" Arthur asked, curiously. "After all the time we've been out in the forest..." A flicker of annoyance. How did you rhyme with forest?

"Rare boss, obviously," Mel said.

"If that's the case, should we be letting him fight it alone?" he asked.

Before she could answer, the tired bear managed to land a punishing swipe on Yao Jing. Missing his block, the man was sent spinning away to roll on the ground, bleeding from the swipe that struck his hip and torso. As he came back to his feet, shaking his head, the bear charged and bowled him over.

"And that's enough," Arthur growled, seeing his friend on his back. He charged forward, triggering both Focused Strike and Heavenly Sage's Mischief. Speed boosted, he crossed the distance within moments to plunge his spear into the spot just behind the front right paw as it rose to crush his friend.

Startled and in pain, the bear twisted off-balance. To Arthur's surprise, Yao Jing was lying on his back, one arm raised in protection but another cocked back and charging up. There was no more light on his protective arm as the man shifted the collected energy to the other hand, launching it forward with an ear-cracking thump as it landed on the monster's jaw and neck, which sent it collapsing over.

Moments later, Jan and Mel arrived, the first just strolling while Mel seemed a little more concerned. The group helped haul the heavy monster off the bleeding and injured Yao Jing, who could not help but grin as he offered them a thumbs-up.

"Told you I could do it," he said, sitting up gingerly.

"Pretty sure I helped," Arthur pointed out.

"I had it without you," Yao Jing said, stiffly. Then, standing up gingerly, taking the hand that Arthur offered to him and being careful not to put weight on his side, he added, "Though the help was nice."

"Uh-huh."

"You two, shut up lah." Pushing over to Yao Jing, Jan began to pour water into the dirty, bleeding side. That elicited a low growl, but before he could say anything, she began cleaning it roughly. He straightened, breath growing tight before she shoved a bandage into his bleeding side. "Hold it there, idiot."

"Me idiot, you—" Already, the woman had stomped off, leaving Yao Jing alone. He shook his head but did continue to put pressure on his wound. Now that he was looking, Arthur could not help but think that the entire thing probably had needed a good wash.

Then again, minor things like infections were much less of a concern in the Tower, and certainly not with their shared healing trait. Yao Jing watched Jan stomp off ahead of them, and Arthur chose not to say anything. If Yao Jing wanted it cleaned further, he would do so.

And if not, it would be a good test to see how fast he healed. As for the other complication...

"You going to do anything about that?" Arthur said, flicking his gaze over to Jan so Yao Jing could clearly note what he meant.

"About what?"

Arthur just looked at the man, waiting for him to get the clue. Yao Jing shrugged, choosing not to comment.

"Whatever." Arthur shook his head. He certainly was not one to criticize. After all, his own minor crush had not gone anywhere, nor did he have the time or desire to pursue it. Never mind the fact that the Yin Body seemed to make the entire arousal and desire thing a little removed for him, he was just too busy.

The need for survival and training seemed to have driven much of that demand away. And it wasn't as though he was one for jumping in bed on the regular. Navigating sex in Malaysia, whether the relationship was casual or serious, was always tricky between cultural expectations, Western ideals, and the practicalities of modern living and shared bedspaces.

There was very little sexy or romantic about alleyway trysts in downtown KL.

"Coming or not?" Mel said, standing up as she finished washing her hand and the bloody core. She slipped the entire thing into her waist pouch, and Arthur dismissed those concerns.

Another time.

Someday, he'd find that time.

Just not today.

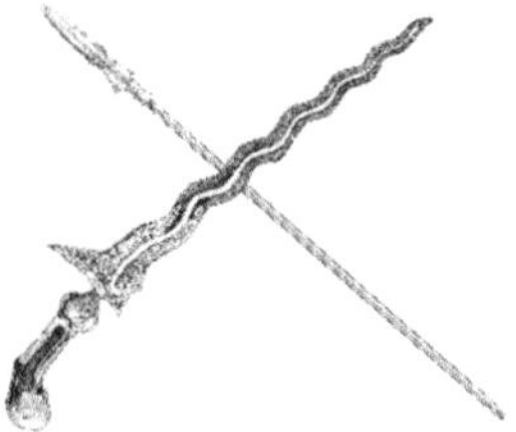

Chapter 114

Their plan had always been to get back to the village late at night. It made sense, since doing so allowed them to get the most out of their hunting—including finding and dealing with some of the more nocturnal monsters—and miss the crush of those who might want to meet and speak with Arthur. Not to mention the potential for violence as well.

On the other hand, Arthur had to admit, moving through the dark always felt like he was creeping back home. A rather stark difference from the proud entry he had envisioned before he ever entered the Tower. Not once had he strode into the village, a conquering hero, lauded by others.

Instead, here he was, moving through the dark, in between tent ropes and around the occasional fireplace, hoping not to wake anyone or run into any real issues. Even if it was a strategic choice, it still made him feel more of a villain than a hero.

One day, perhaps, he might be able to enter with his head held high. Perhaps in a few weeks, now that he had a ready access to cores. But until then, he would grit his teeth and accept the fact that he was going to do this.

Which made it all the more disappointing when a group of five moved to block their way, men holding weapons by their side, wide grins on their faces.

Three of them directly ahead, two on either side coming around the tents that lay in the way.

A quick glance behind showed that Jan was facing off against another two.

"What do you want?" Mel asked, being at the front of the group. Yao Jing by Arthur's side was hesitating, debating between going for the man on the left or adding his weight to the front. Arthur on the other hand was forming a Refined Energy Dart on his brow, having made his own choice.

"Him." One of the men spoke, pointing his parang straight at Arthur.

There was a flicker of light. Instinct reared up and Arthur jerked himself back. A fraction of a moment too slow, such that the energy beam that tore out of the parang burned the right side of his face and body and set him screaming. He managed to dodge most of it, but he was burnt and bloody.

His own Refined Energy Dart dispersed on his brow, causing his own head to pound further. Not that the pain from the backlash was anything compared to the loss of vision and the pain from burnt flesh.

As he fought to control his reactions, he sensed a blurring form charging at him. He thrust with his spear, felt the weapon blocked and found himself stumbling back, half-blinded and working on instinct. Blood spurted, the smell of cooked meat filling his nostrils along with the sudden presence of congealed coconut oil as his attacker ducked in close, sliding a small dagger into his stomach.

Like a needle, it darted in and out, once, twice, then again. On the third time, Arthur gripped the knife hand, holding it still even as he pulled the kris out of his own sheath. Then he cut, slicing against inner thigh, arm, plunging down into thigh again and then ripping sideways. Twisting and cutting, even as the knife in his own stomach twisted and turned.

Coughing in pain, he felt it rip out, but this time he managed to shove his hand into an elbow. Keeping the attacker away, even as he sliced with his own weapon, and the enchanted blade took energy from his opponent. As the curse took effect, his opponent weakened enough that Arthur was able to keep the man's arm away and break free to stab the weapon into his neck and end it.

A dozen seconds, maybe less. It had all happened so fast, but that was the way of fights. Sometimes, an element of surprise was all that was needed to incur death instead of mere injury. Holding the kris up, one eye blinded, his face seared and burnt, he found the fight still going on.

One of the fighters in the front was down, a knife in the back of his neck sufficient reason. Mel was tangling with the leader, his parang against her spear. Mel pushed the leader back and away from Arthur before he could be attacked again. The third and last man in front was fighting Uswah, overbearing the single-armed lady with his greater weight. Using his fist, he struck at her as he held her close with the other hand.

Seeing who he needed to help most, Arthur rushed forward, trusting that the remainder of the team were holding. Adrenaline coursed through him, making the pain fade away. He knew his body was healing, fixing the issues, stemming the blood loss. A glance at Jan and Yao Jing showed that at least they were fine, for now. Hopefully, that would stay the same even as he slipped the kris into a kidney from behind.

The man arched his back, but the last-minute shift of his body was insufficient to stop Arthur from injuring him. The moment his kidney was pierced, his opponent shuddered, the pain overtaking his conscious control. Not to be outdone, Uswah caught his arm with her own and headbutted him across the face as he collapsed.

"Don't kill him!" Arthur cried. Uswah checked her attack and Arthur turned and dashed away, leaving her to deal with the woozy opponent. As a cultivator, he likely wouldn't die immediately, though there was no guarantee of that either. They might be stronger than people outside the Tower but they weren't impervious.

Yao Jing seemed to have had the same idea, having putting his own man in an armlock. His struggling opponent managed to wrench himself all the way around, dislocating his shoulder with a sickening crack as he cut at Yao

Jing's foot. Yao Jing shifted his feet a little, dodging the majority of the attack but still releasing the arm so that he could continue beating his enemy.

Arthur now turned to see Jan. Only to find, to his amusement, that a couple of passersby had appeared to aid her. Her own opponents were dead, while one still alive was clutching his stomach and moaning at having been gutted.

"Save him. I want answers!" But the man had stilled, the pool of blood and effluvia spreading beneath him. Jan, having sheathed her own weapons, bent to check on the others before standing up and shaking her head.

In other places, in the real world, with adrenaline and trauma teams and defibrillators, they might have tried to save him. In the Tower, unless they climbed much higher, perhaps to a new Tower even, there was no point. Dead was dead and no makeshift level of technology would help bring a man back.

"Shit dipped in a zit." Arthur spun about, remembering at last there was one more fight. Only to see Mel extracting her spear from the side of a man who had collapsed onto a tent, the occupants within cursing up a storm. Arthur winced as the burnt flesh of his face broke open again, weeping blood and white water, but he ignored that and whoever managed to clamber out of the damaged tent. That one probably had justifiable grievances against them.

"Search them. Strip them of anything valuable. Then we go," he commanded the group, pointing at Yao Jing's newly recaptured attacker whose arms had been yanked into a painful hold behind his back, strips of leather twisting to lock him in place. "Bring the prisoners."

He looked back at Uswah who nodded, having finished winding a makeshift bandage around the man's back wound. Then Arthur found himself eyeing the pair of passersby who had helped Jan. A man and woman, both bearing remarkably similar features. "Pick him up, will you? We'll talk, after," he told them.

The pair shared a knowing look before they moved to grab Yao Jing's prisoner.

And with that, they were gone. Arthur shoved a bandage onto his stomach, kept one eye squinted shut and focused on moving forward, even through the pain.

By the time the poor occupant of the bloody, thrashed tent managed to squeeze his way out of the collapsed structure, there was little else to see but a series of bodies, including the one still bleeding onto his tent.

Arthur swore he could hear him cry out from behind.

"My tent!"

Chapter 115

The rest of the trip was, thankfully, uneventful. Or as uneventful as you could get when you dragged two bodies on your shoulder towards the beginner village. By the time they reached the edge, the pain had faded for Arthur, his stomach only aching with every step, every breath. Thankfully, the knifing had been more of a shanking, the damage easy to patch for his enhanced healing ability. His eye... well. He could worry about that later.

It was only when they reached the no man's land that they had another problem, though not in the way that Arthur had expected.

"I'm not carrying him in there," the woman said, dropping the body she carried unceremoniously to the ground.

"What now?" Arthur whined, turning around gingerly. He had been keeping an eye on them obliquely, but this sudden change of heart caught him by surprise. Not that he had a lot of attention, but enough for the expected betrayal.

"I'm not bringing him in there." She prodded the man with her boot.

"*Mei mei*..." A long-suffering sigh erupted from her brother. "Explain."

"Guards."

When most people still looked puzzled, the brother smiled. "The guards. Violence. We don't want to get caught up in that." He nodded to the body. "We don't mind helping, but we're not getting into trouble with them."

Firm nod from his sister.

"Doesn't work that way," Mel said, turning around from where she had been leading the group, leaning a little on the spear she held. To Arthur's surprise, he realized that she had a bloody wound running down one side of her body that looked gummy and dark red after drying a little.

"What do you mean?" the young man said.

"The guards stop fighting in the village. And seem to be able to tell if a fight is over, or so it's rumoured. So no assassinations or the like. But if you bring in someone injured, it's fine." She shrugged. "I assume it's because some people use the inn for healing."

"Oh," he said.

Without speaking his sister grabbed hold of the body again and hauled it over her shoulder, the injured man letting out a little groan at the rough handling. She started walking immediately, leaving the brother to catch up.

Arthur eyed the darkness for a second more, noting that they had a few watchers but nothing too onerous. Then, he took off after the group, hoping that he might avoid any additional problems. Thankfully, being a staff wielder, using it to help him walk made the injuries less visible. Though he could not hide the damage of a scarred, burnt face.

They got about halfway there when they were interrupted by two people walking up with wide smiles on their faces. They were a man and woman in their late fifties, and unlike the majority of the cultivators on this floor they were dressed in expensive silks and colourful outerwear, with the woman even bearing some elaborate gold jewelry.

"Clan Head Chua!" the man cried. "Fancy meeting you out here. Oh, your poor thing. Your injuries..."

"Who are you?" Arthur demanded.

"I'm Boss Loh! And this is my wife," the man said as they all eyed the mixed-race couple. "It's fortunate we met, really. I was hoping to speak with you about a merchant contract. Maybe I can provide you something, on the house, for your wounds."

"A merchant." Arthur drawled the last word. Adrenaline had worn off, his breathing had grown less steady, and the pain had increased. The offer of medicine was almost tempting.

Almost.

"The best." Boss Loh slapped his chest. "We might not be the biggest, but we're not that far away from it. And we have access to anything you might want. Beast cores, credits, goods from outside. I have clothing, jewelry, weapons." He lowered his voice, stepping closer as he added. "Cultivation techniques."

Arthur could not help but be interested then. He needed those techniques. That strength. He took a step forward, only to find Mel's hand stopping him. The sudden halt brought a hiss of pain to his lips.

"This one has been trying to speak with you for days now." Mel lips tightened, shaking her head. "I had some people look into him. He's not someone we should make a deal with."

"Why?" Arthur asked curiously. He could see the faltering smile on the other man, but he was not backing down, and Arthur had to admit he admired the man's bravery. Not enough to stand around forever though.

"He's overstretched. Some bad deals outside and a drop in customers on the first floor. Seems like his brother cut him off from outside, because he hasn't sent anything back in a while," Mel said. "So, what he has is what he has."

"Ah, but we are not asking for an exclusive arrangement," Boss Loh said quickly. His wife, standing beside him frowned a little but chose not to say anything. In fact, when Arthur's gaze turned to her, she let a finger slide down from her neck to her bust line, pulling at the silk to part clothing and offer a more generous view of her impressive bosom.

A squeeze on his arm reminded Arthur he was staring. He might not have the instinctive flash of lust common to vigorous young males, but he still enjoyed the views. Pulling his gaze away was easy though. Being in pain, being Yin-bodied, both helped.

"It seems that you are in need of us. And we could use you, so we'll choose you," Boss Loh went on. Now that got a little smirk from Yao Jing. Right. Anime or CCG lover there. He looked at Mel, raising an eyebrow. "Unless we've got other offers?"

"Nothing concrete. Just a few nibbles," she said.

"Then let us talk with him." Glancing back over his shoulder, at the bodies his people were carrying and their exhaustion, assessing their injuries and his own, he added, "Later. Set up an appointment, and we will talk about it later." Arthur's voice grew cold and low. "And make sure to bring the best prices and items you have. You'll only get one chance."

Boss Loh looked a little green at that but sketched a low bow. So did his wife moments later. They stepped aside, allowing Arthur and his group to pass, Mel holding her tongue until they had left the couple behind, and the group threaded the streets of the beginner village.

"Why did you agree to speak with him?" Mel snapped. "He might offer us something now, but he is no partner for the future."

"Maybe not." Arthur paused, then added, "But he has cultivation techniques and those could be useful. And more importantly, he is desperate. He is ready to be taken by others, for his goods, his contacts, all of it."

"How does that help us?"

"Because those who would gobble him up will not want us to help him. And so, they'll come to us with real offers."

Mel blinked, tilting her head and staring at Arthur in surprise. When she made to speak, he cut her off. "I'm not entirely dumb. And I've seen how others handle these things. Copying others isn't hard."

"Maybe. But that's still a good call." She grinned evilly. "And you're right. If we string him out, we can make him and them bleed."

After that, the group limped their way to their clan building. Steeling himself, Arthur opened the doors, knowing that their next steps were going to be less than pleasant. After all, they had a pair of attackers to interrogate.

And he really would have to hold back his own desire to punish them as pain wracked his body.

Chapter 116

"Split them up. Don't let them talk to one another," Arthur said, gesturing to the two as they reached the hallway where individual rooms lay. "Have the wounds looked into. We don't want them dying on us right now, do we?"

Once he confirmed his orders were going to be taken, he gestured for the one that Yao Jing held to be brought into the room alone. "Tie him to the chair, but don't make it too tight. Then let's get something to wake him up. Also, tea and snacks."

Yao Jing had just finished dumping the man onto the chair when Arthur uttered his last request. Surprised, Yao Jing looked back over his shoulder at Arthur. That was when the prisoner made his move, surging out of his chair in an attempt to escape.

Too bad for him, he was still rather beaten and tired. Yao Jing pushed him back down into the chair firmly and wrapped a rope around his arms. Within moments, the man was fully tied.

"Well, we won't need anything to wake him now, will we?" Arthur said, smiling at the prisoner. The man blanched at first, probably because Arthur's burnt face and damaged eye looked positively dreadful. He just hoped he was not blind. He could have washed up, made himself presentable. But not yet.

Once he recovered, the prisoner glared back, and Arthur could not help but note how thin his eyebrows were. It made him look like he was in a perpetual state of startlement.

"What's your name?"

Silence.

"Do you want tea? A snack?" Arthur asked. "If you make a promise not to try to escape for the duration of our conversation, we'll free a hand so you can feed yourself."

"And let you poison me?" the man snorted.

"Why bother? I don't know enough about poisons to carefully regulate a poison to, you know, make you tell the truth or torture you. And if I wanted to kill you, I could just have done it earlier." Arthur tapped the table. "I'm not as incompetent as whoever sent you."

The man growled.

"You certainly didn't bother getting enough people," Arthur said. His face felt tight with dried blood, so he took the water flask from his side and poured the liquid into his hand. He washed his face a little, carefully peeling at the gummed-up blood until his eye was clear. He hissed and growled as he did so, but eventually he had left a mess on the table and his face was clear. "Now, that's better." Grinning savagely, he added, "Sorry. It was bothering me."

More silence.

"Huh. I guess they didn't blind me." Squinting with one eye and then the other, Arthur nodded to himself. "Don't want to think about the scars I'm going to get, but maybe those will go away.

"If I'd been blinded, then I'd be pissed."

A slight shift in the chair, a pressing of lips together to mark impatience.

Arthur ignored it. He leaned forward. "It doesn't matter what happened. If I'd been injured or killed, things might have been different. I wasn't. And we are here."

Silence again, this time more sullen.

"Now, let me be clear. I'm not going to try to torture, beat, or otherwise harm you. I don't believe in that shit and, of course, we're in the beginner village so stuff like that is anathema. Of course, we have more leeway inside this building," Arthur waved his hand around. "But I'd rather not push it.

"Can you imagine the kind of reputation we'd get, if you and your pal were left screaming your head off?"

Still no answer.

"Well, as the boss, I have to think about things like that." Another long shrug. "I am here mostly to talk. I'm really not that interested in you. You're not important, in the overall scheme of things. Who hired you on the other hand... that's more interesting."

Still, the man refused to speak.

"Now, I could keep talking like a monologuing villain. And if you keep quiet like this, I'll start feeling like one. Even if I'm not cutting you apart with a laser." A long pause, then Arthur rubbed his chin. "I wonder if I could even find a laser here. Is there some Tower equivalent of a laser? Some technique?"

This brought a tightening of the lips in the man. However, the answer came from Yao Jing.

"No lasers. But the Sun Phoenix from Iran can use fire. It go whoosh, just like a laser."

"Whoosh?"

"Maybe zwing?"

"I remember those videos. It was more *izzshhh-ooosh.*"

"Yeah, but maybe more *sssssshhhh.*"

Arthur rubbed his chin. "You sure? I remember more *zzzzz.*"

"I would give a good curry for internet connection," Yao Jing said. "Uh, wait. Nope. I'm eating the curry."

"Only if it's really good," Arthur said. "Like there's one in Klang..."

"Which one? And nah, I know better one in SS2."

"Oh, you mean near the Paramount Theatre? The curry *chee cheong fun*?"

"That one? It's just okay, lah. The boss died, and his replacement... I dunno, lah. Not the same anymore. The curry laksa better there."

"Oh, yeah, so good."

"Are you people insane!" roared the prisoner.

"No need to shout, we can hear you, lah," Yao Jing said, disapprovingly.

"You're arguing about what—noises and food?!"

"Well, of course. We're Malaysian," Arthur said. "Which hawker do you like for curry?"

"I don't like curry," the man spat.

Arthur and Yao Jing hissed, staring at the man as though he was an alien creature.

"Why aren't you interrogating me?" the prisoner said.

"I did. I asked you your name. You didn't give it," Arthur said. "I also told you what I wanted to know."

"Then you stopped asking me!"

"Would it help?" Arthur said, cocking his head to the side. "Would you tell me?"

"Of course not!"

"Then, let's talk curry." Arthur paused. "Or not curry in your case. What do you like to eat?"

"You're insane."

"Well, yeah. Ascender. Tower climber." He gestured at the world around, to his damaged face. "We're in a magical Tower that rips us apart to transport us somewhere. We might not even be real anymore, just computer programs or close approximations. And I'm running on adrenaline and other chemicals just to stay awake. If I wasn't insane, I'd be pinning your hand down and chopping your fingers off, one by one."

"We could be souls," Yao Jing pointed out.

"Right, reborn souls." Arthur snorted. "Or aliens or robots or just deluded. Of course we're insane. Why else would we be here?"

"I'm not insane," the prisoner said.

Arthur nodded exaggeratedly. "Sure, sure."

Beside him, Yao Jing had raised a finger and spun it around his head mockingly. Of course, he had not moved far away enough that the prisoner could not see him, so his teasing had the other man growling.

"Anyway. Insane or not. Here we are. And you won't tell me who sent you. So we might as well spend the time chatting about something pleasant."

"Don't you have something better to do?" the prisoner growled.

"Of course I do. Why do you think I'm hiding here?" Before Arthur could continue, the door opened. Drinks and snacks were laid on the table between them and Arthur stood up, snagging a small cookie as he headed for the door.

"Anyway, eat up. I'm going to talk to your friend, see if he tells me anything. Then, if you don't, we'll just keep you here. Awake. Listening to us talk about food." Arthur tapped his nose. "It's weird to say, but all this burnt flesh? Reminds me of siu yuk. So I'm going to go eat for sure. And we'll have a new person come in all the time. Keep you awake and busy. We got the beggars here; they'll be able to help."

"What?"

"Oh, that's my torture. Someone constantly talking to you, never letting you cultivate. Keeping you waiting and underpowered." He grinned. "For weeks. Months. Maybe even years."

"You can't do that."

"Can. Will." Before the man could continue protesting, Arthur stepped the rest of the way out, closing the door after him. Then a moment later he opened it, poking his head around the door and added, "Doing so. Right now. Tah!"

Then he shut the door again before the man could burst out shouting. Smirking to himself, he spun around and almost jumped out of his skin when he spotted Mel staring at him.

"Was there a point to all that?"

"A lot!" Arthur said. "I learned that Yao Jing has no taste in food. And that given enough nonsense, our friend will break." He rubbed his chin. "Also, we've talked long enough that I can now go talk to the other one and see what they have to say."

"Bluff?"

"Yup," Arthur said. "Torture isn't the way to go. Unless you want to. No. No, we won't. So, we talk."

Mel frowned, then shrugged. "I guess we can always pull fingers off later."

"Sometimes, you scare me."

"Awww. That's sweet of you to say so."

Chapter 117

Walking into the infirmary, Arthur frowned as he stared at the unconscious, heavily injured prisoner. He leaned over after he checked that the man was properly tied up, eyeing him to see if he really was still alive. The slow, regular rhythm of his breathing made Arthur nod in gratitude. At least the idiot hadn't died on the way here. As he raised his hand to shake him awake, Amah Si grabbed it.

"Don't," she said.

Arthur tugged his hand free of her strong grip and suppressed a deep wince of pain that moving his torso had brought about. Though the way she was looking at him, leaning on her cane, he doubted he'd fooled her.

"Why not?" he said.

"He lost a lot of blood. And he's fighting off your poison. Good thing it doesn't kill, but he's not going to wake anytime soon." She frowned. "Not without a lot of stimulation, which we won't be using."

"Worried he'll die if we do?"

"Yes. Eventually he'll wake. In a few hours, maybe morning." She hummed in thought. "Probably morning."

"A long time to wait."

Amah Si shrugged. "If you don't want to kill him, then that's what we have to do. Or we could wake him, keep him awake, push him until you get the answers we need." Then she prodded his chest. Very lightly. "In the meantime, we clean you up."

Arthur looked down at his shirt, the movement making him hiss a little. Nodding in acquiescence, he let her guide him over to sit down in a chair.

"I won't heal you," Amah Si said. "I can't waste the energy. None of my people will."

Arthur nodded. He understood that. Especially when he had his own healing ability that worked in the background. He'd probably be fine in a few days, maybe even in one full day. Well, except his good looks. He touched his hair, even as Amah Si finished cutting his shirt off.

Looking down at his stomach, he frowned. It was bloody, but when she had finished washing him the actual puncture wounds were quite small. All but the one where his assailant had yanked the knife out sideways. While she kept washing him down, eyeing the wounds, they returned to the conversation.

Better than sitting there, with nothing to do but focus on the pain.

"I can't tell if you're happy or sad about the entire incident and my choices."

"Why do I have to be either?" she said. "You are the Clan Head as you've said all too often. I serve under you."

"And that means you have no opinion?"

"I have opinions. But in this," she prodded his body a little harder than she had to as she cleaned, "it matters not. You'll choose and we'll work it out."

He sighed. "So you already know what he has to say."

"Not know. I can guess though. Or learn of it a different way," Amah Si said, smiling a little as she looked up. "I do have contacts."

"Yes. You do." He sighed. "All I've done is... useless? Like a pair of nipples on a man."

"Not useless. If you manage it right, we'll learn faster. That could be important, though I'd be hard pressed to guess why." She finished with the cleaning, extracting some green poultices that she dabbed on his wound before wrapping it all in leaves and a rather stained roll of bandages. "Not choosing torture is not a bad thing. It's not a path I would have walked on purpose."

Arthur nodded, then breathed in slowly. Already, the poultice was numbing the wound further, the background ache fading. Thankfully, the damn cultivation technique he had learned seemed to include some degree of pain management.

He still felt a little foolish, having thought of the entire game on the walk over, only to be told that the older woman had it covered. Then again, that was the point wasn't it? He was coming into the game a week late and a core short.

He'd catch up, eventually. Until then, he'd do his best and let others back him up. And anyway, she did say that it wasn't entirely a mistake. He might learn something important, tomorrow. In the meantime, as she stood up, raising more bandages to wash his face down, he made sure to grit his teeth.

This was going to hurt.

"About time," Yao Jing said, yawning the next morning as Arthur wandered in. "This guy eats like an Englishman."

"Some of us have better things to do with our lives than obsess over food!" the prisoner shouted, glaring at Arthur. "And if you think I'll say anything, you're wrong."

"Sure, sure." Arthur raised his remaining, unmarred eyebrow at Yao Jing, hoping that they had managed to get something out of the man. His self-appointed bodyguard waggled his fingers from side to side, indicating some information had indeed been extracted.

Well, some was better than nothing.

"Bedtime." Yao Jing left the room, shutting the door behind him. Arthur took a seat opposite the prisoner, eyeing him and the free hand. All he got in return was an angry glare. Idly, Arthur ran a hand through his hair, wincing a little at the new shortened-hair look. Getting rid of the burnt hair had meant either going with an overcut look or just going short overall. A fade and shorter hair was a much better choice than an overcut.

Still felt weird. But at least his eyesight was fully back, without that slight haziness that one eye had borne last night.

Just as he was about to start speaking, the door swung open again and Jan wandered in. She went and leaned against the door, caressing her knife as she watched. Arthur considered asking why she was here but chose not to. It'd make him look weak and was outside the point.

"I don't need you to say anything, exactly," Arthur began.

"Really," said the prisoner. "You think I'm going to fall for that trick. You going to tell me my friend told you everything you needed to know. As if I'm that dumb."

Arthur winced internally. That had been the initial plan. Before he woke up and found the other man still sleeping.

"No. Nothing that crude. Your friend's still alive. Sleeping. The poison in my kris was rather strong and I stabbed him rather hard," Arthur said. "I don't need you to speak because my people are already looking for information. We'll find out who hired you, soon enough." He smiled, a little grimly. "Or I could poke my head out, let them take another shot at me. And ask the next group."

The other man met Arthur's confident gaze for a long moment until he eventually turned away. For once, Arthur let silence linger in the room. Eventually, the man spoke, his voice soft.

"What do you want from me, then. Why keep me?"

"Not for your taste buds, certainly."

"ENOUGH!" the prisoner roared. "If you really don't need me, then why do you keep me alive?"

"Because I do want your information," Arthur said. "But that information is on a timer. Once my people learn it through other means, then your information is as good as your restaurant recommendations. In other words, not much at all."

"Enough with the food talk. I'm serious!"

"So am I." Arthur sighed. "Once we find out what you know, you're useless. Or if we find out from your friend. From my spies. From someone taking another shot at me."

"Then? What happens to me?"

"What do you think?"

Silence grew between the pair, the man licking his lips. He glanced at the door, at Jan and then back at Arthur. Eventually, he opened his mouth to speak, only for Arthur to cut him off.

"I'll also want you to join our clan."

"What?!" Jan shouted.

"Huh?" the prisoner said.

"I want you to join our clan." Arthur leaned in and smiled tightly. "Because once you start talking, you're in with us. One way or the other."

"You..." Eyes widening, he stared right back at Arthur, willing him to choose something else. However, he gave up and bent his head. "You bastard."

"On the other hand, your friend gets to join you too. So you won't be alone."

"You're going to make us both join you?" the man snarled.

"Yes. You think you're going to be any safer out there? Also, the moment you join, you're kinda stuck. So, in or out."

"You keep raising the stakes."

"Yes."

Silence again and Arthur leaned back, waiting. He knew adding someone who might not want to be there was dangerous. On the other hand, Arthur needed people who could fight. Putting this thug in the outskirts, collecting cores, would benefit them. And it wasn't as though he was inviting him into the inner council.

Not that the inner council would give away much information. You couldn't exactly give away information that wasn't there, for Arthur's clan was newly in the process of building itself. Structures, personnel, and even their resources were constantly fluctuating.

"I hate you."

"I hate you too," Arthur crooned. Then, putting a kibosh on his idiot brain, he continued. "I can accept your feelings. Can you accept that you've lost?" Arthur said softly. Gently. Now was the time to lower the stakes, when the man was ready to give up.

"Yes." He rubbed his face with his free hand, then looked down at the one that was still tied. "You think I could be untied? Stretch a little?"

"Sure." Arthur said, letting his hand brush across the kris's sheath and hilt as he did so. He walked around, undoing the knots even as Jan glared at the back of his head. He finished undoing the arms and then bent down, working the knots around the man's waist and ankles before standing.

All through that, he was tense. Waiting for the man to grab at the kris. It was why he'd slipped the sheath guard over the weapon earlier, making it impossible to draw quickly. If his prisoner was going to try something, he'd need a weapon.

But there was no attempt. The prisoner stood rather unsteadily and using the table to slowly shift his weight. Blood rushed into extremities and he kept making funny faces, even as Arthur made his way back to his own chair.

"Michael. Michael Yeoh."

"Nice to meet you, Michael. Arthur Chua. That's Jan over there. No last name that she's bothered to tell me."

No answer to the obvious provocation.

Michael eyed the pair, before he shook his head, doing a few deep squats before he sighed. "Fine. I'll join. What do I need to know?"

"Just two rules for now." Arthur said, going on to explain them. After that, Arthur added him to the clan and watched the brand sear across

Michael's palm. It was all over quick enough. Then he asked, "Now, who sent you to kill me?"

"I don't know."

"Don't lie!" Jan shouted.

Arthur on the other hand waited patiently. He knew there was more. Had to be, for the man to have been so obtuse.

"I don't *know*," Michael said. "I wasn't one of the boss's friends. But I can guess."

"Then guess."

"The Chin Family."

"Oh god," Jan blurted.

But Arthur could only nod. Because of course things would get worse.

Chapter 118

Arthur watched as his lead team gathered together. It consisted of Yao Jing, Mel and Amah Si. Mohammad Osman was upstairs and indisposed as he cultivated, and Arthur had briefly considered extending the offer to him but chose to decline that option for now. The Sixes were allies, but they weren't of the Durians yet.

Jan was busy settling their newest recruit, with orders to get him out with a fighting group sooner rather than later. Once she was done, she'd likely make her way over, just as Uswah when she made her own appearance.

"The Chin family," Mel repeated once more. "Why them?"

"Because one of their daughters is on this floor," Amah Si said.

"They are? She is?" Mel said, surprised. "When did she arrive?"

"When you were gone," Amah Si explained.

Yao Jing raised a hand a little, looking confused. "Who's this Chin family?"

"Prime Group," Arthur replied.

He could see the light bulb go off in Yao Jing's eyes when that was said. No surprise. Prime Group had started as a simple manufacturing company in the early fifties but had progressed to become one of the biggest manufacturing groups in the early 21st century, having purchased and revolutionized the development of rubber products. They had factories making everything from gloves and tires to condoms, having vertically integrated upwards to purchase dozens of rubber plantations and downstream to add shipping and logistics.

"Why call them the Chins? Why not Prime Group?" Yao Jing said.

"Because the Chins are the family in charge," Arthur said, idly picking at the burnt skin on one side of his face. Stupid fast healing meant that the itching was even worse. "And they have their own mini sect running people in and out of the Tower and building up their management. It's one of the benefits of joining the company. They put you through intensive training in the management program, then guide you through the ascent. Push them up and outwards as fast as they can, so that they can then join middle and upper management."

"Middle management cultivators." Yao Jing shook his head in derision. "Why climb the Tower, just to work for other people?"

"It's stable work. And it makes for loyal employees." Of course, what with automation taking over half the manual labour jobs out there, the need for management had decreased and their job descriptions had changed. Corporate espionage, blackmail, and trade secrets had become even more important, as did working out ways to game the political systems and disrupt the flow of goods from other corporations.

Corporations felt that a more violent resolution was required at times and that idea had become more accepted. What had been the purview of thriller movies, where "accidents" occurred to middle managers or their superiors had become part of the corporate landscape globally.

In America and other 'civilized' countries, the corporations still tried to cover their tracks, to use publicity groups and other forms of propaganda to hide their actions. But in developing countries like Malaysia, where bribery, corruption, and gangs were more visible, the pace of violence had increased significantly since the introduction of the Towers.

Now, being a middle manager was often a difficult and violent job. Survival required not just a degree of corporate wits but also cultivator strength. Which, of course, led to things like the presence of a Chin sect in the Tower and their push for strong members.

"But why target us?" Arthur said, frowning. "We can't be a real threat. We're barely worth a fret."

"Not yet. But if you see an ant crawling beside you, are you going to let it keep crawling or do you squash it?" Amah Si said, making a thumbing motion on the table. "Easier to get it done now, than wait for the ant to bring more of its people."

"So what do you think we should do?" Arthur was not thrilled with the idea of being called an ant, but if they were just targeting him, it seemed that he could just hide away. Of course, if they didn't have an easy target, they might go after the rest of his people too. Which would be even harder to handle. At least he had Grade III Accelerated Healing. Sure, he might end up full of scars and dead ugly, but if he were honest, he was never that good-looking to begin with.

But he still hoped he wasn't too scarred from this recent burn.

"I vote you hide and keep cultivating," Mel said, echoing his own thoughts. "They'll probably forget about what they were doing soon enough."

"Unless they're the kind to get obsessed with killing the ants who won't die. And start pulling the legs off the ant, just to see it squirm," Arthur pointed out. "Not that I ever did that... much."

Amah Si shook her head at that confession. "I worry about that too. But what can we do? Attacking them back will just anger them."

"Ei, why not we just go talk to them?" Yao Jing said.

"Because, um..." Arthur scratched his chin. "I guess we could. But what would we say? 'Please don't try to kill me?'"

"We can find out why they want to. And whether we can somehow work with them," Amah Si pointed out. "We are already making allies with others. If we can make an alliance with them, it could put us in good stead."

"How is that coming along, anyway?" Arthur said curiously. He had left the work of alliances to her, what with his need to cultivate. But he hadn't had much news since then.

She shrugged, a mulish look growing on her face. "They keep asking for things we can't, or don't, have. I don't know if they're just stalling or being fools."

"Well, let's hope for stalling," Arthur said. "We could use more friends. If they demand what we don't have, we'll just end up with more enemies."

That sentence brought everyone's mood down and Arthur could not help but grimace. It sucked, of course, but what could he do? It was the truth.

"So, wanna go talk to the Chins?" Yao Jing said.

"Okay, lah," Arthur sighed, leaning back to cycle his breathing for a moment. The movement had sent a minor twinge along his torso, where muscles had yet to fully join. "I just..." He hesitated, then looked at Mel. "I know you have to cultivate but—"

"But you need to more than me. Especially with all the cores we have," Mel finished for him. "I'll talk to them. Amah?"

"I will help. My people can find the daughter, if she's still around town."

"And if she's not?" Arthur said.

"Then you stay hidden, until she comes back," Mel said firmly.

Nodding, Arthur stood up and pushed back from the table. Taking it as a signal that the meeting was over, the group stood up. There was nothing else to be said, and if he was going to be attacked, he might as well spend the time now absorbing more cores.

Better than worrying about what might come next.

Chapter 119

He knew he should have spent the time speaking with the merchant. He had made the appointment after all. Yet, once he found himself in his room again, Arthur threw away such concerns and focused on draining core after core. He delved deep into his body and senses, the cultivation method that he had been taught by Uswah, seeking ways to improve the flow of energy.

Arthur realized he had been lax. Willing to take the cores as they came, willing to grow, but he had not been driving himself to improve as much as he could have. Despite all those conversations about needing to strengthen himself and the clan—somehow, he thought that he had more time.

He was wrong.

So he lay on the floor, a small blanket underneath to make things a little more comfortable, and stared at the ceiling. Or seemed to. In reality, he was deep within his body, watching the flow of power, understanding how his body took in the energy, how it used some of the ambient energy that was part of the world to heal him.

He'd had to decide which to improve on. Eventually, he'd chosen to focus on the core draining aspect, and how to better make refined energy. How to pull apart a core, transform the Yang energy that was within into

Yin, to strain just for Yin alone and make it his fully. How to extract the full amount of core energy than let any escape wastefully.

The fact that it hurt, that it felt like pouring molten lava into his nerves?

Bugger that.

There was a process of converting Yang into Yin that Uswah had shown him. It worked mostly for cultivated energy, not refined energy. The Tower energy that was around them could be brought into their core, pulled apart, and transformed. For the most part though, she had glossed over it in their lessons. Why bother, when it was easier and faster to just learn to pull only the abundant Yin energy at a faster rate?

Except that didn't work as well when one was working with refined energy from a core. There was a limit to the amount of energy in a core, and most cores were a mixture of Yin and Yang. A generally balanced mixture, with only minor variations.

If he did not learn how to balance the pull, to use all of it, he would only get half as much use. That was still better than merely cultivating and then refining Tower energy, but half as useful than it could be. Twice as long, more importantly. So rather than suffer that, he would take it all first and then convert the Yang into Yin.

The energy entered his body, burning as it was channelled through him. Burning as he used the channels within his body to refine the energy, and his entire body became the transformer. Nerves on fire, even as he shovelled the extra energy into his core, battling the damn Yin energy until he could siphon it away. A bad heartburn, in his bladder, one that threatened to take away his attention.

He sweated and panted but stayed focused. He watched as his body acclimatized to the Yang energy again, converting it over to Yin. He refined the methods, pushing the energy to the full extremities of his body. Yin-soaked cells and bones took the Yang in, using it to fuel them.

After all, a Yin Body was not entirely composed of Yin energy. How could it be? He was no undead. Yang energy was required but in much smaller doses, in tiny increments. That he now used to build upon, to make himself grow stronger.

He sweated and panted, drumming his feet against the ground once in a while and the wounds on his face and stomach began to bleed anew before they closed again. Along the way, Arthur noticed an interaction that he had missed earlier. An interaction between his passive healing and the Yin Body, how it drained Yang energy to fuel itself.

As the beast core crumbled away on his stomach and he reached for another, Arthur chose to activate Accelerated Healing. To divert that river of abundance into the technique, to watch as it reacted to him. All the while pulling Yin chi from the new core, allowing his healing technique to make full use of the Yang energy that came flooding in from the beast core.

At first, there were bumps. Cultivating and healing at the same time were at odds with one another. The pull of energy from the core to his hands interrupted the flow of energy outwards from his dantian to the body. The pair battled, causing blisters and jolts of pain to erupt along his body.

Yet, he persisted. Knowing there had to be a way.

It worked passively. It should be able to work actively.

Struggling through the pain, Arthur focused on what he recalled of the passive healing. He moved the energy around, shifting the flow from the core to only specific channels. At the same time, he shifted the healing energy to other channels. Creating lanes of energy flow, like redirecting cars on a highway.

The process was painful and required his full concentration, which was nearly impossible as surges in the energy flow from the core and from his dantian caused new moments of agony. He had to split his mind, to handle both processes at the same time, and here his Multi-tasking Mind trait aided him. The ability to balance both flows was easier than he had expected, probably because he had, inadvertently, planned for it.

Pain or not, occasional failure or not, he struggled on. He kept channeling the energy into various parts of the body, until he achieved a tentative, excruciating balance. It was not perfect and he had to focus on it entirely, but the energy was flowing correctly. He was healing, rapidly, while also storing more and more Yin energy in his body.

As a bonus, the reduced outflow of Yang energy into his extremities meant that the overburdened organs, skin, and bones were able to make better use of the Yang energy he had shoved into them. He felt his body grow denser, more energy-fueled even as he continued the process.

Of course, he had no idea what all that meant for him when he exited the current cultivation process, but he was kind of looking forward to it. For a short period, he had everything that he wanted and needed. A perfect balance of core energy, healing energy, and Yin storage.

Then, of course, the core burned out. And the balance was thrown off.

Chapter 120

Arthur had just finished pounding out his frustration and pain into the ground when the door opened, revealing a worried-looking Jan.

"Ei. You need something?"

"Nothing. I'm fine. Just *fiiiine.*" Arthur flopped around, brushing the shards of the core crystal off him. They would disappear soon enough. He lay still and stared at her. "Just cultivating."

"Okay, whatever," Jan said. "You look better today. Though your smell got worse."

He would have thrown something at her, if the only things within close reach were not either a pointed weapon or a core. One was too much. The other too precious. So instead, he chose maturity and ignored her. Anyway, there was something much more interesting floating in his vision.

Simultaneous Flow Technique Understanding Begun. Process Reached – 12%

Arthur hummed. It was a little surprising to get updates on how far he'd managed to learn this. He never got that earlier when he was doing the other methods. Then again, he had been studying from a scroll the last few times or making it up as he went along.

If he had failed to figure it out properly, would he still have learned something? Did the Tower give him this data just because he had that new Multi-tasking Mind trait?

Or was it his new status as Clan Head? After all, he was now connected to the Tower in ways that others had not, could not be.

That almost felt like the answer. But he had learned that feeling was not the same thing as knowing, and so he set it aside for further exploration. A series of questions would give him the answer eventually.

Sometimes, he really wished that documentation about people's experiences in the Towers was better. It didn't help, of course, that each Tower was different, even if only marginally. Still, maybe he should have paid more attention to the minor details and not just big-picture knowledge of monsters and levels and how to progress.

Or not. He was still alive, after all.

Moving on.

Yin-Yang Energy Exchange Technique Begun. Process Reached – 25%

Another partial technique. Interesting that it had a name entirely different from the basic Yin Body cultivation technique he had learned previously. Heck, that Yin Body technique had been so simple, the Tower had not even bothered to name it more specifically, even after he had finished learning it.

Nor had the Tower given him a progress percentage then. Which raised the question of whether the technique he was trying now was even a Tower-approved one. He could be doing something the Tower had no idea how to categorise.

That led to questions about the techniques that others had brought in, from martial arts groups and religions that were supposedly working well for cultivators in the Towers. Were they better than Tower techniques but not recognized? Recognized but not spoken about?

Questions, questions, questions. And as usual, no answers.

Even if the process was only partially successful, Arthur found that with his new Mind trait, the process had not been terribly difficult. It wasn't as hard as before to pull and convert Yang chi. Just at the moment, his status sheet appeared unbidden.. Still…

Cultivation Speed: 1.23 Yin
Energy Pool: 12/16 (Yin) (Yang – unusable 0.9)
Refinement Speed: 0.038
Refined Energy: 0.452 (5) (Yang – unusable 0.046)

Attributes and Traits
Mind: 5 (Multi-tasking)
Body: 7 (Enhanced Eyesight, Yin Body)
Spirit: 5 (Sticky Energy)

Techniques
Yin Body – Cultivation Technique
Focused Strike
Accelerated Healing – Refined Energy (Grade III)
Heavenly Sage's Mischief
Refined Energy Dart

Partial Techniques
Simultaneous Flow (12%)
Yin-Yang Energy Exchange (25%)
Bark Skin (0.02%)

"When did that appear?" Arthur growled, rubbing at his face. What the hell was going on? He had wanted to focus on cultivating, but the changing screen was worrying. Pushing himself to his feet, then marveling as he realized his stomach no longer hurt, he stalked over to the door and yanked it open.

Jan looked over, startled. Then, as he explained the problem, she shoved him back into his room.

"Shhhh!"

"What?" Arthur snapped.

"Don't talk so loud. You want more enemies, ah?"

"I... don't. Why?"

"'Cause you special." She waggled her fingers. "You got a better screen, man."

"Better screen?"

She nodded.

"I don't understand, isn't it the same for everyone?"

Jan shook her head. "Tower sometimes, it chooses people it likes. Gives them better status screens. More info. Sometimes even hints." She frowned and whispered even more softly. "Mel might have one."

"How do you know Mel has one?"

"I said *might*. I don't know. She never told me." She shook her head. "Ei. You don't tell anyone, ah. People with good screens, either they become VVIPs or they die quick, you know."

"Shit on a stick."

"Yup."

He rubbed the back of his neck and then nodded. He grabbed her arm and started guiding her out, moving to shoo her when she broke free. "Okay," he said. "Good enough. I got something cool; I'll keep it quiet. Hopefully, there's more cool stuff later."

Made sense why Jan had hushed him. It was a good way of getting killed. Then again, with tell-all books out there, you'd think someone would have mentioned it. Perhaps they had, and then because no one else had backed them up, their works had sunk into obscurity.

Not his problem. He'd look into that when he reached the outside world. Which, at this rate, would be years away. If not decades. So...

"Shoo! I'm going back to cultivate."

Jan narrowed her eyes then nodded, opening the door to take her post outside once more. Arthur shut it firmly, then walked back to his spot on the floor. No more distractions.

Time to cultivate and get himself another damn point.

Chapter 121

Now that he had nothing more to focus on than just drawing the energy, Arthur found himself able to improve the Yin-Yang Exchange at a more efficient and faster rate. The influx of Yang energy into his body, and the way Yin-aspected cells drew Yang in and transformed it, took him a while to understand, to manipulate such that he could speed up the Exchange.

The conversion process was draining. The energetic Yang energy slowly lost its luster, growing slower and cooler, transforming as it did so. The conversion process was a question of redirection, shifting the extreme heat and bled-off energy to another location.

At first, Arthur attempted to contain the energy in one location, bleeding off the dense energy to his dantian. However, all that did was increase the amount of pain he was feeling. In fact, he could almost believe that by adding the energy to the core of his dantian, he was creating a small burning sun within himself.

Useful, perhaps, for another cultivator. Incredibly painful for Arthur such that it had left him curled up, pounding the ground in pain once again until he had it under control.

His next attempt was to shift it to his extremities, to the outer layers of his skin and then his aura. That was somewhat more successful, since there was a constant process of exchange with the outside world, with the Tower. However, it meant that he literally put himself in a sauna, his skin red and flushed as he processed the refined energy into Yin, with a rather significant loss in energy conversion.

He could not, of course, get a proper measurement of how much he lost, but it seemed of the Yang energy—about half of the core in most cases—he only recovered about twenty percent via this method. The rest was either stuck in the growing ball of energy within his dantian, to be converted by his body at a slower rate, or worse, radiated from his skin.

Arthur figured he would need at some point to get a grasp of whether the basic laws of physics were in play here—specifically, that of the conservation of energy. In other words, was everything that was being transformed a matter of eventual loss due to the conversion and transfer, or was there a secondary intake of refined energy happening? What ratio of converted energy was possible, what was the maximum and what was his current rate?

He had no idea, nor did he even understand the nature of the energy that he wielded and pulled into himself. There were, of course, theoretical discussions. Some went esoteric, calling it mana or the lifeblood of the gods or qi. Others spoke of quantum potential and entanglements.

None of it he had understood or cared to study. In the end, for Arthur, the fact that the energy was present, could be cultivated and refined, and then poured into his body to strengthen it was what was important. At least, he had thought so.

Until he found himself actually able to pour that energy into his body directly. Until he started messing with Yin and Yang energy, potential and active, stillness and chaos at the same time. That's when theory became important.

But that was always the trade-off. He could have studied all this, but then how would he have found time to work, to scrounge for food to feed himself? To pay for the lessons that taught him how to fight or that gave him a basic understanding of the Tower?

It was easy for those who had all their needs taken care of, who sat in comfortable chairs and picked at the food that was brought to them. They could discuss theory, talk about optimal methods of cultivation and refinement. In the midst of chaos, when shelter and meals and safety were more the question than whether a girl liked you or a piece of clothing was fashionable, what was optimal gave way to what was expedient.

How many idiots had he come across, who declared themselves rational actors when their so-called rational or correct options presupposed dozens of advantages that many other people were not privileged to possess? Arthur was more like a child who would rather eat a marshmallow now, rather than delay gratification for two marshmallows later, because he'd learned that adults could not be trusted with their word.

"Rational, fractional. Only when one's rich, can you be a bitch," Arthur sung under his breath.

Rational to him was to take the short-term gain because the future was always in question. Stability was a pipe dream, a promise only the advantaged could have.

No. Regret over past choices, taken in an older time and place with previous constraints, could be set aside. He was here, now. He had gained knowledge, experiences.

An understanding of pain, its transitory nature. That allowed him to lie here, as molten metal ran through his meridians and collected in his dantian.

Fine-tuned body awareness allowed him to pick the flow of energy in his meridians, the beat of his heart, the thrum of energy through muscles, and even the ache of his bones as energy passed through him. It allowed him to shift, to divert, to close off portions of himself through trial and error to optimize the path of energy flow.

Knowledge. Not theoretical, but practical knowledge of the Tower. Of Yin and Yang energy as not opposite sides of a coin, but different states of the same energy. He only need convince that energy to transform, to alter itself from one state to the other.

A quantum change, the flip of a switch.

The air burned around Arthur as he drew in energy, pulling the refined power into himself and separating the strands. Yang energy twisted, pouring through his body, priming it for potential change. Excess heat escaped into the air, into the Tower itself and his aura. At the same time, excess chaos, excess potential dissipated. A colder, more steady alteration occurred in those very same muscles and portions of the body.

A priming that Arthur noted. A twisting of potential, which had begun without him realizing it but he now guided and improved upon.

Core after core, the entirety of the team's acquisition minus the tithe, lay in a tiny pile by his side. A pile that diminished as the hours passed, as the guard changed and the air within his room grew chokingly hot.

Until Arthur's hand fell upon empty space by his side and not a single core lay awaiting his grasp.

Only then, exiting his cultivation frenzy, was he aware of the replete, stuffed-to-fullness of his dantian. Of himself. And the notifications awaiting him.

Chapter 122

Arthur could have read the notification immediately. He should have. However, he held off. For a few moments, for his throat was parched, his eyes bloodshot and gummy. His movements sluggish, the skin on his arms and face drawn tight and cracking. Each movement he made, as he stumbled through the oven-hot room, was a struggle. He did not even bother with a glass, instead sticking his head under the tap and slurping down the life-giving liquid.

A small part of him pointed out the paradox of desiring water and yet not needing to drink or eat normally. Why did he feel the need for water now?

Another part of him screamed: magic.

Yet another part noted that what had happened was not within the normal proceedings of existence but a cultivation frenzy wielding the opposite powers of Tower energy, Yin and Yang, in ways that his body was entirely untrained to do.

Of course there could be side effects. He was lucky he was not throwing up or blown up. What he had done was reckless in the extreme.

Another breath. Another dunk of his head under the tap, drinking until he needed to breathe again, and he was sloshing around, feeling like a water jug. He almost sat down then, but chose to stagger over to open the windows, letting in blessed fresh air. Leaning against the window, he wiped at his face that had already begun to steam.

"Steam. Am I in a dream? But if this is a dream, and I am a dream too, should I not be real, so I can cop a feel?"

He frowned, eyeing his body, the way sweat and water he had accidentally splashed on himself rose off him as steam. His lips thinned in thought, as Arthur watched the heat dissipate and then, acting on instinct, dove into his own awareness. It took him only a few moments to verify his initial assumption and a few more after that to curse himself out.

"I should have gotten into a bath first," he muttered to himself. It would have sped up the dispersal of Yang chi, allowing him to speed up his cultivation overall. Because at one point, the problem had not been the rate he could draw energy from cores but the conversion rate of the core energy to his own, which had required him to slow down. In fact, as he cultivated, he had found his refinement speed from the cores increasing. Still well below the theoretical maximum of his new refinement speed but better than before.

"Later. I'm tough. Next time," Arthur said to himself. Right now, as he was beginning to feel more human, between the breeze and the water that he had drunk, he turned his attention to the notifications that had been waiting. He still felt strained, a little off balance, his center of gravity sunk to his overburdened dantian.

Dantian Filled!
Dantian currently filled over recommended amount. Maximum possible energy contained at first transformation – 1.87.
Current amount of Refined Energy: 1.118 (Yang – unusable 0.1712)

Well, that was interesting. There was a maximum his dantian could store. It was not even a full two points but a weird fraction amount. Likely a case of individual growth, though he wondered if it had something to do with his Spirit or Mind attributes. Maybe even Body.

No way to know right now.

Once more, Arthur cursed the way all this knowledge was hidden. Many sects and other organizations had learnt the lesson about patents and the like, instead simply resorting to secrecy. So when secrets did leak, they were scrubbed vigorously, mixed with pure fiction, and the leakers dealt with in a violent and final manner.

Even so, the occasional trickle of information did come through. Governments, NGOs, and the occasional philanthropist released information to the public, giving people like Arthur the ability to at least learn basic cultivation methods or meditative techniques that allowed use of scrolls.

A definite improvement over the first few years, where everyone had been stumbling around completely blindsided by the Towers and how they worked.

"Got another point, where to put it? Do I even need to ask?" Arthur muttered to himself. He moved along the windows, making sure to prop them fully open to cool down the room further before making his way over to the bed.

He stopped himself just before he clambered onto it. While it was much more comfortable to lie on it, it also meant that his sweaty, disgusting skin and clothing would end up touching the new sheets. And even if he was not in charge of cleaning his own laundry—or was he?—he was not going to be that much of an ass.

Anyway, the floor would do.

Lying back down on the stone floor, he shut his eyes, only to realise that there was another notification waiting for him. It had not been pressing on him until now, and only when he was readying himself to apply a new attribute point had the notification come to him.

Body Energy Saturation and Preparation Achieved.

Percentage of Body Saturated – 24.8%

"What the hell does that mean?" He could feel its meaning, of course. The way his entire body felt like an overstuffed balloon, the almost hyperaware sense he had of the breeze, the energy coursing through him that made him want to run and jump and sing.

But what it meant in terms of cultivation, he had no idea.

"In for a penny, in for a pound." He mentally prodded the energy in his dantian into moving, pushing it to start running through him. At the same time, he informed the Tower of his choice, guiding it towards empowering his Body attribute.

There were many reasons for that, but reaching the Body threshold would gain him another trait and, more importantly, improve his overall chances of survival. Perhaps he might have been able to game the numbers a little, improve his Mind such that he could better refine the abundant cores and make more efficient use of clan resources.

But that was assuming his enemies gave him the time. And he'd just learned they weren't willing to do so. So, for now, Body.

Energy coursed through him, as changes were triggered. A waterfall effect of mutation and alteration caused pain once more that made his body arch, his muscles lock, and a strangled scream erupt from his mouth.

No surprise that Yao Jing popped his head in, checked for trouble, and then realizing his boss was busy cultivating and hurting himself again, so the bodyguard closed the door. Yao Jing thought to himself: Some things you just got used to, working for that idiot.

Chapter 123

Downstairs at their canteen, Arthur grabbed a plate of rice and curry. It said something about Malaysians that even when no one needed to eat, there was still a canteen in a building that desperately needed every inch of space.

Arthur eyed the suspiciously watery-looking curry with only a few chunks of meat floating in it, before he shrugged. Curry was curry, and bad curry was still better than no curry.

"Tell me what I missed," Arthur commanded Mel, the woman having appeared soon after he had gotten washed and dressed and exited his room. The fact that it was in the early hours of the morning and she looked a little haggard spoke to how much she had been working—and how important what she had to say was.

"Before that. Any success?" Mel said, gesturing at him to indicate what she meant.

"Decent. Another point in Body," Arthur said. "Thank you all, again. For the cores."

"It's necessary." Mel made a face. "Possibly more than you know." Then before he could ask, she continued. "Anything else?"

Arthur hesitated, mentally calling up his sheet again. There were some changes, but he was uncertain if it would help to tell her about them. Or if he even should.

Cultivation Speed: 1.237 Yin
Energy Pool: 12/17 (Yin) (Yang – unusable 0.9)
Refinement Speed: 0.0387
Refined Energy: 0.274 (6) (Yang – unusable 0.1712)

Attributes and Traits
Mind: 5 (Multi-tasking)
Body: 8 (Enhanced Eyesight, Yin Body)
Spirit: 5 (Sticky Energy)

Techniques
Yin Body – Cultivation Technique
Focused Strike
Accelerated Healing – Refined Energy (Grade III)
Heavenly Sage's Mischief
Refined Energy Dart

Partial Techniques
Simultaneous Flow (12%)
Yin-Yang Energy Exchange (34.1%)
Bark Skin (0.02%)

"A few things. I'm not sure it's useful, certainly not worth discussing here. Or until I figure out the exact details," Arthur said eventually. The minor increase in his cultivation and refinement speed was from his improvement in his Yin Cultivation Technique. He still didn't have a Tower-registered technique, but his homegrown one was nevertheless improving.

The more interesting thing was how a full point had not disappeared. It seemed that being partially primed for change in his Body had allowed him to discount the amount of energy he used to gain an attribute. The negative of that, though, was that he now had exactly none of that priming anymore. And he'd probably spent a lot more cores than he needed to.

A technique for the rich to use—and weirdly enough, he was one of those people, in a small way. And not a technique he'd recommend to anyone else in their struggling clan. Or recommend to himself, if they had any other choice.

"Why sooner?" he asked, before finally burying a spoon in the rice and curry and taking a bite. He made a face. The curry was neither thick, tasty, nor even spicy. Lousy curry. But at least, it was curry.

"Because we heard back from the Chin girl. She'll talk. But only to you." Another beat, before she added. "Outside the village."

"Trap?"

"Probably."

"And are we going to walk into it?" Arthur asked, taking another bite.

Mel looked down at his food, then at Arthur before she shrugged. "Depends on you, doesn't it?"

Arthur sighed. Right. He was the boss.

Yay him, say him.

His meal was halfway done, the curry swallowed and the rice chewed before he gave his answer. "I'd rather walk into an ambush now, than have the rest of you people get caught up in it. And if they intend to bring enough people to kill me right away, I'd like to know."

Mel nodded, looking him up and down again. After a moment, she nodded. "Alright then. But we'll push it to tomorrow or the day after."

"Why?"

"Because you need to familiarize yourself with your new body."

"Oh, right." Arthur smacked himself on the top of his head with his spoon, chuckling a little ruefully. "Forgot about that."

"Try not to?"

"Yeah, yeah." Waving his spoon dismissively, he dug into his meal again and finished the rest of it in short order. He then stood up, picking the plate up and dumping it aside, bidding goodbye to the sleepy-looking attendant.

"We going then?" he said, turning around to look at Mel.

"Right now?" she said, a little startled. She had been cradling a cup of *kopi* in hand, staring into space while he had been doing all that.

"No better time."

She snorted, drained the cup and stood up to join him near where the dirty dishes were placed, dumping her own cup. "You know, a woman needs her beauty sleep too."

"You don't. Pretty enough as it is."

That brought a flush to Mel's cheek, though she chose not to say anything. Instead, she pointed to the exit doors, and Arthur laughed silently as he exited with her.

Time to train.

The best part of training with Mel was that he got to fight another spear user. He liked that even more than getting beaten by her. And no, he wasn't some sadomasochist. Arthur just knew that he learned a lot more by getting beaten in a sparring situation than he did when dominating an opponent.

Sure, there were ways that you could train against juniors. Limiting the kind of movements you made, the techniques you used. Slowing down your reaction speed and movements. Even learning to train specific responses and openings, to guide your opponent into actions that you had pre-set responses towards such that you could hit them with blinding speed, since you were moving into those responses almost as soon as they began the corresponding action.

There were negatives to such training although his sifu had drilled him in those techniques repeatedly. When it was a given that you were going to fight cultivators stronger than you, then not being able to react in time was also a given.

To offset such a disadvantage, the easiest and best method was to program certain responses beforehand. Moving before your opponent, so that you stole time from your opponent. The negative, of course, was the same kind of negative that children playing slaps learned—that if you reacted before your opponent did, you just gave them a free shot.

Against Mel though, Arthur had nothing like that to worry about. Instead, he was pushing himself and his new body to the maximum. He needed to be faster, and so he was. Human bodies were often stronger, faster, and more flexible than people realized, mostly because the mind sets limits. The mind stopped people from tearing themselves apart, injuring themselves when they pushed too far.

Adrenaline, of course, removed those limitations to some extent. Made the body react faster, but also made the mind relax to allow the body to consciously increase speed. However, even then, in most cases, mental limits were still in play, just a little more lenient.

Good, of course, for normal mortals.

Not so great for cultivators who had just increased their Body attribute. Sure, the Tower helped reduce some of those mental blocks, loosening them up. But the Tower could only do much. The hours and hours of practice, learning to dodge by millimetres rather than inches still mattered, no matter how much aid the Tower and its mysterious abilities might offer.

Now, Arthur flinched and twisted, dodged and pushed, faster and harder than he was ever used to. He overjudged his dodges and underjudged his strength, such that he often moved too far and then blocked too hard. Instead of pushing weapons aside, he accidentally sent them spinning away.

The first few hours were frustrating to the extreme, but Mel was a great partner. She often repeated attack sequences, so that Arthur could respond once more to her in the same way, recalibrating his attacks to the proper sequence. Yet, she was faster than him, at the peak of the Body threshold, and thus she forced him back, again and again.

Leaving him sprawling on the ground, panting.

Only for Arthur to get up again and do it all over, because that's what you had to do. It was long past the morning, with the noon sun overhead, that Amah Si finally found them, tiny thunderclouds on her brow.

"Oh shit," Arthur muttered as he saw her, breaking away from Mel as he faced the tiny leader of the defunct Thorned Lotuses.

Seemed like playtime was over.

Chapter 124

Stepping farther away from Mel, just in case, Arthur leaned against his spear and forced himself to breathe slowly and steadily. A part of him wanted to hunch over, but he fought against that fatigue, knowing it would just take longer for him to recover.

Or would it? Hard to say. After all, he was not exactly human any more, but the cultivator body still needed oxygen. So probably? Yeah, probably.

He knew he was distracting himself, concerned about what Amah Si might have to say. When she finally reached him, the triple tap of feet and cane coming to an end, she spoke curtly. "Why did you set up a meeting without asking me beforehand?"

"Because, as it's been so eloquently pointed out to me, I'm the Clan Head," Arthur said. "My choice, my decision. Anyway, I'd think you'd prefer me putting my neck out on the line rather than your people's."

"Your neck is my people's necks, if you still hadn't realized."

"Still the same neck, at the end of the day. And no use to pray." Arthur shrugged. "Guarantee you they'll end up choosing to attack our people if I didn't agree to this meeting."

"Not immediately. We could have stalled, taken longer to talk," Amah Si snapped.

"We could." Then he opened his hand sideways. "But they already tried killing me once. I don't think they're exactly the patient kind. At least not *her*."

Amah Si growled but did not disagree with him. After all, that was true enough. After a moment, she tapped her cane on the ground again. "You should still have asked."

"No. I shouldn't," Arthur said. "I should have informed, but not asked. I know what I'm doing. At least in this case." He pointed to Mel. "And we'd let you know and figure out what was to happen, but I don't have to ask. That's not my place."

Again the older woman glared, before she let out a long breath. "Fine. I don't like it, but fine." She made a face. "I guess you should learn to walk by yourself. Since I won't be coming to the next floor with you."

"You won't?" Mel cried out.

Arthur on the other hand was not surprised.

"Of course not. I haven't gone up in two decades, why would I do so now?" Amah Si said. "I'm too old, too slow to go up again and be the smallest fish in a big pond. I've looked above the well, I know what's out there. I like being down here."

Mel continued to look hurt, while Arthur had a half-smile on his lips. "Mixing metaphors."

"What?" Amah Si said, confused.

"You're mixing metaphors. The fish and pond, frog and the well. They're different metaphors."

In answer, Amah Si raised her cane and prodded him in the stomach. "You. You think you're so smart all the time. Playing your rhyming games to annoy people, see our reactions. You should be careful. Smart doesn't stop a knife in the dark. Or a blade in the gut."

"Well, actually..." Laughing, Arthur backed off before she could prod him again. Then, sobering up a little, he bowed low to her. "I know. And I'm grateful for the advice. But I don't have much going for me. A Yin body and my natural smarts, that's all. Plus the ability to annoy people."

And weren't they glad for the most part that even the "Mind" attribute did not exactly make people smarter. It allowed them to do things like process information faster, or control the Tower energy, or even gain increasingly elaborate methods of memory recall. But the spark that made up creativity or intelligence, that did not seem to be something the Tower could enhance. Being in the Tower was like swapping out different components of a desktop to make it work better, but not touching the actual software.

Of course, it was an imperfect metaphor like most metaphors. But it helped him at least to understand the changes brought by a higher Mind attribute. On the other hand, the Spirit attribute was just a complete morass of contradictory terms, which he wasn't even going to touch. Not when Amah Si was looking at him expectantly.

"What?" he asked.

"Promise you'll keep building upwards. The same way you have here." She tapped the cane end on the ground. "Or better than here. Do it better."

Arthur rolled his eyes. "Can't do it worse now, can I?"

Silence, before Mel started cackling. Arthur frowned, while even Amah Si cracked a small smile. Eventually, Mel choked out a soft, "And whose fault is that?"

"Yours! The stupid Suey Ying. Fate! I never chose to do this," Arthur grumped, fingers tightening on the spear reflexively.

"It's fine. You've done fine," Amah said, a little smile on her lips. "You are not a fool, or as much as I thought. Stubborn, but that can be good." She nodded. "Now, promise."

"Fine, fine!" Arthur said. "I promise to keep the Benevolent Durians the same or build it up better on the next floor." He sniffed. "Why bring it up now anyway? It's going to be months before I have to head up."

Amah Si shrugged. "Call it intuition. Also, we were just talking about it."

There was something in her eyes, the way she spoke, that made Arthur narrow his eyes. He could not place it, but he assumed she knew more than she was saying. Before he could prod her further, she raised her cane and pointed it at him.

"What?" Arthur said, warily. He had backed off already to avoid being poked, but now he stepped away, for the old woman suddenly looked a lot more dangerous with that single motion and a minor shift in stance.

"You're training right?"

"Yeeessss?"

"Then better to train with people who are better, yes?"

Arthur nodded again.

"Good," she said. Springing forward faster than Arthur could have anticipated, she struck the arm that was holding his spear, causing him to lose his grip. Even as the spear fell, she swung the cane again and struck his thigh. As his weight collapsed, she struck the ankle of that leg. Luckily, she chose not to actually break it but hook the ankle and pull, somehow having transitioned to using the other end of her cane in the middle of swinging it.

Landing on his back, arm and thigh aching, Arthur stared up at Amah Si blurrily. Only to find her swinging the cane down, straight for his head. He scrambled to roll out of the way, even as she roared behind him, swinging her cane as she did so.

"Fight! Fight like a man, not scurry like a rat!"

"Rats live longer!" Arthur cried as he dodged, the older woman cackling as she kept swinging. He managed a fakeout that worked, mostly, and on his forward roll, picked up his spear and swung it around. He managed to force her to block, buying him time to take a firmer stance.

Damn evil woman. What was it, with his fate and crazed women? He could swear he was cursed or something.

Chapter 125

Two days passed by quickly, the last half a day spent cultivating and then sleeping made time pass in a blur. Drilling to get his body and techniques synced once more had taken up almost an entire day, most of it being chased around or fighting back against his team for practice.

It seemed nearly everyone had a better Body attribute than him, but thankfully, years spent training prior to the Tower—unlike some of those here—left him with better skills overall. It still did not save him from the constantly accumulating bruises, but all those faded away in hours thanks to the Tower and his Accelerated Healing technique working in conjunction.

All of which meant that, on the day of their meeting, Arthur was as prepared as he could be. He still tugged at the new set of clothing that had made its way to his room, grimacing as he ran his fingers down the black silk.

"I don't know why I have to dress up," Arthur muttered. "I mean, I know why. Got to look the part. But did it have to be like a tart?"

"Ya lah, why this suit?" Jan said, walking beside him. "You look worse than normal."

Yao Jing was on the other side, flanking Arthur and a little behind. The pair who had become his de facto bodyguards were both here for this meeting, as was Mel. Arthur knew that Uswah and a few of the other teams had drifted ahead, and some would be coming from behind to surround the meeting area.

"And why black?" Arthur grumbled. "Couldn't we have a little more splash? A little more pizazz if we're going to make a statement?"

"It's cheaper, it shows blood less well when you inevitably get stabbed, and we can replace the panels more easily," Mel said, ticking each point off with a finger. "Any further questions?"

"Why is everyone thinking I'm going to get stabbed?" Arthur complained.

There was pointed silence, before Jan chose to speak. "I always want to stab you. So why not other people?"

"You know, having your bodyguard say she wants to stab you makes me uncomfortable," Arthur said.

"Makes you careful you don't mess up," she said. "And don't fool around when we all working so hard."

Arthur snorted. "You call cultivating fooling around?"

"Ya lah. Lying around your bedroom all day. Using up all our cores." Jan let that statement linger, watching as Arthur hunched in a little. He really had been hogging a lot of resources lately.

"It's fine. We need you strong, boss. For meetings like this." A clap on the back of his shoulder from Yao Jing brought Arthur's head up and he let out a long breath.

Forcibly straightening himself, he glared at Jan only to catch Mel giving her the death stare too. He almost smirked before choosing to keep that hidden, not wanting to drive the point home too much. He might not get her to stop picking on him, but at least she could learn the proper time and place for it.

Or so he hoped.

"So, we got everything ready for this?" Arthur said, idly. He let his gaze bounce around the beginner village, noting that there weren't more people hanging around than usual. They'd kept word of the meeting quiet it seemed, which meant that they shouldn't have an oversized crowd this time. "I know the other groups haven't chosen to throw in with us just yet, but Mohammad Osman?"

"He's one of those coming from behind," Mel said. "We weren't exactly sure where to put him, so we figured he could play reinforcements. Or, well, not Osman himself but his second-in-command."

Arthur nodded. "Any word on the rest of the Suey Ying?"

"Not really. We know they've joined other groups, but most of them aren't even in the village anymore." Mel chuckled darkly. "Seems like they're all being put to work hard. Maybe to keep them out of sight from us. Maybe just 'cause they're all asses and that's what they deserve."

"Good enough for me." He slowed down a little as they came towards the no man's land between Tower village and tent village. His grip tightened on the black spear he held, and for a moment he felt a flash of uncertainty run through him.

Before he could ask, Mel cut him off. "Your call, remember. We just follow your lead. And it's too late to back out."

"Yeah, yeah. I was actually just going to ask if anyone had any gum," he huffed into his hand and frowned. "Don't want to make a bad impression."

"Too late." Jan pointed with a hand held low. Following her motion, Arthur realized that between his hesitation and him looking at Mel as she spoke, the Chin representative had made her appearance.

"Four of them. Coincidence or spies in our Clan, you think?" Arthur remarked.

Yao Jing was eyeing the bodyguard on the left, another massive bodybuilder who looked like he ate two dozen eggs for breakfast and then had three dozen more for lunch. He even wore a way-too-tight shirt, one that looked to be straining to hold itself together with each breath.

The other bodyguard was clad in a full black suit. The man might have been doing an impersonation of a secret service bodyguard, for all the sunglasses and tie getup he was wearing, but it mostly made him look foolish. While the Tower was cooler than the outside world, it was more a case of a warm twenty-eight degrees Celsius rather than a boiling thirty-eight degrees. Warm enough to make wearing a full suit foolish in the extreme.

Ignoring the guards, Arthur eyed the older man standing right behind the Chin woman, just to the side. He had the look of a real bureaucrat, one who had been here for ages. There were lines in his eyes and a seriously thinned top along with a pair of glasses. Considering the Tower fixed most sight problems when one entered, he must have been doing a lot of reading to require them again.

And, of course, finally, it was the Chin girl. The representative of the infamous, powerful family. The ones who had tried to kill him.

And she was gorgeous.

"You might want to close your mouth before a fly gets in." Mel's voice was chilly. "Try not to sell us out for a pretty face."

Coughing, his face a little flushed with embarrassment, Arthur snapped his mouth shut. He straightened himself out, gave his head a shake, and reminded himself that she had tried to kill him. So. Pretty face or not, she was a killer. It wasn't even as though he was raring to go—the Yin chi in his body kept him calm to some extent. Still, he was a man, and he could look and admire.

Striding over with that refrain in his mind, he met her outside the boundary as agreed, forcing his eyes to keep moving as he searched for treachery or additional danger. Finding none, he found his heartbeat speeding up a little more.

Who knew if these four were the only present? Hidden treachery was the worst kind.

"Arthur Chua?" Her voice was clear, bright, and what Arthur would call sophisticated. British accent. And not a fake one, like some Malaysians got after spending three months overseas. Hers was smooth and without a wrong inflection.

"Yes."

"I am glad you were willing to meet with me." Then, to his utter surprise, she dropped into a deep bow from her waist, hands together. "I apologise for the earlier actions taken against you. They were unconscionable and I can only blame inexperience at managing my personnel."

She added, "I hope you can forgive me."

For the second time in the meeting in as many seconds, Arthur found himself floored.

Chapter 126

"Forgive for trying to kill him? What for!" an outraged Jan blurted out from behind Arthur. For once, he had to admit he was grateful for her lack of decorum, since her words jolted him back into the present. He, however, chose not to answer, curious to see how the Chin girl reacted.

"Yes. It is more complicated than that," the girl said. "If you'd let me explain?"

"Before that. Why are we meeting here?" Mel interrupted, gesturing around them. Her eyes were narrowed in suspicion. "You could have apologized in the village. If you were really contrite, you could have done so in our clan building."

"Ah..." Lips pursed then, a flicker of irritation rising across the pale jade-white skin of the woman. She looked over her shoulder, meeting the other older man's gaze and giving a silent command as she did so.

He stepped forward with ease, bowing low. Similar to the woman, he had a slight British accent. "My niece has been lax in providing introductions. I am Willis Chin, senior member in charge of the first floor. My niece, Casey Chin, is the third daughter of my elder cousin and is in the process of gaining her first Tower progression."

"Arthur Chua. A bit of a bah, that you know that for a fact," Arthur said with a smile.

Mel chimed in with her name, but Arthur's two bodyguards chose not to speak this time and likewise Casey's own guards.

"That doesn't explain why we're meeting here." Arthur purposely looked around, searching for potential trouble or signs from his own people.

"That is my choice." Willis inclined his head to the village behind Arthur. "In there, it can be said that clans hold the advantage. You have not seen the extent of control—of advantage—that you possess, but you should at least understand that it is present."

Arthur frowned a little, casting his mind over the minor advantages they had gained. The guard, the building. Nothing too great. Was he hinting there were other advantages they could gain as a clan? And if so, why tell them? Willis had to know it would only aid Arthur. Unless he assumed Arthur or the Lotuses knew that much already.

"And?" Arthur prompted the man to go on.

"Out here, in this place, lies our strength. We have no clan building here and will not because our Patriarch cannot enter this Tower."

That wasn't new. It was well known that due to the amount of energy present in lower levels of beginner Towers, more powerful cultivators were generally barred from entering. The exact threshold of power was unknown, though it generally ranged between two to three threshold breaks from the average cultivator.

"But we are still the Chin family," Willis continued. "We have our holdings, our alliances. And so, in between those, we find a balance between our strength and yours. A proper place for negotiations, rather than bowing our head to you. Or you to us."

"Negotiate what?" Arthur said, looking increasingly frustrated. "First you try to kill me, then you apologise, then you want to negotiate? You guys are making as much sense as one of my rhymes."

"If you just wait, I can explain," Casey cut in.

"I still don't trust this," Mel faux-whispered to Arthur.

"I know. Me too."

"I JUST TOLD THEM TO TAKE CARE OF YOU WHILE I WENT HUNTING!" Casey shouted, as Mel and Arthur continued talking and ignoring her.

Willis winced, shooting his niece a long glare. Arthur had to wonder about the kind of backroom family politics going on that the older man was basically forced to babysit her. He assumed it had something to do with the reason Willis was relegated to running the lowest floor of the Tower. It was a death sentence for the rest of his life. Or most of it at least.

"My niece is right. The fault was mine. I saw you as a threat. She believes you might be an... opportunity," Willis said, bowing a little. Not much, for the man had his pride after all, but it was a bow.

Arthur's eyes widened, darting between the flush-faced woman—or rather, girl—and her distant uncle. Now that she was blushing and embarrassed, her initial startling beauty had given way to show her true age, her youth. She looked to be in her early twenties at most. Probably just finished her degree in the UK before coming back to run the Tower and take her place among her family.

"Oh." Arthur glanced at Mel. She shrugged and he had to admit that he agreed with her unspoken words. If the Chins were acting or running a trick, then they were wasted as cultivators. Willis and Casey should both take up acting instead. The Malaysian film industry could definitely use more talent.

Arthur chose his words with caution: "Well, you might want to be careful with your words. They seem to carry a lot of weight."

"I know, lah!" Casey snapped, shifting unexpectedly into Manglish a little. She muttered, "*Dai ga jie* won't shut up about that."

Arthur could not help but grin. The initial awe broken, she was no longer the imperial beauty of before but now a softer, more approachable kind. He had to admit that was a little more attractive, but it also meant he could focus better. Mind for the most part clear as the Yin chi pulsed within him, he continued.

"You have use for me, for my clan, it seems. What is it?"

She glanced around, looking at the few passersby who had moved to eavesdrop. She kept staring at the brave fools until they chose to back away and a decent space was cleared around the group. Small gestures from both Willis and Mel had their own people help clear out the space further.

When Casey was finally satisfied, she smiled a little, trying for disenchanting. That disarming beauty flared to being again, but this time around, ready for it, it had little effect on Arthur, allowing him to concentrate on her next words easily.

"An alliance. A safe place to grow and progress." She gestured upwards. "A way to ascend the Tower faster than anyone."

"Faster than anyone?" Arthur said, blinking.

"Yes. Faster than anyone in my family. You know there are prizes for those who clear a Tower quickly?"

Arthur nodded. He also knew that such speedrun awards were useless to someone like him. The time he had spent on this floor so far had seen him already pass the timing for top ten. And even if they gave prizes for the top fifty, he doubted he'd make up enough time no matter how fast they ascended.

"Well, I want one," Casey said. "None in my generation have won such a prize."

With confidence she added, "I intend to change that."

Chapter 127

Contrary to Casey's expectations, her pronouncement did not engender looks of amazement or surprise, much less applause. Instead, the group just stared at her until she flushed and looked down in embarrassment.

"And you want me to help you," Arthur said. "How? I mean, sure, you might join our clan, but I doubt your family is going to like that." There were definitely mulish looks on their faces at that suggestion. "Otherwise, what?"

"I want to use your clan buildings."

He shook his head. "I don't get why it matters. Surely your people have buildings for you to rest, enough cores to push ahead."

"We do." Willis confirmed, his face mostly impassive. But Arthur was beginning to get a sense of the man, and with his keen eyesight, he'd noticed the minor twitches, the micro expressions of unhappiness on his face as Casey had spoken.

"Then?" Arthur said.

"You know how clan buildings provide higher concentrations of energy. Even with enough cores, it's still more efficient to cultivate in a clan building," Casey said. "My second cousin tried a speedrun just using the resources we had, and he still failed."

"He was also not very efficient at the mandatory quests," Willis said. "I am sure, with your abilities, you will be able to finish faster than him."

"And still only get into the top thirty at best," Casey replied. "I ran the numbers. It's not enough."

Willis frowned but Arthur ignored the man, understanding that it was Casey who mattered.

"You do realise I don't have a clan building on higher floors, or the resources to build the next one immediately, right?" Arthur said. "I can't exactly magic one together in higher floors." Or so he had been led to understand. In fact, he heard there were few Tower buildings on the upper floors, unlike on the first floor.

"I know." Casey grinned. "Which is why it's a good deal for you. We'll loan you the money to buy a building, or we'll gift you one from our stock. You make it a clan building and let me—and my people—stay in it and cultivate. You'll also help me progress through the mandatory quests, which will help *you* finish them too." She laughed. "Who knows. You might end up getting a prize too."

"Unlikely," Willis muttered.

Arthur ignored the grumpy old man, looking at Mel for her input. She pursed her lips a little in thought. The entire deal seemed too good to be true, really. Even if the Lotuses had branches further up, they were still a small group, meaning that if they had permanent buildings, they weren't likely to be big. Establishing a clan building on each floor would take a long time.

And while Arthur wasn't exactly against time spent that way, there were obvious advantages to actually reaching the top floor.

"That's a good deal. I'll admit it," Arthur said, making Casey grin. Jan on the other hand winced, knowing he had given up part of his bargaining position by being so upfront. "Only one problem."

"What's that?"

"Well, more than one. But the biggest?" Arthur tapped his chest. "Me."

"What's wrong with you?" Casey said.

"Everything," Jan muttered under her breath.

"Ya lah." Yao Jing muttered.

"Cultivation speed. I can't, I won't, head up without at least having the recommended minimum." Arthur shrugged. "I'm not insane, you know. Those mandatory quests are guaranteed to kill you, if you don't do them right."

Casey paused, then nodded. "We can get you cultivation methods that'll suit you."

"And my people too."

"What?" she snapped.

"And for my people," Arthur repeated.

"You're asking too much, don't you know?"

"I'm not going up and exposing myself to new dangers without my team." He snorted. "That'd be reckless and insane." He paused, then added, "And I'm the only one whose either of those."

"You don't trust me?"

"You tried to kill me."

"It was a mistake!" Casey said.

"And there's no guarantee another 'mistake' wouldn't happen in the future."

She glared at him now, lips pursed. Before she resolved what she intended to say, he added, "My team and I will discuss our conditions. I'll probably want more things, to make sure I'm not being completely betrayed. Like promises of protection. At least for a little while, while the clan sets up on each floor."

"You... you do you know who you're talking to, don't you?"

"Someone who needs me more than I need her, it seems," Arthur said.

"You—! We could crush you and your clan. Make sure you have nothing to ascend to!" Casey spat.

"And now the rich girl comes out." He inclined his head. "You're right. You can crush my fledgling clan with little effort. However, that won't help you now, will it? Cultivation methods for me and my team, that's not a big ask. Not for you guys."

"You would be under oath not to share our techniques with others," Willis snapped, interrupting. "And do not expect a five-star—or even a three-star—technique."

"I'll take whatever I need to keep up with her. My team will need resources too," Arthur said, while Casey continued to fume. "And if we get one for the rest of my team, I'll accept that."

Willis moved to object, but Casey raised a hand. He shut his mouth with a clack. "You said you'll discuss the terms with your team. And then inform us of your full demands. Yes?"

"I also need to know when you intend to go up," Arthur raised a finger. "And don't forget we need those resources to keep up with you." He raised a hand to Willis as the man's eyes bugged out. "I'm not trying to be unreasonable. But if you want me to follow along, to ascend with you, that's what it will take."

"You are not wrong." Casey paused, then added, "But you're also being unreasonable. Financing you is entirely reasonable. But your people as well?" She shook her head. "I might as well be sharpening a dagger in my own back. Who knows if *you* won't betray *us*? My father would not thank me for raising a new competitor."

"Not a competitor," Mel said. "It's not like we're aiming for the corporate arena." She laughed a little ruefully. "Surely you know what it takes to survive in business—knowledge of enchanted items, mining and harvesting cores large-scale... That's beyond our ability. It would take years for us to even come close to any degree of competence in your arena. No matter how desperate we are for cores ourselves."

"All true. But you'd still be a dagger that could be wielded against us," Casey said.

"Unless we are allies," Mel replied.

Now the younger girl fell silent, regarding Arthur and Mel. She hesitated then, looked to the side and met Willis's gaze. The man was visibly wanting to speak but unwilling to do so at the moment. Still, some unspoken message was passed between the pair, before she turned to Arthur and Mel.

"Something for you to consider... I am willing to finance a little more than what it would take for the Clan Head to ascend. But we will not pay for all of you." She paused, then added. "Go back. Make a list of what you want. Then we will decide what we are willing to offer and come to an agreement."

"Still haven't said when you want to go up," Arthur said. "That's important."

"Oh!" Casey laughed ruefully. "Did I not say? In a week. I'm ready to ascend in a week."

Chapter 128

"Completely unfair," Mel muttered, as the group walked back to the clan building. She was idly spinning her spear with each step, burning off nervous energy. "She's barely been in the Tower a month and she wants to ascend?"

"Only three weeks," Jan corrected.

"Exactly!" Mel snapped. "Rich kids, with their infinite resources and cultivation techniques and—aargh!"

"Now, now," Arthur said, only to duck his head a little when Mel glared at him. "If she hands us a proper cultivation technique, our people may have a chance at ascending too."

Beside the group, Yao Jing was counting off fingers held out in front of him. His lips were moving wordlessly. Eventually, his face brightened. And then just as quickly fell.

"What?" Jan asked.

"How, lah? If she just cultivates, it should take at least four months. Even if she only uses cores," Yao Jing said.

"That's using the cultivation methods we currently have," Arthur paused, then smiled a little tightly. "Or well, that most of us have. It's different if you have starred series of techniques."

"Yup," Jan said, and recited: "'One star: twice as good. Two stars: thrice as good.'"

"Four times as good," Arthur idly corrected.

"What?" Jan said.

"It's four times now," Mel chimed in. "They changed the ratings again."

"Why change?" Jan growled.

"Because we keep getting better, of course," Arthur said, his tone taking on a lecturing note. "Did you know that the Seven Rules of Heavenly Breath method that we use was once considered a one-star method? Before that, the basic cultivation system was significantly worse.

"Then, Seven Rules became so widespread because AnonPi released it onto the web again and again that it became a basic method. And once that happened, the cultivation board considered it a zero-level cultivation technique. They shifted the star rating around. And now, a one star is twice, two is four, three is eight and four is twelve. Supposedly a five-star method is twenty times as powerful, but there's no official confirmation that there even is a five-star technique out there."

"There is," Mel said firmly.

"How you know?" Jan said.

"Because they wouldn't create a five-star rating if the cultivation board had not known of one," Mel said. "Eventually, we'll see those methods. I know it."

"I dunno," Yao Jing said. "I feel like we have so little info. The big groups keep hiding what they know."

"But the open-source cultivation forums are getting better," Arthur pointed out. "They've actually improved the Seven Rules of Heavenly Breath by eighteen percent in the last decade. Of course, it doesn't work for everyone exactly but... it'll get there. Especially as they're getting better at keeping stolen cultivation methods up and clean."

"Up and clean?" Jan said.

"Uploaded and clean of manipulation. That's the reason the project has a bad name, for they thrashed the game." Arthur made a face. "People like the Chins or some of the other major players keep altering the information out there, or releasing 'great secrets'. At first they were just blatantly lousy techniques, but—"

"Then they got smart," Mel said, anger in her voice. "They started sneaking in long-term defects. So that you wouldn't harm yourself immediately but slowly in small increments. Eventually though..." She trailed off with a shake of her head.

"It took a long time for the public to find out. It's hard for the outside world to know what's happening in here until someone gets out," Arthur gestured around. "And the people from here who were letting others know outside were being discredited. Eventually, though, there were enough voices it couldn't be denied."

"So, why don't you use their improved methods?" Yao Jing said. "You know a lot, right?"

"I read it over, yes." Arthur shook his head. "But I can't take the chance that their improvements work. I can afford to go slow." He laughed a little softly. "Or I thought I could."

Practical as always, Jan could not help but ask, "You think they gonna give us a bad technique?"

"Who?" Yao Jing said.

"The Chins, lah, who else?"

"Oh! Them."

Arthur snorted. "They could try, but it's easy enough to check."

"If so easy, then..."

"Inside the Tower," Mel said. "It's easy to check a starred cultivation form." She pointed to where the Administrative building stood. "We just need to take the sealed document there and have them create a Tower copy from it. It's expensive but they'll certify the grade when it's done too."

"Ohhh... like that also can, ah?" Jan said. "How come I don't know about this?"

"Have you ever needed to certify a cultivation method? Or even seen one?" Arthur said.

Silence greeted his words as they finally reached the clan building. Arthur walked right in, searching around until his gaze landed on one of the human guards. He barked orders to the girl, sending her scurrying off to find Amah Si. He would have also asked for Uswah, but she arrived moments later, drifting in from the doorway behind them.

"Did you hear?" he asked.

"A little. I'd want to hear it fully later," she said.

"Do you think we can trust her?" Arthur could not help but ask. Of them all, the dispassionate Malay woman probably had a different read of things, being a distance away and all that.

"No additional guards. No backup except one large group that stayed far enough away that it was likely just for an emergency," Uswah answered. "Two scouts, but none of them as good as me."

"I'm not sure what that means."

"She's trusting. Too trusting. Naïve." Uswah paused. "Willis is not. Trust her. Doubt him."

"Thank you," he replied.

"You going to take her up?" she asked.

"I think so. If we can come to a deal." Arthur looked around the building, overcrowded as it was with people. Even now, in the middle of the day, the noise from the indoor population was overwhelming.

They needed more space, more resources, more fighters. More of everything, really, and while time would fix some of it eventually, time was what they had the least of. He could not fix the majority of those matters, but he could improve the clan itself, if he kept climbing the Tower.

So he'd do that. As long as they could get a decent deal from the Chins.

"Then, you cultivate." Uswah pointed to the stairs, making Arthur frown.

"She's not wrong," Mel chimed in. "You're going to need to gather as much strength as you can, especially if she intends to ascend in a few days. You're well behind."

"A few hours won't matter that much," Arthur said. "And we'd be protected by them. Cultivating on the next floor with cores from there—"

"More effective for sure," Mel cut in, "but you'd be significantly weaker. So. Cultivate. It's safer here, and the safer the better." She paused, looked at Jan and Yao Jing and pointed at the both of them in turn. "You two also. I'll find others to take your places."

"And you? What will you do?" Arthur asked.

"I have to talk to Amah Si. And work out what *we* want," Mel said. "You cultivate. We'll handle the negotiations. Unless you want to?" She arched a single eyebrow.

No, he really did not.

"Fine, fine," he grumbled softly. "As though I can't even manage my own life."

The fact that they were all chuckling as he trundled up the stairs did little to placate him.

Chapter 129

With little choice about what he should, or could, do, Arthur chose to spend that time cultivating once more. Since the volume of beast cores had dropped significantly, such that he would likely burn through them in a few moments, he chose to cultivate Tower energy rather than attempt to refine energy from the few cores he had left.

If things went well, the clan would soon have access to many more cores. While he still felt a little guilty for using so many cores over the past few days, he would soon leave the floor entirely and then, they'd have full run of it without him around. In fact...

"I probably should talk to Amah Si about how they're planning to push cores through to me in the real world," Arthur muttered to himself. Then, struck by a random thought, he hummed and sang. "Got to get my moolah, because I'm the... boo-yah?" A violent shake of the head. "Got to get the cash, so I can dash? Get the cash to take care of the rash? No. I have no rash. Don't want people thinking that either..."

Whatever. He'd worry about rhyming later.

That was the normal course of action, where cores owed to the Clan Head would be couriered by members exiting the Tower afterward. Like runners who entered the first floor, a certain level of loss was expected from those failing to complete the exit tests. Even so, there was still a continual flow of beast cores and enchanted items. It was one of the ways that clans managed to solidify their control in the real world. It also allowed family members with the appropriate documentation to draw upon owed amounts inside Tower levels.

It was that kind of debt and balance that Arthur assumed the Chin girl was going to utilize to pay for him. For a large family like theirs, built up over long years, the amounts owed and kept in reserve were likely to be considerable.

As were their expenses when they pushed someone through.

"I can't wait to get another enchanted item," Arthur muttered, glancing over at his black spear. Once again, he pulled up the information for it.

Black Spear (Enchantment Primed)

Enchantments: None

No indicator of damage type, or damage dealt, or anything that would have made it like a real game. Which was great, since it didn't make sense that a glancing blow or a stab to the arm did as much damage as a stab to the head. As Arthur knew, you could better kill someone with a two-inch blade in the right spot as a parang swung badly.

He was initially disappointed that the spear was primed for enchantments but held none. But once he realized why, Arthur had let his disappointment go, instead looking forward to the future. After all, how could his people afford to put a proper enchantment on a weapon on the first floor? They were not rich, they did not have the means to purchase anything extremely powerful. Better to spend the money on equipment that could be primed for use later and simply be patient.

Once he progressed to higher levels, he'd pay for the spear to be enchanted. It'd also help, by that point, to know what he could do and thus fill any gaps he might have with the right enchantment. Anyway, he should not be greedy. He already had one enchanted item.

Hand drifting to the other side, he touched the kris. He called up the information on it, having finally found time between all that cultivating and running around to get it properly identified. Not that what it had to say was particularly surprising.

Cursed Kris of the Lost Warrior

Enchantments: Applies an instance of Toxic Yin Chi when blood is drawn. Effects of Toxic Yin Chi vary depending on resistances and individual factors. The effects include clouding of senses, numbness, paralysis, and respiratory or cardiac arrest.

Not a great name. Arthur would have preferred something like The Kris of Hang Tuah, but that would probably be a reward on the tenth floor, rather than a giveaway on the first. After all, Hang Tuah was one of the greatest legends in Malay literature.

At it stood, Arthur's kris was way too powerful for this floor. Given its toxic effects, most first-floor cultivators who hadn't reached their first threshold break would be finished by three or four hits of this kris. Even a single good strike could infuse enough toxic chi into a fighter to swing the outcome of a battle. As he had learned all too well firsthand.

If he had not already had a Yin Body...

"Not a bin, being Yin."

Arthur shuddered and let that thought sit in his mind for a moment before he pushed it aside. He idly noted that his heart rate had spiked again, and his fingers were trembling a little from the flood of chemicals. No surprise that he was still suffering effects from all the fights, the near-death experiences he had faced.

Even years spent training, working with his master to clear his mind, to help him learn how to handle the expected mental burden of becoming a killer, and nearly dying still had after-effects. And that was on top of the calming influence that hours spent cultivating and meditating had on him—and whatever else the Tower had done to them mentally upon entry.

In fact, there were very clear indications that the Tower did influence or alter those who entered. There was a marked increase in sociopathic traits among those who entered. Or was that psychopathic? He never could get it right, and it didn't help that the damn articles in the paper never got it right either.

It really didn't matter in the end. The point was that people who entered the Tower, who transformed because of it, were almost always a little more callous, a little less empathic. They handled the aftermath of violence better and, frankly, had a tendency to reach for violent solutions as their basic method of handling things. Of course, there was always debate if it was because the Tower made such solutions the most viable ones—thus conditioning said individuals—or because it was an effect of entering the Tower.

Arthur had only a basic understanding of all that discussion, but as his sifu had pointed out, the whys mattered less than the fact that it happened. His goal was to learn how to handle and manage his mind, not figure out why he had a different body.

Pulling his mind back into the present, Arthur breathed, cycling air through his lungs until his hands stopped trembling. Then, and only then, did he begin cultivating. He could have started a little earlier, but the time saved would not be worth the drop in inefficiency.

Anyway, he was close to having a full core of cultivated energy. Once he achieved that, he would need to refine that energy and then repeat the process.

In the meantime, hopefully the negotiations with the Chins would go well. In the end, though, he could only trust his people. Everything, everyone had their place. And his, right now, was cultivating.

Chapter 130

"Eh, boss. I don't wanna sound ungrateful, but can we go hunt, anytime soon?" Yao Jing said, two days later. The group had taken a much-needed break, chilling out with cups of hibiscus water, tucking into plates of nasi lemak that were part of that evening's meal. Not much meat, but the rice itself and the coconuts that were needed to make the dish were simple enough to locate.

"Oi," Jan said, scornfully. "You cannot concentrate for even two days, ah?"

Yao Jing shrugged, not looking at all perturbed. "So, boss?"

"I'm not going anywhere," Arthur said. "If I spend the majority of the hours between now and when we need to ascend cultivating, I should—with the aid of the cores we have coming in—have a chance to break through another point."

"If you keep skipping meetings," Uswah said, teasingly.

"Well, I could come to them but then what would you and Amah Si do?" he said, with a little laugh. Uswah made a face, while the rest of the team laughed at her expense. Since Uswah found her best cultivating time at night, she'd been delegated the early morning meetings, while Mel dealt with the afternoon ones, allowing the pair time to cultivate during the breaks.

Of course, the real heavy lifting was being done by Amah Si and Beggar Joe. The fact that the entire clan had taken to calling him that, and he had not thrown too much of a fit after the first day, meant that was likely going to be his designation from now on.

Surprisingly, after he calmed down, Beggar Joe had turned out to be a very competent administrator. Maybe because he'd actually run a small factory in the real world, before everything had been automated and the need for him and his people had disappeared. It also explained why the older man had chosen to enter the Tower, with no real prospects of finding a good job out there.

"How are things going?" Arthur said. "I know we have a library started, and more information's being recorded. Nothing amazing, of course." Uswah nodded in acknowledgement, having given up her role of library administration to another. "And the treasury is, as always, empty."

Mel snorted. "It's not empty. It's in circulation."

"We do have multiple copies of the manuals right?" Arthur made sure to clarify.

"We do. And I'll be taking one copy with us when we ascend. Updates will come when the next expected ascendee goes up too," Mel said.

The fact that it had been decided to put the cores in circulation, with only a very small number held for emergency, had been Mel's idea. She called it something like fractional reserves, focusing on giving microloans to individuals about to break through. Those individuals would then pay back the clan, allowing them to grow their total, though theoretical, value.

It made sense, of course, to empower his people. Still, Arthur kind of wished there was a room filled with cores. He had seen an old cartoon gif, of a duck swimming through piles of gold coins. It would have been kinda cool to do that with cores.

Highly impractical, of course. But kinda cool to think about.

"And the reporting system?" Arthur said.

"Amah Si is still figuring it out," Mel said with a shrug. "Same with recruiting. You need to designate her as the Clan Head for this floor, by the way."

"I know, I know." Arthur sighed. "The option's not showing up yet, though. I'm guessing it's something that will be offered to me when I actually try to ascend. Or succeed at it."

"Speaking of that," Yao Jing cut in. "To ascend, do you have to do a trial?"

"Or a floor boss?" Jan said. "Do you not listen?"

"Not when it's not necessary," Yao Jing said with a grin, before digging into his food.

"Can I kill him, ah?" Jan said.

"The first floor of the Tower rotates through three different tests," Arthur intoned, as though he was reading from a scroll. Which, in a way, he was. He'd reread the wiki on the first floor so often that he knew a lot of it by heart. "The easiest and most common ascent route is when the Tower judges a cultivator by attributes. A minimum of seven points in each attribute is required. The second most popular method is the individual trial method, and the monsters you're expected to fight aren't much more powerful than what we've fought. The worst case is the *jenglot*, and we've dealt with a bunch of them now."

A lot of nods at that one, all but Yao Jing having been on that ill-fated expedition.

"Lastly, we've got the boss fight. The least preferred trial, since there's a variety of possible boss monsters. In addition, at boss level, a creature is significantly stronger than its counterpart in an individual trial. On the other hand, you can have multiple cultivators fight one boss together. The only negative to fighting as a group is that the total number of people allowed to ascend varies depending on the monster."

"*Ya-lah. Ngo zi!*" Yao Jing said. "What's it now?"

"You've been with us long enough to know our luck," Arthur said, repressingly. "What do you think?"

Silence from the bodyguard. Then the man looked down at his food, up at the group, made a face and started spooning the food into his mouth with haste. Mouth stuffed like a chipmunk, he stumbled off with a wave of his hand to his room to cultivate.

The group held their laughter until he was gone. Jan even went so far as to pound the table, wiping at her eyes after she had gotten the laughter out of her system.

"You going to tell him it's the trials and not a big boss?" Mel said, eyes dancing with humor still.

"Nah," Arthur said. "He needs motivation to cultivate. And I didn't lie, he just left without asking."

The group laughed again and Arthur smiled a little, grateful that things had settled down. For now at least. But, he had to admit to himself, he was a little trepidatious about the trial himself. Getting through sounded easy in theory.

Except nothing in the documents he had read ever discussed what happened when you were a Clan Head. The fact that some Clan Heads disappeared between floors was well known. As a result, many assumed that trials might be a little harder for them.

It was why he intended to push, as hard and as fast as he could. If he had a choice, he'd wait but...

It'd be enough. It had to be. Better to join with the Chins now than wait for someone else with less patience and fewer good intentions to come along and attack them.

Finishing his food, he met Mel's gaze. The older woman—not that much older really—returned his look, understanding in her gaze as he stood. She gave him a firm nod, of support, and of... acknowledgement? He was not sure. But as he returned to cultivate in his room; her nod did lift his spirits a little.

Chapter 131

Strange how time passed, when one moment could stretch for what seemed like an interminable hour. Waiting to get your exam results after school; sitting in a crowded, unairconditioned police station while trying to explain the loss of your identity card. The time between asking a girl out and the answer she would give. Moments that felt like eternity.

Then months which passed in a blur. How fast had he grown up? Under the watchful eye of his sifu and sick mother, finding time to care for her while she slowly died, hunting down the medicines that were in short supply or, worse, often contaminated. You'd think that with the state of 3D printing these days, contaminants would be less of an issue, but it had actually grown worse.

Now, all of a sudden here he was. Time compressing and altering, even as a major change loomed.

Negotiations had gone long into the night each day between Willis and Amah Si, such that the pair had come out of their rooms disheveled with bloodshot eyes, to bark out additional orders for documentation and newly rewritten contracts. They'd grab a drink, a breath, a few hours' sleep before they'd return to argue over another point.

Eventually, a deal had been hammered out. One of mutual cooperation, a contracted series of aid between Clan and Family. More rooms were rented, their previous occupants kicked out. New buildings purchased, near the village border to house those forced to leave. Beast cores and cultivation techniques arrived on the last day, when a rush order for multiple copies of a single-star cultivation technique had been made.

"And why am I not getting my Yin technique now?" Arthur said. He had a pack on his back, the repatched trusty backpack that had seen him through so much wear and tear. Of course, part of the reason he hadn't gotten something new was because of their current state of finances.

Mel, walking beside him as they headed for the village exit and nearby teleportation pads shrugged a little. "They're only giving us one. And since we don't need to verify it's a proper technique, they insisted on handing it over only after you ascended."

"Why, exactly, are we not verifying it ourselves?" Arthur said.

"Because it's Tower-purchased. They're just making a copy of the one they have, so it'll be properly sealed and everything," Mel said. "Anyway, trying to mess with you would likely backfire, considering it's you they need."

"And not the rest of the Clan." He turned his head, taking in his team. There had been some arguments over who was coming, but not too many. More people had wanted to join them, from new recruits to old members of the now-defunct Suey Ying tong. In the end, though, the only people coming with him were his core team: Yao Jing, Mel, Jan, and Uswah.

After all, Arthur's clan still needed fighters on the first floor. Even with the aid being offered by the Chins and Mohammad Osman—and the sudden deluge of offers from other groups, when everyone else realized that the Chins were going to stomp them into kingdom come—the Durians would need to stand on their own feet eventually.

That meant building up an internal base of fighters. Some of whom would stay on the first floor forever, and others who would continue the climb. In fact, if anything, the creation of the clan, the boosts his various

Sigils and Aspects had offered, had sparked ambition that had long lain dormant in older members.

In a few months, maybe a year or two, they'd start seeing people breaking through and ascending. Especially now that the clan had their own copy of a cultivation technique from the Chin's, one that could be used to draw other, unaffiliated individuals in.

They just needed to figure out how to keep the riff-raff out.

Arthur could not help but echo his thoughts out loud. That particular discussion had been ongoing for a while but had dropped off along the way.

"We're trying to figure it out, but penalties and peer pressure seem to be the way to go. I don't think we want to take it to the extreme though..." Mel said, drifting off.

"Extreme?" Yao Jing said.

"Going after those non-affiliated," Mel said. "Families, friends. That kind of thing."

"Yeah, no," Arthur said firmly. "Or maybe, hell no."

"I thought so. So we're working on it. It'd be nice to have a Rod of Binding or something but..." Mel shrugged.

Arthur understood. The Rod was one of the Burning Pixies' main advantages, one of their famed enchanted items. As the fifth most powerful guild, the Burning Pixies were a female-oriented guild, with membership that was only for female-identifying individuals. Or those who were formerly female identifying. They'd had to make that last change due to the way the Rod of Binding worked, since once you were in, you were in.

"Well, we'll figure it out," Arthur said. Or they wouldn't; someone would come in, lay a long-term decades-spanning plan, become part of their management infrastructure, and then, one day in an orgy of revenge would steal, destroy, and betray them all. Because Arthur had killed their brother, lover, father, or mother.

Maybe he had been watching a few too many Korean dramas.

"Arthur? Are you ready for this?" Mel said, just before they passed the boundary. She put a hand on his arm, dark brown eyes searching his for an answer as she held him still. "If you aren't ready to face the trial..."

"Then what?" Arthur said. "We can break our word, make the Chins angry, deal with the fallout and other groups who have been sniffing around and want to take a bite out of us? Did you see that letter I got?"

"What letter?" Jan said, cocking her head to the side.

Yao Jing just grunted while Uswah made a face.

"He received a threatening letter, telling him to not join with the Chins. Promised to kill him, his family, and his friends if he went ahead," Mel explained. "It was, of course, unsigned."

"Cowards," Yao Jing said. "Faceless shorn turtles. I bet they used to hide in their bedrooms before they got kicked into the Tower."

"Why someone like that come to the Tower?" Jan asked.

"Got kicked out by parents, I guess," Yao Jing said. "Or kicked in to the Tower. Hah!"

Arthur made a face. "So. Anyway. I need to get out. Fast. The faster I get up, the higher the chances I can keep my family safe." He nodded to the crowd gathered around Casey Chin, who was waiting for him beyond the village. "She promised to get the word out with her people too. Which will be even faster than what we can do, probably. So. No choice, really. We go ahead. Even if I'm not ready."

There was a long silence, before Jan broke in. "Ei. Sorry, ah."

"For what?" Arthur said.

"This." She shrugged her shoulders. "Pressure. Worry, about family."

"It's not your fault. And you, don't you get soft on me." He laughed, rotating his shoulders to settle the bag more comfortably on his shoulders. That had the others follow suit, checking over their own weapons, their own gear. "I think I'd miss having someone call me stupid every once in a while."

"Okay, stupid."

Laughing, Arthur waved the group forward. Time to meet Casey Chin, the lady with the alliterative name and more money than their entire clan put together and the next floor. Because why not?

Chapter 132

Casey Chin was dressed to ascend. Not only was she in combat fatigues, with a set of green-grey scale mail layered over the top of the camo clothing, but she also had a sword by her side, a long dagger on the other hip, and even a series of throwing knives strapped under her left arm in a holster. She had a helmet reminiscent of medieval ones rather than a modern helmet with a nose guard and leather chin straps. Even at a glance, it was clear that her equipment was of the higher end—even the simple pouch by her side looked of better fabric than Arthur's.

Casey wasn't carrying a backpack but her guards were. They too were armed and armoured in quality. One carried a spear with a boar emblem on its head, while the other guard held a sword and shield. Both wore chainmail on top of brigandine, despite the temperature. So it was no surprise to see the pair sweating a little in the heat and humidity.

As the group neared, Arthur noticed their gaze sweeping over his people. The bodyguards' gaze barely rested on each of them, except to pause at Uswah's missing arm before moving on. There was a dismissive look in their eyes, but they chose not to speak.

"Arthur, you made it!" Casey called out.

"Didn't think I had a choice," Arthur replied. "Or else I might have slept in a little more."

She pouted a little at his joke, then looked over his people. Her lips pursed for a moment, before she continued. "You know we're only providing enough cores for you and two others, right?"

"Yes. We'll split it as we need to," Arthur said. "We won't slow you down, as agreed."

"So long as you keep your portion to yourself, I don't care," she said firmly. "What matters is I succeed in ascending. Don't let your paranoia keep me from achieving my goal."

"Are these the only people you're bringing?" Arthur swept his gaze over the pair of impassive blocks of muscle.

"Of course. It's expensive, doing a speedrun!" Casey said.

Arthur could only grin a little guiltily. She was paying for six people now, instead of three as she had probably planned. Then again, she might not even have tried a speedrun if he hadn't been present.

"My cultivation technique?" Arthur held his hand out.

"On the second floor."

"Do you know how expensive it was, to buy a three-star cultivation technique for a Yin Body?"

"No," Arthur replied. "At the same time, it's not as though your family has much use for a Yin Body technique, do they?"

"Not immediately. But we might in the future," Casey said. "If you pass this trial, I will hand it to you then. If not, I will return the scroll to my family for later use."

"If I die, eh? Not much confidence in me, is there," Arthur said wryly.

She smiled grimly. "Did you think you could hide your weakness until we crossed over? You are lucky I am willing to continue with our agreement. My uncle was all for cancelling it when we learned how new you are to the Tower."

Now, Arthur was frowning. How did they know?

"Your friend, Attendant Lai, was very talkative, when the right inducements were made." To illustrate what she meant, she rubbed finger and thumb together in the universal sign for money.

"Ah." Arthur quickly reassessed his position and the clan's, before he shrugged. "Well, I guess we're just going to have to work on trust for now, then."

"As always," Casey replied. She looked over the team once more, eyes drifting to stop on Yao Jing briefly before moving on. "If you're ready?"

At his assent, the group started walking again, heading for the teleportation pads. Slightly apart from the crowd of bettors and newcomers who were stumbling off the incoming pads, there was a lone pad with only a few bored people in its vicinity on folding chairs.

Arthur frowned as he saw them and the way they perked up as their group approached. More than one nudged a sleeping comrade, though there was one particularly pudgy watcher whose head had lolled all the way back, a dirty cotton handkerchief over his face, and whom no one moved to wake. In fact, there was a wide space around the man and his battered-looking chair.

"Who are they?" Arthur muttered.

"Watchers," Mel replied.

He could not help but roll his eyes a little. "I know that. But who are they watching for?"

"Everyone and anyone who will pay them," Casey said. "They also contract messages and goods upwards, for smaller groups or those who need something urgent." She nodded to the watchers and few of them nodded back to her. "Though you can forget about any of that. We've already picked up what there is." A tight smile. "And I wouldn't recommend taking anything that they might offer. You wouldn't want to be put in the position of not having what was sent up."

"I wouldn't steal," Arthur said, a little affronted at the accusation.

"Not the point. There's nothing to say they can't accuse you of taking what isn't there," Casey pointed out.

Arthur winced, remembering how that scam worked. Send a sucker up with, say, nine cores. When they arrive, the next-floor recipient demands ten. Then you either have to cough up the tenth core or face a fight. Considering you'd normally be outnumbered, most people paid. In the worst case, victims became serfs, unpaid labour until they worked off the cores they "owed." Luckily, since the main method to acquire goods required sending core hunters into the wilderness, the sheer number of escapees and number of watchers required made slavery mostly impractical, except for the most obtuse and sadomasochistic groups.

On the other hand, the minor shakedowns were semi-common. After all, it was a more socially acceptable form of thuggery than the way Suey Ying took goods from newcomers as they arrived.

That was another reason why Arthur had been hesitant about playing runner on entering the Tower. Without any government regulation or central authority keeping an eye on such agreements, it became a matter of honour and reputation. But to trap a Clan Head like himself... well, even a well-reputed organization might be willing to besmirch their honour.

Especially if it also trapped the Chin family.

"Yeah, yeah, I get it." Arthur sighed, dismissing thoughts of making a few cores or credits. Of all things, he probably needed credits the most.

Nothing to it, though. Because while he had been talking and thinking, they'd arrived at the platform. The two bodyguards had separated, staring and waiting. When no one made to move, Casey sighed.

"Well? Go on. It's not as if I'm going to just walk up without you going first." She rolled her eyes.

Arthur bit back comments about "ladies first," knowing she was right. She was relying on him, and if he chickened out at the last moment, she was out of luck. Better to make sure he went, at least this time.

Another breath. Another look over to his team, seeing them nod back at him. And then he took a step up, planting one and then both feet on the platform.

Before the Tower snatched him away to his Trials.

Chapter 133

Once more, Arthur stood in a swirling landscape of mist and clouds. Beneath his feet was solid ground, all around him nothing but the obscuration of his vision. Well, that and the scrolling text within his mind's eye. Without anything better to do, Arthur clutched his spear tighter and read over the text.

Trial Tower Level 1 Test Initiated…

Assessing candidate…

Candidate Arthur Chua verified…

Yin Body identified…

No notable cultivation method identified…

Clan Sigil identified…

Identifying details of Clan Sigil…

Clan Benevolent Durians identified…

Clan Founder of the Benevolent Durians identified…

Special Trial format sub-routine initiated…

Tower Level 1 Trial Test for Clan Founders initiated…

Tiu, Arthur cursed silently. He'd been worried about that. Even assumed it would be a problem he had to face. Now, the mists were churning and his body felt like it was twisting, as if pressed through a particularly tight hole. It was a strange, if somewhat familiar, sensation before he was popped out, into a familiar-looking corridor.

"Really?" Arthur muttered to himself. Still, he wasn't going to complain too much about it. Not managing to acquire sufficient points to increase his Body beforehand meant that he was running on fewer energy points than he would have preferred. Especially if they had increased the difficulty of the trial given his Clan Head status.

Listening to his voice echo back, and then standing still as he tried to ascertain if his words had generated any aggro, he had to forcibly remind himself to breathe properly. Funny how much training was centered around breathing, but it was the easiest, most direct method to tap into the unconscious workings of the body.

No noise. No sign of a monster. Just a straight corridor, leading into the distance.

Arthur eventually started walking, tapping the bottom of his spear before him as he did so. No idea if there were traps in such a place, so he assumed there were. The worst case: he took too long and was penalized. On the other hand, traps meant death.

Arthur wasn't a big fan of death.

For a variety of reasons.

Since the damn corridor was so long, Arthur found himself regarding it with care. The footing was some form of stone, hard and unyielding. Horrible to fall upon, which meant he would have to hope his breakfall techniques were good if he was sent sprawling. More people died from stupid fights on concrete than your average person would know, with so many of them just cracking their head on pavement and never getting back up.

Thus, lesson one of any practical self-defense course when they got to the physical portion of training: Learn how to fall. You couldn't fight if you were dead, stunned, concussed, or had a broken limb because you didn't fall right. Especially bad for women and small-sized individuals.

So.

"Stone floor, roll off. Keep head tucked in, or you'll be..." He trailed off his singing, chuckling to himself. "Got to keep it kid-friendly."

Not that telling himself meant much. The real preparation for all these things was hours upon hours of training in the martial arts halls with sparring partners, repeating the same drill until it became automatic. Well, not just one drill. You varied drills with good partners who knew how to provide just enough resistance and change to stay within the parameters of the drill and stay safe.

"Safe" being the operative word there, what with a single injury putting trainees out of commission for weeks at a time. Oh, sure. You could train some basic techniques while injured, depending on the injury. Arthur had done that more than enough. There was even something to be said about learning to move while in pain.

But mostly, staying uninjured was the goal. Which so many teachers failed to understand.

It was something his own sifu had dictated Arthur learn for himself. Sending his students out to train with others, to learn new techniques and training methods, experience new sparring partners on the regular. So that things never got stale in the martial hall. Bringing the bright ideas of other teachers back, to be disseminated among everyone else.

Talking of illumination.

Diffuse lighting, coming not from any single recess but all around. The stone itself seemed to generate the light, which made for weird shadows. There wasn't any single source of light that overcame any other which meant that his shadow stuck mostly to him, and the light coming from so many sources meant his shadow was just a tiny blob.

Horrible for someone like Uswah who had at least a couple of cultivation techniques that used shadows as a mainstay. Not a problem for him. One reason why he preferred more direct, internally-driven techniques when he had a choice.

Theoretically, there were ways to remove conscious control of a cultivator's body—there were some spiritual and mental techniques that were rumoured to be in play—but it was expensive and confined to more powerful Towers and their upper levels.

"Got light, so bright. Remember: no night, in the Tower. Of POWER!" Raising his voice at the last, laughing a little insanely to himself.

Yeah, maybe the endless corridor was getting to him.

It was a typical hallway, about six feet wide. That meant that whatever monster he might find at the end of this corridor, if it didn't spit out into another hallway, would be confined to relatively normal dimensions. The ceiling was ten feet tall, so it wouldn't even be that big.

Then again, he might have to fight in a larger room. Well, unless it was a six-foot-wide, ten-foot-tall rhinoceros or massive *babi ngepet*—or smaller—Arthur could still retreat back into the corridor and anything larger would be stuck in the doorway.

Which led, of course, to the other forms of speculation. What kind of monsters could he meet? Another *jenglot*? He doubted it'd be a *kuching hitam*, not unless they changed the environment significantly in the room he was walking into. After all, that cat-like creature was an ambush predator. This kind of environment, without ledges or protrusions, without shadows to hide behind, took away the advantages of cat-like and snake-like monsters, leaving the otherwise frail creatures easy prey.

Speculation, which was all that Arthur had to offer, was rife until a shift in light ahead of him had him speed up.

The doorway ahead grew darker, the colours shifting. Arthur had yet to find a single trap, and he was beginning to realize he was likely being over-paranoid. Still, when he finally made it to the doorway at the end, he could not help but shake his head.

What kind of insane Tower chose *that* as a test?

Chapter 134

The room he stared at, on the other side of the doorway, was massive. Easily a few hundred feet across and another sixty or seventy feet wide. The room was darker than the corridor, forcing Arthur to squint as he tried to assess what monsters lay within. Most of all though, what attracted Arthur's attention was the singular hill, formed in a series of staggered slopes that reached a tapered point at the end where a glowing door stood, hanging in mid-air. The entire thing reminded Arthur of a coiled rope, or a snake. Or a turd. Yes, a turd.

"Well, objective seems easy enough. Now, what's the fluff?" Arthur muttered to himself.

His gaze flicked over the surroundings, searching for movement. After a moment, he spotted it. Small, rodent-like creatures near the door. Numerous, with gleaming little fangs that probably were painful to get bitten by. Easy enough to counter, though he'd want to move fast in case they swarmed.

Then, at the base of the hill were the *babi ngepet.* After a few moments of watching, he could pick out at least two sounders patrolling on ground level, constantly circling the base.

After that... nothing. That was worrying. Squint as he might, between the occasional brush and dim lighting, Arthur could not spot other monsters waiting for him there. Probably an ambush predator then.

Looking farther up the hill, he soon spotted monkeys, high enough to throw their offensive—in both senses of the word—armament as he climbed up. Definitely worth heading up at speed then, rather than going slow and getting pelted.

Next up, nothing. The angle was getting steeper, making it harder for him to spot what was waiting from his current vantage point. He assumed it was another ambush predator or something smaller. Not great, but he could deal with it.

Farther up, a flock of birds. Hopefully they weren't all coming down at the same time. If they were, it would be incredibly difficult to fight his way upwards, between dive-bombing birds and flung monkey feces.

Either way, speed would make sense.

"Going to have a need for speed, to minimize bleed…"

Right at the top though, that was the biggest concern. A *jenglot.* And this fellow was the size of the alpha *jenglot* he had fought before. Arms nearly five feet long, hunched over on the second to the last level of the hill. It stared balefully at Arthur as he was silhouetted in the corridor light, as though challenging him to take a run for it.

And run he would have. That was quite clear. This was not something he could play out slowly, taking out each level one at a time. Too many monsters for him to play that game, and no guarantee they wouldn't try to swarm him.

So.

Rush up, killing each monster as he ascended. There were, now that he was staring, small slopes interspersed between each rising level, such that he could either try climbing the steeper twenty-foot levels or take a slope.

He assumed the second was better, especially since he did not have any techniques to pull himself up. If he had, climbing those walls would have been perfect. Again, he had to curse not taking more time to practice parkour or other qinggong methods. With his increased strength, he should theoretically be able to ascend the twenty feet now.

But right now was not the time to try something new. Stay with the tried and true.

Only in movies did you manage to make things work out the first time.

On that cheery thought, Arthur made himself draw a deep breath. He cycled his breath for a few moments, trying to saturate his body with as much oxygen as possible, bouncing a little on his feet. Moments later, resolving himself fully, he tightened the straps on his backpack and dashed forward.

Left foot, right foot. Left foot, push off to jump over that forest rat.

Oops.

He felt the body crunch under his feet, and he skidded a little as the creature ducked in a different direction than anticipated. Another of those rats chose to scramble up his leg, tiny claws piercing through his pants.

Arthur had no time to worry about it though, instead scrambling forward. He needed to keep moving, for as he feared, the entire horde of rats were coming for him now. Speed was going to be his only salvation. Ten, eight, four feet. He kept running, feeling the rat on the side of his leg having managed to make it to his waist. It then stopped, and clamped down on his stomach, eliciting a snarl from Arthur.

He smacked the damn creature aside, feeling skin tear as sharpened fangs sunk into his flesh were ripped out. A notification from the Tower pressed onto his mind but he chose to ignore it, knowing that any distraction would be a problem.

He could probably guess what it said. No damage reports, but poisoning? Or disease? That, the Tower would want to inform him of. A single instance should be a non-issue, his Accelerated Healing easily able to handle the matter.

If more of those monsters managed to injure him though...

Taking a more proactive approach, Arthur started swinging his spear. He used sweeping motions as he flipped, skipped, and jumped forward. He swung his spear, beating aside a pair of rats that had gathered before him.

Another leap took him over the next horde, the creatures spinning about to chase. He did not slow down, spearing one rat through the face as it leapt at him and flicking it away as he swung his spear around, letting the corpse smash into the rushing horde behind.

Forward, always moving forward.

His ears throbbed with the high-pitched chittering of the monsters chasing after him, angling towards him from all sides. Everywhere he looked, a moving carpet of creatures flowed after him, some scrambling up his legs, others biting at his feet the moment they could.

Another half-dozen steps and he threw himself forward, falling upon the pile of squirming creatures and rolling. He felt furry bodies, all too slick and prickly, scratch across his shins, his face, his hands as he rolled, crushing rats. Then, he finished the roll and came up, shedding monsters that had been thrown off by the sudden movement and acquiring a couple more.

Including one clutching at his hair.

He grabbed at the rat, throwing it aside as it squirmed in his hand, tiny tail whipping at him. Then, another motion, to swing his spear at the monsters hanging onto him while he kept running. He hit himself in the leg as he did so, bruising himself but crushing a monster as he did so.

His breathing was fast, and additional notifications pressed upon him. He knew they had bitten him, felt his body slowing down, pain beginning to radiate from his body. The chittering and screeching grew more shrill as he kept running, leaping one last time. Over the carpet that threatened to drag him down.

Landing past the last row of tiny monsters, with a few monsters piled on him and the rest chasing after. But he could outpace them, he knew it.

Which only left the *babi ngepet* ahead.

And then the rest of the hill.

Chapter 135

The *babi ngepet* herd had noticed him. They'd started turning, the biggest of the herd already charging towards Arthur. He reviewed the angles, the direction that he had to move in. Realised that there really weren't a lot of options, not if he wanted to hit one of the slopes.

Any other time, he might have considered wielding his spear, taking at least the largest boar down. But there was an entire fast-moving herd behind the lead monster, and a bunch of jungle rats rushing right after him. Slowing down long enough to set his spear or try anything fancy would mean getting mobbed by them.

So. Run. Like a nun.

At the same time, Arthur was already beginning to understand how this entire trial was meant to go. He had to run, fast, and avoid the herd. He had to keep piling speed on, keep moving so that he would not be injured.

But that also meant he had no time to watch for the ambush predators. Theoretically at least.

Now was the time he realized that his traits were offering him quite a few advantages. Enhanced Eyesight was letting him see into darkness that another cultivator might find blinding. It was because of that singular trait that he could pick out the *kuching hitam* that was waiting for him on the second rise, prowling towards the edge of the ledge that he was most likely to take. It was also that ability that let him spot the flying projectile from the monkeys, reminding him to duck his head a little so that it bounced rather than splattered.

There was still splatter, but a lot less.

"I hate this trial so much," Arthur cursed under his breath, even as he kept running. Good thing another trait was enabling him to do the cursing, while still judging what was coming and spotting how far more he had to go. Multi-tasking at its best, and he definitely needed that trait, because a part of him was also trying to work out the best way around the trial's shanghaied method of guidance.

And boy, was the term shanghai all too appropriate in this case, what with him about to lose his life if he stayed on the rails here.

A snort, a loud squeal. He glanced back, eyes widening as the herd of rats behind him began to glow. Red energy infused the entire herd, gaining in prominence as they ran. He could even swear they were moving faster.

Yep, definitely faster.

"*Hun dan*!" Swearing, Arthur wondered if the Tower was out to get him. Every time he made up his mind not to do something, the Tower would try to make him do it. In this case...

"Time to see, if I can be, a really, really good, jumping bean!" Sing-songing under his breath to get the rhythm and timing right, Arthur switched directions a little. No way to hit the slope on time, never mind the fact that the *kuching* was waiting there.

No. He was not going to risk it. But that didn't mean he shouldn't try to improve his chances. On that note, he made sure to angle his spear down a little. He switched his stance, taking multiple leaps as he built up momentum to the side of the steep slope he was facing.

At the last moment, he plunged his spear down, using it as an impromptu pole vault. It was not as good as his old staff, what with lacking both height and having a spear tip that messed things up, but at least it meant he had a very good pivot point as he threw himself upward.

A little energy was lost, a little momentum as he then yanked his spear out, twisting himself around as he kept flying through the air, launched high. He arced, feet first, before he managed to pull the rest of his body.

As he had expected, the greater strength and the additional energy imparted by the spear vault had let him clear the steepest part of the slope to hit the hill's first level, even as the jungle rats swerved away from the wall at the last moment. Only to meet the thundering herd of *babi ngepet*, who proceeded to trample the entire group of rodents, leading to chaos.

The screams, trumpets, and shrieks of the monsters below him were music to Arthur's ears. Though he had his own problems, for having made it over the edge, he was still turning around and getting his feet positioned for a landing when an unlucky, or skilled, projectile from above caught him on the top of his head.

It knocked him off course a little, but more importantly, it distracted him. Leaving him to crash into the ground in a weird sprawl of limbs, half on the front of his face, half on his knees that he had tucked, pulling him into a spin.

He bounced and rolled before coming to a stop, groaning and spitting out soil and other unmentionables, a little woozy from the diseased poisons and the crap attack and his sudden change in momentum. Movement in the corner of his eyes reminded him that he was not alone up here.

Arthur dropped low, even as the *kuching* leapt at him, nearly taking his head off. He felt claws brush the air, a couple of the sharp implements clipping his hair moments before he spun around. Acting on instinct, the pair twisted around and threw themselves at one another, crashing in a flurry of drawn kris and claws.

One hand against the cat's neck, pushing it and its body sideways so that the more dangerous claws were forced to scrabble for purchase and they lashed and scored at his other arm. Arthur weaved his kris like a sewing needle in and out of the monster's torso. He kept attacking, knowing he couldn't afford to stop until the *kuching* stopped first.

When the cat was finished, Arthur staggered to his feet, worried he was out of time, only to realize that only brief moments had passed. His injuries smarted, blood running down his arm and along the side of his body where the monster had scored against him.

"No time, even to rhyme…" Arthur slipped the kris into its sheath, scooped up the spear and began running for the next slope. As he ran, he angled towards the edge of the cliff where the monkeys stared down at him balefully and kept tossing things at him.

Luckily for him, it seemed the creatures did not have the same volume of projectiles they might have in a forest. The occasional rock or other hardened—or sloppy—mess might arc over to him, but it was not the constant hail that he had feared initially.

That was the good news. The bad? They were angling along the ledge to keep him in sight and intercept him. But he couldn't slow down. For he could hear the drumming of the herds starting up the slope, not so far behind him.

Pouring on more speed, Arthur ran, sucking in deep lungfuls of air as he tried to work out his next move. Caught between the monkey horde and the pig herd.

Definitely a metaphor in there somewhere.

Chapter 136

"Monkey see, monkey kill. Arthur see, very big hill."

Singing under his breath as he ran, Arthur headed for the next easy slope. The ground underneath his feet crunched a little, the footing a mixture of hard earth and occasional stubborn weed. Not the most comfortable thing to land upon, though it had the advantage of soaking up the blood and liquids without leaving a giant mudhole.

Not that he was bleeding that much anymore. The rats didn't puncture deeply with their bites, and the *kuching* had managed to score long wounds along his side but nothing dangerous or anything his Accelerated Healing could not help.

Arthur regretted not practicing healing and moving at the same time, but he definitely was not going to try that now. Pushing his body to the extreme with a flying leap was one thing. Cultivating while moving, while in a fight for his life, was another thing entirely. If he messed up, which was likely, it would leave him crippled and easy prey.

On the other hand...

Arthur began massaging his aura, pulling it apart to form around his third eye. He got the energy ready for a Refined Energy Dart, knowing he was going to need it when he hit the slope. The switchback and the monkeys waiting for him were not going to slow him down, if he had anything to say about it.

He could try lobbing one of the Refined Energy Darts at the monsters above him, but that had the disadvantage of wasting precious energy as well as removing the element of surprise from his attack on the monkeys. Better for the monkeys to think they were the only ones with ranged attacks.

At the same time, he also geared himself up for the use of Heavenly Sage's Mischief. Energy pulsed through his body as he pulled and shoved it into the right meridians, all in anticipation of the increased burn when he ascended the slope.

When he set foot on it, the monkeys unleashed a sudden barrage of stones. Instinctively, Arthur threw himself sideways into the wall, hiding and dodging the majority of stones and hardened feces.

"You are disgusting!" Arthur shouted at them, wiping at himself and then, giving up. He had no time to waste. The *babi ngepet* and the surviving rats had managed to make the first level of the hill and were looking for him. Soon enough, they'd charge up the next slope. He needed as much of a headstart as he could with them in play.

Some of the monkeys had hopped closer to look down from above. A thought sparked through Arthur's mind as he started running, still close to the wall, as the monkeys tried to hit him with angle shots or dropping projectiles on his head.

A dozen feet more and the slope above kept shrinking. The amount of time he had to dodge decreased with each step. Sheltering his head with one raised arm, freely bleeding from a scalp wound that gushed blood down his ear, Arthur kept running.

Biding his time.

Until he judged the monkeys had gotten overconfident, overeager. They reached forward and down, and he jumped. Nearly vertically and only with a little of the built-up momentum of his run, energy pouring into the Heavenly Sage's Mischief to empower his attack.

His spear swung as he ascended, sweeping sideways in a long arc. The highly sharpened edge of tempered steel tore through limbs, chests, and throats with equal measure as the combined momentum and swing injured surprised monsters. Then, as Arthur dropped, he twisted the spear around to strike again. Five of the monkeys dropped, injured or dead, and the others scrambled away in chittering fear.

Landing with a slight stumble, Arthur took off again, heading up the slope at last. The burst of speed from Heavenly Sage's Mischief would only last so long, until he had to pour more energy into it. There were still many monkeys in fit fighting condition, and not to forget the alpha *jenglot* waiting just below the hill's peak.

Once there was only eight feet between him and the next rise, Arthur jumped, grabbed the edge of the next slope with his hand and yanked himself into an upward flip. This time, he only caught a single monkey with the surprise motion, his foot arcing through the air to crack its skull before he landed on the ground.

Around him, the rest of the monkeys had pulled back. With a scream, the largest monkey—the only one with a tuft of red fur on its chest—commanded the rest of its brethren to charge Arthur.

Crouched low, Arthur grinned savagely as he released the Refined Energy Dart at the monkey king. He watched as the glowing object shot from his forehead to strike the leader, who managed to move aside at the last moment so that it only was injured, not killed.

"Arthur see, Arthur kill!"

Not that he was wasting time talking, for he rolled forward and swept his spear low. The attack cut into feet, swept other monkeys off the ground, and broke legs, all while the animals were reacting to the attack on their king. In the chaos, some had rushed to their red-furred leader, others ran away, and a few brave and furious had rushed him.

One managed to clamber up his left side, holding his arm down as it gripped a rock in its hand, banging it against Arthur's torso. Shrugging his shoulder upwards in an attempt to dislodge it, he ducked his head low and ran forward into the crowd, swinging his other spear one-handed to ward off more monsters.

All the while, he felt the pounding fist of the clinging monster, the slavering hot breath as the creature tried to drag him down. Adrenaline and Heavenly Sage's Mischief gave him the strength to power his way through, bouncing monkeys off his body. Sometimes, he even turned to let them crash onto his unwanted passenger.

Finally, his passenger lost grip on its fleshy perch. Arthur's free hand gripped a flailing limb and he finished tearing the simian's body off—also with some of his own skin and cloth. Then, spinning around, he used the creature and his spear to batter those around him before releasing the monkey after a full 360-degree turn.

Brown figures were crushed against their flying brethren, and a new opening broke between the horde. He started running again, heading for the next slope, one leg limping a little from... Well, he wasn't even sure when he picked up that injury.

Both arms ached, and he was covered in blood and bites. Still...

"Monkey bowling, for the win!"

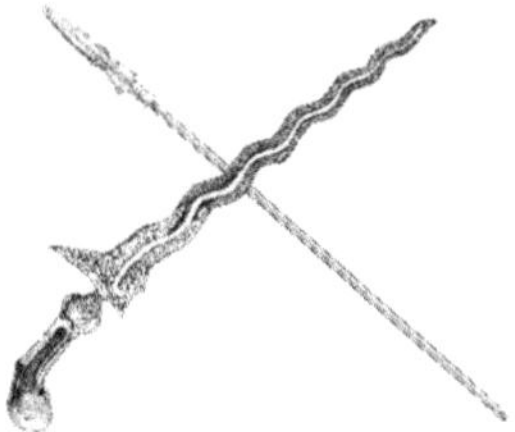

Chapter 137

He nearly made it out of the crowd. Thankfully, there were not that many monkeys. Or there were, but they were also spread out, which meant that instead of having to handle a hundred chittering asses, there were just over a score in near proximity. Now, with the monsters in disarray, their king cradling its injury and not daring to near him, he nearly made it out with a straight run.

Problem was, he never saw the flung projectile. It wasn't aimed at his head, or his torso. Instead, either due to a bad throw or deep cunning, it went for his foot. The upraised foot that, once clogged by the slimy addition, came down unevenly and sent him sprawling to the ground in an undignified fall.

Of course, Arthur rolled with it. He had spent countless hours learning breakfalls and rolling falls, learning how to crash to the earth again and again from different positions. There was embedded muscle memory in his body, just like the muscle memory his sifu had invested in him when he learnt to stab, cut, and otherwise butcher fresh meat.

For that matter, he had spent a number of months working on a nearby farm, cutting chicken necks and bleeding them out before helping to pluck the feathers as well. All to get used to the idea of taking a life. He started when he was twelve and had, for a few years, nightmares of screaming, clucking chickens covered in blood. That was the kind of trauma he had signed up for.

Not so different from running away from hordes of screaming monkeys with poo flung at him from behind and sideways, with a herd of *babi ngepet* were just making their way up from the level below, and a creeping *kuching* that had made its way to the monkey level and started snacking on one of the injured simians a short distance away.

He caught sight of bits and pieces of this as he rolled and came up, swinging his spear to ward off the nearest monkey. Only to realize that the monkeys were now farther away than he had expected. Mostly because they had gone to look for more projectiles to throw at him.

The monkey king in the back was screaming—insults and orders, probably. It seemed no longer willing to risk its people. In the meantime, another troop of monkeys was rushing over, with a leader of their own emitting shrill shrieks. To Arthur's surprise, their arrival split the attention of the troop before him.

"Monkey fight in front of me, and that's when I run rather than be."

Arthur turned and ran, hunkering his head down a little, more in hopes that he could hide himself under his backpack. Thankfully, he never really had anything too precious inside. Pots and pans that got a little banged up, changes of clothing, scrolls or documents that might be useful, canvas tent and bedroll to make sleeping easier. And of course, some food...

"Arse. I bet that's all messed up." He heard a rather wet splat of something striking his backpack from behind and a fresh nasal assault began.

He could not help but let out a long sigh, though he didn't stop running. At least nothing was ahead of him this time, which meant all he had to do was keep moving.

Or so he thought.

Until the other troop drew near enough and began throwing too, and then the ranged barrage came from two directions. Arms held up to cover his face, he felt the impact of projectiles all over his body Arthur felt like he was in the most brutal, most malodorous, most uncivilized game of dodgeball ever.

One impact after the other, causing bruises and pain. He hissed as a particularly strong throw hammered his lower ribs, driving breath from his body. Already, he had been struggling to breathe properly, the stink forcing him to take short sharp breaths even as his nose struggled to reduce the olfactory assault. Lungs burning, his limbs heavy with disease, he hissed and huffed.

Then another stone struck his thigh, punching into the peroneal nerve running along the outside of his thigh. Even though he had trained to take kicks to it, nerves and mind deadened to daily abuse from training, he still collapsed.

This time, there was no artful roll. Just a sudden collapse and slide forward as knee bruised the ground and his front leg kicked forwards. He slid on the slick bottom of his foot, grinding against the dirt underneath his feet. Pants tore, and older, scabbed wounds sprung open.

This time around, he heard it. Monkeys too close. He dropped to his left leg, and his right leg was still not working right after the strike. He rolled over his shoulder and came up to face the opposite direction with his weapon pointed at the incoming horde.

The first monster, launching itself in a brave leap, was pinned by the spear. Its body slid partway off the spear, pulling the tip down. It died coughing and spluttering on the spear even as Arthur yanked the weapon, trying to free it from the corpse.

Another monkey, second in line and smarter, angled itself around the body and spear. It came low, claws extended, and Arthur snarled a little. He poured energy into his fist as he swung it, hammering into the monster's temple and using Focused Strike to crumple the small bones.

Then, it was down.

Legs still burning, Arthur forced himself to stand but the troop of monkeys, though much reduced in number, were surrounding him. He backed off, swinging his spear in arcs to keep them away, eyes flashing.

His breathing was harsh, panting. Every second, he could feel the energy gained from the Heavenly Sage's Mischief running out. Yet he pushed on. He had to. He could not stop, so he backed away, kept swinging his spear.

Each time he swung, he drove one of the monkeys back. Each time he looked aside, another monster crept forward, darting closer. The creatures ducked back and forth, always trying to get closer and past the whirlwind of Arthur's spear. Which was spinning slower and slower.

And then, suddenly the rush from Heavenly Sage's Mischief ran out. The monsters, sensing the shift in pace, charged all at once.

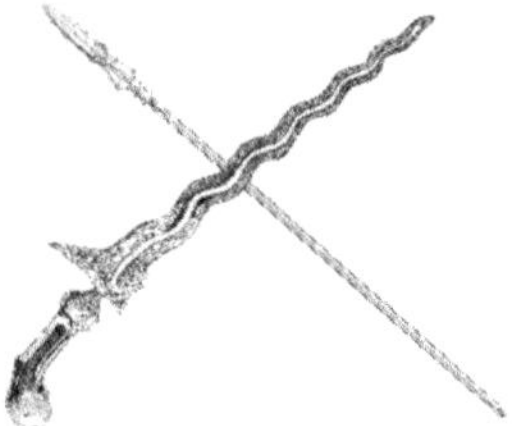

Chapter 138

The first monkey to dart forward was speared in the face. The second took a Refined Energy Dart in the face, leaving it injured and in pain. That left the other five that swarmed him uncontested, the group managing to catch Arthur by surprise as he was still reeling and adjusting to his sudden drop in speed. Even as he swept his foot back to retreat, they were on him.

One grabbed at his spear and arm, dragging the weapon out of alignment from his prepared strike. Another monster took his injured thigh, claws digging into tattered pants and unprotected skin beneath. It ripped and gored at his flesh and muscles, even as a third launched itself past the spear as Arthur tried to twist the entire weapon around to dislodge the monster holding it. Within seconds, the combined strength of the monsters had his weapon stripped from him, even as the final two went for the kill.

The first jumped towards his face, and a last-minute surge by Arthur left the monster's own face smashed and his own head pounding from a bad headbutt. So many stories saw the headbutt as the be-all-and-end-all of surprise attacks, but like any footballer who'd taken a header wrongly, it could also leave you reeling and concussed. Even while dirty mouths and sharp teeth tore at your scalp and left bleeding wounds.

He went reeling, feeling the impact around his torso pushing him back. His body tipped over sideways and without his spear he came down hard, bouncing off a monkey's still scrabbling arm around his torso and cracking it.

Each monster was nowhere as strong as him, but combined, they clambered and grappled, tore and swiped at him. It was in the gaps of their movements that he found space, as they tried to hurt rather than hold him down.

Right hand, free of the spear that had been pulled away, punched a monkey in the side from where it clung to his chest. Another strike freed up space around his belt for him to grab at the kris that had been trapped there. As he rocked back and forth on the uneven surface of the backpack, his balance shifted constantly and the added weight pressed onto him caused sharp metal implement and tent poles to dig into his muscles and elicit shards of pain.

But with kris in hand, Arthur had a weapon now which he wielded swiftly, slicing with the wavy edge of the blade up, sliding the sharpened surface of the enchanted weapon along flesh. He nicked monsters again and again, even as he dodged claws that sought to do more than damage.

One dirty finger plunged towards his eye. Only a last-minute move caused it to dig into his cheek below. Sharp claws tore deep into flesh, even scraping bone. The pain from that was just a portion of the pain all over his body as a monkey clamped down hard on the meaty flesh of his shoulder. But another thrashed as it fell off, dying and poisoned from his kris.

As he rolled aside, a spear—his own spear—plunged into the ground next to him, brushing against his thigh. Eyes wide, he gripped the spear before it was being yanked out by the monkeys.

Thank god that, smart as they were, these monsters were still not highly adept tool users. It would have been incredibly embarrassing to die from one's own weapon at the hand of a mere monkey.

He'd never live it down on his resurrection.

Jerking an elbow into a torso, blinking around the blood covering one eye, he lurched to his feet and kicked out while keeping the kris moving. He scored a shallow slice on furred flesh, barely a light wound. But it didn't matter.

The goal was to damage and open skin, to drop the poison enchantment within. He kept moving, forcing himself into a spin, even as the last free monkey jumped onto him, only to receive a backpack in its face. It still managed to grab on, forcing Arthur to lurch to the side, his breathing coming in ragged breaths as dust and blood and spittle flew through the air.

Then, he cut and cut, sweeping the spear around. In the distance was a thunder of incoming hooves as the fighting monkey troops were bowled over by *babi ngepet*, bringing a new mix of screams and shouts.

Another stab, and the last monkey in front of him was down. Taken with fear, the monkey on his back dropped. Too wounded and tired to finish it off, Arthur just staggered to the wall of the slope, leaning against it as he tried to catch his breath and watched the survivor scurry away.

It took him three tries before he managed to sheath his kris, nearly cutting himself on the second attempt. Maybe he did, but he hurt so much that he was not entirely certain. Well, a little soporific effect from the Yin poison might not be a bad thing.

Transferring the spear over to his right hand, he forced his aching left hand to flex twice by sheer effort of will. Arthur then swiped at the blood on his forehead. He wiped a bloody forearm on the nearby wall, then repeated the process as he sucked in deep breaths. There was something wrong with the last two fingers of his left hand, and when he stared at them he winced. Somewhere along the way, he'd managed to wrench the bottom finger entirely out of place.

It said something about the amount of adrenaline in his body and pain that the actual dislocation was the least of problems. Or that he simply leaned his spear against himself, grabbed hold of his dislocated finger and yanked it back into position with nothing more than a resigned but screaming effort of will.

Then, panting and sweating from exertion and pain, vision blurring from loss of blood, Arthur took in his options. He needed to get moving. But his feet refused to move, and the monsters were—thankfully—in the middle of their tiny war.

He wondered if this was the Tower's plan all along, something for him to exploit. Or if this level was entirely untested, the fighting between the groups an unexpected side result. Regardless, Arthur was finding the entire trial harder than he had expected.

Looking up as he finally caught enough of a breath that he could afford to pay attention to anything else, he looked at the swarm of birds above. He had forgotten about them.

Then, pulling his water bottle free, he chugged down a few mouthfuls, washed the blood from around his eyes a little and wrapped a bandage around his head to soak up any further blood. He left the gummy, bleeding wound on his cheek alone, along with the other myriad wounds on his body.

No time.

Because now, the monsters had settled into an uneasy peace. Monkey troops formed together, the injured monkey king dead and the new king gesturing for the group to back away from the *babi ngepet.* The furious boars, on the other hand, seemed intent on going after him, trotting together in a small group towards him, regaining speed with each moment.

And in between, the rats and the cat were definitely waiting for their own chance.

Which meant...

Time to run.

Again.

Chapter 139

Head raised, Arthur watched the avian monsters wheeling above. They made no move to attack him, and he had managed to make his way up the rest of the slope without a problem. A look along the edge of this level—lined with low-hanging shrubbery—indicated that he was in luck. The next slope up was just a hundred or so feet away, at a diagonal to his left.

But monsters from below were already gaining ground and beginning to charge up to his level. At least the shrubbery would slow the *babi ngepet* down a little. The birds above would likely slow him down too, if they finally chose to attack.

Intuition had Arthur scanning the brush even as he edged himself onto the level fully. He kept moving, knowing he could not stop, but he had yet to catch sight of any monsters on this level. If it was not the birds, it would have to be an ambush predator. And what other creature had he fought on the first floor?

"Snakes. Why does it have to be snakes?" Arthur grumbled, sweeping his spear to slice off some low branches in the brush. His gaze flicked around constantly as he threaded his way.

There.

Rather than attack, he chose to go around. Green and yellow snakes that lay draped on the top of branches, their brilliant scales blending nearly directly into the undergrowth. If not for his Enhanced Eyesight that highlighted the shift in temperature a little, a disparate change that he had not even noticed until now, he might have missed them.

The damn creatures were just a touch cooler, the subtle difference enough to almost highlight them in his eyes as he moved along. He could make his way through this level without an issue.

If a modified, enhanced Iron Skin trait was what was needed to deal with the rats, then here enhanced senses provided him with the edge to survive. A cultivation exercise that expanded his senses in another way would have been just as good...

Moving warily, Arthur did his best to get through without having to kill the snakes. Perhaps they would take their venom out on his pursuers.

If only he could pause between levels.

Time would mean he could heal up a little; his healing technique was already running at full bore. He knew it was replacing blood, fixing up open wounds, and clearing injuries. But it would take hours for a complete healing, and the entire point of this exercise was never to let him stop and rest.

He sighed.

"I got to run again, don't I?" Arthur muttered to himself. No jokes, no rhyming. He was too tired and in pain. He wiped at his face again, coming away bloody and gory before he judged the way forward clear. Then, he started jogging, slowly.

Step by step through the path he eyed.

The first snake that darted forward, wrapping itself around his arm, he managed to disentangle and toss away before it got its coils firmly locked. Thankfully, whoever decided to create this level had gone for a mid-level series of shrubs rather than tall trees from which a constrictor might drop. So the snakes did not have the advantage of height.

They still came at him, though, another dozen feet in. One swinging its head towards him. This time round, he reacted by putting his spear through its head. He shook the corpse aside, but as he ran, he realized there was another noise. A chittering that was rising up around him.

Another nightmare born: The damn rats were flooding upwards from the bottom plain. Rather than taking the walkways, their smaller bodies allowed them to climb directly up the steep hill face. Their sheer numbers let them overwhelm the other monsters, even killing dozens of larger creatures. There were hundreds of rats.

Arthur could not help but stare at the sight.

The rats swiftly reached his level and dealt with the snakes, who were sent bushes shivering as they dropped on their natural prey.

And were in turn overwhelmed by the horde.

Arthur's attention came crashing back down to earth at last, and cold sweat broke out across his body. Dying by rat swarm was the last thing he wanted to do. The disease from earlier rat bites was slowing down his healing technique, making it hard for him to go on. He would be slowly torn to shreds, eaten alive...

Nope, nope, nope.

Rather than dwell on that, Arthur chose to speed up. In his haste he might be ambushed further by snakes, but better that than the rat swarm. Or, frankly, the thundering boars that had survived and were finally on the same level, charging through the underbrush and setting off new fights between the different species.

Head down and on the swivel, he kept running. With a hand, he batted at the underbrush in front of him, hoping to knock or startle the snakes ahead of him into moving before he reached them. The first snake that he managed to bait out, he managed to flip away as it reared back to attack him. Unfortunately, a second creature was just behind it on a lower branch and by the time his spear was dropping back into guard position, the monster had already attacked.

Wrapping itself around his neck and one upraised arm, the slithery serpent snaked its way up his body, clinging to him as it tried to tighten its grip. Arthur plucked the kris from his waist as he kept running, his other hand entangled and still holding the spear above his head a little.

Rushing forward, not daring to stop, he started stabbing into the snake, nearly taking out his own eye as the kris slid off hardened scales. Even so, he managed to pierce it a few times, even as the constrictor kept tightening itself on his body.

Till, finally, it began relaxing as the poison reacted.

Out of breath, forced to breathe in shorter gasps as the monster had tightened itself on him, Arthur shrugged the slow-moving serpent off him as he staggered forward until he finally exited the shrubbery to reach the slope to the next level.

Exhausted, stumbling up the slope which, thankfully, seemed absent of creatures, he made it up one more flight.

Just in time to hear the scream of birds as they descended.

Chapter 140

This was a Malaysian Tower, so these birds weren't large predators like hunting falcons or whirling giers. They also weren't, thankfully, crows—though there were plenty of those in Malaysia—ready to commit grievous, even fatal assault. No, these were sparrows that swooped down on him, in numbers that darkened the sky.

Once again, Arthur wished for protection, for some weapon to wield against a horde. But he had nothing. Nothing but a bag that he hiked up over his head as he bent low and ran, spear held away from his legs.

He aimed for the next slope, knowing that if he reached it, he would meet the *jenglot* in battle. Somehow he would beat it, even as battered and bruised, limping and lethargic, as he was. Because that was the trial. For whoever had designed this trial, had made it such that few were meant to survive—even though it was merely a trial for the first floor of a beginner Tower. The survivors were the lucky, the prepared, the stubborn.

Well, Arthur would take two out of three and hope that was enough, because if he had known it was this hard; he would never have chosen to ascend until he was more ready. Not until he hit the first threshold at least, and damn was that far away.

The whoosh of swooping bodies, the low, almost pleasant cries of tiny swallows enveloped him. Then the impact began, little bodies slamming into the backpack, bouncing off it with beaks and talons ripping into the fabric before they took to the sky once more.

Or at least, the ones that managed to time their landing right. Because those that hit too early, or that missed their descent or came in too hard or struck some of their own friends on the way down, did not get up. Sparrow bodies were not meant for divebombing attacks. Even reinforced by arcane wizardry of the Tower, their tiny fragile bodies were never meant to prey upon others.

So, many died, crushing themselves or being crushed by their brethren. Dozens fell, squashed against the backpack. Others struck his arms and lower back or were accidentally kicked aside as he bulled forward. Like a pelting, moving rain, the bodies crashed down in a never-ending deluge of flesh and blood, their angry chirps encompassing Arthur in a feathery, flickering nightmare.

Trained as he might be, Arthur knew he would someday wake up screaming from this moment. The rats might have mobbed him, clambered on him, tore at him, sent him into convulsions of disgust. But crawling through sewers and cleaning up the damnable port after tides and thunderous storms shook the coast had prepared him in ways for such an occurrence.

This, this never-ending shrieking feathered deluge was entirely new. He had liked birds, sparrows in particular. Thought them cute and beautiful, stared at their occasional foray and smiled at their survival even as damnable crows overflowed the streets.

Now, they sought to kill him, throwing themselves at him in suicidal divebombs that so few survived, all because of...

Something. A Tower test that they probably never even understood, creatures formed from mass and magic and energy, that parodied real life but were obviously not. Because what kind of flock would do this, would suffocate him with their attacks and screams, to pull slivers of pecked flesh?

"Birds on the wire, are really dire." Pushing up and shoving sideways, Arthur made the little corpse pile on his bag bounce off, the pile growing ever higher with each moment. He kept running even when he felt a damn bird plunge deep into his calf, almost causing him to cramp.

Of course, he called it running. But between the assault and damage, he was now doing more of a hard limp than a run. Mind running through his options, he searched for ways out of this. The flock above him was still so dense there was no way he'd ever hit the next rise in time. The rats would eventually come, and then the war of the tinies would begin.

But he had no desire to be around to watch that, even if it might aid him.

On the other hand, he had no traits, no skills that could help. He could form a Refined Energy Dart, but the attack could only kill a single bird. Maybe two if he got really lucky. When the numbers were in hundreds, he was basically helpless.

A shield might have been nice, but his backpack would have to do, even if the pans and tent gear left him bruised from bouncing against it again and again. But he would take what he had. As much as this frenzied attack was a nightmare, he was also still alive. If the birds had just swooped at him from a different angle, instead of arcing down and bouncing off his raised backpack, he would be done.

Not that he was going to tell the damn creatures that. If he did wonder at the lack of strategy, he would keep that thought to himself until he was done. Perhaps it was, really, just a *trial* after all. Not meant to kill everyone, but to push the right people on.

Limping on, arms and body aching as they grew more tired each moment, Arthur kept moving. Blood pooling into his right foot, such that every dragging step was a squish, he kept going. His chest burning with each breath, burning with torso and stomach wounds from monkey bites. He was hunched over, his head swimming, vision fading in and out at the edges.

But Arthur still found himself digging deep into that well of willpower. Not anger, for he was not a raging fool like Jan. No. He had better reasons to go on. He had family that might be disassociated from him on a day-today basis, who did not understand his own drives. But whom he loved. He had a *mei mei* that looked up to him and a mother who did her best, even when most days she found facing the greyness of existence difficult.

He had people he cared for, that he would not abandon entirely. That he would, eventually, go back to. That he intended to give more to.

His sifu who grew older with each day, with each loss of his students to the Tower. Who needed a victory just as much, if not more, than him? Who bled for every single soul that left to find their fortune against his advice, and yet he never stopped training them. No matter the pain their losses caused him.

Let others rage and scream, claw and beg for scraps for their own greed. Arthur just needed to survive, to clear the Tower and go back for his family, for those who needed him. In that deep bedrock of certainty, he kept placing foot in front of foot.

Till, finally, he set it upon the slope and the birds slowed their attacks.

For another had come down to face him. Barring his way.

And the final test was here.

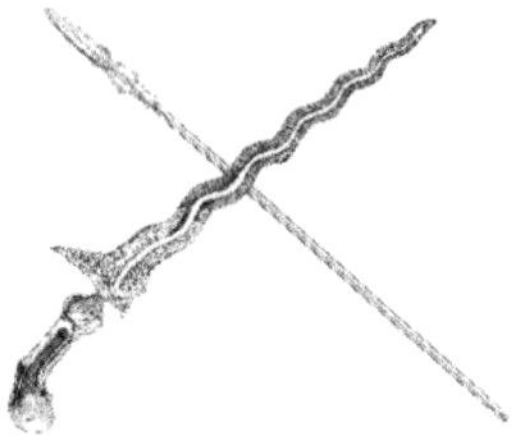

Chapter 141

Jenglot. Thick-haired humanoid creature of the forest. Long arms, dirty fur, and claws that might as well be knives. Long snout with two overarching fangs that were perfect for biting down and punching through armour. If one had armour.

And of course, it had the high ground.

Arthur huffed out a long breath, then immediately sucked in more air. He lowered his backpack, shrugging it back on properly and tightening the straps as he stared at the creature, never letting his gaze shift as he waited and recovered as best he could.

The sparrows might have fled, leaving the creature and him alone; but Arthur could not count on that holding for the more obstinate members of the monster population. Eventually, the *babi ngepet* would make it here. The rat swarm, diminished, would make their way through the snakes and birds and come for him.

Eventually, he would need to move.

Arthur cast a glance at the second-last rise. It was steep, though still no vertical wall. If he had time, he might scramble up it. If his leg was not half-dead, he might be able to take a running leap and somersault himself all the way up.

He'd still have to cross the open ground, much shorter this time, but still cross it. Then ascend one last level to reach the portal. All the while, the *jenglot* would be rushing over.

Arthur had a vision of his body arcing through the air, in a spectacular leap, before his leg was grabbed and he was yanked into the ground. There would be an Arthur-shaped hole in the earth as those big hairy legs came crashing down on his supine form.

He shook those morbid images out of his head, dismissing the entire thing as a bad, bad idea. And not even the cool kind of bad, like biker chicks in leather pants or sex on the beach. No, this was just bad. So no jumping.

His arms had been burning and feeling like they would drop off at any second. But now the pain had slowly decreased. The exhaustion faded a little, allowing him to switch from deep panting breaths to something a little more controlled. His legs ached still, and a glance down showed that blood continued to leak down his wound. Somewhere along the way, the damn sparrow that had lodged itself in his calf had fallen off, leaving a gaping wound behind that refused to clot fully.

His hands were still shaking. Holding the spear at ready, so that he could parry the *jenglot* if it came charging suddenly, he yanked his canteen out with his other hand. He gulped down the water, almost emptying the entire thing between haste and splashing. Then he slipped the canteen away, working the cover until it closed.

All this time, the *jenglot* just chose to stare at him. Behind, raucous fights between the monsters grew in volume, the birds shrieking their unnatural anger as they divebombed new invaders. Still, they left him and the monster alone, another peculiarity of the test.

"You wouldn't be willing to just step aside, would you?" Arthur called out. He wanted to wipe his wet hand dry, but his clothing was either muddy or bloody, leaving him with nothing to use. He settled for just shaking it off and then putting both hands on his spear.

Silence.

Arthur nodded, glanced back to check on the progress of those monsters and made a face. No more delay then.

Back foot still dragging a little, he ascended the slope, spear held steady. He was still tired, his muscles aching, his breathing laboured, and his heart pounding like a machine gun. This was probably the worst timing for him to start a fight, but he had no other options. He was out of time.

Energy coursed through him as he pulled on it, triggering the Heavenly Sage's Mischief. He felt himself lighten a little, his movements ease. It almost seemed like the ache in his body faded to the background as newfound strength poured in.

Even his punctured leg felt steadier, such that he began to ascend faster. On his forehead sat a Refined Energy Dart, ready to be unleashed. Now he wished he practiced making a second one. But one would do well enough.

And anyway, a Focused Strike might be all he required.

A plan was forming, as he neared the stationary monster. As though it could not, or would not, walk down the slope, it stood at the top, its body hunched low, long claws swinging back and forth. Tiny eyes set above a deep muzzle watched every moment of Arthur's, baleful red and yellow eyes glinting with malice.

Nearer now, barely ten feet apart. A long lunge with the spear was possible, if Arthur dared to try it.

He heard a growing rumble from deep within the creature. It was like a bass speaker had been turned up, a stick swirled around the drum, rising and falling each moment. The hands rose a little now, guarding the lower end of its body.

Taunting, tempting a strike to the face.

Another step closer to meet the creature. And then another. Arthur could easily strike with his own raised spear. Stab and thrust, tear and rip. But the much taller monster could do the same if it leaned over.

That last step had been dangerous. Entering a close range was often a striking point for experienced duelists.

But the *jenglot* cared not. It wanted him nearer, it wanted him all the way up there.

And Arthur took the invitation, taking another step in.

Now, he was within the monster's easy reach. It could lash out with its claws. And so could Arthur with his spear.

A micro-second of hesitation, as both watched and waited for the other to move first. Then, both claw and spear in a blur and the fight was on.

Chapter 142

Arthur's spear hissed through the air, the dark wooden shaft and watersteel blade a shadowed emissary of death. He thrust with his backhand, shuffling the weapon through his forehand that steadied, and adjusted the trajectory. On the other side, the *jenglot* swayed as it swung its left arm, seeking to behead Arthur at the same moment, its movement a touch later than Arthur's own. Baited from its position.

Arthur turned his hand, guiding the spear head, aiming at the fast-moving arm that had risen and swung towards him. The motion was meant to intercept the attack, to pin the biceps and upper arm via bone, to tear flesh open whilst stymying the attack.

Simultaneous motion, minute adjustments. Spear striking flesh, tearing into it even as claws struck at hunched head under raised shoulders. He felt the claws clip the top of his scalp, send him reeling a little before the momentum of his spear's stop-thrust broke through and ended the *jenglot*'s attack.

A savage twist of his weapon dislodged it while opening the wound wider and sliced tendons and muscle bands. At the same time, Arthur stepped into the void of the falling arm, using the leverage of his motion as he shuffled up and sideways to gain ground even as the other arm swung at him.

This time, Arthur blocked with the haft of his spear, striking downward. The monster snarled, but had already planned on abandoning the attack, for it moved away from its starting position for the first time. Using its greater height to lean over and bite at his head.

Rather than dodge or lurch backwards, Arthur instead jumped. An inch or half off the ground, pulling his ankles to his butt at the same time. He dropped, faster than the monster expected, as gravity took him and yanked him down, allowing him to fall beneath the attack.

Pain screamed up his legs as he landed, Arthur was forced to grab at the ground with his lead hand to stop himself from collapsing. The wounds along his legs, along his calf woke up, no longer faded to the background and blood gushed anew.

Even so, Arthur could not help but grin as he looked up.

"Gotcha."

Then, from that angle below the monster, he unleashed the Refined Energy Dart. Directly into the monster's groin. The attack was not aimed at the dangling maleness, for not every creature reacted the same way to such an assault.

No. It was targeted just a little higher. Where in a human, the superior pubic ligament connected the pelvis front together and offered stability and control of movement. It was an educated guess that the creature had a similar structure to other humanoids—and similar vulnerability.

No bone in the way. Nothing but flesh and ligaments and tender, tender organs before one reached the spine. Where bundles of nerves and muscles and blood vessels met nearby, and an impactful attack could be agonizing and crippling at the same time.

His Dart burrowed in through coarse, almost metallic fur and impacted. And the creature howled.

Spear pulled close and shortened, he stabbed upward. Not at the part now protected by reflexive hands but at the *jenglot*'s torso. He had no time to get back on his feet, so he stabbed and stabbed, plunging spear into exposed torso, weapon skittering off bone and fur and finally making a puncture.

He had meant to use Focused Strike here, to pin the monster in the head as it bent down. To end the fight in moments. He had intended to do much more damage, but his body had betrayed him.

Then a swinging backhand caught him on the jaw and sent him tumbling away to fetch up against the edge of the slope. His spear fell aside.

As his head rang, the monster lurched towards him in ungainly fashion, stability threatened by the damage to its pelvic area. But it still leapt, seeking his blood, to close the distance and put claws into Arthur and end the battle.

Curled up on his side, Arthur rolled further. No spear, so he tucked his feet in close to his body and took the falling creature on them. His legs screamed, the right foot buckling beneath as claws lashed down, scoring his chest and opening a deep wound.

Rolling backwards even further, so that his feet were literally over his head, tucked into a ball as the monster lashed out, Arthur threw everything that he had into extending his legs entirely. Kicking upward, right leg still lagging, he managed somehow to throw the *jenglot* off. It now sailed over the rise, fingers still.

clawing, unwilling to let a moment pass without trying to end Arthur's life. Only for the monster to realize after a moment that it was dropping past the ledge and to the level below. It twisted in the air then, bestial recognition on its face that it needed to take the impact, the fall, properly.

Then further chaos as the swallows, that had been held at bay until someone crossed an invisible boundary, fell upon the *jenglot*. Pecking at it as the hairy creature fell and crashed to the ground. It was swiftly covered by the furious flock.

In the meantime, Arthur was rocking back from on the edge himself, legs tucked over his head. Only a last minute lurch of his body, and the weird angle of his backpack, that stopped him from sharing the *jenglot*'s fate.

Leaving him bleeding and exhausted on the slope. Alone.

Victorious, if you could call it that.

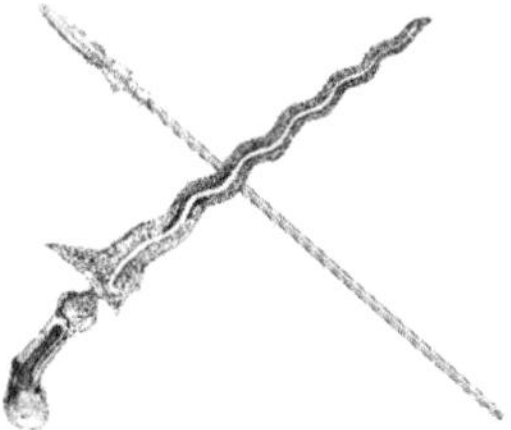

Chapter 143

Crawling towards his spear, and then using it to help him lurch, stumble, and limp towards the portal, every moment was agony, his legs barely functioning as he pushed on. Yet, he refused to let himself stop. A glimpse over the rise had shown him that the *jenglot* was not dead, swarmed as it was by the birds and the rats and a *kuching hitam* that had somehow managed to make its way up and taken a chance to make its mark.

That herd of *babi ngepet* now had riders, for the troop of monkeys somehow managed to corral the creatures to become their unwilling mounts. As the boars charged up relentlessly, the monkeys plucked away snakes and rats, shielding the demonic swine.

All of those creatures gained ground on Arthur, even as he poured unrefined energy into Heavenly Sage's Mischief. The combined increase in his strength, speed, and resilience was all that kept him moving, even as his healing technique strained to patch him together.

Each exhalation saw his vision fade at the edges a little, each laboured inhale saw it come back. Somewhere along the way, he realized that he'd done more than bruise his back. He might have cracked a rib. He felt a spreading numbness from compressed nerves, a dislocated—herniated?—disc or two from repeatedly crashing into hard metal.

His left arm did not want to work properly. He barely could hold onto his spear with his right hand, but it was the only thing helping to push him on. His right foot dragged with each step, nerves and muscles no longer working.

One eye was entirely gummed up, the numerous scalp wounds he'd gained started bleeding again, overwhelming the simple bandana he had used and now dripping down his face, forcing him to blink around it each time.

Behind him, he could hear the monsters coming. The howls, the cries, the shrieks. No birds, not yet, for which he was grateful. If they had come, he was not certain he could have stopped them. He was not even certain how he was moving forward, other than the fact that he refused to stop.

He had beaten the *jenglot.* Maybe not killed it, but beaten it just as surely. He had survived everything this overblown, lopsided test had to throw at him. He would not give up now, just because his body threatened to fall apart with each moment.

He could not. Too much was riding on it.

Breath aching, vision swimming, he pulled himself to the final slope and hauled himself up. The smell of himself, of the congealed blood and the thrown feces that had struck him, the rank stench of dried fear and voided bowels, it all threatened to overwhelm him.

Even then he did not stop, even when he heard a cry from the *jenglot.* How it had recovered so fast and was on its way back up, he could not know. He could feel the thunder of hooves on the ground, hear the panting growls and chittering of rats, and now even the cries of the much diminished flock above as they began their bombing runs again.

Each step, a struggle. Each moment, a threat to his consciousness. The energy within his core had plummeted, Heavenly Sage's Mischief draining his reserve. Thankfully, the final ascent was just a few dozen feet, though it might as well have been a mile long.

Then, his energy was exhausted, the Mischief gone. He crashed to his knees and found himself crawling. Pulling himself through sheer force of will. The glowing doorway of light was hanging right there, waiting for him to cross the threshold.

Inch by inch, he pulled himself toward it, leaving a trail of blood behind. Until he was nearly there, his hand extended and even touched the light. It felt like a snapping, twisting short-circuit of electricity arcing through him.

He grinned, rejoicing. Too soon as a clawed hand grabbed his foot and dragged him back. He twisted about to face the *jenglot*, its snout opened and ready to snap him in half, saliva dripping down too-sharp canines.

"*Cilaka*," Arthur cursed.

It lunged and the fight was back on.

Arthur tumbled through the doorway to land on hard ground. His body ached, his mind ached, his left arm mangled as it had been chewed upon multiple times. His right hand clutched the kris, still moving in a cutting motion. Somewhere along the way, his spear had tumbled through the portal too, dragged along by his feet by accident.

He just lay there for a long time, ignoring the insistent pressure of the Tower demanding that he read the notifications pushing into his head. That pressure was nothing compared to the pain that consisted of his entire being. There was not even an inch that was not cut, bitten, torn, bruised or abraded in some manner.

Arthur could not help but grin.

He had survived the trial. By the skin of his teeth.

Literally.

Turning his head over sideways, he spat out the fur that had already begun dissolving, the taste of decrepit flesh more a memory than reality by now. He smiled even though it hurt.

He had done it. He was on the second floor.

And now it was time to collect his rewards.

"Told you I could do it…" Arthur murmured. "Even if, I almost blew it."

Then, finally, he let the darkness take him as he lay in that liminal space between floors. Victorious.

###

The End of Book 1, Level 1 of Climbing the Ranks

Continue Arthur's adventure by reading Chapter 144 of Climbing the Ranks for free on starlitpublishing.com

A Thousand Li: the First Step
Deluxe Edition

Mark your calendars for April 2024 as *A Thousand Li: the First Step* is getting a deluxe edition to celebrate the series' five-year anniversary!

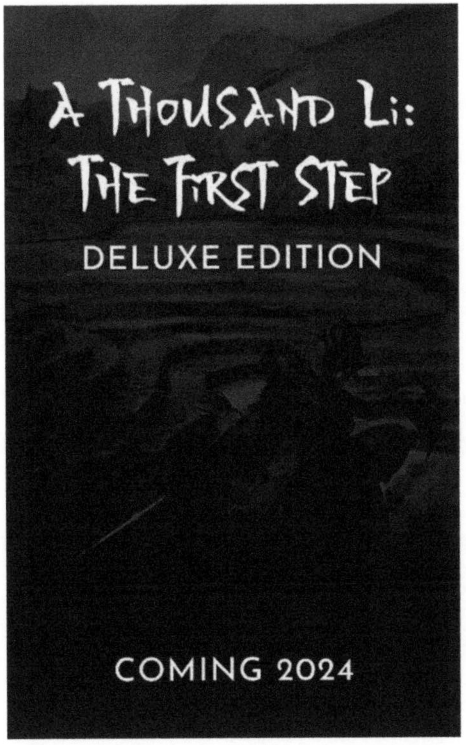

Don't want to miss the launch of this one-of-a-kind edition?

Sign up for notifications on Starlit Publishing.

www.starlitpublishing.com/products/the-first-step-deluxe-edition

The System Apocalypse Series

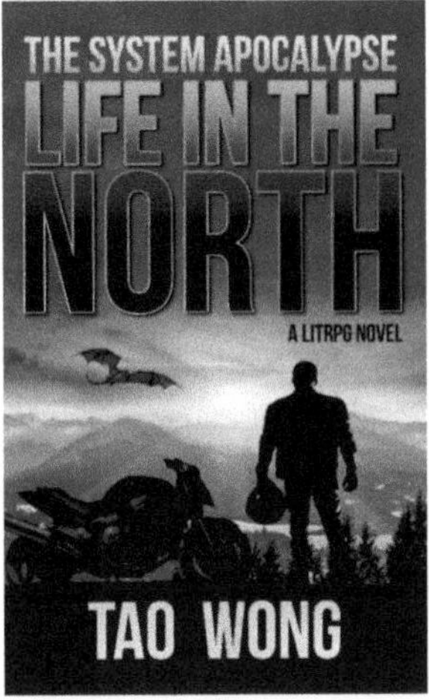

What happens when the apocalypse arrives, not via nuclear weapons or a comet but as Levels and monsters? What if you were camping in the Yukon when the world ended?

All John wanted to do was get away from his life in Kluane National Park for a weekend. Hike, camp and chill. Instead, the world comes to an end in a series of blue boxes. Animals start evolving, monsters start spawning and he has a character sheet and physics defying skills. Now, he has to survive the apocalypse, get back to civilisation and not lose his mind.

The System has arrived and with it, aliens, monsters and a reality that draws upon past legends and game-like reality. John will need to find new friends, deal with his ex and the slavering monsters that keep popping up.

Life in the North is Book 1 of the *System Apocalypse*, a LitRPG Apocalypse series that combines modern day life, science fiction and fantasy elements along with game mechanics. This series contains elements of games like level ups, experience, enchanted materials, a sarcastic spirit, mecha, a beguiling dark elf, monsters, minotaurs, a fiery red head and a semi-realistic view on violence and its effects. Does not include harems.

Author's Note

And that's book one of Climbing the Ranks. Thank you, once again, for reading it. Hopefully the sprinkling of Manglish used throughout the work hasn't put you off too much. Writing Climbing the Ranks started as a side project, to place a work in Malaysia where I grew up. The country itself, is, of course beautiful, though we don't get to see much of it.

Funnily enough, the hardest thing to do was find monsters. In many ways, while we have quite a wide range of supernatural creatures, many of them are supernatural in origin. They make horrible first level monsters, which is why I reached for the more prosaic creatures to begin with. For those looking for more interesting, supernatural creatures – they're coming! Just in higher levels.

As usual, when writing a new work, some of the storylines caught me by surprise. In this case, Arthur's propensity to rhyme and his founding of the Clan. It's certainly required me to adjust some expectations, including lengthening this work more than ever.

Hopefully you enjoyed this book. There's much more to come, including additional chapters on my website and further exploration of the city.

And, as always, do leave a review!

~Tao

About the Author

Tao Wong is a Canadian author based in Toronto who is best known for his System Apocalypse post-apocalyptic LitRPG series and A Thousand Li, a Chinese xianxia fantasy series. His work has been released in audio, paperback, hardcover and ebook formats and translated into German, Spanish, Portuguese, Russian and other languages. He was shortlisted for the UK Kindle Storyteller award in 2021 for his work, A Thousand Li: the Second Sect. When he's not writing and working, he's practicing martial arts, reading and dreaming up new worlds.

Tao became a full-time author in 2019 and is a member of the Science Fiction and Fantasy Writers of America (SFWA) and Novelists Inc.

If you'd like to support Tao directly, he has a Patreon page - benefits include previews of all his new books, full access to series short stories, and other exclusive perks.

- www.patreon.com/taowong

Want updates on upcoming deluxe editions and exclusive merch? Follow Tao on Kickstarter to get notifications on all projects.

- www.kickstarter.com/profile/starlitpublishing

For updates on the series and his other books (and special one-shot stories), please visit the author's website.

- www.mylifemytao.com

Subscribers to Tao's mailing list to receive exclusive access to short stories in the Thousand Li and System Apocalypse universes.

Tao also hosts a Facebook Group for all things cultivation novels. We'd love it if you joined us: Cultivation Novels

www.facebook.com/groups/cultivationnovels

For more great information about LitRPG series, check out the Facebook groups:

GameLit Society

www.facebook.com/groups/LitRPGsociety

LitRPG Books

www.facebook.com/groups/LitRPG.books

LitRPG Legion

www.facebook.com/groups/litrpglegion

Fantasy Nation

www.facebook.com/groups/TheFantasyNation

About the Publisher

Starlit Publishing is wholly owned and operated by Tao Wong. It is a science fiction and fantasy publisher focused on the LitRPG & cultivation genres. Their focus is on promoting new, upcoming authors in the genre whose writing challenges the existing stereotypes while giving a rip-roaring good read. For more information on Starlit Publishing, visit our website!

www.starlitpublishing.com

You can also join Starlit Publishing's mailing list to learn of new, exciting authors and book releases.

LitRPG Group

To learn more about LitRPG, talk to authors including myself, and just have an awesome time, please join the LitRPG Group.

www.facebook.com/groups/LitRPG